"If you need me, sen[...]
to me when you wi[...]
own life, not your sist[...]

Her tears ceased, and she was very firm. "Don't wait for me, Rane. Find a woman you can love and make your life with her. My life is here with my children, with my husband. I do love St. John; not as I love you, but enough so that I will not leave him." If anything changed with St. John, it would be very soon, time enough to go to Rane, but she did not want Rane ruining his own life for her.

It was final. He could feel the strength of her will.

They dressed in silence and then turned to each other in unison to cling for the last time.

"A long and joyful life, how I wish it for you!" she whispered fiercely, and then she pulled away and fled, not looking back.

WILD SWAN

"This is the kind of historical romance that will be most enjoyed read late at night while munching on chocolates and taking an occasional sip of brandy. In short, it is everything the genre should be. The author knows just what she is doing every step of the way and she does it very well indeed, serving up an elegant and exciting tour de force."

—*The Washington Post*

Bantam Books by Celeste De Blasis
Ask your bookseller for the books you have missed

WILD SWAN

Celeste De Blasis

BANTAM BOOKS
NEW YORK · TORONTO · LONDON · SYDNEY · AUCKLAND

WILD SWAN

A Bantam Book
Bantam Hardcover edition / September 1984
Bantam rack-size edition / July 1985

Library of Congress Cataloging in Publication Data

De Blasis, Celeste.
  Wild swan.

  I. Title.
PS3554.E11144W5   1984   813'.54   83-46001
ISBN 0-553-27260-8

Published simultaneously in the United States and Canada

Bantam Books are published by Bantam Books, a division of Bantam
Doubleday Dell Publishing Group, Inc. Its trademark, consisting of the
words "Bantam Books" and the portrayal of a rooster, is Registered in U.S.
Patent and Trademark Office and in other countries. Marca Registrada.
Bantam Books, 666 Fifth Avenue, New York, New York 10103.

PRINTED IN THE UNITED STATES OF AMERICA

KR   15   14   13   12   11   10

*My love and gratitude
to the Parkers—
Geoffrey, Betty, Celie, and Max—
who gave me England.*

❧ Notes and ❧ Acknowledgments

It is of minor importance, I assume, to everyone except me, but I would like to point out that the name, "St. John," is pronounced "Sinjin," emphasis on the first syllable, in this book (in England, the name may also be pronounced "Sinjon," with the emphasis on the second syllable). Alex's nickname for him is "Sinje," again with the stress on the first syllable.

In some circles there is still a dispute over when the word "Thoroughbred" was first used to indicate a particular breed of horse rather than simply a well-schooled animal. However, in original sources of the period, I found it used to refer to the specific breed, and thus feel justified in using it in *Wild Swan*. By 1800, the Thoroughbreds were genetically specific, tracing back to just a few stallions. In fact, when breeding back to Arabian horses was tried, it was found that the two breeds were so separate that the Thoroughbreds were not improved for racing by the addition of Arabian blood, despite the fact that a major factor in the founding of the breed had been the desert imports.

Most of the horse races in the novel were real events, but in some, I have allowed my fictional horses to participate and sometimes to displace the historical winners. To those gallant animals and their descendants, my apologies.

I have consulted hundreds upon hundreds of sources to make the historical background accurate. These works range from periodicals of the past to modern studies, from racing calendars to lists of herbal remedies, from general writings to very specialized treatises. It is impossible to list all of them here. But I would like to mention four that provided unique information: *The Cream of Devon*, published by the Devon Federation of Women's Institutes to celebrate their Diamond Jubilee in 1980; *The Life and Times of Sir Archie*, by Elizabeth Amis Cameron Blanchard and Manly Wade Wellman, published by the University of North Carolina Press; *A New Dictionary of Kent Dialect*, by Alan Major, published by Meresborough Books of Rainham, Kent; and *Racing in America 1665-1865*, by John Hervey, privately published by the Jockey Club, New York. (While the Blanchard and Wellman book spells Sir Archie with an "ie," most sources and many old racing sheets spell it with a "y" which is what I have done. Sir Archy was a horse, not a human, so I doubt he would have minded either way.)

Years ago, my grandmother told me about West Country free traders, or smugglers, in the family and about their connections to Gravesend on the Thames below London. She told me as well about the very strong woman who had managed, almost single-handedly, to bring herself and ten relatives to the United States. *Wild Swan* is fiction, but it grew out of the seeds Grandmother planted with those family histories.

I did extensive research in England and was given generous help along the way. John F. Clausen, rector of St. Mary's Church, Stone, Kent, opened old records for me, and I saw rows and rows of names from the family my grandmother had talked about, including some of the later relatives whom she had met in her youth. Centuries were eclipsed, and the feeling of kinship was at once powerful and strange. It is a way to feel humble in the face of time, for those people lived, loved, and dreamed just as we all do now.

Commander Ballard took me on a tour of Cobham Hall, though it is now a school and closed to the public. Ruth Courtney of Bideford, Devon, first answered questions by mail, though she did not know me, and then we met in England. She is a delightful and intelligent woman and was most helpful. On that same trip, my friend, Susan Bowes Burke, took a day out of her busy schedule to serve as chauffeur through the West Country; I could not have managed to see so much without her. On that and other visits to the West Country, I found the people gave kind greetings to strangers.

The Parkers, to whom this book is dedicated, helped me to locate research sources and made me welcome, as always, in their home. They are so much a part of my days in England, I cannot imagine that country without them.

In addition to visiting historical collections in museums large and small, I also used the services of various libraries, and library staffs on both sides of the Atlantic worked hard to obtain odd bits of information for me. These libraries include, in England, the local history collections in Barnstaple and in Gravesend (where Susan Barton offered special assistance); in London, the British Library, Reference Division, the City of Westminster Central Reference Library, the Guildhall Library, and Lambeth Palace Library (E.G.W. Bill, Librarian); in Maryland, the Enoch Pratt Free Library, Baltimore, Maryland Historical Society Library, Baltimore, and McKeldin Library at the University of Maryland (Suellen M. Towers provided needed information by mail); in California, the California Thoroughbred Association Library in Arcadia, and the Victorville Branch of the San Bernardino County Library System. This last named institution is my local source, and so I have depended heavily on its facilities. The librarians have grown accustomed to my requests for outlandish and hard to find pieces of history and are unfailingly polite and accommodating. Ruth Burch, Joyce Burke, Alice Christiansen, and Mark Sommers, as well as Marjorie Merritt and Helen Tishkoff from headquarters, have been particularly helpful. And Nancy Kuehn deserves a medal for patience and unfailing cheerfulness. She has found and delivered stacks of books in the long work of this novel; and more, she is, as I am, an early morning walker and has accompanied me on many treks, putting up with all manner of moods from me as well as with some nerve-racking encounters with dangerous bulls, bothersome insects, and persistent skunks.

Shirley Baltz gave me a special tour of Belair Mansion, Bowie, Maryland. Though renovations had hardly begun on the house, Ms. Baltz's vivid descriptions refurbished it in the instant and made it easy to see how beautiful it had once been and will be again one day.

My guide for an historical tour of Annapolis, Maryland, was Sylvia Houck, and at the end of the tour, when I explained what I was doing research for, Ms. Houck offered her services as a researcher should I need additional information. She may by now be sorry she made the offer, for I have sent a continual stream of letters asking about this and that, and Ms. Houck has answered them faithfully, often going out of her way to visit special collections at various locations in the state in order to obtain the best material available. In addition she has offered her own keen observations of the flora and fauna of the changing seasons in her state.

Martha Ramsey, another Marylander, has also proved to be an informative correspondent, and I bless the day my friends, Dorothy and Leonard Henderson, introduced me to the Ramseys.

My mother, Jean De Blasis, was once again a willing driver and traveling companion on a research trip to Maryland, and on an historical tour of Virginia, my aunt, Donna Campbell, joined us. Laughter with learning is never amiss, and though we are of different generations, my mother, my aunt, and I enjoy each other's company. They lightened the burden of my work by their presence.

Anna Slavick took on the task of proofreading again and worked frantically to meet my deadline. And she gave the characters a space in her heart and her mind, thus giving me encouragement.

Jane Berkey, who has been my agent from the beginning and my friend for nearly as long, and Linda Grey, who is now my editor and whose involvement in my books goes clear back to *The Night Child*, have given me professional gifts by allowing me to write my novels in my own way and by liking the results.

Many people helped me by sharing their books or their knowledge with me, by putting me in contact with other sources, or by simply making my life easier by performing various tasks for me. I know I will leave someone out, and thus, the following can only be termed a partial list: Buck Abbot, Karen Bojahlian, Joseph B. Campbell, Craig Corder, Harry Cross, Chris Coupe, Susan Dailey, Michael Edgar, Jean Herring, Canon Hultgren, Mildred Kaunas, Madeline MacLaren, John Monteverdi, Nancy Okland, Robert J. Paluzzi, Richard Pusey, Meg Ruley, Zanita Schermerhorn, Rifqa Shahin, Carl Van Burger, Jean Wells, Susan Wells, and Betty Wooster.

To all of you, named and unnamed, my thanks for your contributions to my work.

Celeste N. De Blasis
August 1983

WILD
SWAN

Book One

✥ Chapter 1 ✥

Gravesend, Kent, England, 1813

The air was cool and shadowed in the great oak. Alex took a deep breath, trying to taste its greenness. It did have a taste, an elusive sweetness. Eyes half-closed, legs dangling, she felt the solid trunk against her back, the pull of the earth on her legs. Despite her presence, birds flew in and out of the tree, and her mind went with them, seeking the course of their secret journeys. She was on the edge of knowing exactly how it felt to be one of them when the thud of a horse's hooves brought her back to earth.

She peered through the branches and smiled in delight as she recognized the horse and rider. "Sinje," she called as she started to climb out of the tree.

St. John Aiden Blaine Nigel Carrington grinned and dismounted as he watched the lithe body slither skillfully down the tree, but he managed to don a severe expression by the time she faced him, standing only a few inches shorter than his own bare miss of six feet. "Alexandria Thaine, I should think you had been in trouble often enough for wearing your brother's breeches, and for that matter, for climbing trees, too. Your mother is going to be most displeased."

"She always is, no matter what I do." There was a touch of sadness in the observation but no self-pity.

St. John could not dispute the truth of what she said; he had never seen Margaret Thaine treat this, her youngest child, with kindness. Exasperation bordering on anger was a more likely response. And Caton Thaine, Alexandria's father, was little help; his desire for domestic tranquility often led to what could only be termed a cowardly retreat from his wife's temper.

Eleven years older than she, St. John had known Alexandria all of her life, and he was very fond of her. At thirteen she was still as slender as a boy, having no trouble fitting into her brother Boston's castoff clothing, and yet, it would be hard to mistake her sex. When she was feeling uneasy, she could be awkward, as if the height she had attained in the past year or so still came as a surprise, but when she was happy, she moved with a quick feline grace and her face was undoubtedly as feminine as it was unusual.

If St. John had not been told that she took her coloring from her grandfather, Trahern Thaine, he would have suspected she was a changeling, for she looked nothing like her brothers and sister. Her skin was palest honey, and her hair was such a dark, rich brown, it appeared black in some lights, in others subtle shades of deep gold could be seen. Arched black brows and thick lashes delineated the little outer corner tilt of her big eyes. They, too, contained shades of gold that varied the green of them from the color of new spring leaves to the deepest shadowed emerald of the forest's heart. Her nose was straight, nostrils slightly flared above her generous mouth. Her high cheekbones and the firm line of her jaw were definite though still softened by youth. It was an exotic, arresting face, and St. John suspected she was going to lead some man a merry dance when she grew up.

"Sir Arthur's not limping," she said with pleasure, eyeing his mount.

"No, he's recovered. Your grandmother's poultice did the trick. Would you like to get up on him for a bit?" It was a needless question; she never refused a chance to ride one of the horses from the Carrington stables. It was precisely why she had stationed herself in the tree to wait for him. St. John had been teaching her how to ride for years. Often he wished her sister Florence shared the same passion for fine horseflesh. He smiled to himself as he gave Alex a boost up into the saddle; Florence had other things to offer, not the least of which were curves that would never have fit into the breeches Alex was wearing.

Florence was the most perfectly beautiful young woman

4

he had ever seen, ethereal in the delicately symmetrical features, wide sea blue eyes, and spun gold hair. Having known her since childhood, he had been obsessed with her since he had first made the delightful discovery that males and females differed. That his family disapproved and that Florence seemed to regard him as a great lord rather than an impoverished third son with no prospects, added greatly to her appeal. He felt a rush of warmth at the thought of her lush body. Nonetheless, he watched the horse and rider before him with critical attention, not thinking at all of the fact that he would be late for his tryst with Florence. Passing on his knowledge of and joy in riding and horses was a serious and agreeable business, and he could wish for no more enthusiastic pupil than Alex. He enjoyed her effortless control of the big bay hunter as if he were in the saddle instead of she.

"He's not limping, but he still favors it, doesn't he?" she observed, bringing the horse to an easy halt beside him. "I'm sure it's not pain, just the memory of it."

St. John was pleased by how finely tuned she was to the horse's movement so that she was aware of the slightest hesitation in the stride. "You're right, but he's even jumping quite well again, and I think by hunt season he will have forgotten the injury. There are some advantages to being stupid." As much as he loved them, he had no illusions about horses' intelligence.

Alex slipped down off the horse to stand facing St. John, thinking that she must soon warn him or it would be too late.

He caught the intensity of her look and waited patiently for whatever it was she wanted to say. She was interested in nearly everything, and he had long since given up trying to guess where her quicksilver mind would go next.

She was as nervous as if she were trying to take a horse over too high a wall, but studying St. John's face gave her the courage not to put it off any longer. No matter that he was the youngest Carrington son, he looked the most aristocratic of them all with his high-bridged nose and thin-lipped mouth set in his lean, slightly long face. His hair was heavy gold, his eyes very blue. He could look quite haughty and forbidding, but never had he turned that expression on her. To her, he had always been extraordinarily kind and his features were more dear to her than her own. He was certainly old enough so that he should know what was best, but in the case of Florence, she feared he did not. She took a deep breath and let the words out.

"Sinje, I know how much my mother and my sister want it, but you really mustn't marry Florence. It would be bad for both of you."

He was stunned by the subject she had chosen this time, and he couldn't think of anything to say except, "Why ever so?"

"Because she's not useful!" Alex proclaimed fervently as if that explained everything.

"Not useful for what?" he asked sharply, feeling his patience wearing thin. She really had gone too far this time. "Marriage is not the same as buying a cow or a horse."

"It ought to be! Then perhaps more people would be happy with each other. Florence doesn't even cook very well. She thinks looking beautiful is all she need do. Surely you want a wife who knows how to do more than that." She didn't want to remind him outright that as the youngest son of Sir Ivor Carrington and given the impoverished state of his family's finances, it was widely known that he stood to inherit neither title nor money. Florence would expect the kind of life he could never give her.

St. John had the sudden horrible suspicion that he had badly misread her character, and his anger was very near the surface. "Do you have someone else in mind? Yourself perhaps?"

"Of course not! What a foolish thing to say! I'm just a child."

She was scandalized by the idea which had obviously never occurred to her. St. John's anger receded. He knew Florence got on ill with her sister, but that wasn't unusual; he himself was often at odds with his eldest brother. "Do you really dislike your sister so much?" he inquired quite gently.

She looked at him in surprise. "Most of the time I just ignore her and she ignores me. But that's neither here nor there; it's you who matters and how unhappy you'll be if my mother and Florence have their way. Florence hasn't the sense to know it, but she'll be unhappy, too."

Finally understanding her very real concern for him, he was touched, but he knew he had to set her straight regarding the wisdom of staying out of other people's affairs. The words were never spoken.

So intent had they been on their discussion, they had even ignored Sir Arthur's nervous side-stepping that should have warned them of someone approaching.

"You idiotic, wicked child!" Florence was upon them in the instant, her hand lashing out to slap Alex with great force. "How dare you say such things! Lies, all of it lies, and you so mean and jealous!"

For a moment, St. John had all he could do to control his horse's frightened plunging, but then holding the reins close to the bit in one hand, he grabbed Florence with the other, jerking her back before she could hit Alexandria again.

Alex made no attempt to defend herself. She stood there, her eyes wide and unhappy, the mark of Florence's slap turning from white to red. She had never intended a hideous scene like this. She had hoped St. John would just quietly stop courting Florence and go his own way.

"I think you'd better go, Alexandria," St. John said, though at the moment, he would have preferred that Florence be the one to disappear. He could understand her rage, but still, she was ugly in the grip of it.

Alex saw Florence recollect herself and force tears into her eyes, masking her fury in the guise of heartbroken victim, and she left them there, knowing her continued presence would only make things worse.

She did not go home; she wished she never had to go there again. Once Florence had told her story, there was going to be no end of trouble. She went to her grandmother's house instead, seeking the comfort of the familiar refuge.

Her goal lay to the west on the other side of Gravesend and the contiguous town of Milton, and she took country lanes to get there, skirting the busy port. She had had enough of civilized company for the day. Civilized—as her mother termed her sister. "Florence knows how to behave in a ladylike manner while you remain a little savage. God give me strength, I sometimes think it hopeless."

She could hear the whining tone of her mother's voice all too clearly, and she grinned at the afterimage of Florence screeching her head off. Civilized, was it!

She waved to several farmers on her way and received

kind greetings in return. Despite her hoydenish ways, most of the countryfolk preferred her to her mother whose social pretensions were so rudely obvious. They also viewed Virginia Thaine with respect and affection and knew this child to be the favored granddaughter.

No matter what her mood when she began the journey, Alex never failed to feel comforted at the sight of her grandmother's farm. The old thick-walled house with its crooked windows open to the sun, the neat gardens and well-pruned orchard with the hop fields beyond, all bespoke love and harmony with the earth and the seasons. It was a world away from the discord of the house in Gravesend.

Her grandmother's ginger cat Henry VIII, named for the king with six wives, lay in his usual position in the sun before the front door, and Alex stopped to pay homage before she went on. Henry VIII growled lazily in greeting.

Alex found her grandmother carefully trimming herbs she grew for healing, cooking, and scent, and the air was perfumed by the fresh cutting. It was a magic blend Alex always associated with her grandmother.

Virginia straightened at her approach and smiled wryly. "Your mother won't be pleased if she catches you wearing Boston's clothing again."

Alex shrugged. "She isn't going to be pleased in any case." The story tumbled out, and the expression on her grandmother's face told her the offense was more grave than she had thought.

She did not regard Virginia as old. The spare figure and the white hair were unchanging in the world, and because Virginia continued to work at so many tasks, she retained the energy and quickness of a much younger woman. Her eyes were very dark brown and undimmed by the years, bright and endlessly observant. And her only concession to vanity, the gloves and hat she wore when she was outside, had served her well, leaving her skin soft and scarcely lined over the long, slender hands and the proud bones of her face. But now she looked all of her seventy-two years, her face grave and sad under the shadows cast by the hat brim.

"Oh, Alexandria, this time I fear you have gone too far, much too far. Your mother will be so very angry!" She did not add that the anger would be directed at her as well as

8

at the child. Margaret Thaine kept up a kind of emotional blackmail, wanting nothing to do with her daughter but yet wanting no other influence on her either, particularly that of her mother-in-law. In return for the cherishing Virginia gave Alex, they both paid dearly in the aggravation of bearing Margaret's complaints and accusations of bad behavior, and in threats that they should not be allowed so much of each other's company.

Alex had hoped her grandmother would make light of what she had done, but the hope faded in face of the older woman's gravity. This was the source of all comfort and wisdom in her life. It was Virginia who had taught her to read and to reason, Virginia who had taught her to observe nature and the earth with a keen eye, Virginia who continued to teach her the healing properties of plants and of an understanding heart. If her grandmother considered her offense serious, it was.

"What is wrong with everyone?" she protested. "No one seems to care about St. John or even Florence, for that matter. They do not suit. They will make each other so unhappy!"

"They may indeed. But that is their business, not yours, nor anyone else's. Child, surely you have seen enough to know that people will do as they will, sensible or not. And your mother longs for the marriage because, even though the youngest and poor, St. John is of the nobility. Margaret is not alone in wanting such connections." She detested her daughter-in-law so much, she often found herself stretching to be fair. No good would come of making matters worse between Margaret and her youngest child. "You know you will have to go home sooner or later," she added gently. She could not find it in her heart to scold the child further; she knew her too well to suspect that her motive came from anything other than concern for St. John and, to a lesser extent, for her sister. The bruised mark on Alexandria's face seemed punishment enough.

"I know," Alex agreed reluctantly. "But not yet, Grandmother, please, not yet!" She flinched inwardly, already hearing her mother's voice rising in fury.

Virginia let her stay, seeking to ease her apprehension by invoking their old pattern of teacher and student. Girl child or no, this was the brightest of her grandchildren and the most like her husband, Trahern. The child had not only the look of him, but the same quick intelligence. She had recognized it from the first and had given thanks, having by then all but given up hope that she would find a descendant with whom she could leave her peculiar legacy. Her husband and her two oldest sons had been dead for nearly twenty years, victims of the greedy sea, and while her surviving son, Caton, had scholarly leanings, he was always prone to take the easiest way, in thought and in action, anything to avoid dissension. Privately she considered his fathering of Alexandria as one of the few worthwhile acts of his existence. His wife had been an enemy from the first, and the four children who had come before Alexandria were not suited to what Virginia had had in mind. It was as well for a man to know the healing art as for a woman, but it was more usual now for the herbs to be given by women, "wise-women," as they were often called. Despite the oath they swore, too many of the men of formal medicine did more harm than good to their patients, with their violent treatments, seldom considering that those treatments did as much or more damage than the illnesses. Until that changed, there would be the need for the gentler healers.

Virginia was not a mystic though she never negated the power of human will in life and in death. She regarded her craft as just that—a skill to be learned through long and careful work and the study of new discoveries as well as the old. The potential for harm was ever present, and she was too aware that many who would deal in herbs inflicted as much harm as the worst of the medical profession. Though she indulged Alexandria in other things, in this her teaching was strict and relentless, and she had been rewarded from the beginning by the child's ability to learn.

She offered her comfort now in the old ritual. "What if someone came to you and asked for a draught with the skin of a frog, cat's liver, and rue steeped in wine, saying it had cured the ague before and was needed again from the hand of a wise-woman. What would you do?"

Though Alex grinned at the unlikely ingredients, she did not fall into the old trap. "I would have to consider it very carefully to know whether or not it was a trick, the asking I mean. And if I thought it was not, that the person truly believed in such nonsense, then I would have to go very carefully to persuade him or her to let me treat with Cinchona bark instead."

Virginia nodded in approval. "Well said, but you might do better to call it by the old name, the 'English Remedy,' and relate that it cured Charles the Second's fever. That would give the drug even more power to the superstitious. But what if the patient complained of other sickness, not the ague, and yet you found no signs of aught awry? What would you do then?"

"If I cannot help, I must not harm." The words came automatically. "I might in that case have to give something harmless so that the patient's own will would banish the symptoms."

Satisfied, Virginia moved on, touching a tall stalk of purple flowers. "What is this and what is it used for?"

"Foxglove. It is useful to ease dropsy and trouble with the heart, though it must be used with care," Alex replied. "And your bees are very fond of it."

It was an old joke between them, the passionate interest Virginia had in the hives she kept on the farm. She claimed that the orderly workings of the insects soothed her when humankind was too frenzied.

The two of them stood in the warm shelter of the garden listening to the drone of the bees and the birdsong until the peace was shattered by the cheerful voice of Mrs. Rivers, the woman who came most days of the week to help with the housekeeping, thus giving Virginia more time in the gardens and with the sick.

Mrs. Rivers called her greeting again, and Virginia answered before she turned back to Alex. "A cup of tea before you go, my dear, or are you ready to face the dragon?" They both knew it would do no good for her grandmother to go with her.

"Thank you, no tea today. I've tarried long enough. I might as well get it over with." She gave Virginia a swift kiss on the cheek and was gone, lithe and agile in her brother's clothes.

Watching her depart, Virginia thought of how old Alexandria was in some ways, how young in others, and she wished she could spare her all the pain growing to full womanhood would undoubtedly bring.

❦ *Chapter 2* ❧

"Getting it over with" seemed more and more unlikely. Margaret's rage, fueled by Florence's tearful spasms over the defection of St. John, grew by the day. And Alex's misery was deepened by Margaret's refusal to let her leave the house. After only a couple of days, she longed for the outdoors and her grandmother's company as if she had been a prisoner for years.

The violence of her mother's reaction had stunned her. She had expected anger, but not the screaming hysteria that poured over her, nor the slaps that had bruised flesh already tender from Florence's attack. Only now did she understand how much Margaret had been counting on the match with St. John. It had only made matters worse when Alex pointed out that St. John's family was sure to disapprove the match, thus negating any advantage from it. She had learned that her mother was not rational about this subject—any kind of connection was to be avidly sought. She had not known before the extent of her mother's resentment of being no more than a merchant's wife. Even the favored daughter, Florence, was to be sacrificed to the union, albeit in her ignorance she was a willing sacrifice. Or would have been—St. John seemed to have absented himself from the scene. For that, at least, Alex gave thanks.

She and her mother had never been at ease with each other, but somehow Alex had managed to ignore the full burden of it, taking comfort from her grandmother, and to a lesser degree, from Boston, the one among her siblings who seemed kin in spirit, and from her father, Caton, who though retiring and ineffectual in his domestic role, had always seemed to love her.

But now nothing stood between Alex and the force of her mother's dislike, and she could no longer ignore or deny it. It bowed her spirit with its ugly truth. Nothing she would ever be able to do would make her mother love her. Even knowing that it had never been, she felt as if something precious had died. And she felt unclean, unworthy, diminished in ways she could not understand.

Suddenly her mother looked different to her. Before she had appeared to be a fairly prosperous merchant's wife, a rather handsome woman with even features and dark blond hair slowly fading to white. But now her mouth appeared pinched and mean, her blue eyes cold. Even her voice seemed to have sharpened.

Alex wondered if she herself had similarly changed outwardly, becoming ugly to look upon, mean of countenance. She studied her face in the mirror and could see nothing beyond features so familiar to her. But she found herself slinking about the house, avoiding her family's eyes and their presence as much as possible. Not even her sister's rapid shifts from whining to strident blaming could rouse Alex from the apathy that crept over her.

Beyond offering the mild opinion that he thought the females of the household were making too much of little, Caton Thaine stayed out of it, preferring longer hours at the ship chandlery to the dissension at home. Rome and Paris, Alex's older brothers, had their own wives and households in Gravesend, and once they discovered the stormy weather at their parents' house, they made every excuse to stay away. Only Boston, at eighteen five years older than Alex and divorcing himself more and more from the doings of the household as he sought independence, found himself unable to ignore her plight.

He had always had a special fondness for his younger sister, having found her a good sport from the time she was little, unlike Florence who was two years older than he and had always been too fastidious to enjoy rowdy adventures. And though Boston had long since learned to please his mother by saying the right things and staying out of her way, he could not bear to see Alex looking so wan and defeated, particularly since he thought St. John a good fellow and shared Alex's apprehension should the man marry Florence. But he was not so foolhardy as to confront his mother directly; he went instead, as Alex had done, to his grandmother.

He did not have the close bond with Virginia that his sister had, but he loved and respected her.

"How is Alexandria?" she asked anxiously after the briefest of greetings. "I have not yet tried to find out from Caton. He's no use at all as a source of information. I swear my son lives perpetually in the river fog!"

"I'm truly worried about her," Boston replied. "That's why I've come. There must be something you or Father can do! Lexy looks so sad and lost; Mother and Florence are being beastly."

His unconscious use of his old and long discarded pet name for his little sister told Virginia much about the depth of his distress.

His voice was suddenly young and unsure. "I don't like to believe it, but I don't think Mother loves her at all."

Virginia swallowed the angry words that rose in unbidden confirmation. "Parents and children do not always find each other agreeable. And sometimes it takes a good bit of time before there is understanding." The excuse sounded weak to her own ears, but she sensed Boston's need for reassurance, not only for his sister's sake but for his own; he was discomfitted by his changing view of his mother.

"Sometimes it takes a bit of help, too," she added more strongly. "I've stayed away because I knew how much Margaret would resent my interference—Alexandria is, after all, her child—but I haven't been idle. I think it might serve everyone best if Alexandria were to go away for a time. I've written to relatives in the West Country, and I am sure they will take her in. They're related by distant blood to your grandfather Trahern, and I would trust her to them. I am sure the answer will come soon. And in the meantime, I will talk to Caton. At least he can get her out of that house for a day or so, and maybe your mother's temper will cool." Though I doubt it, she added to herself.

"Don't tell Alexandria of my plans, please, but you can assure her that I have not forsaken her."

Boston left with a lighter heart, but Virginia was of a more sober cast when she finally confronted Caton.

It always amazed her, even after all these years, that this sober, clerkish man who was most happy when he

14

was puttering amid the ships' stores he sold could have come from the fiery mating that had been hers with Trahern. The shop was in the old section of Gravesend, in the maze of buildings crowded on the slopes that led down to the Thames. Tar, hemp, and spices blended their scents with the less pleasant odors of refuse and mud, and the district was busy with the constant traffic of seamen, passengers, and all those who supplied the ships' needs. Gravesend had long been regarded as the "Key to the City of London." It was here that customs officers boarded outgoing ships to make sure wool and other taxed or proscribed cargoes were not being taken out of the country. The fort at Gravesend and the one across the river at Tilbury on the Essex shore could cover river traffic in a deadly crossfire thus protecting that major waterway, the Thames. Gravesend was a convenient place for the friends and families of outgoing passengers to say their last good-byes, and a good place, too, for those coming to England to leave the confines of their vessels. Scores of ships London bound with coal and myriad other cargoes waited down the river at Gravesend Reach for the right combination of wind and tide to carry them upriver. And Gravesend itself boasted two ferries of ancient standing, the Long Ferry whose boats could usually make the trip to and from London in one day, barring adverse winds or dangerously dense fogs, and another that took passengers across to the Essex shore.

It was a town teeming with life and commerce, and yet, Caton Thaine always seemed to his mother to be inhabiting some other place, some slow backwater in his own mind. Virginia sometimes envied him this state, but usually it made her impatient, and she did not bother to hide that now, as she addressed him.

"You must do something for Alexandria. You cannot leave her at the mercy of her mother and her sister. They will break her heart, and I will not allow that. Nor should you be willing to see it done."

Caton blinked at her, shifting his attention to his mother from a list of supplies destined for an outbound merchantman. "I am sure the trouble will pass; it always does," he offered mildly.

"You are blind!" Virginia snapped. "And worse. It was your choice to marry that woman, but your children had no choice in their parents, and you have an obligation to protect them from their mother's cruelty." She lifted her hand, waving away his vague protest with a furious gesture. "Yes, cruelty. There's no other word for it. It's time to cease pretending. The others have fared well enough under Margaret's care, but Alexandria is different. She's a rare child, but her mother does not love her, and she is making that too clear now." Briefly she sketched her plans for her granddaughter and added, "But until I can get her away, you must help. You love her, I know you do. Get her out of the house, away from Margaret, at least for a day or two."

Caton loved his mother even as he sometimes flinched from the force of her personality, and he knew how hard she had tried to stay out of his marriage to a woman she had disliked from the first. He had not wanted to think about it, had in fact purposefully avoided thinking about it, but he was suddenly only too aware of how he, also, had come to dislike his wife. He wondered what he had ever seen in her. She had seemed to be what he needed, a capable, pleasant-looking woman who would make a good wife for a man of his standing. But he had not understood her ambition to rise above the station he found so comfortable, nor had he seen the pettiness of her spirit. And he had known for a long time without admitting it that Margaret had somehow chosen her youngest child as the focus of all of her frustrations and anger. He remembered how dismally she had greeted the fact of that last pregnancy and how disappointed she had been to produce a girl. One daughter had been quite enough for her; she had no interest in her own sex and considered sons the only children worth producing, and even they not overly welcomed, but rather a duty. It was an ugly vision of her and of himself that Caton saw now. He did love Alex; she was his elfin child and for too long he had allowed her to be used as the buffer between himself and Margaret's discontent.

Virginia saw the resolution grow in his eyes and the set of his mouth and thought that he was an attractive man after all when he was roused out of his usual befuddled state. The bones of his face were faintly reminiscent of Trahern's strong visage as were the green lights in his hazel eyes. And his thick brown-blond hair just touched with gray was the color her own had been. Not so lost a cause after all if only he would keep to the course of helping his daughter.

"I suppose you came here unescorted?" he protested affectionately, a matter of form since Virginia always did as she pleased.

"Of course I did. I have not found seamen or the citizens of this town to be driven to crazed action by the sight of an old woman." But there was no bite to her words, and they smiled at each other in a rare moment of complete accord.

Caton found it impossible to concentrate on business once his mother had gone. Instead he saw Alex's face before him, saw how woebegone it had appeared lately, and his guilt was profound. It strengthened his resolve. He and Alex would go to London. There was business enough to warrant the trip, but most of all, he knew how it would delight his daughter. Though the city was only thirty-two miles distant by water or twenty-two by land, a visit to it was a major event for her; Alex had only been to the capital a few times in her life. Caton did not make it a habit to take his family on his business trips, and in London, away from Margaret, he felt quite accomplished. His business contacts were good, and he was well respected as a man who paid promptly and fairly for the goods he ordered.

He had slowly expanded his shop so that he met special needs of the resident populace as well as the ships' needs. His private dream was one day to have a store so general in its merchandise that for convenience alone customers would come to his premises first and would there find what they were looking for at a good price and quality. To be sure, the idea of a general mercantile was not original with him, but it was an idea coming ever more into its own, and he saw the variety offered by a ship chandlery as the perfect beginning. Already he carried a fine line of leather, offering everything from saddles to gloves to dressed skins. To keep the quality high he maintained close contact with the leather market in Bermondsey and with various artisans who made finished products. From London, too, came toiletries purchased by gentlemen and their ladies and even by sea captains anxious to smell sweet during their shore leaves. Proximity to London had not hurt his business; he had found that most people liked the ease of shopping close to home and seldom made the trip to London. The location of his shop had not harmed trade either; the people of Gravesend, Milton, and the surrounding countryside were accustomed to the conditions of a port city and were not overly concerned by the presence of rough sailors and their tavern haunts. The presence of customs officers had a salutary effect on behavior.

Caton sighed wistfully. Sometimes he wondered what would become of what he was building. Though he did not face the fact often, deep inside he knew he would never see his dream fulfilled. He supposed Paris or Rome would take over the shop eventually though both of them were now in trade with their wives' families, in groceries and in coal, respectively, experience all to the good. He knew Boston would not be the one. He could sense in his youngest son the spirit of Trahern and Caton's own dead brothers, a certain restlessness and boldness that had already gotten the boy in more than his share of trouble though he was without meanness. Caton wondered if Virginia knew what a burden it was to be the placid one, the one left after the deaths. He had been nineteen when his father and brothers had perished at sea in 1784, and he remembered them as great hardy men, figures from heroic tales. Even knowing it was a distorted image, he could not alter it. It was the wealth they had gleaned from their voyages that had allowed Virginia to keep the property outside of town and had financed the establishment of his own business.

He had never had that urge for adventure that had run in their veins. He had hated the few voyages forced on him and had proven himself a miserable sailor. His true traveling had been in his mind, and the boldest thing he had ever done was to defy Margaret in his insistence that the children should be named for distant cities. Even Boston was named not for the city in the north of England but for the one in the New World, an important distinction in Caton's mind. Paris, Rome, Florence, Boston, and Alexandria—they were not only his children, they were the conjuring names of faraway places, adventures he would never have.

Ropes, nets, navigation instruments, carpentry tools, sailcloth, ships' biscuits, tea, coffee, sugar, flour, on and on, he surveyed his domain carefully, drawing strength from it before he bid his clerks a polite good day and went home to face Margaret, home to the house he had never cared for much. Spurs of the North Downs reached clear to the shore at Gravesend, giving it a character different from the prevailing low marshy shores along the Thames. And on an elevation higher than the waterfront, the house sat among other residences, removed from the bustle of commerce though still sharing a view of the river. Margaret was not the sort to live above a shop. Caton wished he hadn't taken so long to learn that.

❧ Chapter 3 ❧

Alex began to think that surely her mother knew her well, else she could not have devised so keen a punishment. To have nothing to do was the worst sort of torment. Margaret did not think domestic chores were suitable for her station in life, and she had long since delegated them to daily women who came to cook and clean. They were not unkind, but they could not afford to risk their positions by letting Alex share their work or, indeed, by being too friendly to her. At least Margaret had not thought to take away her books, and so Alex read and studied, but with no access to her grandmother or to her brothers' old tutor, Mr. Buckman, her mind felt curiously dull and unwilling, too sad to stir with its usual curiosity. The same lethargy infected her fingers when she tried to work on the tiny garments for the son or daughter that would be born soon to Paris and his wife, Jane. Her body felt as leaden as her mind. Her mother observed that she was at least beginning to act like a lady; Florence muttered that you couldn't make a silk purse from a sow's ear.

With despairing wonder, Alex began to realize that this

state of inactivity so burdensome to her was to her mother and her sister a mark of social distinction. She recalled going with her grandmother to attend a farmer's wife who complained of various ailments. Virginia's diagnosis had been swift and uncompromising because she had known Mrs. Pennyrose for a long time.

"It's not my simples you need, it's hard work and less food," she had told the woman. "And for your daughters, too. The profits Mr. Pennyrose is making from this war will bury you if you continue to live like a Christmas goose in early December."

Mrs. Pennyrose had actually been relieved by the advice; she was not happy in her idle life. But Virginia had complained all the way home about this new plague. "It's not enough that it's damaged many of those with old wealth, now it must spread to the newly rich, to those who were wont to be honest farmers and merchants whose wives worked as hard as they. What a travesty, to make it fashionable for a woman to be useless! What a mark of gain! Perhaps it would have happened anyway, but I'll blame Napoleon Bonaparte once more. The war with him has gone on so long, there is no sense to the price of grain or anything else!"

Her grandmother was right, Alex thought, idleness was a plague. It had long since claimed her mother and sister though she had only noticed now as it settled over her.

The first ray of light came from Boston. She knew he felt sorry for her, but she didn't expect him to interfere, and she hadn't seen much of him since her incarceration had begun. He had sent her encouraging glances and had managed to sneak little gifts, a new book on flowers and packets of sweetmeats, and she thought that very brave and kind of him. But now, even before he spoke, she sensed his excitement.

Once he had ascertained that his mother and Florence were out visiting neighbors, he spoke urgently. "Grandmother Thaine hasn't forgotten you. She's thinking of something to make things better!"

Alex's reaction was dismay. "Oh, Boston! Mother will be even more angry!"

"Does it really matter?" he asked gently, hating the look of fear in her eyes, bold Alex who had never seemed fearful before. "As long as things change. I don't see how it could be worse for you."

It was there between them, unspoken but clear, the acknowledgment of Margaret's lack of love for her daughter.

"You're right," Alex agreed, her voice low, eyes overly bright. "Thank you for going to Grandmother."

She did not see what her grandmother could do because she had not counted on her father's change of heart. Boston had gone, and her mother and sister had returned by the time Caton charged into the house. There was no other word for the force of his entry, so unlike his usual quiet coming and going, and hours earlier than he normally returned home. There was a new firmness to his stance, and his voice was decidedly grim though still polite when he asked his wife if he might have a word with her in private.

Margaret looked like nothing so much as a startled cat confronted by a mouse suddenly endowed with fangs. Alex and Florence watched wide-eyed as their parents left the room.

And then the shouting began, on one side at least. They could not hear what Caton was saying, but Margaret was using more volume here and there. "London! . . . Take her to . . . You must be mad you . . . She has ruined . . ."

The disjointed phrases continued to filter through, intelligible enough to darken Florence's face with anger and to make Alex doubt what she was hearing.

When the couple emerged, there was no doubt who was the victor. Margaret's face was crimson, and she no longer made any pretense as she glared at Alex with open dislike. "You are to go to London with your father on the morrow. See that you're ready," she snapped, and she left the room followed by a sputtering Florence who couldn't seem to ask the questions she had in mind.

Father and daughter looked at each other for a long moment, and Caton's heart flinched at the conflicting emotions he saw on Alex's face. "It's true," he said. "You are to go with me to London, and we will spend the night there. You did not act in malice when you spoke to St. John, but you have been treated with nothing save malice since. It is unjust, and I want an end to it."

Wordless with gratitude, Alex went to him and felt his arm come around her, strong and warm. Unlikely though it was, he seemed the very perfect knight come to rescue her.

She did not see her mother or her sister before she left,

but she felt the uneasy movement in the house. She and her father ate supper together with Boston who came in just in time to share the meal and could not stop grinning over the turn of events. Florence did not even come to bed in the room she shared with Alex, and Alex imagined her sister and her mother barricaded in her parents' bed chamber, safe behind their wall of outrage. She was quite sure her father had sought his rest in the boys' room, now Boston's.

She lay awake for a long time thinking of how complicated everything had become since her fateful intervention in St. John's affairs. But she was coming to understand that her outburst had only been the flame set to a powder keg that had existed for a long time. That she would never be able to think of her home and family as being secure again was something she did not want to contemplate.

She and her father left with the tide on one of the tilt boats of the Long Ferry, paying the fixed one shilling fare. Though the decks were now secured and had been for decades and more shelter was offered the passengers than in past ages, the old nomenclature was still used. The Thames watermen were a rare breed who did things according to their own traditions. In particular, those of Gravesend had had the privilege of ferrying passengers to and from London since at least 1400 when the monopoly had been given to them to ameliorate the loss caused by the sacking of the town by the French in 1377. The watermen did not take their rights lightly; it was due to their pressure that Gravesend still had no extensive quays for the unloading of passengers and cargo—both were still handled almost entirely by the watermen who brought them ashore from wherever the ships were anchored in the river.

Caton did not resent their power; on the contrary, he admired their independence and knew most of them by name, so the trip to London was pleasant with friendly exchanges between passengers and the small crew.

Alex loved the Thames, and even having been reared so close to it, she had never lost her respect for it. It was the mightiest waterway in the western world because it led to London, the major commercial center of that world. No enemy had reached the city since the Norman Conquest, and thus its safety insured its success as a clearing house for goods coming from and going to countless destinations. Even with the Continent roiling with war and closed to British shipping, business went on in London via the Thames.

The tide in the river flowed for five hours and ebbed back toward the sea for seven before changing again, and the strong current, the sails when useful, and the sturdy backs of the oarsmen carried the boat swiftly toward the city. Alex was rapt with joy as she tried to see everything, from the flowers growing on the river banks to the seemingly endless variety of vessels. Though many of the colliers, the coal-bearing vessels, were unloaded below Gravesend to avoid the tax that extended from London to Gravesend, many carried fuel destined for the city itself, and even in the summer, the greatest number of boats were these. The dark dust that hung over unloading areas and the smoke that often choked the city gave proof of the enormous appetite for fuel in a country where wood had long been in short supply.

Gravesend itself was a port for a considerable fleet of deep-sea fishing boats, and they added to the traffic near the town. For about thirteen miles on this first stretch of river the activity was on the water, not the land which was for the most part desolate marsh with a farmhouse or small riverside town here and there. Here, the voyage was relaxing for the river pilots who boarded the big ships at Gravesend as the depth of water was usually sufficient in all tides, unlike other parts of the river where the depth varied greatly and acute bends of the river necessitated precise navigation to keep ships from running aground.

Alex enjoyed the rather bleak landscape for the flowers and shore birds that livened it in summer, but her interest quickened when they passed Barking, which smelled of tar, pitch, and the fish of its major industry, and then the Royal Docks at Woolwich and past the East India docks at Blackwall. The big East Indiamen could not navigate further upriver and so had permission to unload their dutiable goods here, following strict rules for the disposition of cargoes.

The City of London, the commercial heart of not only London but the whole country, had long guarded her monopolies. The busiest part of the city had had no other bridge than the London Bridge until as late as 1745 simply because the City did not want to lose her control of the traffic across the river. Likewise she had benefitted from severe restrictions on where dutiable goods could be landed. Ships other than the East Indiamen had long been required to come upriver to unload at specified "Legal Quays" or at Sufferance Wharves, the latter allowed little by little to help ease congestion at the former. Covered lighters were also used to unload dutiable goods and take them to Legal Quays and warehouses elsewhere.

But the sheer volume of growth in both the City of London and trade in general was forcing more changes. Just as new bridges were built, new dockyards were springing up along the river and additional sites were being approved for the receiving of dutiable goods. Still, the changes were coming more slowly than the increase in traffic, and the river was crowded with all manner of vessels from launches and lighters, the former to unload passengers from ships in midriver, the latter to handle the cargo from the same, to the deepwater sailing ships. The bulge of the "Isle of Dogs" which was part of the great "S" curve so difficult for big ships to navigate had not been solved by a new project—a canal cut across the Isle to shorten and straighten the journey had already proved of little use for that purpose because of the time it took for vessels to be towed through by gangs of men or rowboats, but at least it had provided sites for yet more docks that were already beginning to be established. The West India Dock, built in 1802, had its own Legal Quays and great success.

On the left bank, opposite the Isle of Dogs, was the lovely palace and town of Greenwich rising steeply from the riverside to the heights of Blackheath. The Queen's House was now a Royal Navy hospital, and work was still going on to build colonnades east and west to provide sheltered areas of play for the children of the Royal Hospital Schools. Alex remembered vividly the time when Caton had taken her on a walk through the park to a high spot from which they had had a magnificent view of London. Boston had been with them for that rare outing, and they had laughed a great deal. It saddened her now to think that even then everything had been better when her mother was not present.

Caton was spending more time watching his daughter than the familiar sights along the Thames. It was as if he were seeing Alexandria clearly for the first time. He wondered how he had missed the stages that had changed her from a small child to this tall slender creature on the verge of womanhood. Her clothes were quite dreadful; it didn't take a woman's eye to discern that, and inwardly he cursed Margaret anew. With all the money that went for fashion in his household, surely Alexandria could have worn something more flattering than the insipid pinkish garment and shabby coat. He doubted Alex cared much, but her mother could easily have provided something better for so striking a girl. Through him she had inherited the blood of his father, the green eyes, the dark hair, the boldly sculpted features, and he suspected something more, the sense of adventure, of facing life in a way he himself never could. He had no illusions. He knew he would not be able to maintain this new sternness with Margaret. In the long run, it would be too hard, take more energy than he had. He knew in a sense that he was saying both hello and good-bye to this the youngest of his children. He knew Virginia was more than right in her plan to spirit Alexandria away from Gravesend, and he was more determined than ever that this time in London would be a delight Alex would long remember.

They passed the Tower, the grim Norman keep that had been built to remind the power of the City that the power of the Crown existed, too. Further on was Billingsgate, long the site of a fish market where the Dutch had free mooring because they had kept bringing eels to the City during the Great Plague centuries before. Alex fancied that even were the fishmongers to quit the place, the smell of their trade would linger for centuries after. From the earthy to the sublime, she raised her eyes to the spires of London's churches, many the work of Sir Christopher Wren, lacing the skyline along with the "Monument," a column erected in 1677 close to the spot where the Great Fire of 1666 had started in Pudding Lane.

She shivered in anticipation as they neared their landing place. She had not been to London enough times in her life to have grown accustomed to the enormous energy that assaulted the senses. Street vendors hawked their wares, offering everything from fish to bread to posies. Dirty urchins darted about with a keen eye to anything dropped or left unattended. Beggars sporting a variety of ailments—some real, some not, and the difference hard to tell—whined their own cries. And everywhere men of business moved briskly in their search for profit. The stench of a large population with only crude means for disposal of waste and refuse was so overwhelming that it quickly numbed the sense of smell, for which Alex was grateful. Even though Gravesend was also on the river and had its fleet of fishing boats, it smelled positively fresh compared to London.

Worst of all was Bermondsey where leather was worked and dog dung was used in the process, supplied by "mudlarks," usually small boys who collected the loathsome stuff. Caton and Alex proceeded there on foot over the London Bridge to the south side of the river after they'd left their small bundles at the narrow-fronted river inn where they would spend the night. Here the stench was so penetrating it was hard to ignore, but Alex did her best because she understood suddenly why they had come.

It was not just that Caton had business to conduct, it was also that he wanted his daughter to see how well respected he was by the people he dealt with in his business world.

The ruse was so transparent, Alex's heart ached for him, but she made sure her comments were enthusiastic and flattering. It was enough just to be with her father. They spent most of the day visiting Caton's various contacts, but their pace was leisurely, and there was no lack of interesting sights to see. Alex felt as if she'd stretched her neck two inches at least simply by gawking at the incredible variety of people that filled London's streets.

And when the perfect summer day seeped into long twilight, Caton paid her the highest compliment by taking her to Vauxhall Gardens just as if she were a young lady of the town. She knew how unsuitable her mother would judge the outing and how envious Florence would be, and that made it all the more fun.

The pleasure gardens were surely the most democratic place in London, for there all classes mixed, judged only by whether or not they had the price of admission. Because Southwark was the area right across the London Bridge from the heart of the City's commerce, this part of the south bank had seen the most development. The Vauxhall Pleasure Gardens, laid out in both formal walks of trees and shrubs and in wilder more secret walks on the outside perimeter for younger people, had begun in 1661. Balls, plays, and musical performances were held in the fanciful buildings in the center, and the popularity of the place sometimes caused huge traffic jams on London Bridge.

It didn't matter to Alex that there were bawds in tawdry dresses selling their dubious wares with a glance and a wiggle or that there were many young couples, who should have known better, stealing off for illicit pleasure on the "dark walks." She took it all in with wide eyes, seeing it in the whirling rainbow colors of a fairytale. She envied no one that night.

The fireworks cast dancing light on her upturned face, and Caton was as enchanted with her as she was with the gardens. She gave him a sense that it had all been worthwhile if only to produce this child. He felt a surge of paternal love that startled him with its intensity.

"No matter what happens, Alexandria, always know that I love you. I would not change a single thing about you," he said softly. "I am very proud of you, Daughter."

She looked at him, unshed tears catching the myriad lights of the evening, and then she hugged him, murmuring, "Thank you, I love you, too. And I've never had so lovely a day." She sensed as he had that they would never be so close again though she was unsure as to why this should be so. She only hoped that he understood the depth of her gratitude for the respite he had given her from her mother's wrath.

They indulged themselves with hot pasties that warmed them against the chill that came from the Thames even in summer, and Caton made Alexandria feel as if she were a grown woman when he allowed her a glass of wine while he drank the dark ale he preferred. They listened to the music coming from various parts of the gardens, and they watched impromptu games of chance and the games of flirtation being played not only by the young but, also, by those long past the first blush.

"Do you ever wish you were from a different sort of family?" Caton asked her. "I mean the sort of family that would have seen that you had your season in London in a few years." Many of the young women they had observed were obviously members of the *ton*, undoubtedly here with their gallants without the permission of chaperones. A wicked adventure for them to come to Vauxhall.

"Never!" Alex answered without hesitation. "I've seen girls like that at the Carringtons', and Father, they don't seem to know anything of use. They have no idea of how to run a house or a farm. And they're sold like cattle at market when they have their season in London; it's for no reason save to be given to a man of their class, just like putting a purebred cow to a purebred bull."

Caton hid a smile. It was unsaid but understood by both that what she had said applied very well to Florence. "Well, I'm glad you don't feel the lack," he commented drily. "And if you remember even half of what your grandmother has taught you, you will always be a useful person to have about."

He thought perhaps he ought to warn her of Virginia's plan for her to go to the West Country, but he decided not to risk the good time they were sharing. And in any case, it was not yet a certainty. He could feel his new forceful self fading and could do nothing to bring it back.

✺ Chapter 4 ✺

The euphoria of the London trip stayed with Alexandria, making her impervious to her mother's continued cold disapproval and Florence's spite. She was no longer confined to the house, and that was all that mattered. Once again her time was spent with her grandmother, learning and working at a plethora of tasks. The summer had been mild and sunny, insuring bountiful crops. All summer long Virginia had been sending vegetables to local markets and to London, and soon the day laborers would come from London to harvest the hops which would then be dried in the oast house before shipment for sale in London. Virginia was more generous than most employers with the workers and allowed them harvest play along with the work so that though her crop was not enormous, those who worked for her were faithful and came to her first. The fruits of the orchards—peaches, plums, cherries, and apples—came in their various seasons, and those Virginia had picked by contract, the contractor leaving a percentage of the crop as payment.

Alex loved the orderly progression of work on Virginia's land; she had always found steady reassurance in one season following another, each one sweet and distinct for its own virtues, and she would not have traded any one of them for all the glories of London.

When she learned she was to trade all that was familiar for exile in the West Country, her immediate reaction was complete disbelief.

"It really will be for the best," Virginia continued in the same gentle voice she had used to broach the subject.

Alex stared at her. "What will be for the best?"

"For you to go to stay with the Falconers in Devonshire," Virginia repeated, watching Alexandria closely. "They are distant cousins on your grandfather's side, and long ago, he and I did a favor for Magnus Falconer and his father. Magnus was only fourteen years old then. We have not had much contact these past years, but there has been word now and then, and I have seen Magnus once or twice." Word about business Alex had no knowledge of; time enough for her to learn of it. "I know Magnus for a good man with a good family. It will be a much better place for you for the time being." She saw that the information was finally registering in her granddaughter's mind, and she steeled herself against the pain she saw rising in the green eyes.

"It is all arranged, and they are prepared to welcome you as soon as we can travel there. I will go with you. We'll take the mail coach. And then I will return here."

"I am to go live with strangers, away from here?" It wasn't really a question. Alex was simply fulfilling the need to hear the awful fact in her own words. The expression on her grandmother's face told her that there was no mistake and no reprieve. The agony of betrayal knifed through her. This place, this person had always been her refuge. Distantly she heard her grandmother assuring her that it was her idea, agreed to by Caton for her good, but she knew that the victory was her mother's and her sister's after all. In her wildest imaginings, she would not have conjured this punishment. She denied the threatening tears and drew inward, blocking out the warmth of the August sun and the sounds of the earth.

Desolation as cold as winter swept through both of them, but Virginia clung fiercely to her conviction that her plan was best for the child. "Dear God," she prayed inwardly, "let her be happy there!"

Virginia and Caton made all the arrangements even to the overseeing of Virginia's land. If she wasn't back in time for the hop harvest, he would see to it. This was something he could do; serving as a buffer between his wife and his daughter was a much harder task and one he knew he was not competent to perform.

Alex took no interest in any of the preparations. Her father insisted she have new clothes and they were hastily made by a well-paid seamstress, but for all Alex cared, they might have been for someone else. The barbs thrown by the sharp voices of her mother and sister failed to penetrate as did the awkward comfort Boston tried to offer. Her older brothers and their wives offered stiff comments about what an adventure it all was, and they might have been strangers for all the notice Alex took of them. She had withdrawn into a cold lonely place, and there she stayed even when she and her grandmother had gone to London by the Long Ferry and were aboard the coach bound for the West Country, going overland because, except for the ride on the ferry, Virginia did not trust ships of any sort; the sea had taken more than she was willing to give. And though the Falconers had offered to come by sea to collect Alex, Virginia wanted the travel time with her.

Caton accompanied them as far as London, spending the day there as they waited for the evening departure. To avoid the crowding at the General Post Office yard, the guards for the West of England mails brought the letter bags from the GPO by pony cart and met their coaches at West End inns such as the Gloucester Coffee House in Piccadilly where the Thaines waited. There passengers and luggage were loaded.

The mail coaches were so punctual, many country people set their clocks by them, and news of victories over Napoleon had been brought to these people throughout the land by these coaches. They were painted maroon, scarlet, and gold, the royal carriage colors, and the guard wore the scarlet royal livery and was armed and prepared to defend the mails. The coachman was not so gaudily decked, being an employee not of the Post Office but of the contractors who provided the horses. Horses were hard used in the mail service, and even with the ever-improving breeding for strength and speed founded on the Yorkshire Cleveland Bay, the horses seldom lasted more than three years on the road. They were raced hard in eight- or ten-mile stages and then replaced by new teams in a relay system.

There were many other vehicles on the road in addition to the mail coaches. Commercial stage coaches were beginning to take some of the mail coaches' business, offering the amenity of stopping for the night at various inns. And in the daylight, the roads were also crowded with carts, riders, private carriages, herds of sheep and cattle, sailors en route to join their ships, soldiers going to help keep watch on the coast, and all manner of other travelers. All in all, being on the road was exciting for Virginia, despite the swaying, jolting motion, and should surely have been for one as young as Alex.

But Alex had simply removed herself from the proceedings. She had neither responded nor drawn away when her father had hugged her before assisting her into the coach. She had regarded him with calm, blank eyes that had made him feel more guilty than had she hurled angry words at him. Squeezed in with her grandmother and other passengers, she took no note of where she was as the coach sped along the Exeter Road through Dorchester. She ate and drank and used the primitive facilities at the brief rest stops, but it was as if her body were a mechanical toy and had no connection with her mind.

Though the coaches were going faster every year with better horses and better road surfaces financed by the toll system of turnpiking, it still took them more than twenty-four hours to reach the cathedral city of Exeter. Virginia was by then thoroughly relieved to leave the coach, though they would board yet another one on the morrow.

She had planned the trip carefully after discovering that there was only one coach a week to Bideford. She had no intention of tarrying in Exeter overlong and was glad now that the next stage of their journey would begin so soon. There was surely no use in trying to interest Alexandria in the sights of this major city of southwest Devon. Virginia clung grimly to her purpose, counting on everything being better once they were safely in Clovelly. But it was difficult not to fear failure in the presence of this dim changeling. She was quite sure that the other passengers on the coach had assumed the child to be simple. She kept expecting to see the real Alexandria peeking out from behind the façade, but the green eyes remained flat and lifeless.

They spent the night in a respectable inn and boarded the coach for Bideford the next day. As fit as she was, Virginia found her bones protesting the long miles of the previous day, and she longed for journey's end. But there was still a good day's travel before them to Bideford, and Clovelly was another jaunt. She turned her attention from her aches and pains to the countryside. She had only been to Clovelly once and that had been by sea on Trahern's ship. Magnus Falconer had only been nine or ten at the time. It was his father they had gone to visit. She studied the rolling terrain and with relief she found Devon pleasing to the eye. They were passing to the north of Dartmoor and further north in the county lay Exmoor, both of these regions worlds unto themselves containing land so harsh that even now it was hardly settled. But their way lay through lush valleys, one after another, the wealth of the land visible in the herds of cattle and sheep grazing there. It was wilder country than the Kent of Gravesend, and Virginia was comforted. From Devon had come great seamen and explorers—Hawkins, the Burrough brothers, Drake, Raleigh, Grenville, and others. It was a land that had room for the adventurous heart; it would have room for Alexandria, too.

She glanced at her granddaughter and still there was no flicker of interest there. But it would come, surely it would.

At Bideford they were met by Seadon, the second Falconer son. He had no trouble identifying them, and Virginia saw at once that it was not only because the combination of an older woman and a young girl was expected. She smiled at him, remembering how much the look of the Thaines Magnus had claimed his wife, Gweneth, had. Seadon was a large, well-muscled man in his late twenties, his hazel eyes merry and kind in his weathered face, his brown hair sun streaked.

He laughed aloud as he introduced himself, adding, "You'll pardon my gawking, I hope, but you, Miss Thaine,

32

have so much the look of my mother and my little brother, it's as if you could be my sister born."

"How interesting," Alex replied politely, feeling shy and ill at ease. But Virginia saw the first spark of life in her eyes as she considered the idea that there were others like her here.

Seadon sensed her unease and turned his attention to Virginia. "Ma'am, it is your choice. We can go along to Clovelly as there's light enough yet on these summer eves, or we can bide here for the night. My brother Elwyn and I married Bideford lasses, Susannah and Barbary, sisters they are, and their parents would be glad to have us if you are too weary to go on now."

Virginia was tempted to take the offered rest, but her anxiety to get Alexandria settled with the Falconers won out. Though he was too well mannered to say so, she suspected Seadon would be just as glad to be going home. She liked the young man more by the minute. He simply ignored Alexandria's lack of response, easing her tense silence by chatting happily about their surroundings as he drove the cart along.

Bideford was a lovely town boasting a twenty-four arch long-bridge over the River Torridge and steepled buildings leading up from the quay.

"This is Bridgeland Street," Seadon said as they moved along a broad, tree-lined avenue by the river. "These fine houses were built by rich merchants, most early in the last century when this was one of the busiest ports in all of England. Great loads of tobacco came in from America and profits, too, from the cod fishery on the Newfoundland Banks and from other goods. Times have changed; the war with the Colonies ended much of the trade, and there's far less traffic up the river now, but it's still a fine town."

Virginia nearly chuckled aloud at the smile he gave as he said it; he was obviously thinking of his Bideford wife. Everything about Seadon reassured her; she could scarcely wait to have Alexandria enfolded by his family.

They went along at a brisk pace, the cart pulled by two horses that showed their mixed blood from Exmoor ponies in the mealy markings on their muzzles.

"They're good beasts, sturdy and enduring. There's hardly a better cross for that than the ponies. Every year they have wild days on Exmoor, bringing them in to sell. I went once and had a grand time." The fondness Seadon had for Devon and every aspect of the land was clear in his words. And he was a sharp young man. He had sensed suddenly that the child was beginning to pay attention even if she wasn't offering anything in return.

"We keep the horses with other livestock on our farm. It's a small bit of land a little way from Clovelly. Barbary and I live there though we have help because I, my brothers, and father are all bound to the sea. Still, the land is there should we need it. My mother is the one who insisted on that. She's not overtrusting of the sea."

"Clever woman; I'm in complete accord with her. But the sea, does it still make the risk worthwhile for you?" Virginia asked.

"The herring shoals have been running less lately, and that's hard on many in Clovelly, but we trade in other goods, so the Falconers have been fortunate." His cryptic reply was clear to Virginia though it meant nothing to Alex. The old trade was still going on. She smiled, remembering how her husband had loved the excitement of it.

They continued west on a rough track that paralleled the sea closely enough so that gulls and other sea birds wheeled over them, crying in the twilight. The countryside was sparsely populated; a couple of tiny villages and a few isolated farmsteads were all that marked the presence of human beings.

Finally they turned north and came in sight of the sea and Clovelly.

Covertly, Virginia watched Alex, and she was not disappointed. The green eyes widened and the sad mouth rounded into a circle of surprise; her dull indifference was no match for the sight before her.

Alex blinked and looked again, but the vision remained. The village spilled six hundred feet down a steep hillside to the quay and the harbor, the trim houses looking as if they clung to their perches by sheer will. A variety of ships dotted the sea, water iridescent in the last of the sun.

"Are you going to drive the cart down there?" Alex asked, her voice sounding rusty from disuse.

Seadon laughed aloud. "Indeed not! There's only the one cobblestone way winding down—'Down-along' it's called going that way, 'Up-along' if you're climbing back up—and though there're donkeys to pull goods up and down on sledges, if you're able to walk, that's what you do in Clovelly. A good pull on the legs it is, too, until you're accustomed to it. Come now, I'll take you to my mother. Don't worry about your belongings, I'll bring them along after."

Alex felt as if she had stepped into the pages of a fairytale. Never had she been in an odder place. But the urge to lean back to keep from falling over as she walked down the angling cobbled lane was real enough as were the voices greeting Seadon from many of the cottages. Doors were open to the balmy night, and the smells of supper drifted out. Much of what was said to Seadon was beyond her understanding, so thick was the West Country burr, changing even a simple word such as "from" into "vrum," but the gist of many of the comments was clear. "Gweneth's got her girl at last," she deciphered from what sounded like, "Gweneth's gurt her gurl art larst."

And then they were stopping at a well-kept house halfway down the hill. Flowers bloomed in profusion in front of it as they did before many, adding their sweet scents to the salt air, and a woman was greeting them, the pleasure clear in her voice. "Oh, I'm so glad you decided to come the rest of the way! I've been so anxious to see you. Welcome, Mrs. Thaine, welcome, Alexandria." She checked in stunned amazement as the soft light inside the cottage illuminated Alex's face. "My soul!" she exclaimed. "It's pure Thaine you are, no doubt! What a delight!" Her face was suddenly bright with mischief. "Wait until you meet my youngest. He and his father will be here shortly; the ship is in."

It was all a blur to Alex, but she could not doubt the genuine welcome being offered nor could she miss the resemblance between herself and Gweneth Falconer. They were much alike in their green eyes and tall slender builds, though Gweneth's hair was streaked with silver and her face was quite different, squarish rather than oval and exotically boned like Alex's.

Quickly on a first name basis, Gweneth and Virginia chatted happily and deliberately, letting Alex make her own adjustment. Matter of factly, Gweneth showed them the necessary house out back and the basin for washing, and then she served them tea and soon had food on the table, too. Seadon reappeared with their luggage, having availed himself of one of the sledges. He bid them good-night and went off to the farm. He gave his mother a quick hug and a kiss as he left, obviously accustomed to displaying his affection and unabashed in the presence of strangers.

Alex studied her surroundings carefully. Everything gleamed with use and care. It was not a lavish display, but neither was it a poor establishment. Even the cooking pots were of good metal brightly polished as was the wood of the furniture and the planked floor. Here and there were bright touches: porcelain from China, Turkey carpets, vessels of beaten brass, and other treasures brought back over distant seas, things that reminded Alex of her grandmother's house.

She found herself eating the food set before her with more appetite than she had had since she had first been told she was to come here.

She heard someone else enter the cottage, and she looked up and knew for certain that she was indeed in some strange kingdom.

Rane Falconer was tired. The voyage to France had been a hard one with winds fickle and the revenue cutters much in evidence. They'd had to hide the goods in caves far down the coast the previous night rather than in the ones convenient to Clovelly. It meant more trouble retrieving them, by land or by sea. But right now, all Rane wanted to do was sleep. He usually felt this way after time on board with his father; Magnus was an exacting taskmaster, and Rane's eighteen-year-old body, tall and lanky, always seemed to crave more food and sleep than were allowed on the ship. He rearranged his plans to include eating anything his mother offered him before he fell into bed.

He had forgotten all about the distant cousin who was coming to stay with them. He had thought little of the matter at all except to consider that it would be nice for his mother to have a girl child to coddle; with three living sons, Gweneth declared herself more than content, but Rane knew she regretted the loss of two infant daughters, both dead at birth years apart and years ago.

He remembered the expected visitors as soon as he entered the house and heard his mother speaking to someone, but nothing eased his shock at his first sight of Alexandria Thaine.

It was like looking into an enchanted mirror that reflected his own image in female form. The planes of their faces were very similar, the dark hair of both framing the features, and green eyes met green eyes in stunned recognition. He heard the older woman gasp, but he and Alexandria remained silent for a long, wondering moment.

Now Alex understood why the various reactions—Seadon's, the villagers', Gweneth's—to her had been so strong. This resemblance went far beyond the similar family traits she shared with Gweneth.

And then Rane smiled at her, a warm welcoming smile that lighted his tired face. "Well, cousin, we would be hard pressed to deny kinship. I'm Rane, R-a-n-e, not R-a-i-n. Welcome to Clovelly." He had a sudden urge to hug her and reassure her as if she were even younger than her age; she looked so scared and somehow fragile, her eyes too big in her thin face and shadows making them seem even larger. She was holding herself stiffly upright, as if only pride were keeping her from bolting though she essayed a small attempt at a smile when he spelled his name.

Even Virginia had lost her composure for a moment, seeing her husband as he had been so many years ago. But the young man had eased the tension in the room, and talk flowed smoothly again though Rane was careful to speak of the recent voyage only in general terms, knowing the child was ignorant of the lucrative trade, for so much her grandmother had told them in her letters.

The cold knot of misery that had gripped Alex since she had first heard of her exile to the West Country began to ease, thawed in some mysterious way by the mere presence of this tall young man. It was hard not to stare at him; it would take time to grow accustomed to this shared image. And she could not begin to understand why the features she found displeasing in herself should be so handsome in him. She had long known that her tall earthy looks had nothing in common with current fashion, her wild dark hair and green eyes so strong and vivid that she seemed out of place even in her own family. But the same in him formed a marvelous symmetry and seemed fitting for an inhabitant of this strange village by the sea.

Her reflections were halted abruptly by the arrival of

Magnus Falconer. He was such a large, hardy man that she shrank back a little, watching him cautiously. He, too, had the look of the Thaine blood. Alex and Rane shared a Thaine great-great-great-great-grandfather, and that same man had been great-great-great grandfather to both Magnus and Gweneth. But in Magnus the Thaine look was changed as it was in Seadon to hazel eyes set in a broad, strong face weathered by the seas, his hair tawny from age and the elements. He reminded Alex of a great roaring lion. His voice seemed too big for the space, and he moved like a large cat, too, with swift economy, not the usual rolling gait of a seaman on land. But then an extraordinary change took place as he greeted the visitors.

"Welcome, ma'am, it's been much too long since I last saw you. And this must be Alexandria. Well, lass, I hope you'll enjoy your time with us. My Gwenny has long wanted a daughter to spoil."

It was not so much the kind words that reassured her as it was the unspoken communication between Magnus and Gweneth. This big, hard man was gentled by the mere presence of his wife, and his wife regarded him as fondly as if he were a small child who had just done something very clever. Love shimmered between them, a nearly visible river of light.

It fascinated Alex. She was so accustomed to the coldness between her own parents, she had not known this warmth could exist. The cold inside her thawed another degree, and for the first time, it occurred to her that this exile might not be so bleak after all.

Virginia saw the bruised wary look in Alexandria's eyes fade to be replaced by alert interest, and she breathed an inward sigh of relief. She knew it was for the best for the child to be here, but she wanted to weep for the fear she had felt in her and had not been able to ease with mere words. The trust between them was so precious to her, her heart could not bear the loss.

✧ Chapter 5 ✧

Alex awakened to the sound of gulls crying and the faintest light of dawn. After a moment of disoriented panic, she remembered where she was, and she lay in bed thinking how odd it was to be in a place where the sun touched later than it did to the east in Gravesend. She pictured it creeping upwards until it was high enough to surmount the cliff that held Clovelly. And then she thought of another oddity; she felt as if a huge burden had been lifted away, as if suddenly she were light enough to fly. She was still unsure of how she would fit into life here, but she was no longer filled with the cold, paralyzing despair. "R-a-n-e, not R-a-i-n," the voice and the image ran through her mind, and she smiled.

Her grandmother was sleeping exhaustedly beside her, and Alex studied the proud face for a moment, all the love for this old woman flooding back through her. Virginia would never do anything to harm her; she felt ashamed for having believed it so.

She slipped out of bed and dressed as quietly as she could, but Virginia was so weary from the long journey that she didn't stir.

The room they shared was one of three on the first floor of the house, and though it was small, everything about it bespoke comfort and simple beauty from the heavy wooden beams of the ceiling to the shining floor. A bowl of flowers had been left on the chest of drawers, and the curtains at the windows as well as the bed linens were sparkling white. A small fireplace would help warm the room in winter. Beeswax, rather than tallow candles, had been provided, and there were books on a stand near the window. Even the closestool was of fine wood and porcelain. Best of all, there was a view of the sea from the window. It was over the rooftop of the next house down, but it could be seen clearly. Alex drew breath softly as she looked out; it was all there as it had been the evening before, this magical place. Already there was activity in the harbor, small boats putting out and some being rowed in, some fair sized vessels near the quay and some larger riding at anchor further out. A mist of smoke hung over the scene from the lime kilns on the beach.

The family's sleeping quarters were above, the rooms made accessible by a stair that twisted up from the end of the hall that divided the ground floor from front to back door. Downstairs on the sea side of the hall were two rooms—a small parlor and the bedroom Alex and Virginia were sharing. And across the hall was the kitchen and dining area, one large room except for a small storage pantry at the back. The kitchen had a window on the street and a couple of small ones faced the houses above and the cliff. It was a house designed for comfort, and the kitchen was the heart of it, not tucked away out of sight, but a gathering place.

After a trip outside, Alex made her way down the hall, stopping when she heard sounds coming from the kitchen. Cautiously she opened the door, calling a soft greeting so as not to startle whoever was within.

She was met by Gweneth's happy voice. "Well, another child of the morning! The tea is hot and the bread fresh. And I'm sinfully proud of my jam."

Rather dazed to discover someone else so alert at this early hour, Alex found herself eating breakfast before she'd even decided whether or not she was hungry.

Gweneth had to curb her impulse to overwhelm the child with love. She wanted to put her arms around the slim shoulders and just hold her. Even though Alexandria was more relaxed than she had been the night before, there was still much of the wood's creature ready to flee. But they would tame her, the Falconers would. Gweneth hid a smile at the aptness of their name.

Her thoughts were not so light when she considered the girl's parents. She did not know all the details, but Virginia had told her enough in the letters and more she could plainly see, and she found it unforgivable that the child should have been made so insecure. She had loved her children fiercely, the living and the dead, from the moment she had known she was carrying each one, and her grief at having no surviving daughter was deep. Alexandria's parents, she judged, were not only callous, but stupid to waste such a gift.

"Please, I would like to know what my duties are."

The soft voice pierced her reverie, and for a moment, she could make no sense of the words, and then she understood. She poured herself a cup of tea, needing time to collect her thoughts. She sat down across from Alex.

"Everyone in this family has tasks to do, and you will, too, when we discover what you do best. But you are not here as a servant, nor as a prisoner. You are here as a member of the family, no more and no less than the rest of our children. If you find you cannot be happy with us, you must tell us honestly so that you can go home."

She watched the doubt give way to wonder, and she saw the big green eyes fill with tears before the child ducked her head. Very calmly she began to talk about Clovelly, giving Alex time to regain her composure.

"The herring are running, and the boats are trying to bring in as many as they can. The shoals aren't so plentiful as they used to be. Sometimes now they're gone after two months or so. The season was much longer in the past. 'Tis hard on many in the village. Most are tenant fishermen and depend on the sea. There're other things to be caught, mackerel in the summer, and sole, hake, and more. But nothing is so valuable as the herring. You'll see them bring the catch up on sledges, and from the top of the hill they load it into carts and take it quick as you please to other towns, even to Barnstaple and beyond. Of course, salted or smoked, it goes to all sorts of markets, even to London." Inwardly she gave thanks for the interest she saw dawning on Alexandria's face and for the absence of tears.

"We're fortunate because we don't depend on the fishing. We're coastal traders, and we deal in many goods." Indeed we do, and this child is very bright; I wonder how long it will take her to suspect? Well, the time would come soon enough, no doubt, and she would know.

Gweneth's voice went on calmly, revealing nothing of her quandary. "My oldest son, Elwyn, and his wife, Susannah, live in Appledore. It's not far from here, and you'll meet them soon. Elwyn studied in Exeter and is a lawyer, as are many men of Devon. It's a useful trade to have in the family. But he's first of all a man of the sea. He has his own ship now. And next will be a ship for Seadon and then for Rane." Her pride was evident but so was the shadow of worry in her eyes.

"It must be difficult to see them sail away," Alex ventured softly, and Gweneth nodded.

"It is, even after all these years it is. I went on many voyages with Magnus when we were younger, but I go no more and am just as glad to stay on land. My mother's family had the Thaine blood, but except for the looks, I seem to take after my father's side. He was a schoolmaster in Barnstaple and no sailor. I met Magnus there. His parents still lived in the town, and they believed even those destined for the sea should be well read. I'm thankful they believed so." The smile that touched her mouth and eyes made her appear suddenly young and very beautiful.

Alex smiled back. "Did you love him even then?" She blushed as soon as the words were out, thinking them too personal, but Gweneth only nodded.

"Almost as soon as I met him, though I was very young indeed, a small child. Even when his family moved to Clovelly, he continued to study in Barnstaple when he wasn't at sea, and then he began to visit just to see me. My parents could scarcely object as we were cousins; though very distant, thank heaven!" She could see that the child was drawn to love as moth to flame, and she was resolved that Alexandria would have the warmth and the light without the harm.

The sound of quick steps thundering down the stairs broadened her smile. "That will be Rane. He is always in a hurry though he and his father were both weary enough last night for a long sleep."

Rane entered the kitchen, checking at the sight of Alex. The slow grin lighted his face again. "Good morning, Mother, good morning, Cousin. It will take some time to grow accustomed to this. It's like coming around a corner to look into a strange mirror."

Alex laughed aloud at the delight of having him saying what she was thinking.

It was a charming sound, and Rane and his mother exchanged a conspiratorial look. Gweneth was thus assured that her son felt as tenderly toward the girl as she

42

herself did, and she was relieved. He would be patient with the child and ease her way. Rane and Seadon both shared a gift for tenderness—children and animals, anything vulnerable seemed to turn to them naturally, sure of kindness and protection. She loved her oldest son Elwyn just as much, but he was different, more aloof except with his wife who had long since tamed him. Magnus, too, was kind, but his manner was so large, just as he was, that he tended to be overwhelming until one knew him. She was glad that Alexandria appeared to have overcome the fear she had felt at first in Magnus's presence.

Rane ate heartily and then, without being prodded to it, asked Alex if she would like to come with him to see a bit of the town. Alex, at Gweneth's urging, accepted gratefully, anxious to see more of the mystical place. And she asked them to call her "Alex"; only two people habitually called her by her full name—her grandmother out of dislike for nicknames of any sort, and her mother out of cold propriety.

Even the earthy odors of fish and donkey dung could not dim her conviction that this place was not quite real. Honeysuckle, jasmine, roses, fuchsias in searing reds and purples, hydrangeas in pink and blue, and a profusion of other flowers spilled their bounty to the eye and nose around every house. And the houses themselves were ornaments in their differences from each other—wood carved this way on one, that on another, this one white, the next soft buff or pink or faint blue, varied even in their basic structure as if the builders had been determined to express their individuality. And on the right hand of the steep street where fresh water ran down in a bright stream, little bridges had been built here and there to allow the tenants access to their houses.

Rane watched her face, tracking the wonder as it dawned in her eyes and brought color to her cheeks. He'd never felt the lack of a sister, but now he thought it not a bad idea at all to have one. He had always been the youngest child and found this distinction tiresome, particularly now when he was so obviously grown and doing a man's work. He could see definite advantages in having Alex assume the role. And he was amused by the incredulous looks they received along with the nods of greeting as they walked down toward the quay. By nightfall every household would be discussing the strength of the Thaine blood producing near twins from a connection that was as distant as great-great-great-great-grandparents.

He could feel her wiggling with excitement beside him and realized that she was humming with questions but too shy to ask them. It did not seem odd to him that he should know so precisely what she was thinking.

"Most of the houses and cottages are owned by the Hamlyn family of Clovelly Court. The manor house is at the top of the village, but it's behind trees so you probably didn't see it last night. Before the Hamlyns were the Carys, but the Hamlyns have had it for more than fifty years. The manor house burned over twenty years ago, but they rebuilt it. It's a bit odd looking for these parts, indeed for anywhere, but the center of the old house from the time of the Tudors remains. They built around that."

"Are they kindly people?" she asked, gathering courage from his obvious willingness to explain things.

"Kind enough. They're good landlords, let people go about their business and charge fair rents depending on how small or grand the house is. And the lord of the manor has been building a long drive for carriages for a few years now. He's given jobs to men out of work as well as using some French prisoners; there are some who don't care for that when Englishmen have no work." He thought he might as well tell the truth since there was some muttering about the French workmen, and Alex would hear it eventually. But her reaction was not what he expected.

"I feel guilty sometimes," she confessed. "I try to understand what's happening in the war, and I'm glad when England wins a victory, but I don't really think of it day to day. It's hard to explain. It ought to be important, but somehow much of the time, it's not. Even soldiers at the forts in Gravesend and nearby don't seem to make it real." She looked at him with a worried frown, afraid he wouldn't understand and would think her rattlebrained, but her fears were groundless.

"The war with France started before I was born; it's been going on for all of my life and all of yours. No wonder it doesn't seem any more special than anything else. Twenty years is a very long time. And now that it's certain Napoleon won't invade England and is, in fact, finally losing the fight, it does make it all seem quite distant." He did not add that he and his family kept close track indeed but not for any direct interest in the war.

They were nearly at the quay when he halted suddenly, his eyes narrowing as he looked out to sea. Alex followed his gaze, saw the sleek ship sailing into view, and recognized it as well as he did. Gravesend was so bound to the sea, Alex knew most vessels. "A revenue cutter. They remind me of sharks, they're so sleek and swift. Are there many in these waters?"

"Enough." Rane just stopped himself from saying "too many." "Your description is apt. A cutter named *Shark* made quite a catch right out there eight years ago. She took the *Dart* out of Fowey and found spirits, tobacco, and pepper aboard from Guernsey. There've been other prizes taken nearby since then, but none so large."

He watched her carefully for her reaction, but she took the story as nothing more or less than added lore about this region that so intrigued her. She was concerned by more immediate things. Turning to look back up the way they had come, she could see that though the village was set on solid rock outcroppings, the cliffs beside were of soft red sandstone sporting falls of tough greenery here and there and adding more color to the already bright scene.

"It's difficult to believe this place exists," she said softly, hugging herself for the welling joy of it.

Rane's focus shifted from the cutter and the problems it brought, to Alex. He was touched by her enthusiasm for the village he loved so well and even more determined that she should enjoy her time with the Falconers.

He took her hand and led her out on the stone quay which was already warming in the sun. "Sir James Hamlyn caused this to be reconstructed years ago. It adds good shelter to the harbor. We're protected anyway, just by the way the village is situated, and the prevailing westerly winds are warm, but sometimes the easterly winds come and can be bitter indeed. And no matter how peaceful it looks out there," he gestured to the wide expanse of sea, "these waters are dangerous for those who don't know them. There have been wrecks aplenty, particularly off of Hartland Point. I'll take you there, by land, someday soon."

The thought of shipwreck held no terror for Alex; the

only thing that mattered was that Rane planned to have time for her beyond this special day.

"The other thing to be wary of is the caves," Rane added. "There are many in the cliffs along this coast, and you mustn't ever go in one by yourself. The rocks could give away, and some believe there is a family of cannibals who eat the unwary who venture too close to their caves. They are said to salt down the extra meat just as if it were fish. They're a mad lot, full of sin and all manner of vice."

"What a wretched tale! Surely you don't believe . . ." Alex's voice trailed off as she studied his serious face.

"No, I don't believe it. I don't think there are enough people missing to feed so large a family." The smile started in his eyes and then curved his mouth at this ridiculous piece of logic. "But there are folk who would swear to the truth of it. They're the same who see the Devil as a black hound chasing them on dark nights, eyes glowing like fire. Gruesome tales to keep children fast in their beds at night."

They continued their survey of the town, Alex finding extra pleasure in the fact that Rane had not classed her as a child.

The beach was heavily pebbled, the stones growing larger on both sides of the shores flanking the quay. It was an active place in the early morning. The lime kilns added haze to the air. There were boats pulled up and nets drying as well as the ones bobbing far out on the water, and Alex watched in fascination as fish were loaded on the sledges and pulled up the hill by the donkeys.

It was such a tiny village, Rane knew everyone, and he introduced Alex often, pretending not to notice the involuntary stares they were receiving. The greetings to Alex were welcoming, but there were sly comments about another subject entirely, references to the cargo that had not come in the night before, subtly made, with only an occasional glance toward the revenue cutter that was now nearly out of sight. Rane could see that Alex was having so much trouble understanding the local accent, it was all she could do to acknowledge words spoken directly to her.

When they were out of earshot of the latest group, Alex started to giggle. "I fear I will say, 'How kind of you,' and then discover I was being told that my dress is unsuitable or that I have a smut on my nose. It's a nice accent, but so

46

new to me," she added hastily. Indeed in the polyglot tongues of Gravesend's waterfront, she had heard nearly every possible dialect, but she had seldom had to respond.

"Aye, naw, zurr durin' well, lass," Rane drawled, and they laughed together.

❧ *Chapter 6* ❧

The first days at Clovelly sped by so swiftly for Alex, she could scarcely keep track of where they began and where they ended; they were a rush of light upon light of new experiences with pauses of nightfall for sleep.

Elwyn and Susannah came from Appledore to meet her, and though she did not feel the same ease with Elwyn as with his brothers, he was nice enough in his reserved way, and his wife was so warm and outgoing, she made up for any chill on his part. And Alex did not judge his manner as anything more than that of a thoughtful and even shy man. Susannah and her sister, Barbary, Seadon's wife, were, despite the several years difference in their ages, very much alike, small and round with bright blue eyes and flaxen hair. Susannah and Elwyn had been married in 1808 and had one son four years old, another two, and a daughter of scarcely a year. Barbary and Seadon had only been married a little more than a year but also had an infant daughter.

The house was merry and filled to bursting with all of them visiting and Magnus seemed to roar even louder. Though she was growing accustomed to him, the sheer noise he made still startled Alex occasionally, and once or twice when she cringed at suddenly being the object of his attention, she noticed how baffled and even hurt he looked. She was touched and amused, seeing him as a lion indeed, but a harmless one who couldn't understand when his friendly overtures were rebuffed.

She felt so enwrapped in her new family, even the pain of her grandmother's departure was dulled. Seadon came with the cart from the farm, but this time Barbary and their baby took up the extra room. It made sense as Barbary would have a chance to visit her parents in Bideford, but Gweneth and Virginia had also decided that it would be easier for Alex to say good-bye here in the village she was growing to love.

Virginia had seen the change even on the first day when Alexandria and Rane had returned to the house. The granddaughter she knew had reappeared—green eyes wide and alert with interest, mouth curved in a smile, and color beginning to show again in her cheeks.

She had come to her grandmother without hesitation, putting her arms around her and murmuring low, "I never should have doubted you! This is a wonderful, magical place! I shall be happy here, I know I shall!"

For Virginia, there was pain and pleasure both in Alexandria's acceptance. It was best for the child, but for the old woman, it meant weeks, months, a very long time without this being who so brightened her days. And she knew that Alexandria, already such a strange mix of young and old, would surely have passed beyond childhood completely by the next time they saw each other. But she had steeled herself against showing anything except approval and had known it would be better were she to leave the following week when she could get the coach from Bideford to Exeter and on to London. To tarry too long would only make it harder for both of them.

For Alex the farewell went as quickly as everything else seemed to in her new life. Virginia filled the last few moments with special charges to Alex to use the herbs she was leaving with great care. Alex was honored by the trust her grandmother was bestowing upon her with the box filled with carefully labeled packets. She barely had time to kiss her grandmother and thank her for everything before Virginia was in the cart and going away.

The pain and sudden longing for life in Gravesend, no matter how complicated, was sharp, but Gweneth was there to tell her that Seadon and Barbary would pick her up on their way back tomorrow for a visit to the farm, and Rane was there, too, with more immediate plans, asking her if she would like to go aboard Magnus's ship, the *Lady Gwen*. He and Magnus had left on a short voyage two days after her arrival, but twenty-four hours later they were home. On the night of their absence, she had gone to sleep thinking how quiet the house was without the two men, but in the morning they were home. She had not heard them return in the darkness, but she thought nothing of it beyond being glad that they were safe and impressed that their skill should allow them to navigate the dangerous waters even in the night.

She had not yet been aboard the graceful ship, and the excitement of Rane's offer did much to banish the sorrow of her grandmother's departure.

Rane rowed her out to the *Lady Gwen*. Though the ship could be brought in close to the quay when tide and wind were right, Magnus preferred to keep her further out for safety.

Alex had been on ships before, at Gravesend when she was quite small, and her father had taken her with him a few times when he was making sure goods he'd supplied were being properly delivered. The *Lady Gwen* was surely one of the trimmest and best kept vessels she had ever seen. Everything from wood to brass gleamed with care. But one thing puzzled her. Though the ship was obviously built for speed, the sleek lines cut down on the cargo space enough so that she noticed. However, she did not register the sly looks the two men on watch exchanged when she questioned Rane about it.

He barely restrained his start of surprise. He had discussed Alex's sharpness with his mother, and they both agreed that she was too quick-witted to be kept in ignorance forever. But Gweneth had insisted that it was better for the child to have time to adjust before she knew all of the Falconers' business, and Magnus had concurred. Still, even Rane had not expected she would question the limited cargo space of the ship. He suppressed his unease and managed to answer calmly.

"We don't deal in large, bulky cargoes such as lime or clay. We carry more precious things, er . . . china, housewares, some foodstuffs. We're paid more for transporting them, and we can do it swiftly with the *Lady Gwen*." He made the details purposefully vague and was relieved to see it made sense to Alex.

Though she found the ship interesting, she was even

more enchanted by the view of Clovelly from out on the water. "I still find it difficult to believe what I'm seeing," she sighed. "It is surely the most beautiful village in all the world. You are very fortunate to live here."

"Indeed I am," Rane agreed gravely. "And now you live here, too." He meant a great deal more than an observation on life in the village. His mother had told him much about Alex's background, and he still could not credit that parents should be so careless with such an appealing child. She made him feel much older than his eighteen years and very protective.

"You don't have to tell me, but if you'd ever like to talk about the trouble at your home, I can listen," he offered gently and was instantly sorry he had.

She stiffened and looked so hurt and lost, he wanted to comfort her as if she were truly a small child, but instead, he listened intently as she told him the story of what she had done. The words tumbled out very quickly, the condemned confessing right before the execution.

"Is that really what happened?" he asked, his voice strangled.

"Yes, but my mother and my sister don't like me very well in any case, so that made it worse." She felt obliged to add this painful bit of information in the interest of honesty, and so intent was she on showing Rane the unvarnished image of herself, at first she didn't understand his reaction and gazed at him as if he had run mad.

Despite his efforts to prevent it, Rane was laughing. He knew it was important and tragic to her, but the image of this grave-faced child creating such havoc for her dull family amused him mightily.

"Oh, Alex, don't you see how foolish they all were?" he gasped. "If this Carrington were any kind of man and your sister any kind of woman, nothing you could have said would have made the slightest difference. It's just our good luck that your mother and sister are so hideously stupid and the rest of the lot so cowardly." He stopped suddenly, appalled by what he had said.

But her reaction was again unexpected. "Not my grandmother," she protested solemnly, and then she was laughing, too, suddenly seeing her mother and sister as red-faced ranting puppets, too small and far away to harm her more. And Rane had called her "Alex" as if they'd been friends for a long time, his voice warm; it gave her an identity beyond the odd relative left to be cared for.

She saw the truth of Rane's contention—if Florence and St. John really cared for each other, neither she nor anyone else would be able to keep them from each other. She thought of Gweneth and Magnus and doubted that any power on earth could have kept them apart. Peace and joy flooded through her; she felt as if she had come home.

In the days that followed, her sense of newness was replaced by a feeling that she had always lived here, and gradually she began to play an active role in Falconer family life, finding her skills appreciated, her help eagerly accepted when she offered it. She loved the farm from the first day she saw it and proved herself useful in milking the cow, collecting eggs from the fowl, and other chores long since familiar because of time spent on Virginia's land. She grew particularly fond of the herd of tough Exmoor ponies and the larger pony-horse crosses. The farm was not as tidy or as productive as her grandmother's, but it provided plenty of fresh food for the tenant farmer and his family and for the Falconers.

In Clovelly she was soon helping Gweneth prepare the meals, and more, she was trusted to treat minor ailments. Magnus was her first patient when he suffered a nasty gash on his forearm. At Gweneth's command, he kept his skepticism to himself and allowed Alex to clean and dress the cut. When he found how much she had eased the discomfort and saw how well the wound healed, he could not have been more generous in his praise had she been one of his own children.

But as much as she was warmed by the kindness of the rest of the family, best of all for Alex were the hours spent with Rane. He took her fishing, and she was soon adept at repairing nets and lines. She applied holystone to the decks of the *Lady Gwen* with a will and polished brass fittings until they shone as brightly as Magnus liked. If Rane were helping out on the farm, she was glad to do any task as long as she was allowed to be with him. The two of them were soon a familiar sight in the district, and because of their likeness, it began to seem to many that Alexandria had always been part of the Falconer family though they remained aware that she did not share the village's secret, and they did not speak of it to her.

Alex began to feel comfortable with the villagers, but

daily she gave thanks she was with the Falconers and not another family. She searched diligently for the right word to describe them and finally realized they were above all else tolerant. Sometimes they went to the Church of England services on Sunday at the church above on the cliffs that served the manor and the surrounding area, but on other Sundays, they did not attend, and nothing was made of it. No excuses, no guilt, and unlike her mother, no show of excessive virtue when they did go. Alex had heard enough about Dissenters to know that she might well have ended up with those who made serious business of religion and life in general. The West Country had more than its share of that sort. Instead she was with people who felt the Lord was not to be feared as long as one treated one's fellow creatures with respect, who loved each other and their life, who rather than being narrow-minded, were well read and enjoyed discussing ideas just for the sake of the exercise. Even Elwyn thawed in the heat of the passionate debates on everything from Napoleon's strategies to the state of Parliament and the Church of England, both of which seemed in grave need of reform. It was ironic, but Alex discovered that the Falconers knew far more about what concerned the country than her own family, in spite of the fact that the Thaines lived so close to London.

"Englishmen are not Frenchmen!" Elwyn declared. "We honor king and country and would not tolerate disorder and revolution even though times are hard."

"Not all men, English or otherwise, have your passion for the House of Hanover," Rane retorted. "The government has surely recognized that, making assemblies illegal, imprisoning writers and publishers. It is more than can be expected for a man to be docile when he and his family are hungry. And few have any voice in the government. Why, consider the mutinies at Spithead and the Nore, those were men sworn to His Majesty's service but forced to such action by the miserable condition of their lives."

"Yes, and they were the same men who rallied to their duty and sailed under Duncan to destroy the Dutch fleet at Camperdown. Surely the able-bodied pay the poor rates just so hunger will not steal bread from too many. We are a reasonable country; we will find reasonable ways to cure the ills that beset us." Elwyn was eloqent in his defense of the rational course, but Alex wondered if time would prove him correct.

They were gathered in the kitchen, and Alex was listening to this latest exchange of ideas with fascination. Through the Falconers she was beginning to understand much more of what was happening in England. Far ahead of other nations in the development of new manufacturing techniques, the country had lost valuable ground due to Napoleon's control of European markets and his banning of English goods, despite the fact that he had had no navy since his defeat at Trafalgar by Nelson in 1805. Indeed, the effect had been severe enough to cause the Czar of Russia to break his alliance with Napoleon when he discovered the hardship brought by the lack of cheap English manufactured goods. It had, though indirectly, led to Napoleon's costly defeat in Russia. But that was a fairly recent development, and no one could foretell what would happen to the Continental markets once Bonaparte's hold was completely broken. And then there was the trouble with the Americans that had stopped trade between England and the United States.

There were too many people now in the cities and towns of England who had found there was no need for their labor and who had no land of their own to grow even the barest minimum of food. And countryfolk were in many cases no better off, barely existing on tired land, or even if they were possessed of profitable farms, and planted as judiciously as possible, they were apt to discover that the crop that had made them rich the year before was bent on ruining them the next since prices fluctuated wildly.

"What do you think, Alex?" Rane asked, wanting her to feel part of the discussion.

She was startled to have all attention suddenly fixed on her, and she swallowed nervously before she found the words she wanted. "I hope Elwyn is correct, but I fear you make too much sense, Rane. I think it is hard to know what people will not risk when their children are hungry, and the poor rates do not seem to be enough any more. Even in Kent where the land is rich, there are too many who cannot find enough work. And it's also true that many do not like the Hanoverians. My grandmother is a loyal Englishwoman, but she knows the old king, Farmer George, is quite mad and the Prince Regent, given power in his father's place, is a wastrel whose private life is often too public. And Parliament doesn't seem to have anything to do with anyone I know. But it is such an awful thing to think of blood running in the streets as it did in France, I pray it never happens here." Her voice trailed away, the image of such carnage too clear.

"Well spoken, lass," Magnus said, and no one tried to make light of the gravity of the problems they had been discussing.

Despite the fair degree of education in her family, Alex could not remember a time when her parents and their offspring had had any exchange of words even faintly resembling the give and take of these conversations. It occurred to her that there were forms of poverty that had nothing to do with physical hunger. Only her grandmother had ever bothered to speak to her as if she were an intelligent human being, but even she did not discuss politics.

Rane watched the changing expressions on her face and marvelled at his own reaction. He was no less fascinated by her than he had been the first time he had seen her. In honest self-appraisal he had expected that he would soon grow weary of having her tagging after him and had been ready to chide himself for lack of patience. But it hadn't happened. He continued to enjoy her company, and he found that once shown how to do it, she was swift and sure help on whatever task they were about. He was glad she wasn't missish. She was so game, often he forgot entirely that she was female. He was growing accustomed to having an extra pair of hands to help him through the chores of the day and to having her face light with pleasure when he returned from sailing with Magnus. So swiftly Alexandria had become an altogether comfortable part of his life. But dull she was not.

The first day she appeared in her brother's knee breeches and stockings and shirt, Rane was completely nonplussed. The day was brisk, and he had not noticed how strangely bulky her clothing was until she began to divest herself of her dress. That caught his interest to be sure.

"What are you . . ." His question died away as he saw what she was wearing beneath her cloak and dress, and he stared, thinking how odd it was that she looked more feminine in boy's clothing than she did in her own—long and lean as she was, there was no mistaking the soft curves.

He swallowed hard and tried again for words. "Alex . . . you, ah, I'm not sure . . ."

"Oh, please don't make a fuss! It is such a bother to wear skirts, they get in the way of everything. I wore these at home," she ended defiantly, unrolling the short jacket she had carried in a tightly rolled bundle.

"And got in trouble for it no doubt," Rane said wryly. "I do see your point. I should hate to wear a dress." Alex's laughter rippled at the picture of him so attired, and he smiled in response to the contagious sound. "Well, I suppose the risk is yours, but you do know someone is bound to see you, and then the secret will be out."

His prediction soon proved true, but his mother's response surprised him.

Magnus was the first to hear that their young ward was cavorting over the countryside in masculine garb, and he came home in high dudgeon.

Gweneth let him sputter, and then very calmly she asked, "What harm is she doing?"

Magnus came to an abrupt stop, peering at her in consternation, trying to work up steam again as he produced his arguments. "It isn't proper. People will talk."

"Let them," Gweneth said. "And, Magnus Falconer, when have we ever cared about what is proper as long as there is no harm? I seem to remember a time at that waterfall . . ." She grinned mischievously at him as his face took on a ruddier hue, but then she sobered again. "I want Alexandria's time with us to be as free and joyful as is possible. She's spent enough time with a family who tried to cage her spirit and make it small. She should have been born to us! She delights my heart."

He enfolded her in his arms and held her against his huge chest. "She's ours now, Gwenny," he said softly, knowing she was thinking of the little infant girls who had not lived. They were buried in the churchyard next to the graves of his parents who had died one winter of pneumonia within a week of each other. "I'll say nothing about the breeches."

Alex had been certain that her freedom would be short-lived. Instead she found a neat stack of masculine clothing on her bed with a note from Gweneth. "My sons have outgrown these. I trust you will wear them with some discretion."

Alex was so pleased, she flew to Gweneth and hugged her, words of thanks tumbling over each other. The older woman's eyes were tear bright as Alex rushed away again to examine her new treasures more closely.

Gweneth's trust was not misplaced. Alex was careful about where she wore her boy's clothes, not flaunting the privilege but confining their use mostly to the farm and to rambles over the sparsely populated countryside. If the lord of Clovelly Court and the people there had heard of the girl who dressed as a boy, still they saw no evidence of it. Winter was drawing in in earnest, and she was grateful for the added protection of the clothing. Even in this part of the country where warm currents from the sea often made the weather milder than in other regions, this particular season had few soft edges. The flowers of Clovelly were gone early this year, and news from the rest of England confirmed lower temperatures than usual. Though she kept it to herself, Alex worried more about the Falconer men, Rane in particular, when they were gone on Magnus's *Lady Gwen* and Elwyn's *Maid of Devon*. The men were all good sailors, and they put out far less often now, but still they did sail even when the weather was foul. She knew that Gweneth did not rest easily until they were back, but the only concession she had asked and long since been granted was that one of her men remain on land while the others were gone. Her nightmare had always been that she would lose them all in a single storm or wreck. It made the evenings when they were all together in the house at Clovelly or at the farm even more precious.

Alex sensed a restlessness in Rane stronger than that in the other men. He was seldom still, but when he was, there was often a faraway look in his eyes, as if he were contemplating horizons he had not yet seen. His need for action was to her advantage because it led to their explorations of the countryside, on foot or sometimes on the ponies. And even in the bitter cold with a knife-edged wind blowing salt spray, one of Rane's favorite haunts was Hartland Point, a jutting red-hued cliff over the sea. Jagged rocks waited some three hundred and fifty feet below to rake the fragile hulls of unwary ships. Alex did not question why it was so, but in spite of the bleakness of the place, she felt exhilarated and washed clean when she came to the Point, and she knew Rane felt the same. Sometimes they would sit for a long time, hunkered down against the cold, sometimes talking lazily, sometimes silent because they could not compete with the roar of the wind and the sea. Even when the elements were wild, here Rane was often at his most peaceful.

On clear days, they could see Lundy, the Norse name meaning "Isle of Puffins," a place rich in legend. It was said that a member of Parliament from Barnstaple had transported convicts there instead of to Virginia in America where they were legally bound. He had used them as slaves to hack out a cave for storing smuggled goods until his malfeasance was discovered and he was arrested.

Alex shivered at the thought of being a prisoner there. "To be confined to so small a piece of land, I would go mad!"

Rane nodded, relieved that the fact of the M.P.'s business seemed to be of no import to her compared to the lot of his victims. "I, too. There is so much of the world to see!"

"If you marry Mary Forthy, she'll understand that. She might even sail with you, being Clovelly born. But then, I suppose the same could be said of the widow from Buck's Mills or any other woman who lives so close to ships and the sea, born here or not."

For a moment, Rane was speechless. It hadn't occurred to him that Alex was aware of his love life, but he saw now that she could scarcely be in ignorance of it. His brothers teased him unmercifully about the accommodating woman at Buck's Mills, and Mary Forthy, a comely blond of seventeen, was less than subtle in her pursuit of him. The widow, ten years older than he, had long since lost her status as an amateur and was not a candidate for marriage, would undoubtedly refuse even were she asked. She was clean, discreet, and skilled, but the favors, physical and otherwise, of one man would never satisfy her. Local wags had it that her husband, years older than she, had died of overwork without leaving the house. Mary, on the other hand, was exactly what most men looked for in a wife. She was pretty, capable of running a household smoothly, and bright enough though not overly educated. But the idea of spending his life with her gave Rane exactly the same feeling he got when he contemplated being a prisoner on Lundy. Mary's adoration was more of an embarrassment than a compliment, and Rane found it very convenient to have Alex beside him as she tended to serve as a buffer against Mary's attentions.

"It seems to me that this is the same sort of interference that got you sent to us," he remarked, and Alex's face clouded, but then she realized he was teasing. To be sure, when he had thought it out, he found that she had amused him again as she so often did in unexpected ways. Her voice had been so practical, neatly tying up his life out of concern, not malice. Whether she was conscious of it or not, he knew she was concerned that he not become embroiled in an unsuitable match like her sister's and the ubiquitous St. John. Sometimes he wondered if she knew how often she mentioned the man's name—he was the final authority on all matters concerning horseflesh and a host of other subjects. But she invoked the name innocently, and he winced away from exploring why it bothered him.

"Mary is a sweet lass, but I haven't any plans in that direction, so please don't make any for me. And as for the widow, well, she is not the sort of woman you ought to be thinking about at all," he added.

Alex blushed, remembering the painted women in London and those she had seen in Gravesend, but she was relieved. She, too, thought Mary a nice enough person, but not good enough for Rane. She hoped he would find someone more like the women his brothers had married. Suddenly she was up and running away from the Point, calling that she would beat him to the ponies.

She just managed to do it because of her head start, and they rode companionably back toward the farm, stopping only to watch a flight of swans pass overhead. These were not the common Mute swans nor yet the Whooper swans but rather smaller foreigners. Their wing beats did not sing as did the Mute's; they passed over in nearly silent grace, the soft *hoo-hoo-hoo* of their voices sounding like nothing more than the wind sighing. And they flew in what seemed a random pattern rather than in the trailing chevron of Whooper swans. They were not native to Britain, nesting instead in more northeasterly countries, some said as far away as Russia, and their coming was an indication of hard weather elsewhere.

"I love them all," Alex said reverently. "These with their soft music when they're feeding, Whooper swans with their loud chorus, and the Mute swans, the royal birds who act as if they own the Thames and every other river and pond in England and are surely not mute! I remember the first time I heard one of them hiss. I was very small, and it frightened me properly. My grandmother explained that it was just warning me not to come too close, and that seemed reasonable once I'd thought about it."

They watched the birds out of sight, sharing their mutual love and knowledge of the wild things. Many were not even aware that these frosty white birds were swans, thinking instead they were geese and thus missing the essential mystery of the birds who wandered so far. Knowing exactly what things were was a way of getting closer to the earth, a skill long taught to Alex by her grandmother and to Rane by both of his parents.

"Perhaps they are swan maidens with fine gold chains around their necks," Rane murmured, whimsy as much a part of his nature as the more rational aspects. "When they settle on secret ponds and lakes, they take off their feather cloaks and are beautiful women, eternally young. That's who I'll wed, one of the swan maidens."

Alex knew the old legend as well as he. "You'll have to take care. Remember that if you do not hide the cloak, she will fly away."

Though he did not remember it, that night Rane dreamed he captured a swan whose feather cloak fell away to reveal not Mary Forthy nor the Buck's Mills' widow, but Alexandria. In his dream she was older, her body more curved, but still she was Alex.

❦ Chapter 7 ❧

Unlike most girls of her age, Alex was normally quite facile with pen and paper, a skill that had been encouraged not only by Virginia, but also by her father, though subtly, as Caton had long known that if he showed too much approval, his wife would disapprove, no matter what the subject. But Alex found it increasingly difficult to write to her family in Gravesend.

Among the last hurried words Virginia had left with her on departure had been pleas that she send word when she could. Expense was no excuse to shirk the duty; Virginia had left money with Gweneth for Alex's keep, and Gweneth had long since declared that Alex was so much help, payment ought to be the other way around. She was gently insistent that Alex keep in touch with her family.

Alex would not have had trouble had it been possible just to write to her grandmother or to her brother, Boston, but she knew that would not do. Her mother was bound to find out, somehow she would. She now understood her mother well enough to know that Margaret would not care whether she heard from her daughter or not, but would not want anyone else to receive special attention from her. Alex doubted she would ever understand that kind of meanness even while knowing it existed.

The only safe course was to write dutiful little letters that said nothing at all. She dared not communicate the overwhelming joy of her new life—that would be enough to cause her mother to summon her home immediately, no matter what opposition. She struggled over the dry missives, hating every sentence, particularly because her grandmother's letters, and even an occasional note from Boston enclosed therein, were so warm.

But near Christmas, Gweneth, who missed so little, offered her a special gift. "I am going to send greetings to your grandmother. No one but she will read my letter; I am sure of it. Would you like to include your own message?" she asked with artful casualness.

Alex accepted gratefully, knowing it was not a privilege to abuse. It was, after all, a way of circumventing her mother even if not presented as such, and Gweneth could not be expected to make a habit of it, no matter what she thought of Margaret Thaine.

It was pure joy to be able to pour out her heart to her grandmother, and she did so in tiny script, making every bit of the page count, crossing the horizontal lines with vertical to crowd twice as much in the space. She wrote of the flowers that had been so bountiful in the village until the cold had come, of the friendly villagers, of the farm, of Hartland Point and the small swans, of the ponies, of the myriad things that had caught her interest, but most of all, of the Falconers and the loving home they had given her. She did not realize that what Rane said and did outweighed all the rest of the family in her account.

Greetings from her family came before her letter had had time to reach Gravesend, but in any case, the letters were predictable—a vague line or two from her father and cold charges of duty from her mother along with a formal assurance that her sister and brothers sent best regards. That she sincerely doubted, except for Boston. Florence surely did not wish her well, and Paris and Rome had scarcely spared her a thought when she was at Gravesend; they could hardly be expected to keep her in mind when she was so far away. That did not trouble her; she felt close to none of the three. But she was touched by the warm, erratically spelled greeting from Boston that was enclosed with her grandmother's witty account of activities on the land and in the town. She could almost feel the love rising from the paper, and for a brief instant, tears threatened. She could sense that Virginia missed her even more with the approach of Christmas. And she missed her grandmother, too, but her life was not in Gravesend any more, and the pain was blunted.

Christmas with the Falconers was as new as everything else had been with them since the beginning. The cold that was gripping all of England continued to deepen, but the house in Clovelly was warm with good food and good cheer, the spirit enhanced by the fine brandy and Madeira Magnus broached for the occasion. The family exchanged gifts they had made for each other—knitted vests, mittens, and scarves, specially baked cakes, handmade toys for the children. Alex was entranced when she learned the Falconer men had done some of the knitting.

"Good thing for a sailor to know," roared Magnus. "Makes the time pass."

Alex had helped with the cooking and had made her own offerings of different combinations of herbs and dried flowers to be added to the bath or brewed for a soothing drink. And the gifts she received left her wide-eyed and stuttering with gratitude. Rane had knitted her a cap so that she could tuck her hair out of sight, thus enhancing her disguise as a boy, but the women of the family had made her a green velvet cloak as soft and feminine as anything she had ever seen, a gentle reminder of her true identity.

The most elaborate gifts were books—poetry from Wordsworth and the wild young Lord Byron, sharply satirical stories by Maria Edgeworth, and volumes on plants, animals, and birds, each with delicate etchings of their subjects—given by Magnus to be enjoyed by the whole family.

Though Gweneth and Magnus had scattered relatives still living, mostly further to the north, they saw none of them on a regular basis, not for any animosity but simply because of lack of familiarity and time. Neither had parents living any more and each was the only surviving child, siblings having died by accidents and disease, most before they reached their majority. It was a circumstance that made them treasure their own children and grandchildren all the more and increased the enjoyment of the time the family spent together.

The house seemed to expand to hold extra people, for though Seadon, Barbary, and their baby daughter went back to the farm to sleep on Christmas Eve, Elwyn and his family stayed in Clovelly, Appledore being too far for quick trips back and forth in their pony cart in such cold.

Alex delighted in the traditions the Falconers maintained with such ceremony, seeing how they bound the family together in celebration. Their yule log was an ashen faggot, a log with smaller branches wrapped all around. It was lighted with great fanfare, and a special lamp was tended as well, kept burning through Christmas Eve because dark legend had it that if it went out, there would be death in the house. In his dogmatic way, Elwyn pointed out that that superstition undoubtedly came from the wish of people to exert some control over fate. Nonetheless, Alex was glad to see the lamp burning merrily.

Toasts were drunk, and songs offered with great zest, if not with skill though Alex noted that Rane, Seadon, and Gweneth had true voices. And Magnus, face perfectly serious, told his grandchildren the tale of the animals kneeling down in reverence at midnight and of pixies that had their own parties. Rane and Alex caught each other's eye as the same thought struck them, and they had to look away to avoid laughing aloud at Magnus's mix of religions.

Most fun of all was the wassailing of the apple trees at the farm. People who followed the custom did so on various nights of the season, but the Falconers had long since celebrated on New Year's Eve. They all, including the tenant farmer and his family, trooped out to the apple trees with the youngest children held in arms, and they sang:

> Here's to thee, old apple tree
> Whence thou may'st bud and whence thou may'st blow
> And whence thou may'st bear apples enow!
> Hats full! Caps full!
> Bushel-bushel-sacks full
> And my pockets full to! Huzza!

They sprinkled cider over the roots and hung cakes on various branches to encourage growth and abundance for cider making in the new year.

It was doubtful that anyone in the family believed in the efficacy of the ritual, but as Rane whispered to Alex, "One never knows. Perhaps the trees do listen, and in any case, Scroggins does believe, and that should make him pay extra attention to the orchard." Scroggins was the tenant farmer, a weathered landsman of indeterminate years and set ways.

Alex didn't care whether it worked or not. It was more than enough for her that the frosty night rang with laughter and celebration. And when the midnight hour came, they all embraced and wished each other the joy of the new year. 1814 might well be a special year indeed because at long last, it seemed as if Napoleon's reign was coming to an end, the allies having scattered his troops at Leipzig, Germany, in October.

But for Alex the best moment came from an unexpected source. Magnus embraced her gently, murmuring gruffly, "You've been a gift to me and Gwenny. You'll always have a home with us, child, for as long as we live."

It happened swiftly, but the memory of it warmed Alex for a long time, and she wondered how she could have feared this man even for a moment.

The new year brought more immediate concerns to the country than the activities of the French tyrant. The deep frosts were joined by howling snowstorms said to be the worst in forty years, and word came that the Thames had frozen hard enough to support a frost fair at the beginning of February, amusements on the ice springing up overnight due to the efforts of a multitude of entrepreneurs. Rane confessed he would very much like to be part of such revelry, but Alex was unmoved. Being there would mean being at Gravesend, and that was no longer something she desired.

The harsh weather made concerns more immediate. Unessential activities outside were curtailed, and more time was spent in the warm kitchen and with the books in the house and the Christmas additions to them. But Alex and Rane were saved from growing too restless by the necessity of helping on the farm when the least break in the weather allowed it, and the same with the constant tasks to be performed aboard the *Lady Gwen* whether she was sailing or not. The single blessing of the terrible weather was that the ship did not put out for days on end.

Late in the month, Alex received two letters from home. The sole purpose of her mother's was to inform her that her attempt at mischief had failed as St. John and Florence were getting married. Her grandmother's letter bore the same news but more kindly. Like Alex, she, too, had grave doubts about the match but cautioned her granddaughter to accept it with good grace. There was, of course, no suggestion that she return home to witness the wedding, and for that she was thankful.

"I'm sorry for Sinje," Alex told Rane, "and even for Florence. But it all seems so far away, as though I've lived in Clovelly forever. Sometimes, I can hardly remember what Sinje and the others looked like. But not Grandmother. When I concentrate very hard I can see her clearly. She's part of my life here; the others aren't."

Observing her carefully, Rane saw that it was true. He was relieved. He wanted her to have as little contact with the people in Gravesend as possible. He squirmed away from examining his own motives too closely, even to suppressing the sparks of jealousy Alex ignited every time she mentioned St. John as an authority on this or that. It was something she still did with vague fondness. Rane had never had a younger sister, and so he tried to assume his feeling was natural, but he could not help noticing that he did not have the same reaction when she mentioned her brother, Boston.

February passed into March, but it was as if spring would never come, and Alex hardly had a thought to spare for Gravesend and the new couple there. The ships were sailing again despite the continued bad weather, and the days and nights when the men were gone seemed to have far more hours than the normal span allowed. Alex knew her face wore the same worried frown as Gweneth's, but from the older woman, she learned the grace of being calmly welcoming when the men returned, as if nothing had disturbed the even pattern of her days.

And then suddenly pieces she had not known she possessed fell together to form the answer to a puzzle she had not known existed.

She had gone to Hartland Point by herself, granted permission by Gweneth because she was too restless to settle to any task and because Mary Forthy had come calling and had been doing her best to establish Alex's place as a child in the family, speaking to her as if she were not a day over six. Alex felt sorry for her, knowing her to be jealous of the time Alex had with Rane, but it would hardly do to tell the young woman that Rane was not interested in Mary in any case. The tension between the two was driving Gweneth to distraction and she had nearly breathed an audible sigh of relief when Alex asked permission to leave. Gweneth gave her a hastily wrapped packet of food and sent her on her way.

Fog shrouded the sea though not the land, a separation often true in Devon. Alex had donned her boy's clothing and topped it with a heavy cloak, so she was well dressed against the cold. She moved briskly, sometimes running for the sheer joy of feeling her body stretching. She pulled the sharp tangy air deep into her lungs and became part of the land, part of every silent stone and crying sea bird, part of every plant and beast. Life pulsed so hard in her veins, she felt as if she would explode with it. She ran with her arms outflung, as if she were flying, the sound of her own laughter surrounding her.

By the time she had covered the miles to the Point, she felt deliciously spent, almost drowsy with the aftereffects of euphoria. She settled down at the favorite lookout and stared out to sea, watching the fog billow and break into drifting tendrils until she could discern Lundy.

> Lundy plain, sign of rain
> Lundy high, sign of dry
> Lundy low, sign of snow.

She chanted the local rhyme Rane had taught her.

The silhouette grew clearer, and her mind wandered from one thought to another. Lundy, fit only for the puffins, kittiwakes, and other birds that nested on the bleak rock ledges, and for the seals that sometimes haunted the cold waters. She considered again the awful punishment the convicts had received when they had been transported to the island and forced to dig the cave for the dishonest M.P. from Barnstaple. Suddenly she remembered what the cave had been used for. She hadn't been curious enough to pursue it. But she was now. Smuggled goods, that's what had been in the cave. And smuggled goods were what undoubtedly filled the caves along the coast, including the one which was said to shelter the family of cannibals, a fair warning to stay away.

The evidence crowded in until she could scarcely breathe. Indeed fish were transported up Clovelly's steep street on sledges, but so were other things, undoubtedly so. The scrape of the sledges and the clatter of the tiny hooves of the donkeys had sounded when no fish had been coming in. The sleek lines of the *Lady Gwen* and of Elwyn's ship,

the odd timings of the voyages, particularly the dangerous night running, the vague listing of cargoes by Rane
on that day she had first gone aboard the *Lady Gwen*, the
grim expressions on most faces when revenue cutters
lurked in Bideford Bay, even the herd of ponies on the
farm—what better way to transport goods all over the
country than by those sturdy little beasts, sure-footed
even at night? There were larger horses for riding, but the
ponies were for night work. It all made clear and terrible
sense.

She felt incredibly stupid and naive. And she felt
betrayed. The central fact of the Falconers' existence, the
essential secret of their lives they had not shared with her.
She felt as much an outsider as she had at Gravesend
when everything had gone wrong. And the last murderous truth was that not only must her grandmother have
known she was sending her to live amongst smugglers,
but it was more than possible that Rane's attention and
friendship had been nothing more than a ploy to keep her
from discovering the smuggling.

The strength that had carried her to the point on such
swift wings had fled. Her legs trembled, and she felt so
dazed and sick, it seemed to take forever to return to
Clovelly. She didn't know where else to go. She was in a
land of dangerous strangers, and there was no safe shelter
anywhere.

Though Alex cautioned herself to behave normally,
Gweneth knew instantly that something was very wrong.
The child's face was bleached white as bone despite being
out in the brisk weather and her eyes were enormous,
pale and yellow-green as cat's eyes.

Gweneth went to her swiftly, putting a hand out to
touch her forehead for signs of malaise, finding deep chill
rather than fever. With great effort, Alex kept herself from
flinching.

"What is it? What's happened?" Gweneth asked frantically, knowing this was something quite beyond the effects of weather.

"The swans, Rane and I saw them long ago, so beautiful,
and today I saw them again, only two of them, but they
were dead. A man had shot them. He was there with
blood on his hands and on the swans . . ." She did not
know where the lie had come from, but she was grateful
for it.

Having raised sons who were kindhearted enough but not overly emotional about such things, Gweneth was at a loss. But she knew Alex's anguish was genuine, and she tucked her into bed with a warm toddy and soft words, hoping the sleep would ease the shock.

Docilely Alex did as she was bid, but inside her mind was beginning to spin with all she suspected and the need to prove it. She had to know for certain before she decided what to do next.

The men came home that night. She heard the soft murmur of voices as Gweneth greeted them. She heard Rane's voice raised enough to carry "Is she all right?" to her with clarity, but the urgency of the words made no impression. He was part of it all.

She lay in her bed, stiff and silent, when she heard him calling outside her room, trying to determine if she were awake without waking her if she slept.

She knew the men were always very tired when they returned from sea, and she had not long to wait before the house was quiet. Still, she let more precious minutes pass to be sure.

When she left the house she felt as if every floorboard had shrieked a message, as if the pierced tin lantern she carried was shining like a star even though it was nearly closed. But there were no sounds or signs of pursuit.

She made her way carefully down the steep street, biting back a nervous giggle at the mental picture of herself rolling down the hill at great speed. It was so cold even most of the village dogs were inside, and those that weren't quickly went back to sleep at her whispered reassurances, accustomed now to her voice and scent. There was still light from a few houses and from the tavern at the base of the hill, but Alex slipped by them all without detection.

The night was murky and moonless, but she didn't dare use the lantern until she was well away along the beach. The eastward going was rough over the rock-strewn ground, but she picked her way cautiously. Some place close by, she was sure of it. There had been no sound tonight of goods being borne up the hill. That meant that nothing had been brought in, or that it was still aboard the *Lady Gwen*, or that it was hidden. She doubted the first circumstance because she could not imagine that Magnus, or Rane for that matter, would fail in a task, and the second because it just seemed too hazardous to allow contraband to float aboard an anchored ship where customs officers might find it. Therefore, it seemed quite logical that the cargo was waiting, hidden nearby for the time when it could be safely moved.

It remained possible that Rane's warning about the caves had been because they were indeed dangerous, but she rejected that idea as she now rejected everything she had thought she knew about Rane. People in the village did not speak of the caves, at least not around her, and the children did not go there to play. The terrain was rough, small pebbles giving way to boulders, and the tides could be treacherous, but there was more to the avoidance than that.

She stopped, peering behind her and straining to hear the sounds of other footsteps above the lap of the sea. But she saw and heard nothing to indicate she was being followed. She needed to be alone, and yet perversely, she had never longed for companionship as much as she did at this instant. The sweep of the cliffs, the sea, and the darkness whirled around her until she felt as if she were already in the depths of a cave, lost and terrified. For a moment a temptation was overwhelming to scurry back to the house and pretend she suspected nothing at all.

She couldn't do it; she had to go on. Everything had changed as she had considered Lundy; she couldn't bear not to know.

Finally she was around a bend, out of sight of the village, and she dared to let a little light seep out of the lantern, keeping it between the land and her body, not wanting it to be sighted from the sea. She could see a few lights out on the water, lanterns on ships, among them no doubt the *Lady Gwen*.

She did not want to go into more fissures in the cliff than she had to. She reasoned that the cave would have to be large, not too far from the village, and would show signs of use.

Despite her care and logic, she nearly missed it. Her first two explorations had yielded nothing more than large cracks in the rocky cliff, and the third at first seemed to be the same until she saw that the feeble lantern light was swallowed by greater darkness rather than reflecting off stone.

It was perfect, a wall of stone set like a partially opened

door making it appear as if there was no sizeable space behind it until one walked around it and found a roomy passage leading inward. Further along the cliff face were more outcroppings of stone; she could see them dimly and guessed that they would block a view of the cave from that direction.

She took a deep breath and swallowed hard. The only way she would ever know was by going inside. A sudden spurt of anger spurred her onward—it was hardly likely that there was anyone guarding the goods; she was probably the only person in the village who had not known what was going on.

She smelled the cargo before she saw it, even over the dank odor of sea and wet rock. There was the sharp tang of brandy, probably from a leaking cask, and other scents— tar, damp rope, and the lingering smoke of fish-oil lamps. She even fancied she could smell the richer, more delicate scents of tea, spices, and tobacco. It came to her that the spices she had enjoyed in the food at the Falconer house, the tea she had sipped from the first day on, the Madeira she had sampled in a Christmas toast, and even the luxurious velvet of the green cloak, had all been brought into England illegally. She had been part of the conspiracy. The depth of her ignorance shocked her anew.

She opened the lantern all the way once she was deep inside the cave, unable to bear the utter darkness and fearful of falling over something. Even expecting it, she drew breath in astonishment.

Stacked as neatly as if the cavern were a store were kegs, barrels, and bales of goods, everything wrapped and sealed against the ravages of damp. The cave walls were stained with the smoke of countless lamps and torches. The very businesslike aspect of it made it more chilling; this had been going on for a very long time. It was certain that they would not let one young girl stand in their way.

They. They were Magnus, Rane, Gweneth, all the Falconers, and the friendly villagers besides. She felt physically sick thinking about it.

And then she felt nothing but terror as the figure loomed beside her, a devil conjured from nowhere because she had been so wrapped in the revelation before her, she had not heard him approach.

She opened her mouth to scream, fear overriding everything else so that she needed beyond all else to make the sound no matter how futile it was. But a hand clamped tightly over her mouth and a strong arm tried to hold the writhing body while her heart beat a furious tattoo.

The words came to her dimly, taking a long time to filter into her numbed mind.

"Alex, stop struggling, please stop! It's Rane, it's all right. Stop it!"

She went suddenly limp in his arms, and he thought she had fainted, but in fact she had merely surrendered. It was impossible to fight Rane now that he was here, holding her. She was too accustomed to his kindness, to the strange kinship that had extended beyond the similarity of their appearance ever since their first sight of each other.

Once sure that she was not unconscious, Rane released her and reached for the lantern he had brought with him, opening it to add its light to the glow cast by the one Alex had brought.

Alex swayed on her feet but remained upright, her green eyes staring at him in dull defeat.

"Don't," he pled softly, "don't look like that."

"How should I look? You lied to me, all of you. And my grandmother knew. You must think I am a very stupid child. It took me so long to understand." Her voice was as leaden as her eyes.

He shook his head doggedly, trying to order his thoughts, knowing that what he said to her now was vitally important. His own heart was still beating too fast, not yet over the fear he had felt when he discovered her gone. He took a deep breath and made himself speak slowly, calmly.

"We didn't lie. Nor did your grandmother. We just did not tell you what we were doing. I knew early on that you would surely guess someday because you notice things. The first time you were aboard the *Lady Gwen* you noticed that her cargo space is limited. In fact, I am surprised that it has taken you this long to find out."

"I trusted you!" There was more life in her voice now, and he welcomed it.

"And we trusted you in turn. You forget what you were like when you came to us. You were hurt and frightened. What would you have thought had your grandmother told you she was taking you to live with a family of West Country free traders?"

"Smugglers!" Alex snapped.

"As you will," Rane returned evenly, "but we call it free trading because that is exactly what it is. If we and others in the trade did not exist, only the wealthy could drink tea or taste brandy and other spirits, use tobacco, or wear silk and other fine cloth, or season their food with good spices. It is foolish and wrong to restrict trade with high duties! It hurts those who can least afford it. There are few enough pleasures in most lives; they should not be made less by a greedy government."

"Then I am to believe you do this out of the goodness of your hearts?" Alex asked sarcastically, looking much older than her years.

"You are to believe whatever you must. But I tell you that the trade is as old as the first tariff and that it is a profitable business when followed with skill. What you must believe without question is that your welcome here is true. We could not love you more if you had been born here and raised with us from the first day of your life."

She studied his face in the flickering, shadowed light, tracing the strong bones, the dark heavy hair framing his features, the thick-lashed eyes regarding her so steadily, and she could no more deny his appeal than cut out her own heart.

He saw her capitulation in the weary bowing of her head, and he gathered her close. "Nothing is changed except that now it will be easier because you know."

She could hardly get the words out, but she had to ask. "Was it all a sham? Was it just to keep me from finding out or to make me biddable when I did?"

At first he didn't understand the soft words murmured against his shoulder, and then he did because in some eerie way he understood things about Alex that went beyond words. It was why he had sought her here tonight. He had tried to keep away, knowing something was wrong beyond the story of the swans, a false tale he had been sure. When he had stood outside her door, he had felt that she was awake even though he could not see her. He had dozed off and then awakened with a start, feeling her absence from the house and her direction as strongly as if he had seen her leave. He was too tired to puzzle it out, and nothing mattered beyond reassuring Alex.

He patted her back in gentle rhythm. "You must never, never think that again. You are part of me as my brothers are, as my parents are, no less, no less since I first saw myself in the strange glass you are to me as I am to you. You have not been here so long, yet I can hardly imagine the time when you were not; it is as if you were born in the same house of the same mother as I and my brothers." Her question had been specifically about the relationship between the two of them, and he hoped desperately that he had banished all her doubts.

With a little sigh, she nestled closer against him, and his arms held her tightly while fierce joy coursed through him at the knowledge she had accepted the truth of his words. She was precious to him in ways he could not fathom. Wryly, he gave inner thanks that he had no other sisters; this feeling of protectiveness was a heavy burden and would be impossible to carry if multiplied beyond the one.

"You are weary and cold. Let us go home."

Carrying their lanterns, hand in hand they left the cave. Relief that nothing was changed between them made Alex giddy, and she scarcely knew that her feet were picking their way over the rocky ground, but she listened to Rane's further explanations of the trade, anxious now to know everything about this new world.

"In the best of times we unload the cargo and carry it out on the same night, but everything has to work perfectly for that. More often, it is as it was tonight—the goods are stored in the cave, and if the weather is right and no customs officers or soldiers are seen in the area, we'll take it up the hill tomorrow night and from there the carriers will take it on by ponies to villages, to various houses, even to Barnstaple and beyond, though by then the goods will be in other hands."

"Everybody must know," Alex ventured, wanting confirmation of what she had surmised earlier in the day.

"Indeed they do. And if they're not helping transport the goods, then they're buying or at the very least simply ignoring what's going on. It's hard to find anyone who does not wish to pay less than the legal price for tea, brandy, and the like. And that includes those at the manor."

"But the revenue men, they must know, too!" Alex's lethargy was lifting as she considered more fully the danger to Rane and the others.

"The trade is vast. There is hardly a place in the country that does not have the night traffic. When so many consider a law unjust and break it, there is little the govern-ment can do. Local men know their own land, their own coasts better than the agents ever will, and few locals will ever tell anything to the agents. It's a sad necessity—talking to a revenue man can be very dangerous unless it's known who can be bribed," he admitted with grim honesty. "And sometimes cargoes are intercepted. It's the risk of it. But we know many places to put in, and at worst, with very little warning time, we can dump the goods into the sea."

He was making every effort to make the trade sound as dull as storekeeping, but Alex had a clear picture in her mind's eye of the sleek revenue cutter cruising the waters so hungrily. The danger involved was rapidly becoming more important than the illegality.

"My grandmother, she knew . . .," her voice trailed off as she struggled with this still painful thought.

Rane hesitated and then decided that concealing the basic truth had already done enough damage. "Your grand-father and your Thaine uncles were free traders, too. You must know that Kent has as much business at night as anywhere."

She did know that; she had simply never connected it with her own life. It was more the stuff of tales of adventure. "Owlers" some called the night travelers, per-haps as a corruption of "woolers" or for the owl's call many used as a signal; others called them "caterpillars" for the fuzzy loads of wool that had been borne by their pack animals to waiting ships for hundreds of years, the heavy tax on exporting wool and at times the outright prohibition of export to protect the home cloth industry having made it a profitable venture to feed the looms of Europe, though now the war on the Continent had dis-rupted cloth production as well as other industries. Still, smuggling went on, goods going out and coming in with-out duty.

The smugglers did not pass right through the town of Gravesend, but Alex found the memory of a particular night spent at her grandmother's house when strange noises had disturbed the quiet. "It is nothing to be afraid of and none of our business," Virginia had assured the little girl.

She remembered more recent things, too—the fine tea and brandy served at her grandmother's house and by her parents as well. Suddenly she doubted that duty was paid on most of it or on the fine materials her mother favored for herself and Florence.

"Are they still smugglers?" she asked bluntly.

Rane let the offensive word pass. "No, your father never felt the same way about the trade as did his father and brothers. I expect though that your grandmother probably misses it. She was known to be a great help to her husband." Involuntarily, they both smiled in the darkness in tribute to Virginia. "And it was lucky for my family that they were part of the brotherhood. My father was quite young, but he was sailing with his father out of Barnstaple, and they roved far. They knew men of Gravesend because they often brought in big cargoes below the town, to avoid the customs agents. Then the goods could be taken overland even to London for good prices, and wool could be shipped out. But this time Magnus, his father, and their men were surprised onshore by the king's men. They might have been hanged for it or transported as convicts, but at great risk to themselves, your grandparents, your uncles, and their crew got them out of the government's clutches, hid them, and then got them back to their ship. It must have been a merry fight, but no one was killed. They'd known each other before, known the family connection, but that night marked a debt my family owed to yours. Virginia chose to collect it in the kindest way, but now I fear my family owes her more than ever before."

The courtly words were balm to the last bruises on Alex's spirit. As he had said he knew her, so she knew him, on some level far deeper than the polite currency of words. Finally, she understood that if anything were changed between them, it was only better because now she could share in the most vital part of the Falconers' lives. And the kindness was surely on Rane's part. She grinned to herself, quite sure that though he had not said so, Rane knew that her family enjoyed the benefit of duty-free goods as well as anyone, probably more due to old connections, even though her father was not actively engaged in smuggling. She could well imagine her grandmother's practical appreciation of purchasing finer goods for less money and making no fuss about it, but the image of her sanctimonious mother enjoying illegal pleasures amused her mightily.

She slept long and deeply that night, awakening to find

that for once even the men were up before her, and the expressions on Magnus's and Gweneth's faces were more eloquent than words. Rane had obviously told them of her discovery, and they had dropped the mantle of authority, waiting instead like anxious children, fearful that Alex would reject them now that she knew. Nothing could have told her more clearly how genuine their love for her was. She went to each of them, hugging them tightly as if she had been born into this warm family instead of to her own coldly reserved mother and faint-hearted father.

Her life changed radically from that day forward. What had seemed like belonging before was pale compared to her involvement now. Even the villagers' attitude changed. Once the need to guard their tongues was gone, so was their last reserve; they called to her now and greeted her as if she were just another child of the village. And more, she became actively involved in the free trading. There was no longer good cause to deny her the work so many shared when the cargoes had to be unloaded on the beach and taken into the cave or loaded on the sledges and taken up to where Seadon and others waited with the ponies. It was most often Seadon who directed the loading operation since of all the Falconers he spent the most time on land. When Seadon sailed with Magnus or Elwyn, Rane usually took his place to await the arrival of the sledges.

Gweneth confessed it was fine to be back on the regular routine, for she had been quietly keeping watch on the busy nights, staying awake after Alex had gone to sleep, waiting until the donkeys had passed by, always alert should Alex awaken and find that more valuable items than fish were streaming past. Normally Gweneth worked right along with the other men and women of Clovelly.

Tremors of excitement ran through Alex as she helped with that first load she had discovered, and even though she knew they had all been at it for a long time, she was amazed by the efficiency with which everything was brought out of the cave and lashed to sledges, a human chain passing the goods along until the sledges could be hitched to the little donkeys who knew the cobbled way of "Up-along" even in the dark, though they were not risked on the treacherous shingle. Alex begged to go with Seadon and the pack animals once everything was at the top of the hill, but her request was firmly refused. It was hazardous duty to run the goods across the land, and a cardinal rule was that no one take extra risks. She was good with the ponies and would be useful if she were needed, but until then her assigned work was what she would do and nothing more. She could not argue with the logic of it. But already she knew the craving for more excitement, as if it were a powerful drug. She could sense the same hunger in Rane and in Magnus and knew as well that it did not exist in Seadon or Elwyn; they simply performed their allotted tasks and were satisfied, neither attracted nor repelled by the danger.

Though Elwyn sailed his ship out of Appledore, most of the cargoes were landed in Clovelly or nearby as that was the territory he knew best and the territory under his father's sway.

Alex grew to understand that the risks were financial as well as physical. There were people to be paid all along the chain. The crew of the ship was paid in rigidly determined percentages from the captain's to the youngest crew member's share, and when there was no profit, they received nothing. Not so with others in the chain; they were paid whether the end result was profit or not. There were bribes to help obtain the best goods from the ports of France, Holland, the Channel Islands, and Ireland, bribes to merchants and port authorities and sometimes to revenue men or soldiers, plus the actual price of the tobacco, tea, coffee, wine, gin, soap, candy, tiles, china, pepper and other spices, madder for dyers, licorice for tobacco manufacturers, and a host of other commodities. Fashion was not neglected either. Silks, linens, laces, and myriad other fine fabrics were run in duty-free, though the risk of choosing something no longer in style tended to make these profits less sure—it took a canny eye and some attention to current modes to discern what would find current favor with ladies and gentlemen. One mark of the smugglers' success was the bandana. These large spotted silk handkerchiefs were in the possession of every fashionable woman in the land, and yet they were prohibited from legal entry.

Though most of the ports offered a variety of goods, some were noted for particular items. Roscoff in Finistère, "end of the world," the westernmost region of Brittany, as well as the Channel Islands of Guernsey and Alderney, were good places to take on wine and spirits. Rotterdam was excellent for brandy and for a wide variety of other goods; there, cargo could be made up of many different kinds of goods in varying weights and measures rather than in huge lots of only a few commodities. The Channel Islands and Ireland provided the best tobacco. Ireland, in particular, had direct connections with companies in New York and Baltimore in the United States, companies specially formed to smuggle tobacco into Ireland in large vessels. And much of that tobacco was in turn smuggled into England. The trade was even somewhat seasonal; for instance, the best time for obtaining wines and spirits began in February and went on for several months.

There were even subsidiary industries that depended wholly on the illicit trade, coopers who made the specially sized casks such as the "half-ankers" or four-gallon size, which could be roped in pairs and slung over a carrier's shoulders, and the eight-gallon "anker" cask for pack horses; men and women who made oilskin pouches to keep tobacco, tea, and cloth dry. And there were endless ways of concealing the goods, from ships with false bottoms and secret panels in their holds to specially sewn coats with deep pockets for holding tea or even small casks of rum. The Falconer ships relied on no such devices, but rather on speed to outrun revenue cutters, but they did carry false flags and false papers for the crew, and each carried a seaman who could sound foreign enough when warranted. Rane made a passable Frenchman, Elwyn a believable Dutchman, and there were others with similar talents. These precautions had allowed them to bluff their way past naval cruisers on a number of occasions, but since they were not prepared to be boarded and searched, they did not abuse the ruse. When a revenue cutter or naval cruiser was too close and all other measures had failed, they jettisoned their cargo. If they could not later locate casks and bales marked by subtle buoys, it meant the ultimate financial loss. It was well that the Falconers lived comfortable but not extravagant lives.

It intrigued Alex that there were gentlemen's rules among many of the free traders. They respected each other's dominions, not intruding on routes or customers. That, however, was not as restricting as it might seem on the surface. Tea, tobacco, and more brought into the West Country might well end up in London, having been transported there by private armies of men and pack animals that moved through the night. But Magnus was not greedy. Only infrequently did he use the old contacts he had had through his father on the east and southeastern coasts of England. They were better patrolled now, and he preferred not to hazard the trade there. He bought contraband from the full range of foreign ports, but he brought almost all of it back to his own bailiwick. And his goods that found their way to London did so only because they had been sold along the way to someone else. Occasionally he did run cargo into Liverpool or Bristol, but only when he judged the customs authorities to be overworked enough to overlook the extra goods. Magnus, for all his great size, was shrewd rather than overconfident, and his sons were like him. They preferred to deal with local people when they brought the cargoes in. Locals who were ready to light warning beacons on the cliffs if soldiers were in the area or if a revenue cutter had been sighted in the waters. Locals who helped unload the cargo, who knew every stone and bush of the area and could guide the night caravans to their various destinations, having woods, concealed pits, and even haystacks picked out along the route in case the goods had to be hidden quickly. Locals who served as informers, routinely reporting the whereabouts of soldiers and revenue men. Magnus shared the belief of many that violence was to be avoided whenever possible. He had nothing but contempt for others, known in various parts of the country, who dealt routinely in mayhem.

"It will ruin the trade for all of us," he declared, face ruddy with anger whenever this particular subject was discussed. "It is the one thing that could set all the people against us. They will not tolerate broken heads or dead bodies for the sake of cheap tea and brandy, any more will I. Why, it is the reason John Wesley bid his followers in the last century to abstain from drinking tea. Called it poison, he did, and just because some were rough who brought it in."

Alex had quickly come to share the Falconers' views. To them smuggling was an old and honorable trade. They did not deny the guilt that came from the fact that buying goods from the French during Napoleon's reign had put gold into the pockets of the enemy. Special forty-foot-long rowing boats manned by thirty-six oarsmen had been called "guinea boats" because, built in Calais, they were used by free traders rowing from Dover, Deal, and Folkstone. And the same was true of the tobacco shipments they bought in roundabout ways from American sources, though it could be said some balance came from selling English goods to the French often enough to make the gold flow back the other way. The Americans, too, showed themselves not above a need for England's manufactured plenty, despite naval blockades and war. They did not deny the guilt, but neither did they dwell on it. Nor did they sell information to the French, an act they considered traitorous, though many others indulged in it for the high rewards it offered. The trade had gone on for too long for it to be suspended for temporary political situations or even wars. The markets and even the goods themselves might vary, but the essential business of avoiding what were considered to be unjust tariffs did not. The Falconers did not consider that business traitorous, only sensible.

And only, as Magnus said, public revulsion against it or truly free trade allowed by the government would stop it. Edmund Burke and William Pitt the Younger had tried in the 1790's to reduce or lift tariffs in addition to tightening restrictions governing importation and storage of tobacco, but the French war had pushed those and other reforms off the stage. The duty on tobacco was now three shillings, two pence a pound; the tax on tea added nearly a hundred percent to the cost.

Alex found herself hoping that it would not all end in Magnus's lifetime. She could not imagine the big man happy with anything less than the freedom and risk he enjoyed so much. His sons were young enough to adjust, but not Magnus. And no matter how much Gweneth worried about him, Alex knew that she would not steal a single voyage from him as long as it made him happy.

So close was she now to the Falconers, Alex had difficulty recalling what her life had truly been like in Gravesend. Sometimes even her grandmother's face was hard to conjure. Of the marriage of St. John and her sister, she hardly thought at all. It was not part of her life.

❧ Chapter 8 ❧

Spring was slow in coming, remaining wet and chill even in northwest Devon, which usually had a more pleasant time of it due to the warm wind and currents from the sea. Steam rose so constantly from wet clothing drying in her kitchen, Gweneth claimed the room was enveloped in its own fog bank.

But spring, foul weathered or not, brought changes to the Continent and thus to England. In June of the previous year, Wellington had at last crossed the Pyrenees from Spain into France. And after Napoleon's defeat at Leipzig in October 1813, an odd assortment of allies including Great Britain, Russia, Germany, Prussia, Austria, Italy, and Spain, bound together only by their hatred (newly discovered in some cases) of Napoleon's rule, managed to unite for long enough to force Napoleon to abdicate in early April. The allies would be settling matters with the government of the restored Bourbons in France, and Napoleon Bonaparte's empire had now shrunk to the small island of Elba between Corsica and Italy. The worst enemies the allies now faced were their own greed and distrust of each other.

But tariffs had not changed even with legal trade opening up as blockades ended, and the free trading went on as if no political upheavals had occurred. The ships brought back news and rumors even faster than the mail coaches and the London papers could spread them, and so there were lively discussions in the Falconer house concerning what changes peace would bring though there were still the hostilities with the Americans to consider. After so many years of war with France, peace was an odd idea.

Elwyn, ever the most pedantic of the family, predicted that the opening markets for British manufactured goods would bring profit because England was so far ahead of other nations that she had an advantage, but that farmers might well suffer once foodstuffs came from the Continent. Farming methods remained primitive due to the refusal in most cases of farmers to relinquish old ways, in spite of the availability of new knowledge.

Alex thought of her grandmother and could see Elwyn's point. Virginia kept her land productive by rotating crops and enriching the soil with marl, dung, and straw ash and was always willing to study new ways and try them if they seemed feasible, but there were many landholders and uncaring tenants even in fertile-earthed Kent who did not feel the same. And closer to hand, Alex had observed the work it took for Seadon to convince Mr. Scroggins that something could be better done this way than the old way Scroggins followed.

Alex thought it just as well that the fate of the country did not rest with her; life was too compelling in its immediacy to fret overlong about the future. She and Rane celebrated spring birthdays, his in early April, hers in early May, turning nineteen and fourteen respectively. She was glad the Falconers did not believe the old Devonshire superstition that cats and children born in May were unlucky; such cats were often drowned so that they would not bring "long-cripples" or vipers into the house—what was done to the children she feared to ask.

On another account entirely, Rane teased her about becoming a young lady whether she willed it or not, and she responded by wearing her breeches even more often.

Outwardly she had changed very little. Her monthly courses had started before she came to Clovelly, but they had not seemed to add the curves her sister had so swiftly acquired at the same age. For that Alex was thankful. She liked her body long and lean and quick, just the way it was, capable of working and playing hard, capable of keeping up with Rane. Because Alex was now part of the secret, she and Rane were more inseparable than before, seeming ever more like a set of twins that had oddly been born in different places at different times. And bright quick youth flowed so strongly in both of them that they celebrated spring with endless energy despite the laggard season.

The ground remained so sodden that it was difficult to get the crops in at the farm, but they lent their backs and hands to whatever work was being done, causing Seadon to complain in mock distress that their overbrimming spirits were causing him to feel ancient. The same willingness made short work of tasks aboard the *Lady Gwen*. And they roamed the countryside in perfect harmony, seldom needing words to mark their mutual pleasure in the life stirring over the land in defiance of the rain.

The orange-red breasts of tiny robins flashed in the brush. Skylarks shot toward the heavens and showered the earth with their long sweet notes. Pied wagtails pursued their busy lives in sharp black and white patterns, their tails in constant jerky motion, earning their name. And the clear loud music of the song thrushes was as sweet to Alex as the nightingales' she had sometimes heard in Kent. The countryside seemed suddenly crowded with bird life, life driven to a joyful crescendo on the days when the sun broke through.

Rane found a badger sett obviously ancient and still occupied, since the various entrances had piles of discarded grass bedding and excavated material from tunnels and well-worn paths led away to the surrounding countryside. He and Alex waited in the dusk one evening and were rewarded by seeing several of the animals waddle out, their broadly black and white striped faces distinct even in the fading light. "Brock" some called the badger, often coupled with a derogatory term, and many killed them on the basis of spurious charges of damage, so it was a gift to see them. But even better was the family of otters discovered in a wynd of water in woodland near the farm. The land rolled steeply enough there so that the water ran over a small fall and pooled. The otters played with the particular comic frenzy of their kind, rippling down a worn mud slide, engaging in intricate games of chase and tag and causing Rane and Alex to rock with silent laughter that exploded once the animals had moved on out of sight.

For once the day was warm, and the little pond was tempting. In one swift motion Rane scooped a handful of water and sent it flashing over Alex. "Too bad you can't swim," he taunted.

"Ah, but I can! I'm no deck-bound sailor! Are you?" she

challenged, secure in the skill Boston and St. John had taught her years before.

Rane was no less prepared than she, having been thrown into the sea by his father at an early age. Magnus was tolerant of most sailors' superstitions and even believed some of them, but he thought it the height of folly to go to sea without being able to swim.

Without thought, as natural as the otters, Rane and Alex raced to peel off their outer clothing and plunged into the water in their undergarments, Alex's only concession to her sex being the cutoff chemise she had worn under her boy's shirt in addition to the drawers beneath her breeches.

The water wasn't very deep, but they made do and, shrieking with laughter, they played like small children, trying to splash and dunk each other, sending up great sweeps of water in the dappled light. Alex grabbed Rane's shoulders and tried to pull him under, but he pushed her backwards so that she submerged instead, coming up sputtering and trying to wipe her heavy wet hair out of her eyes.

"I give up!" she gasped. "Trying to put you under is like pushing over a mountain, a rainy mountain." She giggled at her silly wit, and they both remembered how he had spelled his old Norse name out when he had introduced himself to her.

They drowsed in a patch of sunlight, waiting for hair and undergarments to dry enough so that they could don their clothes, talking little because they needed no words to express the lazy contentment they were sharing. And now that the humans were quiet, the birds filled the air with song.

"I wish this day could last forever," Alex said finally, feeling the edge of sadness that comes when things are too perfectly beautiful to contain.

Rane propped himself up on one elbow and studied her face. "Summer is still to come. There will be many fair days. And if this day went on forever, then you would never grow up. Would you truly want that?" He found he was interested in her answer though he didn't know why.

Eyes staring at the canopy of sky and leaves above her, brow slightly furrowed in thought, Alex considered the question, answering slowly. "I would like some of the things that only come with age. I would like to be as wise as my grandmother and to know as much as she does about everything. And I would like to be old enough so that no one could ever again tell me what to do. I would like the days to be my own. But here, that is so nearly true, I don't have to wish for it," she added hastily, wanting to make it clear that it was the old days in Gravesend that were so restrictive, not her time here in Devon. "But for the rest, I would rather be just as I am now, young and strong enough to swim and run and just *be* on days like this."

"Not everyone becomes a prisoner when older," Rane suggested gently. "Many live lives they choose. I am not saying it is easy, but it is possible."

His experience of young girls was not vast, but it was enough so that he found Alex a sharp contrast; all the others he had known could not wait to grow up and assume the mantle of adulthood. He assumed it must come from the bad relationships she had with her mother and her sister, seeing their womanhood as discontent and cruelty. Whatever the cause, Alex wore her childhood like a protective cloak. Paradoxically he found himself both attracted and frustrated by the disguise. He wanted her to stay the same forever, while he was intrigued to know what kind of woman she would become. He supposed it was the way parents felt about their children, the way brothers felt about younger sisters of whom they were fond. But taking the thought further, he realized that were she simpering and missish, given to mooning over cloyingly sweet verse and impossibly romantic novels and to fussing endlessly over what she wore, he would find her company unbearable. He supposed further that what he wanted was for her to stay essentially the same, just possessed of the accoutrements of adulthood. He let the thought go; the day was too pleasant for mental exercise.

Even their seasonal high spirits were dampened by events in the next week. It had been Rane's turn to sail with Magnus again, Seadon having gone on the last voyage to give Rane a bit more time ashore. From Appledore, Elwyn's ship also sailed, and it was Elwyn who returned first, as overdue as the others, his face set in grim lines.

"We were intercepted by a revenue cutter. Father played cat and mouse with them so that I could go on. It's the hardest thing I've ever done, but I am sworn to it." For a moment his customary composure cracked, and he looked as if he would weep. With visible effort, he regained control. "I don't know whether they were taken or not."

Alex felt as if all the blood had drained out of her body on the instant, but she saw the proud straight set of Gweneth's shoulders and took strength from her calm voice. "You had no choice. It has long been agreed. And do not forget that your father is a wily man when needs be. He's been in the trade for a long time, and he hasn't yet been taken. You go home to Susannah. I will send word when the men are home. And they will be, never doubt it."

Elwyn did as he was bid, not suspecting that his mother was so worried, she could not bear the added burden of his anxious face.

The next forty-eight hours were the longest in Alex's life, and she was sure they seemed even longer to Gweneth. But the woman continued to follow her normal daily routine, allowing no signs of doubt or weakness to show, not even when the sea was shrouded in fog that would make coming home that much more dangerous, if the *Lady Gwen* were coming home at all.

The idea of not seeing Rane again was a pain so acute, Alex could not bear to think about it. She tried to make her mind go blank, and when that did not work, she filled it with images of him—Rane running, laughing; Rane absorbed in a task or a book or a conversation—images so vital that it was impossible he would not return. She knew that other people, the families of Magnus's crew in Clovelly and neighboring hamlets were doing the same thing.

Magnus and Rane arrived home in the middle of the night. The fog had lifted with the wind, and they had ridden the moonlight home.

Gweneth and Alex were awake, sitting in the kitchen drinking tea. Without words they had acknowledged their need for company and the impossibility of sleeping.

A sound outside, and then the house seemed filled to bursting with the smell of the sea, sweat, and healthy man flesh and the sound of male voices.

Their faces were lined with fatigue, dark circles ringing their eyes and making Rane look as old as Magnus. They were unsteady on their feet, and Rane had a bandage around one hand, but they were indisputably alive.

Only then did Alex know how hard the waiting had

been on Gweneth, for the woman, having seen at a glance that her menfolk were basically sound, had a most unexpected reaction. She clenched her fists and wailed, "Magnus Falconer, if you ever frighten me so again, I will kill you myself, I will!" And then she burst into sobs.

Everyone froze, unnerved by this display from the member of the family who was normally the strong, calm one, and then Magnus gathered her into his arms. She beat her fists feebly against his chest, tears still streaming down her cheeks.

He patted her back and stroked her hair, his huge paws unsteady. "Ah, Gwenny, ah love, quiet now. It's all right. We're safely home and the *Lady Gwen*, too. I love you, Gwenny, I love you so." He crooned to his wife in a voice so gentle, Alex felt tears pricking her own eyes and could scarcely swallow past the lump in her throat. The depth of love in this house still had the power to move her unbearably.

To cover her emotion she went to Rane and managed a shaky, "I'm so glad you're both back safely. Now, please, let me see your hand, I'm sure it needs dressing."

He protested that it was all right, but he acquiesced to her request because it gave them both something to do; he, too, was deeply touched by the emotions still swirling around them. He had no awareness that the smile he gave Alex was of such piercing sweetness, she had to bite her lip to keep her own tears from falling.

But it steadied her to tend his injury, focusing all her attention on the old rituals of healing. They had had to do some quick, hard maneuvering with the sails, and one of the lines had cut deeply across Rane's palm. To Alex's relief, he had the use of all his fingers, and the laceration would heal with time and care, but she winced in sympathy as she cleaned it.

In truth, Rane felt little, so dulled were his senses by emotion and fatigue. He was simply instinctively glad she was close, the soft scent of her filling his nostrils as she worked efficiently on his torn hand.

Gweneth, blushing a little because she was as surprised as anyone by her outburst, regained enough control to resume her role as chief comforter of the household, bustling about to set out food, fresh tea, and a bottle of fine brandy.

Magnus eyed the bottle morosely and told the rest of

the tale. He was not ungrateful for their escape, but he was smarting badly from the loss of the cargo. "Heaved every bit of it over the side, had to, the cutter was that close to us. Damned scavengers, that slowed them down! I'll wager they took some of it aboard and not for the king!"

It was a grievous loss, and failure to bring the cargo home was hard on both father and son, but it was difficult for the women to register the same degree of distress—they were too relieved that the men had not been caught.

Gweneth swallowed her misgivings when Magnus and Rane took the ship out a scant two days later. Alex, too, kept her mouth shut, though she wanted to protest that Rane's hand was not fully healed. It was a matter of pride with the men; the failure of the last voyage rankled. The crew was no less resolute, all of them making light of the difficulties they faced, the most basic being that no prear-ranged cargo would await them at Rotterdam, the destina-tion Magnus chose. But it was a vast storehouse of a town with enough for all.

Alex wished desperately that she had sailed with them. She was sure it was worse waiting at home. Even Gweneth's easy temper was frayed and uncertain. Neither of them was convinced of Magnus's theory that the revenue cutter they had run afoul of would consider them too well routed to venture out so soon again. There was, after all, more than one family involved in the trade. Magnus was also convinced that the cutter had not gotten a clear enough view of the ships to know that the home ports were Clovelly and Appledore because they had not followed into the home waters. But he bade Elwyn to remain in port, a circumstance that indicated he was not so certain of his theory as to risk two ships and two sons. Elwyn could not object; he and his crew had not lost their cargo and had nothing to avenge.

The days and nights crawled by until it was reasonable to expect the *Lady Gwen*. Alex's patience was at an end, and she was so twitchy, Gweneth agreed without hesita-tion when she requested permission to keep watch in the cave. It was the first place there would be activity once the *Lady Gwen* had slipped into the vicinity. Waiting there made a certain mad sense in this mad time, and Gweneth was tempted to wait with the child. Her spirits lightened at the thought of how her husband would react if he found her there.

"You must promise to keep close watch. That revenue men have not found it yet does not mean that they never will. There is nothing there now to incriminate you, but it would not be well for you to be discovered."

Alex knew what an act of trust it was for Gweneth to allow her to go. It was a way of acknowledging that Alex had her own pain in the waiting and should thus be allowed the privilege of risk.

The first night nothing happened beyond cramped and chilled limbs that finally sent her home to her warm bed, but the second night, just when she was ready to give up and had emerged onto the beach, she was rewarded by faint sounds over the sea wash, oars moving in muffled oarlocks. Quickly shutting off all light from her lantern, she shrank back into the shadows near the cave entrance and waited, wanting to make sure of identity before she betrayed her presence. She heard the scrape of the keel and then Rane's voice, hushed but audible, giving instructions as he spoke to one of the crew.

She called out low but clear, not wanting to startle them but doing so anyway.

Rane's voice came back sharp and anxious. "Alex! What are you doing, is something wrong?" And then he was before her, looming blessedly tall and strong and whole.

"Nothing is wrong. Everything is right now! I just couldn't bear to wait at the house." Her voice trilled with the same joy as the skylark singing from the heights, and Rane had never felt more welcomed home.

They had seen several revenue cutters but had dodged all confrontations and had come back with a full load. But it was becoming clear that, now that the war with France had ended, more of the government's resources were going to be concentrated on catching the free traders. It was yet another aspect of the shifting political climate. However, as far as Magnus and Rane were concerned, it only meant being more careful, not engaging in less trade. On that note, they stored the night's cargo in the cave, planning to make sure all was clear before they moved it out the next night.

It was as if the war had never been. Rotterdam had been full of luxuries, and the items they had brought back would go a good way to making up for the lost cargo:

silks that under their waterproof wrappings seemed to have sunlight woven through them, the finest grades of tea, coffee, and tobacco, brandy that was soft on the palate and strong in the brain, Madeira of sweet perfection, spices that prickled the nose, and a host of other treasures.

However, the smoothness of the operation in Europe did not continue for the finish of it at home. The next day, Seadon sprained his ankle badly, making it impossible for him to take the ponies cross-country that night, and to compound the problem, another man who knew the route well was also incapacitated, suffering, as Gweneth stated tartly, "from greedy belly. His is more than ample, and he will go on these great bouts of eating and drinking. Gluttony will no doubt be the death of him one day."

The rest of the men who would guide the ponies were ready, but there still must be a leader, and with Seadon and the other unavailable, it meant that Magnus, Rane, or Elwyn must take the pack train.

"Elwyn does enough from Appledore," Rane pointed out. "I'll take it. I'm well rested, and in any case, I would like to see this particular cargo safely away." He and his father exchanged a look of complete understanding.

"I want to go, too," Alex said. "I am very good with the ponies, and I'll do exactly as I'm told."

Three pairs of eyes stared at her, more taken aback by the steely purpose in her quiet voice than by her proposition. She met their looks calmly, chin lifted in defiance.

Magnus's first impulse was to bellow that it was out of the question, but he found himself curiously unable to form the words. Alex and Rane went everywhere together, and the girl was good help at whatever work she did. Suddenly it did not seem so odd to think of her going with Rane tonight. Frowning, he looked to Gweneth for help, but his wife was staying out of it for reasons of her own—they all took risks by engaging in the trade, and as long as one did not jeopardize the operation or one's fellows, it was an individual choice as to how much danger one courted. She knew Rane enjoyed the hazard, enjoyed it quite apart from the business at hand, and she was sure Alex shared the same hunger. She was not sure the child would remain at home tonight even were she ordered to do so.

Rane was amazed by his parents' forbearance as the silence stretched out. As for himself, he was so accustomed now to having Alex by his side it hardly seemed out of the ordinary that she wanted to go tonight. With effort he kept himself from smiling at the image of how his father would react if Alex next insisted that she be included in the crew of the *Lady Gwen*. But that she would not do, no matter how much she might wish it; she was honest and knew she had no special skill or strength to offer in that situation. It was different with the ponies.

"I have no objection," Rane said finally, not wanting his father to feel this was a conspiracy but at the same time compelled to give Alex support.

Magnus studied one young face and then the other. "So be it, but remember your promise, Alexandria, whatever Rane tells you to do, you do without question. He is the captain tonight as much as if he were on the deck of his own ship."

Alex nodded, taking the charge seriously, but nothing could stop the shining of her eyes. Anticipation and excitement coursed through her like rare wine, and it seemed to take extra hours for the day to pass.

The moon was uncertain, hidden off and on by clouds and for that all were grateful though they took the added precaution of blackening their faces. The transportation of the goods from cave to donkey sledges to the ponies went without flaw, and they were on their way, the ponies' hooves wrapped against unnecessary sound. They walked, leading the heavily laden animals because it made them easier to control. Caution was more important than speed. When the cargo was delivered, they could ride.

Their destination was to the east where they would turn everything over to another free trader who would take it on to Exeter. They would earn far more if they took it all the way to the city themselves, but that was not Magnus's way, and his men agreed with him. They were seamen, most comfortable when on the water; they were willing to earn less in order to spend less time being vulnerable on land far from their own corner of the country. It was different on the rare occasions when they ran goods directly into a port such as Liverpool or Bristol. Then the Falconers dealt directly with merchants they knew who were more than eager for the duty-free merchandise. As much as possible in his limited kingdom, Magnus varied the destinations of his shipments as he did the foreign ports he visited to buy the cargoes. Despite occasional losses such as the dumped fortune of the previous voyage, his system worked and provided a good and steady income for families who would otherwise have existed in dire poverty, particularly now that the herring ran so erratically year to year.

Alex's senses were so alert, she could taste the difference in the air as they moved away from the sea, and every night bird's call seemed as loud as thunder. But she walked calmly beside her pony, concentrating on not frightening him with her own nervousness. If there was cause for alarm, Rane or one of the others would tell her. Their route took them through the least populous parts of the countryside, and even when their passing caused dogs to bark at isolated farm houses, no one ventured out to discover who was going by. The people of the area were well trained to ignore the night traffic.

Two young men, chosen because they were swift and wiry, kept well ahead of the ponies, scouting the terrain to make sure there were no soldiers about.

They had been traveling for hours and were only an hour or so from their destination when one of the forward men came running back. There were dragoons up ahead and coming their way. Rane's orders were given swiftly, without panic, and then he was beside her, making sure she knew what to do.

Their route had been planned with just such emergencies in mind. The track they were on now wound through thickets and stunted trees, and in a trice, the patch was abandoned, the free traders and the ponies deep in cover, the ponies' muzzles held so they would not betray their location.

Rane whispered very low, "No questions, no disobedience, if they come in here after us, you climb a tree, and you stay there no matter what happens. You cannot be discovered. The fact that you are a female would not be to the good." His voice did not give away the agony he was suffering at the thought of what they might do to her.

"I will." It was enough that he ordered it; she had sworn to obey. She only hoped she would have the strength to follow the command if she had to. At the moment her blood was roaring in her ears and her knees felt so weak, she wasn't sure she could remain upright, let alone climb anything.

The sounds of the soldiers' approach invaded the thicket,

the thud of hooves, the jingle of harness and sabers, and the voices of the officers. Alex felt Rane relax a little beside her, and she understood—the troop of cavalry would not be making so much noise if they expected to find anyone here. It was a routine patrol, being carried out with sloppy boredom.

Alex was suddenly immensely proud of Rane and his men. They were far more disciplined than the soldiers. There was not a sound, not a cough or sneeze or heavy breath from any of them or from the ponies. It was as if they had become spirits and vanished into the night. Her own heartbeat slowed and slipped back to an even rhythm.

They waited a long time until they were absolutely sure the troop had passed on, so long that the night creatures forgot their presence and rustled and scurried close by without alarm. Then they moved back on the track and continued the journey as though nothing had happened.

"Would you have climbed the tree?" Rane asked, the relief note plain in his soft voice.

"If I could have," Alex replied honestly. "My knees were quite useless for a while."

They smothered their impulse to laugh aloud, but Rane was well satisfied. She had proved as good a companion on this journey as in other situations. Nothing was more useless or dangerous than someone who did not feel fear when it was sensible to do so; fear was part of the excitement, and it helped to keep one alert and alive.

Again the two young men were ahead, but this time they found no soldiers, only the agent who was their objective. The man was well pleased with the contents of the packs as listed by Rane, and he knew there would be no short measures or shoddy goods. He had dealt with the Falconers for a long time; they delivered fairly, and he paid in kind.

Alex was fascinated by a last piece of efficiency. The farmhouse where the man lived (and if he had family there was no sign of them now) had a perfectly innocent looking cellar, but under it was yet another space, the only way in a well-concealed trap door. They unloaded the goods and stored them there, and then they were on their way home. The agent would gather his own secret army and move the merchandise on when he judged it safe. Few words were spoken, and no hospitality was offered; it was best for all concerned that the business be accomplished as swiftly as possible.

On the return trip, they rode the ponies, surefooted even in the dark, and by dawn they were leaving the animals at the farm and trudging home to Clovelly. With sudden grins, the men gave Alex a ragged cheer for having done a good night's work.

"Sartin sure, the lass 'il be vantin' shares vrum us all zoon," one of them grumbled in mock worry, and Alex answered him pertly in his own dialect, "Nay, none o' that, I'll take a dish o' tay an' be glad o' dere ol' Deb'n, needin' nort more," which caused a hearty round of laughter.

Tired to the bone, Alex could not remember a time when she had felt happier.

❧ Chapter 9 ❧

Alex knew it couldn't really make the *Lady Gwen* speed home any faster, but she felt better when she waited at the cave for the men. She was so quietly but determinedly stubborn about her need to be there, the Falconers ceased trying to dissuade her once she promised she would bolt for safety at the first sign of trouble. The fact that she had followed Rane's orders exactly on the night they had nearly run into the soldiers was much in her favor. That she only went to the cave when Rane was aboard the *Lady Gwen* did not seem odd to anyone.

She did not really expect them back this night—more probably it would be tomorrow night—but she decided it wouldn't hurt to wait for a while, just in case.

She approached and entered the cave carefully, reminding herself that it would never do to be too casual about the possibility of running into authorities.

She went from confidence to complete terror so swiftly that she didn't have time to scream before the hand was clamped over her mouth. She tried to hit the huge form that engulfed her with the lantern, but it was wrenched from her grasp. She went wild, wiggling, kicking, and gasping for air.

"Son of a bitch! Young 'un, stop struggling, and I'll stop squeezing. Bargain?"

It was his accent in addition to his rueful tone that made her comply by going still in his arms. Though no words were truly distorted, it wasn't the sound of Devonshire or of any other area in England that she had ever heard. It was a slight, soft drawl that reassured her somehow, making her fear ebb. The man let her go, and she stepped back a little, but stood her ground, staring at him.

He was very tall and very thin with cadaverous hollows in his cheeks and near his temples over an unkempt beard. His golden brown hair was equally ungroomed. But even ringed by shadows, his dark eyes were bright and intelligent, studying her as closely as she was him.

"Caleb Jennings, at your service, ma'am," he said, nearly falling over as he tried to execute a courtly bow. "I knew you weren't a boy early on," he added, his solemnity belied by a slow grin.

For all his height, he was a pitiful sight in the lantern's glow. Shaggy he might be, but he was more or less clean in his tattered clothes, obviously having made the effort in the sea or some stream of fresh water. And he was just as plainly weak, sick, and hungry. He had spent so much of his small store of energy on grabbing her, she was sure that if she pushed him hard, he would fall over like a toppled tree. To cover the surge of maternal tenderness that engulfed her, she responded tartly. "I suppose you've never seen a female in boy's clothing before."

"Wrong," he corrected gravely. "I have two sisters, hellions both, and they tested the freedom of breeches—mine—at one time or another. It's a wonder I wasn't naked as a jaybird for years on end." He was unaware he was swaying on his feet. "By the way, where am I exactly?"

Laughter bubbled up and overflowed in Alex as she listened to his quaint speech. "You're near the village of

Clovelly on the Devonshire coast. Please do sit down before you fall," she said, and he complied gratefully, folding up and sinking down like a peculiarly graceful mechanical toy and placing the still burning lantern carefully beside him.

In that single gesture, Alex saw how much he craved the light, how lonely and afraid he must be here so far from his home—that he was far away from it she had no doubt.

"I am Alexandria Thaine. Where are you from, Mr. Jennings?"

He eyed her gravely. "Late of the prison at Princetown on Dartmoor, sometimes of Ashburton when allowed there on parole, but my home is in Annapolis, Maryland, in the United States."

Alex's eyes widened as she considered what he was telling her. He was an American prisoner of war. She had known vaguely that there were such in the country, taken from ships after sea battles. She had little animosity toward the Americans, indeed many felt as she did. Unlike the French war, the American trouble was far off and seemed a sad and needless confusion between two peoples with at least language in common, even though the Americans had severed their connection with the Crown in the last century. But this was quite another matter, having an escaped prisoner of war sitting before her. He could bring ruin on all of them.

"Are there soldiers pursuing you?" Her voice was less steady than she wished.

"I doubt it very much," he answered honestly. "The prison is a long way from here. I've been walking across the country for days and days. They don't really know what to do with us at the prison. There've been a lot of Frenchmen there, too, and there isn't enough money or food or clothing for all. Officers are allowed to billet in Ashburton if they can afford it. I was there for a time until I couldn't scrape enough together to stay any more. The men are hungry, cold, and sick much of the time. I think even the guards feel somewhat badly about it. They might notice I'm gone, they might even look for me, but I don't think they're going to waste a troop of dragoons scouring the land."

She tried to gather her scattered wits. Without knowing she had done so, she had decided to help him. "I'm sorry, but you'll have to get up again. I don't think the men will be back tonight, but . . ." Her voice trailed away as she realized what she had revealed.

He grinned at her crookedly as he rose to his full height once more. "I thought there must be some smuggling going on. Even the few broken staves I felt in the darkness smell of brandy. My first idea was that there might be food, and my second was that I might stow away on the smugglers' ship. A long chance at best, I know, but I seem to have run out of land."

"Free traders," Alex corrected automatically, and his smile widened.

"I think I like 'moonrakers' best," he announced, as if he had given the matter great thought, and they both laughed. Alex knew the story, too. Rane had told her. The incident had happened in Wiltshire nearly thirty years before, when the authorities discovered the villagers raking the local pond by moonlight. The villagers were actually trying to recover casks of spirits they had secreted there, but they pretended they had gone mad in the moon's light and were raking the water like a field. Nervously the soldiers had moved on, and the story had spread all over England and beyond.

Caleb was unsteady on his feet, and Alex moved to help him, pressing against his side and draping one of his long arms over her shoulder. She could feel the feverish heat radiating from him. "Lean on me, I'm quite strong."

"I believe you are," he murmured.

She left him propped against the cave wall near the entrance while she went outside to check that all was clear, and then they made their way east to the first and smaller cave that Alex had found on the night she went looking for the cache.

"You must stay very quiet, just in case someone comes or the boat lands," she cautioned him. "I'll leave the lantern with you for now, but if I'm not back in an hour, you had better extinguish it just to be safe." She could not bear to deprive him of light so soon.

He looked so sad at her leaving, she hastened to explain further. "I truly will try to come back tonight, but it may not be possible. You need blankets, food, and water so that you don't have to go outside to find it. Please trust me to bring everything as soon as I can, even if it isn't until tomorrow night."

"I do trust you," he said firmly, not adding that he had little choice because, in fact, it went beyond that. It was odd, but it was as if they were old friends despite the fact that they had just met and came from countries thousands of miles apart.

She picked her way back to the bottom of the village, shrinking back into the shadows and waiting with pounding heart as two fishermen came out of the tavern, their voices loud and happy from the pints they'd consumed. The trip up to the house seemed longer than it had ever been, and she prayed that Gweneth had already gone to bed. She could not explain her mission, and yet she couldn't bear the idea of the American spending the night without at least some few comforts.

Her breath escaped in a sigh of relief when she found the house silent, and she suppressed her feelings of guilt as she gathered food, medicine, a stone jar of water, a bottle of brandy, and blankets from her bedroom where she hoped they would not be missed.

She left the house again, feeling as if she'd been climbing up and down the steep street all night long. But she made it back to the cave without detection, and that was a major victory.

Caleb was dozing fretfully but roused when he heard her, and when she gave him the food, it was all he could do not to fall on it like a starving beast. He did not need her warning that if he ate too quickly, he would be sick. The plain nourishing fare and the brandy tasted better than anything he had had in his life, and he told her so.

"That's a measure of your hunger. Even Magnus and Rane, who will eat almost anything, would find this dull on the palate," she retorted, but she was pleased by his appreciation.

He asked her who Magnus and Rane were, and she found herself chattering about coming to Devon and about the Falconer family though she deleted the reason for her exile. She didn't think it made any difference what she said; he was just happy to be at ease with another human being after days of hiding.

At her bidding, he swallowed the contents of the vial she had brought, causing her eyes to widen in surprise as he quoted:

> Come, bitter conduct, come, unsavoury guide!
> Thou desperate pilot, now at once run on
> The dashing rocks thy sea-sick weary bark!
> Here's to my love! O true apothecary!
> Thy drugs are quick. Thus with a kiss I die.

then slumped to his side and closed his eyes dramatically, lids fluttering.

One eye rolled open again. "I wager you didn't know barbaric Americans can be acquainted with the Bard?"

Alex giggled, but the little scene had told her much of about how well read this man was, possessed of a sense of humor that she had already seen earlier, and surely a gentleman even if he was an American.

"The quote is abused, sir," she returned with mock outrage. "I do not poison my patients, only their maladies. You have a fever that would be better gone."

Caleb in turn learned more of her, and he was strangely touched by the odd combination of youth and age she was.

They talked a great deal more because Caleb was as loath to relinquish her company as she was to leave him sick and alone. The effects of the brandy and the infusion she had given him made him talkative, and he opened up a whole new world for her.

When she had thought of America at all, she had vaguely envisioned a vast forbidding land peopled mostly by wild red Indians and uncouth descendants of religious fanatics and convicts, though to be sure the latter two groups had been mostly English. Now she blushed at the thought. This man would not have been out of place in the finest drawing room. And he had parents and two sisters, all of whom he loved and missed dreadfully.

These current troubles with the Americans had been going on for so much of her short life that she could not even remember having seen or heard an American sailor in Gravesend, though there must have been some sailing under other flags. And she had thought little about the war with the Americans, marking it down as more foolish belligerence on their part. Now, she heard the other side.

The trouble had begun with impressment. American ships had been stopped and boarded by press gangs who insisted they were looking for English naval deserters but often took seamen who were nothing of the sort and forced them to serve under brutal discipline on English ships. An American president named Jefferson and the Congress (which Caleb explained was something like Parliament) had passed the Embargo Act of December 27, 1807, to keep American ships off the high seas and thus to deny England and Europe the comfort of American goods, thereby punishing them and preventing war. The plan had worked in reverse, ruining American commerce rather than foreign, and the act was repealed fourteen months later. A new American president, Madison (Caleb pointed out that they had no king and that presidents were to be thought of as something like prime ministers), had tried to press England for concessions through diplomatic channels, but that, too, had failed. And so in 1810, Madison had summoned the American minister in London home and had had the British representatives in the capital city of Washington sent back to England. Thus ended all chances of diplomatic communication. American ships had had trouble with countries other than Britain, but by 1805, Nelson's naval victory at Trafalgar had given Britain control of the seas, and so America's major grievance was with her. The outrages against ships flying the American flag continued, and finally, in June 1812, war had been declared by the Americans.

"It's not as if everyone wanted war," Caleb said. "The northeastern states and the middle states, of which Maryland is one, knew they'd suffer the most being so dependent on shipping, but the frontiersmen, those that live inland and in less settled parts to the west, they wanted the war, and they got it. They tend to fight at the least insult, and they felt England had been insulting for long enough."

Even weak and muzzy-headed, he was an articulate man, and Alex was fascinated by what he had to say. But she feared she had gone too far when she asked how he had been taken prisoner.

He was silent for so long, she hastened to apologize. "You needn't tell me if you don't wish to."

"No, I want to, though there's precious little to tell. I reckon that's what makes it so hard."

As she listened she understood what he meant by that and how helpless he must have felt for too long. His family owned a shipping line. He had been captain of the ship, and it was only his second voyage in full command, though he had been trained all his life in all aspects of the business. Nearly a year ago, they had been taking a cargo of American goods to France and had been outgunned and outmaneuvered by British ships. The battle had been as simple as that, but not the aftermath. Caleb had been knocked unconscious during the fighting but had been thrown overboard and kept afloat by his first mate as the ship burned. The first mate, Charles Bowan, was an older man whom Caleb had known all his life and had been very fond of. The two of them had been picked up by the British, Charlie wounded and in bad shape, Caleb near death. The next time Caleb had been aware of his surroundings, he had found that he and Charlie were in the prison at Princetown with more than fifteen hundred other Americans and eight thousand Frenchmen. But nowhere among them were any other members of Caleb's crew, and he had been unable to find out anything about them at all. The allotment for prisoners was terribly small, but he and Charlie eked out an existence by doing odd jobs at the prison and for the townspeople and even by selling knitted garments and carved wooden toys to kindly buyers. The winter cold had been as deep there as it had been in the rest of the country, and with inadequate food, clothing, and medicine, survival had been hard.

"Charlie kept me alive in the first days, and he made it through until the rains of spring, and then he died. I knew some of the other men and I made a few new friends, but without Charlie, there didn't seem much point in staying," he said dryly. "I tried to get word to my family, but I don't think it ever got through. And when word came that the Frenchmen were going to be released because Napoleon had abdicated, but the Americans were going to have to stay right there, well, that was the last straw. Security wasn't much, and I just drifted off and began walking. I figured it was less civilized westward than to the east and that I'd have a better chance of not getting caught."

He had clung to the vague hope that he would find help from the fellowship of the sea once he reached the coast. And he had been heartened by the bands of night travelers he had seen on his journey, realizing that there was a vast army of smugglers operating in England—if they brought illegal goods in, they surely knew the way out. He had not, however, in his wildest dreams thought that he would be rescued by a slim slip of a girl in boy's breeches.

He peered at her, his vision growing fuzzy, eyelids drooping. Strange, she was a child, but he didn't think of her that way; he felt perfectly confident in placing his life in her hands.

Alex watched sleep overcome him. "I'll have to leave you now, and I fear I must take the lantern. There's too much risk for you to have it here. Rane will be back, probably tomorrow night. God, I hope tomorrow night! And he will help. I promise he will."

He tried to rouse himself to protest, but she forestalled him. "There isn't any other way, believe me! We need him. Now sleep, it is the best thing for you."

He reached out for her hand and brought it to his lips as if she were the finest lady in the land, and then his eyes closed and his hand drifted from hers.

Her legs were trembling with fatigue by the time she reached the house, and she slept soundly from sheer, mindless exhaustion, but she was awake early, instantly aware of the enormous problems ahead. "Well, very tall but not enormous," she corrected herself with wry humor as she thought of Caleb Jennings. She simply could not fail him.

She would have liked more time to consider the best course, but that was not an option she had. It was cold and damp in the cave, the worst place for Caleb Jennings in his enfeebled condition, and she could not count on ferreting enough food out of the house for him without Gweneth noticing. Just the trip back to the house and yet again to the cave the night before had tried her sorely. She had quickly discovered it was one thing to have only one's self at risk, quite another to be responsible for someone else. And tonight the ship would surely come in, and there would be all sorts of activity on the beach. The one good thing about that was that Rane would be home. She wanted him there so badly, she could have wept.

She had considered everyone else. But he was her first and last choice. However the rest of the family felt about the war with the Americans—and the general opinion seemed to be that the Americans had had a just grievance in not wanting their ships stopped and searched, their men impressed for the British navy or taken prisoner— there was a grave difference between understanding and actively helping one of the enemy. The Americans had, after all, declared war on Great Britain and had continued to treat with the French. Helping Caleb Jennings escape might well be viewed in the same light as selling information to the French, something the Falconers had never done.

Gweneth took Alex's increased agitation as an indication of her worry about the *Lady Gwen* returning safely. "Remember, my dear, even though they had that spot of trouble those weeks ago, they lost only the cargo, nothing more." Her eyes were kind with the admission of her own frenzied behavior on that memorable night.

With effort, Alex restrained her impulse to tell Gweneth everything. Instead, she kept her mind on practical matters. She had to trust that Gweneth would not notice the missing blankets; there was little reason she should since Alex took care of her own room. She found that the food wasn't as difficult as it might have been; her own appetite had fled, and it was simply a matter of secreting her own portions throughout the day, plus a bit more. In fact, her appearance of hearty appetite served a good purpose by lulling Gweneth's concern. Nor was it out of the ordinary for her to tell Gweneth she was going to wait at the cave. She even managed to take another bottle of fresh water, which she carried openly, and a bottle of wine which she hid with the food in her bundled coat without arousing Gweneth's suspicions. She gave thanks that it was now part of the established pattern that she go to the cave. It made her feel almost as if there was a preordained rightness to it. But she did not make light of it when she reached Mr. Jennings.

"I am sure the cargo will come in tonight. And that means that all sorts of people will be outside, particularly if it is decided to take it on away. You must keep very, very still or all will be lost."

She frowned at him worriedly. He still looked so sick and gaunt, she wondered if fever might make him babble. She touched his face matter of factly, relieved to find his skin neither too hot nor cold.

He smiled at her. "Whatever you gave me last night has made me feel much better. You're quite the little doctor, ma'am." He had the oddest sense that he had somehow become the younger and was being well looked after by this elfin child-woman. She was the best thing that happened to him since he'd been captured, and he trusted her completely out of need and instinct.

For her part, Alex had lost all fear of him the night before. It was not only that he was sick and in need, there was something essentially courtly and gentle about the man. And she remained fascinated by the slow, charming way he spoke English. His voice alone had been enough to ease much of her anxiety.

"I fear you must stay in the dark. It is too risky otherwise," she told him anxiously as she prepared to go.

"Don't fret. I'll be snug as can be." He patted the wine bottle and began to munch contentedly on the food she'd brought, making her feel easier about leaving him.

But she did not feel so calm as she waited for the ship. She paced back and forth in the cargo cave, finding her own motion nerve-racking, but she was unable to stop. She rehearsed over and over what she would say to Rane when she got the chance. But she did not so forget her situation as to ignore her surroundings. She went outside often to listen, conscious of how ironic it would be if this were the night that the revenue men found the cave. There would be no hope for Caleb Jennings then, for surely they would search where he was, too. She shivered at the memory of the close brush with the soldiers when she had gone with the ponies.

Finally the faint sounds came over the water, and then the soft call of her name. She was too agitated by matters at hand to register that the call indicated how much Rane liked her to be waiting for him.

The men came ashore in high spirits, a full cargo secured and time enough to send it on its way overland as long as nothing was amiss with the land crew. One of the sailors was off posthaste to make sure everything was well and ready. If there was any problem, the goods would be hastily stored in the cave.

The operation went smoothly, people appearing on the beach, sledges swiftly loaded and transfers made at the top of the town to the waiting ponies.

But now that Rane was home, Alex found her control slipping. She hid her agitation in the fierce activity, but Rane was too attuned to her to miss it.

"What is it?" he asked anxiously at one point, his hands firmly capturing hers. "Your hands are cold as ice."

"It's nothing. I was just worried about you and the *Lady Gwen*."

Rane was skeptical, but there was too much work to be done quickly for him to press her further at the moment. However, he resolved to find out what was the matter as soon as possible. Alex's disquiet was his own.

They were both exhausted by the time the cargo had been sent off and they were back at the house, and with Gweneth and Magnus in the kitchen with them, they had no chance of speaking privately. When Alex settled into bed, she had escaped explanation until the next morning, and fatigue made that a good thing as she was no longer sure how she was going to tell Rane. Having him here in the flesh was quite different from planning what to say when he was absent. He had already gone upstairs, and a little later she heard the older Falconers ascend, too. From having thought she would never rest, she found her eyelids drooping and sleep flowing over her in a heavy wave. Thus the soft knock on her door startled her even more than it would have had she been wide awake.

"Alex, open the door!" Rane's command came with urgency despite his hushed voice.

She obeyed, fearful that he would awaken his parents if she delayed.

He was bearing a candle, and his face was limned in gold, his eyes deep caverns with flickers of light within. "Tell me what's wrong, and no excuses, please. I know there's something, and I'm too tired to play guessing games."

Long explanations deserted her. She felt as if she were diving off of Hartland Point as she blurted out, "I've got an American!"

Rane was more at sea than he'd been aboard the *Lady Gwen*. "You've got an American what?"

She started to giggle uncontrollably, trying to be quiet and keep breathing at the same time, causing Rane to think she was either choking or crying until he recognized the laughter and gave her an impatient shake. "This is making less and less sense. Please try to get hold of yourself!"

The exasperation in his voice sobered her enough so that she was able to say it all in a rush. "Not an American *what*, an American *who*. He's an escaped prisoner of war from the prison at Princetown. His name is Caleb Jennings.

He's only a bit older than you, I think, and he's from a place called Annapolis in Maryland in the United States."

Rane was silent, trying to absorb what she was telling him. He was more familiar with place names of the United States than she. Not only did free trading tend to include lessons in geography of the goods' countries of origin, but North Devon had a long history of immigration to the United States and Canada, interrupted only by the present hostilities and the war by which the Americans had wrested their independence from the Crown. Most of those who had gone to the United States had settled in the northeastern part of that country, near Canada, but still, Rane was not unacquainted with the rest of the colonies, now states. He sorted through all of that sensible mental information while remaining totally nonplussed by the most important part of Alex's story. He shook his head, trying to clear the cobwebs of fatigue.

"Where is he?" he asked carefully, suspecting for one awful moment that the man might crawl out from under the bed or tumble out of the wardrobe. He had a vision of his father discovering all and truly losing his temper, a formidable business as Magnus blustered but very seldom expressed real anger. Best to be miles away when that happened.

Mistaking Rane's tone for complete calm, Alex poured out the rest of the story, more than glad to share the burden.

"You mean to tell me that he was nearby the whole time we were working on the beach tonight?" The vision that conjured was horrible. His mind was beginning to work too swiftly rather than too slowly. The villagers were for the most part kindly folk. But they were also very basic in their approach to life. The man, had he been found, most probably would have been killed on the spot and dumped out in the sea, judged and executed as a dangerous witness to the night's activities. On the other hand, alive he was still that witness, capable of bringing the soldiers down on them in exchange for better treatment for himself from the government. "Do you realize what you have done?"

Alex began to sense that what she had taken for calm was in fact disbelief that was rapidly giving way to barely controlled rage, and she met it with her own, seeing Caleb's gaunt face in the lantern light and becoming more determined than ever to help him. "I realize exactly what I've done! He's young, he's hurt, and it wasn't his fault that there is a war going on. How would you like to be sailing on the *Lady Gwen* only to have her burned beneath you? It's a dreadful waste. With a little sense England might have avoided this stupid war with the Americans. They aren't our colonies any more, and they won't have us treating them so." Caleb Jennings had changed forever her view, common to most of the English, that the war with America was simply an adjunct to the French war.

The change stabbed Rane with a sudden hot shard of jealousy, and for a blind instant, he considered killing the man himself.

"Did he touch you?" he demanded harshly.

She did not mistake his meaning, and she totally suppressed the memory of how the man had frightened her at first. "Of course not!" she hissed, quite out of patience with him now. "Haven't you been listening? The man is weak and sick, and all he wants is to go home, not hurt people. I wish I'd never told you, you're being so slow-witted." She knew the attack was unfair, but she had wanted Rane to solve everything the minute she told him.

Rane did not respond in kind. Her need was suddenly quite clear, and in recognizing it, he was committed to help her and thus this American. "I will think of something," he promised tiredly. "But there is nothing to be done tonight. People will still be about, going back to the cave would be too much of a risk. Since he wasn't discovered tonight, he ought to be safe for a while longer."

He turned to go, and the weary slope of his shoulders caught at her heart. "I'm sorry I barked at you," she apologized softly. "I do know how dangerous all of this is, but I couldn't not help him. I just couldn't! And you're the only one I thought would understand."

He turned back and gave her a swift, reassuring one-armed hug, the other hand precariously balancing the candle. "Don't fret any more. It just took me a bit to get accustomed to the problem." A profound understatement, he thought wryly, his mind already beginning to consider and reject one plan after another.

Alex, feeling her burden considerably lightened, slept exhaustedly. Rane slept very little.

Their first chance to speak freely came as they headed

for the farm. They were expected there to lend a hand to various chores, particularly because Seadon would not be back yet from his cross-country trek with the cargo.

"I've thought it all out," Rane announced. "And I can only find one way that might work, and even that's a small chance. But the man can't stay in that cave much longer. Even if he isn't discovered, the cold and damp will finish him. It would be hard enough on a healthy man. And whether you like to admit it or not, he is a danger to us all not only because you've hidden him but because he knows about the free trading. I dare not tell Father. His loyalty must be to the village and his crew." As mine should be, he added to himself.

"The man's name is Caleb Jennings," she pointed out. It was the only protest she made. Rane was in charge now, and that was exactly what she wanted.

"The Irish, or rather a specific Irishman, Sean O'Leary, is the answer. He runs great loads of tobacco from Ireland to Liverpool, Bristol, and when the price is high enough, to London. We passed him on our way home; he was bound for Leigh in the Thames Estuary. Not tonight and not tomorrow night, but the night after he should be rounding our coast, and I think he'd take the American, this Mr. Jennings, aboard. O'Leary would do almost anything to thwart English authorities. The Act of Union was not to his liking."

Rane turned away from the blaze of hope on Alex's face. "Before you consider it done, you must know what a wild chance it is. In the first place, though the weather and winds have been fair enough here, I don't know what kind of weather O'Leary has found on the east coast, nor whether it will hold to bring him back swiftly. And he's an unpredictable fellow. Even if I find him he may refuse the passenger. Nor is there any way to tell if all went well for him in disposing of his cargo. Perhaps the men who were to meet him near Leigh didn't come, or perhaps all were caught. If I take Jennings out on an empty sea, and then have to bring him back it will be much more likely that he'll be discovered." And my part in it, too, he thought.

But Alex was not to be disheartened. "It will not just be you taking him out; I'm going, too." She silenced his objections before he could voice them. "It's your turn to be sensible, Rane Falconer. You are going to need help both going out and coming back. And Mr. Jennings isn't strong enough to be of much use the one way and won't be on the boat returning. Who else do you plan to ask—Seadon or Elwyn?"

She had him there. It was bad enough that he was involved; he shuddered inwardly at the thought of compromising one of his brothers.

"You little vixen," he said, grinning reluctantly. "Oh, you're frightened enough, but you're also looking forward to this, aren't you?"

He didn't need an answer; he could see it in the gleaming fire in her green eyes, in the taut lines of her clean-boned face and long body. She fairly rippled with barely checked excitement, as if she were a highly bred filly pulling to start the race.

He recognized the addiction to hazard; it was a shared trait, and that went a long way toward winning her point. In addition, logic told him that she could not be trusted to stay put were he to leave her ashore. Were their positions reversed, he would be as wild to go.

Barbary told Seadon later that his brother and young cousin had worked as if they were devil possessed. "I don't know where they get the energy," she sighed.

"Ah, youth! I don't care where they get it as long as they spare some of it for the farm," Seadon retorted with a laugh, pleasantly relaxed from a job well done.

Alex and Rane were anything but relaxed. All their attention was fixed on feeding Caleb for the next two nights and on getting him safely away on the third.

The problem of food eased somewhat with Magnus and Rane home because Gweneth always cooked great amounts to feed their enormous appetites, and between the two of them, Rane and Alex managed to steal enough. But getting the food to Jennings was another matter entirely. And despite the shared tension, they were healthy young animals who craved sleep when nightfall came. Half of their battle was staying awake long enough to wait until the elder Falconers slept so they could sneak out of the house.

The first night they slipped down through the village without meeting anyone. Alex was still considering it a good omen when she introduced the two men, but then she had second thoughts about the whole plan.

After barely pretending to shake hands, Caleb and Rane were eyeing each other and bristling like stray dogs. It was so involuntary, neither of the men knew he was doing it until he heard Alex ask in complete bafflement, "Have you met before?" She could think of no other reason for their behavior than previous dislike, which was as unlikely as the moon falling out of the sky.

Caleb and Rane both drew breath and regarded each other warily in the flickering lantern light. Though Caleb was at a disadvantage with his scraggly beard and overall unkempt appearance, it was he who smiled first and put out his hand again. "Pleased to meet you, sir," he said, his voice as firm and polite as if they were being introduced for the first time at a pleasant social function.

Rane relaxed, too, and grinning ruefully, he shook hands, this time meaning it as a cordial greeting. He had no idea why he had behaved in such an unmannerly way when, in truth, he found himself liking the American more by the minute.

Caleb was less confused than Rane. He had had bad times for quite a while now, but they had not dimmed his considerable intelligence and astuteness in judging human nature. That judgment had led him to trust Alexandria so quickly and so completely that he had waited patiently in the cave, as much a prisoner as he had been on Dartmoor. Now, it allowed him to see more about Rane than Rane himself knew.

"The two of you put me in mind of a family I know back home. They, too, carry a strong stamp of one of their lines so that cousins look more like twins than anything else," he offered casually.

"Maybe they're Thaines, too," Alex giggled, relieved that the tension seemed to have dissipated.

But Rane was quick to clarify the relationship. "Our connection is quite distant by blood—the same great-great-great-great-grandfathers—but very close now that Alex is part of our family."

Now Caleb knew a great deal more. So that is indeed the way the wind blows, he thought to himself. Young Rane has far more than cousinly interest in her, and neither of them knows it. It was to his advantage to be careful not to trespass on Rane's territory, but beyond his concern for survival, he found the two very appealing, and the risk they were taking for his sake was a debt he would never be able to repay.

"I haven't anything to offer you," he pointed out,

"though that will change if I can reach home again. If you would rather, I'll go on, and nothing said about that business on the beach, on my word of honor. I'm already stronger for the food and rest."

"You'll go on," Rane agreed, "but it will be aboard an Irish ship if all goes well. The ship's master has direct connections with the tobacco trade from Baltimore in your state. He ought to be able to deliver you almost to your own hearth, though what bargain you will have to strike with him, I don't know." He went on to outline their plans, pretending not to see the tears that glistened suddenly in the American's eyes at the mention of the city so close to his home. Rane's last doubts were gone. He not only liked what he saw of the man, he wanted to do this for Alex.

As Alex had, he listened with interest to Caleb's patient recital of the United States' side of the war. He had never thought much about that country beyond a vague wish to see it someday because it sounded vast and different, and his judgment about their politics had been that they were a churlish people to refuse to help pay for the troops that had protected them from the wild Indians and that perhaps the loss of the colonies in the last century had been all for the best if they were so ungrateful and ungovernable. Despite the free trading, Rane, like the rest of his family, remained at heart loyal to his country, and he had not before imagined that anyone could be better off without the Crown. But now for the first time, he considered that the Americans might have grown to be so different from the mother country that the government of the small island was no longer fitting for them.

He questioned Caleb intently and was fascinated by the answers that came in the slightly drawling voice. Caleb's enthusiasm and love for his country were enough so that Rane began to see the wonder of this country composed of states so different they were almost like sovereign nations yet like enough to band together in a rather quarrelsome but still workable union against a threat from the outside. And the ultimate bond between the two young men was that they had both been raised in the tradition of the sea—Rane in free trading, Caleb in merchant shipping—and that made their differences less than the similarities. The press gangs were loathed enough in England for snatching men for naval service, how much worse it was that they had done the same to foreign nationals. A nation had the right to expect that ships under her flag would be inviolate; any breach of that was piracy or an act of war.

"England seems unwilling to let you grow up," Rane commented.

"But we will, without doubt we will," Caleb returned, and there was no offense on either side.

On the next night, things did not go so smoothly. Rane and Alex found their way impeded by Old Smythe. He was quite suddenly there, a shabby bag of bones rising out of the shadows in the lane. Alex nearly cried out but swallowed the sound in time.

Old Smythe was a rheumy-eyed, rum-soaked old salt who had not adjusted well to the end of his sailing days. His mind faded in and out of the present, and it was difficult to judge where it was located at any given moment.

Rane took the direct approach, assuming it would confuse the old man as much as anything else. He greeted him heartily, albeit softly, and added, "I see you're out for it, too. I wouldn't care to miss it myself."

Swaying back and forth, Old Smythe peered at them uncertainly. "Young Falconers be ye?" he finally asked.

"Indeed we are and a bit late for it, so we must be on our way."

They left him muttering what Rane translated as, "Aye, gone on a jaunt for a fox, everyone gone," jaunt for a fox being a fair distance.

From fear, Alex's mood swung to soaring amusement, and she had to cover her mouth and bite on her fingers to keep from laughing. "That was cruel!" she gasped. "I'm sure he thinks the whole village is away without him."

Rane hushed her, not allowing more speech until they were down on the rocky shore, heading west, the wrong way. "I'm never sure how much Old Smythe knows. Sometimes there's a sharpness to him for all he drinks, and we don't need his company tonight. We'll bide here for a while, to make sure he isn't following."

Finally they were sure neither the old man nor stray fishermen were about, and they hurried east to Jennings.

Though he tried to hide it, Caleb was pathetically glad to see them. His physical hunger appeased by the food of the past days, more food than he had had in months, he was ravenous for friendly human contact. His days and nights of running and hiding had taken a hard toll because he was by nature a gregarious man.

This night, at their urging, he spoke more of his home state, enthralling them with the pictures he painted. Alex had heard much of it already, but she was content to hear it again, particularly because she viewed the growing camaraderie between the two men as necessary to their enterprise.

"It's difficult to capture in words. There is a huge salt bay, the Chesapeake, that divides the eastern from the western shore of Maryland. The Eastern Shore is very flat, but the Western Shore begins the land that rolls soft and green to the Appalachian Mountains, land that raises fine horses, tobacco, grain, and all manner of crops. But the bay is a world unto itself. A special breed, the watermen, harvest its bounty—crab, oysters, and fish to please every palate. And in the winter, ducks, geese, and swans come by the countless thousands, filling the air with their cries."

Rane and Alex exchanged a quick smiling glance, remembering the swans, and Caleb felt their close and special bond even more acutely than before. They had made him feel secure enough so that he could concern himself with affairs beyond his own, and suddenly he did not want to lose contact with them. Part of his charm was that he was genuinely interested in others, and he did not want to miss the end of the story they did not even realize was unfolding.

There was a lack of surface rhythm that might prove a sad discord for all the deep harmony he felt between them. Alex reminded him just a little of his sister, Julia, who had clung to the freedom of sexless childhood to the very last minute, only then bursting forth as a more than passable female. The thought checked him—Julia, after all, had probably been much happier in the former state as the latter had led to a "suitable" marriage that was less than happy due to her husband's demand for an heir and her inability to produce a living child. Perhaps Alex was wise to maintain her forthright stance, more acceptable in a boy than a girl. But whether she willed it or not, Caleb guessed she was going to be a compelling woman. And whether he knew it or not, Rane Falconer was already drawing near to the flame. Caleb could not have wished better for them had he known them for years instead of days.

113

"It's laughable, I know, for me to offer you anything from my present position," he said, his gesturing hand throwing shadows on the stone walls. "But if I get home, I will send word. And if you ever need anything, you must let me know. And if you ever come to my country, it would be my great privilege to welcome you. Your country and mine, they share too many traditions for this war to go on for too much longer. All wars end. I believe the time is not far off when our two countries will finally become allies to our mutual benefit. If nothing else, profit in trade will make it so."

They all nodded solemnly as though sealing a pact. Young as they were, it was more than possible that friendship would come between their countries in their lifetimes.

❧ Chapter 10 ❧

By the time the third night came, Rane and Alex were exhausted from tension and lack of sleep, but they were unaware of it, strung on nerves singing with a great burst of desperate energy. It had to work. There would be no other chances.

Already Gweneth was suspicious, having checked their departure that morning with a worried comment that they both appeared to be sickening with something. She had clucked over them, touching their skin for fever as they stood numbly caught in the net of her love.

"There's little I can do to check your mad starts," she informed her tall son, "but I won't have you making Alex work too hard. A job well done at the farm is all very well, and Seadon says you've been a great help, but you need not do it all in a day. Falling ill would be a sad waste of time."

"Truly, I would know if we were ill," Alex volunteered. That much was true. "It is just that summer is finally beginning after so much rain and cold, and it is hard to waste the fair days." Nature was on her side as the June weather had been pleasant the past few days, despite the hovering threat of more rain.

Rane studiously avoided looking at her as she told this Banbury tale.

That night Rane made a sly show of outfitting himself for a visit to the Buck's Mills widow. This was an area of his life on which his mother did not encroach, having had to admit to herself long since that he was a man, but she did manage a few disapproving sniffs before he set out. Alex's part was to plead an overwhelming need for sleep. This she did with yawns and drooping eyelids.

Her ruse was accepted. "If only sons were as sensible as daughters," Gweneth said. "Rane would do well to be resting, too, rather than going off to see that woman."

"I'm not entirely sure of that," Magnus teased, and the attention shifted away from Alex, who bid them good-night.

Listening from her room, she thought she would scream if they did not go upstairs immediately. She hadn't long to wait. Magnus's teasing had quickly led to other things, and he and Gweneth were lighthearted as they sped up to their room.

Rane, watching from the shadows, was back inside the house as soon as he thought it safe. Alex obediently kept her eyes closed as he changed from his good clothes into more serviceable garments in her bedroom, and then they were off.

It was a nerve-stretching trip down the street this night, for it was earlier, and there were people out. But they had anticipated that they would be unable to avoid friendly interest, and this, too, they had rehearsed. They strolled along, not offering any extra information, but when asked, answering politely that they were going fishing. It was not an unusual occupation on a mild night, but they were warned repeatedly to watch the weather, and received a few muttered comments regarding the foolishness of youth.

The sky was giving its own warning, angry clouds rolling across the moon and the breeze freshening, though the air was still warm. But neither Alex nor Rane was deterred; bad weather seemed a small thing compared to the immediate difficulty of smuggling Caleb Jennings out of the cave.

Rane's skiff was ready, and Alex gave inner thanks that she had spent so many hours helping to sail or row the small craft. They did both to maneuver down the coast, running without so much as a lantern, trusting that they had disappeared from interested eyes nearly as soon as they had put out. At least the looming storm seemed to have discouraged other small boats though they would have to avoid a few larger vessels, including the *Lady Gwen*, further out.

Caleb was more than ready for them. He had spent the hours nervously haunting the entrance to his cave, torn between fear for their risk and the need to go home. As soon as they arrived, he again offered them refusal of the task, but he discovered that Rane was fully in charge now and Alex no less resolute, and gratefully he surrendered.

"No talking at all once we leave this place," Rane ordered, "not until we're well out. It will be difficult, but if we pay attention to the boat and each other, we ought to be able to get her out without words."

Alex wondered if the men's hearts were pounding as hard as hers as they clambered aboard after pushing the boat back into the water. And then she forgot everything except the work at hand.

Despite his best efforts, Caleb was just not in good enough health to row for long. The other two had anticipated that and had simply let him try for pride's sake. Silently, Alex took his place. Her muscles were hard and fit, but nonetheless, she had far less stamina than Rane, and she was trying not to gasp audibly for breath by the time Rane judged they could use the sail. By then they had passed the *Lady Gwen* and another ship, and no one had hailed them.

Though some light filtered through while the clouds flew over the moon, the boat was riding a black sea, and Rane had to concentrate hard not to lose his bearings. He took every sighting he could of the receding shoreline and Lundy when the light allowed it, and he made himself feel the sea in his bones, trying to be alert for every shift in the current beneath him and the air around him, checking his compass when there was light enough, reminding himself this was no new talent but something he had learned from the cradle.

Finally after what seemed like days rather than hours, he judged their position to be as good as any for their enterprise, and it then became a matter of holding it against the sea drift.

"This is daft," he said very low, self-doubt washing over him. "We're a tiny cork floating in vast waters. I don't know how I ever thought we'd find O'Leary's ship. It's against all odds."

"It's not!" Alex whispered furiously, as if an outsider were attacking him. "It is a chance, the only one Caleb has. You know these waters and the trade; if anyone can find O'Leary, you can."

Caleb had the odd fancy that if he put his hand between the two, he would feel a tangible current of warmth running between them as they sought to reassure each other. He, too, recognized the odds against success, but he felt far more confident than his companions. He had come so far and was at long last heading home. In his mind's eye he could see his family quite clearly and then the broad waters of his beloved Chesapeake Bay.

Rane and Alex strained eyes and ears to detect any sign of O'Leary's ship, and Rane cursed softly when the first drops of rain splattered against them as the wind rose. Alex frantically tried to plan what to do next. They could not abandon Caleb nor could they keep him in the cave. But her mind refused to present any alternative. She was so frustrated, tears began to roll down her cheeks, though she was unaware of them.

Rane caught sight of her first, the *Silkie Wife* slipping sleekly through the churning water, and then the three of them were shouting at the top of their lungs, hoping to be heard against the snap of canvas and the singing of the lines on the ship, hoping they wouldn't be fired upon before O'Leary recognized their innocence. The *Silkie Wife* was a large vessel, but she was built for speed and maneuverability, and her crew was skilled. She tacked and altered course gracefully, and finally they heard O'Leary's voice roaring a challenge over the water, the man obviously having ascertained that this was no threat.

"It's Rane Falconer out of Clovelly, Captain O'Leary, with a passenger for you if you'll take him on."

The other vessel was quite close now. Alex could almost feel the astonishment rippling through those on board.

"Aye, an' it's a wild night fer startin' up a ferry service, Rane Falconer. Come alongside."

The three in the little boat relaxed; O'Leary sounded more amused than anything else. They rowed to the side of the *Silkie Wife* and were quickly taken aboard. The soft lantern light looked like the brightest stars to Alex after the hours of darkness.

Sean O'Leary was a dark-eyed, black-haired, fierce-visaged giant of a man. But everything had gone well with this last voyage, and he was in an expansive mood and curious indeed about this strange little band. Rane Falconer he recognized, and there was no doubt that the young Alex introduced as Rane's cousin was of the same stamp though the youth was definitely more slightly built. But the tall lanky Jennings was a surprise even for one as used to the strange offerings of the sea as O'Leary was.

Alex and Caleb let Rane do the explaining, which he did honestly and directly, sure that anything less than the truth would not aid their cause with the captain. It made him nervous enough that Alex was standing in the midst of these hard seamen, and he hoped none would suspect her true sex.

For a long moment, O'Leary said nothing, just stared intently from under bushy brows at the American, missing nothing of his hard used appearance. Caleb met his gaze squarely, betraying no nervousness, just patiently waiting.

Finally O'Leary nodded as if he had just concluded a long conversation with himself. "Americans 've 'elped to make me rich, no reason I shouldn't be returnin' one of their own lost souls. An' more than that, I'd be a lyin' man were I to deny the pleasure it gives me to take somethin' the English'd rather keep, beggin' yer pardon, young Falconers. Welcome aboard, Caleb Jennings, I'll have ye on yer way to Baltimore in a foine short time."

Alex barely stopped herself in time from hugging Caleb and Rane in celebration, contenting herself instead with a broad smile as she thrust the tightly wrapped bundle at Caleb. It contained hastily altered clothing "borrowed" from Magnus because his were the only ones big enough to allow for Caleb's long arms and legs—"in for a penny, in for a pound," Rane and Alex had told each other—and a little sack of gold sovereigns, part of Rane's hard earned hoard that was to go for his own ship after Seadon had his. They had known Caleb would refuse the offering if he were given too much time to think about it.

"Your clothes are so tattered, they won't last much longer. These aren't elegant, but we hope they'll do until you have others," she said, and she pressed his hand hard against the money pouch as he involuntarily took the bundle pushed at him.

His composure began to slip a little with the gifts, and he stuttered, "But I can't take . . . you've done so much."

Rane cut him short. "We haven't time to argue, and we want you to have at least a few good memories of the people of Devon. We must be on our way. A good journey, Caleb." They shook hands in true friendship, far different from when they had first met in what seemed a lifetime ago.

Alex shook hands with him, too, and suddenly she was fighting tears. This was the way she had wanted it to end, and yet she felt very sad to be bidding good-bye to the American. In becoming responsible for him, she had grown to like him very much very quickly. It was doubtful that they would ever see him again.

"Take care, Alex," he murmured huskily. "You have my gratitude forever."

And then they were lowering themselves back over the side into Rane's boat in spite of O'Leary's protests. "It's an angry sea ye be sailin' this night, ye'd be better set to go with me, an' I'll get ye back to Clovelly before too many days."

Politely they refused—the idea of Magnus and Gweneth awaking to find them gone was not to be borne—and O'Leary paid them the tribute of a jaunty salute, feeling a stab of envy for Magnus Falconer. Sean had a lusty wife and five healthy children, but they were all girls.

Doggedly Rane and Alex rowed until they were far away from the *Silkie Wife*, hoisting their own sail as the big ship disappeared in the darkness. The rain that had spattered down on and off began to come more heavily, and Rane mistrusted the heavy roiling motion of the sea under the fretful wind that blew first from one quarter then from another. He didn't have to voice his misgivings aloud; Alex was as aware as he that they were in for heavy going. It was soon a matter of endurance from minute to minute. They had both been tired when they had begun the night's adventure, and now fighting the sea, the wind, and the dropping temperature taxed to the utmost what little energy they had left. Separately they contemplated the very real possibility that they were not going to make it to shore, and separately they discarded the idea as being of no use.

Finally the wind was veering and backing so viciously, they had to reef the sail entirely in order to prevent it from snapping the mast or overturning the boat. They rowed for what seemed an eternity. Her hands were so numbed by the cold and wet, Alex did not know when they blistered and then bled. Her world had shrunk to the grim necessity of bending her back and pulling on the oars one more time and then again, despite the burning in her lungs and every abused muscle.

The great cliff rising out of the rain at the edge of the sea came as a great shock to her. Somewhere along the way she had given up hope of making landfall during the night.

With a last surge of strength, Rane brought them ashore, jumping out to run the boat up the beach the last few yards. When he helped Alex out, she sank to the ground, unable to stand, panting for breath, and he sank down beside her, head bowed, chest heaving until he got enough air to explain.

"We're off course, closer to Hartland Point than to Clovelly, but it's all right. There's a cave here; we can shelter for the night."

It finally hit her. Wrong part of the coast or not, they were safely landed, and Caleb Jennings was on his way home. "We did it!" she crowed, a sudden spurt of energy making her feel even more lightheaded as she threw her arms around Rane. "We did it, we did!"

And then Rane was laughing with her, clinging to her as hard as she was to him. They broke apart and laughed harder when they realized the rain was doing its best to drown them where the sea had failed.

Rane made sure the boat would not wash away, retrieved a small bundle of provisions, and together they staggered to the cave, Rane leading the way until they were sheltered from the storm.

A small, candled lantern, matches and tinderbox, a jug of brandy mixed with water, and a large square of oilcloth these items were wrapped in—that was the sum total of their provisions, bare essentials that seemed like the king's plenty because they were safe on land and not forever lost on the black water.

Rane lit the lantern, and thirstily they drank of the diluted brandy. Alex was beginning to shiver so from reaction and cold, and her hands were so stiff, she could scarcely hold the jug, but she managed to swallow enough to feel a warming trail as it went down.

Rane caught sight of her hands and brought the lantern close for a better look, gasping when he saw what a mess they were. Even his own, toughened from years of rowing, were sore, but they were nothing like hers, blisters on blisters down to open sores, torn and bleeding flesh. Before she could dread what he was going to do, he grasped her hands and poured some of the brandy on them, wincing in sympathy as she jerked in his hold and cried out.

"Sorry, sweetling, sorry," he crooned, gathering her against him. She was so cold, so wet and bedraggled, and so damn gallant, he wanted to enfold her in warmth and keep her safe forever, but he was as chilled as she, and the only warmth there was was generated by their bodies pressed together. Hazily he wondered how that could be when both were cold, but even that thought was beyond him. He settled himself more comfortably against the cave wall and her more securely against himself and drew the oilcloth over them.

Too many sensations, one on the other, plus the brandy on an empty stomach had left Alex feeling distanced from herself. She knew her body was stiff, but the throbbing muscles had ceased to register. Even the sharp pain that had flared in her hands when the liquid was poured over them was now faint and far away. Her mind circled, fluttering like a lost bird, and then settled peacefully in refuge. She was safe in Rane's arms, guarded from all harm, and delicious warmth was beginning to steal through her.

"Why the *Silkie Wife*, why the name?" she asked sleepily, barely able to form the words.

"From the old legend that silkies—seals—are really magical and can become beautiful young men and women when they slip out of their fur cloaks. 'Tis said that a man once saw one of these women playing on the beach. He cast aside her fur pelt before she could reach it, and being a comely man, he persuaded her to come and live with him as his wife in her human form. That she did, and there were even children of the union. But then her silkie lover came to her as a young man bearing her magic cloak and his own, and back to the sea they went, slipping away into the water, silkies again."

On the edge of oblivion, she whispered, "Just like the magic swans. Swans and silkies." She burrowed closer against him and relaxed completely. He followed her, his head bowing over hers, arms still around her.

ꙮ Chapter 11 ꙮ

Morning found the sea calm and the sky clear in sharp contrast to the storm that broke over Rane and Alex when they landed in Clovelly. Boats were being readied to put out to find the two, and Magnus, with Gweneth beside him, was part of the population at the water's edge.

Rane called, "We're all right," even before his feet touched land, but Alex wondered how long that state of health was going to last. Magnus was a truly terrifying figure, standing like a huge statue with his fists clenched and his eyes narrowed to gleaming slits. The villagers faded away, not even curiosity making it worth their while to witness the man's fury.

When the sorry looking pair stood before them, Gweneth's eyes softened a little, but Magnus's did not. "What have you to say for yourselves? Nary a word left with us. We thought you dead. Fishing indeed!" He spat the words out as if they were small stones.

Alex opened her mouth, but she was so frightened, she couldn't make any sound come out. And in any case, Magnus was ignoring her.

Rane faced his father squarely. "We went out to meet

O'Leary's *Silkie Wife*. We had a passenger for him, an escaped American prisoner from Princetown."

Magnus blinked as he considered this outlandish story, and as all the implications dawned on him, his neck corded, and Alex saw the veins pulsing in his temples. She looked to Gweneth but saw there would be no help there; she would abide by whatever her husband did because her own anger was barely in check—it was more subtle than Magnus's, but Alex saw it now in the tight pull of her mouth and the green glitter of her eyes.

"It was my fault. I found the American. I hid him, and I got Rane to help." Alex's voice was light and hollow. At least she got the words out, but it was as if the older Falconers had not heard.

"This is no place to speak of treason," Magnus said, and he marched off to climb the street, the others trailing behind him, and many villagers watching from the safety of their houses.

"They won't stay angry forever," Rane whispered encouragingly, but Alex was too terrified to accept any comfort.

When they reached the house, Gweneth stayed Alex with a firm hand on her arm. Alex stared blankly, not understanding what was going on as Magnus began unbuckling his belt even before he and Rane were in the house.

"I had thought you too old for this, boy, but I see not."

Alex heard the words and saw the moment of rebellion and then the grim acceptance on Rane's face, but none of it made any sense. She stood frozen where she was, devasted by the emotional cataclysm she had brought to this loving household. And then her mind turned backward and she saw again the ominous interchange between father and son as they had gone into the house.

"No-o-o-o!" Her wail of protest took Gweneth completely by surprise as she wrenched away and ran into the house.

Breeches and linen down, shirt up, Rane was bent face down over the table. His body twitched, but he didn't cry out as Magnus's belt sang down and cracked against his back and lean buttocks, laying another white streak that instantly turned red on his skin.

Alex's horrified gaze took in the rising welts and flecks of blood, and the blood expanded until she saw nothing but red as she attacked Magnus in blind flury. "Stop it, stop, you beastly man! He did it for me!"

Magnus dropped his belt and raised his arms in bewildered defense as the slender figure attacked him fearlessly, flailing at him with hands and feet, trying to find any bare skin for her teeth to sink into, shrieking her rage at the injustice.

Rane straightened, turned, and nearly tripped over his clothes before he pulled them up with shaking hands, as taken aback by the intrusion as his father was. But when he saw Magnus begin to swing his arm in self-defense, he shouted, "Touch her, and I'll kill you!" even as he sprang for Alex, grabbing her from behind and pinioning her arms at her sides.

"Alex, quiet now, please, Alex. I'm all right," he crooned in her ear. She went limp so suddenly, he nearly fell over with her in his arms. What fear and cold had failed to do, relief at Rane's deliverance from torment accomplished, and for the first time in her life, Alex fainted.

Rane eased her down to the floor, cradling her head in his lap, before he looked up at his father, expecting to see even more murderous rage than before. Instead Magnus was regarding him with wry humor and something Rane could not name because he couldn't believe it was approval.

Magnus dabbed at a scratch on his chin and nodded at the figure in Rane's arms. "She'll be fine in a bit, but don't get her up too soon else she might be sick." He handed Rane a damp cloth and a cup of water before he stalked out, pulling his wife with him. Rane hadn't even known that his mother had witnessed the battle.

Carefully he wiped Alex's face, watching in relief as her eyelids fluttered and a little color came back into her cheeks. But when she would have started up in confusion, he held her still. "Rest, love, just for a moment." Neither of them noticed this use of the endearment. He held the cup to her lips, and she drank gratefully, feeling as if she'd run a long mile, but then the enormity of what she'd done dawned on her, and she paled again.

"They'll send me back to Gravesend," she murmured, not able to call it home. "I'm sorry. I shouldn't have hit your father, but I couldn't bear it!" She twisted in his arms, her hands patting him anxiously as if she needed the added contact to reassure her that he was safe. "He hurt you dreadfully! How could he do that? I saw the blood."

"And a good deal else," Rane said ruefully, but strangely, he realized that he was not embarrassed that she had seen him in such a humiliating position; her fierce protectiveness made such concerns unimportant. There were other things more vital. "Alex, I'm sore as hell, but I'm all right. Even though we did what we had to do, it was a great risk. I should never have let you go with me. And he was worried about me as well as about you. It was out of love, and nothing else, that he beat me. And it was love for you as well as for me. They won't send you back to Kent, I promise it."

"If ever I have children, I shall find other ways to show them I love them," Alex vowed, still unwilling to forgive the injury to him. Suddenly mindful of how uncomfortable he must be sitting on the floor, she got to her knees and then to her feet with only slight assistance.

In truth, Rane was relieved to get up; his body was beginning to register the punishment it had taken. It had been a long time since his father had whipped him, and never had it been this severe, a measure of the seriousness of the offense. He felt as if streaks of fire were burning over his lower back and buttocks. It was going to be a good while before he would be able to sit in any comfort. He hoped Caleb Jennings of Maryland would make it safely home.

Hand in hand they went outside to Magnus and Gweneth.

His parents had recovered quickly from Alex's attack. When Magnus had led Gweneth outside, they had regarded each other in silence only for an instant before their shock had turned to laughter.

"Ah, Gwenny, she's so like you! Puts me in mind of the time you knocked Matthew Pengilly down for my sake."

"It served him well. Matthew always was a bully, and you didn't have your full growth then," she said, eyes gleaming with remembered victory over the despised Matthew. But then her expression sobered. "Rane's my son, but Alexandria is not my daughter, and that's to the good, I'd say. How would you feel if he took her to wife?"

Magnus blinked in surprise. "But they're just bairns!"

"He's not, he hasn't been for some time, and she'll not be much longer."

Magnus rubbed his right eye gingerly, wondering if it would turn black from the punch Alex had landed. "Her fists are near grown now." He paused and nodded. "I'd like it very well were Rane and Alex to wed. Oft I feel near blind compared to you. It's all there already, isn't it, just waiting for them to understand when the time is right. Why, we knew younger than they." He frowned. "You don't think that Rane . . ."

"You are blind!" she agreed vehemently, cutting him off. "Rane is as protective of her as she is of him, he wouldn't do aught to harm her including taking his pleasure before she is ready. I fear it more the other way, that he will wait too long. Sometimes a treasure under the hand is easily lost. But there's nothing we can do about it save pretend we know nothing and let time do as it will with them. And, husband, there is one more thing. The time for lifting your hand against Rane is past. It is too late to change him now. Whatever sort of man he will be, he already is. It was his grace to you that he accepted the beating at all and did not fight."

Their eyes locked in a brief battle of wills, but then Magnus nodded. "Aye, you're right again. I'm sorry for it now. I hit him too hard, I was that angry, or more to the truth, that frightened. I thought I would not see him and Alex again. I try not to favor him, but I do. Maybe it is always so with the youngest."

"At least in many families," Gweneth amended, thinking of Alex's situation.

Alex and Rane were surprised and relieved by the calm reception they got from his parents. Magnus brushed aside Alex's stammered apology and bid her let Gweneth give her a cup of tea and tend her ill-used hands. Alex looked at her hands in puzzlement, having forgotten all about them, but now the events of the past hours were beginning to catch up with her, and she felt out of focus again. Gweneth bustled her away tenderly.

Magnus put his hand out, and Rane took it without hesitation, noting how gently his father touched him now, Magnus aware that Rane's hands, too, were sore.

"A swim in the cold sea might help what ails you," Magnus offered gruffly, his eyes more tender than he knew as he studied his son's drawn face. "And I would know more of this American, though softly told if you please. 'Twould be better if the rest of the village were not to know. I would give a sovereign to have seen O'Leary's face when you hailed him."

They walked down the hill together, Magnus slowing his gait to match Rane's stiff pace. And when it was time to climb back up again, Magnus put his arm around his son's shoulders, half supporting his tired body, and was grateful that his help was not rejected. He thought how curious it was that a father's greatest hope was that his son should become a fine man, and yet, it was so hard to relinquish the child.

On the surface, nothing seemed to have changed. The daily chores of the Falconer household were still to be done, and the work of the farm and the sea was never finished. For the land, crops, and livestock must always be tended, and for the sea, there were always nets to be mended even for the small bit of fishing the Falconers did, boats to be scraped and caulked, and other equipment to be polished and kept in repair. And though revenue cutters continued to patrol the coast now and again, the free trading continued apace.

At first Alex was so relieved that she had not been sent back to Gravesend, she didn't notice the subtle changes in her relationship with Rane. But when she did take note, she saw that things were sadly awry. Suddenly he had no time for her, not even when she was offering help that would make his load lighter. He made up thin excuses to keep her from going fishing with him or to the farm. The adventures they had had ceased abruptly, and he spent his free time on mysterious pursuits of his own, away from her. Often now he came in late at night or in the early hours of the dawn even when there was no cargo coming in. He took free trading runs when it was not his turn and was gone for days. And she overheard Seadon teasing him about the extra time he was spending with the Buck's Mills widow. She wondered at her own reaction to that. She really had no right to mind, but she worried about him in the clutches of such a creature and felt very young and inadequate in face of his carousing. She kept hoping things would get better and mourned when they worsened. Their estrangement grew until she felt even more lonely than she had when first she arrived in Clovelly She hardly noticed the summer which finally

127

brought long fair days to delight the senses with large blue butterflies hovering over rainbow sweeps of flowers.

Magnus and Gweneth noticed the change and were sorry for the sad, pinched look Alex had now and for the wild unhappy spirit that drove Rane, but they held their peace, knowing that their interference could do no good and might do damage. It was up to the young people to come to their own understanding. Gweneth had to keep reminding herself of that as her maternal instinct rose strongly in spite of her efforts to curb it.

Alex's misery finally spilled over because of the annual fair at Barnstaple. Seadon, Elwyn, and their wives were going, as was Rane, though Magnus and Gweneth were not. No one had gone the year before because the ships had been out, so there was even more anticipation than usual. Alex wanted desperately to go, but she knew it would not be possible unless Rane agreed to escort her. The fair was no place for a young girl alone, and Seadon and Elwyn would have enough to do minding their own families. It would be wrong to ask them to do more.

Alex kept praying that Rane would ask her to go, but as the day neared and he said nothing, she gathered her courage and went looking for him, finding him mending a net with skillful fingers. The sun was warm despite the nip of autumn in the air, and for a moment, she watched the play of light on Rane's brown, calloused hands.

He looked up suddenly, frowning at her. "I didn't hear you. What do you want?"

She nearly lost her nerve at the cold reception, but then she forced the words out. "Please, will you take me to the fair? I shan't trouble you, I promise!"

"No!" he snapped, turning back to his work. "There is too much I want to do there. I don't need a little girl tagging along."

"I'm not a little girl," she protested, but there was no defiance in her voice; it broke on the words as she tried to hold back the tears that would prove his description of her. "Rane, I'm so sorry I caused you a beating! You must believe that. Please, I will do anything you ask. Can't we be friends again?"

For a moment he was completely baffled; it had never occurred to him that she still blamed herself for the aftermath of their aiding the American, but now he realized she had taken on the full burden of his change of attitude toward her. He still might have been able to continue the ploy had she stormed at him or whined about his bad behavior, but he was lost when he glanced up and saw the tears running down her cheeks.

Tears were very rare for Alex, and even when she had first arrived in Clovelly, she had not looked so alone and defeated as she did now. Rane had kept himself from seeing her clearly these past weeks, had kept so fast a pace that he had seen and felt nothing clearly. Now clarity returned with a vengeance. She was no longer the healthy creature who had helped him at myriad chores and accompanied him on various larks. Her cheeks were hollowed, her eyes shadowed, her body much too thin, her shoulders hunched and graceless as if she were trying to shrink inward and take up less space. The loss of that proud carriage was worst of all.

He loved her, not as a cousin or little sister or friend, but as a man loves a woman even though she was not yet so. It had been there when he had held her to warm her that night in the cave though he had not recognized it for what it was until afterward. It had begun to dawn on him in the madness of her assault on his father, and it had hit him full force shortly thereafter when he realized he was looking at her in an entirely new way.

His new view of her appalled him. She was only fourteen years old. That might be all right in some circumstances, but not in his. It made him feel unclean, and it made him think of her even more. Innocent times they had had together no longer seemed innocent—the pale flash of her body when they had gone swimming, the shape of her small rounded bottom and softly developing breasts when she wore her boy's clothing, the vulnerable line of her throat when her head was lifted to him, the ever changing green of her eyes, the thickness of her eyelashes and the heavy springing life of her long hair, all in retrospect became unbearably erotic. Even hearing her speak in her low, throaty voice that seemed so at odds with her age had the power to send chills up and down his spine while it warmed his loins.

So great was his guilt, it never occurred to him that his mother and father had grown to loving adults from an attraction that went nearly back to the cradle, a story he knew well. He had not sought comfort or reason; he had sought punishment for himself. He had inflicted the worst penalty he could—he had denied himself Alex's company and had mourned for what could not be in the arms of a woman for whom he cared nothing at all.

Not until now did he see that the punishment had fallen as heavily on Alex as on himself. He had always had the love of both of his parents and of his brothers, and thus it was difficult for him to imagine how it had been for Alex with a mother who didn't care for her at all and a father who cared only from a safe distance. He didn't doubt that her grandmother's love and that of her favorite brother was important, but they were not enough to balance the other. And he had offered her friendship and cherishing, had made her trust him and love him in her way, and then he had cast her off for no reason she could understand.

Quite simply, Alex wished she could die, just disappear as if she had never existed at all. She was suddenly so weary she couldn't move. The faraway expression on Rane's face was worse than his temper had been. It was as if for him she had indeed ceased to exist. And she could not stop the mortifying tears.

She was so wrapped in misery, she didn't even hear him say her name, didn't see that he had moved until his arms came around her and drew her close.

"Alexandria," he said again, and this time she heard the long, soft sound he made of it. "Don't weep, please don't!" One rough hand stroked the tumble of her hair with infinite care and the other pressed her close to his warmth. "I cannot explain, but it's not your fault that I've been so foul tempered," *not your fault that you were born too many years after I was.* "I'll take you to the fair. How will I stay out of trouble if you're not there to help?" His attempt at lightness failed in the quaver of his own voice, but Alex was so glad that Rane was being kind again, she didn't notice.

He put her away from him and stared down at her, happy to see the tears had stopped. "If we don't take care, we'll have the gossips busy." Perversely he willed her to take the adult view, but she didn't, saying only, "Wouldn't they be foolish then!"

"Come on, help me finish this."

His matter-of-fact tone was the perfect grace note, and in a state of joy bordering on euphoria, Alex settled down beside him, her nimble fingers joining his in the tying and knotting. All was right in her world; Rane had made it so.

Rane's reflections were not so simple, but he was resolved that the burden was his to carry, not hers. In spite of his sometimes wild ways, he had learned discipline from birth; the sea was unforgiving of those who did not learn it. And he trusted now that self-discipline would keep him from frightening Alex until she was old enough to consider whether or not she desired him as a man. That she might then choose another was something he would not allow himself to think about.

❧ Chapter 12 ❧

They could have gone by water to Barnstaple, but it was easier to go overland because Bideford Bar was difficult to navigate, sometimes causing ships to stand off for days on end before they could enter the estuary of the Torridge and Taw rivers. It would also be easier to bring back livestock by land. Tactfully, no one mentioned the fact that another consideration was the fact that Susannah and Barbary were terrible sailors and turned green at the mere thought of stepping aboard a ship despite their husbands' close bonds with the sea.

The balmy September days held in a haze of warmth and sun. Some said it was the fairest autumn they could remember. Alex didn't care about the past history of the month; in harmony with the earth again, she was dazzled by its present glory. Rane smiled at her exuberance and silently approved her straight, easy seat on the rugged little mare she rode. The other women and children were ensconced on bolsters in the cart driven by Elwyn, but Seadon, Rane, and Alex were much happier on horseback.

They had finalized their travel arrangements after meeting Elwyn and his family at Appledore.

"This is surely a royal progress," Alex crowed. "There are Queen Susannah, Princess Barbary, and their court, and we are the knights going to the tourney with them."

"You might just pass as a squire," Seadon teased, eyeing her critically, "but I doubt it."

Alex made a face at him.

It was easier for Rane when she was acting as young as she was today; it was in moments of solemnity or sorrow that she seemed dangerously older than her years.

They spent the night in Bideford with its twenty-four arch long-bridge over the River Torridge and its steeped buildings set on hills. Alex had hardly noticed her surroundings when the coach had brought her and her grandmother here and Seadon had met them, but now she viewed the sights around her with bright eyes.

They visited Susannah and Barbary's parents, other relatives, and friends, but they left very early the next morning so that they were in time to see the white glove put on display in the upper window of the Town Hall in Barnstaple. The glove officially signaled the beginning of the revelry and was an old custom dating from the time of Henry III. At that time, though fairs were held with the king's permission, his men were using them as an excuse to wreak havoc on helpless villagers. Finally the people appealed to the king, and he sent a white gauntlet in token of his promise that any of his men caught misbehaving at the fairs would be punished. The white glove had been displayed at many fairs since that time, and Alex pointed out that it made her fantasy of lords and ladies quite apt.

Seadon swept her an elaborate bow and conceded the point in the joust.

The mayor invited his councillors and the public to "toast and ale," and speeches were made by various people, mostly concerning the past and present glories of Barnstaple or "Barum" as many locals called it for the name on the milestones near it. Many of the words paid flowery tribute to the grand improvements that had been made in the streets and drainage system since 1811. Rane could feel Alex shaking with suppressed mirth beside him and didn't dare look at her.

The spiced ale served with the toast was brewed by the

senior beadle according to a recipe dating back to Elizabethan times and was strong enough to show how hardy those ancestors had been. Preceded by his beadles and mace bearers, the mayor then walked to various key locations in the town, proclaiming the fair open.

The Falconer party watched it all with great enjoyment and then went to call on Thaddeus and Cecily Bromley. Thaddeus was an old merchant friend of Magnus and was glad to offer the hospitality of his household, having been alerted to their coming days before. The Bromley children were long grown and had their own homes in Barnstaple and elsewhere, so there was plenty of room, including stable space for the horses.

Then, before they pursued their separate courses, Elwyn as the eldest in the group, took it upon himself to warn them all of the dangers they faced. "It is not only the potion brewed by the senior beadle that can addle your wits, even the common ale here is strong as well as palatable. It would be well to go carefully with it today. There are surely a fair number of cutpurses and other rascals about."

His brothers listened to him tolerantly, and Alex checked the few coins she had with her, part of the money her grandmother had left with her; they were hardly enough to be worth a thief's while, but they mattered to her. She had already resolved to be no trouble to Rane, but she found it took no effort. He was as willing to enjoy all the sights as she was, and they took their time, peering at the many displays of foods and goods offered for sale. Though the fair had just begun, there was already an air of gaiety throughout as well as the harsher reality of voices raised to bicker over prices. The first day was the Cattle Fair, the second the Horse Fair, and after that the Pleasure Fair. Devon was noted for her improved breeds of cattle, and the Falconers planned to add to the farm stock. That was Seadon's duty as he had the best eye for the beasts. A mare was to be purchased, too, and since Rane was the best judge of horseflesh, he would choose her on the morrow. And that left him free for this day. Elwyn was perfectly satisfied to be in charge of more mundane purchases—cloth, pottery, rope, nets, and various other goods for household and ship. His methodical mind enjoyed the task, and Susannah was a good judge of durability and utility.

Barnstaple was a market town of ancient standing, ruins of its medieval gates and walls still visible here and there, and it, like Bideford, had a long bridge, this with sixteen arches over the River Taw. The rivers of both towns led to the same estuary and thence to the bay beyond. But Barnstaple was built on more level ground and lacked the charm of Bideford's multi-level buildings. The town also lacked the swift current in its river that Bideford had, and thus silt had accumulated, ruining the deep-water trade it had enjoyed for centuries because the ships could no longer make an easy passage. But its status as a great marketing town for all the surrounding area had kept it flourishing, and Alex could find no fault with the town on this festive day. She could even imagine the rich be-wigged merchants of the last century settling their bargains on the Tome, a special stone that still stood, as Bristol merchants paid "on the nail."

Rane felt very old as he escorted Alex and watched her reaction to the bright sights and babble around them, yet he could not help but relax in the glow of her delight. The historical sites fascinated her, and the sellers' wares caught her eyes. She looked at everything from hair ribbons to meat pies with equal interest but without coveting any of it. Rane discovered that when he offered to buy her a pretty little mirror with a cord.

"Oh, no thank you," she responded quickly. "It's much more enjoyable to look and know I don't have to decide."

Rane smiled at this odd point of view and resolved to buy some trinket for her anyway before they left Barnstaple.

The town had had potters for hundreds of years, and their wares were displayed in sometimes graceful, sometimes grotesque profusion. And many of the pieces bore names unique to Devon. A sixteen-pint pitcher was a "Thirty Tale" for reasons unknown to Rane or to the genial potter they questioned. But other pieces bore more evocative names such as "Pinch Gut," "Long Tom," and "Gully Mouth." Milk pans were Big or Little "Bodleys," and one pan was even called a "Bawd." The mathematics of the trade was as obscure as some of the nomenclature. There were "land" and "sea" dozens, the former meaning thirty-nine and the latter sixty. More crucial to Alex and Rane was the delicious taste of the potatoes they purchased to eat, cooked in their jackets and hot from the ashes of a kiln. Alex pronounced them the best thing she had ever tasted.

"There is a solution," Rane announced. "We'll simply build a potter's oven at Clovelly, but we'll use it just for potatoes. Or we could bake them in a limekiln."

Alex made a face of exaggerated distaste at the idea of the delectable food being mixed with the hot, dusty, smoky process that resulted when limestone was poured through a hole in the top to be burned by the culm furnace beneath in order to produce fertilizer. "I think it is a good thing you are not a cook. You have a most indelicate idea of it and would poison us all."

Rane tried to look properly wounded, and they both laughed at their own foolishness. The day slipped by in much laughter over matters of no moment, leaving them both tired and content when they returned to the Bromley household for the night and found the rest of the family.

Seadon was mightily pleased with himself for having purchased two fine cows and a young bull for a reasonable sum. "The best clotted cream in Devon will come from those cows," he boasted, licking his lips at the thought of one of his favorite delicacies, the thick cream that Barbary made with such a sure hand, having learned the scalding and skimming process when she was but a child.

"It would be good on hot potatoes," Rane said, grinning at Alex, and the two of them giggled as if they'd had too much of Barum's strong ale.

"The fair has made the children daft," Elwyn announced, but his eyes were twinkling. In his own quiet way he had enjoyed the day immensely with his wife and children.

Master Bromley and his wife were genial hosts and were glad of the influx of young people in their house; they were used to it from their own children and grandchildren and were very pleased that everyone was having such a good time. Bromley's connection to the Falconers was free trading. He had been skilled at running goods in his youth and had then settled down under the cloak of a respectable merchant, though he still dealt in contraband.

Even after all this time of knowing, Alex found it decidedly strange to listen to such open conversation about breaking the law, yet she listened as respectfully as the rest as Bromley regaled them with tales of daring escapades, his wife regarding him fondly as if she had never heard the stories before.

Unbidden, the image rose in Rane's mind of himself and Alex together with the end of life in sight rather than the beginning, still loving each other as the Bromleys did, as his parents did. Savagely he thrust the thought away only to find that Alex was regarding him worriedly because she had seen the fleeting look of pain. He smiled at her reassuringly and resolved to be more careful; sometimes he still found it unnerving to have another human being as attuned to him as she was. And nothing must spoil her time at the fair.

The next day he was all business and so was Alex. This choosing of a horse was a serious matter. The Falconers, like many others, had long mixed the blood of the Exmoor ponies with other breeds of horses to get animals with better confirmation while retaining the best characteristics of the ponies. In the West Country and elsewhere, Exmoor blood could be found in cart and race horses and those in between.

They arrived early in the area where the horses would be sold, and for a time, they did nothing more than look at the animals and listen to the bargaining. Rane had to deal with the delicate timing of not buying too hastily but still not missing the best animals. And even a keen eye could easily miss the sort of doctoring a sharp dealer might do to make his animals appear better than they were. There were dyes to cover old scars and unsightly markings, and herbs and potions to change temperament. Alex and Rane spent a lot of time just whittling the numbers down until they had picked out six they thought might do and might be affordable. By then, they both felt as if they'd looked at thousands of horses.

The dun they rejected on first close inspection when her owner took them for simpletons and tried to insist the horse was much younger than her teeth proved her to be. Her teeth had been bishopped, filed down to make her look younger. A dark bay was similarly dismissed when Rane found a suspicious swelling on one hock and suspected beaning, the fitting of a small stone under the shoe of the sound foot so that the horse appeared to be only laggard rather than lame. A gray was rejected when Alex whispered to Rane that there was a strong scent of ginger about the seller which probably indicated that he was making his animals appear lively by using it as an irritant, making the poor beasts fidget, sweat, and carry their tails high as if they were finely bred.

Rane looked at her, aghast that she should know about figging, a crude practice since the chewed ginger was applied in the fundament where it was hard to detect.

Interpreting his look correctly, Alex explained, "My grandmother can cure a horse as well as a man, and she knows all the tricks. To be too delicate would be to be of no use to the animals."

Rane had to concede the point.

They both had difficulty resisting the beauty of a black. Her coat glistened in the sun, her lines were clean and sculpted, and she was clearly young enough to have years of foaling ahead of her. But again Alex demurred, drawing Rane aside. "She won't do. For all her flash, she has mean eyes. She'd be nothing but trouble. St. John says you must look at the eyes for temper just as you do with people."

Rane felt a swift pang of jealousy and for a moment wanted to reject the advice, but when he studied the animal more closely, he had to admit the truth of what Alex was saying.

His pique vanished when, in the warmth of conspiratorial agreement, they finally settled on one of two chestnuts. They both schooled their faces to skeptical interest, but Rane could feel Alex's excitement in the nervousness of the slender fingers that slipped into his hand.

This mare had everything they were looking for—strength, youth, good lines, size (necessary for increasing that of the Exmoor pony crosses), and deep calm eyes. The old man who was selling her treated her with affectionate firmness, as if she were a favored child, and he was honest enough to admit she had not been trained to harness though he was sure her sweet nature would accept it. He allowed Rane to try her, and Rane put her through her paces in a small cleared area and found her perfect. She responded well to her rider despite the noise and confusion around her, and Rane and the owner settled down to earnest bargaining that took some time but resulted in satisfaction on both sides. Rane could hardly wait for his family to see the mare.

" 'Er be a gurde 'un, 'er be. Treat 'er kindly an' she do fer ye an' yer wife," the old man bid Rane.

He turned away and did not see Rane blanch, nor did

Alex hear, so busy was she in assuring the mare of how fortunate she was to have been purchased by the Falconers. Rane knew he was overly sensitive, but it bothered him that the man had not mistaken Alex for his sister rather than his wife in spite of how much they looked alike; it made him wonder if he behaved in some betraying way. With effort, he banished the thought.

As he led the horse, Alex skipped beside him, bubbling over with enthusiasm for the new purchase. "She'll have to be named 'Princess,' for the tourney."

Rane was still so lost in his own thoughts, it took him a moment to understand what was happening when he heard Alex gasp.

It happened so fast, she was taken completely by surprise. A man reeking of strong ale lurched out and grabbed her, squeezing the breath out of her with his brawny arms as he clasped her to him and smeared her mouth with his wet lips. "Gie us a kiss, thas a lass," he mumbled, continuing his pursuit.

Rane's momentary paralysis was replaced by a surge of rage that sent him hurtling at the man. He jerked him by the neck, so hard that the man let go of Alex immediately.

She staggered and nearly fell, but friendly hands helped her regain her balance. That was all the aid that was forthcoming; no one wanted to deal with the madman Rane had become.

Alex's attacker was huge, outweighing Rane by at least four stone, but he was drunk, and Rane's fury was totally unexpected. The man managed to land one solid punch, but it was no contest. Rane's pummeling fists and some well-aimed kicks had the man laid out on the ground in short order.

And then to her horror, Alex saw that Rane was not even aware that he had won as he crouched over the fallen man, continuing to punish him.

"Stop it! Oh, Rane, stop it!" she screamed, tugging at his shoulders.

He swung around, and for a moment, she thought he was going to hit her, so crazed were his eyes.

"Please," she whimpered. "He'll do no more harm."

Rane stood and shook his head as if he were coming up from under water. Her fear vanished as he stared at her. She reached up and gently touched his right cheekbone. "You're going to have a bruise and a blackened eye.

Thank you, he shouldn't have grabbed me like that." She wanted to reassure him that though she had stopped it, she understood his violent reaction; it was much like her attack on Magnus in his defense.

Very deliberately, he traced her mouth with his finger, stopping just short of kissing her to erase the imprint of the other man. A queer island of calm and silence seemed to surround them in the crowd.

Alex continued to regard him with such innocent trust that it was Rane who turned away nervously, finding with relief that the mare was being held by one of the onlookers. The man he had downed was sitting up, cradling his aching head, obviously not in the mood to cause any more trouble, and the crowd was dispersing, seeking other sport. Rane drew a deep breath, trying to gain control of his emotions. He realized the excitement of fighting the man on Alex's behalf was as sexual as it was violent. At the moment, he wished Alex was possessed of at least a little of the coquetry her sister must have to have pursued the man St. John so avidly.

They took the new purchase to the Bromley house to stable her with the other beasts and encountered no one but a stableboy, much to Rane's relief—time enough for explanations of his swelling eye. For now, a splash of cold water was his only concession to it.

"I'm hungry," Alex ventured timidly, having difficulty judging his mood, but pressed to it by the gnawing in her stomach.

He looked at her blankly for a moment and then grinned. "So am I!" He was glad to have such a mundane matter to consider after the upheaval of the fight.

The tension flowed out of both of them as they spent the rest of the afternoon wandering about, munching pasties and more potatoes and carefully sipping the strong local ale as they enjoyed the sights.

After close inspection, Alex purchased several little packets of herbs and spices for Gweneth and Magnus, pleased that with the gift she could pass on more of her grandmother's lore. Rane surprised her by presenting her with a figurine of a horse. "To remember choosing the Princess," as the mare was now irrevocably named.

Alex was delighted and touched by the fairing, shaped so cunningly by the potter's art. She kissed Rane on the cheek in her excitement, and he was content.

He persuaded her to have her fortune told, and thinking it would be amusing, she agreed. But she immediately regretted it. The old crone had bright young eyes, neither kind nor malevolent but somehow aloof and watchful, at odds with the lined age of her face. And she smelled quite foul. Her skin had a patina of dirt and grease, her teeth were blackened, and Alex could barely restrain herself from snatching her own hand away when it was taken into the grimy paws with their filthy nails.

The old woman muttered ritual predictions of good fortune, but then a frisson of energy ran through her, and she gripped Alex's hand hard. "Wise child of the wise-woman, you will learn. You are with him now, but you won't be then, until it's time for him again." The words were spoken with eerie clarity, but they made no sense to Alex except for the reference to the "wise-woman," her grandmother. It gave her a shiver of unease that this woman should know that, and then she wondered if it had just been a lucky guess; perhaps the woman had seen her choosing herbs or perhaps the scent of them clung to her, though how the creature could smell anything other than her own odor was a mystery. And perhaps the last lines meant only that if she were not careful, she would be separated from Rane in the seething crowds. She resolved to view it logically, but she pulled her hand away, not wanting to hear any more.

"I saw no more," the old woman said, and there was neither pity nor gloating in the strangely young eyes.

When Rane asked her what the woman had said, Alex assured him that it had just been nonsense and a waste of his coin. She put careful conviction in her words, knowing he could too easily hear what she was not saying.

◆ *Chapter 13* ◆

"You cannot pick blackberries after Michaelmas Day because that's when the Devil comes through Devon and spits on them."

"Ugh! That's disgusting! It's also very silly." Alex studied Rane's face. "Surely you don't believe it? I'm never quite sure."

He held his serious demeanor for another second and then lost it in a wide grin. "No, of course I don't, at least not the Devil part, but the berries just aren't any good after the end of September. Mildew and such steal their sweetness. You're better off not eating them."

Alex changed her mind about picking and eating the late, sheltered berries she had seen in a hedge they passed. October itself was rather like a ripe fruit, not spoiled, just full and sweet. Most of the harvesting was finished at the farm, and the livestock was growing shaggy with the start of winter coats. Foliage, too, was changing, showing gold and brown.

Alex did not find the season sad as many did. She liked the crisp scent coupled with the soft, misty look of it. But she admitted to herself that any season would seem as lovely now that she and Rane were friends again. Sometimes she sensed a reticence in him that had not been there before, but she marked that down to the fact that he was after all, a man and had a life apart from her. Perhaps he was having troubles with the widow.

Very shortly she realized it was not as apart as he might wish it. They were not very far from Buck's Mills, and a woman was coming toward them. Alex would have had no idea who she was were it not for Rane's behavior. The moment he caught sight of the woman, his easy manner vanished to be replaced by the most obvious panic. He looked like a frightened horse, eyes wide and nostrils flared. Alex had to exert savage control on herself to keep from bursting into laughter. She had no doubt that this was the infamous widow. It was as if her own thoughts had conjured the woman.

She was of medium height and fair, unlike many of the inhabitants of Buck's Mills who were dark and partook of the legend that they were descendants of shipwrecked Spanish sailors from the Armada. She probably liked the distinction of her blondness in the dark hamlet, Alex thought, trying not to stare. The woman was so self-conscious, it was rather like watching a bird preening itself. She was rather bright plummaged, too, her walking costume a mix of colors that hadn't much sympathy with each other. Her lashes, lips, and cheeks owed more to artifice than nature, and powder had caught in the tiny creases around her eyes and mouth. The bloom was definitely off this rose and yet her figure had a firm roundness and her clothing was clean.

Though Miranda Griggs was scarcely educated, sense and shrewdness showed in her bright blue eyes. She had long since learned that the hard toil the fisher and farm women of Devon seemed to thrive on was not to her liking, while pleasing men was something she had known how to do well for a long time. Posturing and blinking her eyes for the male species was as natural as breathing. The only major mistake she had made in her life was to marry William Griggs and leave Bristol to live with him in Buck's Mills; she had had to make a great effort to show any regret at all when he died. Even by then she had established particular friendships outside of her marriage, and she had soon found that those seamen were more than willing to give her gifts to ease her way. But she did not flaunt these liaisons, knowing the conservative character of her surroundings. She lived with enough caution to keep her just within the bounds of the community, helping to insure that place by being generous with small loans and other charities which would be missed were she driven away.

All in all, Miranda was content with her lot. She still harbored vague plans of returning to Bristol someday, but in her more honest moments, she admitted to herself that she was probably better off where she was because there was little competition. About Rane Falconer, she harbored no illusions at all. He had a beautiful body and was quite marvelous in bed for one so young, his skill increased to quite a degree, she liked to think, by her teaching. But she had never thought of him as other than a temporary pleasure, and studying the pair before her now, she was more sure than ever of that. She had heard about the cousin who had come to live with the Falconers; she had heard that the girl and Rane had quickly become close, but he had never spoken of her to Miranda, and that had told her a great deal. He had also begun to come to her more often and with a desperation that had not been there before. She learned the rest by simply using her eyes and instinct.

Rane had always had a calm presence despite his youth, but it deserted him now. He was so agitated, he could hardly get through the unavoidable introductions, stammering and stuttering over the names as if they were completely unfamiliar to him. His face was red, and he was unaware that he was clenching and unclenching his hands. He looked as if he wished the sea would rise up and take them all.

Miranda felt an almost overpowering urge to laugh, and she glanced away, catching the girl's eyes and discovering an equal measure of mirth there. For an instant, they communicated in perfect harmony, without words, and completely without Rane's knowledge.

"It has been a pleasure to meet you, Miss Thaine," Miranda managed to say with grave politeness. "And now I must be on my way."

"My pleasure also, Mrs. Griggs," Alex returned, keeping an equally firm grip on herself.

Three different reactions were had from the same meeting. Miranda felt real pity for Rane; if his affection for the girl was cousinly, well, then she, Miranda, knew nothing about men, and that was far from the truth. But Alexandria obviously had no inkling of it. She was still so young, but Miranda had no doubt she would turn many a head in her prime.

As for Alex, she was pleased to have met the widow. She no longer felt that the woman threatened Rane; somehow she was sure there was no real harm in her.

Rane was miserable. And carefully probing the wound,

he realized that worse than the embarrassment of the meeting itself was the fact that Alex had taken no offense. When Alex murmured, "She seems quite nice," he wanted to strangle her. He remained out of sorts for the rest of the day, his mood not helped by the fact that he could sense Alex's continued amusement.

By the next day, he had his temper back on an even keel. He had vowed that the burden was his to carry, and that he would be patient until Alex grew up. And in any case, he could not bear it when things were not well between them. The long summer of avoidance had been more than enough.

He was grateful that Miranda mentioned nothing about the meeting when he saw her again.

In November he received a package that touched both him and Alex and reminded them how closely they were bound. The package was delivered by Sean O'Leary who surprised many in Clovelly by bringing the *Silkie Wife* in quite close and having himself rowed in in the longboat. Sean was a free trader, but he was no thief, and he felt personally responsible for the delivery and was taking the time out on his homeward voyage to accomplish it.

There was no name on the outside of the package, and the inner letter was not personally addressed. Caleb Jennings had done his best to be sure they would not be incriminated were the letter found, taking great care that the package be relayed by trustworthy hands through the tobacco trade from Baltimore to Sean O'Leary in Ireland.

> *31 August 1814*
>
> *Forgive the long delay in my sending word to you. I wanted to be assured that this would reach you safely.*
>
> *The contents are for the two of you alone. Others who carried me have been contacted separately.*
>
> *Because of you, I am home with my family once again. My gratitude is boundless though there is little way I can show it from this distance.*
>
> *The ending of your war with France which has so benefitted your country has proved hard for mine as it has resulted in more British troops coming here. The war will soon end, I still believe that, but I fear there is even more cause for bitterness than previously. The commerce of my*

country is in near ruin from the war, but a worse blow was struck to the heart when our capital city of Washington was burned a week ago by British troops. You must understand, a paltry second it would be in comparison of age and grandeur, but it is our London, the center of our young government. It will not easily be forgiven, and that is not to the good, as it will of a certainty slow the establishment of good relations between our countries. But they will come, they must.

Someday I would like to see both of you again. Perhaps it will be so. The ways of life are strange.

C.J.

The contents were gold sovereigns, four times as many as Rane had given Caleb, a generous offering, but not enough to offend Rane's pride. They were tightly encased in a deerskin pouch and wrapped with the letter in oilcloth.

Rane immediately offered them to Magnus. Seadon's ship was the first priority of the family, and individual shares of earnings were small compared to what went for that. But Magnus shook his head. "No, you earned them, you and Alex. It's a different sort of plunder."

Sean, looking on benevolently, again envied Magnus his sons and the good way he had with them. But maybe daughters weren't so bad. He was still recovering from the shock of discovering that Rane's cousin Alex was a female. Every now and then he chuckled at the memory of her standing so staunchly on the deck of his ship.

When Rane began to divide the coins, Alex, too, refused. "No, it is to go toward your own ship. The money you gave Mr. Jennings was yours, and this is, too."

When he protested, she said, "All right, then consider the coins my share of your ship. A few planks on the deck, a sail, some part of her will be mine, and then I will sail with you wherever you go."

Wives sometimes sail with their husbands, he thought, and his hands closed over the coins; what was his was hers. "So it will be," he said aloud. "Thank you."

Despite offers of hospitality, Captain O'Leary left shortly. His men were waiting for him, and as he pointed out, "Sure an' wouldn't th' Revenue be rejoicin' if they found th' *Silkie Wife* just sittin' there for them." He winked at Alex as he left. "If ever you've a wish t' serve aboard a good ship, I've room for ye." Rane had told him the tale of their wild journey home, and O'Leary had respect for anyone, female or not, who could beat the sea even for a short run.

Alex and Rane were infinitely glad that Caleb Jennings had reached home, and because of their liking for him, they tried to glean what news they could of the war in America. Though the papers were slanted to England's side, it was becoming apparent that the supposition that the Americans could be beaten with the addition of more soldiers, many of them veterans of the Peninsular campaign in Europe, was overly optimistic. There had been more fighting in early September, the Battle of Plattsburg Bay, and the Americans had acquitted themselves well. At least the two sides were finally meeting to discuss peace, though certain boundaries and fishing rights were still in dispute.

Alex had little sympathy for the delay. "You would think it would make better sense to stop the killing now and decide such things later," she sniffed.

"Sense is not normally the weapon that brings wars," Rane replied wryly. "But it's the only one that will stop them, and I think both sides are coming to it."

In December, Alex received news of a more personal nature but found that it held less interest for her than did that of the distant American war. Florence was expecting a baby in January. It did not trouble Alex that even her grandmother had not told her until now. She felt so detached from her old life, her only response to the revelation was a faint twinge of pity—she doubted very much that Florence was ready to be a mother. She wished St. John and even her sister well, but unless things had changed a great deal, she could not imagine that their life together was serene. She remembered her sister's screaming fits of temper and was glad they no longer touched her. It was possible, she supposed, that making a child together might provide a new generosity of spirit, but her mind still refused to picture Florence as a tender woman.

When she told Rane the news from Gravesend, he felt only that anything that made St. John Carrington more inaccessible was fine with him. Neither he nor Alex had any premonition that the birth and its aftermath would affect them profoundly.

They were far more affected by the loss of several fishermen off Clovelly. The wind veered suddenly, blowing so savagely that all were threatened and some boats were smashed as they tried to come in. Alex stood on the beach with Gweneth and other women watching helplessly as Magnus, Rane, and other men tried to put out to help the foundering boats and drowning men, but there was nothing they could do save curse the sea. It was the most grim and basic reminder of how ephemeral life dependent on the sea was.

Alex felt as if the lost men were part of her own family, and she was haunted by the fact that one of them, George Pine, had been scarcely older than Rane, a brawny, cheerful young man who left a wife and two babies among other grieving relatives, and whose body had been milled away by the sea so that there wasn't anything to bury.

> They that go down to the sea in ships, that do business in great waters;
> These see the works of the Lord, and his wonder in the deep
> For he commandeth, and riseth the stormy wind, which lifteth up the waves thereof.
> They mount up to the heaven, they go down again to the depth; their soul is melted because of trouble.
> They reel to and fro, and stagger like drunken men, and are at their wit's end.
> Then they cry unto the Lord in their trouble, and he bringeth them out of their distresses.
> He maketh the storm a calm, so that the waves thereof are still.
> They that are glad because they be quiet; so he bringeth them into their desired haven.

Alex was not comforted by the old words from the Psalms intoned at the funeral. She kept seeing Rane torn apart and stolen away by the dark waters. She was unaware of how clearly she was communicating these thoughts as she gripped his hand so hard that her nails dug into his flesh.

"I am here, safe and whole," he whispered, as if she had asked a question, and then she was comforted and able to give thanks that ships like the *Lady Gwen* that were built for deep water were less vulnerable than small boats.

But it was days before she would go out in Rane's own small craft or let him go without multiple warnings.

Though there was sorrow for the families who had lost so much, their very losses made the Falconers that much more thankful that they were all alive and well to spend Christmas together. It gave a bittersweet edge to all the celebrations.

The Falconer women—Gweneth, Susannah, and Barbary—were all enormously fond of Alex just the way she was. But even for their simple tastes, they found her wardrobe needed additions. In a year, the new dresses she had brought with her had become quite tattered and a trifle short. Alex's figure had changed little, but she was just a bit fuller in the bust and just a little taller. There were fashionable women in Bideford, and in any case, the free trading kept Gweneth and her daughters-in-law informed of current modes, so they were able to produce credible garments.

They had passed the work around, each doing part, getting together a few times to consult or finish off the dresses. Two were everyday smocks with pinafores to wear over them for protection, but the other two were delicate frocks made in the high-waisted fashion of the day, one in a soft green silk to match Alex's eyes, the other in a deep rose because all the jewel colors suited her vivid coloring.

"She will be very grateful, but she will still prefer her boy's clothing," Susannah commented with a good-natured smile. "And yet, she has the perfect form for this style; only the tall and slender appear graceful in these." She patted her own rather plump figure ruefully.

"She scarcely notices what she wears," Gweneth agreed, "but the day will come when that changes."

"I think Rane is in love with her, but I don't think she has any idea of it," Barbary ventured, and there was a little silence because each of the women had decided the same thing, but had thought the observation belonged to her alone.

"We must not make any point of it," Gweneth said, and her voice was serious. "It would hurt them both unbearably were they teased about it. It could well destroy their ease with each other."

Susannah and Barbary agreed, but it did not stop them from contemplating having Alex as a sister-in-law, and they found the idea very pleasing. It seemed as if Alex had been with them forever, and they no longer even considered that she might be summoned home.

The Christmas gift Rane gave Alex confirmed the women's conjecture. It was a necklace delicately wrought in gold in a pattern that at first glance looked like a central heart but on closer inspection revealed two swans, their heads bowed together to form the top of the heart, their breasts meeting to form the bottom. Tiny, gracefully curved gold feathers completed the circle. The swan heart fit precisely in the hollow of Alex's throat.

It was no gift for a child, but when Rane had seen it on one of his trips to France, he had known he had to have it for Alex, in spite of the high price and in spite of the statement it would make.

Alex was speechless with delight as she contemplated the gift, and when she finally spoke, her voice was very soft. "I will remember the day we saw the wild swans forever. Thank you, Rane, I have never seen anything so lovely." She went to him, kissing him on the cheek with spontaneous joy.

Rane found he was perfectly satisfied with her response. He had learned patience over these past months, and he was beginning to believe that mutual memories of special times were as good an approach to love as anything else. He had watched his parents and his brothers with their wives, and he had discovered that they triggered special bonds of feeling with each other by simply asking, "Do you remember when . . ." He had seen that the men reacted much as their wives did, showing sudden tenderness or laughter at the memory. And he had meant for Alex to remember the swans, the magical, lyrical swans who cast aside their cloaks to become lovely maidens, to become what she already was though she knew it not. He had risked revealing much to his family, but he found there was relief in that. Nothing was said; they all pretended to be unsurprised by his generosity to Alex, and he knew by that that they had already considered the matter and were not offended. His sense of being guilty of some crime in loving one so young was greatly eased by their attitude. Now it was only a matter of waiting until Alex was ready.

On New Year's Eve, he held her close for a moment and whispered, "May this be the best year of your life," and she replied, "Every day I am here with you and your family is the best of my life." And she felt warm and safe cradled so gently in his arms.

January brought a rumor that meant a great deal to both of them because of Caleb Jennings. It seemed that the American and British governments were at last close to signing, if they had not already done so, a peace treaty. There were still disputes to be settled over those troublesome boundaries and fishing rights, but the important thing was that the fighting was to cease.

Toward the end of the month, Alex also received word that her sister had given birth to twins, a boy and a girl. "Oh, she and Sinje must be proud!" she exclaimed as she read the news, and she meant it. Surely producing twins was enough of an accomplishment so that the extra praise and attention would please Florence and thus make things better for St. John. She envisioned seeing her niece and nephew someday, but it was a wish without priority; to see them would be to be in Gravesend again, and she had no desire for that.

Rane, in his new mood of optimistic patience and confidence, had stopped minding mentions of St. John, realizing that Alex truly thought of him only as a friend and as the unfortunate husband of her sister. He had even developed a certain sympathy for the man because any woman who could have been so cruel to Alex was undoubtedly a termagant.

In early March, Alex and Rane heard that there had been a terrible battle in America on January 8, at a place called New Orleans. An American named Andrew Jackson had led an improbable mixture of sailors, pirates, and militiamen against General Sir Edward Parkenham's 8,000 veterans of the war against Napoleon. Some 2,000 Englishmen had died; the Americans had lost little more than a score. There was no doubt of the victor. But the tragedy was not only the loss of life, but the fact that the Treaty of Ghent had been finalized the month before, not in time for word to travel widely enough to stop the battle. It was a savage lesson in the differences between an army that fought far from home for the king's shilling and one that fought on and for its own land.

And then in the middle of the month, reliably reported by the *Times* and carried by swift rumor elsewhere, came the news that Napoleon had escaped and was trying to marshal another French army. At first there was complacency, a belief that the French had had enough of Napoleon and of defeat at the hands of the allies and would risk no more.

Because of their free trading connections with the Continent, the Falconers knew the truth sooner than most. Incredible though it was, Napoleon's march to Paris was taking on more and more the trappings of a triumph, and his erstwhile capital was impatiently awaiting the return of the Emperor.

Reports from the Congress of Vienna had made it increasingly clear that the single common motivation of all the allies, Britain included, was selfishness and a desire to return Europe to the shape it had had in 1789—all show of affability the representatives affected at the endless rounds of public entertainments and supposedly secret conferences to the contrary. There was little patience for the new national movements that had emerged in the ensuing years. The old powers wanted back what they considered their own, and a bit more if they could get it. But it seemed now that they might once again have a reason to work together due to Bonaparte's wild postscript to history.

And then with April and the first hints of spring beginning at once and with Rane's twentieth birthday only days away, the focus of Alex's world narrowed radically to the realm of her own spirit. She was summoned back to Gravesend.

❦ Chapter 14 ❧

There were two letters, one from her mother, one from
her grandmother. The terrible news in them was the same:
Florence had never fully recovered from the birth of the
twins, and now she was dead. That was the only similarity in the missives. Her mother's words were so hysterically scrawled, Alex had difficulty reading them at all, but
the message was plain—Margaret wanted Alexandria home
as soon as possible. She had sent a note to Gweneth and
Magnus to the same effect, and it was hardly less erratic
than the letter to her daughter since it was a curt order
without even the pretense of civility.

After stating the bare facts, Virginia had sent quite
different instructions:

My dear Child,

*It is a tragedy, but it is not yours. Florence was as unfit for
marriage as you knew her to be. Her body failed, but her
spirit had given up long before. And your return to Gravesend
will not change anything that has happened. Please consider this very carefully before you decide what you will do.
You have a new life in Clovelly; do not be swift to forsake
it. The twins are not your responsibility. Margaret is quite
capable of taking care of them. And if she will not, then I will.*

*If you decide to stay with the Falconers, I will enlist your
father's aid, and together we will calm Margaret. She is
scarcely rational now, but such a rage of feeling cannot be
sustained indefinitely. If you must return here, send word,
and I will come for you.*

Remember always that I love you and want only your good.

The letters had been sent separately. It was only chance that they had arrived together.

Alex's face had lost all color as she read the mail, but aside from a small mewing sigh, she made no exclamation. Gweneth watched the change with growing apprehension, but she had no idea of what was going on until, wordlessly, Alex handed her the pages, including the note addressed to the Falconers.

As Gweneth read, she found she had to sit down, so weak had her legs become, and she wanted Magnus beside her right now, not off on the *Lady Gwen* picking up a load of tobacco from Ireland. She had grown complacent; they all had. She had ceased to fear that Alex would be taken away from them. It had come to seem as if the child had been with them always, would be with them always.

For a mad instant, she was tempted to burn the letters as if by obliterating them it would be as if they never existed. But Alex's ashen face compelled her to consider the matter rationally and to find a way out, a way for Alex to stay.

She read carefully, but Margaret Thaine's ranting was no more sensible on second consideration than it had been on the first. The gist of it was clearer though, and Gweneth felt a chill sweep over her skin. There was no love, not anywhere on the page was there love. There was duty: "As my sole remaining daughter, it is your responsibility to ease my burden." And there was blame, thinly veiled but surely there: "So much opposition devastated my poor Florence. She was too frail to bear the unkindness." The real intent fairly screamed from the page—your fault, your fault, Alexandria; you helped cause your sister's death.

Gweneth fought to understand why the woman could possibly want the despised child close to her again. And then she knew: "St. John and his kind are of no use, and I am left with the children that should by rights be his responsibility." Bile rose hot and bitter in her throat. Indeed Margaret did need her daughter home. She needed her to give life to the lie that she cared about her new grandchildren. Gweneth could see it too clearly. Margaret did not want the responsibility for the twins, but she did want the credit for doing the right thing, and there could be no better or less expensive way of accomplishing that than summoning Alex to be her unpaid servant. And above all, she wanted to punish Alex.

Gweneth thanked God that Virginia had sent contrary advice. Alex loved her grandmother very much and would surely heed her. Gweneth only wished that Virginia had worded her letter more strongly, had flatly ordered the child to stay in Devon.

"I will have to go, of course." The voice was calm and quiet, and gazing trustingly at Gweneth, Alex added, "My mother needs me. She loves me now."

In those small words, Gweneth understood why Virginia had been so restrained. Alex had never given up hope that her mother would accept and love her as she was.

Gweneth felt completely helpless. She had no weapons to fight this most basic of all needs that the child had. She remembered how loving her own mother had been, and she could not begin to imagine how deep the hurt would have been had that not been so. She, Magnus, Rane, and all the other Falconers had offered the best of their love to Alex, and it had been accepted, love given in return, but it had nothing to do with that first need. She would try, they would all try to persuade Alex to stay with them, but inside, she was already beginning to mourn the loss.

"Give yourself time to think about this," she pled softly. "Your grandmother is wise, please heed her! This is not your fault, and you must not believe it is." With great difficulty she restrained herself from attacking Alex's mother, knowing it would do no good.

"I cannot even remember clearly what my sister looked like. Poor Florence. I should not have been so unkind to her. Poor Mother, she must be so lonely. I don't expect my father is being much use to her." The eerie little voice said the words precisely as the tears slipped down Alex's cheeks.

Gweneth put her arms around her and held her close, but she felt as if the child had already gone.

Rane would forever remember his twentieth birthday as the worst of his life. He had grown so accustomed to having Alex waiting for him in the cave that even though the *Lady Gwen* had come in late, when she was not there on the return from Ireland he was seized by the absolute conviction that something terrible had happened to her.

He had thought in terms of physical injury—the reality, while not physical, was no less devastating.

Magnus was worried as well, and he sent Rane on ahead. "We'll get the cargo stowed in the cave. It's better taken out of Clovelly tomorrow night."

Rane burst into the house with his heart pounding, and his mother's face did not reassure him; she seemed to have aged by years since he had seen her short days before.

He looked wildly around the kitchen. "Where is she? What's happened to her? My God, tell me!"

Gweneth looked into her son's eyes. "She's leaving us. She's going back to Gravesend, back to that bitch out of hell who bore her." She bowed her head against his breast and wept brokenheartedly.

He listened to the gasping words that explained further, but he found only one thing comprehensible. His beloved Alex was leaving. It could not be; he would not allow it.

He held his mother away from him, giving her a little shake. "I'll make her stay. I would have waited, but not now. I'll ask her to marry me. She is young, and I will not force her to be a wife until she is ready, but I will keep her safe in the bond."

Gweneth shook her head, struggling to regain control, waiting until she could speak calmly. "It would only terrify her and add to her burden. She is changed, so changed. She tries on her clothes, first one dress and then another, worrying about which will please that woman most. Her spirit is already gone from here. And it was all I could do to prevent her from traveling to Bideford immediately to start for London. I have told her that you and Magnus will take her back to Gravesend." Gweneth refused to call it home for the child. "Right or wrong, this is something she must do. And if we truly love her, we must allow her to go without blame or anger, you most of all."

He did not want to believe it, did not want to accept it. But the fact was that Alex had not met him at the cave, and she had not come to find him now, though surely she must have heard him arrive. "Is she asleep?"

"I doubt it. I doubt that she has slept since the letters came. Go to her, offer your sympathy but nothing more. Can you do that?"

"I will have to." His face was grimmer than his mother had ever seen it, and inwardly she cursed Margaret Thaine and her dead daughter for the havoc they were wreaking on Alexandria's life.

Rane knew his cause was lost the minute he saw Alex's face. When he knocked on her door, she bade him enter without hesitation, but her manner was so politely distant, all their days together might never have existed.

"I am glad you are returned safely," she said, and it was as if she were speaking to someone she barely knew.

Rane swallowed hard, wanting to rail at her, wanting to weep. Instead he said, "I am sorry for your loss," and left her, carrying with him the image of her young-old face graven by candlelight.

Strangely, Gweneth found it more difficult to get control of Magnus than it had been to make Rane see the truth. She had known her husband loved the child, but she had not fathomed the depth of it. Alex was as much his daughter in his mind as she was Gweneth's in hers, and in addition, Magnus did not want to face the particular pain Alex's leaving would cause his wife and his youngest son. He was suddenly so full of fury and grief, he wanted to lash out at someone.

"I ought to take a stick to her, that would make her see sense!" he roared.

"Can't you understand, she's been beaten since she was a small child. Not with a stick, but beaten just the same," Gweneth countered earnestly, and Magnus's shoulders drooped in defeat because he knew it was so. They clung together like survivors of a shipwreck: though Alex was still alive, this loss was worse than the death of their infant daughters; the babies they had not known so well as Alex.

All the Falconers mourned, down to Elwyn and Susannah's children who understood enough to know that Alex would no longer be there to play with them when they visited their grandparents or the farm. And all of them, even the children, found the new Alex strange and unapproachable. But there was no question of abandonment. Rane and Magnus would take her home aboard the *Lady Gwen* as far as the Medway River, and from there they would trust their free trading contacts to escort her the rest of the way.

Alex did not write to her grandmother or to her mother. There was no need. In a matter of days she would be there.

In the years that followed, Alex could never clearly recall the voyage on the *Lady Gwen*, nor even her final farewells to the Falconers in Clovelly. She was locked away inside of herself, and everything outside was vague and blurred as if her senses had ceased to record anything that might disturb the deep calm that protected her from hurt. Finally her mother needed her, wanted her, loved her. That was all that mattered.

Only when Rane insisted on going all the way to Gravesend with her, did the calm falter.

"I must," Rane told his father.

Magnus could understand his need too well; even he was tempted to see the child all the way home. The ship was safe enough. She carried no contraband and was moored out of the way of the major shipping lines in the Medway River near Hoo. And the first man he had searched for had been there in the desolate house on the edge of marshland. He was an old contact, an owler who knew every inch of Kent and would have no trouble conveying his charge to Gravesend without detection.

"Care well for her and be back as soon as you can," Magnus instructed his son gruffly.

Alex regarded Rane with a puzzled frown as if she were just waking up. "Rane, you are going to Gravesend with me? But there is no need."

"There is," he insisted, but he did not explain. He wondered if it would pierce her protective wall if he added, "Because I cannot bear to surrender these last hours of being close to you." But he did not give voice to the words.

Magnus swept Alex into his arms, mumbling, "Ah, lass, we're there for you if ever you need us. Gwenny and I, we love you like our own." And then he turned and stalked off.

Alex, Rane, and their guide traveled by pack horses, an extra beast loaded with Alex's belongings. And the skill of the man was soon evident. He listened and scented the air like a night creature, leading them with steady confidence as if he could see in the darkness.

It did not seem odd to him that they were transporting a girl rather than contraband across the countryside; he knew it would do no good to have any of the Falconers discovered in the region. Questions led too easily to trouble, and anyone traveling at night was suspect. Being caught

157

even in the most innocent pursuit was dangerous for free traders.

They had less than ten miles crosscountry to cover, and even with their winding route which added some distance, they were in Gravesend in less than three hours. It had already been decided that they would take Alex to her grandmother's house, outside of town, and now Rane was doubly glad. He thought if he came face to face with Margaret Thaine, he might well do her harm.

Virginia opened the door, thinking she was being summoned to someone's sickbed. She blinked in disbelief, and then very softly, she said her granddaughter's name as she opened her arms, and Alex came into them, hugging the spare form.

Rane and Virginia's eyes met and spoke worlds without words. As glad as she was to see her granddaughter again, Virginia already regretted Alex's loss of the good life she had found in Devon. And she saw so much love and grief in Rane's eyes, she looked away first.

"You will stay at least for the night?" she asked him, but he shook his head.

"My thanks, but the ship waits. We must be gone as soon as we unload Alex's trappings."

It was swiftly done, and though he whispered, "Protect her again as you have before," to Virginia, he found he could do no more than bid Alex a stiff good-bye. He was at a loss, afraid to touch her, suddenly wishing himself miles away.

He and the owler were on the way down the road when he heard the running footsteps behind him. He reined his mount and slipped down to the ground.

"For all the days, for all your patience, for the magic seals and swans, for everything—Rane, thank you for all you have given me."

He felt her soft kiss on his cheek, and then she was gone, running back toward her grandmother's house before he could react.

Tremors shook him all the way back to the *Lady Gwen*. The guide wondered if the young man had the fever of the marshes.

Book Two

❧ *Chapter 15* ❧

Gravesend, Kent, England, 1815

In the middle of the night, Alex awakened in panic. She was completely disoriented. She could not hear the sea, and even in the dark, she knew the shape of the room was different from hers in Clovelly. Not even aboard the *Lady Gwen* had she felt this way.

She realized simultaneously that she was at her grandmother's house and that she had awakened herself by calling Rane's name. She could still hear it in the darkness. And in that darkness, the full awareness of what she had done crashed down on her for the first time. She was clear across the country now from the Falconers, from Rane. Suddenly knowing that she would not see Rane in the morning or in the days after made her feel as if part of herself had been severed. She bit her lip against crying out, and her heart pounded wildly. And then she steadied herself with the thought that she could always run away, back to Clovelly if she couldn't bear it in Gravesend. And her mother, her mother needed her now.

She fell into an uneasy sleep haunted by dreams of swans that kept changing shape, swirling in and out of the sea drift.

In the clear light of morning, she was stunned to see how much her grandmother had aged. She was still clear-eyed and straightbacked, but she was even leaner than before, her hands were gnarled and the veins stood out vulnerably beneath the thin skin. Most of all, her face had a look of sadness that not even her smile could wholly lift.

Alex had no way of knowing that most of the sorrow was for her.

She learned that things were even worse than she had supposed.

"Florence was even less prepared to be a wife than you suspected," Virginia said. "She thought her life would become a pleasant fairytale the moment she was married. She thought the Carringtons would change their minds and welcome her into the family. That did not occur. They disinherited St. John for making what they considered an unsuitable match. And when Florence found she was with child, the situation worsened. She loathed the prospect of being a mother." She paused, gathering the courage to go on. She no more than anyone else wanted to speak ill of the dead, and she mourned the waste of her elder granddaughter's passing, but the idea that Florence might reach out from the grave to destroy this bright life was insupportable.

"Alexandria, she did not have to die. It is true that the birth was hard and that she was truly ill, but she could have recovered. She as much as willed herself dead. And she wanted everyone to feel guilty about it, particularly St. John. And your mother was no help. She expected that the connections with the Carringtons would enhance her own social position. When quite the reverse happened, her fury was boundless. She was no help to Florence; she made everything worse by adding her own complaints of injustice and ill usage." She took a deep breath before she could go on. "You must understand, your mother has not changed. She has not become a kind and loving woman, not even the death of one of her children could do that. It is harsh, but it is true. Only I know that you have returned. I can send you back to the Falconers."

"But Mother needs me. She wrote that she did. And the twins, they need me also."

The certainty in Alex's voice grated on Virginia. "Flora and Blaine need a wet nurse which they have. They need to be kept dry and comfortable and little else at the moment. They do not need to destroy your life." Ruthlessly she suppressed the knowledge that babies need a great deal more than basic care, that they need loving at least as much as they need food. All her will was bent on saving this child. There was a new serenity and maturity about Alexandria; the Falconers had given her that with their

162

love. She was poised on the edge of womanhood, just ready to blossom, and Virginia wanted nothing to spoil that flowering. But she had made a fatal mistake in referring to the twins by name. Now they were two individuals, and in that instant she could see Alexandria begin to assume the responsibility of loving them. Her granddaughter wore that same tender expression common to women everywhere when they think of a child with love.

Alex did not recognize the guilt over her sister's death that was part of her response. And she was still certain she would find her mother a changed woman. But most of all there were two children who needed her.

Virginia knew she had lost even before Alex said firmly, "I must stay," and then asked, "Where is Sinje? Even with all that has happened, he must be proud of his children."

"He hardly knows they exist," Virginia snapped, her patience at an end. "England, Prussia, Austria, and Russia have formed a new alliance against Napoleon and have pledged hundreds of thousands of men to the new army. The Duke of Wellington is in command, and one of his men will be St. John. He managed to be aboard one of the ships that sailed from Dover to Ostend on the second of April. Apparently he finds war easier to face than fatherhood—and your mother."

Alex was silent for a long time, considering all her grandmother had told her, and then she announced. "It is time I was on my way. Please, allow me to go alone. I think it would be better. I will send Boston or someone else to fetch my things. And Grandmother, thank you, I know you want what is best for me."

She left Virginia staring unseeingly at the heavy packet Gweneth had sent by Alex. When she opened it, she found the same amount she had left for Alex's keep and a letter:

We are still in your debt. It was not duty to have Alexandria with us. We all love her very much. Thank you for sending her to us. If ever you or she needs us, send word. Our fondest desire is that she return to Clovelly.

Virginia put the coins away carefully; as far as she was concerned, they belonged to Alexandria.

Not even the knowledge that the child would be part of

her life again could lift the sad foreboding that weighed her down and made her feel even older than her long years.

When Alex arrived at the house in Gravesend, she found only the wet nurse and the twins. For years to come, Alex wondered if it would have made a difference had she seen her mother first. But as it was, she saw the tiny girl and boy, both of them fair, perfectly formed, and helpless, and her heart was lost. The boy, Blaine, curled his fingers around one of hers and held on tight, and Alex felt a wonderful current of energy flow from the baby to her, a sensation unlike anything she had ever felt before.

The wet nurse, Mavis Brown, looked on stolidly, her nature apparently as bovine as her form and function.

Alex was still with the babies when her mother returned.

Margaret gave a start of surprise at the sight of her daughter. But there was no light of pleasure in her eyes, no welcoming arms, no comment about her appearance in the green silk dress the Falconer women had made for her. "I see you recognized your Christian duty, though too late to help your sister." Her face was as implacable as her voice. She did not even ask how Alex had gotten from Devon to Kent.

Dizzily Alex wondered if her mother's mouth had always looked so pinched, her eyes so cold and lifeless. She had aged even more than Virginia in the year and a half since Alex had been here. And it was not grief she saw in the face, but rather bitter dissatisfaction.

The rejection was devastating, making it impossible for Alex to offer her own love. It was as if invisible thorns were thrusting her away from her mother. The disappointment and hurt were so profound, she could not accept them. Surely it would change once her mother saw how helpful she would be with the babies, how good a daughter she could be. The protective veil descended again, cushioning her from the shock of what was really happening.

"I will be glad to help care for Flora and Blaine. They are such beautiful children!" she ventured. She did not say that she was sorry about Florence. She knew her mother would not believe it.

"St. John's brats!" her mother hissed, showing emotion

for the first time. "The Carringtons should have the care of them."

Instinctively Alex moved closer to the infants as if to shield them from her mother's venom, but still the unreality persisted—her mother had suffered much, surely she was to be pitied, and surely she would soften with time.

She waited patiently in the days and weeks that followed, but she detected no easing of her mother's attitude, and she saw how it affected the rest of the family. Caton had become even more vague than before, disassociating himself from all conflict to such an extent he hardly seemed to be present. He had greeted Alex with real pleasure, but the focus was not sustained; she had felt him drifting off again almost immediately and knew there was no strength to be counted on there. Her older brothers and their families apparently came to visit even less often than before, and though they did at least pay her the courtesy of coming to see her shortly after her return, she could see the relief in their eyes when they left. Even Paris, who had never seemed to her to be anything but stuffy and self-absorbed, was moved to remark that "Mother has gotten quite odd."

Boston alone of her siblings remained close. He had embraced her exuberantly, told her she looked wonderful, and asked for details of her life in Clovelly. And she had revealed much to him when she had given only spare details, her voice curiously leaden but her eyes alive with pain. She found that talking about the Falconers brought desolation so acute, she was in danger of breaking down completely. She could not afford to have her fragile armor, rather like her father's, pierced, and so she found it safer to suppress all memories of Clovelly. But she could not stop the dreams of Rane and the wild swans.

At least with Boston she could be honest about Florence, and he was even more specific than her grandmother had been.

"I feel so many things at once," she admitted to him. "There is sorrow, but . . . oh, I just don't know how to describe it."

"I know what you mean. It's always sad when someone dies so young, and she was our sister, but she was such a . . . a difficult person. It's a sickening sense of waste as much as anything else that I feel. It's as if with just a few changes, it could have been so different. But it all turned 'round for the worst, not the better. The things that weren't very kind about Florence became more and more a part of her, not less. Instead of behaving like a woman after she married, she got to be more and more like a dreadfully spoilt child. She complained ceaselessly, nothing was good enough for her. And she never stopped telling St. John how horrid his family was, as if he hadn't enough hurt from that quarter. And then when she knew she was with child, her behavior got even more extreme. It seemed she was always either shrieking like a fishwife or crying like an infant. I don't know how St. John stood it; I believe I might have turned her out had I been him. His only fault was in being foolish enough to marry her. Poor fellow, he looked positively haggard before the marriage was very old, but he is a gentleman. He had made a vow, and he did his best to keep it in spite of Florence. I think he kept hoping that having children of her own would make her behave as a woman.

"But it didn't happen that way. After the birth of the twins, she just gave up. She wouldn't do anything Grandmother told her to do to regain her strength; she wouldn't eat properly nor take her medicine. She didn't drink poison, or fall on a sword, but nonetheless, she committed suicide. Alex, she willed herself to die because her life just wasn't what she wanted it to be. And she left St. John to feel terrible, undeserved guilt, and you, too, I expect." He drew a deep shuddering breath. "Florence was not only a selfish person, she was a coward."

They clung together, and Alex knew her tears were more for St. John than for her sister. Sinje suddenly seemed more real than he had since the last time she had seen him. "Take care, Sinje, take care, safe home," she whispered.

Boston, as fond as he was of her, was at twenty a young man with a life of his own. He still lived in the house, but he was seldom there. He worked for his father and was courting a Gravesend girl named Dora Jenkins. Alex remembered her because Boston had plagued her so when they were all children. Now Boston was a comely young man, taller than most, with thick golden-brown hair and the startlingly green Thaine eyes. Dora's coloring was similar though her merry eyes were pansy brown. She had a delicately symmetrical face, a softly rounded figure, and her head just reached Boston's shoulder. They made an attractive couple and obviously adored each other. Dora's father was a grocer, and so there would be no social cataclysm when they married. Alex was happy for them, but their close bond made her feel even more lonely.

Even old Mr. Buckman, who had been such a kind and patient tutor, was gone, having died of a lung complaint the previous winter. It was another source of comfort denied, and Alex would have bolted had it not been for her grandmother and the twins. Virginia kept her from feeling totally abandoned, and Flora and Blaine gave her reason for being alive. Daily they chained her closer to them. Even in their helpless and primary state, she saw the bright reaching out that filled their waking hours, and she saw that they needed her to respond to them, to touch and to talk to them. Margaret continued to avoid such contact, and Mavis seemed incapable of providing anything but milk and basic care.

A farm girl from nearby, Mavis had had a bastard child who had died shortly after birth, but it was impossible to tell if she mourned the child or longed for the father. It seemed impossible that she could feel nothing at all, and yet, she did not seem clever enough to hide her emotions if she had them. Not unkindly, Virginia suggested, "There are people who live lives little different than the beasts, and I don't mean that badly. I mean that they accept whatever happens day to day without struggle or question or regret. To them things just are, like the earth and sky and seasons. In many ways, it must be a comfortable existence."

"It sounds more like being dead," Alex objected.

"Don't worry, it is not a state you will ever enjoy until you are just so," her grandmother assured her wryly.

But Alex was not so sure. She sometimes felt as if she were becoming like Mavis, thinking less and less, feeling less and less. The babies were the only vital part of her life. But there was a tight knot of waiting inside of her; waiting for what, she was not sure, something even beyond a change in her mother.

Margaret did not like the new maturity she sensed in her child; it made her feel she was not in control. So much of her life had slipped beyond her grasp, it baffled and enraged her to feel Alex withdrawing from her influence, just as Caton had done for years. She was tempted to threaten her daughter with the loss of the twins' care, but she realized that would defeat her own purpose. She wanted Alex to have the weight of the burden Florence had left. She would never have admitted it to herself, but Margaret did not miss her older daughter; she mourned only the failed chance to move upward in society. And she truly believed that Alexandria was somehow responsible for much of the failure of Florence's marriage. Alex had poisoned it before it had begun, had sown seeds of doubt in St. John's mind. That Florence and St. John had never been suited was something she would never admit.

Margaret was persistent in her malice, and she discovered that the one thing her daughter would not tolerate was attacks on the Falconers. She began with small pinpricks of disparagement and enjoyed the almost tangible flinching of Alex's spirit, but she did not understand the depth of Alex's devotion to the family who had taken her in, and finally she went too far.

"I don't know what your grandmother was thinking of when she sent you to stay with those people. She and your father, they made it impossible for me to stop it. But relatives or not, the Falconers are surely tainted by their smuggling." Margaret smirked at the look of surprise on Alex's face. "Oh, yes, I know, I heard Caton and Virginia discussing it. The Falconers are dishonest wretches; the authorities ought to know of their ways."

"You unspeakable hypocrite! The tea you drink, the brandy and wine you serve, the silk you wear, all the luxuries you like so well, I'll wager full duty has been paid on none of it." She saw confirmation of that in her mother's face. "And you dare to condemn them! I swear to you now, if you bear witness against them, I will do the same to you. I will tell everyone that you have been receiving illegal goods for years. I have a fair imagination. By the time I'm through, people will not only believe you belong to a family of free traders, they will believe you have had a sure hand in it. They will believe it because women help in the trade and why not you with your love of things so few can afford legally. I will tell them it has been going on since I was a small child. I will bring ruin on this whole family if you dare to harm the Falconers!"

They were both stunned by her fury. Margaret raised her hand and then dropped it, suddenly realizing this was no longer the small child who had always displeased her, as much for the stamp of the Thaines she bore as for any other reason. This was a young woman suddenly grown taller than she and sleekly muscled, capable of doing damage if she chose to retaliate.

Alex watched her, anger still coursing through her, and the detachment that had gotten her through her first days back in Gravesend could not withstand the rush of emotion. She saw her mother with horrifying clarity. Margaret Thaine was not going to change, and she was never going to love her youngest child. Something snapped in Alex, and she advanced on her mother, staring down at her with bright menace. "I will care for Flora and Blaine until their father returns because you are unfit. But you will leave me alone. And you will cease to speak ill of the Falconers. They are warm and loving and do not deserve your malice."

The silence stretched between them as they glared at each other, but it was Margaret who backed down, rustling out of the room.

Very calmly, Alex got her cloak and left the house, knowing Mavis was with the twins. And her control lasted until she had reached the sanctuary of her grandmother's house.

The storm of emotions broke so violently, Alex shook as if in the grip of a seizure as the tears poured down her cheeks. "She will . . . never . . . never . . . love me."

The words were distorted by weeping, but Virginia understood. She cradled Alex against her, stroking her hair. "Margaret doesn't love anyone, not even herself. She tolerates her sons because they give her status and because they do not remind her that she is old and withered inside. You remind her of that, Alexandria, even without meaning to do so. You are so alive! My beloved child, you must not let her change you." But she knew it was too late in many ways; Margaret had caused damage that would never be repaired, no matter how well Alexandria carried on.

"The Falconers want you to return," she said softly. "I have letters from them. They have heard so little from you and they are worried. Magnus and Rane will come for you as soon as you wish."

Alex wrenched herself away from the warm haven of her grandmother's arms and fought visibly for control before she trusted her voice. "I cannot go until Sinje comes back. I cannot leave Flora and Blaine with my mother. And I cannot bear to think of Rane, of all of them."

She had written one terse note of thanks, and she knew continuing guilt for the inadequacy of it and for the letters from Gweneth and Magnus and even from Rane that she had not answered. But she had found she could not dwell on them without wanting to run screaming from the house she had once called home. Even the gold coins Virginia had insisted on giving her for her fifteenth birthday were gifts of pain, the legacy of the Falconers' loving testimony that having her with them had been pleasure, not duty. The coins were also worth more than enough to buy coach passage back to Devon—a constant and immediate temptation, unlike the planning required to bring the *Lady Gwen* back for her.

"Flora and Blaine are not your responsibility!" Virginia protested vehemently.

"But they are, they are because I know how unsuitable my mother is for them, and young as they are, it matters. They have done no wrong. They do not deserve to suffer for merely being born. I will protect them until Sinje can take them. I will make him see that he must."

Virginia knew she was facing a maternal instinct as strong as if the twins had been born to this child, and she could find no solution. Her offer to take the twins herself had been met with blank refusal; Margaret didn't want them, but she also did not want anyone saying she was failing in her "Christian duty." And Virginia had her doubts that St. John would return. There would surely be fighting on the Continent, and if St. John continued in the half-mad state that had made him crave the battlefield, his chances of survival would be diminished. But to tell Alex that would only bind her closer to the twins.

Virginia hated feeling so helpless, and she hated her daughter-in-law for causing such misery. She was even close to hating her own son for being so ineffectual. She clamped on her hat and gloves and marched herself and Alex out into the gardens.

Alex did as she was bid, emotionally exhausted and as ready as her grandmother to seek comfort in the endless demands of the earth.

They pulled weeds with unaccustomed violence until Virginia said, "I see you are imagining, as I am, that your mother grows here." And then they both started to laugh.

It was a little hysterical but also healing, and they continued to work together, reestablishing harmony after the discords of the day.

Alex did not consult with her grandmother before she visited Lady Carrington. It was a last, unlikely chance, but she could not ignore it.

She had been to Carrington Hall several times when she was a child and in the company of the young St. John, but she was more familiar with the gardens and stables than with the house, built of red brick in the time of Elizabeth to replace a more forbidding structure, and not overly distorted by the additions that had been made since. The lands attached to the estate had been rich and extensive, and the Carringtons had been in possession of them for several hundred years despite political and religious upheavals. But it was well known that the family fortunes had dwindled. St. John's grandfather had been and his father still was overly fond of gambling, particularly on horse races. Many acres had been sold, and even as Alex approached the house, she could see the signs of neglect that came from a shortage of funds. But surely there was room and money enough to raise two infants?

The butler pretended not to recognize her though she knew he did, and he was determined that she not see his mistress without an appointment.

"For heaven's sake, Hanley, I am here concerning her grandchildren, Flora and Blaine, and if you don't admit me, I shall stand here and hammer on the door until I am carted way." Desperation gave her courage.

Hanley was clearly taken aback by this outspokenness, but he was also touched, though he did his best to conceal it. He was fond of Master St. John and thought the Carringtons had treated their youngest son badly. And if he had been pressed for the truth, he would have had to admit that Miss Alexandria had always been rather a favorite with him, unlike her sister. He had watched her courageous play with St. John and the other children, and even if her behavior had been unorthodox, it had also amused him.

He led her into the morning room and gruffly bade her to wait.

The room was lovely with the enlarged windows and lightly painted walls that had replaced the dark wood paneling in the last century, expanding and brightening the space. But here, too, there were signs of neglect in the worn upholstery and Turkey carpets.

She had forgotten how much of Lady Carrington there was in St. John's appearance. The eyes were nearly as blue; the hair must once have been as deep a gold as his.

She plunged in before she lost her courage. "Thank you for seeing me, Lady Carrington. It is about your grand-children, Flora and Blaine. Please, you must take them from my mother. She should not have them. Surely you could keep them at least until Sinje returns."

A grimace of pain or distaste, she could not judge which, made Alex wish she had not used St. John's nickname, but there was no help for it now, and she refused to flinch under the cold appraisal of the blue eyes.

"St. John is no longer recognized in this house, nor are his byblows. You should not have come here, Miss Thaine." The words were more terrible for the quiet tone in which they were spoken.

Alex felt the heat rising in her cheeks. "They are legitimate, as you well know, and despite your feelings about Florence, the twins are half Carrington, whatever silly game you choose to play. And I think it is a game. You and your husband had no intention of providing for your youngest son in any case, did you? And his marriage to my sister gave you the final excuse. It is unfortunate that you are not bound to gavelkind as is most of Kent. But then, gambling has taken much of what there was to give, has it not?" Unlike the rules of primogenitor that gave all to the oldest son, gavelkind required that all share and, in Kent, could only be avoided by special provision.

The expression on Lady Carrington's face altered as she studied this outrageous child who was daring to lecture as if she had a degree in law. Where there should have been insult, instead she saw too clearly that Alex was only trying to defend St. John and his offspring. The pain she had held in check for so long flooded through her.

"I cannot do anything to alter the situation! My hus-band will not change his mind. He . . . he detested your sister, and he warned St. John. He will brook no defiance."

And you are afraid of him, Alex thought, knowing it was true, knowing her mission was a failure as soon as she witnessed the change in the woman. She felt a well of pity mixed with anger. At least this woman, unlike her own mother, had the capacity for love even if she lacked the courage for it.

"Do you believe St. John will come back?" Lady Carrington asked softly.

"He must," Alex replied. "He has two children who need him very much. But I will keep them safe until he returns."

Only fifteen years old, Alex felt at least four times that. The carefree childhood days in Clovelly were a lifetime ago.

❧ Chapter 16 ❧

Daily Alex grew more competent in caring for the twins. She had learned something about the handling of infants in her work with her grandmother and more in Clovelly with Elwyn and Seadon's children, but now she looked after the babies with casual ease. Sometimes she chaffed under the tedium of their constant demands—though there were periods when they obliged by being hungry, wet, sleepy, or active at the same time, more often than not they varied their wants as if to make sure there was never too long a peace. But the gratification of seeing them thrive under her care made up for much. Flora and Blaine provided the only continuity in her life; the rest of it seemed to be made of unrelated parts.

The demands of the twins came first, but with Mavis in attendance, Alex was able to take some time away. She began to help her grandmother again when she could, both at the farm and in the rounds of tending the sick. She realized it was not only that Virginia seemed more frail and more in need of help than before, but also that she herself needed the loving contact.

To her shock, she discovered that several young men whom she had known as erstwhile companions in childhood adventures were now approaching her in an entirely new way. She was not interested in being courted by any of them and found their new tendency toward clumsy flattery more an annoyance than anything else. She realized that her long absence and now her charge of her dead sister's children gave them the impression that she had become suitable material for marriage despite her youth. They were mistaken; she had no interest in marriage. And though she was not aware of it, mentally she compared them all to Rane and found them wanting.

In the matter of the Falconers, she had come to see that nothing less than lies would discourage their continuing concern. And so, quite deliberately, she had begun to send letters detailing how happy she was in her new life in Gravesend, as different from the old days as light from dark. She included doting descriptions of the twins' progress, and those were true enough, but she also conjured a totally false picture of her relationship with her mother, and of renewing old and precious friendships in the town and surrounding area. She never forgot to mention and to thank the Falconers for the time she had spent with them, but relentlessly, her letters shut them out. Often she wept as she wrote, but she could not fail in this. She feared that if the *Lady Gwen* appeared at Gravesend or if Rane came stealing through the night to take her back, she would go in spite of her love for Flora and Blaine and her vow to protect them. She trusted that whatever truth was being carried by Virginia's letters would eventually be undermined by her own protestations of contentment.

Some nights she took a great risk by donning her boy's clothing and sneaking out of the house to leave the town and wait on shadowed lanes, and sometimes she was rewarded by the sounds of the owlers passing by. It was a mad thing to do, as she well knew, and she had not even intended to ever wear the clothing again, but Gweneth had secreted the best of the garments among Alex's other belongings as if to say, "Don't let your family take away your freedom."

The night forays into danger were a way of feeling closer to the Falconers when she could no longer bear to shut them out of her mind. But one night when she returned to the house, she was badly startled when she was discovered by Mavis.

The girl said only, "I seed nowt," and Alex knew she would not betray her. There was no slyness in her manner, and it occurred to Alex that Mavis was less than fond of Margaret though she never showed anything but plodding obedience to her employer. There was, after all, more than met the eye with Mavis Brown.

Alex never lost sight of the fact that the way out of Gravesend was St. John, and she gleaned every bit of news she could from the Continent. There was sure to be fighting soon, and if there was any justice at all, the allies would vanquish Napoleon for good and all and St. John would come home.

The early days of June passed with agonizing suspense as the news continued to indicate that the great armies were massing for a confrontation. Out of sheer restlessness, Alex went on her night journeys even more often than before, and though they never spoke directly about it, she was aware that Mavis knew when she was gone, and even kept watch for her. Once when Margaret called out sharply when Alex inadvertently let the door of her room close too loudly, Mavis hastily took the blame for the noise, assuring Margaret that all was well.

When Alex tried to thank her, she just gave a little smile and turned away. She probably assumed that Alex was meeting a young man just as she must once have done, but Alex didn't mind as long as it helped prevent an additional battle with her mother.

On June 22, the *London Times* confirmed the rumors and carried the official account of the Battle of Waterloo. It was a great victory. Napoleon Bonaparte had lost his bid to reign again. The allies were marching on Paris.

The air of celebration was everywhere, but Alex cared only that now St. John would surely hasten home. She understood that it would take some time for him to be released from whatever military duties he had assumed, but surely then . . . She refused even to consider the casualty lists that were being published. And when Margaret observed with relish that "St. John is just the sort of idiot who would get himself killed," Alex rounded on her with such ferocity that she did not repeat it.

When the little man in the shabby uniform appeared at the door, Alex had no premonition of disaster. She regarded him kindly, thinking perhaps he was hungry; he looked as if he'd been hungry all his life. He had the small unhealthy look the poorest children acquired in the big cities and kept all their lives, and when she heard the trace of a Cockney accent, the guess was confirmed.

"Is this th''ouse of th' Thaines?" he asked politely, but there was an air of desperation about him.

"Yes, it is, at least of Caton Thaine and his family. I am his daughter, Alexandria. There are others, my grandmother and my brothers. How may I assist you?"

"Th' babies, St. John Carrington's babies, they be 'ere?"

She still sensed anxiety, not harm, from him, and so she nodded, still having no idea what he wanted or who he was.

Her inquiring look finally registered, and having found the house he was looking for and even recognizing that this girl fit the description St. John had once given of his late wife's sister, he poured out his story with great relief, the accent of his origins slipping through here and there in his agitation. "I'm Timothy Bates, St. John Carrington's batman, an' I'm at me wits end. I brought 'im 'ome, it's what 'e wanted, but I don't know what t'do now. 'E's taken bad an' 'alf off 'is loaf . . . er, 'ead, Miss. Before, 'e says 'is family's got no use for 'im an' 'e'll 'ave nothin' t'do with 'em, but 'e needs 'elp 'e does, an' I thought maybe where 'is babies be, 'e told me that . . . ," his voice trailed off miserably.

Alex stood frozen, trying to take it all in, assimilating the news as if from a great distance. He was home, but he was wounded or ill—those were the bare facts and all that mattered.

"Take me to him," she said, and she tarried only long enough to gather her basket of simples.

Timothy was so grateful to find someone who seemed as concerned about St. John as he that he didn't even question the authority of this young woman.

The trip was a nightmare for Alex; the more information she gleaned from the little man, the worse everything seemed. St. John had taken a serious saber cut on his right arm at the Battle of Waterloo. Doctors had worked on it, but Timothy thought they'd made it worse. St. John had refused to have the arm amputated and had been afraid to sleep or lose consciousness for fear he'd awaken to find the operation had been done. A friend of his, Lord Bettingdon, Duke of Almont, had found him after the battle, and St. John had prevailed on him to bring him back to Gravesend on his way to London where Bettingdon was bound on his yacht. Bettingdon, like many others, had traveled to Belgium to witness the end of Bonaparte, and his private ship had been at Ostend. They had gotten St. John across the land and onto the ship without seeming to do him much damage, and he had still seemed to have some measure of strength when they arrived at Gravesend. Lord Bettingdon had gone on, confident that his friend was on the way to recovery and much better off back in England than he would have been amidst the thousands of wounded in Belgium or in the hold of crowded ships bringing men back. But in the twenty-four hours since his return, St. John's condition had deteriorated so alarmingly, Timothy was terrified he was going to die. It seemed he had used all his strength to get home and then had given up.

Alex wanted to weep for the bleak, unheralded homecoming St. John had had, and it was worse when she discovered that his destination had been a two-story cottage just outside the boundaries of the Carrington estate. She understood instantly that this must have been where he had lived with Florence, and she wondered how he could have tortured himself so by being so close to the lands he loved and yet in exile.

She was somewhat reassured when she entered the house and found that it was neat and clean, obviously having been well looked after while he was gone, and he did have this devoted little man at her side concerned for his welfare. Her hope that things were not so bad after all flickered and died a quick death at her first sight of St. John.

"Oh, Sinje, what have they done to you?" she breathed, and she dug her nails into the palms of her hands to keep from screaming aloud.

It had only been ten days since the Battle of Waterloo, but all the flesh had melted from St. John's bones, making him look like a marble effigy of an old man except for the red flush of fever on his cheekbones. His breathing was shallow and harsh, and worst of all, the sickeningly sweet smell of rotting flesh permeated the room.

Timothy's face was working as he tried not to cry, and his panic steadied Alex. "This is beyond my skill. We need my grandmother. I will go for her. You stay here!"

Timothy nodded dumbly, glad to relinquish authority, even to one so young.

She ran, not caring what anyone thought and not answering any of the people who hailed her, her single thought being that her grandmother must be there.

Everything was a blur from the time she fell gasping into her grandmother's arms until they were back at St. John's bedside, though the taste of the cordial Virginia forced her to drink remained in her mouth, and she knew they'd returned in the pony cart because the hoofbeats continued to sound in her brain.

Alex had tried to believe that once her grandmother saw St. John, everything would be all right, but she quickly began to lose hope.

The dark eyes were full of pity but uncompromising. "The look of him, and the smell, it has already gone too far. I know that without seeing the wound. Child, you know the limits of the art; I have taught you well." Her steady voice did not betray her own sick horror at the wreck of this young man she had known since his infancy.

"Poultices, very hot, hour after hour might . . ."

"No, Alexandria. You know better than that. The arm must be amputated if he is to live. It is his only chance." She did not add that it was a small chance. "Mr. Bates, I want you to summon Mr. Crowley." She gave clear, swift directions plus an ominous list of what he was to bring with him.

" 'E won't 'alf like it, mum. Th' barbers mucked about with 'im enough over there," Timothy protested.

"He doesn't have any choice now," Virginia insisted. "Please go!"

The authoritative voice had its effect. The little man was glad to be taking orders again and made no further protest but scurried off to find the physician.

Virginia turned back to Alex who had remained frozen in place during the exchange. "I would have sent you, but I need your help. Are you able to give it? You will leave when Mr. Crowley arrives."

Alex swallowed hard and her chin came up defiantly. "Of course I'll help, but I won't leave. Sinje is my friend."

Virginia shrugged, recognizing her own stubbornness in her granddaughter. "As you will."

Only concern for St. John kept Alex from bolting once their work had begun. Virginia set her to sponging down his fevered skin while she unwrapped the ghastly wound. The sick sweet odor grew so strong, Alex had to exert all her self-control not to retch, and she bit her lip until it bled when she saw the full extent of the damage.

His arm had been laid open wrist to elbow by a saber, and the cut had closed raggedly over the putrification beneath. The arm was grossly swollen with red streaks reaching toward the shoulder, and the scar leaked evil matter here and there where the swelling had split the thick scab.

"Filth and bone fragments," Virginia murmured, her voice angry now at the loss this would mean for St. John.

He stirred and moaned, pain making him surface from his fevered oblivion. His blue eyes were glazed and sunken, but awareness dawned as he stared at Virginia and then longer at Alex.

"You did grow up," he whispered. His smile failed in a grimace, and Alex could only nod, unable to speak past the lump in her throat.

"St. John, Mr. Crowley is on his way. You must allow us to care for you." Virginia's voice was gentle but firm. "We can't save your arm. I'm sorry, my boy."

St. John's head moved restlessly on the pillow. "No! Let it be!" The effort left him gasping.

"Sinje, you'll die! You can't die, the twins need you! My mother's no good for them. She doesn't like them any better than she likes me. It's your arm, not your mind or your heart! You can't die for that, you just can't! Please, Sinje, please!" The bitter truth poured out of Alex without her volition.

Alex's pain was acute, and even in the hell of his own, St. John could not deny its urgency. He was quite sure he would die anyway. God knew he wanted to. He also wanted to tell Alex that she had been right about his marriage to Florence. Alexandria, the same and yet so changed. Still the same green-gold eyes and dark waving hair, so young, but no longer a child. There was a new maturity about the bones of her face and the set of her body. The new and old images mixed and swirled in his fading consciousness. For Alex, it seemed important to agree for her sake.

"Do what . . . you . . . will," he managed before the mists closed over him again.

The next hour would forever be a scene from hell in

179

Alex's mind, but she did not break and run. Nor did Virginia force her to leave. Both of them knew without acknowledging it aloud that St. John had agreed to the surgery only because of Alex. It seemed only just that she be there.

Mr. Crowley and Virginia were old friends who respected each other's differing approach in the healing of the sick and were seldom adversaries. Neither suffered from false pride nor illusions about the extent of their skills. Virginia particularly liked the physician because he was clean and did not sport the filth-encrusted coat many surgeons wore as a badge of their trade. She knew she did not have the technique and strength to amputate the arm by herself, and Mr. Crowley wasted no time in debating her diagnosis, agreeing at once that there was only one course. Nor did he question Alex's presence. He knew her grandmother had been teaching her almost from the cradle.

The fire in the fireplace was kept burning steadily, not only to ward off any chill which might further endanger their patient, but also to heat the pot of tar that began to fill the room with its heavy burnt scent, stronger even than the smell of diseased flesh. Alex tried not to think about what it was for. She tried not to think at all.

Despite his wasted state, St. John was a tall man, and it took all four of them to move him to the floor before the fire. It was not the best angle for the work, but a firm surface was necessary, and he couldn't thrash about and fall from there. Timothy had long since stripped away St. John's filthy clothes, but the case was too dire for any of them to worry about Alex seeing a man in such a state of undress. Virginia was far more concerned about the sores she could see were already beginning on his thin flanks and back where his bones, uncushioned by extra flesh, were pressing on his skin. She realized St. John must have been much too thin even before the battle. Her hands trembled for an instant of sheer rage against the strutting Corsican who had brought such suffering to so many young men, on both sides.

"Time enough to tend to all of his hurts once this is finished," Mr. Crowley said gruffly, his eyes meeting hers, sharing her thoughts.

In spite of the care they took, St. John roused with a groan at being moved, and Alex, glad of something to do, lifted his head carefully and urged him to drink the draught her grandmother had measured out. "Please drink it, Sinje, it's bitter but will ease your pain. It's made from poppies and other plants." She tried to keep the words steady and soothing.

He drank it obediently, and the sip of water she offered him after, but then his eyes narrowed in concentration as he gathered strength to speak. "Go away . . . not right . . . you here."

"It is right. I won't leave you. Let the medicine work now, Sinje, let go." She stroked his face, oblivious of the others in the room, and he hadn't the strength to contest her will. They wrapped him up to his chest in blankets with linen bands, severely restricting the movement of his legs and good arm to keep him from lashing out. His bad arm was bound outstretched by the wrist to one of the heavy legs of the bed.

Timothy straddled him to keep his body from bucking; Virginia and Alex held his shoulders down. Mr. Crowley picked up a gleaming scalpel and began.

St. John had gone limp as the drug took effect, but as the knife swiftly sliced through flesh and the saw through bone high on his arm, his body came alive, jerking convulsively against the restraints. Inhuman sounds clawed his throat until he opened his clenched jaw and screamed.

Alex jumped to pull his head far back so that he would not swallow his tongue, and she gave thanks when she felt the tension quit his racked frame. She looked up to see her grandmother nod in approval, and she tried to shut her ears against the rasp of metal against bone. It seemed to take so long to accomplish the maiming, though it was in fact swift due to the surgeon's skill.

When it was finished, Mr. Crowley let Virginia take over, and she bathed the stump in a solution made from astringent herbs before they cauterized it with hot tar. The stench of rot and blood and burned flesh filled the room, but St. John was beyond any of it. Even the bleeding was not as much as it could have been from the massive injury.

Alex, Virginia, and the physician all knew what this state meant. It was good that St. John's body had so slowed its pulse and bleeding as protection against a fatal blood loss. It was good as long as it did not go on too long.

His wound was bandaged, and they moved him back to the bed and covered him warmly.

The sudden silence that overtook them was broken by the sound of sobbing. For an instant, Alex wondered if she were making the noise, but then she realized it was Timothy Bates.

"I tried, I did, I kept 'im clean an' fed 'im when I could, but it weren't enough. Poor lad, losin' 'is arm, an' all me fault."

Mr. Crowley didn't hesitate. "Nonsense! You've undoubtedly saved his life. It was war and a saber cut that took his arm. He probably wouldn't even have lived to come home without you. But I warn you, your work has just begun. He's as helpless as a child now, and he'll need constant care."

Again Timothy was reassured by the voice of authority and by a specific task. His tears stopped, and he straightened resolutely. "E'll 'ave th' best I can give 'im."

His courage was further bolstered by Mr. Crowley's promise to look in often and by Virginia and Alex's insistence that they take their turns in watching over the patient. Again, no one in the room questioned Alex's right to be there. She had earned her place by her steady presence during the terrible operation, and there was nothing childlike in her demeanor.

It was quite different at home. Her mother looked at her as if she had sprouted horns.

"It's unseemly, immoral! Your grandmother's foolishness has led you to this, you a child, caring for a fullgrown man. I forbid . . ."

"You will not forbid it!" Alex was too shaken by what she had witnessed to have any patience with her mother's ranting. "You will understand that it is my Christian duty if nothing else." It was sweet to bend the old argument back on her. "And you will pray that our work is not in vain, else you will have the twins for years to come and no payment for it. You, not I, do you hear?" That she herself would never abandon the twins to her mother's care was not something Margaret could know from her own selfish view. "As for the immorality of it, you would have to see St. John to know how daft your words are."

She held her mother's eyes with her own. "He is lying near death. The flesh has wasted from him until he is scarcely more than bones and skin. And we cut his arm off, high, near the shoulder, his good right arm! Perhaps you did not hear me when I first told you. We sawed it off and left a raw stump seared with tar. Tell me, how will he assault my honor in such condition? I would to God he had the strength for it!"

Margaret looked away first, but not until Alex had seen the gleam of fear in her eyes. It gave her an odd jolt, as though their roles were now irrevocably reversed. But she had no time for thoughts that did not concern St. John.

For the next week, she was only home long enough to sleep a little and to check on the twins and praise Mavis for her continued care of them. She saw the rest of her family in a blur though she was vaguely aware of her father's quiet approval and of Boston's in opposition to her mother, who continued to mutter dire predictions of moral ruin, though she avoided another direct confrontation.

The only people in the house who held any interest for Alex were the twins. When she stole a few moments to bask in their innocence and their healthy presence, she assured them silently that their father would not die.

It became a litany in her mind, repeated endlessly as she cared for St. John. In the first days after the surgery, he lay in a stupor broken now and then by bouts of fevered delirium that seemed to leave him weaker each time. Sometimes she had to bend close to be sure he was still breathing. They forced liquids down him and tended to his body's needs as if he were an infant. Timothy was ever faithful, always appearing when it was time to shift the inert body and change the linens, even keeping St. John neatly shaved as if he would care about his appearance. Tim did not flinch no matter how odious the task, and he seemed to exist with almost no sleep. He even did most of the cooking for the little household. Alex and Virginia could not make him do less.

He regarded his care of St. John as much a privilege as a duty. He had been assigned to St. John weeks before the battle, and for the first time he had been treated with respect and affection by a man far above him in social importance. Timothy Bates was a veteran of long service in the French war, and St. John had relied on his expertise from the first while confessing his own ignorance. The praise had been enough to cause Timothy to take on full responsibility for the young man's well-being. If it had been possible, he would have ridden into battle in his place.

But with all the care, Alex lost faith that they would succeed, even though Virginia said it was a good sign that the infection had not spread, the seepage from the wound being natural and not putrid. It just did not seem possible that anyone hovering so near death for so long could draw back from it.

Alex had taken to talking to him as if he were alert, choosing subjects at random so that they ranged from the twins' daily progress to the coming of the pleasure steamer, *Margery*, in service from Gravesend to London since January. "The watermen are surely concerned, but I don't think they have to worry much just yet; the *Margery* is more often stopped for repairs than not," to the changes that would come now that the war was finally over. "Grandmother says that there is not enough work for all the men who will be coming home now, and it will be hard for many."

And one day she told him the story of the wild swans. "The golden chains around their necks are so finely wrought, one can hardly see them, but they catch the sun's light, so if you watch them very carefully you will see that they are the magic ones. Then if you follow them, you will see the beautiful young women they become when they set aside their feathered cloaks."

"I cannot determine whether I am awake or still dreaming."

The words were so weakly spoken, Alex wasn't sure for a moment that she'd heard them at all, but St. John's eyes were open and watching her.

"Oh, Sinje . . ." Her voice was as thready as his. She touched his face and found the fever heat much less.

"Nightmare, I thought . . . but I can feel . . . my arm." His eyes fluttered closed again, and the nightmare was hers as she realized he didn't know his arm was gone.

Virginia was not surprised. "It is often this way; the body is slow to accept the loss. The important thing is that he is recovering."

She then established their new routine which was to feed St. John nourishing broth whenever he awakened. To Alex's question of what to do "if he asked," she replied, "We would have to tell him the truth. But he knows already; somewhere inside he knows. I doubt he'll ask. He'll have to come to acceptance by himself."

Alex found that she was correct. For the next forty-eight hours, St. John was awake on and off. Meekly, he swallowed what they gave him, including the potions to lessen his pain, but he spoke little and asked nothing.

She was there when he summoned the strength to raise his left hand and explore. She watched as slowly, inexorably his hand moved to his right side, confirming what he now knew to be true.

"Why?" he asked softly. "Why didn't you let me die?"

"You have two children who need you very much. And we all love you, Sinje—my grandmother, Timothy Bates, and I. And your friends. Your arm was not worth dying for." Her voice was urgent with the need to make him see the truth, but his only response was to turn his head away.

She was relieved that he did not ask about his family. Virginia had sent word to Lady Carrington, but there had been no direct response from her. Baskets of foods to tempt an invalid—beef jellies, fine claret, and such—were left on the doorstep periodically by a servant who did not tarry to talk, and not so much as a note accompanied the offerings. Alex had confessed her visit to her grandmother, and neither of them had much hope that the Carringtons would rally to St. John's bedside since they had begun to treat him as if he were dead long before he had gone to war. Alex suspected that even the baskets were a great risk on Lady Carrington's part, and she pitied the woman as much as she blamed her for want of courage.

Alex was profoundly grateful that she had her grandmother's strength and knowledge to support her, and she suspected that Timothy Bates felt the same way. Though they spoke of it as little as possible, they were both haunted by St. John's preoccupation with his arm—with the actual missing limb.

For two days after his touching of the stump, he seemed to ignore it entirely, submitting patiently to the care lavished on him, eating when he was bid to do so and swallowing nerve-dulling medicines. He refused to complain about the savage pain that swept over him in waves, as if to acknowledge it would be to acknowledge his crippling, but it was visible in the changes it wrought in him—his face going whiter and whiter as sweat broke out on his skin, his jaw clamping more tightly. Alex wished they could keep him so drugged that the pain would never come, but she knew the dangers of that, the slowing of bodily and mental functions that could lead to death.

And then he asked, as if inquiring about the weather, "Where is my arm?"

Thinking this was a new game of denial, Alex said with gentle insistence, "You know it had to come off; the infection was terrible."

He shook his head restlessly, and then winced at the pain the movement caused. "No, I don't mean that. I mean where is it? Where did you put it afterwards?"

A wave of nausea swept over her as the image of the arm severed from his body rose in her mind. She was torn between hysterical tears and laughter and had to fight the impulse before she could speak. "I truly don't know."

"Find out." It was a command. "Was it buried or was it tossed out on the rubbish heap. Find out."

She was so unnerved, she fled, and when she saw her grandmother entering the house, the tear-choked explanation poured out.

"It's not as insane as it sounds," Virginia assured her."After all, his arm was part of him from birth, a trusted, used part of his body, and now it is gone. It must be a horrid vision to contemplate—part of one's body casually tossed away."

"I buried it," Timothy murmured, "took it out an' dug a grave an' all. Seemed th' proper thing." The Cockney sounded less in his speech now that his initial panic had eased, but both women hoped the odd blend of toughness and sweetness that they had come to know in the wiry little man would never change.

"Thank you, Timothy," Virginia said. "That was well done. I will tell St. John unless you would rather."

"No, mum," Timothy declined hastily. He, like Alex, was more than a little unnerved by the whole subject, even though he had taken care of the matter.

"Alexandria, you go home and get some sleep. Same for you here, Timothy. I will sit with St. John now. I've had a long peaceful rest at the farm."

They complied without question; Virginia's calm assumption of authority had given the mad days and nights a sane pattern. Timothy had muttered to Alex that if her grandmother had been in charge of Bonaparte, he never would have escaped to cause so much more trouble.

Trouble—it seemed to Alex that there was little else in her days now. But she reminded herself that St. John still drew breath and his children flourished. Compared to many, this was great good fortune. All across England there were families who would never see their men again and who would go hungry because there was no one left to provide for them.

✍ Chapter 17 ✍

The house where she had been raised no longer had the slightest feeling of home for Alex. Her parents and even Boston seemed to have shrunk to such insignificance that she was hardly aware of them. They moved as shadowy figures on the periphery of her vision. If the twins had not been there, it would not have seemed a familiar place at all. St. John and the little household held together by his illness had become home. Even thoughts of Rane and the other Falconers assaulted her less often now, memories of what seemed a very long ago time. St. John had become the center of her life; she could no more have left him to flee to the Falconers than she could have deserted his children.

The plan grew in her mind as she watched St. John's slow adjustment to his crippled state. Even as he began to grow stronger, he spoke very little beyond polite thanks for the tasks performed for him. And as the changes he would have to make became clearer by the day, she began to understand that he was repulsed by his own body as it was now and embarrassed that others should see it so. Even shifting him in bed was a problem because he could not lie on his right side and had not yet learned to counterbalance his movements without his right arm. She could feel the rigidity of his flesh when they propped him on his left side or turned him over on his belly to treat the bed sores that had come despite their efforts to prevent them and were so slow in healing. She guessed that it was not the fact that she and Virginia were seeing his nakedness that made him resistant but rather that they were witnesses to his clumsiness and the lack of symmetry of what had once been a perfect male body.

It was worse when he took his first wobbly steps. Alex had just gone downstairs to prepare a tray of food for him, and when she brought it to his room, she found him out of bed, swaying dizzily but determined. She put the tray down and went to him.

"Please be careful, Sinje. You mustn't overdo."

"My dear, my immediate goals are quite reasonable. I would very much like to walk and piss like a man, though not at the same time."

She backed away from the snarling savagery that took all humor from the words. But he had only taken a few steps before he lurched and would have gone down had not Alex been there to prop him up.

A look of unspeakable agony crossed his face, and she glanced at the cut sleeve of his nightshirt, fearing he had torn open the wound. "I swear I could feel my right hand reaching out," he muttered, and then he added a long string of the foulest language Alex had ever heard.

In that instant, his frustration, his sorrow and anger became hers, and the tears poured unheeded down her cheeks as she guided him back to bed.

He reached up and touched the wet tracks. "Oh, Alex, I'm not worth it." This time his voice was infinitely kind, and that made her cry harder. She sniffed and rubbed her eyes like a child, trying to stop. St. John's eyes closed wearily as his harsh breathing eased, and he sought oblivion in sleep.

"He needs to be reminded that there are those weaker than he, he needs to know that he is necessary to someone. The twins should be here. There is room for them and Mavis also. And I can pay Mavis with the coins you gave me. In any case, she is beginning to wean them and soon they can have cow's milk with their food, or so Mavis tells me."

Timothy and Virginia looked at her aghast, thinking of the noise and confusion that would disrupt their quiet routine, but then they began to see the benefits. St. John did need concerns other than himself, and his recovery was what mattered most to all of them.

"I will hire Mavis to come here," Virginia said, "though I'll leave it to you to ask her. Even when the babies are weaned, they will need her care. If it is well with her, then it is done." She and Alex were both wondering what Margaret's reaction to the new arrangement would be, but whatever it was was insignificant compared to St. John's welfare. It was also time and past that he show an interest in his offspring. He had not even asked after them.

Mavis had no hesitation in accepting the change in her circumstances. She liked Alex and Virginia; she did not care at all for Margaret. And it did not trouble her in the least that there might be talk about anyone who joined St. John Carrington's strangely assembled household. She had long suspected that Mrs. Thaine had every intention of turning her out as soon as the infants were weaned (and had indeed been urging the weaning even faster than Mavis would have liked) and giving her daughter charge of them. The offer from Alex was a much better prospect.

Margaret was livid, made more so by the fact that she no longer knew what she wanted. She had thought her only desire was to be free of the burden of Florence's leavings at the expense of Alexandria, and that was almost exactly what was happening. It was the *almost* that spoiled the victory. Though she could not admit it even to herself, Alexandria's ability to adapt and survive roused burning envy that gave Margaret no peace. She wanted the girl humble and obedient—she could see no other use in daughters—and instead, Alexandria grew stronger and more defiant by the day. And more, there was already talk in the town of St. John's return, the continued coldness of his family, and his odd household. Though for the moment it was compassionate, Margaret could not determine yet whether the gossip would eventually be to the advantage or disadvantage of the Thaines. This added to her quandary. And so in the end, her confusion left her muttering more vague threats about impropriety that Alex hardly seemed to hear and which sounded weak even in her own ears. She could not dispute Alex's repeated "They are his children."

There was no doubt of that. Daily Flora and Blaine looked more like St. John, both of them developing his golden hair and his vivid blue eyes, a brighter fairness than their mother had ever had. The doubt was that St. John had room in his life for them.

When Alex brought them in to him, St. John's startled expression quickly gave way to studied indifference. "Do you need other helpless patients to give you enough to do?" he asked cruelly, and he looked away.

She was schooling herself to ignore the barbs of his anger, but this was too much. "These are your children, and like it or not, they are your responsibility. I presume you got these infants on my sister like a man, and if you want to walk and piss like a man, you can damn well learn to take care of your family like a man, too!"

That brought his head around again, and his eyes widened with shock at hearing her speak so. "I can't even hold both of them," he pointed out grimly.

"One at a time will do," she returned, and they glared at each other until, reluctantly, he smiled. "You would have made a good general. Your strategy is boldly executed."

"Grandmother is the general here. Timothy and I are in the lower ranks," she said, and St. John laughed. It was the first time she had heard that sound in so long, she shivered with the pleasure of it, causing the twins to squirm in her arms.

Though it hadn't been the wholehearted response she would have liked, she found it had been a good beginning. Little by little, St. John accepted the twins as part of his days, beginning to notice small signs of their growth. And they in turn regarded this new addition to their world with fearless interest. Alex would put them on the bed beside St. John and deliberately leave the three alone. The first time brought a shout of panicked protest from him, but she was unyielding.

"They aren't old enough to run away yet, and you have a strong arm to haul them back if they wiggle too close to the edge." But she stationed herself close by outside the room just in case there was trouble that first time and was relieved when there was none.

There was no trouble either with the rest of the household. Timothy doted on the children; at first simply because they were St. John's issue and then because they charmed him. Nor did he have difficulty in accepting Mavis Brown. She caused no trouble and cared well for the infants.

Virginia, too, was happy with the new arrangement, not only for the sake of the twins and their father, but also for Alex. It gladdened her heart to see the return of life and confidence in her granddaughter. If she sometimes mourned the disappearance of the child Alex had been, it did not lessen her pride in the competent young woman she had become. Childhood ended for all, and Alexandria had better reasons than most for leaving her own behind.

St. John had existed in a haze since he had taken the saber cut at Waterloo. His journeys out of the mist had been horrific forays into loss and pain. Retreating back into darkness had been the only sane course for days on days, but as clarity began inexorably to return, Alex had become the focus of the world. She had demanded that he live, and he had complied. He did not know why he found her so compelling; she simply was. He knew rationally that Tim and Virginia had shared all the duties of caring for him, but it was Alex's husky voice he listened for, her changeable green eyes and her dark heavy hair that colored his days. Even in anger, he wanted her there, not the others, wanted her there when he struck out to ease the fury inside. And now he found that again she had altered his life, planting his children squarely in the middle of it. And daily he was more drawn to them as he discovered a pride in fatherhood he had never thought to feel. He admitted honestly to himself that the twins were also the lure to keep Alex close. She had always been totally separate from her sister, and now she was even more so, but still that subject lay uneasily between them, could not help but do so with the reality of the twins. It was he who brought it up.

He was playing with his babies, watching them coo and smile as he teased them with a wooden rattle. He thought he could see little of Florence in them and immediately felt guilty; he supposed he would always feel this terrible guilt when he thought of her.

"About Florence, I am sorry. I made her so unhappy. I didn't offer her the right sort of life, the life she wanted.

Oh, God, the words sound so small, and she is dead! My fault, and I can't bear to have it unacknowledged between us."

He took Alex completely by surprise, but she was immediately glad that the subject was out in the open. She chose her words carefully. "Not your fault, and not mine, I am beginning to see, though we will probably both always feel some guilt. Sinje, it's true you made each other unhappy, but it wasn't your fault. It's so hard to say, but Florence had no talent for accepting life, for making the best of things, for being happy. Neither does my mother. It is so difficult to be honest when someone has died; it's as if truth stops at the grave even when the lies continue to hurt the living. But think of what you gave her! You gave her your love, you gave her these two beautiful children, and you gave up your own family for her sake. Though she is the one who died, if there is a victim in all of this, it must be you." Her voice faltered under his intense regard, but she continued, determined to say it all. "When I was a child, I believed that everything would come right one way or another. It was as if time would stop, go back, and all would be done properly. But now I realize that there isn't any going back; things done can't be redone, and some things won't ever be easy or right even in memory, and they just have to be accepted or one would go mad."

Blue eyes held green eyes for a long, strangely charged moment, and then St. John murmured, "How did you grow up so quickly?"

I had to, for your children, and for you, she thought, and the image of him lying so near death rose too clearly. "Everyone grows up, Sinje," she murmured softly, "even these little ones will." She bent over the twins, touching their softness.

The clean female scent of her reached him over the milky smell of the babies, and for the first time since things had gone so sour between him and Florence so early in their marriage, he felt passion stir. Not the mindless lust he had slaked on the bodies of whores in Europe, but the sweet rising current that was as much of the heart and mind as of the loins. And then he remembered that he had felt the same for Florence, and cold memory swept away the heat of the present.

Alex felt his sudden withdrawal and totally misjudged

its cause, thinking that playing with the twins and talking with her had overtired him. "Time for these wee ones to be fed." She picked the babies up with practiced ease and left him.

The heat rose again, Florence's image paling against the reality of Alexandria. He lay there trying to banish the scent of her, the slender curves of her, the tender intimacy of her long hands as she tended his flesh.

His frustration served one useful purpose: it spurred him to greater efforts to regain his strength. With Timothy's help, he was fully dressed and out of bed for longer and longer periods, finding that pushing himself physically to the edge of fatigue helped to quiet his body. His mind was not so easily pacified, veering from hot to cold so that sometimes he treated Alex warmly and then in the next moment with icy formality.

Alex credited his mood changes to his difficult convalescence. Not only was the adjustment hard for him, she also knew he was in constant pain though he did not complain. It gave her endless patience with him, which only added to his restlessness.

He began to prowl the house, but he did not go outside, retaining his awful pallor until Alex confronted him.

"You can't hide forever. The sun is glorious. Come out with me." She extended her hand to him, but he did not take it.

"You are right," she said as if he had spoken his dread aloud. "Someone might well ride by and see you. If not today, then someday soon. And he will see that you have lost your arm. As others have lost their legs, their eyes, parts of their faces. You can still walk out to see the sun."

"Trying to shame me into doing what you want?" he asked nastily.

"Exactly," she retorted. "You look as if you've been in Newgate." Or on Dartmoor in the winter, her mind added, and quite clearly she saw Caleb Jennings and then Rane and the night they had spent on the wild dark sea and in the shelter of the cave.

Suddenly it was as if she were not there at all, and St. John was stunned by the fearful wave of desolation that swept over him. "Alex, what is it? Damn, I'll go out or whatever you wish."

The sharpness of his voice brought her back, and she

blinked at him. "Sorry, it's not your fault. I was thinking of something else."

Someone else, St. John thought. The walls of the cottage seemed to close in with the wave of jealousy he felt. He reminded himself that Alexandria was the only attractive young female he had seen since his return from Waterloo, and so it was natural that she would stir his blood. But his own explanation rang false. Alex was Alex, and no one else had anything to do with it.

To her surprise, St. John strode out of the house without another word. She shrugged—whatever worked. She was still feeling bemused by the vividness of her Clovelly memory. Her attention had been so wholly involved with St. John and the twins these past weeks, Clovelly had faded to the background of her mind, helped by the fact that the letters from the Falconers now came infrequently, due, she knew, to her relentless protestations of contentment. She sighed, accepting the probability that strong surges of memory would occur for a long time—the Falconers had been an important part of her life. She put them firmly in the past tense.

After the overly rainy weather of the previous year, the long fair stretches of 1815 had at first seemed welcome. But now they had run with little break across the country from March to these first days of August, becoming drought instead of pleasure and a grim worry to farmers. However, the sunny days were still deemed a blessing by St. John's household, and most of all by St. John himself.

Even on his first day out, he had felt wondrous changes as the soft air and the warmth had touched his face, stilling much of his restlessness instantly. The cottage had some fine oak and beech trees around it, a small overgrown orchard, and a neglected garden that Alex worked in whenever she got the chance despite the lack of rain. He found it easy to let his mind drift away from troubling thoughts as he sat drowsily in the sun after exercising his legs around the place.

He was fortunate in his first outside encounter, and that helped. An old farmer he had known in what now seemed a previous life stopped on his way past to greet those outside and particularly St. John with great courtesy, not only as if the unpleasantness with his family had never happened but also with grave respect for his having served at Waterloo.

"Arr, dat Bonaparte, 'e know de English soldur now; 'e not be back. Dank 'e, sir," he added, as if St. John had been personally responsible for Napoleon's defeat. He urged his limping cart horse back to a walk as he led him away, explaining politely, "I're gween to de foorge to git de 'oss shod."

St. John smiled as he watched him go. "I like a man who cares well for the beasts who serve him." Eyes still on the departing figures, he added, "That will be hardest of all, I think, not to ride again. I could once use a pistol and a sword with fair skill, and I suppose I will miss that exercise, though I don't plan on fighting any duels, but not riding— that is hard."

His voice was still so soft and musing, so resigned, it sent a chill through Alex; she preferred his anger to this. She glanced over at the twins, crawling around on a blanket under Mavis's stolid gaze and found her inspiration.

"Sinje, there's no reason you can't do all of those things again! Even riding. It is a matter of learning them over, I know, but you can do it. Look at Flora and Blaine; everything they do is something new and difficult, but not too long from now they will walk and run."

"But they, thank God, are whole," St. John pointed out without heat. "I can't even dress myself."

"It's been little more than a month since you lay near death. Give yourself time. You will find new ways to do almost everything you were wont to do before you lost your arm." She still had to steel herself to mention it without a tremor, but somehow she thought directness was necessary. "I am sure of it. And as for riding, it is something you learned almost at birth, and you always told me it is more a matter of balance than of anything else. Your body will remember that balance, changed I know, but if you strengthen your arm, you should be able to control a well-trained mount." She suppressed the tremor of fear that ran through her at the thought of him with only one arm on a horse again. But this was enormously important to him, despite his quiet voice. She sensed that something vital would be irrevocably lost if he accepted that particular limitation. St. John was well enough educated, but his passion had always been fine horseflesh.

He said nothing more about it, and she could not ascertain whether she had made an impression on him or not.

Ironically it was his mother who provided the spur. It was an unexpected and disastrous visit.

They were all outside for another lovely morning, except for Virginia who had resumed much of her normally busy schedule as St. John had needed less of her care.

Timothy spotted Lady Carrington first and so forgot himself as to exclaim, "Cor! Wot's this then?" as the little cart drew near.

Lady Carrington was driving the sturdy pony herself and was accompanied by her maid who stayed in the cart as St. John's mother got down and approached the little group, now a frozen tableau.

St. John recovered first, rising from his favorite wooden bench to greet his mother with cool courtesy.

His eyes were so wary, his face so set, Alex realized the full cost of his family's treatment, though he had said nothing about it, and she had to restrain her impulse to spring at the woman and run her off. Soon she wished she had.

Lady Carrington might have been born and bred to gentility, but she lacked all manner of grace in this situation. She did everything wrong. She barely glanced at her grandchildren, barely acknowledged the others. She bore down on her son with single-minded purpose, tears beginning to roll down her white cheeks even before she reached him.

"Oh, St. John, you are so frail! I wanted to come, truly I did, but your father . . . My poor son, what will you do without . . ."

"Without my arm?" St. John supplied with deceptive gentleness. "I plan to do everything I did before, Mother. It is simply a matter of learning a new way." Now there was no mistaking the ice in his voice, and Lady Carrington stepped back with a little gasp, clearly at a loss.

Alex would not have helped ease the situation for any price. She was seething with rage. How dare this woman moan over St. John's appearance now! She should have been here when he had lain as helpless as a babe, closer to death than life. And then the hopelessness of it all swept over her. Lady Carrington could not help what she was—a foolish, frightened woman who had long since given up her rights to independent thought and action in exchange for her social position.

She reached out and gently took the basket the woman clutched to her bosom. "Thank you, ma'am. Your gifts have been most welcome. I am sure the delicacies you sent helped in Sinje's recovery." It was as kind as she could be, but the last two words, particularly her nickname for him, were clear warning that this was St. John's home now and that his welfare was its purpose. She had a brief battle with panic as she considered what Mavis's reaction might be if Lady Carrington tried to touch the twins. Mavis was looking positively venomous as she stared at the woman, clearly mistrusting her, and the expression on Timothy's face wasn't much better; his normally lively face was blank, and he had drawn his scant height to rigid attention as if he were in the presence of a particularly despised officer. It was St. John's army indeed, ranks closed against all invaders.

Lady Carrington glanced at the babies but did not approach them, murmuring vaguely that they were "coming on well," as if they were parsnips or carrots. Her relief at escaping was evident in the brisk pace she set back to the cart.

St. John broke the tension that bound them all; he laughed until tears stood in his eyes. "My poor mother, she had no idea she would be facing the palace guard!" he choked and was off again. He couldn't explain that Mavis's glaring, silent defense amused him most of all.

Alex was so relieved, her knees nearly gave way. His laughter was genuine. She was grateful that somehow they had managed to surround St. John with enough love so that the loss of his family was beginning to be less painful.

She was not so sure about another development from his mother's visit. Alex wanted him to ride again for his own sake someday when he was strong enough and ready. But his mother's assumption that he could not pushed him to it almost immediately.

A few days after his mother's visit, calmly, as if it were nothing out of the ordinary, St. John asked Timothy to go to the local livery and hire a mount. Tim went directly to Alex.

Her first impulse was to tell St. John that it was much too soon. He still tired so easily, and his wound, though healing cleanly, was still tender and only fragilely covered by new tissue. But then she was trapped by the complexity of things other than his physical well-being. His pride was involved and the very motivation they had all wanted him to have to resume his life.

Hastily she scribbled a note. "Find my grandmother first, pray God she's at the farm, give her this, and then do whatever she says," she told Timothy, both of them glancing around like criminals for fear St. John would catch them in their conspiracy.

Tim returned on horseback, and St. John went out to meet him, his eyes defiantly daring Alex to protest. But her throat was much too dry to allow speech. A surreptitious nod from Tim assured her that her grandmother knew. He slipped the answering note from her to Alex as soon as he dismounted, but she could not read it in front of St. John.

The gelding stood placidly, his ears cocked attentively but not twitching with nervous temper. His eyes were deep and calm. Alex silently blessed Tim; he must have been very specific about what was required.

St. John approached the horse, speaking softly, and then he turned to Tim. "I need a leg up, if you would be so obliging."

Not looking at Alex, Tim did as asked.

Alex watched as if mesmerized. She saw St. John's shoulders bunch with the effort of controlling his balance as he swung up into the saddle, and her stomach clenched with unpleasant vertigo as she saw how vulnerable he was with one hand to hold the reins and no other to help in that task or to brace himself if he needed to. She wanted to close her eyes and couldn't even make herself do that.

He swayed alarmingly when the horse first moved out, but then he righted himself. Alex let her breath out in a long sigh; if his seat was neither as easy nor graceful as it had been, still it was far more competent than she had expected for his first attempt. She glanced at the note from her grandmother. There were only four words: "He is a man." They were enough.

✣ *Chapter 18* ✣

St. John worked with manic energy to strengthen his left arm and his shoulders, flexing the muscles constantly and lifting whatever he could manage. Riding was his salvation. He felt free, swift, and powerful when he was on horseback. He even found it eased the dread of seeing people again and of meeting new ones. As his confidence and endurance grew, he began to range further afield, greeting old friends in such a jovial way that they commented among themselves on how well he was doing. He quickly grew accustomed to the first look that went inevitably to his empty sleeve. He couldn't blame them; he would undoubtedly do the same were the positions reversed, and yet, he had no intention of filling the space with some dead block of wood or metal. What was gone was gone forever, and cosmetic pretense would not bring it back.

He found it harder to accept the praise for his part in the battle. It was true enough that he had acquitted himself well and gallantly, but the images of all those who had lain dead around him were still too clear, and he could still feel his own saber slicing down through sinew and bone even as another's had bitten into his own flesh. And for him it had been no patriotic impulse that had made him prevail upon his friends and connections in the military to find him a place in the campaign; it had simply been to escape the burdens at home.

In his honest moments, he realized that riding served yet another purpose beyond easing his reentry into the company of others: it also eased the sexual tension he now felt around Alexandria. He told himself that she was only a child, but her competent running of his life belied that. And then he told himself that no woman would desire him with the ugly stump of flesh where his arm had been. Nothing could stop the increasing power Alex had over his senses, not even the riding, but it helped dim his response to her. He knew he ought to make her spend less time at the cottage, but she was the heart of his current domestic arrangements, and he could not face having her gone, not yet.

Though sometimes he felt like racing flat out, he restrained himself and the horse. His wound still ached abominably, and he had no wish to submit to further surgery on it should he fall off. Mounting and dismounting were still problems, too, and unless there was someone to help or something to serve as a mounting block, he knew he was going to find it difficult to get back on if he were thrown.

One meeting St. John could have forgone was with his father and his eldest brother. It was certain that his father knew he was getting about now on horseback, and St. John had seen him at a distance with one or the other of his brothers, but neither side had made any attempt at a face-to-face confrontation. However, it was inevitable that they meet since St. John's cottage was so close to the estate, having once been part of it. St. John had recognized his own perversity in renting it right before his marriage from the man who owned it. And he and his father had often passed each other with cold nods after St. John had married Florence.

But this time Sir Ivor Carrington reined his mount to a stop. St. John's brother did likewise, and though St. John was tempted to keep going, he, too, halted. It was a shock to see how much like his father his brother Avery was becoming—both of them pale blonds with light blue eyes, though his father's hair was now nearly white. Noland, his other brother, had much the same look, too, though he had a kinder heart, and for a moment St. John was cynically amused by the idea that perhaps his very proper mother had strayed in the matter of his own conception, thus giving him his deeper coloring. But he knew in fact that all the Carrington men, himself included, shared the same rather long bony faces and lean frames—his father looked positively skeletal now, not frail, but rather tough as old leather. The cold eyes of his sire looked him over.

"St. John, you used to ride a different sort of horse," he barked, the reference to his son's changed social circumstance clear. Not a word about his well-being.

"I used to have a different sort of body, too," St. John replied evenly. "Things change." He stared pointedly at his brother's boots. Avery was reserved to the point of being stiff-necked, very conscious that he would inherit the title, but he was also somewhat of a dandy and would never wear clothing that showed signs of wear if he could help it. His boots were of fine quality and highly polished, but they had obviously seen better days.

St. John raised his eyes to his father's face again. "It would seem the family coffers are hard pressed. I would guess you have not put your wagers on winning cattle lately. Perhaps you would be well to rid yourself of another son."

There was a flicker of admiration in the pale eyes, but it was quickly gone, and the old man urged his horse away, Avery following, looking embarrassed.

St. John heard his own bitter laugh as he watched them out of sight. What unloving seed he had sprung from. He loved the Carrington lands and the fine horseflesh that had been part of the stables off and on, and there was a core of resentment in him that his birth alone as the youngest son had put him outside of the ownership of the estate long before his disastrous marriage, but he had no desire whatsoever to be part again of the bleak chill that passed for family feeling among the Carringtons. It was not, he realized suddenly, a function of social standing; Alex's family was much the same with the exception of her grandmother and Boston. It was another bond drawing him closer to her.

He said nothing about his encounter with his father until he was forced to by the arrival of Sir Arthur. Alex recognized the bay hunter immediately, remembering too clearly the fateful meeting with St. John during which she had not only ridden the horse, but had also warned St. John about Florence and had been overheard.

St. John surveyed the horse expressionlessly for long moments, and then he shook his head. "That old bastard, he never quits." He then told Alex about meeting his father.

She regarded him with a puzzled frown. "But Sir Arthur is a fine gift!" She was, in fact, worried that he was too fine, too fast.

"Oh, his blood lines and his gaits are good enough. But he was soon gelded because he was no good at stud, got poor colts on fine mares. And he still tends to favor his leg when he's feeling tired or lazy, though the injury's long healed. Impotent and slightly crippled, the message seems clear enough from one horseman to another."

Alex wanted to deny such subtle reasoning on Sir Ivor's part, but she knew the old man was more than capable of it.

And then St. John was laughing with real humor. "Well, Sir Arthur, you'll do for all of your faults; I've enough of my own to match you."

The cottage had no provision for livestock, the old sheds having long since fallen into disrepair, but Timothy and St. John soon had a sturdy shelter built for the horse, St. John trying to control his frustration when he found he could no longer do such simple chores as holding a nail and pounding it in with a hammer. More than either of his brothers, he had been interested in the day-to-day work done on the estate, and the workers had been willing enough to teach him, once they discovered he was reliable help. But now what had once been easy tasks were beyond him. Alex could barely stand to witness the hurt she saw in his eyes. She reminded herself that it was all part of the adjustment he was making; some things he would learn to do a different way, and some he would just have to leave to others.

"He is a man," she reminded herself over and over, restraining herself from rushing to help at every turn. Her grandmother came seldom to the cottage these days—even in this year of drought and poor crops, August was a busy month on the farm—but Alex went to her when she needed reassurance that St. John's recovery was going as well as possible.

"It's been scarcely two months since he received the wound," Virginia reminded her. "I think his progress is remarkable. And if he can live with the risks he's taking when he rides, then we must live with them, too." She no longer mentioned Devon or urged Alexandria to return to the Falconers. She thought that would come later when St. John was truly in charge of his life again. Whatever he thought of himself at the moment, he was a winsome young man, and she expected that he would marry again eventually. Surely before too long, some woman would catch his eye. Despite his estrangement from his family, he still had contacts among his own class, and Virginia knew enough about human nature to believe that more than one young woman would find him more rather than less attractive because of his wound.

The heat of August continued until even those who professed to love fair, hot weather tired of it. Alex minded it most of all because it made the babies fussy and uncomfortable, and that in turn tried even Mavis's great well of patience. Not wanting her to grow weary of her employment, Alex sent her out as often as she could so that she would not feel so confined. Mavis, no longer fearful of losing her job, had agreed to weaning the twins to cow's milk, obtained from a farm a short distance away, and other foods, and the babies were thriving even if they did dislike the heat. The new system allowed Mavis more time to herself while enabling Alex to meet all the babies' needs when she had charge of them.

To her secret amusement, Alex noticed that Timothy often accompanied Mavis on her outings. At first, she had thought them a most unlikely couple, but on closer consideration, she began to think they might get on nicely even though Mavis was only nineteen while Tim was over thirty. Timothy cared nothing about Mavis's past, and Mavis looked quite animated, for her, in his company, her soft brown hair and round brown eyes giving her a certain prettiness, and her ample curves leaving no doubt as to her femininity. Tim didn't seem to mind at all that he looked even smaller and more wiry than usual when he stood beside Mavis.

This afternoon she hoped they were enjoying themselves near the river; it was surely the coolest place to be. She fanned her hot face with her hand and gave silent thanks that Flora and Blaine were both finally asleep.

The front door slammed, and she rushed out of the room, heading downstairs to warn whoever it was not to wake the twins. But she stopped dead, eyes going wide at the sight of St. John.

He was dirty and disheveled, his coat dust streaked, his breeches bloodstained and rent at one knee. A bruise had already begun to appear on his jaw, and Alex looked at the pinned sleeve of his jacket, dreading to see evidence of bleeding there, too. She breathed a sigh of relief when she did not.

"Sinje, what on earth happened?" she asked anxiously as she went to him, knowing the words were foolish even as she uttered them; he and Sir Arthur had obviously parted company.

"Just what you would expect, the cripple fell off of his horse," he snarled.

She paused again, held at bay by the force of his rage, but also overwhelmed by the knowledge that the worst had finally happened, and he seemed more or less all right.

His face twisted, the anger supplanted by baffled grief. "Just for an instant, I needed both hands, and I swear I felt my right hand reach forward, but it wasn't there. I came out of the saddle like a child who has never ridden."

She was sure he had been setting a fast pace. The power of Sir Arthur was far more tempting than anything the livery nag had had to offer. Her first impulse was to scold him for pushing too hard, but she stopped herself in time. "Even good riders with two strong arms can be thrown and often are. You were, several times I remember, and there must have been many other falls," she insisted boldly. "You are still learning it all again. Give yourself time. Now, let me see what you've done to your knee."

He was eyeing her oddly, and when she got close, she could smell brandy, but he didn't seem drunk.

"Where're Tim and Mavis?" he demanded suddenly.

His mood shift was hard to follow, but she answered obligingly. "They are off together somewhere. I made them go. They take far too little time to themselves. They seem to be courting, in case you haven't noticed. Now, please, go get out of your clothes!"

"Any time," he muttered as he limped toward the stairs.

Alex gathered the things she needed to tend to him, giving him plenty of time to undress, and then she went upstairs, knocking on his door and waiting until he bid her enter. He was wrapped in his robe, but she hardly thought about it; she was so accustomed to ministering to him, she didn't consider it any more than she did in caring for the twins. But she did understand how helpless he had felt in being so dependent on others' help, and thus how important it had been for him to reclaim the privacy of his own body.

His knee was swollen and badly scraped. She shook her head as she examined it, washed it, and wrapped it as gently as she could. "I fear this is going to be sore for some time, but I don't think there's any permanent injury. Do you hurt anywhere else?"

St. John hardly noticed what she was doing to his knee as she knelt before him. His mind was definitely hazy. To add to his chagrin, he had come out of the saddle not far from an ancient tavern, and several patrons had been standing outside in full witness of his desperate, failed attempt to keep his balance. But there had been no mockery, only solicitude, mostly in the form of brandy which he had gulped not only to ease the aching in his body but also the pain of his embarrassment. His new-found friends had helped him back up on Sir Arthur, who had stopped the instant he had felt his rider leave the saddle.

The brandy had blunted the discomfort, and it had altered other perceptions as well. He wondered if any man had kissed that full mouth or touched her long-limbed body. With great concentration, he studied the gloss of her dark hair and the length of the thick lashes sheltering her green eyes. Her scent came to him, soft, warm, smelling of flowers and sweet herbs. Even on this hot day; how did she manage that? He was startled by the stab of lust. Everything else slipped a little more out of focus with the sharp, exquisite torment of it. If only Tim and Mavis were here to ease the temptation, he thought fleetingly.

"Alexandria, let me . . ."

She glanced up at him questioningly, not understanding the look in his eyes as he suddenly gripped her wrist and pulled her up against him until she was half sprawled across his lap.

"Sinje, what . . ."

Her words were stopped by his mouth plundering hers with hard kisses. "Alex, let me," he repeated. "I need . . ."

She felt his need quite plainly pressing against the cloth of his dressing gown, but she was far more confused than frightened. This was her beloved Sinje who would never hurt her, who had been hurt himself in so many ways. And she could not believe that he wanted her as a woman.

Dimly St. John perceived the wonder in her eyes, and dimly he understood that she trusted him and that he was responsible for her protection. But his need to prove his sex was stronger than any other power on earth.

"Let me love you," he murmured.

Alex froze. She was sure she was strong enough physically to fight him off if she had to, if she wanted to. She did not. It seemed in that moment that she had loved him for a very long time without knowing it was so, perhaps even when she had warned him against her sister. There was no life for her anywhere except with St. John and his children. Her own childhood had ended while she assisted with the surgery that had so changed this man. This was simply the next step away from it, into her womanhood. And most important of all, she knew how St. John had come to doubt everything about himself; if she could help him to restore his pride in his manhood, she could make no greater gift to him.

Fear slipped away before it had time to take root. This was just another part of caring for St. John.

"Yes," she whispered, and she moved her own lips against his timidly, knowing it should be different from a kiss of friendship, but not quite sure how to do it.

He nearly ripped her dress from her in his frustration at his slowness in undoing the fastenings with one hand, but she let him do it, sensing how important it was for him to control everything.

She shivered a little when she stood naked before him, having a horrible vision of her mother pointing at her and naming her whore. But then she lifted her head, straightened her back, and saw by the look in St. John's eyes that he was not disappointed.

"So long and sleek," he whispered huskily, and he pulled her toward the bed.

She sank back, thinking he would discard his robe and follow her, but first he drew the heavy curtains across the small windows and plunged the room into deep shadow. When he came to her, she could hardly see him in the dim light. She realized that that was what he intended; even aware of how intimately she knew his body, he could not bear the thought of her seeing it more. Surely that would change when he once again knew that a woman could desire him; surely desire was the cause of the strange stirrings she felt in her body, prickles of blood and nerves she had not felt before; and surely they would find a way to come together that would banish all doubts and insecurities.

St. John cursed softly as he discovered the difficulty of having only one hand to touch her with, one arm for balance, but despite the awkwardness, his flesh continued to pulse with his need. He ran his hand down the slender form, savoring taut, young skin and finding the subtle curves more erotic than the fuller shapes he had always favored. A last small ghost of conscience warned him that she was very young and a virgin, that she was Alexandria, not Florence, but it was lost in the roaring of his blood and the ache in his loins. Time was disoriented so that it seemed he had been waiting forever to take her.

He knelt between her legs and thrust hard, clumsy with only one arm to support him and with one knee injured, but determined to accomplish his goal. He groaned at the tightness of her, and vaguely he heard her cry out as he battered at her maidenhead, finally piercing the membrane and sinking into her, his way eased by her blood.

Alex was immobilized by the agony he was inflicting. She had known it might hurt the first time, but she had expected nothing like this. He was much too large for her unready flesh; it felt as if she were being torn asunder. Shudders racked St. John, and she felt the hot flood inside before he slumped forward to lie heavily on her. She pushed at him desperately, afraid of suffocating.

He rolled off of her with a mumbled, "That was good, so good," and then he slept.

Alex got out of bed cautiously to stand on unsteady legs, wincing as she moved. She felt his seed spilling from her, and even in the bad light she could see her blood mixed with it. She dipped a piece of the bandage linen in water and scrubbed furiously at the mess, taking some comfort in noting that she was not bleeding hard. She gathered her clothing and dressed as swiftly as she could, putting a pad of linen between her legs to keep the blood from her clothes, feeling as if even the smallest stain would reveal to all what had happened this afternoon. Her mind was too numb to fix on anything more than her need to get out of the darkened room, away from the softly snoring figure on the bed. But she stopped short of leaving the house. The twins still slept, but soon they would awaken and need attention. St. John was in no condition to look after them.

She prayed that Timothy and Mavis would return soon, then she could go. She made herself a cup of tea and cradled the warmth of the cup, feeling chilled despite the hot day. There was comfort in the old ritual, and gradually she allowed herself to think about what had happened. In spite of her training in caring for the sick, she realized she was in fact very ignorant about the finer details of lovemaking between a man and a woman. Even her grandmother had scarcely discussed it, but when she had, it had seemed that the process was quite natural and even enjoyable. On the other hand, Alex had heard her mother hint darkly to Florence that sex was a duty of marriage and that there was little in it for the woman, that her advantages came from other aspects of the bond. It seemed that in this case her mother had been right, and Alex felt more than a little betrayed that her grandmother's wisdom had failed her in such a basic matter.

She shut her eyes tightly, trying to block out the image of how awkward, painful, and without dignity it had been. Surely it could not be that way for all women with all men, else the race would have died out for lack of interest. She was startled by the sharp sound of her own bitter laughter, but she felt better for it.

Gradually her common sense began to reassert itself. It would never hurt so much again; she could only lose her virginity once. It must, like anything else, get better with practice even for St. John, who, though he had had previous sexual experience, had never made love before with his body so changed. And none of the essential things had altered. St. John and the twins still needed her, and she still had no other place she so belonged. She could not imagine returning to the Falconers now.

She wondered if St. John's slurred, "That was good, so good," was really true for him. It was peculiar to consider that, as her mother claimed, the man could so enjoy the act while the woman did not. Nature seemed sadly out of tune.

St. John awakened abruptly with his heart pounding and the foul aftertaste of too much brandy in his mouth. He lay perfectly still, trying to sort out what had happened as he came fully awake, hoping it had been a nightmare, or a dream. But his satiated body told him it had happened. He turned his head, searching for her, and found she had gone. Poor Alexandria. What a way to repay her after all her care of him. He knew he had not been gentle. But he also felt a small stab of resentment, a dark worm of suspicion that he was being maneuvered into marriage just as he had been with Florence, for surely the honorable thing to do was to marry Alex. Perhaps she had not been as unaware of her appeal as he had thought.

Then he snorted derisively. Of course, he was exactly what any young girl would want—a one-armed man who could not even manage his body decently in bed.

He swung out of bed with an angry movement and let the late afternoon light into the room, frowning when he saw the bloodstains on the counterpane. He had to find Alex as quickly as possible. He cursed his infirmity anew as he struggled into his clothes.

He was stunned to find her calmly feeding Flora and Blaine in the kitchen.

"I couldn't leave them alone," she said matter of factly, but he saw the bruised look in her eyes before she turned her attention back to his children, and he saw the effort she was making to keep her hands from trembling.

"I'm sorry, Alexandria. I know I hurt you. It shouldn't have happened at all. It's unfortunate I didn't drink enough to render me incapable. Are you all right?" His voice was taut with self-disgust.

"I could have refused you," she said softly.

"Are you all right?" he asked again.

She nodded but said nothing to elaborate it, talking instead to the children as she picked up first one and then the other, patting each gently on the back.

St. John poured himself a cup of tea, obviously waiting for her to finish with the twins, and she wondered if he were as in need of comfort as she had been. She was glad she had not left the house to have to face him later. She felt curiously calm now, almost as if nothing had changed. But when she had the babies settled on a thin feather tick on the floor where they could roll and crawl about, St. John stunned her by asking, "Will you marry me?"

She stared at him. "Is that what you truly want?" Somehow she had not considered this final step.

A short space before, St. John would have known it was not, but suddenly he felt as if he had desired it for weeks as he had desired her. She was young, growing more beautiful by the day, and not, after all, like Florence. She was marvelous with his children, and she had given him her virginity. His only doubt now was that she would choose him over a whole man.

He went to her, his hand cupping her chin gently, and he was infinitely grateful that she did not flinch from him. "It is what I want, but what of you? You are a beautiful woman, Alex. You can have your pick of any man. I . . ."

"I don't want just any man," she interrupted firmly. "I want you. Already I am far more at home here than in the house where I was born. You, Flora, and Blaine are my family."

He kissed her then, tenderly, not wanting to frighten her with renewed passion even though his body responded to her closeness, and she returned the kiss in the same way.

"Do you mind if we wait a few days before we tell anyone? I'm not quite ready to face my mother," she admitted. "And I would like my grandmother to be the first to know in any case."

"Of course, it will be as you wish. You ask for small concessions." He agreed readily, but he suddenly found he wished he could announce his conquest to the world. They did not mention his family at all, but he would have given much to see his father's face when he learned of this. He might as well be damned for full cause.

❧ Chapter 19 ❧

Alex tried to tell herself that the change in her life was not, after all, so profound, but one that came to most women, simply another step on growing older and leaving childhood behind. But the turmoil in her mind and heart belied her own theory.

For the first few days after her encounter with St. John, she moved through the hours in a daze steadied only by the fact that she still had her work to do at the cottage. She realized she might have stayed away otherwise, as she found it difficult to face him, particularly the first day. It was, she judged, an odd reaction; she should have felt closer to him after being so intimate, but instead, she found it hard to meet his eyes, and her body twinged, reminding her of the lingering soreness. She was acting decidedly missish and was annoyed with herself.

St. John did not share her quandary. His body responded instantly to the sight of her, and it was only with rigid control that he kept himself from trying to get her alone again. Any lingering doubts he had about the marriage were vanquished by the pounding of his blood when she was near; that she was also wonderful with his children was an added benefit. Even her sudden attack of shyness pleased him, making him seem more in charge than he had since his return. Sometimes Alex's competence unnerved him, making him feel years younger than she.

Despite his sore knee, he began riding again immediately, contenting his body with a different exercise than the one it craved. But when a few days had passed, and Alex had said nothing, he began to feel uneasy. It was a new situation. Florence had never shown anything but great enthusiasm for marrying him; had he taken her virginity, she would undoubtedly have been demanding the ring the next day. He wished he need never think of Florence again and knew it would never be so, not with Flora and Blaine to remind him. He was relieved that he was able to love them for their own sakes—Alex's doing.

"Are you having second thoughts?" he finally asked gently. He had had to do some careful maneuvering to get her alone.

Suddenly she wanted to ask him if he truly loved her, just her, without the connection to the twins or to his convalescence. It was a foolish thought. Love was a part of other things always, and there was no way to go back and change the way this had happened. She saw the shadow of doubt in his eyes and recognized again how vulnerable he was.

"No second thoughts, Sinje. It's just so new. But I'll tell Grandmother today."

He looked into her green eyes and thought he might

drown there. Soft, deep-sheltering forest, a loving refuge. He drew her close with his good arm and kissed her, feeling her chaste mouth grow warm and open tentatively under his insistence. He held himself in check, tutoring her carefully as he tasted her sweetness.

Alex felt tendrils of warmth uncoiling deep inside her. The invasion of her mouth was so intimate, she felt as if she were naked before him again, but it was not unpleasant. The man scent of him filled her nostrils and the slightly salt taste of his mouth was in hers. It was hard to think while he was rousing so many sensations in her, but dimly it came to her that this was the goal, this mingling of all into one warm flesh. If they could achieve that, nothing would be strong enough to break them.

When she arrived at her grandmother's house, she was still slightly dizzy with the feelings St. John had aroused. She was also deliriously happy.

Virginia saw that instantly and smiled in response to Alex's expression. "And what marvelous news do you have? Have the twins miraculously begun to speak the king's English?"

Alex hugged her, her joy spilling over. "No, but it's marvelous just the same. Sinje has asked me to marry him, and I've accepted. You're the first to know."

Alex felt her grandmother freeze, and she stumbled back a pace, shocked by the sudden death's mask the beloved face had become.

"Please," she whimpered, "please don't look like that! I know it will be hard for some to understand, but he loves me, and I love him, and the twins need both of us. Please be happy for us!"

Virginia was so devastated, at first she could find no words to speak, though inwardly she cursed herself. It had never occurred to her that St. John and Alexandria would look on each other as man and woman. Now it was so obvious, but she had completely mistaken it, assuming from the time of the surgery on St. John that Alex thought of him just as she thought of her brother Boston, and that St. John would see her only as a little sister. So they had always viewed each other. In this she had failed her granddaughter entirely, refusing to see that the end of childhood had come in all things, not just in some.

"You cannot marry him." She forced the words out with difficulty.

Alex's face changed, the planes subtly tightening, sharpening as if the skin were stretched more tautly over the bones, making her appear haughty and withdrawn. "I thought I wanted your blessing above all things, but I find that is not true. It is St. John I want, with or without your blessing. I will marry him, whether you say I may or not."

Virginia reached out and grasped her shoulders so hard, Alex winced. "It is not what I say or whether you will or not, it is the Church of England that says you may not. It is against the law! You may not marry your dead sister's husband. What the church says about marriage and divorce is the law of the land. Do you understand?"

Alex looked at her as if she had turned into an alien creature. "What care could the church have in such a matter? Florence is dead. And Sinje and I share no blood. I am as closely related to Lord Carrington as I am to Sinje, and that is no closeness at all."

"It is an old, old law, Alexandria. Remember your history, even King Henry VIII had to receive special permission to marry his brother's widow, Catherine of Aragon. And when he set her aside, he said that God had frowned on the union despite the dispensation. And that permission came from the Church of Rome. The Church of England is even more strict about who may marry and who not. I know this is true, Alex, no matter that you are not related, or how much you love."

"Why?" Alex asked desperately, finally beginning to believe her. "Why should the church make such a law?"

"It is one that has caused much pain, but it has also protected many women from being forced into marriages simply because they are useful in the care of the children who are left. The aunt is so often close to her nieces and nephews, particularly if their mother, her sister, had been in ill health. Are you sure, very sure that this is not what has happened to you?"

"I love the twins, but I love Sinje more, and I want to marry him! It is not a case of being forced into anything!" In face of her grandmother's doubts, she had none. "Surely it can be allowed in some cases."

Virginia shook her head. "No, not that I have ever heard of, and you are so young, the authorities would probably be less likely to consider it than ever." She bowed her head wearily for a moment, and then looked squarely at Alex again. "Have you lain with him?"

Alex did not flinch, but she saw the grievous pain her single word "yes" caused her grandmother.

She stood very straight. "And I will again and yet again. He is mine, I his, and no law on earth shall keep us apart." At that moment even the pain of the first encounter faded before her conviction that she and St. John could triumph over any obstacle as long as they were together.

"What about the Falconers?" It was a weak question because Virginia just stopped herself from saying, "What about Rane Falconer who loves you whether you know it or not?" Under the circumstances, she realized, it would horrify rather than reassure Alex. This was no child to be offered one prize in place of another. Young and still uncertain, nonetheless, Alex was a woman now, and Virginia could feel the force of her and was at a loss for how to change her course.

"The Falconers have nothing to do with this. They have done enough for me. This is my life and my decision. I will never forgive you if you involve them in this."

Their eyes locked in a brief, silent battle, and then Virginia nodded, "I will tell them nothing."

It was not Alex's will that won the battle but her love. Virginia did not want to live without it. The bond was too close and too precious to destroy. Alexandria had had little enough love in her life; no wonder she was seeking it and a place of her own with St. John. Virginia felt very old and very sad; in spite of all her efforts to make Alexandria feel cherished, it had not been enough to counteract the malevolent coldness of Margaret Thaine. If St. John could do that, it would be worth the gossip that was sure to come. She was shocked by her own conclusion.

"I wish you were not St. John's lover. I wish your life had not taken this course. I wish you had stayed in Devonshire, away from all of this. I wish you could be spared the trouble that is bound to come. But I love you, and that will never change, no matter what you do, no matter where you go." She thought of all the loss, death, and sorrow she had known in her own long life, and she thought of all the joy and beauty the same years had brought. And she remembered that there was only one lesson worth learning from all her time on earth.

She opened her arms and Alex came to her, cuddling close as if she were a small child again before she drew away. "I love you, too, always."

"Do you wish to spend tonight here?" Virginia knew how unbearable it would be for Alexandria to go home so soon after learning the devastating truth about her future plans.

"No, thank you. I'm going home, to Sinje." It was very clear to her. She was no longer alone. Decisions belonged as much to St. John now as to her.

He was surprised to see her in the long twilight, and he searched her face and knew that something was amiss though she looked gravely resolute. Well, he had not expected that Virginia Thaine would rejoice in the idea.

"I need to speak to you alone, Sinje," she told him softly.

Wordlessly, he led her outside. Timothy and Mavis watched them, conscious of the odd tension between the two.

Making no effort to soften the blow, Alex told St. John about the church law forbidding their marriage, and she saw that he was as stunned as she had been.

"I never thought . . . I . . ." He was desperate to make her believe his offer of marriage had not been a deceit.

She put her fingertips against his mouth, stilling his words. "I know, Sinje, I know. It doesn't matter. I will do what you wish, stay or go."

"If you stay, you will be named my mistress, not my wife, by many. Do you understand what that will mean?" He asked the question urgently, wanting her even more now that the law would prevent them.

"Yes, I understand. The people who think ill of me now will think worse of me. The few who love me will love me still. And I will have you and the twins, my own family, to love."

He felt her calm resolution as much as he heard it in her words, and he knew that once again her well-being was in his hands. On the surface, the right thing to do was to send her home to her family and pretend that nothing had ever passed between them except friendship. But he knew how little joy she had of her family, as cold as his, and he could not bear the loss of her warmth. He reached out and carefully stroked her loosely bound hair. "Poor Alex, you are as much an orphan as I."

She caught his hand and kissed it. "Not together; together we can face anything."

He put his arm around her and drew her to his side.

They stood, warmth touching warmth, and listened to the evensong of the birds, the breeze of the approaching night cool against their faces. For the first time in days, Alex felt utterly content, as if she and St. John had always belonged together and had been married for years.

Finally he returned them both to reality. "We must inform your parents, but first I want to talk to Reverend Tynewater. Perhaps there is a way 'round the law; perhaps your grandmother is wrong." He tried to make his voice sound positive, but his doubt was clear; he no more than Alex could imagine Virginia being misinformed on so important a matter.

"I will go and see the Reverend now. Do you wish to come with me?"

"Do you want me to?" she countered, hoping he could not see how little courage she had for the task. She did not like the clergyman who seemed to her to care more for his food and port than for the well-being of his flock. She detested the idea of the pompous little man passing judgment on whether or not she and St. John could marry.

"You wait here," St. John said, and he planted a fleeting, gentle kiss on her forehead, wishing he could banish the shadows in her eyes.

Alex made no attempt to explain to Timothy and Mavis while she waited for St. John to return, and they did not press her though their worry was plain.

When St. John returned, his face was a mask, the skin pulled tight, his mouth a thin line, and his eyes glittered hotly. "That sanctimonious swine!" he ground out. "Oh, it was all in black and white, but it was the way he told me! He . . ." St. John stopped abruptly, horrified that he had nearly told Alex the whole of it; that he would never do.

The priest had been more concerned about getting to his supper than saving souls, and that had not surprised St. John because he knew the habits of the man. A taste for the bountiful life was shared by many of the Anglican clergy, and St. John was no dissenter to begrudge it. But Tynewater's attitude and advice had been intolerable.

After making it clear that no exceptions to the marriage law had been made in his experience, the priest had gone on to approach St. John as one man with hearty appetites to another. He had pointed out that the law could be seen to be working in St. John's favor as he now knew himself to be unable to marry Alexandria Thaine and was thus freed from onerous duty to her despite his "enjoyment of her favors." He had gone on and on, each sentence leading deeper into the swamp of the man's mind.

St. John had been so shocked and horrified, at first he had not been able to credit what the man was saying. The Carringtons owned the best box pew in the church, and St. John had seen how the clergyman fawned over the Carringtons when they appeared. And now it pleased Tynewater to counsel St. John as if he were an erring younger son who had nothing to do but cast off his lowborn light skirt to be welcomed back into the fold of his own class. Margaret Thaine was proper enough, but everyone knew her youngest child was a wild one, too much like her grandmother.

The words had at last hit St. John with the force of a physical blow, and he had wanted to kill Tynewater for spreading his muck over Alex.

He grinned in sudden savage pleasure at the memory of grabbing Tynewater and nearly strangling the man in his own coat. He might be one-armed now, but it was a strong arm, and he relished the knowledge that he could have done the man real damage had he not realized in time that the creature was not worth the trouble it would cause. He had contented himself with threatening the minister with grevious harm should he dare to make any derogatory statement about Alexandria, or her grandmother.

Alex stepped back a pace, whispering, "Sinje, what have you done?"

The light of battle faded abruptly from his eyes as St. John realized that he was frightening Alex rather than giving her the comfort she needed.

"I lost my temper and we had words, but I doubt the Reverend will miss so much as a bite of his supper over it," he assured her. "There's no use in delay. We must go tell your parents. Or if you prefer, I will do it myself."

Alex was tempted to again take the coward's way, but she knew she could not in this case. She straightened her shoulders. "No, we'll go together."

St. John told Timothy and Mavis first, stating their case baldly. "I have asked Alex to marry me, and she has agreed. But now we find that church law forbids it because I was married to her sister. We intend to live as if we are married despite this law. Alex is to be treated as my wife in all things."

Timothy and Mavis, both basic in their views of life, were not surprised that the two had come to love each other, though they were shocked that the church would have a say in such a thing. Mavis's parents were legally married, and she could not see that it had done her mother any good at all, as overworked and worn-out from childbearing and her husband's ill treatment as she was. Timothy's parents had never been married but had scraped along well enough, selling cockles and winkles from a barrow in London and producing a string of children who were expected to make their own way as soon as possible. But though neither Mavis nor Timothy thought the less of the couple for deciding to live together without benefit of clergy, they both knew that for St. John's class and for Alex's it was an overbold thing to do. And in the strange way of human judgment, it was Alex who would become the object of censure.

A man might take his pleasure where he would and even earn some admiration for his acquisition if she were worth desiring, but the woman was not so privileged. If she possessed great beauty, wealth, and social rank, she just might manage to set her own rules and live as an eccentric, but without those things, she was damned to harsh opinion. Of beauty, Alex had more than her share, but she had no wealth and was only a merchant's daughter. Timothy and Mavis tried to be hearty in their congratulations, but they feared for her.

Alex needed their kind wishes. She knew it was going to go badly when her mother heard their plans, but nothing could have prepared her for the screeching venom that poured over her.

"You've ever been a thankless bitch! I rue the day I bore you! You bring shame on all of us." She advanced on her daughter, hand raised. "A conniving whore, that's what you are!" But St. John stepped between them.

"Madam, that is more than sufficient! Your daughter's only fault is to love, not a fault you've ever had. Touch her and you will regret it."

Margaret backed away hissing, "You, you've ruined both my daughters, murdered one."

"No, Mother, you killed her! You with your plans for what she might get for you from the Carringtons." Alex

218

found her own voice in defense of St. John. "You make it so easy to leave this house."

But it was not as easy to face Caton and Boston. They seemed frozen in place, stunned as much by Margaret's rage as by the couple's announcement. And the tears started to fall on her father's cheeks. He looked so beaten and pathetic, Alex's heart twisted in pity for him, knowing he wept because he could not stand up to Margaret rather than for his daughter's actions.

She went to him, putting her arms around him, murmuring, "It's all right, Father, it truly is. I love Sinje, and he loves me. We'll be fine."

"Always, you will always be my daughter, no matter what you do. Be joyful, Alexandria, be joyful." The words were low and labored, but he got them out.

Boston reacted with more outright courage. He offered his hand to St. John who shook it with his own left. "I hope you'll be very happy. You both deserve it. And I warn you, I plan to visit my nephew and my niece quite often, so I hope Alex is still a good cook." And very low he added, "Don't worry about her clothing and such; I'll see that she gets everything."

St. John thought gratefully that here was one in-law worth having. And Virginia, too, if she ever forgave him. Boston and Virginia, they almost made up for Margaret, Caton, and Alex's older brothers who had never given a damn about her. On balance, his own family didn't fare as well.

There was nothing more to be said. As they made their way back to the cottage, Alex thought how odd it was that it had taken so little time to leave what had been her home since birth; she doubted she would ever enter that house again. Yet, she felt very little beyond sorrow for her father and even that was tinged with the knowledge that she could do him no good even were she to stay in his home. Not hers, not ever again.

The moon was rising, full and yellow. St. John stopped and studied Alex's face in the bleaching light. The long-drawn-out hoot of a tawny owl drifted over them, part of the eerie night chorus carried on the soft stir of air.

Looking up at him, Alex said, "Sinje, I do not care that we cannot be officially married, truly I do not! Please believe that!"

She was all that was sweet and sane in his world, and

for the first time since the confrontation with the minister, he admitted to himself that much of his anger at the man had stemmed from his own guilt for having thought, however briefly, the same awful things about Alex. His voice trembled. "Thank you, Mrs. Carrington, for having so much courage. I love you very much."

His mouth was warm and demanding on hers, and the curls of heat began even more quickly than before, as if she were growing more sensitive to his touch. She put her arms around him and leaned into him, needing the hard contact of his body to reassure her.

They were beyond discretion by the time they reached the cottage, ascending the stairs to St. John's room without stopping, assuming that Mavis and Timothy would understand.

Alex could feel her body tensing in fear that the pain of her first time with St. John would be repeated, but she was also filled with vague yearnings awakened by his kiss, a need to be close to him that they might become one, not pulled apart by the tragedies of their families. She needed to know absolutely that she belonged here with him. Most of all, she needed to please him, to give him what he wanted so that he would never regret loving her.

She was too shy to ask him to light a lamp, but she was saddened when he curtained out the moonlight. Though still very lean, he was firmly muscled again, and she wanted to see him, wanted him to know that he was beautiful to her. Surely soon he would believe that.

They undressed in silence, shedding their clothes in the dark, and she heard him curse softly as he had difficulty with some garment, but she did not dare offer her help.

When they were in bed, he began to nuzzle her flesh hungrily, moving from her mouth to her back and down her breasts, licking and sucking the sensitive nipples until they stood erect and flooded Alex with a host of new sensations.

She ran her hands over his flesh, learning the smooth and the rough where blond hair lightly furred his chest and legs, feeling the difference between that and the silk of the hair on his head. But when she moved to kiss his wounded shoulder, he froze and growled, "Don't!" And then he was covering her body with his own and thrusting into her. She spread her legs trying to accommodate him and began to move her hips involuntarily, instinctively needing to follow him. But he was finished before she learned the harmony.

For an instant she wanted to scream aloud. It was not the acute agony she had felt the first time though there was still pain, it was something she did not understand—an enormous aching pressure that made her feel as if she were going to explode. She whimpered and moved restlessly beneath St. John's weight.

"I'm sorry, I hurt you again," he murmured, as he moved to the side.

"No." She denied it quickly, not wanting the self-doubt she heard in his voice to take hold. "It was much better, Sinje. You will have to be patient with me, it's all so new."

With that he chuckled, "I should hope so."

The tears slipped silently down her cheeks as she listened to his breathing slow and deepen to sleep. She brushed the tears away angrily. She was not sad. It was more like the rage and frustration she had felt as a small child when she could not do something well the first time she tried it. She wondered if all women felt this way at first and if it ever got any better. But she had no one to ask. To admit to Mavis or to her grandmother that all was not perfect between herself and St. John was unthinkable after the step they had taken. Though she tried to thrust it away, the thought rose again and lingered that her mother was correct about the physical relationship between a man and a woman.

Sleep was long in coming, despite her exhaustion.

❧ *Chapter 20* ❧

By the middle of November, Alex knew she was pregnant. At first she thought that the cessation of her monthly courses had been brought on by the mental and physical upheavals of becoming St. John's lover. But now there were other signs—a little more fullness in her breasts, a creeping fatigue she had never experienced before, an unsettled stomach on many mornings, and a feeling that her body was shifting, finding a new center. She suspected she had conceived the first or second time she had lain with St. John.

Her feelings were so contradictory, she despaired of ever sorting them out. She wanted to bear children for St. John. She could not love the twins more, and yet, she was honest enough to realize that she wanted children who were part of her rather than part of Florence. But this was not the time for her to bear them. Of that she was certain. She and St. John still had so many adjustments to make. The realities of "married" life were encroaching more by the day. He had given her a filigreed gold band that had come to him from his grandmother, and sometimes it seemed as heavy as an anchor.

She and St. John loved each other, but she was beginning to learn that that might not be enough to solve all problems. She wondered if all marriages were built on little lies, one on top of the other. It was a wry image, for on a physical level, their love continued as it had begun with St. John on top of her taking his pleasure while she pretended to be pleased also, offering that lie as a gift to his masculinity while her body continued to wait for something that was never found. The discomfort had lessened, and for that she was thankful, but even that held a danger because it freed her mind to wander so that sometimes she was scarcely present as St. John satisfied his hunger in her body.

Not wanting to be like her sister, she never denied him, but she liked it much better when he was too tired to make love and simply lay beside her, sometimes stretching his arm possessively across her as he slept.

It remained a mystery to her how he could be so attentive and kind during the day, showing his affection openly by a word, a touch, a look, even taking the time to bring her leaves or flowers he knew she liked to put about the cottage, a gesture that never failed to move her because she knew how difficult it was for him to manage such a task with one arm. And yet, at night when he made love to her, it was as if she did not exist as an individual at all. She wondered if the women he had had before her sister and herself had had some talent for enjoyment that she and Florence lacked. With Margaret for their mother, she could hardly doubt that it was possible.

She still could not bring herself to seek advice. She worked with her grandmother whenever she could, but she no longer confided in her. In spite of her best efforts to take all in stride, Virginia's sorrow and worry showed whenever she looked at her granddaughter, and Alex could not admit to her that all was not well in her "marriage." She felt the same about Mavis, in addition to knowing that the woman was very loyal to St. John, as well as to her, and would feel torn if she were told he was less than perfect. Part of her wished that either or both of the women would guess that she was pregnant, while another part of her hugged the secret close and knew St. John should be told first.

Telling him was no easy matter. She wanted him to be pleased, but she feared that was not going to be his reaction. He already had two children, and she was beginning to realize that as charming as he was, he was little suited to making his own way. It was a problem she had seen in him before and it had not changed, but now it was of vital concern to her own life. It was not just a matter of his arm, but of the way he had been raised. He knew how to do a variety of things, but none of them consistently or practically. He was a "gentleman." And now even many of these skills he had acquired through his interest in the land were beyond him. Gradually she was coming to know that they were in precarious financial straits and that St. John didn't seem to mind.

He had a small income from a trust left him by his maternal grandmother who had been fond of him when he was a child. His family could not deprive him of it, but neither could he touch the principal. Rent on the cottage had been paid for the year but would be due again in January. Alex suspected they were being charged more because St. John was a Carrington, but there was little they could do about it except move, and Alex wanted to avoid that—it would be difficult to find a place with as much room and in as good repair. Upstairs in addition to the bedchamber she and St. John shared were two smaller rooms, one for the twins and one where Mavis slept, though Alex knew she spent a good deal of time with Timothy in his room downstairs. The kitchen, the larder, and a parlor occupied the rest of the main floor. The spaces had been shaped for function rather than symmetry, and none of the rooms was very large, but it was an adequate house and would be even with the addition of another child. No, she did not want to move. She no longer minded that they were on the border of Carrington land; she would not allow either family to change their lives.

She recognized a nesting instinct in herself, a new concern that life be secure and settled. That was not going to be possible unless she and St. John found a way to increase their income. She was chagrined when she discovered that her grandmother had continued to pay both Mavis and Timothy. Since much of their food came from Virginia's farm, they were indebted to her for that, too. She was angry at herself and at St. John for being so oblivious, but she tried to keep the temper out of her voice when she brought the subject up.

"Sinje, we must decide what we are going to do for a living. We cannot depend forever on Grandmother's charity. It is wrong that she has paid Timothy's and Mavis's wages for so long already. And we cannot live upon credit either."

The calmness in her voice was a wasted effort. St. John glared at her. "Why not live on credit? My family has done it forever."

"Which is how they got into such a muddle! And we are not the high and mighty Carringtons; we are the castoffs of the family, in case you've forgotten! We have no land a creditor could take in place of payment." She was sorry the instant the words were out, but she could not take them back.

St. John's face was suddenly cold and rigid. "I have not forgotten. Nor can I forget how much like your sister you are after all. You've the penny-counting mind of a merchant, and she had it, too." It was the most calculated cruelty he could utter, and she said nothing in return, simply staring after him as he strode away.

Nightfall came, and he was still gone on Sir Arthur. She was frantic with worry and debated sending Timothy to search for him, though she was sure that if something had happened to him, someone would have come to tell her. Sheer exhaustion finally calmed her enough so that she convinced herself it was just as well that he was staying out with his anger. She lay in their bed weeping and missing his warmth beside her until sleep overwhelmed her.

St. John entered the room quietly, and his heart twisted at the sight of her in the candlelight. Her face was pale and tearstained, closed eyes swollen and shadowed. Her dark hair spread out on the pillow, and she had one arm thrown across the place where he should have been.

He awakened her gently, calling her name until she stirred and then leaning over to kiss her. "Oh, my love, you aren't the least like Florence. I said it to hurt you. I am so very sorry."

At first she thought she was dreaming, but then she smelled leather, horse, and sweat, and she nearly laughed aloud for the sheer joy of finding him home safely and rid of his rage. She put her arms around him and kissed him back, murmuring her own apology, feeling his muscles shaking with fatigue under her hands. This time she helped him undress and sponged the grit from his skin, and he accepted her ministrations gratefully, needing the physical contact with her and knowing he was too weary to make love to her. They fell asleep curled spoon fashion, reassured by the shared warmth the length of their bodies.

In the morning, Alex felt so nauseated, she could not lift her head from the pillow without suffering a spinning world. It was the first time the morning sickness had been so violent, the first time St. John had seen her ill at all, and he did not mistake the cause.

"My God, you're pregnant!" he exclaimed, and with surprising efficiency he brought her a basin and a wet cloth. Not surprising, she corrected herself miserably; Florence had undoubtedly suffered the same bouts. She was proving more like her sister than she liked. She waited for him to say something else, but nothing seemed to be forthcoming after his exclamation of discovery. Cautiously she opened her eyes, but she could not read his expression.

"Are you angry?" she asked softly, and he started, trying to pull his scattered thoughts together, knowing the truth would not do. The truth was that the last thing they needed at the moment and for a long time to come was another child. Beyond that, he did not want Alex pregnant under any circumstances; he did not want her to die as Florence had. Pure terror gripped his belly at the thought, but he managed an unsteady laugh.

"Hardly angry, Mrs. Carrington, since I had a great deal to do with this. It's just a bit of a surprise, a grand surprise. When is it due?" He kissed her hand in tribute.

Reassured, she smiled at him in impish humor. "Late May or early June. Sinje, if you were a race horse, you would be well appreciated indeed, quick as you are to get offspring."

His eyes widened, and then he gave a shout of relieved laughter. Here was none of the cringing fear Florence had shown. "That's well enough, my bawdy wife, but if you have anything to say about it, I would prefer just one infant this time."

"Addition rather than multiplication; I'll work on it," she quipped and then wished she hadn't.

But he smiled ruefully. "You were justified in raising the question of our finances. It is a good thing one of us has a head for such matters. I reacted badly because I haven't wanted to think about it, have been too afraid to. Alex, you see before you a perfectly useless man, born and bred that way long before I lost my arm. No, don't defend me, please. Losing my arm has made it worse, but it was hardly better before. The only thing I am truly good at is judging horseflesh. Since I do not own my own stable and see no prospect of that in the immediate future, the only way for me to make a living with my skill is to bet on the races. It is why I had enough to purchase my colors." His face twisted briefly at the thought that good luck at the races had funded his bad luck on the battlefield.

He was watching her so warily, she knew that Florence must have hated his gambling. Only now did she realize that that must have been the way they had paid their bills, for at least there were as yet no creditors demanding payment for past-due accounts. Unless her mother had eased their way; she doubted that the minute she considered it.

Alex was more aware than ever that she was, in truth, a merchant's daughter. Caton was not aggressive enough to aspire to the heights of the princes of commerce, but he had always provided a fair living for his family, including more luxuries than his wife deserved. Alex could see the meticulous figures in the ledgers, figures he could manage so much better than most people. And she realized she craved the same order. She wanted to be able to calculate exactly what she and St. John could afford, and she wanted to pay rent, wages, and bills on time. Of things she did not wish to do, living on the variable proceeds of gambling was close to the top of the list. It had not proved a good way for St. John's family to exist, and in her own social class, only wastrels and miscreants attempted it on more than a casual basis.

But it was something that St. John could do. That had to outweigh all other considerations. She swallowed her misgivings. "I know little about it, Sinje, but if that is what you wish to do, then so be it."

"You must understand, it will mean that I will be gone much of the time. To wager on the horses, I must be where they run."

Still that wary look; she could almost hear the whining Florence must have done. Racing was a gentleman's sport, more a bachelor's world than for the married, and the courses, aside from small rural meets, were no place for women except those of the lowest character. There would be no question of St. John taking her with him.

"Yes, I can see that. As long as you come home to me, I shan't complain." Even as she said it, she vowed to make it true. She allowed herself wry inner amusement; St. John had chosen a clever way to win his will, presenting all the negative arguments almost as if he were against the idea so that she became the one defending it. She was not skilled yet at this marital maneuvering, and she wished it were not necessary. She would much prefer simply talking honestly about how they both felt without fear of injury to either of them. When they were able to do that, she would consider their marriage a success. It was more necessary than ever for her peace of mind to believe that the marriage existed despite the lack of church sanction. Surely it was more important that the marriage lines be written in the hearts of the couple than in the register of the church?

At last St. John relaxed. "Thank you, sweetheart. You'll see, we'll rub along quite well." Gently he brushed her hair back from her face and ran a finger down her cheek. "Do you want to try a cup of tea and a piece of toast?"

Her stomach jumped at the mere mention of food. "Later, please. You go along. I'll call Mavis if I need anything. I don't plan to make a habit of indulging this child." She patted her still flat abdomen, and in that instinctive gesture the baby took on more reality than it had heretofore possessed.

When St. John had gone, she lay there thinking about the child, imagining a little boy or girl with St. John's vivid blue eyes, golden hair, and clear-cut bones. "I do hope you'll look like him," she murmured, and then she giggled, wondering if she were going to be prone to such silly conversations with the unborn until the birth. But she sobered when she contemplated her conversation with St. John. Even she knew that the racing calendar was over for the year and would not begin again until the spring. That left too many months to worry about. She would have to go to her grandmother after all, not to borrow money but to seek her aid in turning the healing skills to profit. She knew it was possible. Many of Virginia's patients paid her in farm products or services if not in money. And many had come to trust Alex as well as her grandmother to treat themselves as well as their beasts. St. John was hardly in a position to object. He had stated how he was going to contribute to their little family; now it was her turn. As soon as she got this damnable morning sickness under control. She groaned in frustration when renewed attempts to get up brought more dizziness. "One thing at a time," she cautioned herself with uncharacteristic patience.

They were certainly not alone in their financial worries. The drought had damaged the hay and turnip crops, though grain had not been so badly hurt. A shortage of fodder had caused a glut of cattle on the market, prices had tumbled, and many farmers were giving up their leases. Manufacturers were overstocked with goods which they could not sell even with the opening of Continental markets because the people in Europe did not have money to buy them. And now there were no longer huge orders for military equipment. Factories were closing, throwing people out of work. In addition, thousands of men returning from the army and navy were finding there were not enough jobs. The Corn Law had been passed to protect farmers, prohibiting the importation of grain until the home price had reached eighty shillings the bushel, famine level. But now there were more people buying bread than raising the grain to make it, and so, many accused the government of starving the poor by policy. Murmurs of unrest and discontent were met with terror that the horrors of the French Revolution would spread to England.

Mindful of the precariousness of everyone's financial state, Alex was absolutely determined that her grandmother not support them any longer. It was a harrowing interview; Alex knew that Virginia was offering out of love and only for love's sake, and that made refusal even harder.

"Child, be sensible! The baby you carry is the most important thing now, and you should not worry about aught else." She was still struggling to accept Alexandria's pregnancy; it terrified and appalled her because Alexandria was so young, and it made her feel even more distant from her granddaughter, particularly because she had not guessed before she was told. Life was rushing in too fast on her granddaughter, and Virginia was feeling less and less in charge, less and less able to ease the way for her.

"I am not refusing all help. Quite the contrary, I need you to help me find a way to earn enough to keep us until Sinje is able to make a living."

There was no use in saying it aloud; they both knew that betting on the horses was, even with St. John's canny perceptions, never going to be a sure living and that much was going to be up to Alex as long as she refused outside financial help.

"Grandmother, I love you dearly, but I cannot continue to come here unless you can accept the fact that Sinje and I are responsible for each other and the children now." Alex closed her eyes and bit her lip hard to keep from crying. The thought of being so close and yet being unable to see her grandmother was horrible.

Virginia was beaten; she no more than Alex could face such a separation. "Some will be too poor to pay anything; others will be able to offer only a little food from their fields and gardens; and some can afford coin. But most will want to pay something. It is human nature to value what has been paid for over what has come without effort; it is the reason I have accepted payment over the years, and the reason will do as well for you. But it will take time for people to trust you because you are so young. You will have to be very careful in judging whether you are able to help or not in this or that case."

Alex nodded, fully aware of how difficult it was going to be and how little room she would have for error. There seemed to be little room for it in her life in general lately; everything was becoming a most delicate balancing act.

Virginia, having bowed to Alexandria's will, set out to make her new plan work. She used her own advancing age to underscore her need for her granddaughter's help, always assuring the patients that she would be available for consultation. Indeed, it was what she had always planned; it was simply happening earlier than she had expected.

Alex began to spend hours poring over the old herbals and the voluminous notes Virginia had kept. Increasingly, she was gone from the cottage, leaving the twins in Mavis's care, as she went with her grandmother on the rounds of visiting the sick. Some days she had to grit her teeth to get out of bed at all since her own sickness of a morning grew worse rather than better, contrary to the usual pattern. Throwing up seemed to have become part of her regular routine. And Virginia was adamant about women taking any soporific drug during pregnancy because she pointed out it must be that whatever the mother ingested, the baby did likewise. She also knew of women who had lost their babies because of taking too much laudanum and other such drugs. Tea and toast and a little salt meat if it would stay down were all she had to prescribe.

St. John was less supportive than Alex needed him to be. Having declared his plans, he had blithely assumed that financial matters were settled. Though it was true they would have some lean months after paying the rent in January, this bothered him less than the idea that Alex was going out to work for payment. The streak of impracticality from his upbringing ran deep and grated hard on Alex's already ragged nerves. The fact that she was probably correct in her calculations that they would not survive without added income fired his resentment and made it difficult for him to be sympathetic about the discomfort of her pregnancy. He longed for the months to pass and the racing season to begin, and in preparation for it, he read all the items he could find on the current crop of colts and fillies, and sought out old cronies who were wise in the ways of the race course. He wandered further and further afield on Sir Arthur and even took the Long Ferry to London for sales at Tattersalls and other activities connected with race horses. Alex would have liked to accompany him to London now and then, but he did not ask her, and her own duties kept her so busy, it would have been hard to find time in any case.

St. John had never been given to much introspection, and he found his mixed feelings hard to interpret. Alex still had the power to move him deeply with her beauty and wit, and when he contemplated life without her, he felt as if he were on the edge of a frightening void. But at the same time, her pregnancy had subtly altered his desire; his blood would rise at the sight or touch or scent of her, even at the sound of her husky voice when he couldn't see her, but then desire seemed to seep away as the reality of her physical state impressed itself on him. Though she did not complain, her queasiness in the morning reminded him too much of the wretched wailing months of Florence's pregnancy, and he felt uneasy when he made love to her and remembered that his child grew inside her. He knew there were men who found that highly erotic, but he was not one of them. Somewhere deep inside was the persistent haunting thought that Alex would die as Florence had, and that was so terrifying, he tried not to acknowledge it at all. It never occurred to him that sharing his fear with Alex might have helped them both.

Alex found comfort from an unexpected source. Though she did not discuss her personal problems with him, she was delighted and grateful that Boston had, from the day he had carted her possessions to the cottage, become a frequent visitor. He staunchly ignored his mother's disapproval, and he provided a link with Caton, assuring Alex that her father did care even if he were unable to show it. Boston adored the twins and got on well with Mavis and Timothy, so his presence was never an intrusion. If he saw problems between his sister and St. John, he never gave any indication of it.

In truth, the cottage was filled with so much more love and warmth than there was at home, Boston was drawn to it like a moth to flame. And sometimes he brought Dora, having made it very clear that if she loved him, she would also accept his sister's way of life. Dora had no problem with this; she was kind and normally easy-going, one of her few strong dislikes being Margaret Thaine. She was prepared on principle to like anyone Margaret had abused, and anyway, she admired Alexandria for what she perceived to be romantic courage.

Boston and Dora helped to make Christmas Eve more festive, and Alex was touched by the gift Boston brought from their father. Though it was money, it was not a cold gift at all. Caton had written:

My dearest Daughter,

Boston has told me that you are carrying a child. I hope he or she will be born with your beauty and courage. No child could ask for more. I have heard from your grandmother how hard you are working, and I know, having set your course, you will do no less, but I beg you allow this gift to ease your way. I would I could do more. May it be a happy Christmas for you and your husband.

The brief words said so much, most of all in his reference to St. John as her husband. And even St. John could not object to the spirit of the gift. Caton had chosen the amount carefully to avoid insult. Briefly Alex remembered Caleb Jennings doing the same thing and then quickly thrust the thought away.

"Why does Father stay with our mother?" Alex asked Boston softly.

"Out of habit, out of a wish to avoid conflict, which there would surely be if he were to try to leave. Mother likes her status as a married woman too much. But most of all I believe because he thinks so little of himself, he thinks he deserves her. Poor Father."

Alex caught St. John's eye and the same thought flashed

between them with eerie clarity—their marriage had its problems, but they were so much better off than their two sets of parents. It was worth fighting to keep and improve what they had. Alex saw the image of St. John as he had been earlier in the evening, sitting on the floor and playing with his children. Both of the twins were very active crawlers now, Flora taking the lead in bold rushes along the floor, and they babbled incessantly, seeming to understand each other. But Blaine had definitely begun to say recognizable words, and "Pa-pa" had caused such a look of loving wonder on St. John's face, Alex turned shivery thinking of it.

St. John felt the warmth of her smile as if she had touched him, and suddenly he wanted her with the old hunger and could scarcely wait until their guests had left.

Alex was very tired and would have preferred that he just hold her, but she accepted his lovemaking with all the enthusiasm she could muster, stroking his lean frame and returning his kisses, opening her body to his hard thrusts. And just for an instant, she felt the strange, building pressure beginning to melt into something different, but whatever it was to have been eluded her as St. John spent himself in her and rolled to the side.

"I love you," he mumbled, and his hand rested on her abdomen, acknowledging the further bond of the child as he fell asleep. For the first time she felt the odd flutter of life moving inside her. It was enough.

✍ Chapter 21 ✍

In late autumn, the drought had given way to bitter gales and threatening floods across the country, and the dawn of the new year brought more of the same.

It infuriated St. John that Alex insisted on going out in the bad weather when she was needed, but he had no effective weapons to fight it. The proof of her success was in much of the food they ate and in the small but growing hoard of coins that kept them from debt.

Sometimes when someone came from an outlying farm, he brought a cart and transported Alex back and forth, but often the trip was on foot in punishing weather. Alex insisted it was keeping her fit; St. John thought it was overtiring her, but again he was forced to concede in the matter of a mount—even up with him on Sir Arthur, she was in more danger than if she walked, for the horse never ceased to shy in the shrieking wind, as indeed most horses did. In fact, Alex would have preferred that he not ride Sir Arthur either under such conditions, and so they had made an uneasy peace about it, each going his or her own way.

Secretly Alex craved his approval, rather than his reluctant tolerance, even more than she was willing to admit to herself. She was working hard to establish herself as a trusted wise-woman in an old tradition, and she was succeeding. At first many had trusted her only with their livestock, presenting their horses and cows with cuts, sores, fevers, and swollen bellies, and patiently she treated them, always being perfectly honest when she could not determine a cause or when an illness or injury was beyond her skill, and always aware that nature was her best ally, so often needing only the proper food, rest, and cleanliness to complete the cure.

Word got about that Alexandria Thaine—and the kindest people added Carrington to her name—was nearly the equal of her grandmother and was not above herself but willing to come and help no matter what the hour or how severe the weather. Many who had been tempted to pity or condemn the girl for her liaison with her dead sister's husband found themselves respecting her instead and remembering that they had liked her even as a child; she had always been more like Virginia Thaine than like her own mother or her sister, they recalled. And as they watched her work with their livestock and then with their children and themselves, they forgot that she was not yet sixteen years old; she became ageless in the tradition of all wise-women.

For Alex, the contacts with people outside her household were very important; they made her feel as if she were not totally cut off from the world by her decision to stay with St. John. Letting Mavis and Tim do any needed shopping there, she seldom ventured into Gravesend unless she was summoned to a patient, which was not often, as many in the town scorned the old ways and used physicians. She would have liked to visit her father, but aside from going to him to thank him for the Christmas gift, she stayed away, knowing that someone would tell her mother if she made a habit of going there, and then it would go hard for her father. She had invited him to come to the cottage whenever he liked, but he had not availed himself of the invitation. He seemed more defeated than ever before.

The countryfolk became not only her patients but her friends, giving her a vital sense of self and worth. And in return, she gave them not only her skill, but her involvement. She cared deeply about their joys and sorrows and made no attempt to ease her burden by developing detachment.

And the joys and sorrows, the triumphs and tragedies seemed to interweave in a strange harmony, some inevitable music beyond judgments of good or evil. It was totally inexplicable to her why Mary Bevil—lovely, valiant, and only twenty-four years old—should die of the consumption she had fought so courageously for years in the same week that Farmer Timmons, an elderly tyrant who had made the lives of his wife, children, and grandchildren miserable for years, should survive a fall from his barn roof that should have proved lethal.

"What cannot be changed must be accepted," the simple words her grandmother had tried to impress on her from the beginning still proved a hard lesson.

Again in the short space of one week, she labored over the Darnell baby, never ceasing the cold bathing and the minute amounts of decoction of white willow bark until the high fever came down and the child slept peacefully. It was the young couple's first child, and they were profoundly grateful. Alex was as proud of the eggs, cider, cheese, and wheaten bread they insisted she take as if she had been paid in gold sovereigns.

Yet three days later Simon Bentley died. Simon had spent most of his life in the coal pits of Northumbria, beginning when he was a small child. But he had dreamed of a softer corner of England and had helped his son, the only surviving child of five, to begin a new life in the Southeast, in the garden shire. Simon had continued to work as a miner until he was sure that his son and daughter-in-law were able to survive on the land, and then he had come to live with them, a welcome addition to their family, endlessly patient with his two young grandchildren and with the orchard and the market garden that were the heart of the dream. But Simon had had less than two years in Kent.

Alex had known he was dying the moment she had met him. She had been summoned to the Bentley home in December, right before Christmas. Simon looked to be in his seventies when in fact he was twenty years younger. Because he had worked in the deep pits, dug as the surface coal gave out, the mines had taken a cruel toll, leaving him emaciated, twisted in his joints, and coughing his lungs away, and yet his faded blue eyes were serene, his manner as kind and courtly as if he were suffering no disability and had all the time in the world.

Hesitantly she had admitted that his illness was quite beyond her skill but that she would be more than willing to summon her grandmother.

Simon had politely refused, saying he liked the look of her, and in any case, he well knew his time was short. Summoning any aid at all had only been for the benefit of his son and daughter-in-law who were having a much harder time accepting the truth than he was.

Alex gave him syrups to ease the coughing and to help him sleep, but more, she gave him her time, sitting with him, listening to his thick dialect when he had the breath to talk, talking in turn when he did not. His family was grateful because he always brightened when Alex visited. She reminded him of his wife, Emma, who had been dead for years, not in the way she looked, Simon explained, but in something of the spirit. Gradually, Alex had come to realize that Simon, despite his humble origins, lived very much in the spirit, viewing life with enjoyment and more than a little amusement, and paying little attention to the weakness of his flesh. He was quite willing to leave his body when it was time, and Alex knew it was fitting, but she, like the younger Bentleys, was less willing than he that he should die.

She was with him and his family until very near the end, and then the faded eyes opened, and he looked right at her. His "Thank 'e" was more the shape of his mouth than the sound of the words, but she understood the benediction and the dismissal. She managed to smile at him before she slipped away.

The night was dark, the wind blowing icy rain, and she knew she should probably wait until young Mr. Bentley could escort her home, but her control was slipping, and more than anything she wanted to be enfolded in St. John's warmth. It was only a few miles. She did not worry about meeting owlers (reported to be more numerous than ever due to the returning military men who could find no work). She would take care, and in any case, she was well known in the district now and would not be suspected of informing.

Tears blinded her more than the rain. She was haunted by the knowledge that Simon, who had so loved the sun and the green growing things of the earth, should have spent nearly all his life below in the darkness of the mines.

"Heard nowt 'bout leavin' this earth alive, 'spect thee'd give me secret did thee know."

She almost laughed thinking of the sly teasing way he had chided her when she had yet again suggested consulting someone else about his condition. It had taken her a moment to translate, for his North Country accent made the words roll together. His expression had been peaceful, even merry, and there had not been the slightest trace of fear.

She reminded herself of that now, but it didn't help, the tears just came faster. Her ankle twisted sharply under her, and she fell.

She was very cold, and she had an odd sensation of floating. Very clearly she heard the heavy rushing of swans' wings and then their loud calling voices. It was very important to distinguish them from the small quiet ones. "But wild swans, all of them," she murmured, satisfied with the observation. "Rane, oh Rane, see them flying!"

"It's more sleet than rain, and the only thing that's gone flying is you." Despite the gentle humor in his voice, she could hear the fear that made it unsteady. "Wake up, Alex! Wake up, sweetheart. I need to know how badly hurt you are."

St. John, not Rane; Rane did not call her sweetheart. She shook her head trying to focus her thoughts, and pain lanced through her skull, making her groan involuntarily.

She heard St. John's gasp of dismay and felt his arm come around her, cradling her as she struggled to sit up.

"Sinje, it's all right. I'm dizzy from hitting my head, but I'm all right. Just give me a moment." She was reassured to feel no cramps that might indicate damage to the baby, but her flexing of various muscles led to another start of pain. She was quite sure her ankle wasn't broken, but neither was it going to support her. It was already beginning to swell, and now that she was more alert, she could feel it throbbing right up her leg.

"I seem to have wrenched my ankle. I remember now, it twisted and I went down. How ever did you find me?" She asked the question to gain time; it occurred to her that it was going to be difficult for St. John to help her if she couldn't stand on her own two feet.

But St. John was no less aware of the difficulties than she, and he dismissed the question with a brief explanation. "It got so late, and the weather was foul. I was worried. I was on my way to the Bentley farm when I saw a heap of rags, or rather, Sir Arthur did." And nearly dumped me on the road with you, he added silently. "Alex, I'm not sure I can manage this. I hate to leave you alone, but I think I ought to get help."

She couldn't bear the anxiety and defeat in his voice. "No, we can do it. If you can help me get up, and if Sir Arthur will behave for a minute or so, until I'm in the saddle, then we can find a step up for you."

If she hadn't been hurting so, she would have laughed. Between them they had three good legs and three arms, which added up to one and a half clumsy people. It was a tricky business for St. John to hold the reins and use the same arm to help her. She came up slowly, clinging to him and getting her sound ankle under her, but the world whirled and tilted so rapidly, she slumped against him until it stopped. Then came the problem of standing on her bad ankle while she stepped up into the saddle.

"Sinje, this is going to take a bit of timing. I fear I won't be able to stand long on my ankle," she admitted, "so give me the reins and then put your hand out, and I'll step up on it."

"Christ, Alex! I don't think this is going to work."

"It is. I don't want to wait in the cold any longer." To emphasize her point, her teeth were beginning to chatter.

Holding onto the reins in one hand and gripping the

saddle with the other, Alex clenched her jaw, and quickly, before she could lose her courage, she stepped up on St. John's hand, throwing her bad leg over the horse at nearly the same instant. She choked back a cry and slumped in the saddle, willing herself not to lose consciousness as her head throbbed in unison with her ankle. Sir Arthur pranced nervously, but St. John was at his head, controlling him, and the horse settled down, seeming to understand that this was not the time for trouble making.

A little way along, St. John found a tumbled stone wall and mounted from there. Alex leaned back against him in relief, and he cradled her as well as he could while using his hand to guide the horse. It was a miserable, wet couple who arrived back at the cottage, but there was triumph in it, too. St. John had not needed help in the rescue, though now he welcomed it from Mavis and Timothy who came on the run at his shout.

Once they were in the house, Alex looked at the three anxious faces and summoned the strength to reassure them. "My head and my ankle ache, but nothing is broken, and the baby is fine." She saw some of the tension ease from St. John's face and knew he had been afraid even to ask. "A hot cup of tea and a warm bed will set me to rights. I do not need my grandmother to be called out in this wicked weather."

The three knew she was prepared to exhaust herself further in stubbornness if they did not comply. And Mavis and Timothy proved quite adept at giving aid. Mavis bathed the ankle in cool water, then Timothy bound it with professional skill, just enough to ease the aching.

In a very short time, Alex found herself warmed from the tea and tucked into bed, having been carried upstairs by St. John and Timothy. Still looking worried, St. John bathed the bruise on her forehead.

"It's only a bad bump, Sinje, not a fracture of the skull. I know quite well who I am, where I am, and who you are. And I'm sleepy for very good reasons. You must be, too; do come to bed." She stayed awake until she felt his familiar weight and warmth against her.

"Thank you for coming to find me, my love," she murmured softly, and felt his gentle kiss on her cheek.

"I could not bear it if something happened to you."

As she drifted off, she thought of how odd it was that she had thought of Rane, not St. John, as she had regained consciousness, and she wondered if there really had been swans going over. She burrowed closer to her husband, and the baby moved quite vigorously inside her.

"It is a strong child indeed." St. John whispered.

The next morning he summoned Virginia who concurred with Alex's own diagnosis but insisted on a week of rest. When Alex protested, her grandmother snapped, "You'll be no use to anyone if you fall ill! And you were tired enough without adding a crack on the head. I don't know what Mr. Bentley was thinking of to let you go wandering off in the dark."

"He didn't. I just left. Old Simon was dying, and we'd already said our own farewell." She caught sight of St. John's face over Virginia's shoulder and was glad she'd explained—she suspected his next visit would have been to the Bentleys to give them hell.

In the days that followed, St. John was as attentive as Alex could have wished, spending much time with her, reading to her because a lingering headache made it hard for her to do it herself, helping to control the enormous energy of the twins when they were in the room, and generally making himself useful. She felt wrapped in his warmth and caring, and privately she admitted to herself that the little accident might have been the best thing that had happened to her in some time. She had been more tired than she knew and found for once in her life, it was pure bliss to stay in bed and rest. The interlude was made even better by St. John's presence.

But by the fifth day she was restless. Her ankle was much better, her headache gone, and she was growing stiff from being in bed. St. John made no protest when she got up because she promised she would still take it easy, but when she began to peruse her and Virginia's notes and to thumb through the worn herbals, his good nature vanished.

"You can't mean to go on with this!" he exclaimed incredulously, the sweep of his arm indicating the books and papers spread around her.

"Of course I mean to go on," she said with quiet resolution. "Sinje, I simply fell down because of my own clumsiness. You surely can't think that would end my work."

"I do indeed, Alexandria, you are carrying my child, and if you don't care about it, I do!"

Her own temper rose to meet his. "That is cruel, and you know it. I do care about the child, very much." She just stopped herself from adding, *much more than you do.* "But it is a natural thing, not an illness. And I care about my work and the people who need me. I need them as much. I have no intention of abandoning them until I am too big to get around easily, and then I shall be back to work as soon as possible."

"Nothing I say will change your mind, will it?" he asked slowly.

She shook her head. He turned on his heel and left her feeling as if something precious had just been shattered. She knew he was in part truly concerned about her health, but the greater part was still his objection to her working to help support the family. And she simply could not allow his foolish notions of pride to threaten what little security she provided. She trusted that once he was back at his "work" at the races, it would not chafe him so that she, too, had duties.

By March she was in her seventh month, and though the high-waisted dresses were well suited to her condition, her pregnancy was quite visible particularly because the rest of her remained slender. Her walks over the countryside and the active play with the twins at home kept her trim despite the hearty meals she consumed, the morning sickness having departed to leave what she judged an enormous appetite in its wake.

There was more talk about her and St. John now; there was bound to be with her swollen belly giving proof of what they had been doing. Her cynical amusement extended to the knowledge that it was certainly a way to sort friends from enemies.

Her mother had left her alone for so long, Alex had ceased to worry about what she might do, but now she discovered her complacency had been naive. She suspected Margaret had felt compelled to do something when she had learned her daughter was pregnant. And obviously what she had done was to spread the word far and wide that she was the injured party, betrayed by a thankless and immoral child.

Alex wondered if her mother was pleased with the meager results she had achieved. The fact was that few liked Margaret Thaine, and those who condemned her daughter as she did had already sided with Margaret when Alex had gone to live with St. John; they were not further shocked by the conception of a child since they already believed Alex wanton and thought this latest development to be no more than the girl's just deserts. They were mostly of the town anyway, and Alex had little to do with them.

And over it all reigned the quietly powerful presence of Virginia Thaine. She was respected even by those who did not like her, and she was feared. She did not seek battles, but she did not back down when they were forced upon her. And she was unrelenting when she thought wrong was being committed. The most powerful weapon she possessed was her immunity. She had lived too long to pay attention to the opinion of others. As long as she was easy with her own conscience, she was satisfied. She cared nothing for the sly innuendos of supposedly civilized encounters. If she had something to say, she said it, and her tongue was too often sharply accurate. Few cared to test their prowess against her. Her saving grace was that she preferred a peaceful existence and did not seek targets.

Alex continued to be grateful that her grandmother was her ally. But she also realized that the withdrawn life she and St. John lived contributed further to their isolation. Only occasionally did she mind. Her work kept her busy, and most of the people on the land were not like the townsfolk.

The farmers were, for the most part, calmly accepting of her altered state. The women of these families continued to toil in house and field while they were pregnant, so it did not seem odd to them that Alex did also. Many were solicitous of her welfare, urging her to have a cup of tea or fresh milk and a bite of this or that while she was visiting their houses. And many of the women offered advice, some of it so outlandish that Alex had to fight not to laugh outright. The list of rhymes and spells to insure an easy delivery and a healthy child seemed endless.

"Where in the world do they all come from?" Alex asked her grandmother, having just related that the current crop of stories she'd been told included the admonitions that to quarrel with her husband would result in an ugly child and to make sure the number of lumps in the umbilical cord were counted so she'd know how many more children she would have.

"Birth and death, they're the most important events in our lives, and yet we have little control over when they happen, and both are inevitable. The old beliefs, silly as most are, help make people think they have some hand in all of it." Virginia was tolerant of superstition, as long as it did not inflict damage or pain, but she had always kept it very separate from what she did. She did not object if someone chanted a supposedly magical rhyme or said a spell to augment a certain treatment, she just did not employ such devices herself. For Virginia, the plants of the earth were to be studied and used with the same careful skill that one applied to farming or doing accounts or any other sort of work. And she was glad she had impressed the same matter-of-factness on Alexandria. As far as she could tell, the various folk beliefs were making no impression on her granddaughter at all, and that was well since so many of them were nothing short of horrific.

Virginia was skilled enough in midwifery, but it was not a frequent part of her practice. There were others, and one in particular close by, who did nothing else and were kind and proficient. Virginia had promised to assist at the birth of Alex's child, but Dame Sally would be in charge. Alex and Dame Sally liked and respected each other, and that would go far to easing matters.

Virginia considered her most important role to be preparing Alex for childbirth before the event. Alex had no training in midwifery; that would have come later had her life unfolded as Virginia had hoped it would. And now Virginia thought it just as well that Alex had not seen the arduous work that too often ended in death for mother and child.

Though she had not witnessed the reality of it, Alex was aware of the risks; she had to be since her own sister had died, though not at the birth. Alex had helped horses and other domestic livestock to bring forth their young, which was all to the good since animals generally had an easier time of it than humans.

Since Alex did not seem overburdened with fear, Virginia approached her training as practically as she did other projects. She told her that there would be pain but that learning to bend with it and to breathe correctly would make it less and that memory would mitigate it further. She gave her salve with blunt instructions to rub it on her abdomen and perineum to avoid severe stretch marks on the former and tears in the latter during birthing. Alex was not embarrassed by the advice. Discussed this way with her grandmother, her own body became something quite apart from herself, a patient to be treated with care and common sense. Even when she did as instructed, she felt no particular intimacy with her own flesh. She took on less reality for herself as the baby took on more.

As Alex's focus shifted inward, St. John's turned outward. He looked forward to the first race meeting at Newmarket as if it were a lifeline. It was not only his wish to contribute toward the support of his household, but also his need to escape from it. He loved Flora and Blaine, and he wanted his child by Alex to be a healthy one, but he felt overwhelmed by the babies and by the domestic routine. And he still resented Alex's stubborn pursuit of her own way.

In early April a visit from Lord Bettingdon made St. John even more aware of how his own life had changed since his marriages to Florence and then to Alex. Charles William Frederick Hugh Bettingdon, Duke of Almont, Hugh to his close friends, was a man of great wealth and urbanity. St. John had admired him since their carefree days in school together, and he owed him his life nearly as much as he owed those who had cared for him in Gravesend. It was Hugh who had brought him and Timothy home. Hugh also had a beautiful sister, Catherine, who was nearly as wild as her brother, though both of them had done fairly well, considering how early their father had died, leaving Hugh to inherit the wealth, the title, and the responsibilities which included a kindhearted but feather-brained mother.

Lord Bettingdon spent the night in Gravesend, staying at an inn so that he and St. John could get an early start for Newmarket in the morning, traveling in the duke's private coach.

The duke came for dinner at the cottage, and Alex could not have sensed the danger more clearly had he been pointing a pistol at her. In the first place, it was clear that St. John would have preferred that his friend never visit his home at all, but he could think of no way to avoid it without breaching the rules of civility. And in the second, it was equally clear that Lord Bettingdon had already judged Alex a scheming bitch like her sister.

Tall, dark in contrast to St. John's fairness, well muscled and dressed in impeccably tailored clothes, Hugh Bettingdon was a handsome man. The same chronological age as St. John, he was years older in experience; his arrogant features already had a hard cast of cynicism as if nothing would ever surprise him again. And when he was introduced to Alex, his black eyes were still and cold though his mouth smiled.

Alex immediately felt shabbily dressed and grotesquely pregnant, and she thought that while both were true, she would not have been so conscious of her state had he been warm in his greeting. And then she was furious that he had so thoroughly judged and condemned her before they even met. The gold wedding band she wore meant nothing to him.

She straightened her weary shoulders and gave him the same up-and-down perusal he had given her. She had the satisfaction of seeing a flicker of reaction in his eyes.

"It is kind of you to have me in your home, Mrs. Carrington," he said, and ever so slightly his voice hesitated on the "Mrs." Either he had known of the law preventing their legal marriage or St. John had told him, and either way it was unspeakably rude of him to betray his knowledge.

"Any friend of my husband is welcome here, my Lord Duke," Alex replied. She emphasized "husband" and inclined her head with exaggerated graciousness as if he were not the sort who would normally be allowed in the house but was being granted a special privilege on account of St. John.

Again his eyes flickered, and the faintest trace of a smile curved his mouth before it was quickly gone.

You wish to duel, very well, my Lord Duke, Alex thought, and she looked forward to it with grim relish.

They treated each other with elaborate politeness, each aware of what the other was doing, while St. John felt only relief that his friend and Alex seemed to be getting along quite well.

But both Hugh and Alex dropped their guards when the discussion turned to Hugh's stable, which was extensive and full of race course champions. And Hugh's face lost its aloof cast as Alex offered remedies for various ailments in his horses. The basic good sense of the recommendations impressed him greatly; he was only too familiar with the outlandish and often dangerous treatments too often offered by those who professed to know how to heal the beasts.

When he bid the Carringtons good-night, his attitude was radically different from when he had arrived. "I am pleased to find my friend in such good hands," he said, and now his courtliness was not a sham. It was, Alex guessed, as close as Lord Bettingdon would ever come to an apology.

"And I am pleased to know he will be in your company when he leaves here tomorrow," she returned with equal grace. They smiled at each other in perfect accord.

Knowing that St. John would be with the duke did make it easier for Alex to bid him a calm farewell the next morning. And she tried very hard not to resent the fact that he was going off so happily, leaving her when she was so heavily pregnant with his child.

St. John was conscious of little else except that he was reentering the world he had been born to, a sporting gentleman among other sporting gentlemen. He had not felt so content since his return from Waterloo. He did not notice the thoughtful study Hugh was making of him.

✺ Chapter 22 ✺

Though the baby was not due until the end of May, by the beginning of the month Alex had drastically curtailed her activities. She was just too big, clumsy, and short of breath to be much use, and Virginia was caring for most of her patients.

Alex spent much of her time playing with the twins,

though she was glad Mavis and Timothy were there to chase after the pair when necessary. Flora and Blaine chattered incessantly now, sometimes in recognizable language, sometimes in their own, and having more or less acquired the skill of walking, they seemed to be everywhere at once, in constant motion from the time they awakened until they slept. Despite the fact that they were not identical and had distinct personalities, they played so much in unison, Alex wondered how separate they really were. Sometimes it seemed as if they thought as one child instead of two. Having no twin and no sibling closer than Boston, she could not imagine what it was like. And then she remembered how close she had sometimes felt to Rane. But thoughts of the Falconers were not to be dwelt upon, for memories of those carefree days in Clovelly were too apt to make her feel discontent. Correspondence with the Falconers had become so infrequent as to be nearly nonexistent. They knew nothing of her new status, and that was the way she wanted it.

The twins were healthy, she was healthy, and the household was well run. Alex knew there were many reasons to be grateful, but the discontent persisted and with it resentment against St. John. She felt limited by her condition and too often bored despite the antics of the twins. She longed to be going about the countryside again. And the picture of St. John enjoying himself with his titled friends did not please her. He had gone to the Newmarket Craven Meeting which had begun on April 15, to run a week, and because the distance was too great for traveling back and forth, he had stayed on for the Newmarket First Spring Meeting which commenced on April 29. It was as planned, but Alex had secretly hoped he would return early.

He was not there when she went into labor early on the second day of May. The baby was not due for several weeks, but with the first contraction, Alex had no doubt that it was coming. She was more relieved than anything else. She was tired of being so big and uncomfortable, and she calmly did as her grandmother and Dame Sally told her, reassured by their insistence that the baby would be fine even though it was coming early. That it might not have turned properly was something they did not tell her.

It was a long labor, and it hurt more than Alex had thought possible, but she breathed as her grandmother bade her and flowed with the pain until she was so much a part of it, it no longer seemed to be a separate entity attacking her. And in the morning of the third of May she drifted into a sky of swans, the small, quietly musical ones of faraway, and was soothed and charmed by their presence until her grandmother called her back sharply. "Alexandria, pay attention, bear down now!"

Virginia had begun to fear that Alex was growing too exhausted to deliver the child and had felt her slipping away to some other place, but the baby presented itself properly, head and shoulders quickly followed by the perfectly formed body of a girl.

"You have a daughter," Virginia announced, laying the baby on Alex's stomach as Dame Sally cut and tied the cord and beamed as if this was the first child she had ever helped into the world.

There had been no tearing, the afterbirth was delivered easily, and aside from feeling sore and exhausted, Alex had suffered no damage from the delivery. The baby was a trifle small, but she was breathing well, and Alex fell asleep still marveling that she had produced such a child. She was already quite sure the baby was going to look like her father, and at that moment she even forgave St. John his absence.

However, her euphoria diminished when she discovered she could not nurse her child. She simply did not have an adequate supply of milk, and all she achieved from her efforts to feed the infant were sore nipples and a squalling daughter. Mavis grumbled that if she herself had kept nursing the twins there would be milk for the newborn, but since that wasn't the case, Alex snapped at her to hold her tongue unless she had something useful to offer. She immediately apologized, but Mavis had taken no offense; she had eyes to see that Alex was disappointed in not being able to feed the wee one and more by the fact that her husband wasn't with her.

None of them liked the idea of bringing a stranger into the house, so they tried cow's milk, knowing they would have to find a wet nurse immediately if that didn't work. But to everyone's relief, the baby thrived on her new diet.

St. John arrived home a week after the birth and was stunned to find that his new daughter had preceded him. He felt more than a little guilt for the extra time he had spent at the course socializing at the close of the meeting, but he had also won his wagers on several races. That he was not returning empty handed buoyed his spirits.

Alex was already up and nearly back to her usual level of energy, and she greeted him without reproach, having decided the recriminations would only prove her to be too much like Florence. She was rewarded by St. John's obvious relief and his gentle welcome of his new daughter.

Lord Bettingdon had remained in the background for the reunion between the couple, but when he came to be presented to the new Carrington, Alex was stunned by the warm approval she saw in his eyes. It was so different from the coldness of their first meeting. She realized that little escaped the duke's notice, and he had fully expected Alex to rage at St. John for not being there at the birth. She was doubly glad she had not.

They named the child Christiana Virginia, the Christiana for St. John's maternal grandmother who had gifted him with Alex's ring and the small inheritance they so needed. It was a wry tribute to the two relatives who had proved the most helpful to them. And Lord Bettingdon professed himself more than ready to stand as godparent. Since the church would not sanctify their marriage, Alex could have foregone the christening altogether, but St. John did not feel that way, and so again she refrained from saying what she really felt. Boston and Dora, soon to be married, were pleased to be the other godparents. Neither of the Carringtons minded that usually there were two godmothers and one godfather for a girl child, vice versa for a boy.

Money and power certainly had their uses, Alex discovered. Lord Bettingdon provided the clergyman for the ceremony, a priest who was indebted to Hugh for his living. And the christening was recorded in the register of Stone Church, six miles from Gravesend. It was where Virginia had been married and where she still went to worship when she felt in need of the old traditions. It was a grand edifice for so small a village as Stone, and even though its days of glory were long past, it still had a stately beauty. And best of all, it was not the church in Gravesend where Margaret Thaine worshipped and Reverend Tynewater officiated.

But not even Hugh's influence could force the church to allow Alex and St. John to marry. Watching Alex dress Christiana for the christening, St. John said, "Hugh pled our case with the highest authority, the Archbishop of Canterbury, but no dispensation was granted."

Alex looked at him inquiringly, thinking that for some odd reason he had waited this long to tell her that the christening would not go forward after all, but then it dawned on her that he was speaking of their marriage. Suddenly he looked as angry as he had after his interview with the Reverend Tynewater. He was not only furiously angry, but beyond that she could sense his feeling of betrayal. Even though he had been disinherited, he still cared about the trappings of his class, and he expected institutions such as the church to serve, not thwart him.

Cradling Christiana in her arms, Alex spoke softly in counterpoint to St. John's rage. "The archbishop is not the highest authority. You and I and this child, all of us bound together by love, we are higher. And above us whatever God there is surely cannot be limited in His benevolence by manmade rules. My love, I told you before and I will tell you again and again, I do not need the church's sanction to be your wife." She did not say it aloud, but inwardly the thought ran on that it was he who needed the church's approval. She wished it were not so.

St. John's anger faded in face of Alex's calm and his daughter's happy gurgling. He gave each of them a kiss and his smile was easy. "Two beautiful ladies to escort; it would be difficult to find a more fortunate man in all the land," he announced with laughing gallantry.

Hugh presented Alex with a set of exquisitely wrought silver cups as a christening gift, and she suspected he would have liked to do a good deal more. He was a complex man but she sensed in him a real attraction to the simple life of the cottage. He doted on the children and was always gravely polite to Mavis and Timothy, not failing to see them as individuals despite his lofty position. And sometimes she thought he was subtly trying to alter St. John's behavior, deliberately drawing attention to Alex when he thought St. John was neglecting her.

When she tried to thank Hugh for his intervention with the archbishop he would have none of it. "I was hardly successful," he pointed out ruefully. "Clerkish minds are difficult to move be they in the church or the state. If they will be so obdurate and uncharitable, it is on their heads, not on yours or St. John's."

It would, she thought, be the best of all possible worlds if St. John could share Hugh's attitude.

Too often now, Alex wondered whether St. John thought of her apart from the rest of the household at all. More and more he seemed to regard her as just another part of the routine that cared for his children and provided him with a home between races. It was as if their closeness at the baby's christening had never been. She suspected that the knowledge that the highest authority of the church had refused permission for the marriage had subtly preyed on St. John's mind until he was beginning to see the marriage itself, rather than the law against it, as the offense. And beyond continuing to love him, she could not see a way to change his attitude.

Her birthday had slipped by in the birth of Christiana Virginia, but her grandmother and Boston had remembered it by presenting her with some much needed dress lengths. And though he still remained apart, her father had paid for the services of a local dressmaker who would come at Alex's convenience to measure her and discuss styles. She was not only touched by the gifts, she was grateful, for the clothing was much needed to replenish her depleted wardrobe. St. John's winnings did not amount to enough for any luxuries. Aside from his vague assurances that matters would improve as the season went on, they did not discuss it. Alex realized how ignorant he was regarding the cost of everything these days; his only concern was that he had won more than he lost. His contribution to the communal purse would never have been enough without her earnings. And when he belatedly added a lovely length of apricot silk to her birthday gifts, she was sure that Hugh had been responsible; she hoped he had not also helped to pay for it. Clearly she remembered the suddenly intent look on his face when Boston had teased her about the uselessness of dress goods if one did not take the time to have them made into clothing.

Hugh presented her with a perfectly proper gift of books that nonetheless seemed even more intimate than the apricot silk from her husband. There was a beautifully printed and illustrated herbal, poems by Coleridge and Byron, as well as some current novels. Obviously each book had been carefully chosen for her.

She wished St. John was showing her the same attention. As the summer progressed she felt more and more lonesome for him, even when he was home, and that was seldom enough as he was at Epsom for the Woodcot, the Coburg, the Oaks, the Hedley Stakes, and the Derby at the end of May and early June, and at Ascot Heath by the second week of June. July brought the Newmarket July Meeting at the beginning of the month and the Goodwood races at the end.

Alex's days were an exhausting round of caring for her patients and giving attention to Christiana and the twins, and she tried to use the fatigue to cease thinking. But the thoughts still seeped through the blur. The race courses were like a drug to St. John, something quite beyond his professed purpose of making a living. It was not the gambling; it was the return to people of his own kind. Disinherited third son he might be, but at the race courses he was still entitled to associate with others of the nobility, and he thrived on it. His luck and skill at picking winning horses, while not phenomenal because he did not have a fortune to risk, allowed him to stay ahead of the game, but more and more of his winnings were swallowed by bills from London tailors and bootmakers, by the inns he stayed in when no invitations to private homes were forthcoming, and by the hospitality at taverns where he entertained friends and acquaintances who had treated him in kind. He never said it aloud, but it was as if he had announced, "You want to work and count the pennies, so be it. You be responsible for this household. My life is elsewhere."

The prospect of shouldering that responsibility alone terrified Alex, for the agricultural depression had continued to deepen, aggravated by a cold, wet summer that was bound to ruin harvests. Even the food payments she received had diminished, and few of the people who summoned her had coins to pay.

She did not want to consider it, but deep inside she wrestled with the prospect of ending her "marriage" to St. John. She kept telling herself that he simply needed time to find his place in the scheme of things. But eleven years younger than he, she felt decades older, and she was not sure she could wait for him to grow up. The bitter irony of it all was that beyond the need of the children for a home and family, the greatest impetus for her to stay with St. John was her mother's conviction that it was a sinful union doomed to failure. The thought of Margaret's gloating was enough to make Alex redouble her efforts to hold on.

But in August, she began to doubt that even the specter of a self-satisfied Margaret could sustain her. When St. John had resumed his marital privileges some six weeks after the birth, there had been in his lovemaking, as in all other aspects of his life at home, an abstracted air, as if his mind and his interest lay elsewhere. Alex had had to forgive him that since she often felt the same way about it. But now it took on a new dimension, an air of insult that was no less wounding for its subtlety. Nothing was said openly, but small aspects of their lives were altered. There were no longer endearments from him, and when he had taken his pleasure, he slept slightly apart, the heat of him but not his flesh touching her. He no longer brought her flowers. And when she spoke to him, he seemed impatient, as if something of much greater importance was demanding his attention. It made it more and more difficult for her to approach him on anything but the most important matters, and that led to less communication between them than there had ever been before. But worst of all was the attitude of his friends.

St. John, having seen that Hugh was charmed by the rustic life rather than being appalled by the reduced circumstances, felt emboldened to invite other friends to visit. But his casual attitude toward Alex led many of his friends to assume that despite the children involved, St. John saw this as only a temporary arrangement that could be abandoned when he tired of his young mistress. Some were too polite to make use of the knowledge, but others were not so restrained.

Alex was slow to understand the full import of what was going on, for she did nothing to encourage any advances and was abstracted by the amount of work she had to do, a load made heavier when St. John's friends were visiting.

It was Mr. Dodds who brought everything into focus. Alex detested him on sight. Education had failed to make him a gentleman. He dressed and acted the part of the tasteless dandy. He was the wealthy son of a cotton mill owner in Lancashire, and he made up for a vast lack of presence by the equally vast expenditure of ready coin. His oily blond hair and splotchy skin were offensive enough, but his dirty fingernails fixed Alex's attention even more. She could not imagine what he did to acquire such grime since work was obviously not part of his routine. She was appalled that St. John would have anything to do with him, but when she timidly broached the subject, St. John brushed her off.

"He's a good enough fellow. And he pays his debts. I won a good sum from him on a wager at Goodwood."

"And that is all you require of those you invite into our home?" She wished she could take the words back the instant she said them.

"I didn't realize there were specific requirements for those I would invite here. Would you care to tell me what they are?"

"Reasonable civility and clean fingernails!" Alex retorted, suddenly goaded beyond endurance, and her answer was so ridiculous she was tempted to laugh, but the impulse died as she saw that no warmth flickered in St. John's cold eyes.

And because of that exchange, she was afraid to tell him that from the first day of his visit, Mr. Dodds had looked at her too long, crowded her too closely. As he extended his time in Gravesend from a brief stopover to several days, she began to suspect that she was the reason. She was out seeing patients for most of the day and tried to avoid him when he visited at night and took supper with them. But it was increasingly difficult, though St. John seemed not to notice at all. She wished she could seek shelter with Mavis and Timothy, who refused to eat with them when there were guests, but she didn't want to involve them.

She saw the unheralded arrival of Lord Bettingdon as a miracle of deliverance, sure that even Mr. Dodds would behave in his august presence.

"It is so good to see you, Hugh!" she exclaimed, long since on a first name basis with him. He had not been to Gravesend since the middle of July.

"I have to make certain my godchild is well," he replied easily, but his eyes searched Alex's face intently, and she blushed under his scrutiny, afraid that he would read the full measure of her distress.

When Hugh learned that they had another guest due for supper and that he was Mr. Dodds, his manner turned distant, and he suggested he not add to the numbers this night. But Alex pled that he reconsider, assuring him that it would not add to the work of preparing the meal. St. John added his own encouragement, but it was Alex whom Hugh heeded.

Mr. Dodds did not seem at all discomfitted by the presence of the duke, rather he greeted him as if they were the best of friends. Alex could see Hugh bristle with dislike, and under the cloak of formal good manners, his speech was barbed when he addressed Mr. Dodds, which was as seldom as possible.

The twins were not on their best behavior, having started quarreling early in the day and having resumed the battle after their naps. And they were still going at it though they should have been settled for the night, and their voices were whiny with fatigue. Alex was sure at this point Mavis would gladly murder the twins, and she excused herself from the men, leaving them to linger over their port while she went upstairs to the children.

Christiana, sleeping peacefully in spite of the din from her siblings, appeared quite angelic compared to the twins. Alex's private feeling of awe had grown rather than diminished since the birth of her daughter; she still found it difficult to believe she had produced this beautiful scrap of humanity. But she loved the twins as well, even with their faces blotched red from the long siege of shrieking, pinching, and hitting. And she thought how frustrating it must be to be so full of angry feelings even though the initial cause was long forgotten.

"You go on down and have some supper," she told Mavis, who agreed with alacrity, admitting, "I're fair worn out by dem."

Flora and Blaine eyed Alex suspiciously, looking for a new enemy. Alex couldn't help smiling at them. "Well, it's very late, my dears. Would you rather fuss and cry or should I tell you a story?" Mavis was no hand at story-telling.

The twins eyed each other for a moment, and then Blaine nodded gravely. "Story!" he crowed, adding, "Now!" to show that he was still in control.

They loved nursery rhymes and even tried to sing along, so Alex did verse after verse of "London Bridge is Broken Down" for them, and by the time she got to:

Build it up with silver and gold,
    Silver and gold, silver and gold,

Build it up with silver and gold,
  My fair lady.

Silver and gold will be stolen away,
  Stolen away, stolen away,
Silver and gold will be stolen away,
  My fair lady.

their two thin voices had ceased to chirp along with her
and their eyes were closed. Very softly she sang:

Rock-a-bye, Baby;
  Thy cradle is green,
Father's a nobleman,
  Mother's a queen;
And Betty's a lady,
  And wears a gold ring;
And Johnny's a drummer
And drums for the king.

She felt a great well of contentment, finding life so
sweet in that instant that all the rushes and starts of the
day became unimportant when measured against the wondrous presence of the three sleeping children.

She was still dazed by the tide of maternal love as she
left the room, and it took her a startled instant to realize
that Mr. Dodds was waiting for her in the shadowy passage.

"Very pretty," he purred, and there was nothing com-
plimentary in the words.

She made a move to brush past him, unable to credit
that he would try anything with St. John and Lord
Bettingdon just downstairs. But he reached out and grabbed
her, pulling her into a clumsy embrace and smearing her
mouth with his wet lips. She was frozen with revulsion
and incredulity, and then she pushed against him frantically, trying to kick at the same time and finding he was
far stronger than he looked.

He was wrenched from her, and Alex backed away as
Hugh shook Mr. Dodds like a terrier with a rat. She could
hear the man's teeth rattling together, and Hugh's voice
pouring over him, low and vicious. "If you ever come to
this house again or bother Mrs. Carrington in any fashion,
I will kill you. I will find you, and I will kill you. Do you

understand?" He stepped back from the man, waiting for his answer.

Mr. Dodds was not accustomed to being thwarted, and he made a grave error in trying to defend his action. "But she's not Mrs. Carrington, wedding ring or not. She's just his . . ."

Hugh's fist connected with his jaw and sent Mr. Dodds sprawling into unconsciousness.

"Thank you, Hugh, oh, please don't tell St. John!" The words came out in a breathless rush quite unlike her normal voice.

Hugh stared at her in the shadowed light and shook his head to clear it of the rage that had engulfed him. "Why not tell your husband?"

Silently she blessed him for calling St. John her husband with no hesitation, but she could not explain her reluctance for St. John to know what had happened. It was not only that he was one-armed and thus less able than other men to defend his honor; it was also the fear that he would not defend her at all. The shock of Dodds's attack had brought too much clarity. What she had considered innocent flirtatious remarks made by other friends of St. John were in retrospect hardly less insulting than Dodds's physical attack. Somehow St. John had given them leave to treat her as far less than his wife.

"I just do not want any more trouble," she mumbled.

Hugh continued to stare at her, dark eyes glinting, but then he nodded. "If he doesn't catch me disposing of this rubbish, it shall be as you wish."

As easily as if he were lifting no weight at all, he slung Dodds over his shoulder and headed downstairs with him and outside.

Alex found St. John in the little parlor where Hugh had left him. St. John was pleasantly foxed on the port he had consumed. Alex suppressed a shudder at the memory of the liquor on Mr. Dodds's breath.

"Seem to have been deserted," St. John said vaguely, and Alex felt a rush of anger so strong, she had to clamp her jaw tightly to keep from screaming at him.

But Hugh was suddenly behind her, saying smoothly, "Mr. Dodds wasn't feeling quite the thing; he's gone back to his lodgings."

"Thought he stepped out for rather a long time," St. John observed, but he was clearly not interested in the whereabouts of Mr. Dodds, as he immediately launched into a dissertation on the prospects of one of Hugh's horses at Doncaster in September.

Hugh ignored him. "Alexandria, you are looking a trifle pale. May I offer you a glass of port?" He saw her face go even whiter, her green eyes her only color, and he guessed the reason. "Brandy then." His manner brooked no refusal as he poured a stiff measure from the decanter and handed it to her.

She could hardly swallow past the lump in her throat. Undoubtedly this brandy had come from free traders somewhere; she could not imagine Timothy paying full duty prices. Suddenly she wished she were with Rane again, roaming wild and free over the land of Devon. And she knew the wish was cowardice, and there was guilt, for to return to her own childhood would be to leave the twins motherless and Christiana unborn.

❦ Chapter 23 ❦

Rane Falconer felt a great sense of freedom and exhilaration. It was over. He had waited long enough. Alex had been sixteen in May. It was September now, and he was discarding his heavy burden of patience. Alex would surely want time to make up her mind, and he was willing to wait until she was eighteen or even older, but from now on, she would know that he wanted her for his wife.

He had worked hard in the year and a half since his last sight of her, and he had played hard, too, but his love for her had not wavered. He smiled at the inner sound of her name. Alexandria Thaine Falconer.

It was odd to be on a ship making her way so openly

toward London. He had boarded her at Appledore, and she had legitimate business in London, so there was no objection to being boarded by the tidesmen from the customs house at Gravesend should they so choose. This ship had no secret compartments or illegal cargo; she was simply part of the busy river traffic.

Rane had his plan firmly in mind. After leaving his portmanteau at a local inn, he would seek out Virginia Thaine, despite his impatience to see Alex. He had liked the old woman when he met her, and he knew her to be the person closest to Alex. He did not want to speak to Alex's parents yet—he did not like what he knew of how they had treated their youngest child—but he did want an ally, someone with authority in Alex's life to give sanction to the match.

He found Virginia's house with ease and was immediately charmed by the sight of it in daylight, by the gracious trees and the wealth of plants in the gardens around it, by the contented drone of bees and the bird song. The front door was ajar, and a marmalade cat on the doorstep blinked impassively at Rane as he knocked and called out. Hearing no answer, he went in and found warmth and welcome in the wooden floors and furnishings and a pervasive spicy scent of herbs and flowers that reminded him of Alex. But there was no sign of Virginia.

He went outside again and found her in the back gardens, her face shadowed by a broad-brimmed hat as she meticulously trimmed the plants before her. The results of her labors lay in neat piles.

He called to her softly, and she turned, studying him calmly for a moment before she said, "Rane Falconer. You are far from Clovelly. How may I help you?"

He understood that she had immediately thought of free trading and the help she and her husband had given his father and grandfather so many years ago; now she was forthrightly offering aid again.

He grinned at her. "Indeed you may help, Mrs. Thaine, but not in the way you suppose." Suddenly there didn't seem to be any use in approaching the subject obliquely. "I've come to see if Alex will have me to wed. Of course, I realize she is still very young, and I will not press my suit until she's ready, but I want her to . . ."

"The two of you have not corresponded for a long time, have you?" Her voice was strained as she interrupted him, and he was aware that his first impression was wrong; she did not look as ageless and indomitable as she had been three years before. At the moment she looked very old, frail, and sad.

His heart was beating much too fast. "She's not . . . nothing's happened?"

"She's alive and well," she hastened to reassure him, but Rane heard the peculiar twist to the last word.

She drew a deep breath. "Come inside; this will take some telling, and I serve a stout cup of tea."

"From a reliable supplier, I trust," Rane commented, trying to aid in her attempt to lighten the mood, but he knew something was terribly wrong.

The water was already hot in the kettle she kept on the hob, and she brewed a fresh pot of tea and served two cups of it with great concentration, obviously gathering her thoughts. Rane steeled himself to continued patience with great effort.

Finally Virginia shook her head. "I have thought of no way to soften this. Alexandria is married to St. John Carrington and has a child, a daughter, Christiana, born this past May." She could not bring herself to admit that the marriage was not sanctioned by the church; if Rane didn't know that point of law, she was not going to enlighten him. She saw the blank incomprehension on his face swiftly chased by denial.

"She can't be," he stated flatly. "She can't be married. I've waited because she was a child, not yet fifteen when she left Clovelly. She is scarce more now."

"She is not a child any longer. As it is with many women, she left childhood behind quickly for another's need." Her voice was very weary now. "It is hard to tell you how it was when she came home, her sister dead, St. John off to war, and the twins in Margaret's care. Alexandria loved the babes first, and then St. John came home, wounded, from Waterloo. We almost lost him. I think he lived only because Alexandria bade him do so. But he is not the same. He lost an arm and much more because of it. It has made him different, harsher. He was always a man to think more with his body than his mind. But I believe he cares for my granddaughter, perhaps only her, and she is the one who keeps the father with the children."

The silence built between them as Rane tried to assimilate what she had said. The unthinkable had happened. There was no young Alex waiting for him. Another man had taken her, and she had borne his child.

His shock began to give way to a deep corrosive anger, slow burning in his gut. But his face was impassive when he asked, "Will you try to keep me from seeing her?"

Virginia spoke slowly. "No, I doubt it would do much good. And even if your delay has come to this, it was meant to aid her. I do believe you love her. I know you treated her with great kindness in Devon. I will trust that that same kindness will keep you from harming her now."

Their eyes locked, and he nodded his agreement. He didn't know what he was going to do, but he would have shaken hands with the Devil to gain access to Alex.

"You'll not have long to wait. She is due here to help me in the garden." And to keep her own sanity, Virginia added to herself. She knew she might have contrived to keep the two young people apart, but she also knew her efforts would most likely have come to naught. Rane had approached her honorably, but she could sense the force of the man. Man he certainly was, full grown from the youngster she had met previously. He had an added advantage in her presence; he looked so much like her husband, Trahern. How enduring was the Thaine blood to show so clearly, but then, Rane had it on both sides though far back, and his mother bore the strong imprint. Trahern, Gweneth, Rane, and Alexandria—all of them shared the exotic green-eyed, dark-haired beauty. Sometimes Virginia wished she were the witch some of the country folk thought her; she would like to see the future now. She felt a strange sense of foreboding, as if there were some deep tie between her beloved granddaughter and this man, a tie that might be stronger than other loyalties. She remembered how arrested she had been by her first sight of them together. And she wished life could have turned out differently for Alexandria, wished Rane had come back much, much sooner.

Rane heard her voice calling, "Grandmother, are you here? I saw a lovely patch of . . ." And then she was standing before him, her voice trailing off in shock. She stood absolutely still for an instant, and then she launched herself at him, his name a glad cry as she hugged him. Her straw hat fell back on its ribbons, and her hair tumbled down.

"Oh, why are you here? How are Magnus, Gweneth, Seadon, Elwyn, all of them? Tell me everything!" She stepped back, straightening her plain muslin gown and blushing a little for being so exuberant in her greeting. But it was so good to see Rane. It was as if she had conjured him. She felt young and carefree just because of his presence.

For a moment Rane was speechless, trying to take in all that was the same, all that was changed. In her greeting, he had seen the same Alex that his mind and heart had carried all this time of waiting, but the differences were profound. Even her face had subtly changed shape as if the softness of childhood had been completely honed away to leave the fine bones in high relief. There were hollows under the high curved cheekbones and shadows under the tilted green eyes, but the generous mouth was the same, and luxuriant deep brown hair was still going its own stubborn way and looked almost too heavy for the slender neck to support. He had expected childbearing would have added flesh to her frame, but it had not. She was too thin, not with the coltish leanness she had had at Clovelly, but with an under-nourished look, definitely a woman but one who worked too hard, worried too much, and slept too little. It was another version of how she had looked when he had stayed distant from her after he had first realized he loved her.

From what Virginia had told him about Alex's new life, he had grasped at the hope that she would be so altered, he would find that his feelings, too, had changed. To his despair, he found they had, but only in intensity. It swept over him in a vast wave—the urge to protect her from all care, to love her as she had never been loved. He was amazed to hear his voice giving brief prosaic details of the Falconers' well-being. He did not mention that of his family, only Seadon knew where he was.

"Why don't you go out in the garden?" Virginia asked, feeling as if the room were suddenly too small to contain the currents swirling around them.

"Yes, please, Rane, let us go! It's lovely out, and there is still much to be done before the first hard frost; there has already been a light one." As they went out into the warm afternoon, she wanted to run and dance and sing all at once and had to remind herself that she was a married woman with children. She contented herself with swinging the basket she had grabbed from the kitchen.

She didn't have to remind Rane of her new status.

"Your grandmother tells me you have a daughter." His voice was as steady as he could have wished it. And Alex knew he believed her married.

"Christiana Virginia. She's quite marvelous though a bit delicate. I know I worry about her too much, but I suppose one does with the first children. Of course, Flora and Blaine, the twins, are mine, too." She said it with fierce maternal pride, unconsciously turning her ring around and around.

Rane had hoped, too, that hearing her talk about the children would lessen the magic, and again the ploy failed. All he could think of was that the child should have been his, sprung from his loins, nurtured in her womb.

Alex began to pick bright red rose hips. "These are just right for jelly or syrup, though if you wait until they go soft with frost, you can make a lovely wine. This is a dog rose. Grandmother has a wonderful mixture of wild and domestic plants in her gardens. I'm planting mine bit by bit, but it will take years for it to be right." She stopped, suddenly realizing she was chattering nervously. She had to remind herself that this was the same Rane she had known so well, but it was difficult. The young thinness was completely vanished, replaced by a lean strength that showed even when he reached out to touch one of the rose haws. She had grown accustomed to St. John's comfortable height, only a few inches more than her own; she did not remember Rane being so tall and broad-shouldered, so male. That was it, she discovered, and a strange ripple ran through her. She had never before perceived Rane as a man. He had been friend, companion, brother, but not this raw force. As sweet to her as the perfume of the flowers was his scent, borne to her on the soft warm air, a clean smell, a blend of sea air and an almost herbal tartness, his own particular essence.

She remembered the man he had fought for kissing her at the Barnstaple Fair, remembered how wild he had been in her defense. She remembered the endless hours he had spent with her, the skills, the information, the laughter he had shared with her. She remembered the time after his father had beaten him, and he had been so distant until she had asked him to take her to the fair and had cried when he refused. She remembered how she had welcomed his renewed warmth toward her, and how his face had looked when he had bid her good-bye. She remembered how the swans had appeared in her mind and how she had called out to Rane. In memory, the images were clearer than they had been in their own present.

The truth of it burst on her with such force, she swayed, and Rane put out his hand to steady her. She looked at the lean brown fingers gripping the fabric of her sleeve and her arm beneath, and she asked very softly, "Why are you here?"

She watched his hand as if her life depended on it and did not flinch when his grip tightened.

It was a last chance to leave all between them as it had been, a last chance to avoid trouble. But he had waited too long and dreamed too much. He had nothing more to lose. "I came because I love you. I loved you in Clovelly, but you were too young, or so I thought." His hand fell away from her arm.

She suffered so many emotions at once, she couldn't sort them out. She was terribly sorry for him, for his broken dreams, and for herself, for the choice she had never known she had, for the loss she felt in being unable to turn to him. She knew how easy it would be. Just the warmth of him standing beside her was enough to draw her, and the image of being sheltered by him and taken away from the drudgery of her present life flowed into her mind without effort. With the sorrow, there was joy, joy that such a magnificent man should love her and with so little cause. But most of all, she was disoriented, incapable of truly understanding what his declaration meant.

"I must go home now. I don't like to leave the children for too long." Her voice was a quavery whisper, the excuse transparently thin since she had come with the intention of working with her grandmother for several hours. But sanity lay at home in the milky smell of Christiana and the consuming energy of the twins. She wished that St. John were there instead of at the Doncaster races far to the north in Yorkshire.

Rane curbed his frustration because he could hear the panic in her voice and see the pain in her eyes. He didn't even know what he expected her to say, but he knew he couldn't leave it like this. He wanted to know more about the woman she had become, more about her life even were he to have no part in it. "When and where can I see you again?"

He thought she was going to flee, but she murmured, "The wood you passed on your way here, I will meet you there tomorrow afternoon, at two o'clock, by the big oak with the lightning burn. The afternoon is the only time I will have to myself." And that will have to be stolen from time with my patients and the children, she thought as she contemplated the next day's demands, though she did not say it aloud.

It was more than Rane had hoped for; he did not expect her to invite him to her home. He watched as she left him, going into the house to bid her grandmother good-day.

The words Virginia was going to say died unspoken. She could see that Alexandria was frightened, but she also looked more alive and joyful than she had in months. She contented herself with, "Go carefully, child; you have had so much trouble to bear already."

Alex didn't answer. She kissed her grandmother's cheek and was gone. Virginia had felt her trembling.

She was not so reticent when Rane came in to take his leave.

"It has not been easy for Alexandria. I will not forgive you if you make it harder for her," she said harshly.

His expression was quite gentle as he looked at her. "All I have done to this point was intended to make it easier for her. I will never want less than her happiness."

She had to be content with his ambiguous answer. Her own feelings were still mixed. Even though she knew that only complications could come from Rane intruding on Alexandria's life, still she judged that one of those might be to the good, that Alexandria might learn to see herself as a desirable woman instead of everyone's servant.

She was startled by the sudden streak of anger that ran through her. She had not realized how much she resented St. John's treatment of her granddaughter. Alex never said anything about difficulties between herself and St. John, but Virginia saw only too clearly that things were not well. Virginia had forgiven St. John much because of his difficult situation, but if he didn't begin to appreciate his wife more, and soon, he was going to extinguish the bright flame of her forever. Despite the fact that Virginia made herself regard Alexandria as married, the treacherous thought was there that she was not legally bound. She could leave St. John if she chose.

She looked Rane squarely in the eye. "Please come to see me again before you leave Gravesend. I will send some of my garden's yield to your mother." It was not a very subtle way of telling him she knew he was not leaving Gravesend immediately.

"I will, ma'am," he agreed courteously, but his eyes gleamed with challenge and sardonic humor.

A formidable man indeed, Virginia thought as she watched him out of sight down the road. "I have wicked thoughts, Henry," she confessed to the cat rubbing against her skirt, "but curse or blessing, I think Alexandria needs him in her life. And it is, in any case, for them to decide."

❧ Chapter 24 ❧

Rane kept his business to himself at the inn, not mentioning the Thaine name at all and professing to have an interest in the shipping that daily passed the town. He was careful to keep his face well shadowed by his hat brim most of the time, and to the occasional comment that he looked much like part of a certain local family, he answered only that he had no relatives in the region. He did not use his own name, but rather "Fletcher," which had enough of a similar sound so that he remembered to answer to it. He reasoned that his manner might well suggest involvement with free trading and knew that as widespread as the trade was here, there were few who objected to the cheaper goods offered. Certainly the innkeeper had not paid full tariff on his well-stocked cellar, in spite of the fact that customs officers might take a drink here. He did not hire a horse, not only because he did not really need one, but also because the animal checked in and out of the livery would make his comings and goings easier to track. He doubted very much that anyone would regard his careful behavior as having more to do with the heart than the pocket.

He watched the infrequently traveled lane until his eyes ached and the conviction grew in him that she was not coming. When he finally caught sight of her, it took him a moment to believe it wasn't a trick of his imagination.

He stepped out of the shadow of the scarred oak and waited for her, not wanting to crowd her, though his impulse was to run to her.

She came to him slowly, her eyes shadowed under the shelter of her straw hat. It was a hat made only for shelter, not for any hope of fashion, and it made her look very young. The gold necklace he had given her was around her neck; her wedding band was not on her finger.

"Thank you for coming," he said simply.

"I almost did not. I should not be here. Everything is changed. But I could not stay away." She sounded dazed and looked more tired than she had the day before.

He could not resist the longing a second more. He took her hand and pulled her into the shadow of the trees and deeper into the wood until no one could see them from the lane. And then he put his arms around her and held her close.

She did not resist; she listened to the beat of his heart and felt the strength of him enfolding her. She was exhausted, and she felt as if she were floating in a place she had never been before. She had not slept at all. She had lain awake all night, alternately wishing St. John were beside her and giving thanks that he was not there to witness her turmoil. It was madness to have come to Rane, but she hadn't the courage to stay away. She craved him as the earth did rain after a drought, and she felt that parched, as if she had been slowly drying up and withering in the past months. And now there was a storm building, a wild and wonderful storm beating in her heart beneath his. She did not know what would happen, though she did know she would not leave St. John, not like this, not with him so far away and everything so unresolved between them. That was absolute. But for now, the minutes were hers, stolen out of weary days.

"Come," he commanded softly, and he led her deeper

into the woods to a small clearing, soft with grass not yet frost damaged and bordered by a small brook.

"It's one of my favorite places," she murmured, and then she laughed aloud for the sheer pleasure of knowing he had looked on this place and had seen the same beauty she had enjoyed since childhood.

"On whose land are we trespassing?" he asked as they settled down on the grass, and she laughed again, pure music to him.

"On Grandmother's. Grandfather Trahern left it to her; it had been in the Thaine family for generations, as had her house and the farmland. I suppose it will eventually go to my father, but it is truly Grandmother's to do with as she wills. Grandfather loved her a great deal. And Grandmother loves this land. There is a farmer, a man named William Each, who has been trying to buy these acres for years. Grandmother refuses to sell. She knows he would clear the trees."

Rane wondered which was the stronger of her motives. The wood offered them privacy; but because it belonged to Virginia, it was as if the old woman were watching them. He doubted that Alex knew. She was still bemused by his sudden appearance and declaration. But he could sense her need for cherishing as if she were pleading for it aloud.

"Will your husband wonder where you are?" It had to be asked.

"No, he is not here," she answered dully, not adding that even were he, he did not pay much attention to her daily routine any more.

Rane's wish that Carrington had left for good was quickly dashed by Alex's explanation of his attendance at the Doncaster races. The day he was to return was the same day Rane's ship was due.

"It is a difficult way to earn a living, but Sinje is truly trying. His family has had nothing to do with him since he married my sister. He has had to learn a new way of survival." Compassion and doubt were mixed in her tone, and Rane wondered whether she were trying to convince him or herself.

Suddenly he wanted to know everything about her life. "Tell me about your days, tell me how it is for you now!" he demanded urgently. He felt her stiffen beside him, and he drew her against his side. "Please, Alex."

After a long pause, she sighed. "It is a most ordinary life. Mavis Brown helps care for the children and is wonderful at it, but I am their mother, and the household is mine to manage. It keeps me busy. It is the same surely for most mothers with young children. There are never enough hours in the day. Often I feel guilty, but I am gone from the house a great deal because I have patients of my own now to treat. And I try to have time each week with Grandmother; there is still so much I need to learn." She went on with small, unimportant details of her domestic routine, but Rane heard more in what she did not say.

He began to understand how precarious was their financial situation, and he wondered at the rejection by both families. Even though the marriage had clearly not been approved, it seemed unduly harsh to him that the censure continued. He was thankful that Virginia Thaine had not seen fit to join the cruelty. His heart ached for Alex. There seemed to be so little love in her life. He could hear the underlying insecurity even as she spoke of everyday things. St. John Carrington seemed to have given her a child, care of his twins, and little else. Rane's guilt eased.

"Your turn now. I have said quite enough."

He acquiesced to her command, sharing his excitement at being close to owning his own ship at last as Seadon now had his, the trade having been very profitable in the past year, telling her of his parents, his brothers and their wives and children, and all the while he thought of what he knew about her now. Though no one would miss her at her house, he doubted very much that her grandmother would remain ignorant of Alex's time with him for long. The old and the young lives were too intertwined. He knew how much her grandmother's love meant to her; he thought of what she was risking for him, and he was humbled.

His voice trailed away, and he looked down at her head resting against his shoulder. She was fast asleep, long lashes lying in dark crescents above her cheekbones. He smiled tenderly, dropped a light kiss on her hair, and let her sleep. She would come to him again.

He awakened her gently when he thought she could afford no more time away.

She did not flutter in dismay. She blinked, smiled at him, and stretched like a contented cat. "I'm sorry that I fell asleep, but it was a lovely rest! Thank you."

"My pleasure, ma'am. And now I think you ought to go. You will come tomorrow?"

She studied him for a long moment. She had not intended to repeat this. One afternoon stolen to be with him had seemed enough. Now she knew it was not. As she put her hat on again, she murmured, "I'll come."

He did not walk back to the town until she was long out of sight.

Alex moved through the hours until the next meeting in a haze, grateful that Mavis was not given to chatter. And when she found Rane waiting for her again, she ran to him, and his kiss was as warm as sunlight.

He wanted to brand her with his mouth and make love to her right there, but he restrained himself, savoring her sweetness with a light teasing touch. Her husband would come home, and he himself would have to go, but she would come with him, she and the children. He schooled himself to patience once again, knowing that he must go slowly even with time so short. He saw the joy he kindled in her, he saw the sorrow of her life, and he was resolved that she would never regret going away with him to Clovelly, or even out of England if they must.

Hand in hand they wandered through the woods, not needing words, content to be with each other. Alex could still feel Rane's mouth on her own, and the wonder of it continued to flow through her. Even by such soft, momentary contact he had awakened sensations she had never experienced before. It was as if all her nerves had stirred from sleep so that every inch of her skin felt Rane's touch. She had never known this with St. John.

When their time was gone, it was she who asked, "If I come tomorrow, will you be here?"

Rane nodded and drew her close, kissing her with the same gentleness as before, and released her. They had four more days, no time at all—a lifetime.

The next morning, the baby had a fever, and Flora and Blaine were fretful as if sensing Christiana's discontent or their mother's. Alex knew it wasn't serious, and just as well she knew she could not leave the baby. She was as frantic as she was helpless; she could not even send a message to Rane explaining her absence. And the cold wet that had plagued the summer and the beginning of September was descending again. She tried to shut her mind to the image of Rane shivering as he waited for her in the wood.

Timothy and Mavis noticed Alex's agitation, but they put it down to the wrong cause and hastened to assure her that the baby would be fine with all the loving care she was receiving from her mother. And Timothy added that St. John would be home in no time at all.

Alex had to grit her teeth to keep from snapping in response to their tender and misguided concern, but she reminded herself of how loyal they both were and of how shocked they would be if they knew the true source of her distress.

She continued to fix her mind grimly on domestic matters. She played games with the twins and took comfort in their lively warmth as they ceased to bleat with the morning's bad temper. But when they were put down for their afternoon nap, she wanted to scream aloud for the time wasted without Rane.

He waited in the cold; he waited until he knew it was far too late for her to come, and then he walked slowly back to Gravesend. He considered seeking her out at her home and immediately knew he could not so jeopardize her. He did not even know where the house was; it was better so.

When he got back to the inn, he drank far more brandy than he needed to warm himself and thought of all the things that might have kept her from the wood, and still he could not rid himself of the conviction that she had chosen not to come.

He awakened the next morning with a headache and even less hope. He felt like the day looked, flat and gray, but in the afternoon, he duly trudged out the lane and waited to see which would come first, his good sense or the rain.

The first drops were beginning to fall when he saw her cloaked figure. She ran to him, and it took him an instant to understand that it was not rain but tears that glistened on her cheeks.

"The baby had a fever yesterday. And Mavis thought I was mad to go out today. Oh, God! I thought you would be gone!" She began to tremble so hard with the relief of seeing him, she could not continue, and her tears fell faster.

He wrapped her in his arms, crooning as he had long ago in Clovelly, "Don't cry, please don't." Only now he no longer had to hide his feelings. "My love, hush, it's all right. We're here together."

She raised her head and kissed him, her mouth demanding more than gentleness because fear was still coursing through her. He responded, his tongue exploring her mouth, tasting her, miming the patterns his loins ached to dance. And even in his rising passion, he learned another secret of her marriage from her willing but tentative response, and he damned her husband anew for caring so little for so much warmth. This slow prelude to lovemaking was obviously unusual for her.

They sought shelter deep in the wood under the heavy branches of an ancient oak, and heedless of the cold, they worked feverishly to undress each other. Alex could scarcely comprehend her eagerness. Sex was unpleasant, something to be endured to please the man; St. John had taught her that, and she was willing to please Rane this way because she could feel his need. It was her response she did not understand; all the sensations were so new.

Rane made a bed of her cloak and his coat, and he laid her down tenderly, his eyes taking in the pale, smooth honey of her skin and every line of her long body. She was too thin, her belly and hip bones hollowed, her breasts hardly more than small swells beneath the dark upstanding nipples, but to him, she was more beautiful than any other woman. Her half-closed eyes appeared to be the deepest forest green in the storm shadow, and her lips were full and rosy from his kissing.

He leaned over her and began to worship her with his mouth and his hands, touching her everywhere, learning her body as if it were the last secret he would ever need to know.

Alex was stunned by the onslaught of sensations, fire and ice everywhere, from the hands kneading her breasts and stroking down her belly to tease with feather light touches on inner thighs and between her legs, from the mouth kissing and licking her flesh on the angle of her jaw, the hollow of her throat, and everywhere his hands had been. She touched him anywhere she could reach, her passion heightened by her perception of his different textures, here rough with the pelt of manhood, there as smooth as ivory, all of him structured of long muscle, lean strength beneath the skin. How beautiful he was to look at, to touch, to love. A small distant voice mourned that St. John tried never to let her see him naked, had never made love to her nor let her love him so freely. Indeed at all. Only now did she understand that.

And then the voice was silent, and there was no one else on earth except Rane, over her, coming into her. She tensed for an instant, the habit of discomfort tightening her muscles and making new pain.

Rane held himself still, amazed that not even childbirth had altered the virginal feel of her. "Easy, sweetling, easy. Let me pleasure you, love you," he whispered, and he felt her open to him. Velvety muscles sheathed and caressed him as he thrust into her, and he moaned with the effort of tempering his passion to her need.

Alex did not recognize the cries as her own. She no longer felt as though her body belonged to her at all. It had become magic, at once as deep as the earth and as light as the heavens. Early flutters of sensation were transmuted into endless waves of heat and pulsing muscles and nerves until she felt as if she were soaring and must reach the unknown destination else die of it.

She found that destination in the heart of her own universe, spirals of flight leading back to the center so that she cried out at the exquisite release and let herself sink into the warm, soft sea, feeling Rane's own flight ending in the shuddering release of his seed.

She made no move to cover herself against the cold. It was Rane who maneuvered her rain-splashed body into her clothes. "Come, help me," he urged. "I don't want you to take a chill."

She gazed at him in wonder. "Can it always be like that?"

He chuckled and kissed the tip of her nose. "Always if the two parties are willing and take some time and care."

His mirth deserted him abruptly as he remembered that she was no virgin, but a married woman who had never known sexual joy with her husband. He hugged her to him convulsively, afraid he would weep. It would change for her, it must. She would come with him. He had no remorse for using the added bond of shared physical love to make it so. Their time was running short, but he did not press her, not wanting to spoil what she had just experienced.

"I love you," he said, and he contented himself with a last kiss before he sent her on her way.

❧ *Chapter 25* ❧

Alex had lost her bearings on an uncharted sea. She nearly went to her parents' house instead of to her own home, as if her life with St. John had never been.

Mavis exclaimed over her wet clothing; Alex ignored her. She floated blankly through the hours, wrapped in wonder, unable to believe that so much glory could exist in her own body at a man's touch. No, at Rane's touch. All she need do was close her eyes, and she could see him in every detail and feel the heavy warmth beginning in the center of her. The only thing she had ever felt before that was like it had been when Christiana had begun to suckle, albeit futilely, at her breast.

The hours until their next meeting passed as slowly as if each had grown into a day, and yet she found her eagerness tempered by fear that it would never be so wonderful again. But the fear fled at Rane's first touch as Alex felt her body come alive in expectation, already sensitized by just one time with him.

He had brought a piece of heavy oilcloth and blankets, and Alex giggled at the domestic incongruity of making their bed in the forest. "Adam and Eve could have used your foresight."

"Adam and Eve lived in a warmer climate," he retorted, and reaching for her, he nuzzled her neck as he let her hair down and worked at the buttons of her dress. He refused to let the weather reduce them to furtive fumbling through half-unfastened layers of clothing. He wanted to see her, wanted her to see him.

This time Alex touched him with more purpose than she had the day before, fascinated to feel his nipples grow as hard as hers over the flexing muscles of his chest, enthralled by the responsiveness of his body everywhere she touched until he groaned in both pleasure and warning as her hands closed over his swelling manhood. It pleased her deeply to know he was as vulnerable to her touch as she to his. And then he took control from her, arousing her pliant flesh with seeking mouth and hands until she cried aloud for him to take her.

His strong arms lifted her easily and placed her astride him, and her eyes flared golden-green in surprise as he pulled her down on his shaft. A long purr of pleasure rippled her throat as she experienced the new power and freedom of movement.

Rane watched the delight and passion reflected in her expression as she moved on him, leaning forward to kiss him, long tendrils of hair brushing his skin, until she closed her eyes and threw her head back, baring the long line of her neck. He rolled them over, taking back the dominance, bringing her to completion before he allowed himself release.

They lay in silence, this time warmly covered, and listened to the patter of rain on the dying leaves.

She spoke first. "There has hardly been any summer, and now it seems that winter is coming early."

Her voice was infinitely sad, and he knew she was not talking about the weather, but about the shortness of their time together. There would be no better opportunity. He drew a deep breath. "You will come with me, you and the children. I will take you to Clovelly or anywhere we must go to be together. The day after tomorrow the ship will be here, or I could take you to London tomorrow, whichever is best for you. I will find a wet nurse or cow's milk for the baby; you aren't to worry about it."

She shivered but said nothing for a long moment, and he thought she was considering his plan, but when she spoke, he realized she had simply been gathering courage. "I cannot leave St. John, nor can I take his children from him. We are all he has."

Rane was hard pressed to control the fierce burst of angry fear that coursed through him. He forced himself to speak reasonably. "But you love me as I love you. I know it is so. And your marriage has been a mistake. I know that, too. I know how little he has loved you. How can

275

you return to him after this? You might even be carrying my child."

"I will not conceive." She said it with a certainty she didn't feel, dismissing the issue. "I cannot forsake St. John. You must think me evil to have spent this time with you, but I don't feel guilty, not yet. I do love you, I expect I always will, and I wanted everything you have given me, wanted it without even knowing it existed. But there's an end to it. I know you are strong enough to go on without me and certainly without the complication of another man's children. St. John is not strong enough. He cannot even hold me with two good arms as you can. That cannot be helped. It is sadder that he cannot love himself in order to love me. You've made me realize that. You are so sure of your love and your strength, you can share both. Sinje cannot. Perhaps someday he will be able to, perhaps not, but if I leave him, it will never happen. If he choses to leave me, that is another matter."

"Would it change your mind if I shot my foot off or broke my neck?" The surly words were out before he could stop them; it was particularly bitter to hear her slip back into calling the man by her nickname for him, such an intimate little gesture.

"How would you like it, Rane, if you could never put two good arms around a woman again? I cannot tell you how different it has been to have been held by you, loved by you with no thought of what you can and cannot do." Her voice was flat and hard. "How would you like it if you were clumsy at making love and at everything else because your body was maimed? And how would you like it if you married a woman who not only turned out to be unsuited for marriage, but also died weeping and wailing so that you would feel guilty for the rest of your life because your love hadn't been enough?"

She was still and resistant when he drew her close. "God, I'm sorry, forgive me! I didn't want to think about St. John at all, I still don't. But I see I must. You are too kind and loyal. Any man who has you should want for nothing else, not even two good arms. What a damnable coil!"

She could not bear the broken sound of his voice; even if he didn't know it, the beginning of resignation was there. She pressed closer for a moment, kissing his shoulder and stroking his soft, thick hair. Then she pulled away and began to dress, conscious of time passing.

"There is one more day," she said softly, not looking at him. "I will not change my mind, but I will come to you tomorrow if you wish it."

"I will be here. I would never give up time I might have with you." His tone was as soft as hers.

They were already beginning to say good-bye, and she wondered how she would bear it.

The magic, separate world was already beginning to unravel. When she arrived home, Mavis was too concerned to leave her alone.

"Ye be chilled through, ye be! It be daft for 'e t' be out on days like dis. Yer granny'd not be mindin' did ye not come now an' den."

"I would mind," Alex replied tightly, having almost forgotten that Virginia was the excuse she had used. "I love my children, but the hours I have away from them are important to me, rain or not, and I am not so delicate that I will dissolve in it." *R-a-n-e, not R-a-i-n,* her mind supplied hysterically; *I could dissolve in him forever.*

Mavis mumbled quite audibly about how some women went mad while their husbands were gone.

And then Boston came to call, eager to extoll the new virtues he'd discovered in his beloved, whom he would be marrying in two weeks. "She's a splendid cook. Imagine, I never thought of that."

"How extraordinary she is," Alex said sarcastically and was instantly repentant because of his hurt look. "I apologize. I'm out of sorts today. Would you like to stay for supper and tell me more about the divine Dora?"

Boston, never one to hold a grudge, agreed and added wisely, "I expect you're missing St. John. When is he coming home?"

"Day after tomorrow," she managed, and she was relieved when he turned his attention to his nephew and nieces.

Now the hours ran too quickly toward farewell. And she did not even have the comfort of being able to wish Rane had never come to her. Not for the world would she give up what she had experienced in his arms.

The afternoon was draped in cold, wet misery.

Rane searched her face for some sign that she had

relented, and his own expression darkened. "You are sure? Nothing will change your mind?"

"Nothing." She did not want to give him false hope by telling him it was possible St. John would want her to go; that was something only Sinje could settle.

They came together with an urgency that bordered on violence as if each was trying to leave an image with the other. And with hardly a respite, they melded into each other again, this time with strange slow gentleness as if they were already ghosts of themselves.

When it was over, Alex wept, hopeless tears acknowledging all she was losing, and she found Rane's tears mixing with her own. His face was twisted, and deep shudders wrenched his body as he tried to control his grief. Alex reached up and touched his cheek gently.

"I will hear you in the sails of the ships. I will taste you in the spice and brandy of free traders. I will see you always. When sunlight touches my face, you will touch me, and when I see the wild swans flying, I will see you. I will never forget you, not as I knew you in Clovelly; not as I know you now." The words were a clear vow despite her crying.

"If you need me, send for me," he pled. "You are not responsible for what your sister was or for the wreckage she left behind, Alex, you're not! Come to me when you will and you will have your own life, not her leavings."

Her tears ceased, and she was very firm. "Don't wait for me, Rane. Find a woman you can love and make your life with her. My life is here with my children, with my husband. I do love him; not as I love you, but enough so that I will not leave him." If anything changed with St. John, it would be very soon, time enough to go to Rane, but she did not want Rane ruining his own life for her.

It was final. He could feel the strength of her will.

They dressed in silence and then turned to each other in unison to cling together for the last time.

"A long and joyful life, how I wish it for you!" she whispered fiercely, and then she pulled away and fled, not looking back.

He remained in the wood for a long time, simply staring at the gray-green space where she had vanished. And when finally he left, he went toward Virginia's house, not the town. He knew it was unwise, but he could not deny the last contact with someone close to Alex.

He left the bundle of the forest bed some distance from the house and straightened his clothing again before he knocked on the door.

Virginia regarded him expressionlessly before she nodded and bid him enter.

"I am leaving tomorrow. I said I would come again before I departed."

Their eyes met and locked in silent challenge, and then Virginia's expression softened. "I have some fine brandy. I think you need that more than tea." She led him to the kitchen where a fire burned merrily and the air was fragrant with the smell of bread baking.

Her sudden kindness undid him. "I asked her to come with me. She refused."

Virginia poured the brandy and handed him the glass with a steady hand. "I have done many odd things in my life, but this is surely the oddest of all—to be serving the finest untaxed brandy to my granddaughter's seducer. But you look as if you've been to hell and can't find the way home again. If it weren't for the children, you would abduct her, wouldn't you?"

He nodded grimly. "The thought has occurred to me."

"Trahern did just that to me." With satisfaction, she noted Rane's start of surprise and interest. "I wasn't sure soon enough for him. He lost patience and took me off on his ship for a week. Fortunately, I discovered he was indeed the man for me. Otherwise, I would have stabbed him in his overeager heart or elsewhere. Trahern's crew would have died before they betrayed him, and both families pretended the marriage had been planned all along, so there was no scandal."

She sighed. "Part of me wishes you could have done the same for Alexandria. But it is impossible, and she has made her will known. She is very strong, you know, and very loyal. I only hope you have not hurt her."

He had no reassurance for her because if Alex's pain was even half of his own, then he had hurt her deeply indeed.

When he would have left, Virginia asked him to stay for supper, and he complied, the two of them drawing comfort from each other in their different but mutual love for Alex.

When finally he took his leave, she gave him the herbs

for Gweneth, and then she stood on tiptoe so that she could kiss him on the cheek. "Don't waste your life, young Falconer," she said, and there were tears in her eyes as she watched him disappear into the night.

❧ Chapter 26 ❧

Alex did not go to the river to watch the departure of Rane's ship. She worked at keeping her mind blank because her thoughts spun so dizzily when she allowed them, she could make no sense of anything. It all hinged on St. John now. She waited for him, wondering if he would bring another Mr. Dodds with him, another sign he held her in contempt. Though she wore her wedding ring again, another such visitor would be signal enough to confront him, to ask him if he no longer wished their marriage to continue.

But he came home alone that night, his face so gray and worn, she feared he was ill and immediately reached out to touch his forehead, checking for fever.

He grasped her hand so hard she winced, and he brought it to his lips, kissing it fervently. She froze, unable to comprehend.

"Is there still time? Can you forgive me? I love you, Alexandria, I love you. Hugh, my best friend, he . . ."

She was still totally baffled, but now fear gripped her. "Hugh, what happened to him? What's wrong?" His talk of love had not registered at all.

St. John saw her fear and confusion, and he willed himself to explain calmly. He led her into the little parlor.

"Hugh is all right. Do you love him?" He asked the question steadily, but his eyes searched her face anxiously.

She sank down in a chair, finding her legs too weak to

support her. "Love Hugh?" she asked. "Have you lost your mind?" Hugh, not Rane; the whirling was starting in her head again; it was she who was losing her mind. She had to concentrate fiercely to understand what he was saying.

"I have been crazed. Hugh made me see that, though I could have killed him for it." He told the story without sparing himself.

Hugh's sister, Lady Catherine, had been at the Doncaster races, defying convention with the excuse that horses she owned were running. And St. John had found her particular attention flattering. She had viewed his loss of an arm as perversely attractive and had made that clear since they had first renewed their acquaintance after Waterloo. But at Doncaster her approach had been even more direct. And St. John had basked in the flirtation, feeling carefree and expansive because his wagers had gone well and he was plump in the pocket. Alexandria and the children had seemed a thousand miles and a lifetime away. He had become a bachelor among bachelors and had not even defended Alex from coarse remarks made by some of his set. He had not only allowed them to think she was no more than his light-skirt, he had encouraged it with suggestive comments of his own. Until Hugh had made his offer.

He had been very calm, even casual about it. They had been having a pint of ale when Hugh said, "Before you return to dancing attendance on my sister, I have a bit of business to conduct with you. It's obvious you're tiring of Alexandria. I think it would make it easier for all if I took her under my protection. I know Christiana is a problem, but if you will allow it, she, too, will have the best I can provide for her."

St. John's throat was as dry as sand despite the ale. "Make her your mistress?" he choked.

"As you have done, only with more kindness, I should hope," Hugh replied evenly. "I am very fond of her. She will want for nothing. I might even marry her. Despite her origins, she would make a fine duchess. People would talk, but then, they already do, and I've never listened before, so why should I now? She would look magnificent in the family emeralds." He finished on a musing note, but his eyes were very bright as he waited for St. John's reaction.

St. John felt as if he'd been trampled. His whole body hurt, and he found it difficult to draw enough air into his lungs. Suddenly the world around him dissolved, leaving only the agonizingly clear image of Alexandria. He could smell the sweet scent of her, could taste her mouth, could feel the softness of her young skin, could hear the husky voice. She had given him her virginity, her love, a child, and his very life. And in return he had treated her with contempt and had allowed his friends to do the same. Hugh, whom he regarded as his closest friend, was coolly offering for her as if she were a prize horse. And yet, Hugh was prepared to treat her with far more respect than he himself had. The blame was his own, not Hugh's, though at the moment he wanted to kill him.

"It is my fault; I acknowledge that. But if you ever speak of my wife in such terms again, I will kill you." He raised his left hand and flexed it. "I will find a way if I need to. I was once quite good with a pistol or a sword; I can learn to be so again. Alexandria is mine. I love her, and I hope that she still has love left for me."

Only then did he see that Hugh was looking very pleased with himself and that a small smile curved his mouth.

"You did it on purpose!" St. John gasped, and then he confessed, "And I deserved it. God help me, I hope there is still time for me to make it up to Alex."

"I do, too, because I know she loves you. But, St. John, don't mistake me. My offer stands." His expression was still affable, but St. John had known him for too long to miss the implacable determination in his eyes.

St. John had planned to linger at Doncaster for the after-race festivities, but now all he could think of was getting home to Alex. It was as if his whole life had spun around in an instant. Hugh wisely let him go alone.

Now facing her, he tried to explain why he had treated her so badly, finding it excruciatingly difficult to express his innermost thoughts, a process that had never been part of his nature.

"I have leant on your strength and resented it at the same time. My Alex, so calm, so sensible . . . so useful. I am more like Florence than I would want to be, more decorative than anything else. And I pretended—I pretended that everything would suddenly change. I would be the first, not the third son, and not estranged from my family. Wealth and position would somehow come to me, and I would not have to deal with the realities of life and of having a family of my own. You reminded me that life is indeed real and must be dealt with on all the small levels—rent to meet, servants to pay, children to feed and clothe." He saw the look of hurt in her eyes. "No, it is not a fault, it is a virtue to face life squarely, and bit by bit, I mean to learn."

He drew a deep breath. "Even my very life I owe to you; I would not have survived had you not asked me to. I am sure of that now. And I think part of me wished for that honorable death, a way out, a good soldier—few would have known that I simply did not want to take up the responsibilities of my life. But I did not return today to tell you that I will be a good husband to repay a debt, though it surely must sound that way. I am so bad at this! Of course I am grateful for your care of my children and my household, for your gift of our daughter, for so many things, but most of all, I love you, Alexandria Thaine Carrington, my beautiful, compassionate, wise wise-woman. Can you forgive me?"

It was more than she had dreamed of; his heart and soul were stripped bare and laid before her, the ultimate offering. And she was terrified. His change had followed so swiftly on her own, there was no space between them for understanding and deciding. She felt as if she were on a very high ledge where one misstep would send her plunging into the void. And yet, delay would be just as fatal. St. John had so humbled himself that he was completely vulnerable, and no one could bear to be in that state for long. He would surely freeze and draw inward, and the chance of reconciliation between them would be lost.

In the instant of decision, she said a more profound farewell to Rane than had marked their physical parting, and she rose and stretched her arms out to St. John. The wings lost forever; swans' flight denied; the mythical golden chain around her neck binding her to earth and this man, not to Rane.

He came to her gratefully, bowing his head on her shoulder, and she enfolded him in her youth and strength. "I love you, too, Sinje, always. There is no forgiveness involved. It is enough that you have come to me, really come home. We'll be all right, we will. It will be a good marriage."

It was as strong a marriage vow as ever witnessed by a clergyman. And Alex hoped St. John would never know the sacrifice it entailed.

He led her upstairs and when she would have blown out the candles in their room, St. John stopped her. "I want to see you," he said softly, and she knew how profound the change in him was that he would expose his imperfect body to her eyes even as he looked at her.

It had not seemed wanton to lie naked with Rane and make love with him, but now with St. John, she felt as abandoned as her mother accused her of being. And she felt wonderful.

Slowly she undressed for him, and his eyes caressed her as if he were seeing her for the first time. She went to him, carrying herself proudly, refusing to flinch or cower in her nakedness, and she undressed him in turn, feeling him tremble under her ministrations.

She saw the bright gleam of his blue eyes before he drew her against him and just held her for a moment against his pounding heart. "We begin again, Alex, all over again."

He led her to their bed and followed her down. "I am surely damned as a cradle robber, you are so young, so sweet." He braced himself on his arm and leaned over her, his mouth kissing and laving her flesh with exquisite care and concentration. She could feel the heat of his love and desire, and her body answered with radiating warmth. She knew what the feeling was now, she knew what could come of it, and she blocked from her mind the knowledge of who had taught her.

He sucked gently at her breasts and then grazed the nipples with his teeth, and her body arched in response to the pleasurable shocks he generated. She shivered when he found the sensitive skin beneath her ears, and her ardor matched his when his mouth captured hers, his tongue moving inside.

He lay on his side, drawing her with him, and then his hand moved to stroke the soft skin of her inner thighs and upward to tease the swelling bud of her sex until she was moving convulsively against his fingers and uttering soft cries. Her own eyes closed, she could yet feel the intensity of his watching. She wanted to ask him how she could please him in turn, but she was drifting out of control on the wave of passion he had created, and it seemed he needed no encouragement, for she could feel his staff hot and hard probing and then thrusting into her own slick heat.

There was no discomfort, no unresolved energy this time, just the great twisting tide of fulfillment that washed over her and lifted her up until her cry blended with St. John's as he emptied his own sea of creation into her.

"I love you, wife," he whispered, and he kissed her before he fell asleep, part of his body still covering hers, one leg entwined with her own.

She lay awake, watching the candles guttering down, her hands stroking St. John's thick gilt hair and the smooth skin of his back as she tried to absorb all that had happened.

It was different from being with Rane; it would always be so, for Rane had no physical adjustments to make and could depend on the strength and grace of a whole body. There would always be moments of awkwardness with St. John and more effort needed by him to balance his body. And as much as he had aroused her, still he lacked the practiced ease Rane had long since learned in lovemaking. Though St. John was the elder, he was the innocent in this compared to Rane. Despite his marriage to her sister and despite the light-skirts who had surely initiated him into manhood, Alex doubted that St. John had ever been very focused on the woman's pleasure. Until now. For her. Together they would both learn.

She searched for guilt and found none. She had lain with two men in so short a space, and yet she felt nothing beyond a lingering sorrow that she and Rane had been destined to have only a short passage of sweet song together out of the general disharmony of their lives. But it was he who had made her a woman and glad to be one. She was not even sure she could have responded as she had to St. John if Rane had not shown her what her body could do. She was more changed now than she had been by the loss of her virginity or the birth of Christiana.

Wanton she must surely be to contemplate all of this so calmly. And wanton to find so much pleasure in her body. And wantonness would be the gift she would give to St. John, loving him so lavishly that he would never stray to Lady Catherine or any other woman and so well that he would always feel strong and whole, and the bitter days between them would fade to the palest memories.

St. John awakened in the night and reached for her, and when she pressed him down on his back and proceeded to make love to him as he had to her, he sighed in pleasure and murmured, "That's good, Alex, oh, sweetheart, yes, just there," encouraging her and letting her know what he liked. He had possessed her so thoroughly before, it seemed only just that the tables should be turned, and as it seemed she was only doing to him what he had done to her, it never occurred to him that another man had taught her this.

They drifted through the following days so obviously in love and so drugged with the satisfaction they were discovering in each other, it was hard for those around them to restrain their knowing looks.

Alex continued to work hard caring for her patients, but the nights were hers with St. John unless an emergency called her away, and then she always found him waiting up for her, no matter what the hour, his former resentment gone, his welcome warm and patient.

In short days they had learned a sensuality that extended beyond lovemaking, so that simply holding each other was often as satisfying as the deeper physical joining. Alex remembered when she had found comfort in the embrace because she had liked it better than the lovemaking. But now it was all part of the same thing, part of the loving that bound their hearts, minds, spirits, and their bodies. Alex suggested to St. John that perhaps all marriages would be better for a bad start.

"Perhaps not a bad start but surely patience," he replied, testing her own patience sorely by raining teasing kisses everywhere except on her lips until she claimed his mouth with her own.

They did not attend Boston's wedding, but they had a supper for the couple that night, thus sharing in the celebration without having to confront Margaret. And Virginia was there, too, making the party seem more complete for the addition of one of the older generation.

Virginia would have agreed with St. John's theory of patience. It had been difficult, but over the years, she had learned it. Alexandria had told her nothing more than that she and St. John had reached a new understanding, and that Virginia had known from the moment her granddaughter had come to her after St. John's return. She also knew that there was much, much more to the story.

Alexandria had not mentioned Rane since his departure, but he was surely part of it all. And Virginia knew that even her patient waiting might never be rewarded with further explanation. Alexandria had not confided in her when her marriage was going badly; it was likely she would give as few details when it was going well. As close as she was to her grandmother, she had always had a part of herself that was intensely private. Virginia respected that and saw her role as simply being there if her granddaughter needed her. And she knew a contentment deeper than she had felt in a long time; it was no sham, Alexandria and St. John were truly joyful and openly adoring of each other. It was enough for any marriage.

Alex did not mind when St. John left for the Houghton Meeting at Newmarket toward the end of October. She was secure enough in his love now not to care even if Lady Catherine was there. He had done well at Doncaster and most of his winnings had gone into the household fund. It was only just that he pursue his chosen profession as he now allowed her with good grace to follow hers. And they were bound too closely now for distance and a little time apart to come between them. Alex even discussed the horses with him, delighting in the exotic names such as Equator by Zodiac and Milton by Waxy and trying to store up all the information he gave her regarding odds and bloodlines.

St. John was more worried by the parting than Alex. He still harbored the last memories of Florence's raging protests. But gradually it dawned on him that Alex loved him enough to trust him.

"Let Hugh know he is still welcome here," she admonished him as he departed. "We both owe him a great deal." She gave him an impish smile, and he nearly gave up his plans to attend the Houghton Meeting.

Alex was grateful for the time without him. It was too early to be sure, but nonetheless, she strongly suspected she was pregnant again. And suddenly she found that she could not sort it all out alone. She felt as if she would go insane if she could not confide in someone. But when she went to her grandmother, she recognized the possibility that Virginia would be so horrified by her confession that she would never again look on her with the same generous love she had shown in the past.

Virginia saw the white misery in her face and was

immediately alarmed. "Has something happened to St. John, to one of the children?"

Alex shook her head. "No, to me."

She related everything as if it had happened to someone else and had nothing to do with her until she came to the end.

"Even though it is very early yet, I know I am with child. And I can't explain how I know, but I do know it is Rane's, not Sinje's. Even though I told him it would not happen, I think I knew the instant the baby was conceived."

She searched her grandmother's face for the expression of disgust she expected to find there. Instead, Virginia looked placid and a little distant.

"I taught you how to read when you were very young, but you never asked me how I learned, and I never told you. I think now would be a good time," she said.

"There was no firm tradition of learning in my family, and certainly not for girls. But I cannot remember a time when I did not lust after knowledge, and I choose the word 'lust' with a will because nothing else can describe the driving hunger I had even as a small child. I wanted to know what was inside books. I wanted to read the broadsides in public places and even the small daily lines of ledgers. The years went by, and I learned a little here and there but not nearly enough. I could read scarcely better than a product of the poorest dame school. And then when I was twelve years old, a new clergyman came to the parish. He was a poorly set up young man, wan, frail, and ill adapted to social ease. But he could read and write Latin and Greek as well as English, and though his personal possessions were for the most part few and shabby, he had books, oh, so many books! But he, no more than many others, had no interest in tutoring a female. It was as if he were an alchemist and would impart his knowledge only to a special apprentice. It was the only thing that gave him any distinction."

Alex was regarding her grandmother with more than a little apprehension, wondering if her own confession had so shocked her that it had made her irrational, but Virginia's next words shocked Alex in turn and showed her there was indeed a point to be made.

"I seduced him for his knowledge. I gave him everything except the membrane of my virginity, and that, too, I would have given had he been bold enough to take it, but he was so much more of the mind than the flesh, guilt and cowardice kept him from taking the final prize. It was a matter of awkward fumbling and poking." She grimaced in remembered distaste. "I am sure he had never had a woman before, and I doubt he ever did. But I got from him what I wanted, nearly a year of education that could not have been surpassed by the greatest university in the land. My family despaired of the sulky, secretive child I had become, but the time was well spent with books. And when your grandfather came along, he was a man who, praise be, believed in all the passions, physical and mental, not just for himself, but for others. In pursuit of those passions, he took me off on his ship until I consented to marriage. My family had no concern beyond the fact that no scandal came of it and an impressive man had deigned to take a troublesome child off their hands. Mind, they did love me, they just didn't understand me."

She fixed Alex with her dark eyes. "I offered everything for the knowledge I craved; you offered everything for love of Rane. Of the two, I would say your motive was more virtuous than mine. And the fact is that women often have only themselves with which to bargain. It has been going on for a very long time. You are not alone; you are part of a vast sisterhood. And no matter what anyone tells you, you—your flesh, your spirit, your heart, and your mind—belong to yourself, not to the church nor the state nor even to your husband. And what bargains you strike with life must be of your own choice, though I would always trust that you would not harm another for your own gain."

"Have I not done that already?" Alex questioned softly. "I am bearing another man's child."

"The harm will come only if you tell St. John. The child will look like you; there is no trouble in that. It may be true that Rane will suffer unknowing hurt for having a child of whom he knows nothing, but the risk was there for him in his possession of you. Alexandria, you love them both in different ways and in the same way and for good reason."

"You are sure I should not tell Sinje?" It was as much a plea as a question.

"Ah, that is the punishment, if there is any in his, not thunder from the pulpit or shrieks from your mother. You must carry this secret alone as you alone can carry the child. To tell St. John might relieve your burden in some paroxysm of self-abasement and confession, but it would do only hurt to him."

Alex bowed her head in acceptance, knowing that her grandmother was right, knowing that her own urge to tell Sinje had not been for his sake but for hers.

"How do you go on loving me despite the things I've done to disappoint you?"

"You haven't disappointed me!" Virginia corrected her sharply. "You weren't listening closely enough. Your life is your own, not mine. And there is nothing on earth you would be capable of doing that could make me love you less, not anything, not ever. I've loved you from the day you were born, and I will love you until the day I die." She gathered Alex into her arms and let her be, just for a little time, a sheltered child again. And she gave thanks that Alexandria had not once mentioned ridding herself of the baby, a dangerous procedure whenever done. There was more love in Alexandria for Rane than even she knew. And though Virginia could only be glad that St. John had become such a loving spouse, she could not rid herself of the feeling that destiny had somehow gone sadly awry.

❦ Chapter 27 ❧

Carrying his child, it was impossible not to think of Rane now. Alex's words to him had proved prophetic. She did sense him in so many daily things; even the sound of Blaine's name was enough to send a start through her for its rhyming with Rane, something that had never bothered her before. But she learned to live with it because she had to. St. John was the reality in her life, and gradually she began to accept the fact that perfect harmony between two people was not only not always possible, it was not always desirable.

Once awakened, St. John's love for her seemed to grow like a flower finding the sun. He returned from the races with such eagerness that she could well believe his admission that he had been hard pressed to keep his mind on matters at hand at the course.

"Though the horse Milton had something to do with this, you are my luck as well as my love," he told her as he proudly presented her with enough money to pay the next year's rent.

They were learning the interdependence of love together. It was a sweet lesson, and she was not going to let the memories of Rane or even the presence of his child spoil this. She wondered how other women lived such dual lives and then realized the numbers made no difference; it was a solitary journey of the heart and the body, apart from other women, essentially apart from both St. John and Rane.

When St. John possessed her with his new and anxious care for her pleasure, she responded with all of the ardor she could summon even when she was so tired she wanted only to sleep, but she did not have to do that very often because he was growing very sensitive to her moods.

She had not planned to tell him about her pregnancy until it was a little further on, but one night as they lay in the languorous aftermath of loving, St. John's hand continued to idly stroke her, running down the curve of waist to hip and over the softness of her breasts and belly until it suddenly stilled. "Are you increasing?" he asked softly.

For an instant she felt as if she were riding too fast toward a wall that was too high, but then she was over it, soaring free, glad that it was out, willing to accept whatever happened next.

"Yes, I am, but how in the world do you know? My figure has not changed yet."

His hand began to move again, love and acceptance in the gentle stroking even before the words. "I cannot touch the difference yet, but nonetheless, I can feel it, as if your body is mine. This time I will be here when our son or daughter is born." He nuzzled her shoulder, and she held him close, vowing that this child would prove only joyful for him.

But the ironies did not escape her. He had been absent for the birth of his own child but would be here for the birth of Rane's. And the changes in her body that had repulsed him before, now intrigued and pleased him. His passion did not dim, but he touched her with an almost reverent intensity, as if he would learn through her what it was to be female.

St. John in love wanted the world to be in love, too, and Alex found this aspect of him utterly charming. It made Boston and Dora feel even more welcome at the cottage than they had before, and so they were there more often. And it brought to light a problem Alex had not even suspected.

St. John had been teasing Timothy gently about whether or not his intentions toward Mavis were honorable.

"We rub along all right, we do," Tim had protested. "Me mum an' da never 'ad—had—a paper an' they was foine."

But St. John pressed him further, sensing there was more to this matter, and the true state of things amazed him.

"It never occurred to me," he told Alex, "but they have decided it is not proper for them to marry when we cannot. They say that they haven't seen that marriage has improved many people, but still, I think they want it."

Alex was at once touched and horrified. "Oh, Sinje! I hope you persuaded him that that is not the case at all! They must marry immediately if that is what they wish. Perhaps it isn't so important to Tim, but I do think Mavis cares. I should have been paying more attention. I recall now that one day she mentioned her parents, saying only that she had finally come to know that their unhappiness wasn't from being wed to each other but from being unhappy people down to the bone. I should have guessed she was thinking of herself and Tim." She had come to like Mavis very much and to know that there was great depth to the woman beneath the placid exterior. She was instantly busy with plans to celebrate the match, and so she nearly missed St. John's hesitant question.

"Do you mind terribly that we are not married in the eyes of the law?"

"I have never cared about it as you have. And I am so well loved by you, how then could I mind?" She was rewarded by the bright leap of fire in his blue eyes, and she reached out and ruffled his silky hair just because she needed the contact.

It was a small but joyful wedding. Mavis did not care to have her family there as they had had nothing but spite for her since her fall from grace, but both she and Tim were flattered by the attendance of Lord Bettingdon.

Alex had eased any constraint on Hugh's part by going to him the minute he arrived. Despite his high station, she hugged him and murmured, "Hugh, we owe you so much. Thank you with all my heart."

He had not known until that moment how much it mattered to him that he had not lost her friendship, and only then did he admit to himself how very willing he would indeed have been to take St. John's place. But that was something she need never know. Even without her gracious attitude for what, after all, had been a grievous insult, he would have known how well things were going between her and his friend; they both glowed with it. But he sensed depths in Alexandria that would never be in St. John, and he thought how ironic it was that with all his wealth and power, he could so envy his supposedly less fortunate friend.

At Christmas, they had another visitor, an unexpected gift for Alex.

Boston and Dora were perfectly content living in the old quarters over the shop. It was convenient since Boston was taking on more and more responsibility from his father, and it saved them the cost of renting a separate house. Margaret, probably to retain some control over Boston, had wanted them to live in the Thaine house, but Boston had been firm in his refusal, and Alex applauded his stand. The more he and Dora could stay away from Margaret, the better off they would be. She was beginning to learn that under Dora's sweet exterior there was more than a little will, but it was fortunately dedicated to Boston's well-being. They had made their obligatory call at the Thaine house on Christmas Eve, but when they came on to the cottage, they brought Caton with them.

Alex froze at the sight of him, and Caton, too, paused uncertainly in the doorway, obviously unsure of his welcome. And then Alex flew to him, tears beginning to run unchecked down her cheeks.

"Welcome, Father, welcome to our home. I have so longed for you to come to us!" It did not matter that he had not come before nor that he looked so old and frail; nothing mattered except his presence now.

St. John stepped forward to add his own warm welcome, and Virginia beamed at this unexpected show of courage by her son.

Boston finally managed to draw Alex aside to explain that their father had left with them, letting his wife think he was returning to the store for bookwork. "Paris and Rome and their families are with Mother, and a grim, stuffy group it is, too. They have no need of us."

It was one of the loveliest evenings Alex could remember. Though the children were soon to bed, it was not before Caton had held each of them, his eyes bright with tears as he admired his grandchildren. Inwardly Alex gave thanks that the children accepted his presence with wide-eyed interest and little fuss. For his sake, she could not have borne it had they howled in rejection.

They sang old carols and toasted their good fortune in being together, and St. John, looking very proud, made the announcement of the expected new child. He had asked Alex if he might share the news, and so she was not shocked and accepted the congratulations with a smile.

Virginia's eyes were warm with approval, and as she kissed her granddaughter's cheek, she whispered, "Well done. No amount of truth could be worth more than St. John's joy."

"I do love you very much, my darling," Alex murmured to her husband when they were finally settled for the night. The warmth flowed between them, wrapping them both in their own small, safe world.

St. John felt himself more and more a part of that world, less and less part of that he had come from. Alex's concerns were becoming his own. He knew this only too clearly when Alex returned late one cold January day, her temper at white heat.

"I couldn't help him! I had to send for Mr. Crowley. And even he was hard pressed to do much for the man. He will probably lose his foot, and only because he wanted to feed his family. Damn your father to hell!"

She was so horrified by what she had seen, she did not see St. John flinch at the mention of amputation, but his voice was terrible when he asked what she was talking about.

"Oh, God! It isn't your fault," she moaned, "but I just

feel so helpless! The man's a farm laborer who, like so many others, has had trouble getting enough work or help from the poor rates. He and his wife have four children, and they have had no meat for so long, he grew desperate enough to poach for it. He was trying to take rabbits on your father's land, and he got his ankle caught in a trap. It took both him and his oldest son to get it off, and the metal had bitten deep by then, nearly into the bone. That was the boy who came for me."

He was glad that people saw him as separate enough from his family to come for aid to his wife. Rage to match Alex's poured through him. He had heard rumors that many landowners were setting vicious traps and employing armed patrols to keep people from poaching their game, but he had not known his own father was doing so. Most game on the Carrington land had not been naturally plentiful for a long time, but his father had stocked partridge and pheasant off and on, and the rabbits and brown hares had always kept up their numbers.

Because of his life with Alex, St. John had seen how hungry and impoverished many were, and the idea that his family would mangle or even kill those so in need made him feel physically ill. The agony of having his arm cut off seared through him again so sharply that he grasped his shoulder.

Alex understood the gesture too well. "I'm sorry! I should not have brought this home with me. There is nothing you can do." She pushed his hand away and gently massaged the old wound and then subsided gratefully against him when he pulled her close.

"That is the worst of it, that I can do nothing. The law is on my father's side. There is such injustice in that, but were I to tell my father that, it would only make him glory in his cruelty. We must do what we can to help the man and his family." He tipped her chin up. "And you must remember that you already do the best you can to help so many, you cannot allow what you can't change to burden you too heavily." He moved his hand down to touch her slightly rounded abdomen. "You already have a burden to carry."

More than you know, she thought, but she said, "You sound very like Grandmother."

"I could do much worse. I could be like my father."

"Or my mother."

It was a strange but strong bond between them—this need to be better than the worst of their blood.

She thought of it when her father came to visit. He came quite often now as if his wife's cold had finally seeped too deeply into his bones and he longed for the warmth of the cottage. Alex sensed that it was not altogether a good change. It was not as if he had gained an extra measure of courage, but rather that he simply did not care any more. It was not her observation alone; Boston confirmed it. He told his sister that quite often their father spent the whole day buried in a book, and seemed unaware of the bustle around him while Boston ran the chandlery. Boston insisted that it was fine with him. "Paris and Rome seem perfectly content with their work and their families; they hardly seem to remember that the ship chandlery exists. Dora and I have a good life this way."

Inwardly Alex mourned the loss of the adventurous spirit that had seemed too much a part of Boston when he was younger, but she had to concede that it was well he was grown so suddenly mature and capable, given the way things were.

"At least Father has proved to be a splendid grandfather. The children adore him, and he is endlessly patient with them. Mavis told me that if he came to them more often, she would have no job to do."

But to her, Caton in many ways was more child than parent. She hated the thought, but she saw that he shared with Florence the inability to take responsibility for life. In him the result was kinder because he was essentially kind, but it was still a vast lack in a grown man. It made her more determined than ever to be responsible for her own life.

But she didn't know what she would have done without help from Mavis and Timothy. The twins at two seemed to have become a small army of mischief. There was no meanness in either child, but they seemed to encourage each other in endless new adventures. And of the two, it was usually Flora who led while Blaine came along happily to assist.

One afternoon when they were supposed to be napping, they had instead gone roving and had ended up in their parents' bedchamber. The maneuver was not discovered until St. John was interrupted in his perusal of Weatherby's

Racing Calendar by an ominous thump from above. Tim was out, but St. John and Mavis headed upstairs at the same time and discovered the twins playing in the midst of splendid disarray. Everything they could reach had been pulled out of drawers or off tables; even the bedclothes were part of the heap.

Mavis went for them, scolding in her thickest Kentish dialect. "Yer tants wull be de death o' me!" was followed by an unintelligible burr; at least St. John couldn't understand it, though the twins seemed to.

He had to turn away for a moment in the interest of discipline. What the children had done was wrong, but they looked so funny he had to bite back laughter. Flora's angelic face was smeared with black ash from the hearth, and Blaine was draped in one of Alex's petticoats. They had obviously had a wonderful time, but now they were regarding Mavis with wide eyes. She was so seldom cross with them, they had no doubt of the trouble they were in.

St. John turned back to help clean up the mess and found his children looking to him for assistance. "Papa . . . ," Flora began with her most beguiling look, but he shook his head severely. "No, you have both been naughty; you mustn't touch other people's things." He was baffled by the further process of discipline, being unwilling to tyrannize his offspring, and was relieved to see that Mavis's displeasure was having all the effect he could wish for. Flora and Blaine were very subdued as they were led back to their room and told to stay there.

St. John helped Mavis tidy the room, though he was much slower than she, having to put things down to fold them neatly, but she was grateful for his efforts as she felt compelled to check often on the twins to make sure they were not bothering Christiana or thinking up new mischief. Both of the adults were thinking Alex would be tired when she got home, and they did not want her to have to face the mess.

St. John stopped to pick up the gleaming gold necklace, noting how artfully crafted it was. He put it on the bureau wondering in passing why Alex never wore it and then forgetting all about it as the task of setting the room to rights went on. Luckily nothing was broken, the thump having been caused by a stack of books toppling.

Alex wasn't home until late that afternoon, and she had to laugh at St. John's description of the twins, but then she sobered. "We probably aren't strict enough with them, but they're usually quite good, all things considered. And I loathe the idea of beating them into obedience when reason should suffice."

St. John's face reflected her own horror of the idea, but more clearly she was seeing the red streaks on Rane's flanks when Magnus had taken the belt to him.

She managed a shaky laugh. "Well, given our reactions to the thought, I don't think the children are in any danger of cruel treatment."

"Even if they're spoilt for a while, I prefer that to showing them what they already know—that we are bigger and stronger than they. I remember a great deal of hitting when I was a child, sometimes by governesses, later by my father and schoolmasters, and all it did for my character was to make me damn careful that no one knew much about what I was up to."

Alex's eyes were deep and tender as she looked at him. "I never knew; you never said a thing about it when we were children."

"I suppose I thought it was the lot of every child. But even so, my parents treated me better than yours treated you, my love."

Caton had not abused her, but nor had he interfered. St. John could not remember hearing a single kind word from Margaret to her daughter, and that had been worse than the occasional physical penalties he had had to endure.

"Come here, orphan mine," he said, and she curled gratefully into his lap, closing her eyes. It had been a long day of treating various ailments, including a case of the ague that still plagued too many people, especially those who came from very marshy areas. Peruvian bark, Cinchona, was a marvelous treatment for the symptoms, but it would be a better day when the fevers disappeared altogether. The effects were so debilitating, hardworking souls lost much precious strength and time to them. Storms and floods had begun this year, and she hoped they were not harbingers of another wet summer and spoiled grain and hay harvest. The economy of the country was so in need of a good year, and so were so many of the farm families Alex treated.

The concerns of the day blotted out all thought of Rane, but he was swiftly in focus again when she found the swan necklace on the bureau when she and St. John went up to bed.

Her heart gave a queer jump against her ribs as she stared at the piece, and then realizing she was hesitating too long, she said, "I presume one of the twins found this. I had it in a bottom drawer, I think."

"Yes. It's a fine bit of work. Why do you never wear it?" There was no suspicion in his voice, just curiosity, and it would stay that way, she hoped.

"The relatives in Devon, the Falconers, the ones who took me in, they were very generous. The green velvet cloak was a gift from them, too."

"Hardly humble fisherfolk, were they?"

His interest was heightened, not dispelled, and she chose her words carefully. "No, they own their own ships and some land besides. Sinje, they're free traders. They do very well at it, too, and have for a long time. Does that make you hate them because you fought at Waterloo?" Anything, anything, even this admission to keep him from finding out about Rane.

"No, truly it doesn't," he assured her after a moment's thought. "One thing hardly seems to have anything to do with the other, though I know one could argue the gold helped Bonaparte. I'm hardly in a position to object as I doubt I've had many glasses of wine or brandy or cups of tea that had full duty paid on them. No wonder you never speak of your time with them; a casual word could easily bring them to grief. The government is trying harder than ever to control free trading now that so many returned soldiers and sailors are taking to it. With the income tax being repealed and duties going up to compensate, it's no wonder the trade continues to be so lucrative. Did you take part?"

Suddenly it was a relief to talk about it. She kept Rane out of it except in passing mention of the Falconers, but she told St. John about unloading the cargoes at night, about the Exmoor ponies and Barnstaple Fair, about wassailing the apple trees, and about the wild swans.

"You loved the swans even when you were very small," St. John mused, his mind on other things as he began to understand. "You were so happy in Devon, but you came back. It was for Flora and Blaine, wasn't it?" He didn't need her confirmation. "And because of that I am alive and with my love. Dear heart, you will never be sorry again that you returned to Kent."

"I am not sorry now," she whispered, and it was true.

ᴥ Chapter 28 ᴥ

Morgan Carrington was born late in June, 1817. He was a healthy, squalling boy with a cap of dark hair and eyes that were sure to turn green. Even though Morgan was a larger baby than Christiana had been, his birth was swifter and easier than hers. True to his word, St. John was home, making, as Virginia claimed, "a perfect nuisance of himself," as he insisted on checking on Alex while she labored though he turned paler with each visit.

Irony on irony to have St. John so involved in this pregnancy. Even the prescribed practice of rubbing the salve over the skin of her abdomen and perineum in the last weeks had ceased to be a detached precaution and had become an erotic ritual performed by St. John.

She had kept the secret even while she labored, drifting only once to the place of the swans and then speaking only of them. St. John thought he understood perfectly; he knew how enchanted she had always been by those magnificent birds.

Only Virginia understood Alexandria's determination to name the child Morgan, which meant in the old Celtic tongue, "from the sea." As set as Alex was on making sure St. John never suffered for what she had done, so she was also resolved that Morgan would never be slighted for the truth of his conception. Even her body seemed to agree, for this time, she had enough milk to nurse her child even as in the course of the pregnancy she had suffered little discomfort. She found it not only satisfying but also a strange sensation as if the rest of the world ceased to exist while the child suckled, and they were both wrapped in an aura of calm.

Far from being jealous of this bond, St. John found himself drinking in the sight as thirstily as Morgan took life from Alex and feeling utterly content. Loving Alex had expanded his capacity for feeling until it was almost as if she had given birth to him as well as to the children. He noticed things that had never been important to him before, from the sunlight illuminating the edges of leaves to the texture of the clothes Alex wore. All his senses were heightened and so was his care for others. He had not been raised to notice those less fortunate than he except in a general way as his mother sometimes dispensed baskets of food or alms out of duty, not out of love or personal interest. But now he saw the lives behind the worn faces and chaffed against his inability to do much for them.

Spring had been chill and wet, and then a brief heat wave in June had given way to bad weather that was sure to damage the harvest once again. He wondered if the orderly habits of English life could withstand the misery of so many who had no work and little food. In the previous December, there had been serious trouble at Spa Fields, London, when a crowd, gathered to hear an address on parliamentary reform, had turned to acts of violence resulting in a riot. In March, the government had responded by passing the Coercion Acts which among other things suspended habeas corpus and were generally reactionary. St. John felt the failure of his own class keenly. Too many of the nobility cared too little and governed badly, and no one seemed able to deal with the changes taking place in the country as the population gradually moved to the cities to become more and more dependent on factory work and more and more vulnerable to the lack of it when the work shut down for want of buyers for the products. And with crops bad, those left on the land were so often little better off. Many families had meat no more than once a week, if that often, and no fuel for a warm hearth, the wood famine already of long standing over much of the land, and coal too dear for many to buy.

Short of massive reform, St. John could see no way out, and certainly he was not the stuff of the Baptist crying out in the wilderness. He suspected his reaction was that of many; he feared for his country and sorrowed for the suffering, but his energies were concentrated on keeping his own family secure. At least he managed to give money to the man who had been lamed poaching on Carrington land.

Timothy had carried out the mission, leaving the packet of coins on the family's doorstep without being detected. If they did not know where the money came from, they could not return it. But the man's foot had been amputated, and nothing would ever make him whole again. The stump of St. John's arm ached every time he thought of it. The last time he had seen his father and brothers, he had cut them dead before they could do the same to him. It was childish; nonetheless, it gave him some small satisfaction.

Most of his energy was concentrated on keeping track of all the up-and-coming colts and fillies and their various bloodlines. Overall he was winning more than he lost, but it was never a sure thing. Handicapping, a fairly recent development, had changed the face of the sport forever. Though its virtue was that it allowed the field of horses to be widened in that inferior horses could make a better showing when carrying less weight than their more capable opponents, its vice was the same in that the best horse was no longer bound to be the winner. And everything was further complicated by the wide opportunity handicapping allowed for cheating—shaving the weight for this horse, increasing it for that, so easily could the outcome of a race be altered.

Alex found it wholly frustrating. "I think it is completely unjust," she protested. "When a horse is the very best, it ought to be able to win fairly."

"Yes, it was simpler that way," St. John agreed. "But don't you see, often one finds an animal that is so swift, few if any other horses can race against him, and that spoils the sport." He smiled at her frown of doubt. "Yet to be honest, it does seem a pity to slow him down."

Alex saw more clearly now how skilled St. John was at his betting, not because he was a superior gambler, though that was part of it, but because he had been learning about fine horseflesh nearly from the cradle. And in addition to the acquired knowledge, he had an excellent, instinctive eye for it. He did not credit horses with superior intelligence; he had always judged them to be quite stupid. But this in no way diminished his admiration for them. He loved the beauty of their confirmation and the strength of spirit that would keep a champion running to win long after exhaustion set in. And his single dream was to someday own a stable of the finest horses in the land.

Alex did not protest that such an establishment would, barring a miracle, be forever out of their reach. The best racing stables were the providence of kings and other high nobles or extremely rich merchants. The funds required to buy and maintain fine bloodstock were enormous, and few horses ever won consistently enough to recoup the outlay. If money were to be made, it was in the breeding and selling of the offspring of those animals who proved themselves to be the swiftest. And even that was a chancy business at best; a mare or stallion might prove to be a bad breeder or the foals might show none of the promise of their sires and dams. The best combination of speed, temperament, and endurance was a delicate one, easily lost by just a shade of difference in any of the elements. But it didn't matter; if St. John wanted to dream of racing horses under his own colors some day, so be it.

With four children, it was too easy for the two of them to become too distracted to have time for each other, and they both worked hard to prevent it. Alex told him about her patients; he told her about the current racing crop; and they shared time with the children.

St. John was enchanted by each of the four. Flora and Blaine were daily becoming more individual, though their lives were still deeply intertwined. But it was easy to see that Flora was the instigator, Blaine the happy follower. When Flora announced that she "don't want new baby," St. John cleverly deflected Blaine's alliance with his sister by pointing out that it would be fun for him to have a brother to play with when the infant Morgan got a little older. Blaine pondered this for quite a time before he decided he liked the idea, and then his parents discovered an interesting fact. Blaine was so easygoing, they had not been aware before that when he did want something different from what Flora wanted, he got it by sheer, immovable stubbornness. Morgan became, proudly, "my bruver," and Flora, not wanting to be excluded, ceased to view Morgan with such animosity.

Christiana, over a year old now, charmed her father by

her mere existence. She was such a fragile little girl, as fair as he, but possessed of green-blue eyes that tilted just like her mother's. In repose, her face was very solemn, but she was quick to laugh, and then it was like a burst of sunlight, startling in its intensity.

"I shall be a madman when she comes of age," St. John confessed to Alex. "I am sure I will not find a man in all of England who is good enough for her."

"I fear she may have ideas about finding her own man," Alex retorted with a smile, and St. John looked so worried, she burst out laughing. "You don't have to worry about it yet, dear heart."

For Morgan, he felt such a depth of love, it sometimes frightened him. Even in so small and new a personage, the old stamp of the Thaines was completely clear. To look at Morgan was to see Alexandria, and this pleased St. John endlessly.

Often he was amused by his own behavior. Never in his wildest imaginings as a youth would he have pictured himself as a devoted father with a brood of four. He had grown up assuming he would father children eventually and know them only in the vague way his parents had done, at the distance of servants caring for them and allowing only brief parental visits. In a perverse way he had even grown to be grateful for his infatuation with Florence. Without it, he would never have had either the twins or Alexandria. Sometimes when Alex turned her head a certain way or was just caught in sunlight for a moment, her emerging beauty would stun him anew, and he would feel a twinge of guilt for having made her a woman when she was so young. He knew that she would have had a wide choice of young men were it not for him. And that only made him more determined that she should always be loved as much as any woman had ever been loved by any man.

Though she sometimes felt overwhelmed by the amount of attention demanded of her by patients and her own family, Alex never ceased to give thanks that what had begun so badly had come so right. Everywhere there were reminders that others were not so fortunate, one of those reminders in her own household.

She had snapped at the twins and was even cross with Christiana because the children were being very fractious on a morning when she herself was so tired, she wished she'd stayed in bed. Taking up her practice again while still nursing Morgan required extra precision with her time, for if she could not manage to visit a patient and return in time for Morgan's next feeding, she had to carry him with her even while she made sure he did not distract her mind from the problems of the ill. She did not have a maid trailing after her to share the burden.

When a small measure of order had been restored, Alex sighed, "Sometimes I think children are as much a curse as a blessing."

"I'd gie all t'ave just one," Mavis murmured.

"Surely you will have them," Alex assured her, mindful of the baby Mavis had already had.

But Mavis shook her head, and the rest of the story poured out. There had been damage, and the midwife had told her she doubted she'd conceive again. She had told Tim before their marriage, and he had said it didn't matter, but she wasn't so sure.

"Midwives aren't always correct," Alex pointed out, thinking this particular one should never have told Mavis such a thing and thinking, too, of how sick and sad Mavis must have felt when she'd first taken over the suckling of the twins. "But even if it is true, I'm sure Timothy told you the truth about how he feels. He loves you very much." Words were hardly compensation for empty arms. Suddenly her own children seemed even more precious to Alex, and she was more grateful than ever for Mavis's loving care of them.

The early new year of 1818 brought news of yet another child on the way; this time Boston and Dora's.

"All in all the Thaines are proving a fertile lot," Boston observed to his sister. "Even Paris and Rome have done their part, though I find it difficult to imagine them involved in such basic work."

Alex giggled and shocked Boston in turn. "Cautiously, with their eyes closed, and most of their clothes on."

St. John came over, attracted by the sound of their laughter.

"Your wife is developing a very bawdy sense of humor," Boston told him.

"Thank heaven for that," St. John said fervently, and that set them off again.

But in June, the laughter was gone. St. John returned from Epsom Downs to find Alex looking so ill and tired, he immediately feared something awful had befallen one of the children or Mavis or Timothy, who did not seem to be in evidence.

He found that Mavis and Tim had taken his perfectly healthy children out for a time to give Alex a respite, and it was Dora's name Alex sobbed as he held her.

"No warning, there was none, and . . . nothing to do for her. So close to term, but the . . . the baby was born dead and Dora bled to death. They were buried nearly a week ago."

St. John's first thought was purely selfish and caused his arm to tighten with fierce strength around her. As it had been with Florence, so this time it could have been Alexandria and one of his own children who were lost. But then his heart contracted for Boston who had been so joyful with his wife. And for Dora with the merry brown eyes and the good heart that had not slighted the Carringtons despite the illegality of their marriage.

He held Alex until she gained control, and then he asked, "Boston, how is he?"

She bit her lip against fresh tears. "He does nothing but work. Father says he's gone over the same figures countless times to no purpose. I don't think he's slept or eaten a decent meal since it happened. And he hasn't wept; his face looks carved of stone. I can't help him. My heart is breaking for him, but I can't help him! I'm so worried about him!"

"It may just be a matter of time, love, but I'll go see him, and if I can, I'll bring him back here. You should have sent for me. Someone could have found me."

There was no censure in his voice, just love overflowing for her, and she was so grateful for his strong presence that she wanted to weep anew for her brother's loss.

The children and even Tim and Mavis were all abed by the time St. John returned late in the evening. He had Boston in tow, a very drunk Boston.

Alex had never seen her brother inebriated. He was hard pressed to walk under his own power, but he made it to the parlor before he collapsed in a chair. St. John had had a time even luring him away from the ledgers, but he had persisted, using every stratagem, including his added years and his plea that Alex was worrying herself sick over her brother.

In truth, St. John had been stunned by the change in

the young man. In the short time since he had last seen him, Boston had been stripped down to mere skin and bones, his green eyes muddy and vacant. St. John had begun to ply him with brandy at the first opportunity, bespeaking a private room at a local tavern. While urging him to drink, he had rattled on about nothing in particular, covering his intent with innocuous words that apparently made as much sense to Boston as anything had lately. Boston had no hard head for drinking, and in his weakened state, he had quickly lost his bearings on a sea of brandy. St. John had timed it neatly to get him home before he fell over.

Alex's eyes were wide and questioning, and St. John murmured, "If nothing else, he'll sleep. But I think he's about ready to give way, and that's the best thing for him."

Alex approached her brother, speaking gently as she put her arms around him. "Boston, Dora loved you so much, she would hate to see you so diminished. I know it's not the same, but we're here for you, and we love you."

A convulsive shudder ran through his lanky frame, and then he began to weep harshly, tortured words of guilt and loss pouring from him.

Alex hung on to him, stroking his hair. "That's it, weep for her, but you mustn't blame yourself. It happens, God knows it happens too often. But it's a risk we all take to have children."

St. John stayed with them until Boston had fallen into a sodden sleep, and then he led Alex up to their bed, and they held each other tightly all through the night.

Slowly Boston picked up the threads of his life again, claiming with a flash of his old humor that he dared do no less since his brother-in-law had employed such drastic methods of healing. But though he spent much time at the cottage and was as tender with the children as he had ever been, he was profoundly changed. His old fire was gone; he had an air of patient acceptance that reminded Alex too much of their father. But St. John kept reminding her that whatever final adjustments Boston made in his life, they were a private matter.

For his own part, St. John found himself wanting more time alone with Alex, away from the daily cares of their life. Her responsibilities made it difficult for her to get away for more than a few hours at a time, but in early August, he took her to the annual swan-upping.

Once she realized they were really going, she was as giddy as a child. She had heard of the ceremony but had never witnessed it. Even the trip by steamer ferry (Gravesend now had two in alternating service) to London made her wide-eyed and a little fearful, and St. John teased that perhaps that was excitement enough.

Lord Bettingdon met them with a private launch manned by stout oarsmen, and they followed the procession on the river from Southwark. Hugh and St. John were more fascinated by Alex's reactions than by the colorful pageant.

Mute swans privately owned were required to be marked on the bill, unmarked swans belonging to the Crown, the mute swan being considered the royal bird. There were various marks throughout the country, but in an area of some thirty miles, from Blackfriars Bridge to Henley, the swans belonged either to the Crown or to the Vintners or Dyers, old city guilds.

On their barges, the participants were dressed in bright liveries—blue and white for the Vintners, blue for the Dyers—and rowed by uniformed oarsmen. The royal swanmaster and his men wore scarlet. At long last England was having a fair summer that promised a fine harvest, and the weather held for the vivid ceremony.

Alex discovered that she liked everything about it except the actual work, which was to mark the half-grown cygnets with a notch on the side of the bill if it belonged to the Dyers, with a double chevron if it was property of the Vintners, the ownership established by the marks—or lack of them in the case of the royal birds—on the parents' bills. The swans struggled mightily, but even though the cygnets at this stage were large enough to inflict a bonebreaking blow with their wings, the "uppers" were skillful in catching them and folding their feet back over their wings to immobilize them.

When they were close enough to see the bills being punctured, Alex winced in sympathy.

"I don't think swans have very long memories," Hugh pointed out. "By tomorrow they will undoubtedly be unaware that their bills are marked." But he noted that she did not look convinced and was glad he had not included in his commentary an account of the annual swan roasting held by the guilds.

"It's rather better to be a royal bird than not, isn't it? Here as elsewhere," Alex remarked tartly, and the two men exchanged a look of such surprise that she laughed and added, "Even simple country lasses have heard of Mrs. Fitzherbert." Mrs. Fitzherbert was the Prince Regent's longtime mistress, whom many suspected he had married in secret before he wed his cousin Caroline, daughter of the Duke of Brunswick-Wolfenbüttel, for purely political reasons. There was no proof of the first marriage, but Mrs. Fitzherbert was a Roman Catholic and rumored to have strong feelings about an illicit union.

"Simple I doubt you have ever been," Hugh protested, and then he roared with laughter, as much for the startled look on St. John's face as for what Alex had said. "St. John, you will have to dance lightly to keep ahead of this one."

In the afternoon, Hugh took them outside London for a ride in his phaeton pulled by a magnificent pair of matched grays, fast driving being all the rage now that England's roads were being improved. It was possible to survive in vehicles much lighter and swifter than the lumbering coaches of old that had been necessary for survival on very bad surfaces.

Alex watched St. John surreptitiously, worrying that the skill with which Hugh handled the ribbons would make him conscious of his own lack of two strong hands, but he was perfectly at ease and genuinely admiring of the high-bred grays.

Suddenly he caught her anxious look and whispered, "Ah, but I do other things very well, or so my wife tells me."

"Your wife is a very honest woman," she retorted, and they didn't mind that they were smiling at each other like besotted youngsters.

They had supper at Hugh's elegant London residence and then went out to enjoy the soft summer evening under London's gaslight. Treating her with elaborate and silly courtliness, the men escorted Alex to Vauxhall Pleasure Gardens where they listened to a concert and observed all the mischief going on, Hugh giving a wicked though restrained account of who was doing what to whom. The men stayed close to Alex, aware of the hungry glances of other men though she took no notice at all, enchanted with her companions and needing no other attention.

She remembered her visit here with her father before her exile to Devon, and there was only joy in the memory, a sweet echo of a childhood that seemed a lifetime before. Taking advantage of a deep patch of shadow, she tugged St. John's head down and gave him a swift kiss. "That's just because I love you," she whispered, and later as they lay together in the grand bed of the exquisite room Hugh had given them in his house, St. John managed to murmur, "I must take you to Vauxhall more often, it had a marvelous effect on you," before coherent speech deserted him as Alex began to tease his groin with knowing hands and delicate mouth.

They were both deeply grateful to Hugh for making their stay with him so easy and private, for had he invited his usual friends to join them, Alex knew she would have been self-conscious about her simple wardrobe and lack of polish, no matter how well she might have been able to cope. And even St. John, who had the social graces, wore clothing that was slightly out of date and worn now that he had shouldered his share of the family's financial burden. The servants, who could have shown their disapproval in subtle but noticeable ways, had been kind, helpful, and unobtrusive, another measure of Hugh's skill as a host.

But when the Carringtons tried to thank him, Hugh cut them short. "Do you really believe that anything in this house or all of it together could equal the sum of Flora, Blaine, Christiana, and Morgan, whom you so generously share with me?"

"We will have to play matchmakers and find you a lovely lady," Alex told him as she bid him farewell.

Your twin would do nicely, Hugh thought, but none of his longing showed on his face.

❧ *Chapter 29* ❧

One still night in autumn, Alex heard wild swans passing overhead on their way to warmer climes for the winter, their calls and the rhythmic beat of their great wings made clear by some trick of air. She thought of the August outing with St. John and Hugh and smiled—the swans flying over were free and unmarked. She snuggled closer to St. John's warmth, glad that he was home between race meetings. Even the swans had now become part of her life with him, not with Rane, and she felt gain, not loss, in that.

The fair weather held for so long, it was as if the sweet days of summer were going to last forever. Confused spring flowers bloomed here and there, and it was said that in Devon strawberries and raspberries were being picked even in December. In a fit of whimsy, Alex wondered if the Devil had come through to spit on the blackberries on Michaelmas Day or had been as seduced by the mild weather as everyone else.

The halcyon days ended in pain so acute it was to remain part of Alex forever. The weather in January and February of 1819 was less inclement than it had been in the two previous years, but there were still the usual outbreaks of earaches, colds, and various other ailments. Alex spent long hours treating a family whose six children had putrid sore throats and whose mother was simply too worn out to cope and received little help from her husband. It was hard going for the youngest for a couple of days as he ran a very high fever, but he began to recover swiftly once the fever had broken.

Alex was not even particularly concerned when Christiana

began to develop the same symptoms, though she felt a severe twinge of guilt for having brought the infection home with her despite her efforts to wash thoroughly before she got close to the children. But no matter what one did, children contracted various ailments; it was part of childhood.

Her calm approach began to desert her rapidly as Christiana's condition grew worse at an alarming rate.

"I don't seem to be doing very well with this. Will you go for Grandmother?" she asked St. John, and he went immediately, already at his wit's end because he could not bear to see any of his children suffering.

Alex expected to feel more confident the moment Virginia arrived, but her grandmother had nothing good to tell her. "Christiana is very ill indeed. Her throat is so swollen, she can hardly breathe. I think Mr. Crowley ought to be summoned."

This time Timothy went, remembering too clearly when he had gone to find the man for St. John. But then, St. John had lived, surely the little one would, too.

They labored over her for hours, trying to reduce her fever, trying to control the swelling in her throat. Alex crooned to her continuously until her own throat was raw, her normally husky voice reduced to a dry whisper. But her daughter was lost in her own feverish nightmares, croaking unintelligible terrors of the young—things crawling on the walls and on her skin, animals of vast size tearing at her—until her throat was too swollen for the words to escape.

As a last resort, Mr. Crowley cut into the frail throat, seeking to give Christiana a new airway, but it was no use. Her little body convulsed violently, and then she was still, utterly still.

"I killed her," Alex said in a light, conversational tone. "I brought the contagion home to her."

Virginia, Mr. Crowley, and St. John froze, and then Virginia snapped, "Nonsense! These things happen. Christiana has been delicate and prone to fevers since she was born." She held her own grief at bay by sheer willpower.

"Of course," Alex agreed, and they all knew she did not believe it.

"We have the twins and Morgan." St. John forced the

futile words past the tightness of his own throat and then began to sob.

The deep wrenching sounds of grief penetrated the fog that was beginning to enshroud Alex. She put her arms around St. John, but no tears of her own came. *Sinje, you do not know, but this is our only child, the only child you and I have made together. The twins were Florence's, and Morgan is not your son. Why couldn't it have been one of the twins, not my child, but hers?* She was instantly appalled by the thought and wondered for an awful instant if she had said any of it aloud. She knew she had not by the lack of reaction in those around her.

The fierce inner voice came again. *I do not mean it. I love Flora and Blaine more than my own life. I will never love them less than my own flesh; I swear it on my soul.*

She knew Christiana was dead, but she could not feel her own pain, only the pulse of it in St. John who was in worse agony than when he had lost his arm. He kept gasping his daughter's name over and over, his voice so lost and broken that he became the lost child.

She was needed. It was her job to look after St. John and the children. Her own grief slipped further out of focus. Not even at the graveside did she weep. Christiana was buried in the yard of St. Mary's, Stone Church, where she had been christened. Alex saw that many of the stones were weathered away and did not think of it any more. She could hear Mavis weeping again, and she wished the woman would stop. It was an annoying sound. Beside Alex, St. John trembled, and she moved closer to him in case he needed her support.

Across the grave, Hugh watched them, his own misery so great for the loss of his godchild, he might have lost a child of his own. He had stood godfather to Morgan, too, and was relieved that neither Morgan nor the twins showed any signs of illness, only baffled restlessness at the strange behavior of those around them. Timothy was with them now.

Hugh tried to keep his mind on the others, but his thoughts kept coming back to Alexandria. He knew St. John was going to be all right; he was working through his grief by acknowledging it, even giving in to it. But not Alex. St. John had told him she had not even cried, and he believed it. Her face had an inhuman pallor, her green eyes were as big as the world and as unfathomable, and there was a stillness about her that made him realize how animated she usually was, always in swift motion. He had talked to Virginia about her, and her answer haunted him.

"She will break. She cannot go on like this forever. And once she is broken, she can begin to put the pieces back one by one. She will never be the same—a woman cannot be after the burial of her child—but she will be something new and stronger. Or she will be nothing at all."

"Let go, Alex, let go!" he wanted to scream at her, but instead he observed all the rules of good breeding, expressing his condolences as best he could and feeling more useless than he ever had before.

Boston felt the same and murmured to Hugh, "I wish I believed that dosing her with brandy as St. John did me would open the gates, but I know it wouldn't do the slightest bit of good. Alex is very strong, but now she's using her strength against herself."

St. John, who was closest to her in the loss, was as helpless as the others. When he held her and finally made desperate love to her, and even felt her body respond to his, it was as if she were not there. An endlessly kind and patient Alex met his needs and those of the children who were baffled and frightened by the disappearance of their sister, but the essential Alex was hidden away so well that he could not even glimpse her. Her patients found the same thing. They were surprised when she continued to visit the sick even after what had happened, but for her, it was a simple decision. People still needed her, so she must go. She gave the same competent care as before, but her patients, too, missed the lively lass they had known and hoped for her return.

It was an ugly vicious rumor that made the Carringtons' friends feel ashamed even to have heard it. The rumor said that the child's death was a judgment on St. John's and Alex's unsanctioned union. It said that Alexandria could not even cure her own child, so what use was she to others. Those who knew her skill defended her hotly, but Alex herself said nothing at all about it. When St. John asked her hesitantly if she had heard certain gossip, her face did not change expression as she repeated the hideous lies.

St. John had enough rage for both of them, and he knew where the venom was coming from.

He had not been to the Thaine house since the night he had gone with Alex to tell her parents of their intentions. And he did not want to be there now, but he could not stay away. He made sure Caton was at the store before he sought out Margaret.

Whatever beauty the woman had once possessed was totally eclipsed by her sour spirit, but her eyes gleamed with malice when she saw who her visitor was.

St. John wasted no time in pleasantries. "I know what you have been saying about Alexandria, about me, and about the death of our daughter. You are a hag out of hell, and that cannot be changed. But I warn you now, if I ever hear of you saying even one more word against my wife, I will kill you or have it done. It would be wise of you to let your gossips know that you spoke unwisely out of grief for the loss of your granddaughter. Do you understand?"

Margaret's head wagged assent as her defiance gave way to pure terror. He had only one arm, and his voice was quite low and controlled, but she felt the enormous force behind his threat and saw her own death in his vivid blue eyes. She was accustomed to dealing in barbed words, but not in physical violence, and she knew defeat. Boston was out of her control now, and even Caton, she was sure, had been seeing Alex and St. John and their children. He had met her questions with a blank stare that was unnerving. She considered herself a righteous woman who knew the cost of virtue and was baffled by her failure to triumph. Alexandria had caused all her misery; she fixed on that fact but knew it was no use. This man was her daughter's slave and would keep his vow.

When word of her mother's supposed change of heart filtered through to Alex, she knew instantly that St. John was responsible, and she thanked him politely for defending her, but with a sinking heart, he realized that it mattered to her no more than the cruel rumors had. She was drifting in some private space where nothing touched her.

When he would have foregone the spring racing season, St. John found that Alex would have none of it. "Staying here will not bring Christiana back," she told him bluntly. "And we need your winnings."

More than you know, she thought. The idea had formed and grown steadily, the only definite shape in the mist that had swirled around her since Christiana's death. She wanted to leave, to go far away and start a completely new life. Maryland. It had become a talisman against the madness she felt waiting at the edges of her mind. Caleb Jennings's descriptions had come back to her so clearly that she felt as if she could see the great salt bay and the thriving life it contained, and the green land stretching to great mountains.

The irony of the change in herself did not escape her. Once Devon had seemed exile at the end of the earth, and now she wanted to sail far beyond the West Country. She wanted to be with her family in a place where the old social distinctions did not matter, where St. John's family and her own mother did not exist. She twisted away from admitting to herself that she did not want to be where she could see her daughter's name scrubbed by rain and wind from the headstone over the years.

But to go would mean a great expense—money to travel to America and money to start a new life there. Pennies and shillings, even farthings, took on new meaning. The Bateses, Timothy and Mavis, would have been insulted by her cheeseparing ways had they not believed the change was somehow connected with the loss of her child, for after all, they were very careful in the way they shopped for the family's needs.

St. John unfortunately remained unaware of Alex's new preoccupation until it was too late. He knew how much she valued security, and so he did the best he could to provide it, concentrating more intensely on the horses and his wagers than he ever had before and gratefully accepting Hugh's help when the duke offered inside tips on various horses and jockeys and even his suspicions when the handicapping of a certain race did not seem honest.

Unable to risk enough to make a huge amount, still St. John stayed a little ahead and was able to give money to Alex when he was home. He was more and more reluctant to leave her, and yet, she remained completely in control on the surface, and he could not pierce the darkness beneath. He felt lonely even when he was with her, and it made him realize how much he depended on her spirit freely given to him. But in June, when he returned from the races at Epsom, he brought with him a surprise he was sure would not only cheer Alex but would also give her a new interest.

The mare was glorious—a sleek chestnut with startlingly beautiful conformation, her wide-set dark eyes and sculptured head hinting of her Arabian forebears. She was high-strung but sweet tempered. In her coursed the blood of some of the best racehorses England had ever known, among them Herod who traced back to the Byerley Turk and Eclipse who had descended from the Darley Arabian. And she was carrying a foal whose sire had the blood of Matchem, who in turn had been of the blood of both the Byerley Turk and the Godolphin Arabian.

The Byerley Turk, the Darley Arabian, the Godolphin Arabian—St. John savored the names and the promise. Those three from the last century, and in the case of the Byerley Turk, from the late years of the seventeenth century, were the founding sires of all the great race horses of the day. And though the mare and the stallion she had been bred to had not done terribly well in their own racing days, the strains of speed and endurance were there, marked by winners in previous generations.

The mare's name was Leda which St. John thought would please Alex with its allusion to the myth of the woman visited by Zeus disguised as a swan. She was seven years old, and she was lame, having fallen shortly after she had been bred. The best care had not improved her condition. It was the only reason St. John owned her now.

He had won a heavy wager with the owner. It had been the biggest risk he had ever taken because he had not had the money to pay had he lost, but he had felt very sure and had acted on his instinct even while knowing it was the same seductive sense that even had proved the ruin of many gamblers, his family included. Hugh's frown had shown his disapproval when he was told about the bet, but he had had the restraint to keep his thoughts to himself. His thoughts had been mostly of Alexandria because he had known that if St. John lost, the sum that was bet would beggar the Carringtons for years to come. But he had also spared a thought for his friend. He suspected that St. John was feeling some of the same numbness Alex displayed and that this enormous risk was a way of feeling more alive.

Hugh had not kept silent when St. John's victory had been converted to yet another gamble. Lord Sharbrowley, the loser, was known to be short of the ready, but he did

have a fine stable. And he had given St. John a choice—
the money or the mare.

"For God's sake, St. John, make him pay you the money!"
Hugh had urged. "The mare is lame. He's made no secret
of that. And because of that you know as well as I that
she may not even be able to carry the foal to term. Even if
she does, and even with all her good blood, there is no
way to be sure that the foal will inherit the desired
characteristics. It might well turn out to be a bleeder with
no speed."

The argument was not specious. Herod himself had
burst a blood vessel while running at York in 1766 and
had bled so profusely that his life had been in danger.
Among the good characteristics he had passed on to his
descendants had been this unfortunate one. And for that
matter, the Eclipse blood could produce, along with great
speed, excitability to the point of making the horse very
difficult to control.

St. John had replied without heat. "Everything you say
is true. If it were not, nothing on earth could make
Sharbrowley part with the mare. Nothing is sure in racing;
nothing is sure in anything."

The sudden shadow of grief in the blue eyes undid
Hugh, and he ceased to argue, but he could not shake his
misgivings about what Alex's reaction would be. Somehow he just did not think that she would welcome the
crippled mare in place of the hundred guineas her husband could have brought home.

Because Leda had to be brought along slowly from
Sharbrowley's stables, St. John and Hugh took several
extra days to reach Gravesend. But Alex had felt no particular worry; indeed, she hardly kept track of the days
anymore, but rather went from one to the next trying not
to think, trying to be like those people her grandmother
had once described as living lives little different from the
beasts.

Maryland. It was now the single goal, the chance for
renewal, and nothing else mattered, not even the now
familiar changes in her own body.

Until she saw the mare. Until St. John, his voice full of
remembered excitement, told her of the wager and how
he had foregone one hundred guineas.

Timothy was already crooning to the beast as Hugh's
groom held her, and Mavis had her hands full keeping

the four-year-old twins and two-year-old Morgan from running to the horse.

One hundred guineas. It was a small fortune. The rage swept through Alex in a tidal wave, the hot blood roaring in her ears and blinding her eyes.

"You swyving bastard! Have you no sense at all? The money could have taken us a good way toward Maryland. A goddamn crippled mare . . ."

The shrieking voice was totally unlike her, and even the children were frozen in place, their eyes wide with horror as they stared at their mother. The horses backed and danced in agitation.

Hugh understood first what was happening. "Get her inside," he barked at St. John. "Keep the children out of the house," he ordered Timothy and Mavis.

The heritage of centuries of giving orders and expecting to be obeyed were in his demeanor, and no one questioned his right. Driving his phaeton as if in a race, Hugh went for Virginia Thaine, and he was so thankful when he found her, that he burst out, "Thank God!"

Alex continued to curse as St. John led her inside, but she did not resist him, and then the strident note died to a strange soft keening. "We'll never go, I know we'll never go. But I want to. God, how I want to be gone from this place! Another child, I carry another child. I don't want another child in her place, another child to die. My mother's right, I am cursed. Guilt, so much guilt. I brought the sickness home." She babbled on, St. John receiving one shock after another as he listened, but some small measure of sanity kept Rane's name locked deep inside of Alex.

And then the tears came, great hot rivers of them as her whole body heaved with strangled sobs.

St. John looked up desperately as Virginia and Hugh came in, but he took heart when Virginia said, "This has needed to happen for months. It's all right, St. John, just hold on to her. She'll know you're there eventually."

Her calm voice reassured him, but it seemed like forever before Alex slumped against him in exhausted sleep. Hugh carried her upstairs to bed, and St. John helped Virginia undress her, his voice breaking a little as he said, "I've gotten quite good at untying and unbuttoning with one hand."

"You've gotten quite good at most things," Virginia

said warmly. "And you mustn't think this is your fault. It has been coming ever since Christiana died. It was time and past for her to weep. If it hadn't been the mare, it would have been something else. Now we let her rest."

Virginia told him that the children and the Bateses had already been taken by Hugh to her house. "It's best that they're out from underfoot." She did not need to add that she and Mavis would do their best to convince the children that their mother was recovered. "Hugh will take me home, and then he will stay here with you, just in case you need someone. Pray allow him to do so; he is very fond of you and Alexandria."

St. John was immensely grateful to all of them for taking charge; he had little thought to spare for anyone except the woman sleeping upstairs.

"Has she spoken to you of Maryland?" he asked Virginia before she departed.

"No," she looked as puzzled as he felt. "Maryland in the United States?"

"I presume so, but I really don't know. I never heard her mention it before." He shivered at the memory of Alex's mad screaming.

Virginia was suddenly sure that it had something to do with Falconers. Maryland tobacco was an old part of the trade. But she was also sure that even in her uncontrolled state, Alex had not mentioned Rane. St. John was stunned, but he did not have the look of a man who had just discovered that he had been betrayed by his wife.

"You will know why she mentioned the place soon enough. I promise you, she has not gone insane. She is very, very strong, and that is a curse as well as a blessing because it takes her such a very long time to bend. But I would rather have that than the way of my son. Caton bends so easily, he is scarcely ever upright." The tart note brought a smile from St. John, just as she had intended.

She pulled his head down and kissed him on the cheek. "Just go on loving her, my boy. It is enough."

Hugh stayed with St. John until near dawn. They talked in a desultory fashion, but both of them had all their senses trained on the room upstairs. St. John checked on Alex frequently, but she lay perfectly still, her pale face looking bruised from her weeping.

The only time St. John truly focused on their conversation was when he again brought up the subject of Maryland and was startled by Hugh's reaction.

"What if she means it? What if she really wants to leave England?" Hugh asked. "It must be something deeply felt to come out at such a time."

"Leave England? She can't mean . . . ," his voice trailed away.

Hugh pressed his advantage. "Why not? This is the country where you have no rights because you are a younger son and disinherited. And this is the country where Alexandria cannot marry the father of her children, the man she loves. It is not so strange that she would want to make a new beginning. St. John, Alex is like the wild swans she loves so much. She needs to be free, not tame and marked." His voice died away, and he prayed that St. John would never know how much he had come to love Alex.

❧ Chapter 30 ❧

When Alex stirred and opened her eyes, she found St. John watching her, his eyes so anxious and full of love that weak tears began to trickle down her cheeks.

"Now that I've started to weep, I can't seem to stop. Oh, Sinje, I'm so sorry! I didn't mean any of the things I said. Of course we'll care for the mare—Leda, isn't it? —and she'll have a fine colt." Her voice faded for a moment, and she had to make a concentrated effort to go on. She felt so battered, as if she'd been in an awful fight and had lost. "Our dreams just went in different directions."

"Yours to Maryland, in the United States? Why?" he asked gently.

She told him the story of Caleb Jennings, changing only

Rane's part to "my cousins," as if Seadon and Elwyn had been involved, too, and not only was St. John struck by the adventure of it, but also by the liveliness that came to Alex's eyes. How he had missed that!

"I know how crazed it must sound, but I truly have thought about it. Life will never change for us here, never. We will always be just on the edge of dreams, yours or mine, and our children, too, as long as we remain here." Her hands moved involuntarily to cover her abdomen, and St. John leaned down to kiss her, asking, "When is it due?"

"November." The word held a world of pain, and counting back he understood why; the new baby must have been conceived very near to the time of Christiana's death.

She reached for his hand and held it very tightly. "I knew the instant Christiana died, I did know. But somehow I haven't believed it. And I knew she was being buried; I can still see that dry sheaf of wheat on the little coffin. But somehow, I haven't believed it. I've expected to see her coming to me with her funny little walk. I've almost heard her voice a thousand times. I saw a butterfly the other day, and I could see Christiana gazing at it in pure delight, just barely keeping herself from trying to touch it. Once she told me that 'fluttabies bweak.' I do know she is dead. I know with every bone and drop of blood in my body now. And I want to go from this place where she died."

Tears glistening on her cheeks, she fell asleep again, and St. John eased himself down beside her, suddenly intolerably weary. But in the days that followed, he was haunted by her wish to leave England. He offered to sell the mare even though he knew it would be difficult to find someone as willing as he to take a risk on her, but Alex refused.

"No, she is your dream, at least a beginning for it. And she needs good care. Poor Leda, my outburst wasn't her fault; she was an innocent victim."

The fact that she did not mention Maryland again made St. John consider it more. He thought of what Hugh had said, and he explained the reference to Virginia, wincing at the pain he saw in her eyes when she considered what it would mean to her if her granddaughter left.

"You could come with us," St. John proposed sincerely, though he knew she would never leave her farm.

But she did not dismiss the idea out of hand. She, too, saw the reasons for Alex's desire to be gone. "Many have emigrated for less," she observed thoughtfully. "But the important thing now is Alexandria's health and that of her unborn child. You would not be able to leave until next spring."

St. John knew that the carefully practical words were a benediction; Virginia would, as always, stand with them, not against.

And then Hugh gave even more shape to the dream St. John was not sure he could share.

"It's all hearsay, of course, but I've done some checking on Maryland. While it's true that the tobacco lands of the more settled eastern parts of the state seem to be suffering from depleted soil, it sounds to me that if one were to use the land with more care and enrich the soil, it would still have possibilities. And in any case, you would probably not be going into the tobacco business. There are other things being raised in Maryland, fruits, vegetables, and grain among them, and horses, fine horses. Some of the best studs have moved south and west, but Maryland is still noted for good bloodstock. And there is no law against your marriage in America; they broke with the Church of England when they rebelled against the Crown. St. John, there is no state church in the United States!" Hugh's efforts to sound offhand failed utterly with his last bit of information.

"Has Alex spoken to you?" St. John asked. "Is that why you're urging us to go?"

"No, she hasn't said a word," Hugh replied firmly. "And I'm not urging you to go. That has to be your decision and will be my loss if you do go, but I am urging you to consider it. I would be less than a friend if I did not want what is best for you, your wife, and your children. And Alex is not the same as she was before Christiana died. Maybe she never will be again, but she might have a better chance of life in a new setting. And it is not as if the course of life is running that smoothly here in England."

St. John had to agree with Hugh's observation, though he wished he could deny it. He felt closer to Alex again, but much of her spirit still seemed to be lacking. She had not regained her old look of health, and often when she was unaware of his scrutiny, he saw a well of sadness in her eyes that tore at his heart. Hugh was no less astute in his view of the general situation in the country. The good harvest of the previous year had not been enough to turn things around as it might have done in an older and simpler time. Economic depression was settling on the country again, hurting the workers in the coal mines and in the weaving industry the worst, leaving them in cruel conditions with scant wages, or without work at all. The tremors of discontent were being met by reactionary growls from the government rather than any helpful measures. Even in Gravesend, still a prosperous port, there were signs of trouble. Though the cornerstone had been laid for improvements on the market and town hall and work had begun, there were rumors that funds would be insufficient for completion.

Too often for his peace of mind, St. John found himself thinking that his beloved England had grown too old to support the dreams of the young.

In August the awful account of the "Peterloo Massacre" spread across the land. A crowd had gathered at St. Peter's Fields, Manchester, to hear a speech on the repeal of the Corn Laws and the need for parliamentary reform. Things had swiftly gotten disastrously out of hand. Soldiers ordered to arrest the speaker charged the crowd in the process, and pandemonium reigned. Several people were killed and hundreds injured. And the greatest shame of all was that many of the soldiers had served at Waterloo, hence "Peterloo." The idea that the returned heroes had turned on the citizenry appalled many people, even as the idea of a great crowd of workers, men and women, demanding changes horrified others.

St. John could not help but see it as another sign of life unraveling in England. But still he did not discuss it with Alex, and she did not raise the subject either. One of the most obvious things that kept them both silent was the financial impossibility of leaving. In that their thoughts were parallel, and they did not want to harp on each other about a lack of funds. St. John further had to caution himself from seeking another bet such as the one that had brought him the mare. He did not want to invite the grim possibility of debt. His father and brothers were clear reminders of that danger. Though he avoided them at the race meetings when they attended, and though they were as relieved not to see him, still he was aware that their credit was very poor, their stables depleted, and he suffered a nearly physical pain when he learned that they were trying to sell off yet more of the Carrington lands.

Alex did not relinquish her dream, but she accepted the pain as well as the hope of it. Someday, someday she would find a way for them to go. The pain was in the reality of knowing that the someday was by all current measure a very long way off. Her immediate task and dream was to produce a healthy baby.

Despite all that had happened, she did not have a difficult time with this pregnancy, and so she was stunned by the violence of the onslaught of labor. One moment she was listening to St. John and Hugh tell her how they had done at the Houghton Meeting at Newmarket from which they had just returned, and in the next, she was doubled over, sinking to the floor in the grip of the worst pain she had ever felt.

She heard her own choking cry, and then knew nothing more until she opened her eyes to see her grandmother, Dame Sally, and St. John leaning over her as she lay in bed.

"Sorry, I . . ." She got no further as the great claws tore at her belly again, and she writhed violently, trying to escape.

She wanted to tell St. John that she did want this child, that she would never do anything to harm it. She wanted to tell him that she loved him. She wanted to tell him that it didn't matter whether they went to Maryland or not, as long as they were together with their children. But none of the words would come, only screams when she opened her mouth, and so she concentrated on keeping her jaws locked against any sound at all. She wondered if she were being punished for Christiana's death or Morgan's birth, and finally she began to wonder how St. John was going to fare without her because she was surely dying.

It was hot, red, and huge, this agony filling her, tearing, smothering the beat of her heart, and choking the air out of her lungs. It was a beast outside and within, consuming her.

Virginia tried to send St. John away but gave up in the face of his determination and her own terror. She was beyond pretense. It was a race between Alexandria's endurance and the birth, and her granddaughter was losing. That became more apparent as the hours passed, and the birth seemed no closer even when the baby seemed to be in the proper position for it. Virginia and Dame Sally had done everything they knew. Virginia thought she had suffered the most acute pain she would ever know when her husband and two sons had died, but this was far worse. To see Alexandria racked and helpless, her cries reduced to animal moans, was enough to make Virginia wish she herself had died rather than witness this. She shivered as St. John's voice, pitched very low, suddenly filled all the air.

"Alex, listen to me, listen, please! We can't go to Maryland without you, we can't. My love, unless you live to take us there, we will be here forever. Live, Alex, for me, for our children. And we will go, I swear it! Somehow we will go when the spring sailings begin. Hear me, next spring, not years from now. And we'll raise fine horses and fine children in your Maryland; we will! I know it hurts, but the hurting will stop if you just hold on. I lived for you; now live for me!"

She had no strength to separate it. She was St. John and he was she, and the pain was the same for both, and she could not die because he had not. Miraculously the pain moved away for long enough to allow her to see the swans. High and wild they flew, cool sweet air singing in their heavy wings, over the sea, over the wide, wide sea.

She was pinned to the earth again as the baby boy, weary and purpled from his struggle but strong and whole, left her body. But then she drifted away again, at peace at last after almost two days of hell.

St. John hardly noticed his son. His concentration was on his wife as the women worked over her, delivering the afterbirth and still working frantically because the bleeding did not stop. The room stank of blood. St. John held Alex's hand and would not let go, willing his life to flow into her, his voice hoarse and broken now as he repeated his promise.

It was one of the hardest things she had ever done, but Virginia left him alone in his vigil. And she knew that one way or the other, it was the beginning of saying good-bye to her granddaughter because even if she lived, Alexandria was not going to stay in this place; Virginia was going to make sure of it.

Alex returned to full awareness slowly, opening her eyes to brief periods of consciousness over the next three days, gradually understanding that she had produced a healthy son and that her body was beginning to produce milk for him despite the battle it had been through. Virginia and Dame Sally had wanted the baby to suckle because they knew that the process somehow inhibited bleeding in the mother. Alex wanted to feed the child herself because she never wanted him to doubt his welcome; she still felt guilty for having said she did not want this new child in place of Christiana. She understood now that the one had nothing to do with the other. She also knew that St. John was there every time she awakened.

"You look horrid, like a fight," she finally managed to whisper and was rewarded by St. John's wide smile.

"Sweetheart, were I a cruel man, I would bring you a mirror." His smile wavered, and he leaned over to kiss her cheeks, her eyelids, and her mouth before he hid his face against her neck, and she felt his tears.

When Hugh was allowed a brief visit, he looked as worn as her husband, and she marvelled at the love and concern that had been expended on her behalf.

"You made old men of us overnight," Hugh scolded gently. "Nigel Carrington had better grow up to be a special man."

"He will, he's Sinje's son," Alex declared. St. John was flattered by her choice of one of his names for their new son. To Alex it was absolutely necessary. This was his son; no one else's.

St. John was with her when Virginia brought the gift that changed their lives. She put the heavy pouch on the counterpane of Alex's bed, opened it to reveal a small fortune in gold and silver coins and bank notes, and took advantage of their stunned expressions.

"Not a word, please, until I have spoken my piece. I have sold the wood to Mr. Each. He has coveted it for long enough, and he is a shrewd man who has money to spend even in these hard times. It is done and cannot be changed. It is for you—for your life in Maryland. And I think I have found a reliable ship to carry you to Canada in the spring. From there a coastal vessel can take you south to Maryland. I do not doubt that you would have found a way to go someday. But the building of a new life in a new land is for the young."

"He will sell the trees!" Alex protested in shock.

"Yes, he undoubtedly will. He can sell the oaks for shipbuilding; they are worth five pounds or more each, and he will still have the coppices for hop poles." Her voice was utterly serene. "Life is a matter of exchanges. Youth for age, ignorance for knowledge. Endless exchanges. It is entirely my choice to exchange the wood for this gift to both of you. Alexandria, in time it would have been yours in any case. Someday plant a small wood, or better yet an orchard, for me in the New World, and the exchange will be complete."

St. John lifted her hand and kissed it with a courtly gesture. He could feel no insult to his pride because Virginia's gift was one of pure love. His heart ached for her when he thought of how she would part from Alex and then see the wood disappear tree by tree, reminding her that she would never see her granddaughter again.

"You will not come with us?" he asked softly.

She shook her head. "I am as English as the oaks. My roots are very deep here. But I will expect to hear from you often so that I may become a traveler of the mind."

In her weakened state, tears came easily to Alex, and St. John had all he could do to keep from weeping with her as she forced the words out. "Thank you. All my life you have given me gift after gift . . ." She could not go on.

"And you have been a gift to me from the day you were born. I pray that someday you have a special grandchild of your own, a child who will give you love when you think there can be no more love in your life, a child who will give you youth when your own is over. Only then will you understand what a small gift it is I give you today."

❦ Chapter 31 ❧

The days began to race by with breathtaking speed for Alex. There was so much to do before they left, and she felt more positive about the move by the day because St. John seemed so certain now of its rightness, not just of a promise he had made to her under extreme circumstances.

And their little family would not be going alone. The Bateses were accompanying them. To the Carringtons' joy, there had been no hesitation. In fact, Timothy had seemed more than a little put out that St. John and Alex would even consider trying to cope without them.

Alex overheard him grumbling to Mavis, "Lud, can't you jus' see it, them with all th' children tryin' to do without us."

But the most startling development was Boston's determination to go to Maryland also.

He asked diffidently and mistook Alex's hesitation for refusal. "Of course, if you think it would make things too difficult to have me along, I'll . . ."

"God, no!" she stopped him. "I was just surprised. We would all love to have you with us. But are you quite sure? Boston, you're almost completely in charge of the ship chandlery now. I expect someday Father will leave it to you, with provision for Mother, of course. But Paris and Rome don't seem interested."

"They will have to be," he countered. "I feel guilty, but I don't want to become like Father, so lost and vague. Alex, I'm dying here, bit by bit. Everything reminds me of Dora and the baby. I see them everywhere."

"You don't have to explain that to me," Alex said gently. "It is not that I will ever forget Christiana, or even that I

329

want to, but I do want to forget the pain of losing her. And I can't seem to do that here. We can use your strong arms and clear head in Maryland."

Alex had no doubt that Margaret had raised hell at Boston's plan to leave, but Caton was more understanding than she expected him to be.

"Paris or Rome will come into the business if I make it attractive enough for him; both of those boys have a good bit of greed in them," he observed with uncharacteristic cynicism. And he managed to hide the deep sorrow he felt at the impending departure of his two favorite children. The only reference he made to it was when he told Alex, "I have always known that the more adventurous blood of my father would surely exist somewhere in my children. It's the legacy of the Thaines as much as your green eyes and dark hair are."

Alex blessed him for letting them go so graciously.

In addition, Caton concerned himself with the supplies they would take to their new life, happy that this was a skill he could share. It also gave him extra time with the children at the Carrington cottage as he, St. John, Alex, and Boston pored over various lists with occasional anxious comments from Timothy and Mavis who feared that certain practical items might be overlooked.

"I think they fear we will sail off without a pound of flour or an ounce of sugar if they don't remind us," St. John complained.

"Despite their eagerness to accompany us, they must feel that we are setting off for a land of savages," Alex reminded him. "And who knows, it might be true. I doubt that every American is as civilized as Caleb Jennings."

St. John growled in mock anger, "I hope this paragon of virtue is by now fat and bald."

Alex laughed, but inwardly she thought, how far from the truth you are, not Caleb at all, but Rane. With Morgan before her eyes, thoughts of Rane would also always be part of her. But they no longer hurt or startled her. Her life had become so strongly interwoven with St. John's that the fabric of it was proof against not only the daily problems they faced, but also the pull of old memories and loyalties. There was even a certain justice in the fact that the wood where she and Rane had loved would now vanish to provide a new life for her and St. John.

Virginia's gifts had not stopped with the money, for she

was determined that Alex take with her the best cuttings and seeds for everything from fruit trees to roses to herbs and medicinal plants.

"You will, I know, find rich flora in America and many plants unfamiliar to you. Some of them will undoubtedly prove very useful, but go carefully until you are sure," she cautioned her granddaughter. "Remember, many that heal can also kill."

Alex did not mind the unnecessary repetition of lessons long since learned; it was comforting to be back in the old teacher-pupil relationship. And they were both exquisitely careful to keep their emotions under control as if the final days were not approaching so swiftly. But sometimes it was difficult as emotions slipped out unbidden.

"Will you tell the bees?" Alex asked one day and was sorry the instant she said it. It was an old custom to knock on the hive and then turn it around three times and tell the inhabitants of great events in the family, of births, marriages, deaths, and leave-takings. Virginia, despite her matter-of-fact approach to life and her dislike of superstition, maintained that certain old rituals worked and thus should be followed whether they were understood or not.

Bees Virginia judged to be eerily intelligent insects, and if sharing the news of the family would keep them from deserting the hive, then so be it. Alex had always been secretly amused by this, but she was not now. She could barely swallow past the lump in her throat as her grandmother answered. "Of course, I shall tell them. I told them of your marriage and of the births of your children and the death of Christiana. And I shall tell them of your journey."

Her eyes were suspiciously bright, but then she added with a wicked start of mischief, "I think I shall have His Grace, the Duke of Almont, assist me. I should like to see his dignified approach to the task." The image she conjured eased the tension for both of them.

Hugh's gift to them was spectacular without seeming like charity. The mare Leda under Alex's and St. John's care had improved greatly by the time she foaled in January. Leda would never be sound enough to race or even ride again, but she withstood the strain of carrying her foal to full term without mishap, and in February, she was bred back to one of Hugh's prize-winning stallions. A winner of major races, including the Derby at Epsom some years before, the animal was proving himself a fine stud as the first of his progeny appeared on the race courses.

The colt Leda had produced from the breeding to Sharbrowley's stud was as beautiful a chestnut as his mother. St. John named him "Wild Swan," quickly shortened simply to "Swan," defending the odd name by pointing out that it was perfectly logical since the colt's dam was Leda. "It sounds better than 'Son of Zeus,'" he teased, but Alex was touched by the gift to her in the name: St. John knew how much she loved the birds.

The *Paul and Sarah*, named by the owner for his two children, was the ship that would take them as far as Nova Scotia. She was a hundred and sixteen feet long, and her captain and crew were skilled seamen who had made many safe voyages to and from Canada in the past few years. She did not run a regular passenger service but would have ample room for the Carrington party and the horses as she would carry little cargo on the outward voyage, returning with a full hold of timber from Canada.

Captain Gaites was an irascible man who didn't care much for having civilians on his ship, but he owed Virginia Thaine more than one favor from his free-trading days and from more recent times when she had treated him and his family in Gravesend for various ailments, and that was an end to it, particularly because the Carringtons would be paying well for the passage. Grudgingly he gave orders for the stalls that would be built on deck to shelter the mare, her foal, and the gelding, Sir Arthur, whom St. John was insisting on taking. Captain Gaites took some comfort from the fact that the Carringtons would provide their own food and fodder for the horses; he detested the extra fuss passengers caused.

The last few days in Gravesend were the hardest for everyone. They were filled with last-minute tasks, but there was still enough time for the adults to realize that all that was familiar was soon to be left behind and for the children to fret over the disruption of their lives even though they did not fully understand what was going on.

To Alex the daffodils and other flowers of the April days seemed to be more vivid and fragrant than ever before, and she wondered sadly if she would ever see such lovely flowers again, and if the new tenants of the cottage would care for the plantings she had done so carefully since she had come to live here five years before.

Resolutely, she kept her mind from the people she was leaving, particularly from her father and from her grandmother. But she made one journey deliberately and by herself, taking the silver christening cups Hugh had presented for Christiana's birth to Stone Church.

"Sell them or instruct your successor to do so when funds are needed for the upkeep of my daughter's grave," she told the priest. "I do not want the weeds to grow and the stone to wear away."

She told St. John what she had done with the silver, and he understood. He made his own pilgrimage, trespassing boldly on his father's lands, seeing old retainers who greeted him shyly, but no sign of his family. The love he had felt for these acres flooded through him anew, but he acknowledged that even were he to stay in Gravesend, the land would never be his. And he felt no sorrow to be leaving a family that no longer recognized him as their own and had not even seen his children by Alex.

When the sailing day came, all had been previously loaded aboard the *Paul and Sarah* except the horses, and that final task was so diverting in its tension that Alex almost got through the last moments numb to all but the excitement of it. But quite suddenly, the blindfolded horses were safely aboard, and Alex was face to face with her grandmother.

It all came back to her, the endless patience Virginia had shown in the teaching of everything that was best in Alex's life—the love of books and learning, and of all the bright life of the earth and sky, the healing skill, and most of all, the ability of one person to love another. All she would ever know of loving was possible because this old woman, standing so straight and brave before her, had taught her the first steps in the most complicated dance of all. Love for St. John, love for her children, even love for herself—all of it had flowed from the fathomless well of her grandmother's love for her.

In that instant, she was ready to forsake her dream of the New World in payment of her debt to the old, but her grandmother spoke first.

"Alexandria, for your sake and mine, we must pretend for just a little longer that we will see each other again. Don't think about it, don't, child. Be joyful!" Her voice was fierce.

Alex put her arms around her, hugging the spare frame, trying to do as she was bid, trying not to acknowledge that this would be the last time. "Grandmother, you will be with me always, all the days of my life. Everything I know of value is from you. I will not forget you, nor will my children or their children. Wherever we are, you will be with us."

She was blind to the sorrow on her father's face and to the misery in Hugh's eyes as she made her last farewells, the wrenching pain of parting from her grandmother dulling other perceptions. She hardly noticed the disapproving expressions on her older brothers' faces as they bid her a dutiful farewell.

Virginia maintained her calm face and upright posture until the ship was making its way down the river, and then she said to her son and to Hugh, "Gentlemen, as unseemly as it may be, I propose to go home and get quite inebriated on the best brandy my house provides. Will you join me?"

Hugh looked into her eyes and realized she knew perfectly well how much he loved Alexandria, and it eased his misery to have the knowledge shared. "It would be an honor, ma'am," he said, and when Virginia informed him that he was to help her turn the bees, he almost managed to smile. "It sounds," he said, "as if that were better done before rather than after the brandy."

❧ Chapter 32 ❧

At first, Alex had been so busy catering to everyone else's needs, she had been able to avoid thinking. But by the time the ship lost sight of Ireland in the heavy mist, both horses and humans had found their sea legs. And watching the gray wall swallowing the land, the full import of what they were doing hit Alex, paralyzing her as she gripped the ship's rail. Suddenly she could smell the ripe warm odor of the drying hops in her grandmother's oast house and the scent of the flowers in her own garden, could see the windmills of Kent, their sweeps turning gracefully, and the busy traffic on the Thames, could hear the heavy drone of bees on a warm day, and could touch all of her life at Gravesend as if it were right before her. The images were eclipsed in the vastness of the chill waters.

"My God, what have I done?" she breathed softly.

St. John had come to stand beside her, and he had watched the changes in her, knowing she was not even aware of his presence. He reached out to cover her white knuckles with his own hand. "You have done well, managing everything with your usual competence."

"Managing. Yes, maybe too much. What if I have managed everyone into a bad choice? Things have not been easy in America either these past few years, from what Hugh told us."

"I should not have said managing. I didn't mean it that way. This is as much my decision as yours, even if it was your idea originally. Alexandria, all the reasons we had for leaving remain the same. And we are going to be buyers, not sellers, in Maryland, at least at first, and that means we should be able to make shrewd bargains and pay low prices for land or anything else we purchase. It's a hard fact of life that what hurts some, benefits others in difficult times. It is the same in England. With the old king dead, and the Prince Regent coming to the throne, I fear it will take a very long time for conditions to improve." He paused, knowing her thoughts were not of economic or political conditions but of the small everyday things and the people who made life familiar. "Together we can do anything and build everything anew," he said softly, and she looked up at him, her eyes bright with unshed tears and gratitude for his understanding. But mentally she reproached herself; this was her doing whatever he said, and to grow fainthearted now was to be of no use to anyone.

Alex had thought days aboard ship would quickly prove boring, and there were such stretches of time, but there was also much to see. Sometimes they sighted other ves-

sels in the distance, and closer to, they enjoyed the wild-
life of the sea and sky—the stormy petrels the sailors
called "Mother Carey's chickens," the dolphins, or "sea
pigs," that sometimes behaved very much as if they were
playing with the hull of the ship, racing beside it, leaping,
and looking as if they were laughing. They even sighted
whales now and then. Morgan called them "up down
boats" until Blaine, with dogged persistence, convinced
him that they were not overturned ships at all.

The twins as well as Mavis had been pitifully seasick at
first, but Morgan had been fine, quickly finding a wide-
straddled walk that swayed his body side to side but kept
him upright most of the time.

"He could have been born to this," St. John had observed proudly, and Alex's inner voice had said, *He was,
indeed he was born to this.*

She had worried most of all about St. John. Though he
was not seasick, the rolling motion of the ship had thrown
him off balance for the first days. He did not have two
good arms to brace himself when the vessel lurched with
sudden violence. Alex had pretended not to notice when
he slammed against things as he lost his balance, and
finally he had given in to Morgan's way of spread-leg
walking.

Even the horses, after their first misery, had adjusted as
well as possible to their confining deck stalls and the
movement of the ship.

Alex was grateful to Captain Gaites and his crew for
helping to make the voyage more pleasant. Once the
captain had discovered that Mavis and Alex were willing
to help liven the normally bland cooking served aboard
ship and that, in addition, Alex was capable of treating all
manner of ailments, his rather gruff manner had eased
and he had instructed his crew to extend every courtesy
to the passengers. The sailors good-naturedly kept watch
on the children and patiently answered their many
questions.

The captain even arranged a special evening of celebration for Alex's birthday, the twins having informed him of
this important event. The sailors played their hornpipes
and did nimble jigs, delighting their audience. But Alex
was most touched by the books St. John had hidden away
for this day.

They all spent as much time as possible on deck when

the weather permitted as well as using those days to air their clothing and bedding. Most of their bathing was done in salt water, but whenever it rained hard, they used the extra for the luxury of fresh water washing. And when it was very calm, they exercised the horses as well as they could, leading them blindfolded, sailors serving as extra guards alongside in case the animal started to slip or fall. But even with all the care, the horses suffered bouts of bad digestion and lost much of the glossy look they had had in England.

When they ran into bad weather, they all simply had to adjust and wait for it to pass, spending the time in the hold, out of the crew's way. But when they were thirty-three days out and near the Banks of Newfoundland, they realized how fortunate they had been in their passage so far.

Ugly swells gave way to choppier water as the wind rose and then the full fury of the storm enveloped them. The *Paul and Sarah* that had slipped so gracefully through the water was suddenly a wallowing old lady, tossed violently from side to side and up and down at the whim of the sea. And over the shrieking wind and the thunder of the water, the ship's timbers groaned in torment.

Mavis and the twins were too terrified to be sick; Nigel was fretful, and Morgan was round-eyed with wonder, more exhilarated than frightened. Alex knew the same feeling, a rushing of the blood as if her body was riding the storm independently of the laboring ship.

St. John, Boston, and Tim were working in the shadows trying to lash down part of their cargo when Alex suddenly remembered how awful it must be for the horses on deck. She grabbed her cloak and was gone before Mavis could protest.

The ship was bucking so violently, she had to cling to something the whole way. She was blinded by the lashing rain, but nearly crawling, she followed the high-pitched screams of the horses until she was clinging to the mare's stall.

"There, there, lovely Leda, I'm here, love," she crooned, trying to get close enough so that the mare would hear her voice, feeling helpless as she heard the thump of their bodies. She called Sir Arthur's name, too, and at least he seemed to settle a little, though the mare continued to fret until Alex was afraid she would harm the colt.

337

"What in the hell do you think you're doing!" St. John's hand clamped down roughly on her shoulder as Alex jumped at the sound of his voice so close to her ear.

"Trying to reassure them," she said, as calmly as if they were standing on dry land in no danger themselves.

St. John saw that she was not the least bit afraid and marvelled. His own heart was pumping wildly at the mere sight of her on the treacherous, heaving deck.

And then Boston was with them, Timothy having been delegated to stay with Mavis and the children, and among the three of them, they managed to keep the horses from injuring themselves, losing track of the cold wet hours that passed until the storm had moved on. Shaking with fatigue and reaction, they stared at each other numbly until Boston muttered hoarsely that he'd better go tell the others they were still alive. St. John and Alex didn't notice his going nor the swirl of weary sailors around them.

"You were not afraid. Why?" St. John asked, searching her face.

She blinked at him, exhaustion beginning to claim her. "Nothing could happen to us, not when we've come so far." She stated it as if it were a deeply held religious conviction, but then she realized how ridiculous it was—everyone who ever crossed the sea to this point had come this far, but not all of them had made it beyond to safe harbor. She started to laugh, hysteria beginning to overwhelm her now that the need for her strength was gone.

Oblivious of grinning sailors, St. John kissed her into quiet, feeling her trembling subside against him.

Because of their victory over the storm, the ceremony of crossing the Newfoundland Banks was even more joyous than it might have been.

Captain Gaites looked on benignly as Mark, a young crewman, played the part of Father Neptune. Draped in rags to represent seaweed and wearing a false beard and a paper crown that sat askew, Mark demanded that the passengers pay their footing or submit to being shaved with a piece of hoop iron.

St. John gave the coins to the twins and Morgan to pay Father Neptune, and they did so solemnly, Morgan looking brave but nervous until Mark muttered something to him, and the child recognized his friend. Morgan clapped his hands over his mouth to stifle his giggle, obviously pleased that he knew a secret. In that instant, he looked exactly as Rane had looked when he had told her about the Devil and the blackberries. Alex's heart skipped a beat, but her face betrayed nothing; she was growing more and more accustomed to seeing the father in the son.

The Banks were known for sudden weather changes and for the danger of floating ice, and so the crew was doubly watchful, and St. John, Boston, and Timothy took their turns standing watch at the bow. But aside from some mist that cut visibility and ice floes that they watched carefully, they ran into no great hazard. Compared to the storm they had survived, this seemed quite mild. It was an eerie world of ice and water, and one night it was breathtakingly beautiful as the moon turned a great school of fish floating around the ship into a river of silver.

They smelled it before they saw it, the heady perfume of pine and damp earth born on the wind, and on the forty-first day out, after a night that began with rough seas and ended with calmer waters, the ship came about from north to south, and at midday under a bright sun, they saw Cape Breton Island, which Mark told them was the most easterly part of Nova Scotia and separated from the mainland by the Gut of Canso.

Alex felt like dancing on the deck at the sight of the heavily wooded land because they were at last nearing the continent of their dreams, but she contented herself with standing close against her husband as they watched the children hopping madly about.

They had to navigate carefully through a perilous field of icebergs; twice the ice could not be avoided, and the ship was momentarily halted by the impact that reverberated like thunder. But being in sight of land made the ice less frightening even though they knew that cold water could kill. The children didn't fear the ice at all and crowed with delight as they watched a whale spout quite close to the ship.

They continued on past Cape Breton Island to the port of Halifax, Nova Scotia, and their days on the *Paul and Sarah* were at an end. It was an odd feeling, at once joyful and sad. The crew felt like part of their family now, and even the dark quarters in the hold were at least familiar. They had no definite plans for proceeding from here to the United States and had to face the prospect of a long wait if no ships were available.

Captain Gaites came to their rescue. He had become fond of them, and he didn't feel his job would be complete were he just to leave them without knowing what happened to them next. He suggested that they leave the bulk of their belongings aboard his ship for the time being, gave them directions to reasonably priced lodgings, and told them he would meet them there later. And when he did, he was smiling. He had found a ship bound for the West Indies in five days, and the captain had agreed to take the Carringtons and their horses.

"Captain Gaites, we will be forever in your debt. My grandmother certainly put us in good hands when she consigned us to your care," Alex told him, and St. John claimed afterwards that the captain actually blushed above his beard.

It was unsettling at first to be on land again. They all tended to stagger when they walked, and Alex felt dizzier than she had aboard ship. But she insisted everyone walk as much as possible. The men found stabling for the horses, and they saw to their exercise and feeding, ever mindful of how short a time five days was to improve the animals' condition.

Halifax was a much more civilized city than Alex had expected. In 1739, it had been established as a naval and army base and supplied with a population of English civilians. The intention had been to create a military stronghold supplied by farmers who would grow food for the sailors and soldiers. However, though the military objective was gained, the settlers were mostly poor cockneys from London's streets, farming was not their skill or desire, and cold and disease took a grievous toll of them. Over the years, they had been replaced by Germans, American Loyalists, and New Englanders.

Over Halifax rose Citadel Hill with fortifications on top and the town clock on a tower partway down the slope. The town boasted public gardens as well as quite a number of impressive residences, churches, government buildings, and businesses, many of brick or blocks of stone. Nonetheless, it, too, was suffering from the current economic difficulties of Europe and America. Since its creation, Halifax had always done better in times of war when it had served as a base for troops or, as in the case of the last conflict with the United States, as a place where captured privateers and other ships had been auctioned off, so many in fact that permission had been asked to sell some of them back to the American market.

But for all its aspects of civilization, Alex felt no desire to stay. The forest still seemed to press from every side, as if the days of attacks by wild Indians were not so far away, and she suspected that winters here could be harsh indeed. It was, as far as she was concerned, just a necessary stop on the way to Maryland. It made it easier to board the *Sibylla* and set sail again.

Alex watched the children anxiously but found they were more content than the adults to be on a ship once more. They had grown accustomed to the small life there. And small it was on the Halifax-built *Sibylla*; she was carrying a good cargo of timber, and thus space for the passengers was makeshift and limited. But the horses were secure again in temporary but sturdy stalls on deck, and with a straight face belied by the twinkle in his eye, St. John announced that that was all that mattered.

"I can well imagine the horses comfortably stabled in Maryland while I and the children wander in the wilderness," Alex retorted.

"A stable warm with hay and horses wouldn't be so bad right now," he muttered, "more private than this." The longing in his voice was plain, and Alex shared it; they had had no time and no room to themselves since they'd left England; even in Halifax they had been crowded with the children, Boston, and the Bateses.

"Patience, my love," she whispered.

Aside from a few rain squalls, the weather held for them as they made their way along the coast of the United States. They spent much time studying other vessels and the many harbors when they were in sight, but it was hard to form any valid opinion. The overall impression was of an enormity outside of their experience. Here, too, great forests crowded right to the edge of the coastal towns, but it was the image of the land stretching forever behind them that was so difficult to comprehend for a mind accustomed to the well-known perimeters of the British Isles. It was both a threat and a promise, but Alex felt her heart lift as they neared their goal—surely so wide a world had room for them.

Captain Cronin was jolly. His high spirits were enhanced by the good sum he was getting from the Carringtons for their passage. He made it as pleasant as possible, but they did not feel the closeness to him and the crew that they had had on the *Paul and Sarah*. All their attention was focused on Annapolis, and in slightly over a week, they were sailing up Chesapeake Bay, past the divided shores of Virginia—just the name of that state was enough to bring a misty smile to Alex as she thought of her grandmother—into Maryland's waters with the flat Eastern Shore on one hand and the Western Shore, the edge of the great continent, on the other.

Memory threatened to overwhelm Alex. She could hear Caleb Jennings's lyrical description of this vast body of water even as she gazed upon it and saw he had not exaggerated. Six full years ago she and Rane had helped him return to his home. She felt suddenly as if she had completed some mystic circle whose existence she had not known until it closed around her.

"I believe I'm going to like it here," Boston said in an awed voice, and beyond words, Alex gripped his hand.

"I think we all will," St. John said from the other side of her, and she felt more certain of her course than she had in a very long time.

Book Three

❧ Chapter 33 ❧

Annapolis, Maryland, United States, 1820

Made the seat of the provincial government in 1696 when the power had been moved from St. Mary's city in southern Maryland, Annapolis was an elegantly planned city of streets radiating out from two major circles on a hill, one with the State House, the other with a church, a prominent setting in the otherwise flat land. The town boasted fine red and salmon brick houses, most of them built in the halcyon days of the past century before the colonies had rebelled against the mother country. The city was on the south bank of the Severn River near its mouth on the bay, and there was a view of water from many points.

By English standards, it was a very young place, and even the grandest houses were like miniatures of great English manors, but Alex fell in love with the look of it. Like Halifax, it was much more civilized than she had expected, and there were many beautiful gardens sure to win her heart. St. John teased that she could be bewitched by any square foot of earth as long as it sported at least one bloom and was close to water.

But it was not paradise. Despite the names of streets such as Cornhill and Fleet, reminiscent of London, and the name of the town itself which had been chosen to honor the then Princess Anne who had later become queen, Annapolis was not England nor was it free of problems. Though it remained the state capital and the seat of Anne Arundel County, the golden era was over for Annapolis. In the previous century it had been not only a center of government, but also, according to many foreign observers, the most charming and cosmopolitan city in the United States. Wealthy tobacco planters had built their town houses and had come in from their plantations to spend the season in the city, enjoying balls, social clubs, horse racing, and other amusements. During the Revolution, Maryland had not been the site of battles, but both French and American troops had passed through Annapolis. And in 1783, the Continental Congress had met there because it lacked a place of its own, and that was when George Washington had formally resigned his commission as commander in chief of the Continental Army.

But Annapolis had not become the nation's capital; in fact, it had nearly lost its position as state capital to another city, Baltimore, thirty miles to the north on the bay. Annapolis had retained her importance in the state by will and wrangling, but much else she had lost, and much of that to Baltimore.

The last war with England had damaged the Chesapeake Bay region more than the Revolution had. The stoppage of trade for so long had been a severe blow, and even the cessation of hostilities had not cured the ills as many had hoped. The West Indies trade which had been so vital in the past, was terribly uncertain now as England alternately allowed and disallowed it, and even the resumption of direct trade with England seemed to be creating more problems than it was solving.

In the past, English merchants had simply shipped what they pleased to the goods-hungry markets of the eastern seaboard of North America, but this time when they attempted to reestablish the same practice, they had begun to discover that hard times and financial failure had drastically reduced the demand for their manufactured goods, of which vast quantities had been stockpiled during the Napoleonic war years. The lack of uniform and stable currency in the United States had deepened the confusion. Farmers and traders from the western parts of the states and from the territories too often found that bank notes from their regions were not acceptable on the coast, and thus they required long terms of credit. This in turn left the seaboard merchants short of cash to pay for English goods.

What prosperity there was seemed to be gravitating to New York, which was closer sailing distance to Liverpool, thus making the transport cost of goods less than it was for more distant cities such as Baltimore and Annapolis. And of the latter two, Baltimore now had the bulk of Maryland's commerce. Baltimore had a bigger harbor as Annapolis's had silt problems, and Baltimore had been expanding at a much greater rate than Annapolis since the close of the last century. Shipbuilding and other trades had moved there, leaving Annapolis in the backwater.

Alex and St. John felt as if they were young students desperately trying to learn all they could in days with too few hours. Their best source of information was Mrs. Perkins, the woman who ran the boardinghouse where they were staying. Small and past sixty, she was rather abrupt in her manner, but she was a mine of blunt information about Maryland, having all the fervor of a convert. She had been born in England, had married her American sea captain on the eve of the Revolution, and had spent the war years in Annapolis. Despite his love for an English girl, Captain Perkins had been no royalist, and that had helped his wife's situation, but she well knew what it was like to be regarded as one of the enemy. In her tart way, she offered advice and sympathy to the newly arrived English. Her husband had been dead for many years, but she had done well with what he had left her and had made a modest success of her boardinghouse. She thought of herself as a woman of business and kept abreast of the news, though she was no gossip. Alex had cause later to wish she were.

On meeting the Carringtons through Captain Cronin, Mrs. Perkins had been civil enough, but her bright blue eyes had studied Alex the longest. "Have you relatives in this country?" she asked.

Alex answered honestly that they had none and worried that there was some requirement for entry into the United States that they could not meet. For an instant, she was tempted to mention Caleb Jennings, but she refrained; she had no intention of imposing on him, having long since decided that it would be well enough if their paths crossed but that she would make no effort to establish contact. She did not want him to feel that her brood had come to be his responsibility.

Mrs. Perkins saw her apprehension and hastened to reassure her. "It's no matter. For all that you're English, you have money to pay your way, healthy children, and from what Captain Cronin tells me, some good horseflesh." She did not add that Mr. Carrington's missing arm would glean more than a little sympathy no matter how he had lost it. "Altogether it is more than enough to convince the natives that you're not here to start up the war again on the bay. This is not even a port of entry any more, but there'll be no trouble. Captain Cronin is a welcome visitor; he manages now and then to take on a little cargo for the West Indies trade."

The information amused Alex when she realized its full import. Captain Cronin's ship was of British, not American, registry, so the West Indies trade remained open to him even when it was closed to Americans. Official clearances did not seem to concern him. In effect, they had sailed down the coast in a smuggler's vessel. But Alex kept her amusement to herself, for St. John hadn't looked the least pleased with the information.

She felt more attuned to him than ever before. The strangeness of the new land pressed against them, making the familiarity of each other more precious and reassuring. After the cramped quarters of the ships, it was pure bliss for them to have a bedchamber to themselves again.

St. John watched with enjoyment as Alex brushed her long hair, her face made a mystery of high relief and shadow by the soft candlelight; even her plain white bed gown seemed to have the sheen of silk against her golden skin.

"Will you marry me?" he asked softly.

Alex stared at him, wondering what kind of jest this was, then saw that he was perfectly serious. She put the brush down very carefully, studying it as if it had suddenly changed into something quite different. "We are married," she said quietly, and she could not understand why his question so discomfitted her.

"I know we are. By all measure that makes a marriage valuable and true, we are. But we have no legal document to prove it, and we have children to whom we owe all the security we can provide, and that includes proof of their legitimacy. Here we can be legally married; there is no bar of kinship."

His reasonable discourse told her that he had given the matter much thought, and more, that it mattered to him. She knew her own reaction was irrational, but it was there nonetheless. She did not want the official sanction. They had faced the contempt of her mother and others at home, and they had survived without their approval. She felt as if seeking that official status now was an admission of defeat and of wrongdoing.

She couldn't put any of it into words. She went to him, wrapping her arms around him, and the warm strength of him reminded her that this was, after all, all that mattered.

St. John took his answer from her offering of herself, nuzzling his mouth against her throat, feeling her pulse leap in response as her hands urged him to shed his robe.

They fell together on the bed, and Alex was the aggressor, kissing him feverishly and running her hands over his body until he could bear no more and thrust deep to find his relief.

Alex ceased at that moment to be the children's mother, the family manager, or anything else except St. John's lover. The hard shaft of his flesh invading her softness became her universe, her muscles alternately tightening and surrendering to the intruder, her body arching against his until all spiraled into oblivion.

The new boundaries of earth and sky did not matter; home was wherever they were together. When St. John made slow love to her again in the night, she whispered, "I'll marry you today, tomorrow, forever," and he chuckled against her throat, "I should hope so!" She no longer minded his need for legal approval so much; he had come from a background that demanded such things, while her attitudes were quite different, stemming mostly from her grandmother's tolerance of the vagaries of life, and yet she and St. John fit together.

In the morning the aura of contentment lingered around them as Alex nursed Nigel and St. John watched, his eyes heavy-lidded with tenderness.

But Alex, as loath as she was to break the spell, knew there were vital decisions to be made. She waited until Nigel was replete, and she gained more time by fussing over him a little longer before settling him in his cradle. Then she returned to St. John.

She could find no delicate way to approach the subject, and so the words came out more bluntly than she intended. "I was foolish not to consider it. Can we live here with slavery all around us? I cannot forget . . . ," her voice trailed away and she shuddered.

Vaguely they had known that there were slave and free states in the United States, but they had not expected to see so many black faces among the white nor to discover that nearly all of the blacks were slaves.

And then within a few days of arrival in Annapolis, Alex had witnessed a scene that haunted her still.

She had been on one side of the street near Mrs. Perkins's house and a white woman and her servant had been coming down the other side.

The Negro had been carrying a multitude of parcels for the woman and keeping a careful distance behind her. And then he had dropped one of the bundles and had had to move quickly to avoid losing them all. He'd managed to balance the remainder and retrieve the one before Alex could start across the street to help him. And as casually as if she'd been swatting a fly, the woman had turned and cuffed the man.

"You lazy fool, I told you to bring the basket! If any dirt got on my new gloves, I'll have your hide."

The two of them had walked on as if nothing had happened.

Alex had been frozen in place. Even had the incident not happened so quickly, she doubted she could have intervened. There had been something self-contained about the action, as if it were a well-rehearsed theatrical set piece, neither actor having to think as the scene unfolded.

The ugliness of it had washed over her, making her feel physically ill. Those few seconds had revealed more about slavery than the high drama of a crackling whip and bellowed orders would have. She had no doubt that the white woman owned the black man and felt no shame for the ownership. There had been nothing furtive in the slap that had stripped all right of manhood from the black. And worse, the man was part of it, so accustomed to his position of servitude and humility that he had shown no reaction to the abuse.

If he had shown resistance or resentment, he could be sold to a worse owner. Blood and bone, heart and spirit, all that he was as a human being was negated by his color. He was as much an object of commerce as the dropped package. The truth of it chilled Alex to the bone though the day was warm.

When she had told St. John, he had understood more from the lingering horror in her eyes than from her terse words, and he had comforted her as best he could with his presence and soft words. But they had not fully discussed the impact slavery would have on their lives, though silently and separately they had both been considering it.

It was an insidious system. Though Mrs. Perkins owned no slaves, she did hire a couple who belonged to someone else for work in her house. Part of their wages was theirs to keep; the rest went to their owner. It made Mrs. Perkins part of the system, and yet she seemed a morally upright, even kind, woman. Her attitude that all was well as long as the slaves were well cared for and not needlessly abused seemed to be shared by most whites.

"Even though we never own slaves, will it not make us part of it just by being here?" Alex asked now, determined that they delay the discussion no longer.

St. John regarded her gravely for a long moment before he spoke. "You saw the rocky shores of many of the states north of here and the forests, and I've made inquiries; those states are no place to raise race horses. Racing hardly exists there and is forbidden by law in many places. And if we go further south, I know we will find the slavery problem is even worse. This is a border state, between north and south, not quite either one, but further south there is no doubt. I'm told there are vast plantations of cotton, rice, and tobacco there that depend entirely on slave labor. And yet that is where much of the racing is. And some of it is moving to the west far across the mountains, to a place called Kentucky, but I don't think you want to live so far from the sea."

She shook her head slowly thinking of it, thinking of being miles and mountains away from salt water, away from the cry of sea birds and the passing of ships. Even with its exotic name, she doubted very much that Kentucky had many swans. Thinking of them, she could suddenly hear their passage overhead as she had in Gravesend and could see the small, quiet birds as she had seen them in Devon.

"I don't really know the answer to your question," St. John continued. "Perhaps it is true that to witness injustice is to be guilty of it, but I doubt there is a place on earth where there is only justice."

They both knew the facts of slavery in England. Though slavery itself had been illegal for some time in their country, the trade had not been outlawed for Englishmen until

1807, as it had been for Americans in 1808, and there were still many slaves in bondage in English territories. In addition, there were many people in England who were bound fast by circumstances if not by chains.

Alex took a deep breath. "We stay," she said, needing to hear the words aloud, but she wondered how long it would be before home meant Maryland, not England. Slavery made Maryland even more alien than it would otherwise have been, but there was nothing she could do about this evil that marred the land.

She fixed her mind on more immediate problems. They could not just wait for Leda's foal, Wild Swan, to grow into a fine race horse; the money from the sale of the oak wood would not sustain them forever. They had used a good amount of it already to come this far; they needed to invest in something soon that would generate income. She didn't want to upset St. John by arguing that the purchase of land might not be in their best interest at the moment. It seemed that tobacco was a harsh crop that depleted the land, and much of the prime acreage of Maryland had been so harmed. She had no doubt that the land could be reborn using the methods of fertilizing and crop rotation she had learned from her grandmother, but that would take time. Eventually they certainly must have their own farm if they were to raise their horses. For the time being, Alex had something quite different in mind.

She had discussed her plan with Mavis who, after first expressing shock, had begun to see the merits. But broaching the subject with St. John was another matter. She was searching for the right words when she was saved by the boisterous demands for attention from the twins and Morgan, signalling that the day had truly begun. And then the way was opened for her by unforeseen assistance.

Leda, Swan, and Sir Arthur were all being cared for at a local livery stable, but the colt particularly needed room to romp so that he might develop speed and stamina. Thus it was imperative that St. John find a more spacious place for the horses as soon as possible, and to that end he began investigating properties outside of Annapolis.

He returned from one foray looking so stunned that Alex hastened to ask him what was amiss, sure that something dreadful had happened though she could see no signs of injury.

"My God! I feel as untutored as Nigel! With all the

foreignness here, still I expected racing to be the same as it is at home. But it is so different! I spoke with a Mr. Hawlington today, an elderly man who has raised and raced the finest stock for years, though he has few at his farm now. He knew me for an ignorant Englishman at once."

He ran his hand through his heavy gilt hair, shaking his head as if he'd received a blow. "Dash racing is hardly known here. They breed horses for the 'heroic distance,' for four-mile heats three of five in some cases or two out of three in others. A horse must be four or five years old to stand such a test, so the racing of two-year-olds is virtually nonexistent, and many of the best horses are five years or older, though they may have been tested at three years old over shorter distances. And it is not a sport of kings here where there are no crowns; everyone must see all of the race in this democratic land, so their courses are all oval or circular. They do not race on the straight. There is no organized betting, though Mr. Hawlington assured me great sums do change hands; if they handicap at all, it's weight for age; and I suppose because of their love of hurry, they have begun to keep time records, as if it matters how many minutes and seconds it takes a horse to win a race. They even race geldings!" His voice died way, and Alex had to force her own to steadiness as she saw too clearly the image of all of them boarding the ship again to slink back to England in defeat.

"Does this mean we had better reconsider life in England?"

Despite her efforts, he heard the despair in her voice, and it goaded his own determination. "No, it simply means we must be even more patient than I thought." He searched her green eyes deeply. "Sweetheart, you do understand, we may never have horses that win. It may not work even with care and patience."

Nothing mattered except that they did not have to take ship again. "It will work! You'll see, it will! You are a marvelous judge of horseflesh, British or American. And we will make the land yield other things when we have it. We'll have other livestock and orchards, fields, and gardens. And in the meantime, I have a plan for us to earn enough to buy the land when it is time.

"I've found a house, a lovely big house, and it's to let. It would make a marvelous tavern and inn. And one room could be for ladies only, for afternoon tea and coffee, and we could live in the house, too." She said the words quickly and then came to an abrupt halt.

St. John was studying her as if she had sprouted horns and a tail. "A tavern? A public house? We have come all this way for that?"

The disdain in his voice tapped a sudden freshet of anger in her. "No, we came to start a new life, eventually to have land of our own and to raise fine Thoroughbred horses. But it is foolish to think we can do all of that now, particularly since you yourself have said that racing is so different here. And even with all the financial problems of this region, people will still pay for good food and drink and for a clean bed when they are far from their own. If we offer only the best quality of everything, we will not lack for customers. There are no noble families here; we must work like everyone else." She glared at him defiantly.

"Everyone here seems to be a shopkeeper of one sort or another," St. John observed with quiet contempt. "You must feel very much at home. Even Florence would not have stooped this low."

"Florence never did a full day's work in her life, and she hadn't the sense God gave a goose!" Alex exploded. "You aren't married to me yet! Remember that. You can still sail back to England and claim that this common trollop tempted you. There might yet be an heiress who would take you on and pay your way. Or perhaps you could live on the debts and credit like your family." She was so angry, she wasn't sorry for the hateful words until long minutes after he had stalked out. And then she discovered that their quarrel had not been confined to their room. She could hear the uneasiness in Boston's voice even as he asked permission to come in.

"St. John shot past me without even seeing me, and you look like the very devil. Is there anything I can do?" he asked worriedly. He didn't like bad feelings between his sister and her husband, particularly now when they were the glue that held everyone together.

Alex shook her head, misery fast replacing her rage. "Not unless you can make one of us into an entirely different person." Tersely she explained what the argument had been about. "I do have a shopkeeper's mind! I like the practical side of things as well as dreams; I like things to work in an orderly fashion. Sinje still fancies somewhere inside that he'll be lord of the manor someday by some natural process rather than hard work. Oh, damn! He would have been better off without ever knowing any of the Thaines." She buried her face in her hands, and Boston saw the tears leaking through.

He was nearly as taken aback by her suggestion of a tavern as St. John had been, but he quickly saw the possibilities of the idea. He put his arm around her and gave her a brotherly hug. "You're quite wrong, you know. Florence was no good for him though there were the twins to prove some worth, but you are entirely different. You saved his life. You've loved him right through," he said, though he knew there had been a rough patch some years before. "And you've made beautiful children together. I don't think it's such a bad thing to have two different people in a marriage—he the dreamer and you the one who will find the way to make the dreams come true."

She sniffed and took the handkerchief he offered, mopping her face, blowing her nose, and then managing a shaky giggle. "I even use a handkerchief like a shopkeeper, no grace, just to dry off. Boston, you're very wise, and I'm very glad you came with us." It was not only blood ties between them; it was the shared bond of having lost loved ones, he his wife and child, she her daughter.

St. John was gone for the whole day, and by nightfall, Alex would have agreed to immediate sailing for England or anything else as long as he returned safely. She fought unsuccessfully to block out visions of him lying helpless and injured somewhere after riding too hard. To the children's inquiries, she answered only that their father was away on business, and to Mavis and Timothy, she said nothing at all.

Though the night was warm and humid, the bed felt cold without St. John to share it, and Alex lay wide awake, starting at every sound in Mrs. Perkins's house.

When St. John entered the room, the last tallow candle Alex had left lighted was sputtering greasily, but there was enough light for her to see that he was carrying something large and flat under his arm.

She flew out of bed. "Oh, Sinje, where have you been? I've been so worried! Whatever you want, we'll do . . ."

He put his burden down and quieted Alex by drawing her against him, his arm a comforting band of strength. "I'm sorry. My business took me longer than I expected."

He kissed her deeply, as if he'd been long away instead of a matter of hours. "Forgive me for being such a stupid clod? I didn't mean any of the dreadful things I said."

"I didn't either," she murmured, breathing in the essence of him and of his day, finding comfort even in the scent of horse and leather.

He put her away from him gently. "I have peace offerings."

They were far more than that; they were three gifts of the future—a plain gold band, her own wedding ring to add to the chased gold circlet that had belonged to his grandmother; the bill of sale and pedigree of a Thoroughbred mare so that she could ride out with St. John; and the piece of wood he had been carrying. It was freshly carved and had yet to be painted. "The Wild Swan" it read, and in addition to the lettering bore a graceful rendition of the bird.

"I thought it would be a good name for our new establishment," St. John said, and Alex clung to him, her tears of gratitude salting their kiss.

❦ Chapter 34 ❦

Alex was sublimely happy. Not even the heavy humid heat of the Maryland summer could dampen her spirits. A breeze from the bay often alleviated it, and even when it did not, her mind was so taken up with all the work to be done, she hardly noticed anything else. Except St. John. She never ceased to be thankful for his approval of their new venture. Since the night he had brought her the sign, he had shown nothing but enthusiasm for The Wild Swan. Sometimes she wondered if he was truly reconciled to being a publican and innkeeper; if he still recoiled from it, he gave no evidence.

Though he had negotiated the lease, it was Alex who had insisted on a long term. So sure was she of success that she did not want the owner of the house to capitalize on their hard work a few years later by taking back the premises and continuing the tavern. There was little dispute. The owner had long since retired to his exhausted acreage on the Eastern Shore across the bay from Annapolis and had little use for a town house where no social season survived and funds for upkeep were severely limited. Previous tenants had not lasted long but had managed to leave the house in some disrepair. But he had a feeling that, at the very least, the Carringtons would make sure the place was well kept.

Nor did they have any trouble obtaining the necessary licenses to serve spirits and harbor guests; Annapolis was in dire need of people willing to start new businesses.

The house, executed in Flemish bond, a pattern of side and end bricklaying, followed the elegant geometric lines of many of the great residences built in the last century. It was reputed to have been designed by the famous architect, William Buckland, who had originally come from England to Virginia on an indenture agreement. The five-part plan had a central building flanked by two one-story "hyphen" passages leading to two-story dependencies with semi-octagonal ends. The central block was two-and-a-half stories. It was only two main rooms deep and two plus a wide passage long, the rooms large and airy, the reason for the design evident in the relative comfort of the temperature in the house even on the hottest days. A dense cluster of rooms would have been suffocating. The kitchen was in one of the wings with servants quarters above, but the other could be used for four guest chambers. Alex had already decided that guests would be very limited because the rooms above stairs in the main building would be given over to her own family. The meals and spirits served at The Wild Swan would be the main business.

The house had several unique features, including the main staircase which, rather than being the dominant feature at the center back of the hall, was screened off in its own space to the left, thus taking less space from the back rooms. And best of all to Alex's mind was a large garden at the back of the house. Now sadly overgrown and neglected, with work, it would provide her with kitchen and healing herbs in addition to fruits and flowers. The cuttings she had brought with her from England were already in tubs and could be planted more permanently later to produce shoots for the next setting. And from the garden side, there was a view of the water, partially obscured now by other buildings, but visible from the top story.

She and St. John made a brief trip to Baltimore before signing the lease on the house. Having heard that it was a much livelier and progressive city, they felt they owed it to themselves at least to take a look at it. They found it was indeed much busier, its harbor far better suited to shipping than Annapolis's, and noticeable building and expansion was going on despite the hard financial climate.

"Our chances for making a good living would probably be much better here," St. John said.

"Yes, and it seems more . . . I don't know, busier, more American, I suppose. Even the way they say it, 'Balimore' . . ." Nigel shifted restlessly in her arms, sensing her disquiet as her voice trailed away.

"Too American." St. John was suddenly very firm. "I would rather the children grew up in a quieter place until we can remove them to the country."

Alex beamed with relief. She did not think they were ready for Baltimore.

After the trip, one memory of the city stayed with her longer than anything else. As they had gazed at the ships in the harbor, she had seen one with a flag depicting the silhouette of a golden falcon on a crimson ground. The Falconers had flown no such device on their ships in Devon, but still, it gave her an odd start to see it as it conjured the name and the memories instantly. She wondered whose ships flew the flag, and then dismissed it from her mind, assuming that eventually much of the traffic on the bay would become familiar to her.

There was much to be done to the house before it would be open for business. The kitchen was large enough as the house had once seen great entertainments, but it had to be equipped with all the cooking ware necessary to prepare meals for numbers once again. And the walls in most of the rooms needed repainting as well, as did the delicate woodwork and plaster trim. Here and there the wooden floors had been gouged and must be sanded, but as they had never been varnished, there was no stripping to be done. Throughout there was a dearth of good furniture, the best of it having long since been removed by the owner or damaged by previous tenants.

Mavis, Timothy, Boston, St. John, and Alex all worked feverishly, but they also had to hire outside help, and in so doing, they gave the town clear notice of how they felt about slavery. When word got around that they were looking for hired help, several slave owners offered their people for a fee. Politely but firmly, the Carringtons turned them down. And they acknowledged anew that nothing would ever be simple when dealing with the peculiar institution, for the slaves in most cases would have been allowed to keep part of the money paid for their labor. They finally managed to hire a mixed crew to do a variety of jobs, the Negroes showing their papers to prove they were free and not escaped slaves. The necessity of such documents was yet another mark of the pervasiveness of the injustice.

"I won't ever understand," Alex confided to St. John. "Caesar, for instance, is skilled at all he does. He knows how to do carpentry, gardening, whatever task is required of him, and there must be many, many like him; intelligent, capable human beings who happen to be dark skinned. And yet, slave owners insist the blacks are not quite human, or at least no more developed than very young and stupid children to be guided and, not incidentally, used. The same people who so believe, trust their children, their houses, indeed all they own to the care of their slaves. How can they see it both ways?"

"They don't," St. John returned quietly. "They don't see it clearly at all because they're afraid to look. You know our stand on this may hurt our business, don't you?"

She nodded. "But I hope if what we offer is good enough, people will come to The Wild Swan anyway. Perhaps they will mark us down as odd English. Do you think Caesar would stay on? We could use his skill." She did not say that Tim could not be expected to do all of the heavy work himself. St. John had learned to be surprisingly dexterous with his one arm and hand, but there were many tasks that still took him an inordinate amount of time or were impossible without help.

"I'll speak to him," St. John promised and did so promptly, finding that the man seemed pleased with the idea of continued employment. It was from Mrs. Perkins that he learned the man's history. Caesar had been born a slave but had been freed on his master's death by the man's will. It was not that rare a situation and had been particularly practiced by Quakers when they had come to the conclusion that slavery was incompatible with their religious beliefs, but many whites objected to the process because they feared the specter of more and more free blacks in the state. Some hoped that free blacks could be encouraged to emigrate to Africa, but it did not seem to be an idea with wide appeal, as many Negroes had been born in America, not Africa.

St. John and Alex could not help but notice the excessive deference with which the blacks, free and slave, treated whites, but gradually they became aware of other currents as well—the shifting of glances, the sudden flashes of expression quickly suppressed, the reluctance to offer any information unless it was demanded—and they realized that there was an entirely separate life that most blacks led, hidden from the eyes of whites.

"I don't think it is much different from what goes on below stairs at home," St. John observed. "When I reflect on it, I am quite certain that the servants at Carrington Hall had a world apart from ours."

"Yes, but in dire straits they could leave without being hunted down," Alex pointed out.

"In the case of Carrington Hall, they could, but there are other places where leaving is not so easy, where the servants are virtually slaves. And remember, a servant taken on at a hiring fair is bound for a year." He sighed and ran his hand through his hair, his characteristic gesture leaving the thick gold in disarray. "I am finding that age brings more confusion, not less."

"A veritable greybeard, that's what you are," Alex teased, breaking the tension and kissing him soundly.

They tried not to lose sight of each other in the demands of the children and of all the work to be accomplished. They were well and truly married now. Alex had not felt that the simple civil ceremony would make any difference, but she discovered in some subtle way it had because St. John continued to need that official seal on the union. He simply seemed more at ease and more committed to his role as husband and father now that the gold circle on her finger was there by decree. She had conceded the point for his need, but inwardly she still regarded it with the wry realization that he would always need society's approval more than she did.

He had the grace to grin sheepishly when she first saw the mare he had purchased for her. Mab's Maid carried blood that could be traced back to Queen Mab, an English mare brought to Maryland by Governor Ogle in 1747. Mab's Maid was a seven-year-old bay built on clean, strong lines. She was a trifle skittish but capable of giving a good ride once she settled down. St. John had been able to afford her impeccable Thoroughbred lines for two reasons—she had proved herself completely unwilling to race on demand though she showed bursts of speed when it suited her and because though several attempts had been made to breed her, she had proved barren.

"I suspect you have plans for this animal beyond her ability to carry me and a saddle," Alex accused good-naturedly when St. John explained the conditions that had made the sale price lower.

"You know me too well. We don't need her for racing; we can't afford to enter races now and haven't the connections for the big ones in any case. But she seems very fit, and I suspect though she may be slow in conceiving, she might yet bear fine colts. When it is time, we'll put Swan to her. And we will try her with some good stallions before that. Obviously we can't afford to buy winning horses in their prime, but we can gamble on the unproven young and the discredited older animals, and I think we'll win more than we lose."

He looked so happy when he talked about his plans for the horses, she could not help but share his enthusiasm. And whatever her future purpose, Mab's Maid, quickly nicknamed "Mabbie" by the children, gave Alex more freedom than she had had since leaving England. They didn't have much time free from work, but when they could steal a few hours, she and St. John rode out of Annapolis to check on Leda and Swan and to explore the surrounding countryside. And the more they saw of the gently rolling green land, the more they liked it and longed for their own acres.

Though many women nursed their children beyond a year or even two, Alex weaned Nigel of necessity as she fully expected to work long hours when The Wild Swan opened, and she wanted someone other than herself to be able to feed the baby. Nigel didn't seem to mind his new routine at all; it was his father who objected.

"There is more of a chance that you will conceive again if you aren't nursing him, isn't there?" St. John demanded bluntly.

His voice was harsh, but the fear was so plain in his eyes, she knew instantly that he was picturing her struggles to give birth to Nigel. "Did you plan to cease loving me whenever Nigel no longer fed at my breast?" she asked softly.

"The thought occurred to me," he admitted grimly. "Alex, I love you and I love possessing your body. But I could live without that more readily than I could live without you."

"So we could become distant as so many couples are, as my parents are? I understand it better now, the coldness between them. Oh, no, Sinje! Never that. It is your fault, you know; you have made me want your touch at least as much as you want mine. And I want another daughter."

The silence stretched between them as they endured their separate memories of Christiana, and Alex knew the victory of willingness to have another child was shared. Another daughter would not replace the little girl but would ease the loss.

By the middle of August, they had achieved a great deal for the short time they had been there, and they planned to open in two weeks. They were living at The Wild Swan now, though they still visited Mrs. Perkins quite often. She remained their only close contact. Their attitude regarding slavery undoubtedly had something to do with it, but the very fact of their being English was probably as much to blame for the rather chilly reception they received in many quarters. Even though they knew the truth of it now, it was difficult to credit that what had been only a side issue of the war with France for the English had been a major conflict for the Americans. The English had not even named the actions, while the Americans called it the War of 1812.

The frosty attitude simply made Alex more determined than ever that the food and service at the tavern should be so fine that even the reluctant would be attracted.

Mrs. Perkins unbent enough to observe, "With your green eyes and fine looks and Mr. Carrington's dashing ways, people will come for curiosity if naught else." She personally thought the Carringtons' stand on slavery was too righteous for sense, but she had grown fond of them and liked to hear the sounds of her long forsaken native land in their voices. She was pleased to share her knowledge of local markets and various sources for fresh seafood and produce, and she was willing as well to help Alex in matters of staff. It made her feel quite motherly to have the young woman heeding her advice.

In addition to Caesar, Alex had hired a young black woman, Tillie Carter, who, though she said very little and that so drawled the Carringtons could hardly understand her, was a hard worker. She was the daughter of sharecroppers, which Alex translated to mean tenant farmers, and she much preferred living in town to the farm. With the five adults in their own family, plus the two extra sets of hands, they could manage, but Alex still thought an extra woman who knew something about cooking would be a help.

Timothy and Mavis could both produce good plain meals, and Alex herself had a wide knowledge of making dishes savory with herbs and spices, but none of them knew about local taste beyond the dishes they had eaten at Mrs. Perkins's table. And it was Mrs. Perkins who found Della.

"I think I know a woman who might prove to be exactly what you need," Mrs. Perkins ventured, an odd look in her eyes. "She has a mind of her own, does Della Johnson, but she's a very good cook. She's worked for me from time to time when I needed extra help, and she's been in more than one of the richest houses here, doing the same thing. She might like a term of steady employment, and then again, she might not. She's very independent; some say uppity."

Alex knew the minute Mrs. Perkins used the word "uppity" that the woman in question was black, but she let it pass. "I would be grateful if you would tell me how to contact her."

"Something you ought to know first. Her father was a white man in his late years when he developed a fondness for one of his slaves, her mother. The child and the mother were freed on his death. Della's mother worked as a laundress and cook until her death a few years ago. I know Della loved her mother, but I don't think she's ever cared for anyone else, black or white. She holds herself aloof from both, being neither one nor the other. It's hard for her, I know, but you may find her difficult to deal with."

Alex felt a twist of disgust for Della's father. It might even have been that he loved the woman, but it seemed he had not freed her and given her a choice of whether or not she would be his lover, had loosened his hold on her only when he was in his grave. No wonder his daughter was bitter. She realized now that Mrs. Perkins had been curious about what her reaction would be to the tale of mixed blood; she let nothing show on her face.

She had a harder time controlling her emotions when Della came to inquire about the job.

Alex judged her to be a few years beyond her own age of twenty. Of less than medium height, the woman held herself regally upright; so much so that it was as if she were looking down her nose at all around her. Black and white blood had forged a unique beauty, further enchanced by the snowy kerchief she wore wrapped around her head. Her nose was strongly sculpted with open high-arching nostrils, and her brows curved perfectly over large, deep brown eyes in a pale brown, oval face. But her full, even mouth was held in a taut line and her eyes were sullen.

"It is true you hire no slaves?" she asked abruptly, her voice precise, with none of the drawl Alex was growing accustomed to.

Alex nodded, taken aback by the way the interview was beginning. "My husband and I do not believe in slavery and want no part of it."

"What kind of work did you have in mind for me?" There was still no warmth in her manner, and Alex felt her temper begin to rise.

"None at all if you cannot be civil," she retorted. "Miss Johnson, I am sure you have had difficulties in your life, but I am not responsible for them, and we are working too hard here to allow anyone to disrupt our days. What I had in mind was for you to help us with the cooking and perhaps with other tasks as well. We do not yet know everything that will need to be done. My husband and I have never run a public house before."

They stared at each other until Della allowed herself a faint smile. "You'll do, Mrs. Carrington. You know what you want and how to get it. I like that in a person. Do you still want to hire me?"

Alex smiled back. "Indeed I do. Mrs. Perkins is not given to exaggeration, and she says you're one of the best cooks in Annapolis."

"In all of Maryland, I expect," Della offered blandly, and then they both laughed and settled amicably to discuss terms. Only after the woman had departed did Alex consider what a courageous person she was. Her defiant pride must have cost her dearly along the way, had surely cost her jobs and might even have endangered her. It was hardly the way to make friends, but it was a way of insisting that she was an individual and worthy of consideration on her own terms.

Alex sighed. It was going to take a bit of explaining as far as Mavis Bates was concerned. Timothy seemed to be adapting very well, as if his time with the army had given him a broad view of life, but Mavis was decidedly provincial, and working with blacks had been as alien to her as if she'd been asked to associate with creatures from the nether world.

" 'Ow do I talk to dem?" she asked plaintively, and Alex curbed her exasperation and forebore pointing out that in the matter of language, though the cadence was different, Mavis's own speech was more kin to Tillie Carter's and Caesar's than to Alex's. "Talk to them as you would to any English-speaking human being and remember that there are regions in England where the dialect is far more incomprehensible," she told Mavis. "At least people here speak slowly."

Alex suspected it would take Mavis a long while to adjust. Though she ceased to start like a nervous horse every time one of the blacks was near, Alex doubted that Mavis and Della would ever establish more than an armed truce. Della was obviously better educated than Mavis, something the Englishwoman could hardly tolerate. Choosing the coward's way, Alex decided they could work it out on their own.

The more Alex learned about Della, the more pleased she was that the woman had consented to work for them. They worked in harmony, testing the quality of everything from flour to sugar to spices, tea, and coffee, and discussing the best prices of meats and fowl, domestic and wild. Mavis had charge of the children so they would not be underfoot.

Alex found that she and Della spoke the same language

when it came to the quality of food, various seasonings, and cleanliness in the kitchen. She felt a great surge of contentment. It would work; she would make sure of it. Once again, she gave thanks for all the skills her grandmother had taught her.

"You would like my grandmother," she remarked to Della. "You and she are a great deal alike, forthright, strong, and knowledgeable."

Della eyed her skeptically. "Seems to me that you just described yourself."

They both laughed, and Alex protested, "No, not yet, but I would like to be like that eventually." She began to tell the other woman about Virginia's many projects but paused as she heard people approaching through the passage from the main part of the house. Caesar's normally soft voice was raised in alarm as he insisted that Mrs. Carrington might not want to be bothered even if it was a relation.

Alex was vexed that Tim wasn't there; he had a knack for keeping insistent tradesmen at bay. Then she heard the two male voices, muffled but vaguely familiar, one American, one English.

"I tell you, it can't be," said the Englishman.

"Stranger things have happened; you're here. I'm sure it's she. The description is too close. And the name," said the American.

The shock was so great when she saw him, Alex nearly fell to her knees. Caleb Jennings she had thought she might see one day, but not Rane Falconer, not ever again.

❧ *Chapter 35* ❧

He was changed, so changed. Only five years older than she, he looked far more mature than that, as if the years since she had seen him had not treated him kindly. His tanned face had lines graven beside his mouth and at the corners of his eyes. The last trace of boyhood had left the rest of his body, too. He would always be lean, but it was a man's leanness now, showing in every line from his broad shoulders to the muscular legs displayed by tight breeches. He seemed so much taller and larger than she remembered. Even his hands looked bigger and stronger, calloused and capable. Involuntarily images rose of the younger version of those hands going nimbly about many tasks. She forced herself to meet his gaze. The thick, dark, faintly wavy hair and the vivid green eyes were the same, the eyes registering as much shock and wariness as her own must be, but still Rane's.

The moment for easy greeting had long since passed. Vaguely she was aware of Caesar easing himself from the room, and of Della's hushed, "Lord in heaven!" as she studied first one face and then the other and then left as well.

It was not going at all as Caleb had thought it would. He felt responsible for the meeting because it was he who had heard of the new arrivals in Annapolis and guessed that it was Alexandria, no matter how unlikely. His mother's maid, who was a dependable source of gossip, had confirmed the great resemblance between Mrs. Carrington and Mr. Falconer, having seen the newcomer recently in the town and having known Rane since his first visit to the Jenningses' Annapolis residence. Caleb had incorrectly assumed that whatever youthful passion had stirred them was long over and that they would be glad of a reunion. Instead, the current flowed between them as strongly as the spring flood tides.

The heat that Alex had borne without real distress until now suddenly seemed to engulf her so that she felt as if she were suffocating, and for a moment, the room and its occupants swung dizzily before her eyes, coming into focus again as she saw Rane reaching out for her. She took a step back, feeling terror and a host of other unreasonable emotions. Just by existing, he threatened everything she had. That the threat was as much from her own response to him as from anything else did not comfort her. The sound of the children's voices as they scurried toward the kitchen in search of something to eat completed her nightmare.

Flora, Blaine, and Morgan checked at the sight of the visitors, and Mavis, with Nigel in her arms, came to a stop behind them, looking no less startled. Alex could feel their eyes taking in the astonishing fact of a strange man who looked very like their mother.

"Like Mummy, like me!" Morgan crowed after he had carefully scrutinized Rane, and Alex thought her heart would stop as she saw Rane's eyes avidly taking in every detail of the little boy's appearance.

The children were her life now, the children and St. John, and whatever had happened in the past was better left there. Strength flowed through her again.

"I would like you to meet my children," she said calmly, offering their names and introducing Mavis as well, as if the tense time moments before had never happened.

"Children, this is Caleb Jennings, an American I met in England, and Rane Falconer is my cousin from Devonshire."

"That's the West Country," Blaine announced, pleased that he knew.

"Yes, it is. It's good to know your geography," Rane said, drawing his attention with effort away from Morgan.

"Your mother and Rane helped me to escape from soldiers and come home to my own country." Caleb was relieved to have found a subject which so instantly drew the children's interest and set the stage for further storytelling, giving Alex and Rane time to gain more control, though at the moment, it seemed Rane needed it more than she; Caleb could feel the effort the man was making to keep from paying undue attention to the little boy Morgan, and he could not help but wonder. Rane had given only the briefest account of Alex when Caleb had inquired after her. He had said that she had returned to her home in Kent, had married, and had a family of her own. Now Caleb suspected there was far more to the story than that and surely Morgan was part of it. The twins baffled him completely since they were certainly too old to be Alex's. Still wondering about it, he did his best to make the story of his escape from England as exciting as possible and was rewarded by the enthusiasm of the children.

"Mummy, you were very brave!" Flora exclaimed, adding, "And you, too, Mr. Rain. That's a funny name, like snow or wind or something."

"It's spelt R-a-n-e, not R-a-i-n," he explained, and he managed to smile as he remembered telling Alex the same thing when she had first come to Clovelly. For a moment, he felt an overwhelming hatred for the twins—without them, Alex surely would not have been so bound to St. John Carrington. Alex, even with a smear of flour on her cheek, her hair in a loose tumble, and her dress damp with perspiration, was more lovely than he remembered.

The resemblance between them now was only superficial. As he knew his full power as a man, so she had come into her own as a woman. She was still slender despite the birth of her children and could never be termed voluptuous, but the uncertain angles of youth were gone. Now that she was recovering from the shock of seeing him, she moved with graceful assurance. But the greatest change was in her eyes. In addition to the quick intelligence that had always been there, now there was maturity and a well of sorrow along with the joy. She had lived much since he had seen her. He felt more than the urge of his body to possess hers; he ached to enfold her in his arms and hold her close and safe against his heart. As he thought it, he recognized the impossibility of giving life to the past in the present. He touched the gold band on his finger; familiar pain moved through him.

Alex saw him touch the ring, and she saw that Caleb was wearing a wedding band as well. It steadied her further to know they all had domestic concerns apart from any past bonds even as she felt elusive pain at the idea of Rane married to another woman. It was what she had wanted for him, and yet, it was hard to swallow the reality. And she could not help but wonder about the woman because Rane did not look like a happy, contented man. She was not arrogant enough to believe that the graven lines in his face had anything to do with her.

The gathering moved into a strange twilight of civility. Rane and Caleb entertained the children with stories about ships until the little ones had had their snack and went willingly out to play in the garden under the watchful eye of Mavis. Gazing after them, Alex explained to Caleb that the twins were her stepchildren, as if that were the only confusion in the meeting.

She took the men on a tour of the house, drawing added strength and pride from being able to show what she, St. John, and the others had accomplished in brief weeks. And casually she asked Caleb and Rane about their lives.

Caleb was now sole head of the Jennings shipping company. His parents had elected to stay in Annapolis though they had shared in the decision to move the company to Baltimore. Caleb had married a woman named Penelope in early 1815 and was the proud father of a three-year-old, John. Despite the current hard times for shipping, Caleb was obviously delighted in his life.

In 1817, Rane had come to the United States via Canada, purchasing his first ship in Nova Scotia with the money he would have used for the same purpose in England. Through a series of profitable ventures, described with no more detail than that, he had acquired two more ships and a share in a fourth. And he and Caleb were sharing the risks and profits of their newly established shipyard, concentrating at the moment on coastal vessels, but planning to build swift deepwater ships as soon as the market for them improved.

"Do your ships fly a flag with a golden falcon on a crimson ground?" Alex asked, and he nodded.

"St. John and I saw a ship with such a flag in Baltimore's harbor," she explained, "and it brought your family to mind, though I could not believe at the time that there was any connection. It is a good device."

There was a gleam of satisfaction in his eyes that told her he was not fooled by her reference to his family; he knew she had thought chiefly of him when she had seen the flag, and it pleased him.

"Your wife, is she American?" she asked quietly, carefully adding to the wall between them.

His face changed perceptibly, the lines becoming more deeply graven, the green eyes suddenly dull and lifeless. "She is," he said and offered nothing more about her.

"Would you care to come for supper this evening? My husband and my brother will be home by then, and I would like you to meet them. Your wives are welcome, too, of course."

Caleb didn't know what to say. There were so many things being said without words between the two, he felt the odd man out. He was relieved when Rane answered for both of them.

"Our wives are in Baltimore. Caleb, if it is agreeable with you, I would like to join the Carringtons tonight."

Caleb agreed, wondering if they even heard him.

Alex knew that she and Rane were at cross purposes; she wanted to show him how close she and St. John were; he expected to find the same discord that had driven her into his arms. She was soothed by the fact that that was no longer the case.

It was a caculated risk to invite the men to dine with them. St. John had never seen Rane before, and he could not miss the resemblance between Morgan and Rane. But he knew the strength of the Thaine blood, and he did not know that Rane had come to Gravesend in 1816. If there was to be any chance of a normal life in Maryland, it must be settled now. Boundaries must be secured. Alex refused to contemplate dreading the meeting of Rane and St. John every day of her life. She was fully aware of the act of trust involved. Rane could tell St. John that he had been in Gravesend after Alex had left Clovelly, but she was absolutely certain he would not. No matter what had happened between them, she trusted that he would want only the best for her, as she wanted the same for him.

But courage faltered as Rane took his leave, waiting until Caleb was out of earshot.

"Is Morgan my son?"

She had known the question would come, but she had not expected it so soon or so bluntly asked. She swallowed hard and met his gaze squarely. "I do not know." The words fell like stones between them, and she winced inwardly at the raw pain that flared in his eyes.

"When Sinje returned after you left, all was changed.

He and I came to a new understanding, and things have been well between us since then. Rane, I love him dearly. And we have shared much together. Our little girl, Christiana, died last year," even now her voice quavered at the memory, "and Nigel was born. There is so much between us, and so much yet to be. I would not have him hurt for all the world."

The pain was still there; he doubted that it would ever be completely gone. Alex had gone from his arms into St. John's so swiftly, she did not even know the paternity of her son for certain. His son. Despite all, he was sure of it. And it changed nothing. He loved her. Bemused as he was by finding her in the same place where he had sought refuge from memories of her, still he felt the old love for her pulsing through him as intimately as the beat of his heart. To love was to protect from harm.

"As you would not hurt your husband, so I would not hurt you, not for all the world," he said softly, deliberately repeating her words.

She watched him leave with Caleb, and she wondered how they were ever going to get through the evening. She half expected, half feared the arrival of a messenger saying the men would not be able to return for the meal. Part of her longed for the reprieve and part of her knew the sooner over, the better.

No messenger arrived. Mavis and Della in a rare mood of truce took over preparation of the meal, and Alex took a deep breath and swept into the performance of her lifetime when St. John and Boston arrived home.

"The most marvelous thing has occurred! I've just discovered that my cousin, Rane Falconer, from Clovelly, is here, and so is Caleb Jennings, the American we helped to escape from England. I've invited them for supper so you can meet them. Rane shows the Thaine blood as clearly as I do, just as his mother does." The words tumbled out too quickly, but St. John seemed to find nothing amiss in her excitement.

"That is news! It's not such a vast world after all." He gave her a quick kiss.

St. John's basic innocence and a certain degree of ignorance he still maintained about women served as his armor. With relief and amazement, Alex saw that he did not suspect, not even for a moment.

He greeted Caleb and Rane with real warmth, and the

three plus Boston discussed a wide variety of subjects from shipping to racing and the current financial distress in the United States and Europe. Alex said little, her heart continuing to beat so fast that breath for speech was limited.

The men seemed genuinely at ease with each other, even Caleb and St. John who had fought on opposite sides of the war. And there was neither contempt nor dislike in Rane's eyes as he looked at her husband. St. John at his most charming was charming indeed, open and affable. And she gave full credit to Rane who was, for love of her, willing to be civil.

Watching him, she was more certain than ever that Morgan was his son. She had forgotten little gestures characteristic of Rane—the certain way he tilted his head when he was interested in something, even the way his hands curved at rest. Morgan was the mirror image.

Mirrors in mirrors. That was what her life had become. She realized suddenly that it was possible that the certain way Rane moved could be as much an inheritance as the green eyes and dark hair. So perhaps after all, Morgan's inheritance was from her, not from Rane. And the looks she and Rane shared lulled St. John more than anything else. Even though he understood that their kinship was distant, the sight of them together seemed as natural as seeing Alex and Boston; in fact, to St. John, Alex and Rane looked more like brother and sister than did Alex and Boston.

St. John was speaking enthusiastically of his plans to found a line of fine race horses. "It's too early to tell for certain, of course, but Swan has all the marks of a magnificent future. His legs are long and sturdy, and he has the promise of a deep chest. He's of sweet temperament and quick to learn. If only horses bred as true as the Thaines," he added, his blue eyes merry.

Nothing changed in Rane's face as he answered easily, "Ah, but perhaps we would be considered throwbacks," eliciting a bark of laughter from St. John.

Caleb managed to smile, but Alex caught the sudden stillness in Boston as he let the conversation flow over him. He was very fond of Morgan, and he had known how sad Alex had been to leave Clovelly. She could see him sorting through seemingly unrelated facts, and then she saw the flare of alarmed suspicion in his green eyes, followed by the little shake of his head as if he sought physically to clear his mind. He no more than St. John knew that Rane had come to Gravesend to see her.

Alex kept her face carefully blank as Boston's eyes flickered from her to Rane. Whatever conclusion he came to, she knew that he, as much as Rane, would do nothing to hurt her. "Oh, what a tangled web we weave when first we practice to deceive." She wished the poet's words were not so apt, wished that the line had not risen to haunt her now.

She was thankful at least that the children had been fed and put to bed before the guests arrived; to have Morgan before them now would have been unbearable.

Though the men continued to enjoy themselves, for Alex the minutes stretched endlessly, and she could not wait for the evening to end. She tried to keep her relief from showing when the time finally came to bid the guests good-night, but Rane, even after the long separation, knew her too well.

"We both survived rather well, I think," he murmured softly as he took his leave of her. "You have a good husband and fine children; I envy you." The summer night swallowed him as he walked away.

Dimly she heard Caleb saying to St. John, "I have found my friends, Alexandria and Rane, to be very independent since they gave me no warning of their emigration to this country nor asked my assistance once here. I hope you will be more flexible than they and call upon me should you need my help. The United States has need of people willing to commit their fortunes to her. And for all the trouble there has been between England and my country, there is yet more cause for friendship than for enmity."

"We appreciate your offer," St. John replied as Alex stepped to his side. "I wish I could say that we will never need your help, but life is so different here, we are bound to need it one day or another."

Alex added her thanks, but all the while she was seeing again Rane's tall, broad-shouldered form disappearing into the dark.

"It's been a pleasurable evening, sweetheart. I like both your American friend and your cousin." St. John's arm came around her waist, hugging her to him for a moment, and she leaned against his solid body, grateful for the closeness, willing him to banish the image of Rane.

It had been a long day for both of them, but when St. John would have settled down to sleep, Alex moved against him so restlessly that he asked, "What is it, love?"

"Just that," she murmured, "just love, for you."

As his hand began to stroke her body in languorous patterns, Alex straddled him, teasing him with long tresses of her hair, with her hands and with swift light kisses, filling her senses with the differing textures of him, rough to smooth, with the scent of him, fresh and masculine, uniquely his, with the salt taste of him and the sound of his quickened breathing. Even in the darkness she could see his shining fairness.

St. John groaned and bucked beneath her as she guided his hard shaft into her waiting softness, loving him, loving the fit of his flesh in hers.

Afterwards when she thought he had fallen asleep, his voice startled her. "I begin to see more clearly what you gave up to return to Gravesend to care for the twins and then for me. Your cousin is a fine man, and I am sure his family welcomed you warmly. I am so glad you did not stay in Devon!"

She had thought her heart would stop at his first words, sure that he suspected her relationship with Rane, but then she realized his innocent view was unchanged.

"I am glad, too, my darling," she whispered. And silently, she vowed anew that he would never have cause to regret their marriage.

❧ *Chapter 36* ❧

They soon discovered that Caleb Jennings had not waited
for them to ask for his help; though he had swiftly returned to Baltimore, he had accomplished much before he
left. That Alexandria Thaine Carrington had been another
who had helped Caleb Jennings escape from England was
suddenly common knowledge in Annapolis. And it did
not stop there. Caleb had also let it be known that St.
John had lost his arm in honorable combat for his country,
no matter that the battle had been against the French,
America's allies. Further, Mr. Carrington had given up all
of the advantages of his aristocratic family in order to
marry the woman he loved. That slight twisting of facts
was a touch of genius, Alex came to realize, for Americans,
as much as they disdained the Crown, still had a sneaking
admiration for titles, and Caleb's version of St. John suited
their every desire—his blood was blue, but his choice had
been democratic. Nor had Alex suffered in the legend.
She had not only braved the militia to help an American
in need, she had also defied stiff convention to become a
devoted wife and mother.

Among the many overtures of interest and friendship
was an invitation from Caleb's parents for the Carringtons
to call. They complied and found it easy to like the older
couple. They were as open and cordial as their son, and
they were both so grateful to Alex that she was moved to
insist that Caleb would surely have survived without her
help.

Tears in her eyes, Mrs. Jennings shook her head. "No,
child, he told us how ill and lost he was. I believe he

would have died in that cave were it not for you. Whatever we can do for you, consider it done."

"But Caleb paid Rane and me well for our help," Alex protested, and then gave up when Mr. Jennings said gruffly, "A few gold coins are scarce the value of our son."

When they had finally pieced all the new attention together with a good deal of help from Mrs. Perkins, Alex laughed until she cried. "Oh, Sinje, we sound like escapees from a royal family, deposed but unbowed!"

"Mr. Jennings's version of my family is far better than the reality," St. John said, "even though both exile me for my luck in having you. Sweet exile!" He did not seem to take any notice of the fact that the true story of Caleb's escape included only Rane and Alex, not Seadon or Elwyn.

Neither Alex nor St. John was foolish enough to resent Caleb's interference. They were too aware of how easily their stand on slavery and their nationality might have ruined their chance of success. Instead, The Wild Swan was successful from the day it opened. They knew that most people came to the establishment the first time out of curiosity, but they returned for good food and good service.

In addition to meat pies, savories, and a host of other dishes Alex had learned to make in England, the tavern offered local favorites made according to Della's recipes. Among those were beaten biscuits (the name earned by the long period of beating with a stick that the dough required before baking) and dishes that included such things as sweet potatoes, peanuts, and cornmeal, not common ingredients in cooking as Alex knew it. She confessed to Della that cornmeal in particular had had her baffled until she discovered that Americans called a specific grain "corn" unlike the English who used it as a general term for various cereal crops.

Ladies who came to partake of afternoon tea or coffee, fast becoming a popular beverage in the United States, found that they had a wide choice of delicate cakes, biscuits, and sandwiches from which to choose. One of the two rooms on the street side of the house had been set aside for ladies' use from the beginning so that it would not carry the scent of liquor or tobacco, and the afternoon offerings proved as popular as the rest of the business.

Women had quickly taken to the idea of having a place to meet for a bite to eat and a visit.

For the main meals served at the tavern, the bay yielded oysters, crab, various succulent fishes, and waterfowl of every description from ducks to geese to ortolans, or sora rails, and reed birds, or bobolinks, long considered delicacies. Rabbit, muskrat, turkey, chicken, pork, and beef were easily purchased, as well as venison as the autumn deepened. Despite the name of the place, Alex put her foot down in the matter of serving swan. The birds were coming in in vast flights to winter on the bay, not only the small whistling swans but also the huge trumpeters, prized for their feathers and skins as well as their meat. But none of them would die to improve the bill of fare at The Wild Swan.

The swans made Alex feel more at peace, more at home than ever since landing in Maryland. She loved the grace of the great white wings and the varied cries. And one day when she was out riding with St. John, they witnessed the truth of a sad legend. A whistling swan shot by a hunter uttered a long musical note totally unlike its usual call of high-pitched, melodious laughter. Alex shivered as if the sound had pierced her as the bullet had the swan, and St. John's voice was not quite steady as he said, "I have never heard such a mournful cry, as if she were calling to her own to come to her." He did not tease her again for her reluctance to serve the fowl at her table.

Even in the press of work, Alex continued to thrive on the beauty of her new country. She loved the skeins of geese that moved across the sky, their cries sounding like the faraway baying of hounds. She loved the changing of the foliage to browns, golds, and reds as the sultry heat was vanquished by chill nights and crisp days, and an early storm in November gave warning of how severe winter could be. The bright red of the male cardinal's feathers delighted her, and she was even willing to concede the name "robin" to what was obviously some sort of thrush and bore no similarity to the plump little robin of England. "I think Americans like even their birds larger than ours," she told St. John.

"But their tutors smaller," he replied, and they laughed guiltily.

They had hired a man named Horace Whittleby to instruct the children. In his late twenties, he was well read, patient, and had no objection to teaching Flora as well as Blaine and even Morgan despite the child's extreme youth. He earned his living by various tutoring and clerkish jobs, and it was hard to imagine a more colorless and reserved man. His narrow face topped by thinning hair was not improved by the spectacles perched on his beaky nose. And not even his neat clothes disguised legs as bowed as any jockey's though he professed a great dislike of riding, a personal distaste he promised not to impose upon the children. He was, in fact, about the size of a jockey and made Alex feel like a giant when she stood near him. He seemed altogether gray until he had something of interest to impart to the children, and then he came alive, his voice rumbling and his gestures grand as if he were a much larger man.

Alex wished she had the time to continue teaching the children herself, but the burden of duties at The Wild Swan prevented it, and she had to content herself with making the most of the time she did have to spend with her offspring. They seemed to be adjusting very well to life in the New World and had even begun to make friends with other children, though most of their time was spent with each other. They were too young to have long lessons with Mr. Whittleby as yet, but even short sessions were improving their knowledge of letters and numbers. Her grandmother had started to teach her at such a young age, Alex knew very well how possible it was for children to learn nearly from the day they were born.

"I wonder what language they will speak when they're grown," she mused. "From Mavis they have learned to call ants 'ammets' in addition to other Kentish oddities; it took me quite a time the other day to convince Blaine that 'bliv' is not the same as 'believe.' And now, even though Mr. Whittleby is quite precise in his speech, I hear a noticeable drawl invading theirs."

"They seem to have no difficulty in making their wants known," St. John replied and nuzzled her throat, making his own wants clear. "Have I told you how glad I would be anywhere with you?"

Their time together was made more precious by the knowledge that in the early spring of the new year, St. John would begin to travel to various race meetings. It was mutually agreed. He had become a popular figure as host at the tavern, even deigning to learn a certain dexterity in the one-handed drawing of ale and wine, but their future lay with the horses.

Alex shared his excitement over the prospects of Leda's foal, due in January from her breeding to Hugh's prize stud. The birth date would be fortuitous as they had learned that many of the southern racing regions considered May 1 to be the official birth date of foals born in any given year. That meant that those born earlier had the advantage of several months' more growth over those born on May 1 or after. In the first trials of young horses, that added age could make a vital difference.

St. John planned to make arrangements to breed Alex's mare, Mabbie, in late February for a January foal, and Alex hoped as much as he that the breeding would be successful. Little by little they would build their stock.

Their lives were so taken up by work, they gave little thought to any social life, but in late November they received an invitation from Caleb to join him and his wife for a party at his parents' home in early December. A missive to the same effect also came from his parents.

They saw the elder Jenningses now and again, particularly because they had developed an undisguised fondness for the Carrington children, their own children and grandchildren being less accessible since their son lived in Baltimore and their two daughters had been transplanted by their husbands to New York where business opportunities were better.

St. John was instantly enthusiastic about attending the party, pointing out that many of their customers would undoubtedly be there, plus others who might be future customers, and so it would be good for business, as well as enjoyable.

"Now who has the shopkeeper's mind?" Alex teased, but she, too, was excited as well as apprehensive; social occasions such as this had never been a part of her life. She had attended various country celebrations with her grandmother when she was young, but she had never been to anything even approaching the Jenningses' party.

Her disquiet was so plainly reflected in her eyes, St. John noticed and was puzzled until the cause dawned on him, and he felt a ripple of pain; so much she had given up for him. When she should have been dancing and attending various routs, she had already been tied to him and his children. "You mustn't fret, you will be the most beautiful woman there," he said gently. "To begin this campaign, you will have a new dress made, no arguments about it. And perhaps Boston can teach you some of the dances."

With that she looked even more panicked. "Surely I won't have to dance since you . . ."

"Don't be sorry you said it; it's perfectly true that I shan't be dancing. But I can think of nothing I would rather watch than you gliding to the music. You are a very graceful woman, Alex. I expect dancing will come easily to you."

It came instead with a great deal of laughter as Boston demonstrated various steps, protesting all the while that dancing was not his forte and blushing uncomfortably as he stepped wrong for the countless time.

"I'm beginning to believe you," Alex said and went off in peals of laughter as they nearly toppled over while Boston attempted a waltz turn.

"Perhaps they don't permit the waltz anyway," Boston suggested hopefully as he regained his balance.

It didn't help the learning process any when the children arrived on the scene to share the hilarity and fell about laughing at their elders' antics.

Help came from an unexpected source. Without change of his sober expression, Mr. Whittleby announced that he was not unfamiliar with dancing and might be of aid.

Alex was desperate enough to accept help from any quarter, and privately she thought if she could survive the embarrassment of towering over Horace as they went through various patterns, the Jenningses' party would be easy. The children were banished by a firm word from their tutor, but St. John and Boston were hardly more sober witnesses. Even as she concentrated on the steps, she was aware of both men struggling mightily to control their mirth.

But though his somewhat prim expression never altered, Mr. Whittleby turned out to be a credible dancer and a good teacher, and Alex's thanks for his instruction were sincere.

"It just goes to show you that one should never judge people too quickly. Who would ever have thought that Horace Whittleby would know how to dance!"

"God knows what other hidden talents he has," St. John said, trying to keep a straight face. "I shall have to watch him when he's around you." He grunted as he received an elbow in his ribs.

The night of the party, they drew a whistle of approval from Boston who was going with them. "My, my, the honor of England will be upheld tonight on appearance alone. Alex, you're lovely, even if you are my sister. And St. John, the gossips will have you a duke at the very least before the evening is over."

Alex's dress was of creamy satin, high-waisted with sleeves that puffed at the shoulders and fit at the wrist. The skirt was overlaid by gauze decorated with a delicate pattern of roses near the hem. Her hair was piled on her head in soft curls circled by a rose ribbon. Her eyes glowed golden green, and her cheeks were flushed with excitement.

St. John looked very handsome in his black knee breeches and coat which contrasted so well with his fairness and made his eyes look as blue as sapphires. He offered Alex his arm. "On to battle, Britannia."

The night was clear and chill but less so than the weather had been a month ago when a sudden cold spell had hit the eastern seaboard, bringing unseasonably hard frost and even snow. The natives had complained about it, but the Carringtons, having no previous experience of Maryland's cycle of seasons, had taken it more in stride, finding the cold easier to bear than some of the extremely hot days of summer.

It was no distance at all to the Jenningses' house, Annapolis being a compact town, and the three of them were soon bathed in the light and babble of the festivities.

Caleb was greeting guests with his parents, and beside him stood his wife, Penelope. Alex felt Boston's start of surprise and understood; at first glance, Penelope bore more than a small resemblance to Boston's dead wife. She, too, was small and round with big brown eyes and an obvious adoration of her husband. And when Caleb introduced Alex to her, Penelope's face was instantly alight.

"Mrs. Carrington, I have so longed to meet you! I owe you so much! I will never cease to be grateful for what you did for Caleb. Without you and Rane, I would not have my family." One hand unconsciously brushed the front of her dress, and she and Caleb exchanged a brief smile, and though it did not show yet, Alex was sure she was expecting another child. "Please feel free to call on me or Caleb for anything you might need."

"The Jenningses have already done much for us," Alex pointed out. "Your husband enhanced our welcome so that we went from being treated as suspicious strangers to part of the community overnight." She smiled at Caleb who looked like a small boy caught stealing sweets. "You helped our business a great deal," she assured him, taking pity on him.

"From what I've heard, you didn't need much help. It seems that half of the government depends on The Wild Swan for food and drink." He debated warning Alex of the other guests, but the moment was lost as the Carringtons and Boston moved on to allow their hosts to greet new arrivals. Caleb sighed inwardly, hoping the evening would be enjoyable for everyone.

Buoyed by the warm welcome they had received, Alex and St. John were at ease from the beginning, finding they knew many of the people in attendance and were recipients of many friendly overtures and admiring glances. Alex watched with amusement as Boston dealt courteously with a great deal of obvious female interest.

"I still think of Boston simply as my brother, but I can see he's a force to be reckoned with among the young ladies of Annapolis," she told St. John, her eyes fond as she continued to observe her brother.

"Yes, we might well acquire an American sister-in-law."

"I'd like that for him. He deserves a new beginning . . ." All thought of Boston's future marital bliss fled her mind as she caught sight of Rane. Fortunately, St. John shared her shock.

"Good God! Your cousin surely has fine taste in women! I presume that is his wife."

Rane's eyes met Alex's over the crowd, but the expression in his was cool and aloof as if he didn't see her clearly, though his face was set in a polite smile as he greeted people he knew.

The meeting was unavoidable. "Claire, I would like you to meet St. John Carrington and his wife, my cousin, Alexandria Carrington."

Alex heard the peculiar emphasis Rane put on their kinship, and she knew she was making the properly civil responses to the introduction, but the truth overwhelmed her.

Rane's wife was the most exquisite woman Alex had ever seen. She was small and silvery fair with pale blue eyes and delicately symmetrical features. She was the image of the fairytale princess, the ghost of men's dreams.

Alex wondered if Rane were as conscious as she of how she loomed over Claire. Small, fair, perfect—everything Alex was not. She was startled by the stab of pain the knowledge brought. It was only just that Rane have his love as she had hers. She had no right to anger because he had chosen someone so different from herself. After all, St. John was different from Rane. But she was baffled by the misery he had revealed when he first mentioned his wife, nor did she understand the anxiety she felt in him now.

Eyes. Rane's so worried and his wife's so . . . mad. Another truth far more agonizing than the first and as undeniable. She saw the strange, frenzied light moving in the woman's eyes as if it were a separate creature, a razor-toothed ferret wild to slash its way out.

Then it was gone, extinguished as though it had never been. Claire was greeting her graciously, remarking on how pleasant it must be for her and Rane to have found familiar faces from England on these foreign shores, particularly since they looked so alike, far more so than most cousins. There seemed to be no rancor in her observation.

Alex found her own tongue. "Yes, though Clovelly and my childhood seem quite distant, Rane and his family made me very welcome when I stayed with them." She was pleased with the way she expressd it, relegating any contact with Rane to the past, and she was relieved that Claire apparently thought their blood kinship far closer than it was. Safer that way. But the chill remained in Alex's blood. She was sure of what she had seen, however briefly. She would have liked to move away from the Falconers, but Claire and circumstance prevented it as musicians began to play and couples began to move to the music—a waltz guaranteed to add excitement to the party as there were still many who considered the dance immoral. Alex could just imagine Caleb's mother choosing it with deliberate mischief; Mrs. Jennings, for all her propriety, liked things lively.

"Rane, dance with your cousin. I'll entertain Mr. Carrington," Claire ordered, steel and sweetness so mixed in her voice, they were hard to distinguish.

"I've just learned. I'm . . . I'm not . . . ," Alex tried to protest, suddenly terrified of this closeness to Rane, but she found herself swept into the dance as Rane muttered grimly, "What Claire wants, she must have."

He kept his proper distance, one hand lightly at her waist, the other against her hand, but it made no difference; Alex felt as if their bodies were fused together head to toe. She was so disconcerted, she faltered, regaining her balance only because of Rane's quick steps.

"One dance, you can surely survive that," he said bitterly.

She raised her eyes swiftly to his, the other whirling couples disappearing.

"I'm sorry, Alex, forgive my foul mood. Claire is . . . well, sometimes she is difficult and not her best in crowds, though she will not miss any social function if she can help it."

Alex's heart twisted at the unthinkable truth. Rane was afraid of his wife's behavior, so afraid that he would do her bidding rather than risk crossing her.

"Don't!" he commanded sharply, "don't you dare pity me!" And then his gaze softened again. "You look beautiful, so beautiful tonight, and happy, but tired as well. Do you ever take time for yourself, just to be wild and free again as you were in Devon?"

With effort she suppressed the shiver that rose from the center of her. "Those days are a world away," she murmured and was infinitely thankful that the music was ending. She felt dazed as he led her back to her husband. Rane's words had touched her as intimately as if his hands had run over her body. Yet, she knew that he had not done it deliberately, and that made it all the worse.

Rane offered his arm politely to his wife, and they moved away. Alex barely prevented a sigh of relief from escaping.

"Damned if there isn't something very peculiar about that woman. I didn't understand half of what she said while you were dancing. Her sentences seemed to be in odd pieces," St. John confided to Alex, and there was grim comfort in knowing he had noticed it, too.

Though she danced again and again and managed to keep up her end of the conversation when she and St. John joined other couples for supper, the joy had gone out of the evening, and she was relieved when St. John suggested they go home, leaving Boston to enjoy the party to its end.

As they walked along, St. John tucked his arm in hers.

"You were the most beautiful woman there, just as I knew you would be. And bless you for your marvelous, practical mind! Your cousin's wife has made me truly thankful."

Despite her efforts to deny it to herself, sorrow for Rane continued to well in her as she lay against the warm comfort of St. John's body.

✺ *Chapter 37* ✾

Caleb brought Penelope to see The Wild Swan, and with them came their little boy who looked exactly like his father except for having his mother's eyes. After close scrutiny on both sides, Johnny was soon playing with the Carrington children, and the two women were easily calling each other "Pen" and "Alex" as they exchanged information about a variety of domestic subjects, including Pen's pregnancy which she spoke of without embarrassment or fear and with great joy.

"My only problem is Caleb, who frets too much and restricts my activities with his mournful complaints. If we have another child after this one, I will try not to tell him until I am delivered of the babe." She giggled. "Of course, not telling him would do little good, as I get very plump. At least I did with Johnny and expect I shall again." She patted her stomach. "This one I hope will be a girl. Caleb would love a daughter, I know, though all he says is that he wants us both to be healthy."

So would I love a daughter, Alex thought, but she pushed away the sad thoughts of Christiana, not wanting to dim Pen's bright spirits. It was Pen, however, who switched the conversation to a more serious matter.

"How did you find Rane's wife?" she asked, watching Alex closely.

For a moment, Alex was tempted to pretend she had noticed nothing at all, but Pen's eyes were too bright and honest to tolerate the lie.

"Sinje and I found her rather odd, or perhaps she is just highly nervous."

Pen sighed. "We all pretend it isn't so, but I think Claire is going quite insane, and I feel very, very sorry for your cousin. He met and married her in all innocence. Claire had been the darling of Baltimore society since the day she first put her hair up. Her father was very rich and very indulgent, and most thought that accounted for the erratic way Claire sometimes behaved. Rane seemed a sadly driven man when he first arrived in this country, and I suppose Claire seemed to him a bright patch of sunlight."

A driven man, Alex thought, *driven by me from England?* She shied away from the idea and concentrated again on Penelope's words.

"Claire became very dependent on Rane very quickly, and they married. And then her father died, and she was more in need than ever. And it wasn't as if there was any financial gain for Rane before or after the marriage. His death revealed that he had, like so many others, miscalculated the changes brought on by the war. There was little left after his debts were paid. And then the rumors started, rumors that say Claire's mother died not of fever as had been reported, but hopelessly mad and by her own hand. Claire's father had been powerful enough to enforce silence about it while he lived but not beyond the grave."

Alex suppressed a shudder. Madness, sorrow, and death—what a hideous exchange Rane had made for his old life in England.

"Rane never complains," Pen said, "and I have never seen him treat her with anything but courtesy, but I believe it is very difficult for him. I fear the only peace he ever has is when he sails on one of his ships, and even then, he must wonder what he will find on his return."

"Poor Rane!" Alex breathed. "He deserves so much better than that."

They began to speak of other things, both knowing there was nothing they could do for Rane Falconer or for his self-tormented wife. And for Alex, it was dangerous to think of him so tenderly.

Caleb came to collect his wife and suggested a ride the next morning. "St. John, I would like to see your horses, and if you are free, I will have time as we don't return to Baltimore until the following day."

"I, of course, will not be invited, as you would never allow me such activity in my condition. It's fine to risk wallowing up and down in a boat on the bay, but not on a horse." Pen scowled at her husband with mock ferocity, and Caleb looked so distraught that his wife and Alex burst out laughing.

"Just as I told you," Pen said sweetly to Alex and then relented toward her spouse. "Caleb, you needn't look so miserable. You know I don't care for riding that much in any case. I shall play the martyr and keep Claire busy if you wish to include Rane in your outing. Poor dear, I expect he could use the fresh air."

Alex thought of how difficult it must be for Rane to bear his friends' pity.

The next morning was crystal clear and quite cold. For the first quarter of an hour, Alex concentrated on controlling Mabbie. The mare was in need of exercise and seemed intent on getting it all at once. She danced and tried a little buck now and then, as if she had decided the race course appealed to her after all and wanted to run at top speed.

St. John smiled at Alex, and though he said nothing, she could see the approval in his eyes for the way she managed the fretful animal.

Rane and Caleb on hired hacks did not sit their mounts with the same grace that St. John managed even one-armed now, but they were practical, competent riders who did not need to be coddled. Alex remembered that Rane's basic style had been the same back in Devon with the animals used in smuggling. She remembered Barnstaple Fair, too, and the mare they had chosen there, as well as the man Rane had attacked for her sake. She gave her head a little shake, banishing the old images, and brought her attention back to her horse, who had chosen the moment of inattention to gather herself for a little bucking hop.

"Oh, no you don't, Mabbie, my girl," Alex said, her

voice as firm as her hands on the reins as she shifted her weight to thwart the mare's movements.

"Would a brisker pace be acceptable?" St. John asked their company. "Mabbie and Sir Arthur could use a run, and this open stretch goes on for quite a distance."

The men nodded, and the four urged their mounts forward. Mabbie needed no encouragement. Her long, low stride devoured the ground in great lengths, and Alex felt like shrieking aloud for the joy of it. Nothing on earth was like this feeling of enormous power beneath her, the great muscles working in sleek harmony to generate the speed the mare had been bred for.

When they finally slowed down, Alex and St. John were a good distance ahead of the others, and Alex ahead of St. John. She guided her mare back to him, and they walked the horses in circles, cooling them down.

"Now she's ready to be a perfect lady," Alex told St. John, and they laughed together at the docile patience the mare now displayed.

When the others caught up to them, Caleb wore a wide smile. "I can now understand your dynastic hopes—that mare goes like lightning!"

"When it suits her," Alex responded. "We're hoping her offspring will have her speed as well as more willingness. Mabbie runs for herself."

The party split naturally in two as Caleb and St. John began to discuss various aspects of the racing world in America, St. John asking eager questions and Caleb answering them knowledgeably. Though Caleb was a better sailor than rider, he shared the love of horse racing that so many Marylanders had and had many acquaintances in the racing world.

Alex turned to Rane, prepared to speak pleasantly with him, but she found his face tight-lipped with rage, his eyes glaring hotly at her, and she was completely baffled.

"You are in a bad mood for such a glorious morning. What is amiss?" she asked tentatively.

"Your husband is out of his mind! I wouldn't expect you to have any sense, but he ought to know better!" Rane exploded.

"I haven't any idea of what you are talking about," Alex snapped, fast losing patience with him.

"I'm talking about that horse you're riding. That's a

goddamn race horse! You have no business riding her at all, let alone perched on that ridiculous sidesaddle!"

"Sinje gave me this mare because he knows I am an extremely good rider; he taught me. And you've seen me ride before, so you ought to know the truth of it. Mabbie is very well mannered for all her hot blood. She was only skittish at first because I haven't taken her out for several days, and the morning is very brisk." Her temper began to cool as she realized that his anger came only from concern for her, and she tried to coax a smile from him. "Actually if she were a good race horse, I probably wouldn't be riding her so casually; she'd have more serious training to do. But she's a failure on the course; she only runs at her best speed when it pleases her. Shows she has more sense than most horses. And as for this saddle, I am already resolved to return to the comfort of breeches and riding astride as soon as we have land of our own and the privacy of it."

Reluctantly he let his anger go, but it left him even more vulnerable to her, and he heard himself saying words he never meant to voice aloud. "I am trying to keep my proper place with you, Alex, but it is hard, so hard. I even find that I like your St. John, but that doesn't seem to help much. I still love you."

Alex's first impulse was to deny that she had heard him, but the words were as crisp and clear as the winter morning. And then protective platitudes leapt to mind—"You don't mean that, those are old feelings, we don't really know each other any more"—and they wound in a useless tangle in her head, none of them true. She glanced around to see that St. John and Caleb were still riding side by side, deep in conversation. She took a deep breath and raised her eyes to Rane's.

"I will not deny what you say, what you feel. I feel it, too. When I see you, it is as if time stands still in a place where only you and I exist. There is some special love in me for you that does not seem to change. Perhaps it is some ancient bond of kinship beyond our will. But I ceased to belong wholly to myself the day I took responsibility for Sinje and the twins, and you ceased to belong wholly to yourself the day you committed yourself to Claire. And though part of me loves you and perhaps always will, I love St. John, too, and he is my husband."

"Is he? He wears no wedding band."

She did not flinch; she knew his knowledge went beyond the lack of ring. "Yes, we are married, legally now as well as morally. We were officially married here. When did you find out?"

He wished now that he had not betrayed that he knew; it was to no purpose. "When Elwyn, always the lawyer, let his knowledge of marriage law show before he had time to think better of it."

"How you must have hated me!"

"No, never hate, not even for an instant. Bitterness and jealousy, but not hate."

"Your family, will they ever forgive me?" Her voice trembled. "It was so hard to cut them deliberately out of my life, but I could not do it any other way."

"They were sorry for me and for you, Alex, but they, no more than I, never hated you. They love you still."

She bit back tears, swept by a sudden longing to turn back the years and be a child in Devon again with the strength and love of Gweneth, Magnus, and the other Falconers shielding her.

Mabbie sidled uneasily beneath her, and Alex straightened her back and her will. "We must learn to be at ease with each other, as if the past never was. I cannot bear to live in dread of seeing you. If you and I cannot find some ease together, sooner or later I will betray myself and wound Sinje, and you will do the same to your wife. We must only be cousins as they think us, nothing more, nothing less. Can you do that?"

The old urge to protect her from all harm, even from the hurt of his love, rose in him as strongly as it had when she was still a child. And beyond that, he sensed her desperation and knew that she would contrive some way to avoid seeing him again, even if it meant leaving Maryland, if she were not sure her husband would be protected. At first Rane had not been certain he could bear having her so close and yet so out of his reach, but now he knew that the pleasure of having her back in his life on any terms outweighed the torment. "I promise you; it will be as you wish." *And I will be able to watch over you and my son*, he added silently.

She felt as if they had just exchanged vows, vows as binding and demanding as those that united her in marriage to St. John. And though she tried to deny it, deep inside there was a warm glow of comfort from the fact that her world and Rane's had come together again. Not the same, never to be the same again, and with a host of new rules—she would not ask about Claire; he would not question her again about Morgan—but still healing, as if a missing part of her had been restored. Suddenly she wished that Claire were different, that she were like Penelope Jennings, a lively, loving woman. Undeniably everything would be easier if Rane were content in his marriage.

Having ridden quite a distance from Rane and Alex, the two ahead halted, and St. John called, "Everything all right back there?"

Alex urged Mabbie ahead. "Perfectly fine. I've been begging news of Rane's family."

Oh, what a tangled web . . . the words wafted through her head again.

When they were close enough for normal conversation, St. John said to Rane, "I shall always be grateful for the time Alex had with you and your family. I know how important those days were to her."

"It was to our benefit," Rane replied without a trace of irony. It was Caleb who looked momentarily discomfitted, but only Alex noticed, and she pretended not to, thinking what a loyal friend he had turned out to be. He obviously knew or suspected much, and yet he kept it to himself and offered steadfast support to both Rane and her, though he ran the risk of being caught in the middle. It was unlikely company for him, but nonetheless, his position reminded her of Mavis.

She had long since learned that Mavis was as keen and thoughtful as anyone, despite her placid façade, and she had more than a little suspicion that the woman had begun to wonder about those days when Alex had been so distracted and away from the house while St. John was off at the races, nine months before Morgan's birth. Another thread in the tangled weave. Mavis would never have wondered if she had not met Rane here, for she had never seen him in Gravesend. But now she had seen him, and she had helped raise Morgan from the day of his birth. And yet, she treated Alex no differently, and had been polite to Rane when he had come to the house this day. From her bitter past experience with the lover who had left her, Mavis had her own reasons for not condemning the behavior of others, and Timothy was as nonjudgmental as his wife. Alex counted them both among her blessings.

Her mind wandered further to her brother. Boston was another matter, and she didn't regret that he had not accompanied them today. He treated her with no less courtesy and love than was his habit, but some of the old ease was gone, and a few times she had caught him studying her with such a lost, puzzled look as if the suspicion that had slipped into his mind could not be dislodged despite the fact that he had no proof and loved his sister. He was a just man. He was as cordial to Rane as Alex could wish, but she was too close to him to be unaware of his new unease. For a moment, she thought of what a relief it would be to simply tell him the whole story, but as quickly, she dismissed the idea. It would serve only to ease her burden while it would tear at Boston's loyalties, for he had grown very close to St. John. There was no help for it except to give him no cause for further doubt of her.

It felt good to have another run on Mabbie, and she ignored the anxiety that still showed in Rane's eyes when the party reassembled.

Leda and her colt were duly admired, and Mr. Hawlington assured the Carringtons that Leda was doing very well though she was heavy with foal. She limped slightly when she moved, due to the added weight she carried, but it did not seem to impede her progress; she was much better than when St. John had first seen her. She was eating well and looking healthy and content.

Swan greeted the visitors with a friendly nicker and stretched his neck out to have his head and throat scratched. Mr. Hawlington had grown quite fond of him and worked the colt himself, putting him through his paces on a line and making sure he was handled often and gently. It was the best training program possible for a colt because it might well help prevent some of the vicious behavior many studs showed when they matured.

"He's a goer!" Mr. Hawlington said enthusiastically. "Likes nothin' better'n a good run in th' meadow. I think you'll have yourself a winner in a few years' time."

"I hope you're correct!" St. John said fervently.

The discussion proceeded to the strong and weak points of stallions standing at various farms, mostly in the state of Virginia and further south, though some notables were still in Maryland. Seriously, they considered which might be suitable as mates for Mabbie and Leda. At first Mr. Hawlington was uncomfortable discussing such matters before Alex, but when St. John made it clear that his wife was as much a part of the business as he, Mr. Hawlington forgot his inhibitions. "You want t' breed to Sir Archy's blood if not t' th' horse himself. His get are near unbeatable."

"It's not a bad idea," Caleb said slowly. "I believe Sir Archy is still standing at Moorfield Plantation, or Mowfield, as some call it, in North Carolina. You could transport Leda most of the way by ship so that she wouldn't have to walk so far. The fee is high, probably fifty or sixty dollars with more to insure, but you couldn't breed to a better stallion in the United States, and it might as well be Leda as she's surer to breed and won't be missed for riding if she stays in North Carolina for a time."

"For someone who deals in shipping, you certainly know a great deal about Thoroughbred horses," Alex teased.

Caleb grinned. "Sir Archy is a legend; anyone who follows racing with even a small interest knows about him. His sire was Diomed, his dam a blind mare named Castianira, and Diomed was twenty-seven years old when he sired Sir Archy."

"Diomed." St. John said the name with reverence and described the horse for Alex's benefit. "His grandsire was Herod, his sire Florizel, and Diomed, as a three-year-old, won the first running of the twelfth Earl of Derby's race at Epsom in 1780. He was said to be a splendid animal, a chestnut sixteen hands high with no white except a spot on the heel of his right hind foot. But he got a reputation for being a bad foal getter and was sold to an American."

"Yes, to Colonel Hoomes who brought him to Virginia. Diomed started his first season at stud in this country at the age of twenty-one." Caleb picked up the story. "Actually, our best Thoroughbred lines have come from horses that slipped through English fingers for one cause or another; it isn't as if England has wanted to stock our stables with the finest." He pretended umbrage at this, but his eyes twinkled with satisfaction at the history of English mistakes, and none of the English standing beside him took offense, all thinking that any who tried to pass off bad horses ought to get his comeuppance one way or another.

"Sir Archy was born in 1805," Caleb went on. "He was

raced a few times when he was a three-year-old and lost, but after that he proved nearly impossible to beat except when he was run unfit. And since the first of his offspring appeared on the courses six years ago, his fame has grown enormously, for just as Mr. Hawlington says, his get are hard to beat. There is only one drawback I can see—a vicious rumor that insists Sir Archy was got by a teaser stallion rather than Diomed. Proof is said to be in the fact that Sir Archy is a bay while Diomed was a chestnut. But I believe the claim is completely spurious, for despite the color difference, the white mark is the same. Sir Archy, too, has no white except for a spot of it near the heel of his right rear foot."

Alex didn't need St. John to tell her that he was highly interested in the prospect of a colt by Sir Archy; she could see the excitement glittering in his blue eyes. Fifty or sixty dollars; it was a great deal for a chance, but she resolved to make no protest when St. John broached the subject. The Wild Swan had been her chance; the horses were St. John's and ultimately the best chance for all of them.

The immediate concern of the added expense centered her again on her own family, and she was too abstracted to feel any continued unease in Rane's presence. It was, she realized afterwards, the best way for things to be. She was totally unaware that Rane had watched the changing expression on her face with enormous pain, guessing her dilemma and wishing fruitlessly that Claire were capable of dealing with the practical side of life. He wondered if St. John knew how fortunate he was to have a wife who was involved in the daily business and the future planning of his life.

He made his mind go blank as another thought intruded. It was still immeasurably painful to think of Alex, his Alex, married to St. John, sharing St. John's bed.

❧ Chapter 38 ☙

Christmas was an odd time, happy because the children enjoyed it, but with passages of sadness because Virginia and Caton seemed very far away. The two had shipped greetings and small gifts weeks before so that they might arrive in time, but still Alex wished that just for a moment, she could reach out and touch her grandmother and reassure her father. A packet of potpourri raised the summer scent of an English garden so vividly, tears pricked her eyes.

St. John was particularly attentive. "We are beginning our own traditions, and I think that is good for every family," he told her gently, and she knew he was right. They were doing very well in establishing their new life. She reminded herself of that every time she winced away from the money that would soon be spent to breed Leda to Sir Archy, Mabbie to another, and the added outlay that would surely come with St. John's first season of attendance at the American races.

For Christmas, Alex gave St. John a wedding band, and though he was not a man who wore jewelry, he was infinitely pleased that she had thought of it. "I will never take it off," he promised, holding her close.

"I don't want any American women getting ideas about my handsome husband; they seem quite forward," she said teasingly, but she knew her motive was deeper than that; Rane wore the token of his marriage to Claire, and it had become important that St. John wear her own and that Rane see it. She did not feel guilty about it; marriage, she was learning, was made up of many small ties, visible and invisible.

Early one morning in the first week of January, a messenger came from Mr. Hawlington to tell them that Leda was close to foaling, despite the fact that she wasn't due for two weeks or so.

The weather was foul, the sky ominously luminous even though it was before dawn, and snow was already beginning to fall. St. John looked at Alex as if she were spouting gibberish when she insisted that she was going with him.

"We're wasting time! I'm not asking you; I'm telling you. Leda's foal is as important to me as it is to you, and I'm useful in situations such as this, as you well know!"

They glared at each other for a moment until St. John gave in with a reluctant grin. "I don't know what even made me think I could dissuade you."

Though they were willing to brave the storm, they bid the young man who had brought the message to stay at the tavern until the weather improved. Chilled to the bone, he accepted gratefully.

St. John's eyes widened when Alex appeared in breeches, but he did not protest.

"I couldn't bring myself to throw them away," she said. "And scandalous or not, I am going to ride astride today."

Though they were dressed warmly, the cold was insidious, seeming to be mild as it often does with snowfall, but creeping into the bones nonetheless. Sir Arthur and Mabbie were both nervous in the storm, but they settled down fairly well to ploughing through the drifts that were already forming. As Mabbie slid a little under her, it occurred too vividly to Alex that neither horse was specially shod for ice, but she put the thought away resolutely because there was nothing to be done.

She was glad they had gone regularly to Hawlington's farm because the snow was fast erasing familiar landmarks, and a good deal of instinct was needed to keep in the right direction. She was feeling pleased with their progress when she heard St. John's sharp curse. It happened so quickly, that was all there was to warn her that Sir Arthur was going down.

This is very odd, she thought; now everything is slowing down. She saw Sir Arthur falling very, very slowly, trying to keep his balance but toppling sideways. And very, very slowly, she saw St. John give up the effort of keeping his mount's head up and throw his body free of the saddle, rolling as he landed.

Sir Arthur had long been schooled to halt when he felt his rider leave the saddle, particularly since St. John had lost his arm, but the animal was panicked by the fall and was lunging into a run even as he regained his footing.

This, too, Alex saw as a long, slow stretch into space, and she nudged Mabbie forward, time and place snapping back into proper perspective as she grabbed Sir Arthur's bridle and felt her arm wrenched as he plunged once more before coming to a stop.

St. John was immediately beside them, still cursing as he took the gelding's reins. Blinking at him through the snowflakes obscuring her vision, Alex began to laugh helplessly, her teeth chattering as reaction set in.

"Alex, stop it! I haven't a hand free to slap you, but by God, I'll manage." The desperation in his voice jolted her as effectively as a slap would have done, and her hysteria died abruptly, leaving her with a lump in her throat and a very sane urge to cry. She watched as he managed the extreme feat of hoisting himself into the saddle without a mounting block, and she bit her lip to keep the tears back. She was so accustomed to his one-armed state, she had forgotten how many adjustments he had to make. And a moment ago he could have been crippled further or killed.

"I love you so much." She didn't know she had said the words aloud until he responded, "I love you, too, but unless we continue, someone will discover us here as frozen equestrian statues." His voice was light, but even in the snow-filled air, she could see how tender his eyes were. It was a mark of how far they had come together that he no longer resented her fear for him.

Wet, cold, but triumphant, they arrived at the farm to be greeted by Mr. Hawlington, who was calm about Leda's progress, but frantic about them. "Started snowin' right after th' boy left, wished I'd never sent 'im, but you did ask to be told."

They assured him that he had done exactly the right thing and that his messenger was safe and warm. Leda, they found, was doing a good job on her own. She had begun to labor in earnest only a short time before, and now she was going about her business calmly, though Alex and St. John helped her when she heaved herself up to shift the position of the foal.

Alex had seen it before, but that in no way lessened the thrill of witnessing the silvery sack of life slipping from the mare. When the wet membrane had been cleaned away, the foal was revealed as a perfect filly, true black like her sire with a white star on her forehead.

"Black Swan, I presume," St. John murmured as they watched Leda nudging her baby into nursing position.

"Of course." Alex tipped her head up, and he kissed her, both of them oblivious of the fact that Mr. Hawlington and two stablemen were observing the process with great interest.

It was afternoon, but the storm raged on, making it seem like perpetual twilight. There was no chance of returning to Annapolis yet, and Mr. Hawlington persuaded the Carringtons to leave the barn for a hot meal and a wash at his house, but when he pressed them further to remain there, Alex demurred.

"I expect you will think us addlebrained, but if you will allow it, we will spend the night in the barn. You see, Mr. Carrington and I hardly ever have time to ourselves anymore." The blood rose to her cheeks, and she hurried on, "And the new foal is very important to us both. It just seems . . ." She felt St. John's fingers curling around her hand and knew without looking that he was amused.

Mr. Hawlington took pity on her out of the kindness of his own memories. "My Mary, she would've thought of somethin' jus' like that, she would." He looked years younger as he said it, and Alex saw him in a new light. She knew he had been a widower for some years and that he had two sons who had gone to settle in the western part of the state, but now the bare facts were given life by his words.

He not only provided them with blankets, but he insisted on presenting them with a jug of strong cider. "Medicine for th' cold," he explained, his eyes twinkling, and he gave them a packet of food as well. "No one'll disturb you 'til early mornin' when the cows have t' be milked again," he added, giving them the most precious gift of all in their people-crowded lives.

Leda and her new foal were content, as were the other livestock sheltered in the barn, including a few cows and horses. Among the latter was Swan who stretched his head out of his stall for attention before he went back to his feed. The barn was well built and, despite the frigid temperature outside, it was warm enough for comfort, the beasts within adding their heat to the air redolent with the scents of straw, grain, and well-tended animals.

St. John was bruised from his fall, and Alex's arm and shoulder were stiff from the wrench Sir Arthur had given them, but neither noticed. He put his arm around her and drew her close. "You are a romantic, not so practical after all, sweetheart, and I give thanks for it." His lips trailed down her cheek to find her mouth and wandered again to the hollow beneath her ear while his hand found the firm curve of her buttocks. "Ummm, there are definite advantages to this garb."

She shivered with the sensations his delicate touch was causing and sank down with him on the blankets they had spread over the straw. She felt boneless, as if she were melting into his body, slipping the boundaries of her own. She tried to rouse herself enough to pleasure him with her touch in return, but when they had stripped away their clothes, he murmured, "No, let me love you," and she did.

She writhed under the gentle onslaught, the tantalizing soft stroking of his hand seeking every curve and hollow, his mouth following until he teased between her legs, and she cried, "Please, Sinje, please now!"

His fingers slipped in and out of her, miming possession, but he withheld his sex.

"Damn you!" she gasped, and her eyes flew open at the sound of her own cursing.

St. John's eyes were deep, glittering blue in the lantern light, and he was half smiling, suffused with pleasure at the response he was conjuring from her.

"So impatient, my love," he chided mockingly and thrust into her, his shaft full, hard, and satisfying, their cries melding into one ancient song swallowed in the high vault of their shelter.

Good nights, sweet nights followed, but she thought most often of the night in the barn in the days and nights that St. John was absent.

Though they had managed to struggle back to Annapolis the following day, the storm left phenomenal cold in its wake for the remainder of the month. Up and down the Atlantic seaboard, harbors were frozen, including Baltimore's, and the temperatures in many places dropped below zero. The sight of ice in Chesapeake Bay was extraordinary for the Carringtons. But it was a view St. John could have forgone, as it delayed his departure for North Carolina until February and made the timing of Leda's breeding even more delicate for an early colt in the next year.

Boston went with St. John and the horses—Leda, the suckling Black Swan, and Sir Arthur. Boston was an indifferent rider, and they would hire a hack for him when needed, but Sir Arthur, despite his mishap in the snow, was a dependable mount and accustomed to his one-armed rider. He seemed to have left his tendency to lameness back in England.

It made sense for Boston to go instead of Timothy because Tim was not only vital to the running of The Wild Swan, having quietly assumed many duties, but also to Mavis. It was only just that one of the husbands stay home, if possible.

It was all very sensible, but Alex hoped that Boston's eagerness stemmed from the desire to see new places, and not, as she suspected, from the need to be away from her. She hugged him hard before he left, but he didn't quite meet her eyes.

Somewhere deep inside rose a small, defiant voice: "Not as I am now, but as I was then, I would do it all again." But when she and St. John said their last good-byes, she thought of nothing but him, hardly even noticing the clamor of the children as they hopped about excitedly.

"Take good care of yourself, and send word as often as you can," she bade him.

"I will. Don't worry. I have Boston, and we'll be fine. It is you I worry about. Don't do too much. Let the others help." His eyes suddenly gleamed with mischief. "Find another barn for when I come home."

She had to smile at that.

She watched the ship until it was out of sight. Winter sky, winter bay, winter land; she thought she would feel less desolate if it were a kinder season.

February was almost over before the intense cold began to weaken, but business at the tavern had not been hurt except for a few days when the snowstorm had made travel difficult. Generous helpings of hot meals and potent cider and punches made bubbling hot by a poker from the fire kept the steady stream of customers content. And word had gotten about that no matter what one discussed at The Wild Swan, it went no further. Members of the state government, and even the governor, Samuel Sprigg, an intelligent and energetic man and wealthy landowner, made the tavern a popular place. Visitors from Washington City and those from further afield passing through the state capital and county seat patronized the tavern as well.

Alex's polite demeanor and rather reserved manner never changed, but she found herself paying close attention to some discussions, particularly those concerning slavery. Many spoke of an inevitable end to slavery, but some were not so moderate. It fascinated as well as repelled her to witness otherwise rational men passionately asserting their rights to own slaves, never seeming to notice the presence of Della, Caesar, or others. And the game worked both ways; the black faces were carefully blank.

She had nearly interrupted the first round she had witnessed, her polite hostess's façade beginning to slip as she listened to a man whine, "The way things are, I would be much better off if I sold some of my people, but my wife objects. She hasn't any idea of business matters and her sensibilities are too delicate. She thinks they'll pine for each other, but I know they'd settle right down before long. It isn't as if they remember as we do."

He said it with absolute conviction, and it carried added offense for Alex because there was the trace of an English accent in his voice, no doubt from a long-past education at university there.

She wasn't quite clear what action she was going to take, though she wanted to throw him out bodily; if nothing else, she could shame him publicly, make him realize what he had just said. A firm grip on her arm stayed her forward march.

"Something needs your attention in the kitchen, Mrs. Carrington," Della insisted politely, her grip tightening until it was painful.

Baffled, Alex did as she was bid, not speaking until they were away from the customers. Then she burst out angrily, "He had no right to speak that way, at least not here. I want him out of my house."

"If you throw out every man and woman who owns slaves or believes in slavery, you will have no business at all, and we will have no work." Della's voice was harsh. "I know your heart is in the right place, but your head has some traveling to do. You've been forgiven for your feelings about slavery; Mr. Jennings helped that to happen, but you start telling other folks what to do, things will change. Abolitionists aren't popular in this part of the country."

Still unwilling to make the compromise, Alex asked, "How can you stand it? How can you say such things, as if the man is right?"

"I can say them because this is my home, and I want to keep living here without fear of being murdered for my color." Della's tone was suddenly strident with anger. "We all keep to the rules, blacks and whites, so that we can go on living. It's the only way."

The "rules" were long established, Alex realized, and to call attention to the foolishness and cruelty of them was to cause useless trouble. It was what she had feared from the beginning. One could not live in a slave state without compromise. Suddenly she felt very weary; compromise upon compromise, it seemed to be the heart of growing older.

"My father broke the rules." The softness in Della's voice now was more startling than the anger had been. "He loved my mother; in his way, he really loved her. And he loved me enough to risk educating me as well as he would have any white child of his loins. His wife was dead when he took my mother to his bed, and he had no legal issue. I think my mother loved him, too, though she hadn't any choice. But they were not just two people minding their own lives. He was white, and she was black, and that is against the rules. My kind, neither one nor the other, is the most fearful thing a slave owner can see, even though it's mostly slave owners who create us, because we make it too clear that there isn't enough difference after all."

It was such an intensely personal view of Della, Alex had trouble finding anything to say. Finally she settled for a weak smile and, "I'll behave myself, I promise."

Della's face was once again impassive, but Alex knew that they had taken a large step toward being closer friends.

She kept her word, her face revealing as little as those of the blacks when slavery was defended or slave sales discussed, but she paid closer attention than ever to the issue.

Generally politics in the United States baffled her. Political parties seemed to change their names by the day, making it difficult to keep track of who was involved. But she was beginning to see that sectional differences were pervasive. In the North where manufacturing was growing and farms had always been for the most part small and rocky, slavery was not part of the economic life except as it had brought wealth from ships that had imported slaves and some that still did, albeit illegally. In the South, particularly on the vast plantations that encompassed swampy, heat-ridden land, slavery was an integral part of the agrarian economy.

Perhaps the Americans themselves had not realized how divided their country was becoming—after all, they had adopted the phrase "era of good feeling" to describe the supposedly unified nationalism of the United States under President Monroe—but they knew it now. The Missouri Compromise had passed in Congress the previous year, and the dragon had risen, fully fanged and undeniable.

In 1819 there had been an equal number of slave and free states, but when Missouri had wanted to come in as a slave state, there had been fear on both sides that the balance would be lost. An amendment had been proposed that would have forbidden the further importation of slaves into Missouri and would have freed all children born of slaves when those children were twenty-five. The House had passed it, but the Senate had rejected it, and Southern interests had waited in fear to see what would happen to territories embracing the "peculiar institution."

Then Maine had framed a constitution and asked for admission to the Union. After bargaining back and forth, a compromise was reached whereby Missouri would be admitted as a slave state with no restrictions on slavery, and Maine would come in as a free state. This made the region of the Louisiana purchase above 36° 30' north latitude free except for the state of Missouri.

But there was still bitter debate in Congress due to the fact that Missouri had drafted a constitution which would enable its legislature to ban mulattoes and free blacks from the state. This meant tampering with the rights of free citizens of the United States, no matter how low their status in most minds. Another compromise was in progress by which the state constitution would not abridge such rights, and most agreed that Missouri would be a state before the year was out.

Though she did not voice her opinion aloud, Alex thought the United States had been better off in many ways when there was a common enemy, England, to be faced. Now that those years of conflict were over, Americans were discovering that they might well be their own worst enemy. It was a disquieting thought, for to live here was to be part of the forces that would give the young nation its final shape. Sometimes when she heard the harsh voices arguing over rights and privileges of this region over that, and of states over the Union, and vice versa; and when she saw the angry blood in the faces, she wondered if the country would always be able to solve the disputes by compromises signed in Congress rather than on the battlefield. Civil war was, sadly, not unimaginable. The scars from the one nearly two centuries before in England were still tender in some regions.

As she went about her varied duties, Alex felt increasingly more competent in her new life, but there were still frequent moments when everything was totally alien, so much so that she wondered if the day would ever come when she ceased to feel so essentially English. And then she wondered if she wanted to make that adjustment at all. Patience, she cautioned herself, patience; all things in their season. She could hear her grandmother's voice.

The swans and geese began to fly north, and that made her even more lonesome. She missed St. John fiercely and awaited word anxiously, having to be content with rare, briefly scrawled missives. Writing was still difficult for him with his left hand because he did little of it, but he was too proud to have Boston or someone else write at more length for him. And Boston was simply no letter writer. His messages were more neatly written, but no longer than St. John's. Still, she was able to chart their progress as they delivered Leda to Moorfield, ascertained that "Sir Archy is a magnificent stud," left the mare there, and went further south to race courses in South Carolina and Georgia.

In the meantime, Mabbie had been taken by Mr. Hawlington to another farm in Maryland where one of Sir Archy's sons was standing at stud. Alex hardly missed the mare because she had so little free time for riding, but she was ever conscious of the enormous outlay in stud fees and in the financing of St. John's trip to the race courses. These projects had taken every spare penny they had, and the only recourse was to make The Wild Swan produce as much profit as possible without acquiring a reputation for unfair prices. To Alex, that meant pleasing their patrons so that others were told and traffic increased to the optimum.

Though it made their financial state even more finely balanced, Alex and St. John had decided that the income from his small trust would be set aside for the children's education. The arrangement pleased Alex because it gave her the image of a stable future, and caused her to push herself even harder.

"You'd better slow down before you fall down," Della suggested one day, but Alex had no sense of how tired she was; one day was simply a repetition of the last. However, she paid attention when Caleb put it more forcefully.

She saw his parents now and again, and once the grip of winter loosened a little, and after he had attended President Monroe's second inauguration in Washington, D.C., on March 5, Caleb paid a brief visit to Annapolis. He came again in early April, and on both visits, he dropped by The Wild Swan.

"Pen sends love and wishes she could come, but she's finding herself content to stay at home these days," Caleb said as he greeted Alex in April, but then he checked and peered at her more closely. "Good God! What have you been doing to yourself? I thought you looked pale the last time I saw you, but nothing like this!"

She shrugged indifferently. "The children and I shared some cold-weather malady, but some of my grandmother's brews soon set us right." And a score of other people as well, she thought wearily, remembering the others she had tended when word of her remedies had gotten about, courtesy of the staff of The Wild Swan.

"If the cure leaves one looking as you do, I'd rather have the disease," Caleb barked, genuinely upset by her neglect of herself. "You've got ugly circles clear around your eyes, and you look about as lively as a stick. Do you want St. John to feel guilty when he comes home and finds you like this?"

That got her attention. It wasn't at all what she wanted. She wanted St. John to know how competent she was.

Caleb pressed his advantage. "You're coming with me to my parents' house. Bring your night clothes and whatever else you need because you won't be allowed back here for at least two days."

"The children, the work here . . ."

He cut her off. "Will be looked after by Mavis, Della, Timothy, and the rest of your excellent staff."

It was as if there was an instant conspiracy, Mavis and Della rushing about to pack a few things for her despite her protests that she could do it herself if she wanted to do it at all, and even the children let her go willingly after having been crassly bribed by Della with the promise of anything they wanted for supper, including gingerbread, a general favorite.

Once she had surrendered, Alex's defeat was entire. A fog of weariness enveloped her so thickly that she could scarcely move or see. Caleb wondered what Annapolis would say were he to be seen carrying Mrs. Carrington down the street, but she managed to make it to his parents' house, and then he turned her over to his mother. "She's worn out, and I've kidnapped her for a rest," he explained, and Mrs. Jennings had Alex undressed and tucked warmly in bed in no time.

"She's already fast asleep," she reported to her son. "Poor child, she was dead on her feet. I'm so glad you brought her to me. I should have been paying more attention to her, but she is very independent, and I don't want her to feel we're patronizing her."

Caleb kissed a softly rounded cheek affectionately. "Don't fret about it, Mother, all she needs is a little time to herself."

Alex slept for nearly twenty-four hours and awakened hungrier than she had been in weeks. She soon discovered that protesting against further pampering was wasted breath. Caleb had promised his mother that she would have the care of their visitor for at least two nights, and Mrs. Jennings was not about to settle for less. She welcomed Alex so warmly and anxiously, and Mr. Jennings was so cordial as well, Alex couldn't bring herself to refuse their hospitality.

After supper that night, Alex was still bright eyed from the long rest she'd had, and she and Caleb stayed up to talk after the elders had retired.

They now had the ease of long friendship, and when Alex asked after his sisters, he answered honestly. "Julie's the one I worry about. Things have never been easy between her and her husband, though it was her choice to marry him; there was no pressure from our parents. Julie's a gentle soul, and her husband, Kenneth, is too forceful. She has always seemed rather afraid of him." He shook his head, considering it anew. "I could not bear it if Pen looked at me with fear."

"You needn't worry about that," Alex said, thinking of the affection that flowed so obviously between the two and feeling more lonesome than ever for St. John.

They discussed the shipping business and how long it was taking for recovery, and Alex knew that to ignore Rane's existence was to call undue attention, so as casually as she could, she mentioned him.

"His business prospers," Caleb said, "but it is equally difficult for him to leave on his ships or to remain at home. Claire is . . . well, she seems more unstable than ever." For an instant Caleb was tempted to tell Alex the details of the woman's erratic behavior, how she could be sweet and sane one moment and in the next so crazed, at once fearful and accusatory, so that he suspected Rane would be happier were she to become one thing or another, even totally insane. He wished Rane had someone he could confide in, but he realized Alex was not a suitable choice. They were too close, and whatever peace they had made with their feelings was undoubtedly fragile.

Caleb stepped back from the abyss of burdening Alex with Rane's domestic tragedy and inadvertently fell into another trap as he answered her questions about Rane's shipping interests.

Alex didn't want to know anything more about Claire; she didn't want to feel any sorrier for Rane than she already did. She asked about Rane's business in order to shift the focus from his tangled marriage, but even as she asked, she realized she'd been wondering for a long time how Rane had done so well in such a short time while more experienced men had lost fortunes.

"Is trade with the West Indies always so profitable?" she asked smoothly.

"It's long been so, but it is particularly true now with Britain's policy of closing the ports . . ." Caleb's voice trailed away as he heard his own words.

Alex's laughter rang out, and there was true delight in her voice as she crowed, "Of course, he's still a smuggler—no, a free trader! Don't look so guilty, I should have suspected it long before this. Oh, Caleb, it's hard to explain, but I'm glad. It makes him seem more like the old Rane I knew." The image of him waiting fearfully to see what his wife would do next was not one either liked.

"I want you to know that Rane does not deal in slaves. But then, you know him well enough to know he never would," he amended hastily at her frown. "There are profits enough to be made without dealing in those poor wretches. Many planters and merchants need to ship their goods to that market without running the risk of getting caught. And many in the West Indies are anxious to buy Rane's cargoes. He takes the risk for everyone."

Alex had thought she would surely not sleep soundly after her long rest, but she did, and she dreamed joyful dreams of Rane free and wild on the deck of his ship.

Her thanks to the Jenningses for the respite were heartfelt but unnecessary. Their reward was in the renewed sparkle in her green eyes and the color returning to her cheeks.

"I will keep a better eye on you in the future, my dear," Mrs. Jennings warned her with mock severity, and Alex went back to The Wild Swan feeling deliciously well cared for. And on her return, she discovered not only that things had not fallen apart in her absence, but Della and Mavis seemed to have reached a new understanding.

"My Mavis, she's not quick to change, but little by little she comes about. She's comin' to see that Della's no different from 'er, no matter the brown skin," Tim declared.

❧ Chapter 39 ❧

In the middle of April, a late season storm swept through beginning with rain and ending at nightfall with snow showers, but the earth began to bloom in earnest after that, and the early pink splashes of the redbud or Judas trees in the woods were followed by the unfurling of leaves and blossoms of a grand variety of wild and domestic plants, including the waxy white perfection of dogwood flowers.

St. John and Boston returned in time for Alex's birthday, and their reactions to their travels were different but complementary. Boston was full of the strangeness of the places he'd seen—vast plantations with many slaves, Indians in Georgia, English spoken but so drawled that he swore it bore little resemblance to the mother tongue, and a host of other phenomena that had delighted his senses. St. John had noticed little else except the racing stock, but that, after all, had been the purpose of the trip.

"For all the roughness of the sport here in comparison with racing in England, the horses are marvelous!" he told her. "Magnificent animals capable of incredible endurance. I saw Sir Charles win in Georgia, and though he was beaten once last month in three-mile heats, he's already winning everything again. He's one of Sir Archy's sons. Though the maternal pedigree is questioned by some—there seems to be a great deal of that sort of controversy here—I would not fault him on any count. He's a bright chestnut, built closer to the ground than his sire and with greater length, all to the good for speed, and his confirmation is most pleasing. He's a five-year-old now, and here that means he still has years of racing ahead. Why, another of Sir Archy's offspring, Lady Lightfoot, is nine years old and still runs like the wind. She was foaled right here in Maryland, at Belair Stud, only some sixteen miles from here, when the stable was still one of the finest in the country. She's brown with no white and very muscular, though as feminine as any mare I've ever seen. She's aptly named, sweet tempered and charming."

Alex couldn't help it; she burst out laughing. "Oh, Sinje! I vow if you ever spoke of me or our children in such glowing terms, I would suspect you were feverish."

For a moment he looked affronted, and then he laughed with her. "I do sound overly fond, don't I? But think, with luck, we will have the same fine blood in our horses as I have seen in my travels."

They had every hope that Leda, safely back at Hawlington's farm, was carrying Sir Archy's foal. Mabbie, on the other hand, showed no signs of having been successfully bred. They were disappointed, but willing to have patience. And in the meantime, she was back for Alex to ride.

The nebulous dream of raising fine racing horses was taking on reality more quickly than Alex had thought possible, and her own excitement was growing to match St. John's, but the practical problem stretched in a vast sea before them. The more horses they had, the more imperative it was that they acquire acres to accommodate them. And all of it must be financed.

St. John had not done much betting since this trip had been to learn the ways of American race courses, and in the wagers he had placed, he had come out just slightly ahead, the extra dollars going to help defray the costs of the trip.

The tavern was turning a tidy profit and would in the long run provide enough for expansion on the land, but only if it were done by slow degrees. Alex did not want St. John to lose his enthusiasm, but she feared that things might not continue to happen as fast as he wished. She was, she realized, in many ways as protective of St. John as she was of the children, and it occurred to her that a little of that was not amiss, but that too much of it took something from him; he had to have the strength to succeed and fail. At the same time, she felt nothing but gratitude when St. John told her that the Jenningses' influence had extended far beyond Annapolis.

"Almost all the races with a purse of any size are limited to entries nominated or owned by jockey club owners, and many owners belong to all of the major jockey clubs. I'm sure it would be difficult for a foreigner of limited means to join under normal circumstances, but I received a host of kind offers of sponsorship for memberships and invitations to race our horses under other people's colors when it is time. We were treated royally, invited into several grand houses, and all of it was courtesy of Caleb and his family." He reached out to tuck an errant strand of hair behind her ear. "I did tell everyone that my wife is the heroine of the piece, not I, but that didn't seem to matter except that I have promised they will meet you soon. Many women attend the races, and at some of the meetings there are even special entertainments, balls and such for their particular enjoyment."

He was as good as his word. Though races were scheduled for the near future in Annapolis, these races were no longer held with frequency, lacked most of their past glamor, and were subject to cancellation. But the city of Washington was increasingly popular for race meetings, the prestige of being the nation's capital rubbing off on the sport.

It was Alex's first view of the capital even though it was only thirty miles west of Annapolis. She and St. John made the journey on horseback, and Alex knew delight every mile of the way. The rolling countryside was coming into full bloom, the scent of spring heavy on the air, and Mabbie's jaunty pace reflected Alex's mood.

Many made jokes about the dismal aspects of Washington, the unfinished look of it, the dust in summer and mud in winter, but Alex was peculiarly touched by it and sorry her countrymen had tried to burn it down seven years before. It was not London, to be sure, but it was the sign of a young nation trying to build a lasting center for its government. And though there was a certain strangeness about the plans for wide avenues and classically designed buildings to rise up on land that not long before had been the province of Indians and wild forest creatures and had never felt the tramp of Roman legions, it was also a tribute to the ideals of justice and law, the best of an ancient inheritance from Britain and from Rome before her. But in those civilizations there had been misrule and excess; here it was all changed and expanded in a brave

412

attempt to determine if a people could live in order without crowns and scepters over them.

Deep inside, Alex had harbored a sense of superiority because she was English, in spite of the fact that she had left her country for a better life here. Now, she felt that conviction slipping.

"I believe I've just suffered my first attack of American patriotism," she confided to St. John as they gazed at the unfinished Capitol. She wondered if he would understand at all and was inordinately pleased when he did.

"Damned gallant, isn't it?" he said.

After engaging a hotel room, they hired a landau in order to have comfortable seats at the National Race Course and joined a host of other vehicles of various sorts as well as many people on horseback. St. John handled the reins very well, using his knees for added control when he needed to, but though it was not acknowledged aloud between them, Alex was ready to grab the ribbons if more dexterity was needed. She was glad they were not dealing in the same class of horseflesh as had pulled Hugh's phaeton on that day in London. The memory seemed at once very fresh and very far away.

She had been to only a few races and those roughly staged matches at harvest festivals and such. This was an entirely new experience, and her wonder and excitement showed in her wide eyes and rosy cheeks. St. John drew as much pleasure from watching her as from observing the races.

Alex tried to absorb everything at once, from the well-dressed ladies and gentlemen visiting with each other much as people did on fair days in Hyde Park in London, to the horses being led out, most of them ridden by black jockeys in various silks, the time of the gentleman rider being much of the past. The horses were glorious—chestnuts, browns, bays, duns, roans, a few blacks and grays—their coats gleaming in the sun as they carried themselves with proud, hot eagerness.

A tap of a drum was the starting signal for the heats, and once the racing started, Alex lost interest in all else.

She felt the drumming of the hooves in her own veins. She could feel the air being sucked into the deep chests as if her own lungs were pumping it in with each stride, could feel the wild reaching for victory. She wasn't even aware that she was gripping St. John's hand as if she needed a stationary center in the swirl of sensation.

When the first heat was over, she turned to St. John with dazed eyes. "Is it always this thrilling?" she whispered, and he nodded. "Always, if love for the sport is in your blood, and I would say it is definitely in yours." His look was at once tender and intense, and he kissed her with total disregard for spectators.

Alex understood; at the instant of the birth of this new enthusiasm in her, a profound change had taken place in her relationship with St. John. His dream was now truly hers, not accepted for love of him, but embraced for its own sake, for the sheer heart-pounding excitement of it.

The two- and three-mile heat races were not the important events of the few days of the meeting; it was the four-mile heats, the "heroic distance," that drew the most attention, the heaviest wagers, and the biggest, most prestigious purses.

The youngest horses in these heats were four-year-olds, but most were older, needing the added time to build up the muscle and stamina required, and this was a part of American racing that Alex knew from the first time she witnessed it she would never thoroughly enjoy as she did the shorter contests.

It was at once impressive and cruel, so much a part of both, that her heart was torn as she watched the horses struggling valiantly to maintain top speed even when they had to face the ultimate test: as many as five four-mile heats with only a half hour or so between each until one of the field had won three heats out of five, as opposed to the two-out-of-three heat victories in shorter contests. Their coats were lathered with white foam, their mouths dripped saliva and even blood, their breath came in great rasping heaves of effort. As in the shorter races, the blood of Sir Archy dominated.

Now St. John watched Alex anxiously, fearful that the brief union of hope was lost between them.

"Don't fret," she said slowly. "Things are different in this country; harsher and wilder even though there is a veneer of gentility. I must accept that as part of this new life. I will not promise that I will ever like these punishing contests. But I do see the reason—only the very best animals can withstand such demands—and I promise I will not let it spoil my enjoyment of the rest."

"I married a wise woman," he said, and they laughed at his pun on the old term for a woman who dealt in herbs and simples.

At Annapolis, St. John took her to races that also featured offspring of Sir Archy. Beggar Girl, a five-year-old, won the three-mile heats, Duchess of Marlborough, four years old, won the two-mile heats, and Alex forced herself to watch Ratler, a six-year-old chestnut, survive the four-mile heats to beat Chance, Medley, and three other entries. As expected, the Annapolis races were not quite as glamorous as Washington's, and Alex was glad the latter had been her initiation.

It was easier to see St. John off again in the autumn because now she understood the fascination, and he returned in time to take her with him to the races in Baltimore.

They had seen neither Caleb nor Rane during the summer, though the elder Jenningses had kept in touch and had given news of Penelope's safe delivery of a girl in June. The Carringtons had sent heartfelt congratulations and a christening gift. Alex was genuinely happy for the couple, but she longed more than ever for another daughter and fretted at her inability to conceive again. It was a worry she kept from St. John, thinking with a wry twist of humor that he was doing his best in the matter. She knew she had much to be thankful for; her four children were healthy and bright, and St. John had become as considerate a lover and devoted a husband as she could wish.

When they went to Baltimore, it was natural to send word to Caleb and Pen and to Rane as well, for it would have been odd had Alex omitted him from their plans. They had every intention of staying in a hotel but the Jenningses wouldn't hear of it, and so they stayed in their fashionable brick house.

Pen was in the full blossom of healthy motherhood, feeling, as she freely confessed, remarkably pleased with herself for having produced the baby Elizabeth whom Caleb doted on as "Liza."

It had been a busy summer for Caleb as he worked hard to engage enough coastal shipping business to keep the line solvent, and he was still hard at it. But he graciously took the time to attend some of the races with the Carringtons and to entertain them in his home. Rane, he informed them, would join them for dinner on the second night, being due back from Philadelphia on the morrow. It was Pen who told Alex more personal details.

"I believe he's trying to find another doctor to treat Claire. But it seems a hopeless cause. Those who say they can help propose to use cruel methods or harmful opiates, and Rane does not want her tortured, but rather helped."

For a moment, Alex wanted to screech at her to stop and never to tell her anything personal about Rane again, but instead she kept her expression sympathetic and reminded herself that Pen obviously had no suspicion that Alex's relationship with Rane was anything more than cousinly. "And it's not," she told herself fiercely, "it's not anything but that!"

But it was hard not to show her distress when she saw Rane. He looked terrible, face so lined and gray with weariness, Alex wanted to reach out and magically sooth away the marks of suffering. But that was not her right. She made her eyes shift away from his, and she joined the idle chatter.

"You should have told me," St. John chided gently later when they were settled for the night, and her heart jumped in her throat for fear it had something to do with Rane.

"Told you what?" she asked, pleased with the steadiness of her voice.

"That you were ill while I was away last spring. Caleb told me."

"He shouldn't have! If Della, Mavis, and the children could say nothing about it, he could have held his tongue, too. And I wasn't ill, just tired. It was soon remedied by a good sleep."

"You mustn't blame Caleb; it slipped out because he is a good friend and wishes us well."

Alex conceded the point by moving against him in slow, languorous patterns, murmuring throatily, "As you can judge, I am very, very healthy."

Having thought so much about it, Alex was afraid to believe at first that she was pregnant, but by Christmas, she was well along. In fact, she was quite sure she had conceived the child clear back in August though it had taken her until nearly the end of November to believe it. St. John guessed before she told him. Returning in early December from race meetings far to the south, he was so hungry for her that he felt as if all his perceptions of her were heightened as he made fierce love to her.

He was falling asleep when it all registered, and he sat up abruptly. "Alex, you're different! That is . . . either you've been eating more or . . ." His hand traced the slightly fuller contours of her breasts, the subtle difference in the curve of her belly, and she giggled. "It's the 'or'. You are to be a father again, in May, I think."

His worry and his pleasure at the news were as tangible as his kiss, his heart beating hard against her breast.

The Jenningses were delighted for them and glad to see Alex looking and feeling so well.

Though none of them voiced it aloud, it was a guilty relief that the Falconers did not attend the Jenningses' party this year. Claire had continued unwell for most of the autumn, and the thought of having to cope with her in the midst of such joyful celebration was not a pleasant one.

In January, Leda presented them with another beautiful foal by Sir Archy, a colt they named "Bay Swan" with some amusement, playing on his color and on the great flocks of swans that had again come to winter on Chesapeake Bay. As soon as the mare and foal were strong enough to travel, St. John and Boston left to take her back to North Carolina to be bred again to the famous stallion while Mabbie was once more put to a Maryland stud. St. John and Boston were going on to the race courses again, and this Alex considered her personal victory, for St. John had been so reluctant to leave her for an extended period that she had her hands full convincing him that it was vital for him to go.

It was not hard to see him off this time because she was feeling complete and centered in herself and the coming child. She had no morning sickness and felt very energetic. In some ways, it was more difficult to say good-bye to Boston. He had congratulated them both heartily on the expected child, but there was still a distance between him and his sister. Alex felt it keenly, but could not seem to bridge it. And the restlessness she had sensed in him seemed to be growing rather than lessening. He continued to be a willing and useful part of their business, but Alex was beginning to suspect he had more than a little of the Thaine craving for far-off horizons. She hoped that was the case rather than that she was driving him away.

She had passages of wishing desperately that she could talk about all of it with her grandmother. But that was not possible, and since arriving in Maryland, she had made it a habit to write to Virginia only of the joyful things in her life. It seemed a very small exchange for the enormous gift of freedom to begin again that Virginia had given them. For that reason and for an almost superstitious fear of committing it to paper where the wrong eyes might see it, Alex had not written a single word about Rane. She doubted that he had written to his family about her either, and Boston had apparently made no mention of Rane. She sighed as she penned the latest news to her grandmother, limiting her news to word of the new colt, the men's trip, and her own joy in the prospect of the coming child.

Do not fear that I view this child as a replacement for Christiana. No one will ever take her place. And I will be as happy to welcome another son as a daughter as long as the babe is healthy. But I do confess that a little girl would delight my heart.

She continued with news of the children, feeling perfectly justified in bragging of their progress:

Flora and Blaine will soon be seven years old. How swiftly time does pass. They are flourishing here, both being of sweet and even temper most of the time, though Flora is, I know, too sure of having her own way and too enchanting to cross. Morgan—it is so difficult to believe that it has been nearly five years since his birth—terrifies me because he has no fear. Grandmother, you would find it hard to credit how bold he is for one so young! He flies in boldly no matter what the adventure and gleans more than his share of bumps and bruises to no effect. I would not teach him to be timid, so must swallow many words of caution. I think perhaps it is so for many mothers with sons; what we most admire in the man, we fear in the child. Nigel is altogether different, quiet and most content when he is busy with his hands. I often wonder what he believes he is building when he piles one stick or stone upon another. His hero is not, alas, either of his parents, but rather Caesar, who is most patient with him. Caesar can turn his hand at many a task, which is all to the good for Nigel's learning, but I fear my son speaks with the decided drawl possessed by Caesar. I suspect Timothy is a bit jealous.

Odd to think that in a year's time, I shall be writing to you of another child, who will by then be quite his or her own person.

Soon the swans and geese will rise on their strong wings to go northward, and spring will be on the land again. How much I wish you could come to us with the same swift ease. I think of you with love every day of my life.

She smiled ruefully as she put away her writing materials. Despite the necessity for it, she was sure her grandmother would have some crisp words to say about the tiny criss-crossed script.

Her smiles and laughter ended abruptly in the middle of February. It began as such an ordinary day, at first she denied the nightmare was happening.

She and Della were working together in the kitchen, arguing facetiously over how many thousands of individual meat pasties like the ones they were making now they had made before. Alex insisted the number had to be equal at least to the stars in the sky, while Della, pretending great seriousness, objected that so many would have fed the whole continent and, though they had served many, it was not quite equal to that.

"When one considers how many pies Mr. Cronmer eats all by himself every time he comes here . . . Oh!" Alex grabbed her swollen abdomen with flour-smeared hands as the pain rippled through her.

"Baby kicking hard? Maybe it doesn't have a taste for nonsense," Della teased, but then the pan she was holding clattered to the floor, scattering little pasties everywhere as she grabbed for Alex's sagging form.

"No-o-o!" It came out as a scream instead of a protest, as Alex fell, not even aware that Della had kept her from hitting the floor. The agony was too familiar; so had the labor with Nigel started. But Nigel had had enough time in her womb to be born; the baby she carried now had not.

The pains came in piercing waves; she could not get her breath. She heard the terrible, panting animal noises she was making but could not stop them. She was dimly aware of Della's screaming and of faces floating over her— Timothy's, Mavis's, others', and then Caesar's as he lifted her as carefully as he could, his dark face creased with reflected pain.

And then there was nothing but the searing contractions attacking without mercy until the hot reds and oranges faded to black.

"Love, sweet love, it's over now. Stay with us, stay, Alex."

There were other voices, but that one deep male chant of love and sorrow and fear for her penetrated and stayed with her as the others did not. And she began to listen for its repetition.

A big, gentle hand touched her forehead and her cheek, followed by a cool cloth. Her head was lifted and a cup was pressed to her lips. She swallowed the cool water gratefully, her raw throat too clear a reminder of the awful sounds she had made.

"So . . . rry." It took incalculable effort to form the word badly.

"Hush, sweetling, don't try to talk, just rest now, stay with us and rest." The male voice came again, wrapping her in protective strength.

She concentrated all her energy on opening her eyes. At first everything was a blur, and she gritted her teeth as she tried to focus.

Green eyes so like hers, looking down at her. Rane's face so alive with tormented love that she gasped aloud and her own eyes flared in alarm. The pieces were coming back, but they did not fit. The baby. She knew she had lost it. But it had been St. John's child, not Rane's. When she had borne Rane's child—her mind did not doubt the paternity at this moment—St. John had been there, but now she had lost his baby and Rane was here instead. Everyone would know, and so many would be hurt. Her body jerked convulsively as she tried to rise, and pain clutched at her again.

Rane held her down easily with one hand and sponged her face. "Easy, easy, lie still. Everything's taken care of. We've sent for St. John. I fear it might take some time to find him, but it will be done. Timothy did the right thing. He went to the Jenningses' house for help. Caleb and I had just arrived."

And I was just passing through and had no intention of seeking you out this time because seeing you is getting harder, not easier. Instead I nearly witnessed your death, held on to you while the blood poured from your body, called you back. And all notions of propriety were cast aside by all of us for the single purpose of keeping you alive. I think Timothy and Mavis already knew and now Della knows, too, but it doesn't matter, nothing matters except that you still breathe. We will all go back to our proper roles when it is safe to do so. He said none of this aloud, but he turned her head carefully so that she could see Della on the other side of the bed.

"Della has been watching over you, too. Everyone has," he told her, and had the satisfaction of seeing her apprehension ease.

"Girl?" The single word was low and hoarse, but he understood her question and her right to know.

"Yes, it was a little girl," he told her, his throat tight with pity. "Caleb had her buried in the churchyard." *Because we could not simply dispose of her like refuse,* he thought, his throat tight, and he was grateful to Caleb for having arranged the burial in consecrated ground even though there had been no baptism.

Alex heard Della's stifled sob, but she herself was too weary for tears. She fell asleep again, only vaguely aware that Rane held one of her hands in both of his, his fingers tracing the delicate structure to reassure himself that she still existed in his world. He forgot that Della was in the room. Watching the naked love on his face with troubled sympathy, she hoped that St. John would come home soon.

❦ Chapter 40 ❧

Alex had lost a great deal of blood, and it was several days before she was fully conscious of what was going on around her. Then she understood how much care and love had gone into saving her life. Even Mrs. Jennings, who had been feeling unwell and thus had been the reason for Caleb's and Rane's visit to Annapolis, gathered her strength as soon as she could and came to sit with Alex for a while, though Alex told her bluntly that she looked too frail for such duty. "I would feel far worse than I do were you to collapse."

Mrs. Jennings waved her hand in airy dismissal. "It was all a fuss for nothing. My husband panicked and sent for Caleb, foolish man. At my age, indispositions simply show more. But as it turns out, I am glad the young men were here in your time of trouble. Did you know that your cousin nearly threw Dr. Bartley out bodily?"

Alex shook her head, and Mrs. Jennings's eyes sparkled with grim amusement. "That man is scarcely fit to be called a physician, but he was available when they needed help for you. However, when Bartley suggested purging and bloodletting to rid you of 'ill humors,' Caleb tells me Rane roared like a madman and chased him away. Oh, I should have liked to have seen that! Dr. Bartley is a pompous ass."

Hearing the dignified old woman use such language coaxed a small smile from Alex, and Mrs. Jennings was well satisfied.

In fact, Alex was biddable. She smiled when it was appropriate, ate when she was offered food, made the proper responses when spoken to, reassured the children that she was all right, just very tired, and inside she felt numb, as if everything was happening to someone else. Even the words of love spoken by Rane became something distant and dreamlike.

She had advanced to the stage of sitting up in a chair for part of the day by the time St. John and Boston returned.

St. John's appearance was a terrible shock. He looked as if he rather than she had nearly bled to death. His skin was sickly gray, his eyes muddy and red-rimmed. He tried to maintain some control at his first sight of her, but he failed, sinking to his knees and burying his face in her lap as great sobs racked his lean body. "My God, Alex, I thought I would not be in time. I thought I would never see you again!"

The tears began to pour down her cheeks as if some secret well of sorrow had broken its boundaries. "It was a girl," she choked, but she wept as much for St. John's terror and love as she did for the lost child.

They clung to each other until the storm had passed, and when St. John would have blamed himself for not being there when she needed him, she stopped the words with a hand to his mouth. "It just happened. It was not your fault, nor was it mine. And our friends gave me the best of care."

Despite her reassurances, he nearly drove her insane in the next days, constantly hovering to prevent her from the least exertion, watching her with hawklike intensity lest she eat too little or attempt too much, even holding her too tightly as he slept, as if he feared she would slip away from him forever in the night.

Finally she confronted him. "I cannot bear any more of this! You must trust that I am well again. You must let me go about my life, and you must go about yours. We have so much work to do! You've got to go back for Leda eventually in any case, and the races are important to our future." He still looked so stubbornly unconvinced that she used her final weapon. "Do you remember how you chafed to ride again, to go your own way again after the loss of your arm? I feel the same way."

Silence stretched between them until reluctantly he nodded. "I will try."

To further insure a return to normalcy, she enlisted Boston's aid. Things were still not as they had once been between brother and sister, but Boston, no less than St. John, had feared for her life, and he was anxious to aid her in any way he could.

"Persuade him to get on with the horses and to stop hovering over me," she implored him, and Boston complied, working with stubborn subtlety to reassure St. John that it was his duty to Alex as much as to himself to go traveling again.

It was the end of March by the time they left, and by then Alex was able to see them off with the glow of true health about her. The loss of the child was a constant ache, and together she and St. John had visited the small grave, but it was not like losing Christiana, who had become an individual, fully realized in her young life before her death. And Alex had proof of the value of her own life in the daily sight of her four living children, the twins no less hers in her heart than the other two. To fail to make peace with this new loss would be a waste of time and energy Alex knew she could not afford. She worried more about her husband than herself. He had slept beside her every night, but he had not made love to her before his departure. She had not pressed the issue, knowing he needed time to adjust, but she had no intention of tolerating a platonic marriage for long. When he returned, things would change.

Following the pattern of the previous year, he was back for her birthday and took her to the races again at the National Course. She watched the sleek bodies reaching for ultimate speed, but rather than odds and wagers, she thought about making love with St. John. She nearly giggled aloud at the incongruity of it, keeping her face properly polite as St. John introduced her to various acquaintances met at other race courses. And all the while she was fully conscious of the way the sun turned his hair to molten silver gold when he doffed his hat and how the blue of the sky seemed to be captured in his eyes. She could hardly repress a shiver of anticipation as she studied his capable fingers handling the reins of the horse hitched to the landau. He allowed her to take the ribbons now and again, but his left hand was ever stronger and more skillful, exerting perfect control. She wanted that hand touching her, and it was all she could do to wait until they were alone in their hotel room that night.

"You seemed preoccupied today," he observed as he began to undress. "Has racing paled so soon?"

"No, but I was thinking of other things." Her thrill of warm laughter caught his attention, and he froze in place as she came to him, her hands cupping his face. "I was thinking of you." She pulled his head down to nibble softly at his mouth, planting small kisses over his face, returning to his mouth to press her suit more fiercely.

"Alex, I . . . ," he began to mumble against her mouth.

"I don't want to hear it! I told you once before that I would not settle for the sort of marriage you seem to have in mind, not after my body has learned to love yours so well."

She began to tug impatiently at the rest of his clothing, dropping her head to rub her cheek against his lightly furred chest, feeling his flat nipples harden even as her own breasts were swelling with desire.

St. John was lost. He knew it absolutely in the swelling of his manhood in hunger for her. And there was relief in the knowledge that she had taken the responsibility and the initiative in this.

He nuzzled her throat, taking in the scent and taste of her, letting the restraints he had imposed on himself slip away.

They crashed on the bed, both of them laughing now at their haste, and ripples of sheer joy were still vibrating in Alex when St. John came into her, his need so great by then that he was writhing in both pain and pleasure. Alex wrapped her legs around him and met his thrust with wild abandon until she gained her own pleasure and felt his.

They lay still locked together as their hearts eased the frantic gallop and their breathing eased. Peace flowed through Alex as if she were drifting on a wide, warm river, the first real peace she had known since losing the baby, and she considered how much a part of her life loving St. John had become. The physical joining was simply an expression of what that loving entailed. And married people, she was beginning to discover, could not take for granted that things well established between them at one point would continue so.

They didn't speak often of the lost baby, but it was another bond twining one life to the other, and in reasserting their love for each other, they were stronger for the loss.

The fact that Alex was more interested in the horses than ever before formed an added closeness between them. They laughed at the realization that even knowing the limitations of the beasts, they thought of them almost as extensions of their family rather than solely as investments. As the twins and Morgan were now receiving more serious training in riding with the aid of two steady old nags and a pony at Hawlington's farm, so did the education of Leda's offspring continue.

They tried to keep their expectations within reasonable bounds, but Swan, at two years old, was rapidly becoming a miracle of motion. Even Mr. Hawlington, who had seen many winners and losers in his time and might be expected to be more objective, waxed lyrical when he watched Swan run. The colt ran when he was bid to run, and he ran when he was free in the pasture. He ran with a long, low, ground-eating stride. He ran effortlessly, his legs, lungs, and heart increasing their capacity by the day.

And he kept his sweet temperament though now his light colt's voice gave way periodically to the harsh scream he would have as a stallion.

Though they planned to start him in shorter races the following year, they cautioned themselves against hoping too much; many things could happen between now and then and in the actual racing.

Leda's second foal, the filly, Black Swan, showed promise, too, of great speed even though she was only a yearling, but she also had a fractious temperament—not malevolent, but erratic—that might cause trouble on a race course were it not controlled. It was just too early to tell.

The new year would bring not only another foal from Leda, but also one from Mabbie who had conceived this year, much to the Carringtons' joy.

Life felt so rich and full that summer, Alex moved through the damp heat with a spring in her step and ready laughter. It was as if coming close to death had sharpened her appreciation for life. And when Penelope Jennings came to visit, Alex's heightened perceptions told her instantly that something was drastically wrong.

Her heart twisted painfully in sudden fear as she wondered if Pen brought bad news about Rane. "What is it? I haven't seen you for months and months, and now you come looking as if something dreadful has occurred. Has it?"

Pen looked as if she were going to burst into tears, but she drew a deep breath and steadied herself. "Caleb said this was how you'd be, but I didn't believe him. Oh, Alex, I was afraid you wouldn't want to see me, that I would remind you that my daughter lives while your daughters . . ."

Alex stared at her in amazement. "Penelope Jennings, no wonder Caleb adores you! You've got a very soft heart. Think what a foolish waste of time and tears it would be if I resented every mother whose daughters have survived, most particularly you who are such a good friend. I miss Christiana still, I always will, and I wish the new baby had lived, but I have two fine sons and two stepchildren who seem so much my own, it is often hard to remember I did not bear them."

As they quickly returned to their old ease with each other, Alex realized how much she had missed seeing

Pen. She had never before had a close female friend near her own age, and she found the friendship was a source of special joy. They chatted happily, and Pen promised to bring the children to visit the next day, but then her expression grew serious, and Alex knew that she had news of Rane. Unconsciously she had been waiting for it all along, both dreading and wanting word of him.

"Rane and Caleb are working harder than ever on building and selling their ships and on the coastal business, and that part of Rane's life continues to go well, but I do worry so about him. Claire seemed to be doing quite well, but then a few weeks ago, she took a pair of shears and cut all of her clothes, every stitch, to shreds. It must have taken her a long time. She claimed someone else did it. Maybe she even believes it's so, but poor Rane, he must fear she might next take the blades to his heart."

Alex stared at her in horror. "What has he done about it?"

"There is little he can do as long as he keeps her at home and does not commit her to a madhouse. He has hired an attendant who seems kind enough and is very strongly built. When he is not there, Claire is closely watched."

"My God, how dreadful! Their home must be like a prison!"

"Very like, I fear. But if Claire follows her old pattern, she will be all right for a while." Both of them wondered how long the calm would last for Rane this time.

The heat gave way to the cool days of autumn, and St. John and Boston once more went south, but in November, they were back and on the twenty-fifth, Alex accompanied St. John to the National Course in Washington, D.C., for a special match for the national championship. Sir Charles, a son of Sir Archy born in 1816, and a horse with a dazzling record of races won, was to represent the South in the race against the Northern representative, American Eclipse, whose sire was Diomed, as was Sir Archy's.

Privately, Alex wondered if formalizing the sectional rivalry of the country in this manner was really such a good idea, but the excitement of the event was undeniable.

And the result was a fiasco. Eclipse, a light chestnut with flaxen mane and tail, was led out by smartly clothed attendants; his jockey was wearing vivid new silks, and the horse himself looked ready to take on any contender. In contrast, Sir Charles limped out, his covering blanket worn, his attendant looking nearly as frayed as the blanket. The poor beast had gone lame in the spring, though he seemed to have recovered enough for the fall meets and had added four more races to his string of victories, the last of these having resulted in the challenge. But he was far from fit now.

It was announced that forfeit had been paid for Sir Charles, but most of the spectators did not share the Carringtons' relief at this news. Their disappointment was so vociferous that another announcement was made and applauded—Sir Charles and American Eclipse would race one four-mile heat.

Alex felt a lump forming in her throat and could barely hold back her tears. She wished she could go out and take the horse away from the cruelty of making him run in such deplorable condition.

The tears did overflow as she watched Sir Charles struggling valiantly to keep running until his bad leg failed him completely in the last mile, and he came to a trembling stop, giving Eclipse a worthless victory.

"Never, ever will we race any of our horses in such condition!" Alex swore, and then she buried her face against St. John's chest and sobbed.

St. John patted her back comfortingly. "Of course not; it is unthinkable." Having seen Sir Charles race in all his glory, St. John wanted to cry with Alex over this travesty.

But out of that shameful match came an event that changed the Carringtons' lives. On the evening of the twenty-fifth, William R. Johnson, nicknamed the "Napoleon of the Turf," issued another challenge against Eclipse. Johnson said he would produce a horse on the last Tuesday in May of the following year, 1823, to run against the Northern champion at the Union Course on Long Island. The Union had been built in 1821 when regulations against racing in the North had begun to ease, and the course was enjoying increasing popularity.

At the Jenningses' Christmas party, there was much talk of the race. Annapolis was essentially a Southern town, much more so than Baltimore, and many of the guests discussed Johnson's challenge with glee, pointing out that he had all the South and most of Sir Archy's progeny to choose from, while American Eclipse was the only choice for the North. Many were already planning to attend the race.

The Falconers were there, and Alex was trying to listen to talk of the upcoming race and ignore Claire. But it was difficult. This night Claire looked bewitching, her deep blue gown a perfect foil for her blue-eyed fairness. Alex tried to suppress the bitchy thought that perhaps Claire had destroyed her old wardrobe simply to gain a new one. At least the woman seemed to be behaving with perfect normalcy, and for Rane's sake, Alex was thankful.

It was Caleb who proposed the trip north, addressing the Carringtons. "Why don't we all go? I think it might be quite exciting to be there. And it would be interesting for you to see New York. It is quite different from any city in Maryland."

"What do you say, Alex?" St. John asked. "It sounds like quite an adventure, and I am sure there will be no repetition of that awful match at the National."

Alex thought of what fun it would be to travel with the Jenningses and to see another part of America. She nodded. "I think it a grand plan."

"So do I! Of course, Rane and I would hate to intrude if you think we would add too many to your party." Claire's cloyingly demure voice startled them all into awkward silence.

Alex was suddenly aware of Rane standing behind his wife, his face flushed with embarrassment. "I don't think . . . ," he began, but Caleb, deeply distressed for him, cut him short. "You must come!"

St. John added his own encouragement, and Rane had no graceful way to refuse. "Well then, I will provide the ship to carry us north."

Alex had to look away from him because she could see too clearly his conflict. He genuinely wanted to be with his friends, but he dreaded how Claire might behave. With sudden savagery, Alex wished he were cruel enough to lock his wife away. She felt instant remorse for the thought, but could not rid her mind of it.

By the time May arrived, she and St. John were more than ready for a break from the press of daily life. In January Mabbie had presented them with a splendid bay colt which they named "Oberon" for the mythical king of fairyland, Queen Mab being a fairy queen who governed people's dreams. It seemed a fitting choice as the colt was of Mabbie's line, not the Swan line. Leda's new foal was not so promising. The chestnut filly was so undersized and frail, they feared for her life. Harder and more practical souls would have gone on with the regular breeding process, letting the new baby take her chances on the journey with her mother, but St. John and Alex decided not to breed Leda back that year.

"Perhaps a year without carrying a foal will result in a stronger one next time," Alex suggested.

"A woman's view to be sure," St. John replied, "and probably the heart of the matter."

With more than a little sad irony, they named the filly "Swan Song" and tried to condition themselves not to mind should they lose her. It was Mabbie who went to Sir Archy this year, and Alex, when she wanted to ride, had to use one of the children's mounts or hire a nag from the livery, but neither option held much charm.

Remembering what trouble there had been in locating him the year before, St. John sent word of his whereabouts much more often this year, and Alex was deeply grateful that he had when she sent for him in a panic. The "bastard strangles" swept through their young herd with savage force. It began with the horses appearing out of sorts and off their feed and went on to the dread signs of stiff, sore neck, the hot tender swelling between the branches of the jaw, and the discharge from the nose. The horses were thoroughly miserable, and worst of all to see was Swan who went so swiftly from eager health to a shadow of his former vigor. The only good thing was that Mabbie and her new colt were away from the contagion, and Leda, being older, was not affected.

With the help of Mr. Hawlington, Alex set on a course of treatment that consumed the hours and left no time for anything else. They rubbed and wrapped the horses' legs and fed them bran mashes, boiled oats, and other nourishing foods, softened to pass easily down the sore throats. And they kept up a round of hot fomentations and poultices applied to the swellings to bring the matter to a head.

St. John and Boston arrived to find Alex and Mr. Hawlington looking nearly as worn as the horses. Their hands were as raw and red as if they'd been dipped in acid.

St. John was sure they would lose Swan Song, and worse, he feared Swan would not recover either. The latter could scarcely draw breath, his throat was so swollen. St. John tried to help Alex to accept the possibility, but she refused, snapping angrily, "I don't want to discuss it!"

When they were finally able to lance the huge knot under Swan's jaw, they were relieved to see the thick pus from the wound. It was Swan's only chance to live, and finally they knew he would, though he was a poor imitation of the strong horse he had been, his coat dull, his bones jutting out from all the weight he had dropped.

"Well, they've put up th' framework, someday they'll build a horse on this spot," Mr. Hawlington observed wryly, shaking his head as he looked at Swan. There was a moment of silence, and then they were all laughing, fatigue and relief forcing emotions near the surface. Waves of weakness flowing over her, Alex leaned against St. John.

"A long sleep is what you need," he said, hugging her gently. "You saved them all, sweetheart, even Swan Song."

It was a setback that Swan would not be able to race this spring, and perhaps not at all for the year. But St. John pointed out that while that would have ended his best chances as a race horse in England where dash racing of young horses was the style, here in America the blow was far less severe because the heat racing required the strength of older horses.

Easter at the end of March brought a severe snowstorm which made the signs of spring that came with April even more welcome, and Alex began to look forward with keen anticipation to the trip to New York, longing to get away from the round of duties that crowded her life and even from the children who, bright and biddable as she could wish, were still capable of causing small wars among themselves and battles that spilled over to include everyone else.

St. John and Boston, who had gone back to the racing circuit, returned with Mabbie in early May, and this time, St. John had a tidy pile of winnings to show for his efforts. "I'm beginning to know the horses here as I did in England," he announced, and Alex loved the high spirits in his voice.

The only sad note in their planned trip to New York was Boston's quiet but stubborn refusal to go with them.

"But you've loved seeing new places in this country," Alex protested.

"Yes, and I will continue to do so, but this is just not a trip I want to make."

She realized it might well be that he felt odd man out among all the married couples, but she suspected that it was more a matter of her brother not wanting to accept Rane's hospitality aboard ship. It was galling to have this dark, unacknowledged current separating them, and she was tempted to confront him. But the impulse died in face of the possibility that a confrontation might make everything worse rather than better, might widen the rift between them irrevocably. She did not press him further about his decison.

❧ Chapter 41 ❧

Though it was a longer route than going up the Delaware River and then overland, the Carringtons went by ship with the Jenningses and the Falconers down the bay and then north to New York on one of Rane's ships. Their quarters were well appointed for comfort, and the weather continued fair for the days of the voyage.

Thousands of people were traveling from various parts of the country, particularly the South, by road and water to witness the race, and the general excitement of the event pervaded everyone, including the crew of Rane's ship. Rumor had it that thousands of dollars were being wagered in addition to the $20,000 a side, $3,000 for forfeit, established as the official stakes. The names of the

Northern backers were known, but the Southern contributors were not listed.

Had Alex not been so nervous about being near Claire Falconer again, she would have noticed that St. John wore an abstracted expression every time wagers were discussed.

Alex could not fully understand her attitude toward Rane's wife. She had met her only twice, though she had certainly heard enough about her erratic temperament and had glimpsed it in the woman herself. But she feared her discomfort came from guilt, as if Rane's feelings for her were stolen from what belonged to his wife. And it was as if all the twisting of Claire's mind had brought a peculiar clarity of vision to the woman. Since they had boarded the ship, Alex had been conscious of Claire's brittle, speculative gaze too often fixed on her.

"I am glad to see you continue in such robust good health," Claire had said in greeting. "Rane and dear Caleb were quite worried about you last year."

There should have been no offense in the words, but there was, an intimation that Alex had used trickery to bring the men to her side. She had been tempted to reply in kind, but she feared verbal dueling with Claire; if the woman were really so unstable, she did not want to be the one to push her over the edge again.

She did her best to avoid Claire's company during the voyage and found that Rane aided her in this, appearing to steer Claire away or to join the conversation whenever his wife managed to find Alex apart from the others.

Finally, thwarted once again, Claire snapped, "Always protective, aren't you, Rane?"

"Of you? Of course, my dear," he replied smoothly, but a muscle twitched angrily in his jaw.

At last his interference seemed to wear his wife down, and she ceased to stalk Alex on the ship and turned instead to striking lonely poses that would have been laughable had they not been so pathetic.

Alex knew she had not imagined it all when Pen whispered to her, "I see Claire has relinquished her pursuit. She usually does once Rane calls her off. She tends to test people rather rudely."

She was somewhat comforted by Pen's description of this as Claire's usual behavior. Anything to make Claire's behavior seem less personal.

New York was an immediate assault on the senses, a port with far more commercial activity than Baltimore as ties with Liverpool were strengthening. The city was overflowing with race spectators, and so it was fortunate that Caleb's sisters had room for guests in their homes. The Carringtons were to stay with Julia and Kenneth, while Caleb, Pen, and the Falconers would stay with Peggy and Lawrence.

Though Julia had all the domestic comfort one could wish, Alex was immediately aware that Caleb's assessment was correct—Julia was afraid of her husband because she felt inadequate. Her humble attitude toward the man made Alex want to shake her. In fact, she wanted to shake them both. Kenneth, for all his superior air, still bore some obvious affection for his wife, but was put on edge by her timid attitude and her continual need for reassurance. Perhaps being able to bear children would have helped, but as that did not seem to be Julia's option, it would be a better course for her to make the best of what she had.

"I would much rather be in our marriage than in theirs," Alex confided to St. John, and only later did she realize that normally he would have responded with a jest but was so abstracted that he hardly heard what she said.

The trip took on the aspect of a fairytale for Alex when they dined at a fine restaurant and then went to the Park Theater in Park Row. The theater had been rebuilt in 1821 after a fire had destroyed it, and the old pink and gold decor had been replaced with rather drab green baize seats, the back of the boxes being whitewashed and the iron columns covered in burnished gold. Alex didn't mind at all; she found this theater that could seat 2500 quite impressive. Having never been to a real theater before, she made no comparisons and watched the English guest star, Charles Mathews, a hugely popular comedian, with great enjoyment, her eyes shining and her laughter frequent. Mathews performed his unique monologues and impersonations, which he called "At Homes," with great zest.

Alex, enthralled, did not notice that St. John was so lost in his own thoughts, he was paying no attention to the performance. Nor did she notice that Rane was watching her instead of Charles Mathews.

But the diversions of New York were not the reason for

their being in the city, and on the twenty-third, they left before dawn, ten of them in three landaus that would serve as their seats at the race. Alex gave thanks that Pen and Caleb were the Carringtons' companions rather than Claire and Rane.

"Claire looks as nervous as if she's going to run in the race," Pen remarked at one point when there was light enough to see, and Alex saw the truth of it: the woman was fidgeting so in her seat beside Rane, it looked as if she were going to jump out. Rane's face looked stone graven. But to give his wife her due, she had not behaved badly in New York, to everyone's relief.

It was well they had left early. Many people had gathered in and around the course the previous evening, and all the roads leading toward the Union Course on Long Island were congested with vehicles, people on horseback, and people on foot, all hoping for a good view of the match at 1:00 P.M.

All morning the infield and most of the area around the course, both by the inner and outer rails, was packed tighter and tighter with humanity. By starting time, it did not seem there would be a square foot left anywhere. And yet, friends did manage to find each other in the confusion. Rumor had it that fully 20,000 people had come from the South alone, many with their families in tow.

Alex recognized Mr. Ralston of Virginia, one of the people she had met at the National Course races the previous autumn, as he approached them on horseback, and she welcomed him with a friendly smile. He had seemed a courtly and intelligent man on first meeting.

He smiled in return, but there was a reckless glint in his eyes as he greeted St. John. "I hope to own a fine flock of swans before long," he said genially.

"And I hope to own a good Virginian profit," St. John returned with equal grace.

The cold dread clutching Alex's heart was intensified by the anxious look on Caleb's face; it confirmed better than words that some monstrous wager had been made between Ralston and St. John. Suddenly aware that Alex knew nothing of the bet, and flustered out of his normal sophistication, Ralston bid them all a hasty good day and moved away.

Eyes blazing green fire, Alex turned on her husband.

"What have you done?" she hissed, ignoring the presence of Caleb and Pen entirely.

"I've wagered Leda, Swan, and Black Swan against $5,000 in gold and silver coin that American Eclipse will defeat the Southern entry," he said with such defiant matter-of-factness, Alex had difficulty believing she was hearing correctly.

Suddenly she was aware of how abstracted he had been on this trip, and then she knew that without consulting her at all, he had risked much of their future on a horse race. Just like his father and brothers. She felt an awful kinship with his mother. The food she had eaten from the generous basket they had brought along threatened to come back up, and she swallowed convulsively. She felt utterly betrayed, not only by St. John, but by Caleb and Rane, too, for she was certain all the men had known. Damn their sense of honor!

In the midst of the great press of spectators gathered under the warm sky, she felt as cold as death. She wondered fleetingly what they would do, all these nattily dressed racing enthusiasts, if she were to give in to the impulse to scream like a harpy.

Instead she stayed where she was, gazing at her husband with eyes full of pain and anger.

St. John did not soften despite her white-faced misery. It was done; there was no way to beg off the wager. If there was to be regret it would come later. Now he was in the grip of feverish excitement. "How could I miss a chance to bet against a man named Napoleon?" he said, but there was no levity in the words.

She knew that St. John was saying much more than a mere reference to William R. Johnson's nickname. It was as if he had said, "This is something I have to do as I had to go to war. This is men's work, and no business of yours." And it infuriated her further.

She wanted to tell him that he was no better than his father, but instead, she turned the statistics of the race against him. She knew them as well as anyone, had considered them with great interest when she had looked forward to this day with such excitement. It seemed a lifetime ago.

"You don't even know which horse will race against American Eclipse. There is a field of five against him, and he is the oldest and has raced only three times in the last four years. And if he carries the same blood as Sir Archy back to Diomed, so do the others. How can he hope to win?"

"No matter what care has been taken to bring those horses north, no matter how the journey has been eased by water and easy stages, they have still had a long trip, and most of them have raced a good deal, perhaps too much, perhaps enough to give Eclipse the advantage he needs. And beyond that, I cannot tell you how, but I know he will be the victor."

"You are quite mad," she said, and she turned away from him, ignoring the distress on Caleb's and Pen's faces.

She sat frozen, waiting for this awful day to end, trying unsuccessfully to banish images of the precious horses from her mind. Leda and Swan, those two she would miss most of all, not just for the future they had promised, but for the animals themselves, who had, as she, begun in England and come to this country. She thought of the great speed Swan had already shown by his third year and of his sweet nature. She thought of how hard she had fought to save his life, and she did not think she could bear having him led away to become part of Ralston's stable.

It was no great surprise when Henry was led out to represent the Southern interests. Most had felt he would be the choice, and as it turned out, two of the other four had been injured, narrowing the field considerably. Considered a four-year-old, though he was somewhat short of that, Henry was carrying one hundred and eight pounds while Eclipse was forced to carry one hundred and twenty-six pounds as an aged horse. Both were ridden by white jockeys, Henry's in sky blue, and Eclipse's in crimson. Eclipse had the pole position, and Henry's jockey had his mount some twenty-five feet away.

At the tap of the drum, Henry sprinted away, passing Eclipse and taking the lower turn at the rail. At the quarter, he was three lengths ahead, and he kept up a searing pace, maintaining his lead for the first three circuits of the course. Crafts, Eclipse's jockey, made his move on the far turn of the fourth circuit. By the time they were on the home stretch, Eclipse had cut Henry's lead to no more than a length and a half, but at what cost!

Suddenly nothing mattered to Alex except the older horse, and she cried aloud, the sound blending with a multitude of voices raised in dismay. While Henry was running with no punishment, Eclipse's jockey was spurring and beating the horse unmercifully and swayed so wildly in the saddle, he nearly lost control. Eclipse threw his tail up as if he were vanquished, but the cruel beating went on, and he finished only a length behind Henry.

The Southern faction roared with approval, and the sound grew even louder when 7:37 was hung out as the official time—the first time 7:40 had been reached or bettered in America, the accuracy guaranteed by three split-second chronometers, specially imported from France for this race and held by three of the most honorable turfmen of the country.

"That man ought to be shot," St. John said. "Not for anything on earth would I see a horse so abused. Crafts should not have been chosen in the first place; he weighs only a hundred pounds, and that means Eclipse is carrying twenty-six pounds of dead weight. Crafts is not strong enough for such a contest."

Alex's heart softened a little toward him because his distress was equal to hers.

The four of them sat in frozen misery waiting for the next heat, wondering if Eclipse would even be able to run it. They could not leave the course; the spectators were packed too tightly to allow it. Caleb wished he could pick Pen up and fly away with her; the trouble between the Carringtons distressing him even more than the cruelty on the course.

The news swept through the crowd. Samuel Purdy, once the best rider in the North but now, at thirty-eight, retired and a family man, had been persuaded to take Crafts's place. There was a sigh of relief from those who cared about Eclipse, but it still seemed doubtful that the horse could come back. While Henry had left the track in good shape, Eclipse had been beaten so badly and so far back on his body that both his sheath and his testicles had been cut, which explained why the poor beast had thrown his tail up in pain and protest.

As soon as the drum tap started the next heat, Purdy pushed Eclipse at Henry and kept him at it, using whip and spur, not with the same vicious abandon that had characterized Crafts's ride but rather in the judicial way Eclipse had always needed to run his best. In the back-stretch of the final mile, Eclipse cleared Henry and increased his speed until he won the heat by an open length.

The roar of the crowd—the Northerners cheering their champion and the Southerners urging theirs on—was as loud as the voice of war. Alex clapped her hands over her ears and felt the vibrations of the waves of sound shaking her.

The tables were turned. Eclipse was now the favorite. His time was 7:49, the first accurately recorded instant of a second four-mile heat being run in 7:50 or better. Betting on Henry diminished, and now a new jockey was requested for the younger horse. When the horses come on the course again, Henry was being ridden by Arthur Taylor, who had not ridden for years, but had been notable in his day.

But Purdy kept after Eclipse with whip and spur from the beginning, and when Taylor tried to urge Henry to the lead at the end of the race, the younger horse simply could not pass his elder and fell back to be defeated by three lengths.

The ovation rising to the skies for Eclipse was not of the North alone; many of the Southerners, even those who had lost money on the race, joined in tribute to the sheer gallantry of the older horse.

Alex found herself standing and clapping while tears streamed down her face. It had not even hit her yet that St. John had won his bet; she had no room to feel anything except relief that Eclipse was no longer under the whip and had competed with such great heart.

Reality came with St. John's painfully tight grip on her arm. "I had to do it!" he said fiercely. "Without this, it would have been years before we could buy land of our own. Now we can do it. Now, Alex!"

Reaction was setting in, and she began to tremble, but she kept her voice steady. "I am glad you were so astute, glad for all of us. But if you ever do such a thing again without consulting me, win or lose, I will leave you."

She willed him to understand that the betrayal she felt was more important than the small fortune he had won.

His anger flared and then died as he took note of the signs of strain in her face, from the unnatural pallor of her skin to the bruised look in her eyes. Ignoring the seething hordes around them, he kissed her tremulous mouth. "I promise. To be honest, I don't think I could stand the strain of such a secret again in any case."

"Amen," she heard Caleb say with heartfelt relief, and when her eyes met Rane's across the way, she saw that he looked relaxed and happy and realized that the tension she had seen that morning had been worry for her because of St. John's wager, not concern over his wife's behavior. Claire was still fidgeting and posturing in their carriage, but Rane seemed not to notice.

Years later, Alex was to wonder what course their lives would have taken had American Eclipse not beaten Henry in the famous match race.

Book Four

❧ Chapter 42 ❧

Alex exchanged a look with St. John, and his smile answered hers, and for a moment, it was as if they were alone rather than surrounded by their New Year's Eve guests. Pride in each other and in what they had accomplished in so short a time flowed between them without words.

They had looked at land on the Eastern Shore, land in counties with the sound of England in them—Kent, Somerset, and the like—but much of the acreage was exhausted from years of tobacco crops, and the land was so flat that the wind seemed to blow from one side to the other without hindrance.

It was Caleb who had heard about the property in Prince George's County, midway between Annapolis and Washington, D. C., that was to be sold at auction because of the owner's death.

What had been a dream of opulence more than seventy years before had degenerated into the nightmare of Job for Mr. Philip Bladen, who had received the estate as a gift from his father some fifty years before when the young Bladen had been in his early twenties and newly married. What promise he must have seen in the princely legacy, when for a time, abundance had graced the land and his family. Tobacco had been their money crop and fine Thoroughbred horses, too. Gardens had surrounded the house, and four sons had been born to the Bladens of Bladensfield.

But then the long decline had begun. His wife had died

443

trying to give birth to a daughter who had perished with her. One son had died in a freakish accident while timber was being cleared from the wood on the land, and another had drowned when a storm on the Chesapeake had capsized the boat on which he was a passenger crossing to the Eastern Shore. Neither of these sons had left any issue. By 1800, Mr. Bladen's parents were dead as well as his one sibling, a sister who had been ailing all of her life. Another son he lost to a lung complaint, and the final blow fell when his last son broke his neck in a riding accident.

There were no daughters-in-law, no grandchildren to liven Mr. Bladen's days, and he had, by all accounts, spent his last years in bitter memory and long bouts of drunkenness. The land had suffered as he had, played out with nothing offered to enrich it. Over the years, the horses had been sold off and most of the slaves as well until only those as feeble as the old man were left, clinging to half as many acres as he had had in the beginning.

Fences began to sag back to earth, paint peeled from window sills, repairs to the dependencies of the great house were never made. Death had come to Bladensfield long before Mr. Bladen had died in the early summer of 1823, leaving no heirs except the state, which demanded back taxes.

The Carringtons had had no competition for their bid of $20,000. Money was still very short in the state, and the dilapidated condition of the property tempted few. But the Carringtons saw how it could be with work and love. Alex never confessed it to St. John, but sometimes she had a sense of being there to heal the lost dreams of Mr. Bladen.

They were fortunate in the fact that no expense had been spared in the initial construction of Bladensfield. Even the dependencies, the outbuildings used for laundry, summer kitchen, salting meats, sheltering the well, storing ice, and various other purposes, had been built to last, and were made usable again with a minimum of repair. And the main house with its big central block flanked by two "hyphens" connecting two smaller blocks, in the same symmetrical style of their Annapolis rental, was of rosy brick, as were the stables.

The stables and barns pleased St. John most of all, and to Alex's wry amusement, he had been far more concerned about repairs to the shelters for the horses than to the house. There was also a half-mile practice "track" (as many Americans called race courses), overgrown now, but it, too, could be renovated.

The Carringtons renamed the estate "Wild Swan" and vowed from the first to take each day as it came.

Tillie Carter had remained to work at the tavern, but two of her sisters, Polly and Cassie, had joined the staff on the estate, proving themselves willing workers though their speech was as slow-drawled as their sister's. Caesar, too, had remained in town, though he and Timothy Bates had come out often to help with various tasks. Calvin, a young man courting Polly Carter, had come to work for the Carringtons, too, in order that he might be close to Polly, and he had married her. Jed and Mabel Barlow, a white couple in their late twenties, were also employed at Wild Swan. They were both rawboned and capable of hard work, but somehow they lacked the luck and drive to make it on their own. Their attempt to farm their rented land had ended in dismal failure, and they needed steady pay to feed their four sons.

Of the slaves Mr. Bladen had once owned, only an old couple was left: Marcus, who still tottered about the house in a brave attempt to maintain the illusion that he was head houseman, and his wife, Octavia, who insisted that no one could produce cleaner laundry than she, but was content most of the time to doze in patches of sun that eased her arthritic joints. The two were so old and frail, there had been no question of a separate sale; they had come with the acres, and though the first thing the Carringtons had done was to grant them their freedom, it was soon apparent that there was no place for the couple to go; they were a liability to be cared for just as the ravaged land was. It had taken them a while to regard the new owners with any trust, but now, though they subscribed to the old rules of aloof separateness, they seemed quite content with the changes at Bladensfield, now Wild Swan.

Additional hands, young men whom St. John was training, had been hired to work with the horses.

It was a rather motley mix of people, but they seemed to get on well enough with each other and with the extra hands hired for seasonal work. The rules had been made clear from the first—there were to be no slaves at Wild

Swan, and blacks and whites would work peaceably together or find somewhere else to go. There had been a few failures, blacks and whites too surly to remain, and their swift dismissal had served as a lesson to those who stayed.

Alex did not confess her fears to St. John, but she was continually conscious of how much she was expected to know and oversee. The raising, preparation, and preservation of various foodstuffs by drying, by treating with salt or sugar, or by storing in the coolness of the root cellar, the treatment of various ailments among the humans and the livestock, the settlement of various disputes among the servants and among the children, the thrifty ordering of supplies, the smooth running of the house, even the keeping of the accounts had become her province because she did it better than St. John. His major interest and skill lay with the horses.

She did not resent the fullness of her days; she had never felt more alive or more necessary to the lives of the people she loved; it was only that she feared she would prove inadequate in some important task. She was continually grateful that Della had moved out to the country with them.

It had been a totally unexpected gift. The adjustments to the new life on the land had in many ways been as profound as had been the move from England to the United States. And in the reordering of their lives, it had become apparent that Timothy and Mavis, though too loyal to press the point, would much prefer to stay in town and run the tavern. It was a life they both liked. Tim was city bred, and Mavis had never missed her parents' farm from the day she had left it. It was finally decided that the Bateses would stay on to run the tavern, sharing in much needed profits. It was very logical. The land would not pay for itself for some time, and in the interval, there was an enormous mortgage on which payments would be due for years to come. But logic did not account for the desperation Alex had felt at the idea of being without Mavis's help with the children. And Mavis, though she didn't put it in such blunt terms, was not at all sure Alex could cope without her or that she herself could bear the separation even with the promise of frequent contact. They had fussed and fretted about it together and separately.

And then Della had calmly announced, "I am going with you to the new Wild Swan. Mavis is a good cook now; she can arrange matters here. But you and the children need someone to look after you."

Alex had been flabbergasted. "I fear to question your offer, but I must. What of your life here? What of your former customers?" It was true that Della had not cooked for anyone else since coming to the tavern, but Alex had always thought the independent Della would go back to being her own mistress eventually.

"I've thought about it carefully, and I have come to see that there is little for me here, no family, and what friends there are will be friends even if I live out in the country. I like working for you and Mr. Carrington."

There was a world of pain and loneliness behind the quietly spoken words, and Alex was fully aware of how profound an act it was for Della to admit to any kind of affection for a white family. And she had had continued reason to be thankful ever since the move had been made, and Della had proven to be so helpful with all manner of work. Alex sometimes suspected that Della was also managing her with subtle efficiency, but knowing it was for her own good, she could not resent it.

Horace Whittleby had also established his place in the Carringtons' lives by accepting the gentle mount they found for him. Despite his dislike of riding, he came regularly to spend part of the week at Wild Swan so that the children would not, in his words, "revert to the wilds." Under Alex's gentle insistence, the Barlow boys were also receiving at least a minimal education.

Alex felt a renewed burst of confidence and contentment. They were well and truly anchored here now, tied to these acres and buildings that so needed their love and care. And if they were no longer in sight of salt water, still the geese and swans passed overhead and sometimes stopped in the small pond formed from the stream that flowed through the property. And the broad expanse of the Chesapeake was less than a day's ride away.

Now, as the New Year neared, she surveyed their guests: Penelope, Caleb, and Caleb's parents, Mrs. Perkins, Rane and Claire, a few neighbors, and some of the horse racing set, mostly from Virginia and including Mr. Ralston, who in good grace claimed to have more than a little to do with the establishment of Wild Swan since his loss had provided the first payment. Mavis and Timothy were there, too, but at their own insistence they were with Della and the others in the kitchen.

The talk had turned to the new president, John Quincy Adams, sixth president and "The Second Adams," son of John Adams who had been the second president of the United States, the only non-Virginians who had so far served. There had been much ill feeling surrounding the election of John Quincy as Andrew Jackson, who had been born in South Carolina and was now from Tennessee, had received the most votes both at the polls and in the state electoral colleges, but had lacked a constitutional majority. Thus, the House of Representatives had chosen Adams over Jackson. Sectionalism was ever more apparent as many feared that Adams's fondness for national power to achieve internal improvements in such things as canals, roads, education, and exploration might lead in turn to the abolition of slavery. Adams's outlook was that of a New Englander; Jackson was of the South.

Alex caught Rane's rueful look. He had confessed that he shared her disaffection for American politics. Even though what happened in this country concerned them all now, still it was difficult to follow the twists and turns of the American contests.

She would never be at ease with Claire Falconer, but now she knew that no one was, including Rane, and so she no longer took the burden so much to heart. There were times when Claire seemed not only wholly sane but quite charming, when a flash of humor would light her face and her laughter would ring out, charming and infectious; then it was easy to see why Rane had fallen in love with her. But more often, the woman was in a middle state, not quite mad and not quite sane. She moved in a kind of pettish haze that saw slights where none existed and followed a train of thought that was usually at odds with the company's. Alex had learned to deal with her as they all did, with forebearance until Claire sighted another target. And all of them tried not to think about what the future would bring for the woman and for Rane.

At the moment, Claire was trying to attract attention by pointing out with false sympathy how brave "dear Alexandria is to make do with so little furniture," and then proceeding to enumerate the splendid pieces her own husband had provided for her comfort in their Baltimore home.

Alex was secretly amused. It was true that the rooms at Wild Swan were not overly adorned—furniture was not high on the Carrington list of priorities—but the lack of clutter pleased Alex, and she was not, in any case, house proud. Her vulnerability lay with the children, and Claire was so uninterested in children in general that she hardly seemed aware that they existed and never remarked on the uncanny likeness between Morgan and Rane. That, Alex would have found unbearable.

She caught the flash of anger in Rane's eyes and saw that he was not pleased by his wife's antics. As he moved toward Claire, Alex put her hand on his arm. "It doesn't matter. She's doing no harm by commenting on the obvious," she said softly.

She felt the muscles of his arm tense and then relax beneath the cloth of his coat, and her hand dropped away.

She and Rane seemed further away than ever from the brief lovers they had been, but they were in many ways closer as friends, having achieved an ease that was much like her relationship with Caleb Jennings. It suited her very well, and she hoped he felt the same. She suspected that he visited Wild Swan more to see Morgan than her. Though he was scrupulously attentive to the other children, she had grown accustomed to seeing them together, the little boy and the man, cut from the same cloth. The fear of discovery had eased as St. John had never shown any suspicion of the resemblance, but had rather professed himself as glad of Rane Falconer's friendship as he was of Caleb's.

Caleb—how very good a friend he had proven himself to be! It was he who had stood as guarantor for the loans that had provided the balance of the payment on the land. At first both Alex and St. John had protested such a risk, but he had been inexorable, pointing out that it was in fact little risk as he expected they would work hard to hold on to it, and that even if they failed, the property was more valuable than what was still owed on it.

And Penelope had proved herself no less vital a part of the Carringtons' lives. Though the two women did not see each other as often as they would have liked, they sent letters back and forth and made the most of the visits they did manage. Pen was expecting another child in the spring and was looking softly radiant while Caleb had once again assumed his attitude of fiercely protective husband. Pen had suggested good-naturedly that things would be a deal simpler were Caleb able to bear the child as well as worry about it.

Alex suppressed the little flicker of pain. She did not begrudge the Jenningses their good fortune, but she still longed for a daughter though she had begun to learn resignation. As St. John had pointed out, they were doing the best they could to remedy the problem. Though Alex had tried to share his humorous acceptance, she realized that their feelings were quite different: he feared the danger of pregnancy more than he wanted another child, while she was fully willing to take the risk, particularly because she found herself enjoying her children more by the day.

She focused again on the conversation as she heard St. John say, "We still have hope that Swan will prove himself at four miles. The problem has not been his speed or his willingness, but rather his pacing. He has a great heart and needs a strong hand to keep him from running too hard too soon."

There was a murmur of understanding from the horse owners. It was a common problem, finding jockeys who were at once light enough to race and yet strong enough to control the great horses for as many as five four-mile heats in order to win three out of five. It was not uncommon for horses to veer off the tracks, injuring themselves and their riders, out of control simply because their ninety-pound jockeys, many of them scarcely more than boys, could no longer hold them.

And in the South where most of the racing in the United States was done, most of the jockeys were slaves. It was a stone wall Alex and St. John had found well nigh impassable. They had tried not to compromise their opposition to slavery. They had searched hard for white and free black riders who were available for hire or willing to race for more than one owner. And sometimes they had found a rider for their horses, but for the most part, it had proved a futile quest. They had agonized over the decision, but in the end, they had given in and accepted the offers of slave jockeys from friends in the racing fraternity. They had done it on the condition that the jockeys would receive direct payment from them, but they had only the owners' word that the slaves' earnings were not confiscated later. And they had done it with the firm determination that the practice would end as soon as they could hire and train their own riders. But nothing could change the knowledge that they had compromised their principles, and nothing was more important now than getting their own riders. Alex had the uncomfortable feeling that no matter how gracious some of the slave owners were, they were secretly pleased that the Carringtons had been forced to admit the necessity of slaves. And that, of course, was not the point at all, for if there were no slaves, there would be a system of free jockeys from which to choose, as there was in England.

Alex knew how fortunate they were that St. John knew so much about the training of race horses, for here, too, the finding of the right free man was difficult. Some had hired trainers from England and Ireland, and some had free white men in the position, but most used skilled slaves. So far the Carringtons had tried three men. The first had known a great deal about horses but more about drinking rum; the second had proven himself as fond of wandering as of working and had been on his way in far too short a time; and the third, Mr. Beaker, presently at Wild Swan, was not, in Alex's opinion, going to last very long. She had not caught him at anything yet, but she sensed an unease in the horses, a sudden skittishness that made her suspect he was too severe with his charges when there were no witnesses. St. John did not discount her suspicion, but he wanted proof before he resumed the full burden of the horses' schooling.

The horses—they remained the center of the dream for St. John and thus for Alex. She had every hope that other enterprises—vegetables, fruits, grains, garden stock, poultry, swine, and cattle—would eventually provide added income for the property, but with the horses lay the greatest chance of fame and fortune.

They had done well so far with their small stable. Of Leda's foals, in addition to her first, Wild Swan, her second, the mare Black Swan who was within days of being five years old, had proven herself to be a swift and spirited runner though her fractious temper was not always dependable. She was good-natured with humans but a virago with her own species, capable of attempting to savage other horses in a race if she were not carefully handled. She got on well with her stablemates, however, reserving her aggression for strangers. They had not yet tested her at the "heroic distance" and doubted that they would. She was so good at shorter distances, and they wanted to breed her soon, so it seemed foolish to risk injury in the longer races. Bay Swan, Leda's third foal, was, at nearly four years old, a great strapping young stallion of willing heart, but so far in practice runs, he had fallen short of his sire's, Sir Archy, speed. Bay Swan could be depended on to run a good race whenever challenged, though it was unlikely that he would ever beat the best. Swan Song, who had begun life in such a frail state, was healthy now, but still an unknown quantity at three years old.

Mabbie's offspring had not yet been tested in real races, but both the colt, Oberon, born in 1823, and the filly, Titania, born in 1824 and nicknamed "Taney" by the children, showed every sign of possessing Sir Archy's endurance and speed.

But the burden of proof remained with Wild Swan, and not just because he was the oldest of their racing stock. He was English bred, and both Alex and St. John wanted him to prove that the preference for dash racing there had not lessened the strength of the bloodlines.

"It's childish to feel this way," St. John had pointed out.

"I know," Alex had agreed. "And that doesn't change a thing, does it?"

They had laughed at themselves and continued to hope that Swan would triumph at four miles. Though they had left England for a better life, they remained essentially English and had come to accept that fact. Part of the feeling came simply from having been born and raised in that country, but it was also reinforced by the way many Americans treated them.

They had encountered very little outright rudeness, but there was often a chill when their accents were first heard. Common interests such as the horses and the problems of the land usually thawed the unease, but the differences were still there. It would take a long while for all the resentment the Americans felt for England's treatment of their country to fade. And on a personal level, the Americans seemed to fear that they would be judged uncouth and culturally wanting for not having been raised in the mother country. The irony did not escape Alex. St. John's connection with the nobility had both helped and hurt them, impressing on the one hand and frightening away on the other. She was glad she could call Pen, Della, Mrs. Perkins, and Mavis her friends, for it certainly did not seem that any of her neighbors were going to be close. Few were any longer part of the racing world and most were struggling on tired land, as unwilling to try new methods as they were to lose their old way of life, the men and women equally disheartened. She knew they called her the "Englishwoman," marking her as an outsider, and though more and more came to her for various remedies, they did not extend social invitations. The few overtures in that direction that she had made had led to disastrously stiff meetings which left her convinced that she and these people had little in common.

A few couples who were at the party tonight were exceptions, but even they could not be counted close friends. The lack of slaves and the new agricultural methods they were trying did not add to the popularity of the Carringtons. And they had been hurt as well by their aloofness from the festivities when the Marquis de Lafayette had been welcomed in Annapolis and elsewhere on his long visit to the United States, a visit that had begun in July, 1824, and lasted for fifteen months. Alex had not blamed St. John for his reluctance to be part of the festivities in honor of the famous Frenchman. Despite the fact that Lafayette was not to blame, it was all too reminiscent of France's antagonism to England and of the battle that had cost St. John his arm. Alex blessed the Jenningses for being so understanding, for while they had been deeply involved in the celebration of Lafayette, they had understood the Carringtons' lack of enthusiasm.

As midnight drew near, Caleb raised his glass in a toast. "May 1826 be a good year for all of us and particularly for our friends and hosts, the Carringtons, who have so bravely committed themselves to Maryland."

They paused to listen to the high, clear chime of the mantel clock bringing in the New Year. Alex caught Boston's eye and was grateful for the slow, sweet smile he gave her. They were closer than they had been for some time because together they had mourned the death of their father when the news had reached them in September. It was a sad, haunting thought that he had already been dead for weeks by the time Virginia's letter had arrived.

Caton's heart had simply given out, something that could have happened to anyone, but even in the brief words her grandmother had written, Alex had known how much the old woman blamed herself for somehow never having been able to instill enough strength and courage in her only surviving child. "It is bitter indeed to outlive the last of one's children, but I think of you both building your new lives in the new land and am comforted," she had written, and then she had, typically, gone on to more practical matters:

> *Your mother is enjoying her role of widow, more I judge than she ever did that of wife. She is well provided for, as Caton left the store to Paris and Rome with the provision that they take care of their mother. Paris will soon take over the store's management. This may all sound mean spirited, but I give you warning, Margaret has, I believe, some plan afoot to disrupt your lives. I bid you remember that she has not changed.*

They were glad of her warning when Boston received the letter from his mother, the first since he had left England. It was full of pleas for him, "her favorite son," to return to her. Paris and Rome did not love her enough. Now that her "beloved husband" was gone, only Boston could truly understand her deep sorrow.

To Alex's relief, Boston burned the letter, as disgusted as she by the hypocrisy of the words. She knew that her mother's chief motive had been to separate Boston and Alex.

The paradox was that it was going to be accomplished, Alex was sure of it, though not in the way her mother intended. She and her brother were closer, yes, but at the same time, she could feel him getting ready to leave. He had said nothing about it and had continued to be of great help in all the Carrington projects, but there were many small signs. He read everything he could find concerning various regions of the United States, and he listened to those from the frontier who came in to trade, listened to the cackling, twanging voices as if they were enchanting music. Even the intense and loving way he entertained his nephews and his niece gave Alex warning that he was storing memories for when he would no longer be with them.

Several times she thought to broach the subject, but restrained the impulse, fearful that she would push him into earlier action. And somehow she knew it was all connected now with their father's death, as if that quiet failure of a life had given Boston the added impetus he needed to set his own course. There was a measure of peace in that because she no longer felt entirely responsible for whatever direction he might take.

"May it be a very good year for you," she said to her brother as she kissed him for luck in the new year.

"And for you," he replied, and she could see both sorrow and excitement in his green Thaine eyes.

Despite the late hour that everyone had retired, most of them were up early the next morning to ride. St. John took the three Virginians and Boston, who had developed into a fine rider, in his party, while Alex took her children and John Jennings, who, going on nine, was Morgan's age, out on mounts ranging from ponies to full-grown horses for Morgan and the twins. The other ladies of the party and Caleb's father remained at the house, but Caleb and Rane accompanied Alex, both of them cheerfully admitting the pace she and the children would set was more to their liking than St. John's would be.

The twins and Morgan were accomplished riders who could well keep up with the faster party, but they were mollified when they learned Caleb and Rane, two favorites with them, were coming along.

Alex sighed inwardly as she watched Flora's antics. The twins would celebrate their eleventh birthdays soon, and already Flora was a flirt, smiling prettily and preening the minute she was in the company of men, though her body was still in the stick-thin stage. She had certainly not learned such behavior from her stepmother, and Alex had decided it was inborn, a natural talent or liability, depending on one's point of view. But she couldn't be cross with her. Though Flora liked to get her way and liked to charm, she was without malice and easily brought to heel by her twin.

It was an odd relationship. Blaine was so much less forward, so easygoing most of the time, but he was also the self-appointed guardian of his sister, very patient but capable of quelling Flora with a few words or a look.

"I think Flora has delegated the work of her conscience to her brother," Rane said as he rode beside Alex, startling her with his perception of her thoughts. "And he does the job admirably."

Alex nodded, her eyes returning to the slim, straight figures of the twins. With their golden brown hair, vivid blue eyes, and aristocratic features, they looked much like St. John though they were not quite so fair as he. "It's all right now, but someday they will not have each other to depend on so closely, and I do worry about what will happen then."

Rane did not dismiss her fears. "I expect there will be some pain depending on who falls in love first; that must always be painful for the other twin. I remember when I was a child and saw twins for the first time. At first I thought it would be marvelous to have one, and then I was glad I didn't when I considered how birthdays and everything else would have to be shared. Selfish little bastard, wasn't I?"

Alex giggled. "No, just practical." But her mood sobered as she watched Morgan and knew that Rane watched, too. Morgan with his green, green eyes and dark hair; Morgan with the indelible stamp of the Thaines. He was the reckless one, born with a sense of balance and daring so intertwined that no physical feat dismayed him, not even when it brought him to the edge of disaster. It was Morgan who climbed highest in the trees, who ran along the fence tops as if they were broad avenues, who loved to ride at breakneck speed, and it was Morgan, as mentally agile as he was physically, who learned so effortlessly that Mr. Whittleby was hard pressed to keep the boy's interest fixed. Often Alex feared that everything came too easily to him, and yet Morgan was generous with his siblings and patient when they could not keep up.

It occurred to her that Rane must have been very like Morgan at the same age, indeed had had many of the same characteristics when she had first known him and still did. She wrenched her thoughts away from Morgan, fearful she would say something she should not.

"Nigel is the one I worry about most often. He is the most self-contained little person! It seems I've been wondering what he's thinking since the day he was born. He seems to enjoy himself well enough but everything he does has a purpose; he can't really be said to play. He informed me quite solemnly the other day that he did not think it was fair that there is so much to put in such a small place as the mind. I assured him that as far as I knew, the human mind can learn all manner of things without becoming overcrowded. But I must say, I can't remember worrying about such matters when I was less than seven years old."

They laughed companionably, and inwardly Rane congratulated himself. He had come to like St. John very much, and most of all, he would not do anything to hurt Alex. But he loved her more fiercely with each passing year. He loved the timbre of her voice and the way she laughed. He loved the changing shadow and light in her green eyes. He loved her long slender hands and the still vulnerable curve of her neck where it met her shoulders. He loved the tenderness when she looked at her children and the patience she showed to them. Though he worried about her, he loved her sure, strong grace when she rode modestly sidesaddle as now or boldly astride as she often did at Wild Swan. He loved the way she thought and even the way she loved her husband—even that was part of the whole that enchanted him anew every time he saw her.

He had faced his love, his desire, and his options. He could see her as seldom as possible or he could assume a new role in her life, a role similar to the one he had had at first with her, the friendly relative with her and the unofficial uncle with the children. He had chosen the latter course because he could not bear the first.

Claire had taught him a great deal about dissembling. His life with her was a matter of never showing her where his true affections lay. It was not just Alex who had to be protected, it was the Jenningses and other friends as well. He explained all of them to Claire in ways totally devoid of truth. Alex was his cousin, nothing more than that, and he judged that she and her husband might well be very prominent one day, given the love of racing there was in this part of the country; it never hurt to have a good connection in that world. That Claire could understand as she understood that the Jenningses were highly useful business contacts. To Claire, people were to be used; she had no sense of them existing as she herself did. Hers was forever the view of a very young child, so totally self-centered that it was inconceivable to her that others had desires, wishes, and rights equal to hers.

It would have been simpler for him if he could have

blamed Claire for the hell of their marriage, but he could not. If he were unhappy, she was well and truly damned. Unable to give to and take from others, she was totally dependent on herself to gratify all her needs, and she was inadequate to the task. As she could not love others, so she did not love herself in any healing way. She was the most desolately lonely soul he had ever known. And he had married her for all the wrong reasons. He had thought himself in love at the time, attracted to the blithe, bright flame Claire had seemed to be, attracted to her seeming need for him.

Now he knew it all for a lie. He had used Claire to try to eradicate the image of Alex, and the sentence for his failure was his marriage. He was resolved to live one day at a time, caring for Claire as well as he could, knowing the day would come when she would be so imprisoned in her strange mind that no one would be able to reach her at all. He did not look forward to that day; he dreaded it for the failure of all that was good and human that it would mean.

"If ever you need us, Sinje and I are here for you."

Alex's soft voice broke his reverie, and he realized anew how careful he had to be around her. "Thank you," he said quietly and left it at that, turning his attention back to the children. Not just Morgan, but any one of them I would take for my own, he thought, but his longing was not revealed on his face.

Caleb guided his mount over to them. "I fear you are a bad influence," he announced to Alex. "I'm feeling quite shaken. My son has just informed me that he intends to be a jockey despite the fact that as yet his seat on a horse is a precarious thing."

Alex chuckled. "I don't think you have anything to worry about. Young John appears to be heading for your height, and swiftly, too. I doubt he will be the proper size for a jockey for very long."

Nigel pointed, and the other children responded with gasps of delight as a flock of wild swans passed overhead. Rane and Alex watched the birds, both of them remembering long ago in Clovelly, neither of them saying anything. Caleb was so used to feeling the current that often passed between them, he hardly noticed it now.

They returned to the house at the same time as the swifter riders, and Alex and St. John were immediately together, surrounded by the children as they compared notes on their separate routes.

"Did you see the swans?" St. John asked, and Alex let the clamor of the children answer him. In a gesture so habitual that he was unaware of it, St. John reached out and tucked the ever errant strand of Alex's dark hair behind her ear, and for an instant, she leaned against him, smiling for the beauty of the winter morning and her family. The intimate proprietary gestures said more than words ever could about the Carringtons' marriage.

Rane closed his eyes for an instant, bracing himself against the pain that coursed through him, then, calmly, he turned to face his wife.

❧ Chapter 43 ❧

St. John and Boston left in January in order to attend the races in Charleston, South Carolina, taking Swan and Black Swan by water to enter them in the early February races. They allowed themselves enough time so that the horses would have some days to regain their balance after being on board ship. Lacking better transportation, horses still had to travel to races either by ship or by walking all the way.

St. John was already gone when Leda gave birth to a bright chestnut filly out of Sir Archy that Alex and the children named "Fire Swan." Though Sir Archy's previous owner had died, the old stallion was still standing at stud at Moorfield, his status undiminished under new ownership and his get winning races wherever they ran. But Alex and St. John remained convinced that it was better for Leda, now fourteen, to bear a foal every other year rather than every year, so they had no plans to breed her back to Sir Archy this year. Though they were grateful for the two foals, Oberon and Taney, they had gotten from Mabbie, she continued to be an uncertain brood mare, having failed to conceive for the past two years, so this year they had made arrangements for her to be bred again to a Sir Archy son in Maryland rather than to the patriarch himself in North Carolina. That plan had allowed St. John to leave earlier. But it also made it clear to them that they were going to have to acquire more help with the horses; St. John couldn't be everywhere at once.

Alex considered the problem as she put Swan Song through her paces one cold January morning. While Mabbie was being bred, Alex was schooling the three-year-olds, sometimes Swan Song and sometimes Oberon, enjoying the challenge of working the spirited animals. Swan Song remained too lightly built for very long races, but she was capable of fierce bursts of speed as well as sudden starts that could easily dump an unwary rider.

As she brought her back this morning, Alex patted her with grudging admiration. The horse had had a hard workout and was yet willing to try a few sidesteps and bucks, her high spirits still intact.

"You might make a four-miler after all," Alex chuckled.

Swan Song rolled her eyes and tried to sidle away as she was turned over to Mr. Beaker, but she quieted down as Alex admonished her, "Easy, lass, easy, you've had enough exercise for one morning."

She was aware of Mr. Beaker's disapproval of her riding the racing stock, but she ignored it and hardly blamed him for sharing a common attitude. But as she entered the house, she turned back, suddenly struck by the thought that she was fully in charge with St. John away, and that Mr. Beaker had better be aware enough of that so that he treated the horses as she wished. She didn't like the way Swan Song had acted around him; it was different from the filly's usual behavior.

She rounded the corner in time to see the man give Swan Song such a vicious clout on the nose as he yanked her reins down hard, that the horse nearly fell to her knees. One of the stableboys looked on sullenly, not approving, but also not willing to cross his superior.

Hot red rage poured through Alex as she remembered and understood all the strange little lapses in good behavior that had afflicted the horses lately.

"Give her to me," she said with as much calm as she could muster, not wanting to startle the filly further. For an instant, Beaker seemed ready to refuse, but Alex's demeanor persuaded him otherwise.

She led the trembling horse over to the stableboy. "Can you cool her out gently?"

His face had brightened with the new developments, and he nodded enthusiastically and led Swan Song away, talking to her reassuringly.

Alex turned back to the trainer. "Your services are no longer required here. Please be off the property within twenty-four hours. I will pay you for the full month, which is more than you deserve."

The man grinned at her insolently. "You cain't do that. Your man ain't even here, an' he's the one thet hired me."

"And I'm the one who is letting you go. I am in charge here in my husband's absence. If you do not leave willingly, I will have the authorities escort you off the premises." Her voice was deceptively quiet, but her eyes smoldered. Beaker raised his hand as if he was going to strike her, but it was he who backed down. She heard a sound behind her and looked back to find most of the staff of Wild Swan assembling at the scene, summoned by the stableboy.

Suddenly the man changed tactics, whining, "Now, you know how shorthanded you are, you cain't hardly do without me."

"We can do very well indeed without you," Alex returned coldly. "And we will. Your kind of training can make perfectly good horses intractable." But even as she said the words and knew them to be true, she also knew that this further development was going to render their training program that much more understaffed and overworked, in addition to being leaderless. But there was no help for it, and she felt no regret when she handed Beaker his pay and watched him out of sight. She did not think he would return to cause any trouble; she suspected the mention of the authorities meant more to him than she knew, and she did not think he was anxious to confront them.

In the next days, the children, who already had chores about the place, helped their mother by taking on more work just as she did, and together with the remaining stablehands and the other workers, they managed to keep

461

up the schedule of feeding, grooming, mucking out, exercising, and generally keeping the horses in top condition. In addition to the Thoroughbreds, there were the children's less hotly bred mounts and the farm team, but the load was lightened by the fact that Sir Arthur, Mabbie, Swan, and Black Swan were not on the property. Still, the system was makeshift at best and emphasized the need for a new trainer. Alex would have preferred to wait until St. John returned before trying to hire a new man, but she wasn't sure she could. And then the man appeared.

Alex's first reaction was bone-jarring fear. One minute she was alone as she rode Swan Song down a path through the woods, and in the next, the way was blocked by an enormous black man. Even with the superior height of being on horseback, she felt intimidated by the sheer size of the man. He towered well over six feet, and though he looked ragged and hungry, nonetheless, he radiated strength and power. They stared at each other for a long instant, and then he spoke first, doffing his battered felt hat.

"I been watchin', you gots hosses need work. I kin do dat." His words were neither threatening nor subservient, just a statement of the facts as he saw them. He had a broad flat-planed face. His right cheek was marred by a scar and part of his right earlobe was missing. His skin was deep brown.

Alex swallowed, further unnerved by the idea that he had been lurking about without any of them being aware of it. It occurred to her much too vividly that he could easily drag her from her horse. And then an odd fact struck her. Swan Song had not shied at the man's appearance, nor was she acting skittish now. Quite the contrary, she was thrusting her muzzle at him in the friendliest of gestures, and the man responded by gently stroking the filly's nose and scratching under her jaw. Swan Song gave a breathy little sigh of pure bliss.

Involuntarily Alex smiled, breaking the tension between herself and the man.

"You know I must see your papers first." She heard her own words with wonder and thought that this was surely the last way she had expected to find added help for Wild Swan.

His face did not change nor did his hands fumble as he

brought out the paper and handed it to her, but Swan Song's sudden snort of displeasure betrayed the man's tension. Alex kept her own expression calm as she read the paper that proclaimed him a free man, or rather, proclaimed a man named "Freddy" free.

The description fit only in the most general sense; the particulars of the man before her and the man described on paper did not match. Both men were tall, though the paper said six feet two inches, and Alex was sure this man was at least two inches taller than that, and both men were dark brown. But there was no mention of the scar nor the tooth missing near the lower front of an otherwise full mouth of white teeth. No mention either of the scarred bracelets of flesh on his wrists or of the scars she suspected marred his back under the old shirt and patched coat.

Her stomach turned with sick pity. He was a runaway. She had no doubt of it. She was quite sure he could not read and so did not know how far off the description on the paper was. Somehow, that pulled at her heart more than anything else. Despite his great size, he was, because of the peculiar institution, desperately vulnerable. He could be hunted down by men and dogs, whipped, maimed, even killed for his offense.

She thought of the compromise of the slave jockeys, and she felt as if she had been given a chance at redemption. If he could work the horses, she would give him the job and persuade St. John to let him keep it.

She handed the paper back. "It suits me well enough." He did not mistake her emphasis on "me." He raised his eyes and looked at her squarely, each of them acknowledging what the other knew. She felt obligated to give him some warning; she did not want him to think the papers would pass every scrutiny. She was not the only person in this country capable of reading.

"If your work proves suitable, you have the job. What wage are you asking?"

For a moment, he was taken aback by the question, but then he collected himself. "Food, a place fo' sleepin', an' mebbe anudder suit a clothes."

"Certainly not!" she exclaimed, feeling close to tears as she imagined how people had taken advantage of him on his journey. She had no doubt that many had gotten hard labor from him for little or nothing, knowing full well he was in no position to object.

"Den no clothes," he offered hastily, sure he'd demanded too much.

Alex wiped furiously at her eyes. "Of course you will have some new clothes! I didn't mean that. I meant that you will also be paid a wage like everyone else at Wild Swan. There are no slaves here! And no one is treated so." She named the same wage they had been paying Beaker.

It was swiftly gone, but the image lingered—a smile stretching his mouth wide and illuminating his dark face so that she could see all the humanity that had survived in this man no matter what his past had been. The smile banished the last of her doubts.

She rode ahead humming softly to herself, already feeling a load lifted from her, so sure was she that Freddy, for want of his true name, would prove useful.

She was not disappointed. Freddy was a miracle worker with the horses. It was as though he cast a spell on them. They not only trusted him, they seemed to perform better when it was he who asked them to go through their paces. He cossetted them and coaxed them, seldom needing to discipline them and then only seeking to fix their attention and remind rather than hurt, treating them like great children. The Carrington and Barlow children received the same treatment, and from their initial timidity due to his size, they swiftly moved to behaving like a pack of puppies eager for his praise. And once Freddy knew that Alex wanted and expected the children to be useful, he set them to various tasks, always shrewdly judging their capabilities so that they were challenged without feeling defeated.

The horses, the children, and Alex: those were the denizens of Freddy's charmed circle; everyone else was held at a firm distance. He was no bully nor was he surly, he just locked himself off in some private inner place where no one could enter without his permission. If the others resented it, they were careful not to show it and left him alone. It was to their advantage to do so because he worked harder than anyone else at Wild Swan. It would, Alex hoped, be enough to insure his safety. She did not think she had to worry much in any case. She was aware that every once in a while extra mouths were fed, and she was quite certain more than one escaped slave had stopped to rest briefly at Wild Swan. It made sense as she and St. John were openly antislavery, and she had not questioned the situation because it was another way of making up for being involved in slavery, even peripherally. The white workers seemed so content with their lot that she did not expect trouble from them either, particularly since she had stated boldly to everyone that Freddy's papers were in order.

Opposition came from such an unexpected quarter, Alex was stunned.

"It's time he moves along," Della announced one morning.

"Who?" Alex asked, completely at sea.

"That Freddy or whatever his real name is!" Della snapped.

"Freddy is one of the best things that has happened to Wild Swan. He's worth three workers at least, and not only is he a fine horse trainer, but he is also a competent farrier, a nearly priceless skill for us."

"He's an escaped slave, and you know it!"

"I presume you have proof of that." Alex's voice was degrees cooler.

"He never goes off the place, not for any reason. And he's got scars on his back, on his wrists and ankles. There's only one thing that can mean. That and the fact that he never says anything about where he's from. Oh, it's foolish for me to be standing here telling you all of this when you know it already. You're breaking the law by letting him stay here!"

Alex made no effort to conceal her disgust. "Your lack of compassion does you little credit. I would find it difficult to manage without you, but I could do it. And though you might like your position here, indeed I hope you do, I know you could survive very well without us as you have before. Freddy could not. The marks you speak of are proof enough of the abuse he has already suffered; I do not intend that he endure any more." Her attitude softened again as she sought to understand this inexplicable harshness in her friend. "Of course, all of this changes if Freddy has offered some insult to your person. Has he?"

Della's look of defiance broke and tears poured down her cheeks. "No, he hasn't. Dumb buck nigger, can't read, can't write, but I know he'd die for you or one of the children, I know . . . ," her voice trailed off in sobs, and she looked so young and forlorn, so shaken out of her normal self-possession, that Alex's anger vanished as comprehension dawned.

Della had worked very hard all her life and had made a place for herself, but she was still neither black nor white. Alex had already seen how careful she was in her personal relationships, in many ways as self-contained as Freddy. And now Della was attracted to a runaway slave whose skin was many shades darker than her own and who lacked any of the formal education that was so much a part of her. It must be galling to find her instincts moving so strongly against her usual rational way of life.

With difficulty, Alex hid a smile of relief at the discovery that it was not some horrible unkindness in Della that had caused her outburst. "Do you think you can adjust to his being here and just let me worry about any problems with his papers?" she asked gently.

Della scrubbed at her face with her apron and nodded, her expression still woebegone. "I don't know what got into me. I have no business speaking so about that man. He has done me no harm."

Alex did not enlighten her, saying only, "I hope you will always speak honestly to me."

In the following days, observation confirmed her suspicion. If anything, Freddy was even more distantly polite and withdrawn around Della than he was around the others, treating her as if she were a white woman who had nothing at all in common with him. And Della started and dropped things when he was near, stuttered and was totally unlike her normally calm self. Alex wondered where it would all lead. She judged Freddy to be in his early thirties, a few years older than Della, and old enough to have left a family wherever he had run from. It was a mystery she could not solve without Freddy's past, and she had a good deal of dread about that subject.

FIFTY DOLLARS REWARD: Ran away from the Subscriber, living near Port Tobacco, in Charles County, Maryland, on the 17th Dec., negro Man MADISON, calls himself Madison Butler. This is a likely young fellow, about twenty-one or -two years of age, about five feet ten inches high, handsome and well proportioned, his color light black, high forehead and sharp nose; the beard on his chin is becoming stiff, and, like that of negroes generally at matured manhood, that on his upper lip is yet soft and young; his countenance is pleasant, and he is apt to smile, when spoken to civilly; he has been accustomed to waiting, gardening, and driving a carriage, but prior to his running away, he stole some clothes and 5 dols. He is well acquainted through the whole Western Shore of Maryland, and somewhat in the back parts of Pennsylvania and Virginia, having traveled a good deal with me. I think it probable he may be in Georgetown or Washington, as he has very many acquaintances in both these places, particularly the latter, where he has a mother who is the property of Dr. N. P. Nausin, on Pennsylvania Avenue. I will give the above reward of fifty dollars, if taken in the District of Columbia, or anywhere beyond Prince George's County, and secured in any jail, so that I get him again. Or if taken in Charles, St. Mary's, or Prince George's counties, 25 dols. for apprehending and securing him in jail, or 25 dols. and all reasonable charges for bringing him home.

FIFTY DOLLARS REWARD: Ran away from the Subscriber, in Fauquier County, Virginia, on the morning of the 9th, a negro named BILL, who calls himself William Hampton. Bill is a black negro, twenty-four years of age, about five feet ten inches high, well made and rather handsome; has long slender fingers, is a polite, gentle, plausible fellow, and talks and laughs loud, is fond of show and parade; he is extensively known, as he has traveled about a good deal in the capacity of a waiter, is an excellent hand with horses. The cause of Bill's elopement is, he stole ten dollars, and was detected in it, and broke from the guard; he may have procured free papers.

The notices were myriad in the various periodicals the Carringtons subscribed to, advertisements in columns which also listed new imports by various shops, lost coats, and horses for sale. Women as well as men were listed as runaways, and in almost every case some infraction such as stealing money was listed and scars were nearly always explained as being the result of an accident. Alex viewed such details as transparent ploys to persuade those who might sympathize with the slaves that the slaves were no better than common criminals. The notices that appeared in the papers printed in Washington and Annapolis listed slaves escaped from states further south than Maryland and Virginia, though most were from these two states.

The papers carried news of horses and races which was of interest to the Carringtons, but Alex had from the beginning read the runaway descriptions with wondering disgust, hoping in each case that the man or woman had gotten well away. Now, it became a terrifying process. Each time mention was made of a man being good with horses, her heart beat erratically until she was sure it was not Freddy. And yet, she was sure the notice must be printed somewhere and might well appear locally, as the man was obviously a valuable possession. It was becoming increasingly frustrating not to know where he had come from or how long he had been on the run. But short of challenging Freddy, there was nothing to do but wait.

The first word from St. John was encouraging, and each message after was better. The Swan line was earning a name for itself this year. Swan was roaring to victory time after time despite the heavier weight he carried now for his age, though the four-mile victories still eluded him. But even there, St. John was encouraged as Swan was consistently second or third, staying in the race rather than breaking down or being distanced as many were. And Black Swan was eradicating her competition in two- and three-mile heats, running in her characteristic breakneck way, and, as St. John confessed in his private missives to Alex, threatening opponents with a fine show of teeth when necessary:

> She is not, by any means, a lady, and I feel like the parent of a slightly wicked child, too fond even though I know it would be better were she sweeter natured. I find there are many who admire her determination to have her own way, fair or foul. There are more than a few champions in Sir Archy's line who display more than a little temper, and though Black Swan is no kin to him, this seems a mark in her favor. It would be too complicated for me to point out to those who hold that

468

*opinion that the horses we have of Sir Archy and Leda
have so far proved themselves much more amenable
than Black Swan. English perversity, no doubt.*

I miss you, sweet wife.

The closing made Alex misty-eyed. Even the improvement in his left-handed script touched her. She missed St.
John, too, sometimes so fiercely that her body ached for
him, and she knew it was a good thing that her days were
so crowded with tasks to be accomplished. But loving and
missing him did not preclude some subtlety on her part
regarding the subject of their new trainer. In each of her
letters, she noted how skilled Freddy was, but she did not
mention the fact that he was a runaway. She wanted St.
John to be accustomed to the idea of the man working at
Wild Swan before the rest of the situation was made
known to him.

Daily it was getting more impossible to imagine life
without Freddy, not only for the care he gave the horses,
but also for the strong male presence he was for the
children. Little Horace Whittleby was providing their formal education, but what Freddy taught was no less
important. He knew the birds, beasts, and plants in all
their seasons. He taught the children how to judge the
fury of a coming storm by the actions of the livestock and
the wild beasts; he showed them where burrows and
nests were and taught them to respect the inhabitants; he
taught them stillness in the woods that allowed them to
blend in with their surroundings and thus see more, and
more important, feel more a part of all around them; he
promised that when summer came, he would teach them
to tell the temperature by the music of the crickets.

Nigel could hardly wait for this demonstration, and
Alex shared his enthusiasm because it meant Freddy was
not planning to move on, at least not yet. Alex knew he
would never make a promise to the children that he did
not intend to keep.

Freddy seldom came to her with any problems; he was
too competent to have many, but one day in February, he
sought her out, and she knew instantly that something
was seriously amiss.

"Has one of the horses been injured?" she asked
anxiously.

"No, not 'zactly," Freddy murmured, and then he took a deep breath and launched into his story. "Dat mare, dat Mabbie you done sent off fo' breedin', wahl, dere might be some big trouble gettin' a colt on her by dat stud 'cause dat dere Beaker man you had here befo' me, he done put Bay Swan to 'er. I doan like bearin' tales 'bout a man who not here to talk fo' hisself, but one o' de hands, he been frettin' 'bout it since it happen. Not his fault, he had to do what dat Beaker man say." A world of contempt was in Freddy's voice for a trainer who would breed two prize horses so carelessly and without permission.

"Mabbie is very hard to breed in any case," Alex said slowly, her mind racing to consider all the possibilities. "And at least it is not a close breeding; Mabbie and Bay Swan are not related. But damn that man! How dare he do such a thing! Mabbie could have been badly hurt. And now Bay Swan knows what mounting a mare is like; it is a wonder that he has remained so well behaved!" She gritted her teeth to control her rising fury. "I want to speak with the young man who witnessed this. Tell him no blame attaches to him."

The young man was obviously terrified despite Freddy's assurances that he was not being held responsible, and Alex had to speak calmly to him for some minutes before he believed no punishment was planned. "Please, this is very important! I must know how Bay Swan behaved and whether or not he truly bred with Mabbie."

She had to repress her impatience when she realized that the man's fear had given way to embarrassment at speaking of such matters with a woman, and she was more grateful than ever for Freddy's acceptance of her knowledge of and interest in the workings of the farm.

Finally, seeing no way around it, the young man gave his account. "The hosses, they doan like Mr. Beaker, so they was a little skittish on account of that, but that Bay Swan even after he been teased by Mabbie, he still doan hurt her none, an' the mare, she doan try nuthin' fancy, just 'cepts it 'cause she be ready. Was a day when you an' the childun done gone to 'napolis."

So there it was. Mabbie had come into season, and Mr. Beaker had amused himself by putting an untried stallion to her. If they were lucky, Mabbie had not conceived by the time she had gone to the Sir Archy son. But at least if she were in foal, there was a witness to the breeding so there could be no claim of an inferior sire. It was not a bad cross and might well have been in their future plans; it was simply a very young age to have bred Bay Swan when they wanted him for a well-mannered race horse, not one who strayed after every mare that went by.

She sighed, thinking of having to tell St. John about this and decided it could wait until he returned.

Soon Freddy approached her on another matter. "Dem Barlow boys, Jim an' Georgy, dey jus' might be good jockeys we learn dem how. Jim, he be twelve dis year, an' Georgy eleben, an' dey both scrawny little kids. I bet dey neber be too big. An' mebbe later Tad an' Billy, too, when dey's older."

Alex stared at him in dawning hope. The idea had not occurred to her, but what he said was true—the Barlow children were all so little and undernourished, she doubted that even the good food they were getting now would make up for the years of want. But they were tough; she had seen that in their wiry parents and in the children, as if they were all honed down to the bare essentials of bone and muscle for labor. Of course, many conditions had to be met. Their parents had to agree; the boys had to be willing; and they had to have the mental as well as the physical capacity to be good riders.

The Barlows proved to be so enthusiastic about the idea, Alex found herself feeling obliged to argue against her own best interests. "Please understand. Jim and Georgy might not prove suitable, which would be very disappointing for them. And even if they do become skilled, you must remember that it is a dangerous sport; there is always the chance of serious injury or death."

Jed and Mabel had married at sixteen, thirteen years before, and had had their first son, Jim, in 1814, within the first year of their marriage. The four living sons were not the only children Mabel had borne; there had been one nearly every year, but they had died either at birth or shortly thereafter. At twenty-nine, Mabel looked closer to forty, pale and worn, and her husband appeared no younger. But for all the disappointment they had experienced, they still shared a deep and abiding affection for each other. It showed in the wordless communication that passed between them now. A slight nod from Mabel, and Jed spoke for both of them.

The Barlows would never be at ease with Alex as were Della, Mavis, and Tim. To Jed and Mabel, Alex was a real "lady," an exotic foreign lady at that, in addition to being the wife of St. John, their benefactor. But in spite of his awe, Jed stood firm, not cringing, speaking his piece firmly.

"Ma'am, ain't no way my boys are goin' to amount to nuthin' special 'less some big piece a luck drops right on 'em. Oh, they'se good boys, they is, an' their ma an' me wouldn't take no others fer 'em, but still, they'se jes' headed fer bein' dirt farmers like their pa. Ridin' th' hosses, now thet would put 'em right up there 'bove that dirt, even if they come down to it now an' agin. An' as fer wantin' it, heck, they already think Freddy cain't do nuthin' wrong. They'd fly iffen he axed 'em to."

Alex appreciated the ghost of humor in his words. "All right then, we'll give it a try. I'll rely on you to ask Jim and Georgy."

There was no doubt of the boys' willingness to try the experiment. Alex had never seen them so animated and joyful. As though his days were not full enough, Freddy took on the task of teaching them from the beginning.

He started them off on logs rigged with reins, and he gave them exercises to strengthen their muscles, not just in their arms and legs, but in their backs and necks, so that they might eventually have the stamina to keep enormously powerful Thoroughbreds under control. They had already bounced around on the backs of the farm team and on the children's mounts, but now Freddy watched every move they made and corrected them with steady patience.

Alex saw Freddy's elusive smile once again when he announced, "Dey be fine, so fine! Like dey's born to be ridin'! Got good hands, no bad habits, an' no fear I kin see. De younger ones, little Tad an' Billy, dey takin' to it, too. You be habin' a whole fambly a jockeys."

Watching them one bright morning as they rode around the practice track, she shared Freddy's vision and could hardly wait until St. John got home. This was a surprise she wanted him to see, so she sent him no word of it.

So engrossed was she in watching Jim and Georgy handling their mounts, she did not hear the stranger approach until he addressed her.

"Mrs. Carrington of Wild Swan, I would guess. And I am Alastair Cameron, physician. Good day, ma'am."

The name—and the faintest suggestion of a burr in his voice—told Alex that he had spent at least part of his life in Scotland. They stared at each other in frank appraisal and not a little challenge.

He had arrived on an indifferent horse, unusual as most doctors took pride in their mounts, and his clothing, though of fine cloth, was exceedingly plain and casually worn. Under his hat, his hair was a shaggy, sandy thatch with a hint of red, his eyes were deep blue, and his skin was freckled and creased with little crow's-feet at the corners of his eyes and mouth, though he couldn't be much more than thirty years old. He had craggy bones that made his brows, nose, and jaw jut aggressively and gave him big-knuckled hands, though he was less than six feet tall. Despite his unheralded arrival and rather abrupt manner, Alex found herself smiling with more welcome as she studied him.

"The Jenningses said we'd rub along well enough," he announced. "The older pair in Annapolis. I gather you're acquainted with their son and daughter-in-law as well. How do you judge sassafras?"

The unlikely course of the conversation made Alex want to laugh aloud, but she kept her face straight as she answered, "I think it has a pleasant aroma and little else."

"Wormwood?"

"Mixed with rhubarb and garlic, it kills worms and loosens the bowels, but it must be used with care; too much can cause madness. And you, how do you judge bloodletting, blistering, and violent purging?"

His mouth twitched into a smile and his eyes twinkled. "Exactly the way you do, that they are violent crimes against innocent sufferers. It is a testament to the strength of the species that any survive. And while I'm at it, I'll thank you for concurring in my diagnosis of Mrs. Pradner's complaint, though I confess myself jealous of your success where I failed."

This time Alex did laugh aloud. Mrs. Pradner, who lived about midway between Wild Swan and Annapolis, had come to her in high dudgeon, not mentioning the physician's name but furious that she had been told there was no drug or treatment he would recommend beyond eating more slowly and eating less. Mrs. Pradner was acquiring vast proportions pound by pound, meal by meal, but she made no connection between her habits and her condition.

"I fear you were too harsh," Alex chided, and then she was quite serious. "You must understand, it is very difficult for her. She is hungry all the time and moves about very little, so each day it gets worse. You made her feel that she had to change all at once, and she knew she couldn't do that. I simply told her to do it as well as she could each day and consider the change there would be a year from now, not tomorrow."

She stopped, suddenly aware that the doctor might feel she was insulting him, but he nodded, looking more pleased with her by the minute. "You are quite correct. I tend to be abrasive when tact would be a better course. A gentle Alexander and a rough one; the sick may have a mix of both."

Alex smiled at him, understanding the reference, for Alastair is the Scots for Alexander, just as hers was the feminine form of the same. With that, it was as if a professional pact had been sealed. Doctor Cameron (for unlike the English, Americans called their physicians by that title) spent the afternoon at Wild Swan, and he and Alex found many treatments to discuss, sometimes disagreeing vigorously, but more often discovering yet another area of agreement. She learned that he had gotten his medical training at Edinburgh, though he had been born in America of expatriot Scots, his father having also been a physician trained at Edinburgh—a last loyalty, Alastair called it.

She did not have to ask him why he had moved his practice from Baltimore to quieter Annapolis; he offered the information. "If you listen to gossip at all, you will hear that I'm to be pitied, left by my wild young wife. The story followed me to Annapolis even though she didn't. There's not a word of truth in it. I should never have married, drove the poor dear to distraction, never on time for meals or anything else, left her to her own mischief too much of the time. And mischief she found aplenty, with a traveling player of all things! I can't say I approve of her choice, but I certainly can't blame her motives."

He related the story with such good humor, Alex could not be embarrassed by it. And she could detect absolutely no regret in him for having lost his wife.

When she showed him Virginia's notes, he was soon

handling the pages with reverence. "You could not have had a better teacher," he murmured. "There's a lifetime of wisdom here." And as an added compliment to her grandmother, he asked for writing materials that he might take some notes from the clear, fine script.

When he had gone on his way with promises to visit again, Alex was aware of yet another kindness Mrs. Jennings had done in sending the man to her. After nearly losing her own life along with the life of the fetus, Alex had wondered where they might find good medical attention for fractures and wounds that were beyond her skill. And now they had Alastair Cameron. She thought St. John would like him as well as she did.

It was not a conscious goal, but while St. John was gone, she strove continually to keep things running so smoothly that he could step back into life at Wild Swan without first confronting a multitude of problems to be solved. Alastair Cameron was a mark in favor of this scheme, but two entirely unrelated other matters were not.

Mabbie had come back from the breeding farm without having been bred to the Sir Archy stallion there. The owner of the stallion was not certain, but he suspected that Mabbie, even as difficult to breed as she was, was already in foal. Alex had wearily confirmed the possibility of his guess by telling him about Mr. Beaker's unauthorized breeding of Bay Swan to Mabbie.

The horseman had considered this at length and then observed, "Might not be a bad cross at all. That's a colt I'll want to see." And Alex had felt better about the matter, though she still didn't relish telling her husband.

For the other problem, Alex intended immediate resolution. As the Barlow boys daily grew into more competent riders, her own children became more and more sullen about it.

At first she had not noticed. There were so many things to consider each day. But then it became too obvious to miss. Her children began treating the Barlow children with cold superiority, no longer sharing their play or anything else and mocking the less educated children in the classroom, much to Mr. Whittleby's disgust. Alex was appalled by their behavior, but she also suspected its cause.

Once they saw their mother's face, the children had no

doubt that they were in trouble; Alex was so seldom cross with them.

"I would like to know the meaning of your cruelty to the Barlow boys," she said without preamble. "And do not begin with denials. Where you were wont to offer friendship, you now treat them shamefully. All four of you are guilty of being rude, selfish, and greedy. What do you have to say for yourselves?"

Their faces were already gloomy due to the unflattering terms their mother had used, but Morgan still felt compelled to speak in their defense. "Well, we haven't been very nice, I guess, but it doesn't seem fair that them Barlow boys get to be jockeys an' we don't. We're good riders!"

"It's 'those,' not 'them,' " Alex corrected automatically. "And I would like you to tell me what else the Barlows have to look forward to in their lives."

Blank silence greeted this.

"Let me tell you, then. You have never been hungry. You have always had enough clothing and good shelter, as well as books and lessons for your minds. Your father and I are pleased to provide for you because we love you, but neither of us ever wants you to forget that there are many who are not so fortunate. The Barlows have known hunger and want, and for the boys to become jockeys is one chance for them to have a little more and see a little more of the country than they would otherwise. And finally, look at each other and see yourselves; you are all growing into tall people. Good food has kept your growth from being stunted. None of you is going to be the proper size for a jockey, not even you, Flora, were girls allowed to ride in races."

There was a long pause while the children digested this, and then Blaine spoke for all of them. "I think we've been mean and very foolish." He looked at his brothers and his sister and received nods of agreement. "It won't happen any more."

"Thank you, that is far more like the children I know." She smiled at them and hugged each one, knowing they would be as good as Blaine's word. In fact, in the following days, Alex often had to hide her amusement; the Barlows were in danger of being overwhelmed by the new rush of kindness. But they were as calmly accepting as their parents, taking the good with the bad, questioning

476

neither, and the situation soon settled down into the normal give and take of any pack of children.

Alex was relieved; she did not want St. John to arrive home in the midst of civil war among the children.

❧ Chapter 44 ❧

From Charleston, South Carolina, to Halifax, North Carolina, and at Lawrenceville, Belfield, the New Market course at Petersburg, and Tree Hill in Richmond, all in Virginia, sometimes racing in the Carrington silks, sometimes racing under another's colors where race entries were restricted and St. John did not belong to the jockey club—all the way, Swan and Black Swan won one victoy after another; Swan in all distances except the four-mile where he continued to finish consistently second at least. With borrowed jockeys and courses in various states of repair, the horses had left the imprint of new blood and victory. There were already a multitude of inquiries about when Swan would be standing at stud.

St. John came home nearly three thousand dollars plumper in pocket, not only from the stakes the horses had won, which were generally small, but from private wagers on the races. Two thousand dollars of it he turned over to Alex; it would not only allow payment on their loan, but would also help to cover the many expenses that Wild Swan now generated in upkeep and staff.

St. John was so flushed with joy and triumph, Alex had to smile every time she looked at him. He appeared years younger and as excited as she had ever seen him.

"For the good of Thoroughbreds in general, they need another line to compete with Sir Archy's. With one so strong, horses are being bred closer and closer, and that will surely hurt the animals in the long run if other blood isn't brought in by outcrosses. And Leda's foals are being looked to for that. She is the common factor, since Swan and Black Swan had different sires."

Alex let him run on, content to drink in the sight of him, until he stopped suddenly, touched by the intensity of her gaze. "I've missed you, too," he murmured. But they had no more than a few minutes alone until the day was long over. The children had missed their father and their uncle as well, and the men let them come along on their rounds of the property. Alex sensed that Boston went only to be with the children; he was clearly deferring to St. John as Lord of the Manor. He was gently, gently disengaging himself from Carrington affairs.

The most important event of the day for Alex was St. John's meeting Freddy, and she knew a vast swell of relief as soon as the two men faced each other. In spite of how much St. John's approval meant to the security of his job, Freddy was neither overly bold nor subservient but rather stood quietly and answered St. John's questions honestly and in detail, so that St. John immediately knew that this was no novice in the handling of fine horseflesh. And though it was late in the day, Alex had the Barlow boys show off some of their new skills, and now her own children watched as if it were something they had had a hand in creating.

"My God, I think they have a chance to be among the best!" St. John marveled, turning to Alex.

"It is all Freddy's doing," she assured him. "He saw the promise and he's training them."

When they were finally alone, Alex did not want to think of horses, crops, children, or anything else except having her husband home again. She saw the same glitter of desire light his blue eyes as they undressed. When she started to snuff out the candles, he growled, "Don't. I want to see you as well as touch you."

Thinking of how far they had come from that first rude coupling, she came to him without her gown and shivered at the sensation of his skin against hers, rougher than hers, and drew a deep breath of his scent and tasted his flesh with her tongue.

"I'm not sure I can wait," he groaned as they sank down on the bed, and she could feel his shaft swelling hard and ready against her belly.

"Don't wait," she murmured against his lips, taking his tongue inside her mouth as she spread her legs and arched her hips to meet his thrust, moaning at the mingled pain and pleasure of the sudden invasion.

He held himself still for an instant, gasping her name, but she urged him on, "I want . . . Sinje, don't stop . . . I want . . ." Her body began to move and buck under him, more eloquent than her words, and St. John let himself go, thrusting in and out with no slow build-up of rhythm, frenzied in his need to spend himself in the tight pulsing warmth of her.

Alex felt totally out of control, her body roiling and seething in savage counterpoint to St. John's, wanting to devour his sex and make him whole at the same time, just as he sought to give and take of his pleasure. She heard the rising wail of their joined voices as the great hot trembling took her body and his.

There was nothing of the slow gentle pattern of familiarity in this harsh spending of long denied passion, and nothing less than this would have so satisfied them both. They lay panting together like two beasts slaked on a kill, hearts pounding hard until they slipped back to normal beat, bodies still joined.

Alex ran her hands through his heavy, damp hair and down his back to his lean buttocks, relearning the textures of him, savoring the security of his weight on top of her, carefully balanced to comfort without crushing. His mouth began to move in a soft caress over the hollow of her throat. She felt the renewed stirring of his manhood inside her, and she worked her hand between them until she could stroke the heavy sack of his sex and touch the place of their joining. She shivered with the heightened awareness of the two of them as one, and as St. John grew ready, he began to make love to her again, this time with slow deliberation.

Afterward, she would have slipped into sleep and expected he already had after his day of travel and his recent exertions.

"Why are we so fortunate as to have this Freddy working for us? He has the skill to work anywhere. His talent as an ironsmith alone is enough to make him a valuable asset to any horse farm."

His question startled her so much, her lethargy fled instantly. St. John, propped on his elbow, was watching her in the soft glow of the still burning candle stubs, and Alex knew there was nothing for it but the truth.

She related her first meeting with Freddy, and then she took a deep breath and admitted. "His papers list the name Freddy, but the description differs in too many particulars."

"Then he is a runaway slave." It was not a question.

She decided it might as well all be told, and she poured out the story of Mr. Beaker's perfidy that had resulted in the unscheduled breeding of Mabbie and in the man's general lack of fitness for the job he had held. "Freddy, or whatever his name is, was a godsend! He came at just the time we needed him the most. And no one could be a better trainer than he." She went on to sing his praises for the handling of the children as well as the horses, for his infinite capacity for hard work, and for his lack of complaint about any condition of his employment.

"None of that is in question," St. John pointed out calmly. "It is against the law to shelter a slave, considered here to be another man's property. Have you thought of the risk in that?"

"Yes, I have. And I know there will be other problems we would not have with a free man. Freddy will not be able to go with you. He has not left Wild Swan since he arrived. I am sure he fears detection. And since he knows so much about horses, it is probable that his owner raises and even races them. The racing world is small; he could be seen by his owner were he to go to the courses. But he is a very good teacher. The Barlow boys are proof of that, and the stablehands, too, have improved under his guidance. I am sure he could train a fine staff to go to the races in his place if you thought it necessary."

"Is this a way of easing your guilt over the slave jockeys we use?"

"You know me too well," she accused. "I admit it is partly that, but even that would make no difference were he not so good at his job. Sinje, the horses mean a great deal to me, too, and I cannot imagine anyone who would be better with them. It has all been a gamble, hasn't it? Why not one more hazard?"

"Why not indeed?" St. John lay back and closed his eyes, suddenly overwhelmed by weariness, but he did manage to add a final condition. "If we see a description of him in one of the papers, we will have to confront him and learn more of the truth. . . . A colt from Mabbie and Bay Swan; it might turn out well. . . ." His voice trailed off as sleep captured him.

Alex managed to savor the comfort of having him back beside her again before she, too, slept.

St. John spent only a few days at Wild Swan before he set off again, but this time Alex was with him as well as Boston, Jed Barlow, and one of the stablehands, and the horses—Swan, Black Swan, and Bay Swan, all entered in races at Washington. Freddy watched the parade leave, his dark face revealing nothing, but Alex could feel how much he wanted to go with them.

She was torn between excitement and apprehension; it was one thing to simply attend the races; it was quite another to have to watch one's own horses compete. On the first day of the three-day meet, Black Swan won in the mile heats against an inferior field, and on the second, she had to work harder but won again in two-mile heats. On the third day, Bay Swan finished second in the three-mile heats, unwilling to exert himself unduly despite the urging of his jockey.

St. John shook his head ruefully. "That horse has everything but the will to win. He is a very lazy fellow, and short of a cruel beating, I don't think he'll ever bestir himself. You know, I'm almost glad Beaker bred him to Mabbie; he may prove a better sire than racer." St. John did not feel too badly about the outcome of the race; he had done modestly well betting on Black Swan and had not risked anything on Bay Swan.

Alex had kept her eyes closed for most of Black Swan's first race, particularly because the mare was partially lathered before the race ever began, piqued over not being allowed to attack another horse that had ventured too close. By the second day, Alex had managed to watch at least part of the race. And when Bay Swan ran she watched the whole event with scarcely a qualm because she knew Bay Swan's lazy tendencies and, not expecting much of him, was not disappointed.

It was all child's play compared to witnessing Swan's attempt to win the four-mile heats. That was the major reason for their attendance at the meet. And time was running out. In the past year and in the present season, Swan and Black Swan had done well in establishing the standing of the Carringtons' Swan line, but proof of extraordinary worth remained, in the United States, the heroic distance. If Swan could assert himself there, particularly against Sir Archy's blood, mares would be brought from far afield to be bred to him.

Though Boston had watched the other races with them, he slipped away before the start of Swan's four-mile challenge. Win or lose, this was a special occasion that he wanted Alex and St. John to share without his interference. And for his own sake as well as theirs, he dearly hoped Swan would win. The more secure St. John and his sister were, the easier it would be for Boston to be on his way. He had not discussed it with Alex, but he was sure she suspected. She was too perceptive to miss the signs. Nonetheless, he dreaded making it official.

Alex was hardly aware that Boston was not with them, hardly noticed as wellwishers stopped at their vehicles for a few words. After all her control during the other races, she now found herself unraveling, breathing so quickly she felt faint. St. John had wagered heavily on this race, and that didn't make her feel any calmer.

"You can't help him run any faster by making yourself ill," St. John pointed out gently, seeing her pallor, and she relaxed a little under his concerned gaze. He was right; it was Swan who had to run the course, not she. She even managed to giggle at the sudden picture of herself galloping along with the horses.

Today, though the jockey was borrowed, the silks were the Carringtons' own, the vivid blue and green chosen by the children with much self-congratulatory laughter for their cleverness at combining the colors of their parents' eyes as well as the sea and the land wild swans flew over.

The first heat went so easily for Swan, Alex watched the whole thing with diminishing panic. Swan ran the mile course four times with ease, always keeping just ahead of the five other entries, even Sir Thomas, a big bay son of Sir Archy. And after a forty-five minute rest, Swan again stepped onto the course, looking as fresh as he had before. But this time, Sir Thomas edged him out by a nose after a tearing run down the homestretch.

St. John heard Alex's little mew of protest. "No, don't despair. The jockey is doing a good job with Swan. The race is going too fast; the jockey's trying to save Swan from himself." His voice hardened. "My suspicion is that the roan is being used to keep the pace too fast so that the big brown colt can win."

Alex looked at him inquiringly, needing more of an explanation.

"Sir Thomas and Swan are running honest races and obviously doing well. Barring breakdown or injury, it should continue to be a match between the two of them. But the pace has been very fast. The roan is what some call a 'rabbit,' put in to help another horse. He has forced it every mile, but I don't think he has the stamina to finish, let alone win, and any horse that doesn't win at least one out of three is not allowed to go on. I think the big brown colt has the endurance, but he's been laying back so far, conserving his energy though not allowing enough of a lag to be distanced. If what I guess is true, the roan will be out after this next heat while the brown takes it."

"Isn't that illegal?" Alex questioned, outraged that such a scheme should push Swan harder than need be.

"It is certainly against jockey club rules for any sort of agreement to be made between owners or jockeys, but in this case, how would one prove it? And remember, it is also against the rules for there to be betting on the premises, but I haven't noticed that that has dissuaded anyone." He was leaving the landau as he spoke, going to speak to their jockey.

The bright day lost its luster for Alex, and suddenly she just wanted the race to be over, win or lose, with Swan uninjured. St. John returned just before the third heat commenced. His face was grim.

"I've told him to go ahead and push Swan to win this one if the brown colt challenges. It's important that he not be allowed to stay in the race."

Alex dug her nails into the palms of her hands as the heat began. Sir Thomas and Swan were again in the lead, but this time the roan was visibly faltering, dropping back and finally trailing so far behind that he would be considered disqualified when the heat was over. And the brown colt started moving up in the third mile and was at Swan's tail by the time the final mile commenced. Just that slightly slower pace the brown had been able to enjoy in the previous heats was enough to give him an edge of energy now, and Alex could see Swan beginning to labor in his effort to pull further ahead of the brown as both of them passed Sir Thomas.

"Come on, Swan, come on now, you can do it, you can win." She murmured the words over and over without knowing, and then she was urging Sir Thomas on as well, as he seemed to take offense at being passed by the brown interloper and found his own burst of speed. They approached the finish in a tight wedge of pounding muscle, but it was Swan and Sir Thomas who finished first and second, thus disqualifying all the others who had won no heats out of the three run.

Alex barely kept herself from tumbling out of the carriage as she rose to cheer with the rest of the onlookers, and her praise was as much for Sir Thomas as for Swan.

St. John knew there would be no way to dissuade her from joining him in going to see the condition of their horse, so he found a young man to mind their carriage.

Alex gasped when she saw how exhausted Swan was. His head hung down as he stumbled along, cooling out at a walk. He was blanketed, but even the hair of his neck and head lay in wet whorls.

"Oh, my God, Sinje, how can he possibly run any more?"

"Sweetheart, Sir Thomas is as weary as he." He gestured to where the other horse was receiving the same attention. "It is why it is called the 'heroic distance.' And I believe Swan can win. But bet or no, I'll forfeit if you want him out of the race." St. John was acknowledging her as more than an equal partner; he was giving her the means to change their future.

She considered the option and the consequences for a long moment. It would spare Swan for the day, but in all other ways, it would be destructive. Swan had been bred and raised to race, and he was today showing exactly how fine and valuable his bloodline was, a bloodline that could be continued in other horses. "He races," she said softly, and before they went back to the landau, she went to Swan.

He blew softly at her and stretched his lips in a funny welcoming gesture as he recognized her. "You can do it, love. Take this one, and you've won the day and so much more," she whispered.

Swan, in his usual way when not actually racing, was so calm, he looked too lazy to run. Stealing another look at Sir Thomas, Alex saw that he was sidling clumsily in crazed weariness, making it difficult for his grooms to get him cooled out as he wasted precious energy.

The crowd was highly appreciative now of the contest they were witnessing. This was proof of greatness, and there was added interest as they were calling Swan the "English horse" and betting heavily against him.

Only by the rigid set of his jaw did St. John betray how much this heat meant to him, and Alex hoped she appeared as collected. Friends came by to wish them well, but still she felt very much as if it were just the two of them alone in the big crowd. Swan had pushed the speed in the last heat to beat the brown colt; now it was imperative that he win again rather than having to run yet another four miles.

Despite the distance they had already run, they started fast, neither horse giving ground to the other, and by the third lap they were both being ridden under the whip. Alex winced at the thought of it coming down on Swan's hide even though she could see that the jockey was skillful enough to be using the whip more to keep the horse into top speed than to hurt him. Neck and neck they came down the homestretch, both of them showing the effects of the long contest in strides that were no longer smooth. For an instant, Swan veered dangerously, but his tired jockey checked him in time to keep him on the course. The wasted motion had cost him dearly; there was now visible distance between the two with Sir Thomas ahead.

Alex wanted to close her eyes, but she made herself watch, and she saw Swan suddenly leap forward in a final burst of speed as he closed the distance and then finished nearly a full body length in front of his opponent.

Even though many had wagered against the English entry, the crowd went wild over the courageous finish, clapping and cheering. Alex turned her face into St. John's chest and rested against him, trembling violently.

Her bonnet had been knocked askew, and St. John pushed it further back and then tilted her face up so he could see it. Taking his time about it, he kissed her until a warm blush colored her cheeks.

"I'm not sure I could survive many days like this one," she confessed.

"No day will ever be quite like this one again," St. John remarked with sudden gravity. "How far we and Swan have come! You must send word to your grandmother; she has much to do with this."

Alex felt an enormous well of gratitude for his recognition of that fact. "Indeed she did. But it has been your dream all along, and it was you who brought Leda home."

She found it fitting that their first big victory should be won in the city on the shores of the Potomac; some said the Indian word meant "River of the Swans."

It seemed as if they had stepped into a charmed circle with that victory. At the Canton Course in Baltimore, their horses again triumphed, even Bay Swan who seemed to take a sudden interest in the business at hand and bestirred himself enough to win heats at three miles. But again it was Swan who drew the most attention with his speed and endurance in the four-mile contest.

They stayed with Pen and Caleb, and the Jenningses were particularly happy to see them, as it was their first chance to show off the newest addition to the family, Blake Jennings, born in early May. He was a beautiful and good-natured baby; Caleb, trying to keep a straight face, claimed these were specifically Jennings traits.

They did not see the Falconers. Rane was gone on one of his ships on a run to the West Indies, Caleb admitted to Alex when she pressed him, and the news of Claire was not good. She had retreated further into the mad recesses of her mind lately and was virtually imprisoned, guarded day and night by well-paid companions.

When Pen inquired about Boston, who had not come with them, it brought its own sorrow. "He has not said anything outright, but I am quite sure he will be on his way soon. He does not mean to settle with us permanently, or even in Maryland." She heard the resignation in her own voice and knew the reason for Pen's puzzled look.

"There, I've said it aloud and calmly, too. And I find I do not mind as much as I once did, though I know it will be very hard indeed to see him go."

"It is still the promise of this country that young men can find their own way to new lives," Pen suggested gently. "And from what I have seen of your brother, he has his own quiet strength and an easy manner with people. I think he will do well in whatever he chooses."

Having discussed it openly with Pen made it easier for

Alex when Boston finally spoke to her and St. John, though there was no doubt it was difficult for Boston himself.

"St. John, you and Alex have been wonderful to me, and the children seem like my own. All of you brought me through a dark time in my life when I lost Dora and nothing seemed to matter. And without you, I would never have come to this country. But now I want to see more of it. And you have such good people working for you, I don't fear that my going will cause great inconvenience."

He twisted his hands in a sudden nervous gesture. "I wish I could explain what draws me to see more of this land. It is almost like talking about a lover, hard to do without sounding too foolish and indulgent. I do see many things wrong here. A country that established itself in the name of liberty has a huge slave market in its capital city. A country which preaches equality of rights for every man seems engaged in a policy of moving the native population forever from their ancestral lands. And in the name of making one's way, every sort of sharp practice is employed. And yet, the land is so vast and so varied! I have seen land completely different from this further to the south, and I have heard tales of huge mountains and valleys where wild creatures still roam in abundance. I want to see it all! I want to hear the different ways of speaking and know the different ways of thinking. I want to wander while I still have the strength and youth to do it. If this nation does not run aground on its differences, I think it will one day be greater even than England." When he finished, his cheeks were as flushed as if he had indeed been speaking of a love, and his eyes implored them to understand.

St. John got up and went to his brother-in-law. "Boston, I could not care more for you were you my own brother. In fact, you are far dearer to me than those of my own blood. And you have been of great value to your sister and me. To you we will always owe much for the help you have given so freely in the work of establishing our new life here. Send word of your progress when you can. I wish you every success in your travels." He put his hand out, and gratefully Boston took it.

St. John left them, casting one glance at Alex that told her he trusted her not to be too hard on her brother.

Boston and Alex faced each other, and Alex saw all the

kindness he had meant in her life, the fine man he had become, and over it all, the face of her grandmother when Virginia had relinquished all her own claims of love and need to send them away from her.

"I have dreaded this day for so long, and now I find the dreading was worse than the reality." Alex was happy to see his face relax with her admission. "What an eloquent man you have become, Boston Thaine. Not just my brother, but someone quite apart and very special. And how can I blame you, for the Thaine blood that has set men to wandering, at least one in every generation, and surely the women, too, for here I am so far from where I was born. It is as Sinje said, you have already done so much for us; we would not be so well settled had you not been here to work with us and for us. Now I hope you find your own life, wherever it waits for you. But one thing I must know. Is it all true, this love you profess for this country? It is not a kind deceit to cover a need to escape from me?"

The question shimmered between them for an instant, and then Boston took her in his arms, hugging her tightly. "I love you, Lexy, and I'm proud of you for all the strength you've shown in building your own life. It is just that I need to do the same now. It has nothing to do with you."

All the things unsaid. He didn't want confirmation of what he suspected. He knew it had nothing to do with her life now. She realized that sometimes less than the truth acknowledged was better for all concerned, and the impulse to tell him all that had happened, to justify what she had done so long ago, died. His use of his old pet name for her told her the depth of his need that she remain as he wanted her to be in his mind. She stepped back, fixing her thoughts on practical matters and promising herself she would not cry.

"How shall you manage?" She knew he had inherited a small sum from their father just as she had and that he had probably saved at least some of the money they had paid him for his work, but his savings would not last forever.

He smiled widely, glad to be away from dangerous ground. "I paid more attention than you might have guessed to the leather goods Father sold. And I have become quite a hand at repairing saddlery. I liked the smell of good leather and the texture of it even when I was a small boy. With a few basic tools, I can make myself useful almost anywhere. Even these self-reliant Americans have some tasks better done by an expert, which is, of course, how I will present myself—Boston Thaine, Esquire, English leather specialist, repairing and refurbishing. I think I might even be able to fashion a fair pair of gloves were it necessary."

Alex giggled, suddenly enchanted by the picture of her brother as a traveling huckster.

"Ah, madam, you laugh! But being with the Carringtons has been an education in all manner of practical tasks." He sobered again. "Alex, how proud Grandmother would be if she could see how well all the things she taught you have been put to use."

"I am grateful to her every day," Alex said. "Will you write to her of your travels or should I?"

"As poor a correspondent as I am, still I will do it. And I promise I will send word to you now and again, but do not fret if some time passes without, for I plan to be in places where the post is probably very primitive." His eyes glittered with the vision of those wild vistas, and Alex knew that having decided to go, he was in a sense already on his way.

"Will you take one of our horses? You'll have need of a good mount."

"As soon as I would steal one of your children," he answered promptly. "For you or St. John, such a mount is a necessity; for me, despite all I've learnt about them, a Thoroughbred would be a liability. If it got so much as a bruised foot, I would feel unbearable guilt. Better for me to go from one dependable nag to the next."

Alex did not press him; the new Boston was a man who knew what he wanted and what he did not. "Do you ever think of returning to England?"

"I used to, but after Father died, it was as if I turned in another direction. I would have liked to see Grandmother again, but that's all. And you?"

"Only when I am feeling extremely cowardly," she confessed. "And then I remember how it really was for me at Gravesend. You, Grandmother, and St. John were the only ones who made it bearable, and then Timothy and Mavis, and save for Grandmother, all of you are here. Even with you wandering, I will know you are somewhere in the same land as I." Her voice was still steady, and the two of them talked companionably until very late, but when Alex slipped into bed beside St. John, the tears began to pour down her cheeks despite her efforts to prevent them. St. John awakened and wordlessly drew her close.

"I didn't cr . . . cry in front of him," Alex sniffed.

St. John did not try to comfort her with meaningless words, he just held her, his arm strong across her back, his warmth and the heated air of the June night gradually banishing the chill from her flesh.

He was beside her as she saw Boston off with a smile and a kiss for good luck. The children took their lead from her, and in any case, they were accustomed to their uncle's comings and goings and had not grasped the fact that it might be a very long time before they saw him again, if ever. Alex and St. John made no point of it. And one of the ways Alex got through the leave-taking was to pretend that the parting was just for a little while.

❧ Chapter 45 ❧

On July 4, 1826, fifty years to the day after the adoption of the Declaration of Independence, John Adams, the second president, and Thomas Jefferson, the third president, died. Though the former was from New England and the latter from Virginia, and though they had been political rivals, in their youth they had both helped create the Declaration. Old age had mellowed their animosity somewhat, and death was surely the final equalizer. It was rumored that shortly before his passing, Adams had said, "Jefferson still lives," with wry determination to outlive his old rival, having no way of knowing that Jefferson had died earlier in the day. When the news of the two deaths got about, the country not only mourned, it seemed to reflect as well that its childhood was over.

Alex and St. John were not touched in the same way the Americans were, and yet, the strange coincidence of the two men dying on the same Independence Day was enough to give anyone pause. And Alex was intrigued by what she learned of Jefferson in particular.

He had been an extremely erudite man whose intelligence seemed to have had no limits. Music, literature, history, the arts and sciences, all interested him, and nothing was too insignificant for his attention. He had moved easily from such grandiose projects as the idea of a classical look for the government buildings of Washington to such minutiae as which fruits, vegetables, and flowers would yield the best produce from his Monticello acres in Virginia. And yet the fatal flaw of the republic was also his own. It was no secret that he had grave doubts about slavery, but he had also owned slaves, and Alex had heard that he had had a black slave mistress of whom he was very fond.

She tried to explain to St. John why that so distressed her. "Don't you see, if a man of such stature could not solve his own dilemma, what hope is there for a country comprised of so many lesser mortals?"

St. John was not as given to abstract considerations as she was, but this was a problem he well recognized as being crucial to the future of the country and to their own. "I fear that history shows people and thus countries do not learn the harder lessons until forced to it. Consider how England lost her colonies here; there were warnings aplenty that things must change steadily or else would be overturned radically. France, too, has suffered the same kind of storm. Whatever slavery and sectional differences there are will be resolved in time. . . ." His voice trailed away and Alex knew he was seeing the same awful vision she was—all the promise of a nation born in defiance of tyranny breaking apart violently because of the tyranny within.

"It is selfish, I know, but I hope it does not happen in my lifetime, nor in that of our children," Alex murmured.

"But generation follows generation, and there is no escape," St. John observed sadly.

Both of them were too aware of the growing conflict between the pro- and antislavery factions. The year before eight Northern state legislatures had proposed that all slaves be freed with the federal government paying the owners. The Southern states had flatly rejected the idea. And now Pennsylvania was passing a law that would largely nullify the Fugitive Slave Act of 1793 by making kidnapping a crime. It might indeed prevent state officials from participating in slave catching, but it would surely not stop the private agents paid for that purpose. Little skirmishes back and forth, little skirmishes that could too easily lead to bigger battles in the future.

As if the other shoe had dropped, it was a horrible sort of relief when Alex found the notice in the *National Intelligencer*, printed in Washington and widely circulated:

100 DOLLARS REWARD—RAN AWAY from Floralgate near Savannah County, Georgia in Oct. 1825, a negro man named **THOMAS.** He is about 31 or 32 years of age, very big, 6 feet 3 or 4 inches high, dark brown, with a tooth missing near low front, scars on wrists, ankles, back, right cheek, and part of right earlobe missing from punishments for past disobedience. Had on when he went away rough brown pantaloons and coat, old hat. He is an excellent horseman and blacksmith, and may endeavor to get employment in those ways. I suspect he has worked his way north of this state by searching out fine horseflesh. All are cautioned against employing him at their peril as he can be of violent temper. He speaks slowly and clearly and does not drop his eyes. 50 Dollars will be given for apprehending and securing said negro in jail so that I can get him again. If brought here to me, 100 Dollars and all reasonable charges.

WILLARD D. HUTCHINS

Without comment, Alex handed the advertisement to St. John.

"There's no doubt, he and Freddy are the same man," he said flatly. "Do you want me to talk to him?"

She shook her head. "No. I hired him, and I knew even then. It's up to me."

Taking the paper with her, she sought out Freddy, making sure no one else was in earshot. No task was too small for his attention; at this moment he was carefully oiling the leather of a little halter used for the foals' first lessons. But he put the work down and stood when she approached.

"Freddy, I don't believe you can read, can you?" she asked gently.

"No, Miz Alex, I doan be readin'," he agreed politely, but she caught the flicker of apprehension in his eyes as he saw the newspaper.

Word for word she read the advertisement, and when she had finished, an awful silence enshrouded them, seeming to block out even the normal sounds of the stables until Freddy spoke.

"You gib me time to move on or you turn me in? I done save mos' all de money you pays me. I gib you dat fo' ma own ree-ward."

"Oh, do stop! I can't bear it! I would never on this earth turn a slave back to his master, let alone you who have worked so hard for Wild Swan. It is just a matter of deciding what to do next. I've known since the beginning that you are a runaway; your papers do not exactly fit. But now I know that it is this Hutchins creature who is searching for you, and he has guessed correctly that you would find work with horses on your northward progress. Other people will have read this, and Hutchins has undoubtedly advertised elsewhere as well these past months; it can only grow more dangerous for you. I do not understand why you haven't gone on to a safer place, even to Canada. Was it a matter of not being able to get through?"

Freddy shook his head, finding it difficult to speak, overwhelmed by her concern. "I doan try. I gots reasons fo' not goin' furder. I be sorry, but I doan be tellin' you why." He was clearly miserable at the decision, but determined to stick by it. "Mo' dan anythin' in dis worl' I be wantin' to be here, but dat make trouble fo' you. Bes' I be on ma way. But I thanks you fo' all you done fo' me."

He turned away, but not before Alex saw the gleam of tears in his eyes. A shudder moved the massive shoulders, and then they were still. Alex could not bear his vulnerability.

She supposed the decision had been made the day she had hired him or even before, at the time when she had faced her full aversion to the institution of slavery. It was not enough to hate it in theory while compromising in so many small ways; sooner or later a stand had to be made, even when it was against the law of the region.

"Freddy, Thomas, . . . Oh, I don't even know what to call you now! But if you wish to stay here, stay you shall. I know there are problems; you will have to be very careful around the horse owners when they visit, and you won't be able to go to the race courses, but we've known that all along. St. John knows of your situation as well as I. There may come a time when we cannot protect you, but if you wish to risk it, I would very much like you to remain with us."

He turned back to her, and now tears overflowed and left glistening trails on his dark skin. His hands worked helplessly as he fought to find the words.

Alex reached out and took one of his huge hands in both of hers, patting it as she would to comfort one of the children. "There, there, you mustn't think it is all onesided. You are the finest trainer St. John and I have ever seen. Because of you, our horses will win far more than they would have otherwise. And it is not only that. The children adore you, and for good reason. You teach them so much about the earth, things like my grandmother taught me in England. You will stay?"

"I stay. Someday I mebbe hab to go 'tend to some business, but dis ma home." He paused and then announced. "Freddy, dat was de name of a man I tries to help. He lib on his own patch of land, an' he let me stay fo' a time, but he done cuts his foot real bad an' gets de stiffen'n sickness. Can't do nuthin' fo' him an' he die. But he gib me his papers 'cause we looks somethin' de same. Guess not enough de same. An' Thomas, dat ma slabe name, gib me by de massa. Ma real name gib to me by ma mama is 'Samson' 'cause she want me to grow up strong like de man in de Bible."

Alex beamed at him. "Samson! It is a perfect name for you. I think I will rechristen you so that it may be used here. Is that all right?"

"Dat's right fine!" Samson's shoulders straightened and broadened before her eyes. It was as if strength indeed came from the fable and from the name given him by his own mother, rather than by his white slave master.

"Mista Carrington," (he still had to remind himself it was "mister" not "master"), "he say yes to dis?" He asked the question, but his faith in Alex was so boundless, he did not doubt that she would somehow make it right.

"It's fine with him," she said firmly and was inwardly resolved to make it so.

St. John was less resistant than she had thought he would be. He studied her set face. "I haven't even objected yet, but you are ready to do battle, aren't you? I presume you have thought what the consequences might be. It was one thing to suspect it; it is quite another to see the notice demanding his return."

"The consequence of letting him stay I can face. The consequence of turning him out or giving him back I could not live with for so much as an instant, let alone the rest of my life."

"Nor, I fear, could I," St. John agreed. "It is as you once said: it is all a hazard in any case. But I think a vague suggestion that I bought him and gave him his freedom might be in order if there are too many inquiries from locals who might wonder about his presence."

Alex threw her arms around him and rained kisses all over his face until he was laughing with the exuberance of her attack. He could have given her no more precious gift than his own involvement.

The renaming was as smoothly done as a Christmas play. Alex saw Samson lifting a heavy load of feed, and she observed, "Why, you should have been called 'Samson,'" in the clear hearing of the children, who immediately took to the idea and danced around the big man giggling and calling him by his new name. To them, he had become a dark-visaged god who lightened their days with wisdom and a special kind of rough tenderness they received from no one else.

"Suits dis man jus' fine." He laughed, a deep rumbling of pure joy, and Freddy disappeared; it was to be hoped that he took Thomas with him.

All of them watched over the horses, but it was Samson who sensed the slightest change in any of the animals. The grass of summer was keeping the horses fit with little additional feeding, but as autumn approached, Samson put the ones who would race back into training, giving them from eight to twelve quarts of oats a day, depending on their needs, and putting them through their paces with a keen eye to any sign of their strides being off. He worked the Barlow boys as well. They were to go to some of the fall meetings with St. John in order to see real races run, and Samson thought there was a chance that Jim would be ready to ride, though he was only twelve years old.

It was a busy season with full crops of everything from grain to fruit being harvested, and after the fact, Alex found she had not been paying as close attention to the children as she thought.

"Have we adopted a child?" St. John asked her one morning as they prepared to go about their separate tasks.

She regarded him blankly. "What are you talking about?"

"About someone named 'Sam' who seems to have joined the ranks of our young army, and it isn't Samson."

Alex thought a minute, suddenly putting together sessions of whispers and giggles that had afflicted the children lately and remembering Nigel's comment about "telling Sam." Morgan had eyed him fiercely and reminded him that one did not tell things to invisible people.

"I presume you mean the invisible companion they seem to have acquired for the summer, as if the four of them plus the Barlow brood aren't enough."

St. John's eyes were twinkling now. "Actually, I think this person is quite substantial, if the flash of arms and legs I saw is anything to go on. He, she, or it was waiting for them at the edge of the wood as they went off."

Alex considered additional evidence. Nigel, who could be a very picky eater, had not been lately. In fact, all of them had seemed to consume whatever was put before them much more readily than before. Now she suspected they had established a provisioning system for their secret friend. Undoubtedly, this unfortunate had been plied with mounds of various vegetables that were not the Carrington children's favorites. She hoped her offspring had been generous enough to include more tempting fare as well.

"The more I consider it, the more I believe you're right. Dear lord! I am not nearly as careful a mother as I thought."

They burst out laughing at the same time, mutually amused by their children's adventure. When she could draw a breath again, Alex wiped her eyes and said, "We really must do something about it. Someone must be missing a child."

"Not very much, or else we would surely have heard," St. John pointed out. "After all, we've let the children run rather freely these past few weeks. Maybe someone else has done the same."

They had decided the children should have time out of training just as the horses did, and though they were still responsible for chores, lessons with Mr. Whittleby had been suspended for two months. The tutor had been as enthusiastic as the children, though he had tried not to appear so. Dr. Cameron, who had gotten on well with St. John from the first meeting and who visited now and then, had insisted with great seriousness that playing probably taught children as much as books did.

"That's an odd idea for a hard-working Scot," Alex had teased.

"Ah, but I was very good at playing, too," he announced, his solemnity ruined by the twinkle in his eyes.

Alex and St. John went together in search of the elusive Sam. There was a place in the woods where the water ran through that Alex knew was a favored haunt on hot summer days, and she and St. John heard the voices long before they saw the brood—their four, the Barlow four, and the stranger.

Sam was a very grubby little girl. Her brown hair in two straggling and uneven braids was shot with golden-red highlights. There was a smear of dirt across her straight little nose and on one rounded cheek. Her eyes, a light-filled combination of green, brown, and gold, were huge and startled as she caught sight of the interlopers. All the children froze in place.

Alex fell in love at first sight. She wanted to take the child in her arms and just hold her. She could not have explained how she knew, but she had no doubt that this was a child as devoid of mother love as she herself had been. It was not the tattered appearance—any child could get dirty and disheveled in hard play—it was something quite apart from that. It was the way the child quickly recovered from her surprise and drew into herself, holding her small form rigidly erect, her face suddenly closed and watchful, strangely adult.

"How do you do?" Alex said politely. "I am Alex Carrington, and this is my husband, St. John."

The child blinked at her, considering this offer with visible suspicion. Alex heard Morgan whisper, "Mama's really very nice, and Papa, too," and his word seemed to carry weight as the child gave a funny little curtsy and said, "My name is Samantha Elisa Sheldon-Burke, but I like just plain Sam better." No more information was forthcoming.

"Do your parents know where you are?" St. John asked gently.

"They don't care as long as I don't get into trouble." The absolute honesty of it struck at Alex's heart; she remembered carrying the same knowledge of her own mother's lack of concern.

"And I'm not supposed to bother the neighbors," Samantha added with grudging honesty, and it was clear why her presence had been kept secret.

"Well, you certainly haven't done that," St. John commented with a smile. "Until this morning we thought you were invisible."

Sam considered this for a moment, and then she laughed, revealing new front teeth not quite grown in. The merry sound pealed through the small glade, and the other children joined in, energy added by their relief at no longer having to keep the secret and at discovering that they were not to be punished for it.

Gloom descended when Alex informed them that Samantha's parents really had to be told where their daughter was spending her days. "But we'll tell them that it is fine with us if she visits, and if they give their permission, nothing need change."

The children could not dispute the justice of this, and Alex and St. John could see no reason to delay, so they set out at once on horseback for Brookhaven, the Sheldon-Burke plantation. They did not take the child with them. As Alex said to her husband, "At least she'll have one more day in case her parents refuse permission."

Brookhaven was a good four miles from Wild Swan; it said a great deal about Samantha's tenacity that she made the trip so regularly on foot and back again.

"No wonder she's such a sturdily built little thing," St. John remarked.

Though a change from tobacco to grain was obviously in process at Brookhaven, it showed the decline of former glories in a slightly unkempt look, and there did not seem to be many workers on hand.

Nevertheless, they were greeted politely enough by an old black houseman and shown into an airy room to await Mrs. Sheldon-Burke. Far away, Alex heard the wail of a baby and wondered if it was a brother or sister of Samantha or the child of a servant.

Not just Mrs. Sheldon-Burke but her husband also came to greet them, and Alex was instantly struck by the fact that while Samantha had a vague look of her father in the reddish tint of her hair and the hazel of her eyes, there was no resemblance to the woman before her with the flower petal skin and the ebony hair. Despite the heat of the day, Mrs. Sheldon-Burke was wearing a heavy and elaborate morning dress of a blue to match her eyes, the eyes that flickered over Alex and made an immediate and derogatory judgment about the simple riding habit Alex was wearing. Alex kept her own expression blandly genial; she did not want to ruin Sam's chances. Alex was already becoming familiar with this breed of female—exquisitely soft on the outside, cold metal beneath. She appeared to be in her midtwenties, her husband not yet thirty.

After introductions had been made, St. John took charge in his most courtly manner.

"I do hope you will pardon us for calling on you without prior warning. It is not something we would normally do, but we seem to have acquired an extra child, your daughter, Samantha. And we wanted to make certain you were not worried about her."

Mrs. Sheldon-Burke's moue of impatience and distaste said worlds about how she regarded the child, though it was her husband who spoke.

"I do apologize. Samantha does wander off and finds more than her share of trouble. Since her pony has not been out, I assumed she had not been going far. But I believe you have the old Bladen place, a good distance from here. I will make certain it does not happen again." There was no particular anger in his voice, but there was no special concern either.

"Please, that's not at all what we meant!" Alex protested. "We would be glad to have Samantha spend time with us. You see, we have four children, but only one girl, and I would very much like to have Flora know another girl, even though there are a few years between them. Flora is eleven."

Whatever the man thought about the plan, his wife looked as if she'd just been given a gift. "Samantha is eight, and a very difficult child, but if you truly don't mind her being with your children, we would be very grateful." She sighed and smiled sadly. "Samantha is from my husband's first marriage; her mother died in childbirth, poor dear. But now we have two little babies of our own, a boy and a girl, and Samantha just doesn't seem to fit in. I fear it is often so with stepchildren." Her voice carried the soft cultured sound of tidewater Virginia.

Neither Alex nor St. John felt obligated to inform the woman that Alex, too, had stepchildren. Alex felt physically ill watching the woman's posturing and her husband's doting response; the man was obviously besotted with the woman to the detriment of his daughter.

St. John, his smile a trifle fixed, made the motions of leaving. "Then it is settled. And though the children are having no lessons at the moment, when their tutor returns, your daughter is welcome to join them in their lessons as well."

Mr. Sheldon-Burke thanked them quite warmly, following his wife's lead and finding his own relief in the plan. "It really has been difficult for Lydia," he confided to the Carringtons, as he saw them on their way. "She and Samantha don't get along at all. You must, of course, inform me if my daughter proves to be a problem."

"Of course," Alex replied, knowing she would never do any such thing.

She and St. John rode in silence for some time; then St. John drew several deep breaths as if he were trying to clear his lungs of any air that might have been left from the visit to Brookhaven. "They made me realize more clearly than ever before how truly harmful your mother was to you."

"But I had Grandmother and in another way, you and Boston, to show me affection. Sam seems to have no one there."

"She has someone now, several someones in fact."

When the children were told of the now official sanction of their friendship, they went wild with the victory except for Sam herself, who stood absolutely still for a moment gazing at Alex and St. John, her eyes shining with near worship, her smile wide.

Though it was hardly the name for a little girl, Samantha remained "Sam," liking her nickname even more when she discovered that Alex, too, had a longer name that was seldom used. There was no confusion with Samson as no one ever shortened his name; it would have been overly familiar to do so, for he was a man of great dignity.

Sometimes it seemed to Alex that Sam had always been with them. She was not a substitute for the longed-for daughter; rather it was as if she fit right into a special place that had been reserved for her. Contrary to her parents' predictions of difficulty, Sam did everything she could to make sure she would not lose her welcome, pitching in with the chores and treating all adults with such painstaking and anxious courtesy that Alex finally had a talk with her.

"Sam, I appreciate everything you do to help at Wild Swan, and I expect you to go on helping, just like the rest of the children. But I don't want you to think that that is the only reason we like having you here. We love you just for you, just because you are, not for the things you do. Do you understand?"

Sam gazed at her wordlessly, her eyes huge. "My new mama doesn't like me at all, but now that's all right," she said, and then the tears came despite her efforts to hold them back.

Alex drew her into her arms and held her tightly, rocking her back and forth. "It's all right indeed, sweetling, and everyone cries sometimes. There will always be people here to love you." She knew it would never fully make up for the coldness in Sam's own family, but at least she would never feel alone again.

Suddenly Alex could hear Gweneth Falconer saying almost the same words to her that she had just said to Sam. She had an eerie sense of the love from Gweneth passing from her to Sam, as if once given, the gift continued to flow from one generation in need to the next.

❧ Chapter 46 ❧

The autumn brought an increased flurry of activity as last harvests were brought in, though in Maryland's climate where winters were not as brutal as further north, some vegetables could be raised during the cold months and others started under glass and put out early.

Classes for the children began again, and Sam proved to be woefully uneducated compared to the Carrington children. Morgan received a bloody nose for unchivalrously pointing out this fact. Sam gave as good as she got among the children, and in this case, Morgan conceded that he probably deserved it.

Sam's mind was as quick as her fists, and Mr. Whittleby was pleased to report that she was rapidly catching up. She treated this experience as she did everything at Wild Swan—with wide-eyed enthusiasm. Having access to so many books was to her something akin to magic, and even better to her mind were the lessons from Alex on everything from managing an estate to brewing simples. The stillroom was her favorite place, the smell of drying plants the headiest perfume.

Flora had shown no interest in such matters, and she showed none now. She was not jealous of Sam, whom she regarded more as another brother than any sort of competition. It was just as well, but Alex did wish her eldest had the will to learn Virginia's legacy. There was no use in trying to force it on anyone who was unwilling; too much depended on keen attention and a great deal of caring. It was to her advantage that the Sheldon-Burkes had so forsaken Sam, but she still felt a start of anger when she saw Sam arriving unescorted on her pony, the transportation now allowed since the visits were out in the open. Alex made sure someone at least went most of the way home with the child as the daylight shortened.

No matter what other activities the change of season brought, the fall race meetings were the most important, with the horses from Wild Swan already entered in various races from Maryland to South Carolina. There was irony in their spring successes—very few would want to wager against Swan or Black Swan, so little added income would come from that quarter. If they continued to win, their worth would be in the breeding. Bay Swan was another matter, but St. John had no intention of risking large sums on him. In a poor field, he was competent, but his innate laziness was not to be trusted. Mabbie's bay colt, Oberon, was an unknown quantity, but they had decided to test him this fall as a three-year-old rather than wait for the added strength of his next year's growth. In his trial runs, he had proved to be very fast, worthy of the Sir Archy blood he carried, but no one could predict how he would do at a formal race meeting. Though he tended to be excitable and to lather before he ran, once he was racing, he was tractable and businesslike. One horse with Black Swan's mean temper was enough, but much to Samson's pleasure, Jim Barlow had proven himself adept at keeping her aggressive tendencies under control. Black Swan seemed to pay more attention to Jim than to anyone else, and that was all to the good, as he was to ride her.

It would never be easy for Samson to see his charges leave without him. But it was a necessity, and he respected St. John's knowledge of horses and to a lesser degree, Jed Barlow's. Jed had been learning from Samson, and he did so willingly and without prejudice, but blood horses were new in his experience. It would be some time before he possessed true expertise. But he was calm, steady, and hard working, exactly the sort of help St. John needed now that Boston was gone.

It was sad and odd to be commencing the racing season without Boston. But in the two messages the Carringtons had received from him, it was clear that he was having a marvelous time. He had drifted far south but was now contemplating heading west. It was frustrating that he did not write more often and at greater length, but even the descriptions he had sent so far were ablaze with the wonders he was seeing:

*New Orleans might well be another country, so for-
eign is it with a strangely mixed populace of French,
German, Spanish, and English speaking peoples who
have little to do with each other. Gaming of all sorts is
popular, horse racing, too, though the Creoles, as the
descendants of the first French settlers are called, have
little to do with it, leaving it to rougher folk.*

*There are many slaves here but also those of mixed
blood, particularly quadroon women of exotic demeanor who are guarded by fierce chaperones until a
bargain is made with a protector; I cannot think of a
more delicate way to explain.*

*The river traffic on the Mississippi is ever compelling;
I believe my wandering will follow the river soon.*

Alex particularly missed her brother when she and St.
John took the children to the races; she knew Boston
would have enjoyed the day with them. In order to make
it more palatable for the other children that the two older
Barlow boys would be on the racing circuit, the rest were
taken on a special outing to Washington City to see the
races there. Alex and St. John chose the opening day with
its one- and two-mile heats, not only because the crowds
would be less but because they decided witnessing the
grueling three- and four-mile races, so different from training sessions, could wait for another time.

They left before dawn, a cavalcade of horses and people,
the children loaded in a wagon with Jed Barlow at the
reins. Sam went with them, and Alex doubted the child
had slept at all the night before. She had had permission
to stay over at Wild Swan so as not to miss the early
departure. Though Alex had learned that the slaves at
Brookhaven were kind enough to Sam and ever indulgent,
there was no one specifically concerned with her welfare.
She doubted that anyone there ever so much as looked
closely at the child. Sam's usual apparel was a succession
of worn smocks that served well enough for the hard play
she enjoyed and shoes that were more off than on as long
as it was not too cold. But today she was wearing what
was presumably her best, an extremely ill-fitting dress in
mustard yellow with droopy pantalettes underneath. Only
her hair, braided for her by Alex, looked neat.

No one at her home seemed to have noticed that Sam was growing, changing from the round little shape Alex had first seen to a skinny slip of a child. Alex would have been willing to bet a substantial sum that Sam was going to be a stunning woman someday, once she'd gotten through all the gawky states and grown into her strangely adult face. But for now she had absolutely no awareness of her appeal and had admired Flora's dress without a trace of envy or the thought that she herself might have been better dressed.

Alex had seen Morgan's quick frown at the ugly dress, but to her relief, he had said nothing. Sam was the friend of all the children, but Morgan seemed to have appointed himself her special guardian and watched over her much as Blaine did over Flora, sometimes to the point of sharpness when he thought she was behaving too recklessly, a privilege he reserved for himself. Sam, for her part, was more patient by the day with this interference, seldom roused to retaliation unless Morgan was being intolerably overbearing.

It was a long, tiring, and blissful day for all of them. The children were awed by their first sight of the capital and found it fine indeed. The traffic on the Potomac enthralled them, and seeing Oberon win his maiden race in two-mile heats was almost more excitement than they could bear. Jim Barlow rode the young horse with skill far beyond his years; Samson had schooled both the horse and the boy to perfection.

The children were so content with the day they'd had, they did not even protest when they were loaded into the wagon for Jed to take them back to Wild Swan in the afternoon.

"This is the very best day I have ever had in my whole life!" Sam proclaimed with utter conviction. "Thank you, Mr. and Mrs. Carrington."

Alex stayed in Washington with St. John, one of the stablehands, the horses, and Jim and Georgy Barlow, and Jed rejoined them the next day for the two remaining days of the meet.

Bay Swan ran a disappointing third in his race, but Black Swan won the three-mile heats, and on the final day, Swan once again won the Proprietor's Purse at four miles, this time with much of the crowd cheering him on. They did not allow Jim to ride in either race; the following season would be time enough to tax his strength at the longer distances.

Now when people asked about breeding their mares to Swan, they were told he would be standing at stud from February to June, fifty dollars to breed, seventy to insure. The first bookings were arranged, and as the season progressed, Swan continued to win and to remain sound, and more mares were scheduled to be brought to him despite the high price. Alex went to Baltimore to see him win there and later received word from St. John of his various other victories further south. Black Swan, too, was doing her part for their fame, and most encouraging of all, Oberon was quickly making a name for himself, though he had not yet been tested at the longer distances and would not be until the following year. Bay Swan, due to his poor record the previous season, was left at home.

In October, there were two more sectional contests held at the Union Course, Long Island. In the first, Ariel, a gray mare foaled in 1822 out of Young Empress by American Eclipse, beat the Southern entry, W. R. Johnson's colt, Lafayette. But in the second, Ariel was beaten by Flirtilla, a bay mare foaled in 1820 by Robin Mare out of Sir Archy. Nonetheless, Mr. Johnson knew the value of Ariel and brought her south with him.

Though Alex could not help but be interested in the results of these races, the sectional rivalry involved still did not sit easily with her, and she wished the races could be run on some other basis.

The December party at the Jenningses' house in Annapolis was particularly festive this year because it had been such a good year for both Jennings families and the Carringtons, and they enjoyed celebrating together. The only unease came from the Falconers' presence, though Claire seemed once again in some control of herself.

In some ways, being with the Falconers had grown easier over the years for Alex, but it was never easy for her to see how marriage to Claire was aging Rane. His face had a graven look even in repose, and his eyes were shuttered, betraying less and less of the inner man, even to the people he trusted.

Christmas at Wild Swan was brightened by exotic gifts Boston had sent—a beautifully crafted leather bridle for St. John, a luxurious cape of beaver fur for Alex, and braided leather riding crops for the children. The presents told them that Boston was thinking of them, and that helped to ease the sorrow of not having him with them.

There were messages, too, from Virginia and from Hugh in England. Alex found it difficult to explain, but though she still had times when vivid memories of Devon or Kent would sweep before her eyes, in many ways it seemed another lifetime entirely, as if the continual newness of America was sweeping all else away. But the unsteadiness of her grandmother's writing was very real, a clear indication that the woman, as strong as she was, was not immune to the passing of the years. It helped that she still wrote with the same clarity of mind and lively involvement in the world around her. And when they had planted new trees in the old orchards at Wild Swan, they had thought of the wood Virginia had sacrificed for them; even the children called the new growth "Grandmother's Gift." With the trees growing and yielding their seasonal bounty, it was as if Virginia's spirit was with them.

The news from Hugh made Alex and St. John chuckle. After years of seeming impervious to the arrows of Cupid, Hugh had married, and not solely for the purpose of continuing his line. He was, he confessed, "quite foolishly in love with Angelica, who is much more sensible than her name would imply. She reminds me in many ways of you, Alexandria, and I can pay her no higher compliment. Someday I hope she will have the chance to meet you." Though it didn't seem a very likely chance, Alex and St. John thought of the pleasure it would be to welcome Hugh and his bride to Wild Swan.

Mavis and Timothy spent Christmas with them, and they both looked so contented and prosperous, there was little doubt that life in the new land suited them well. They had brought sacks of sweets for the children, and Alex was pleased that the Barlow boys and Sam were included. The Bateses had taken to the little girl instantly, and Sam numbered them among the securities of her life at Wild Swan.

The food was delicious, the house gleamed, the children had been extraordinarily well behaved when they had made their appearance at the party and had gone off to bed when they were bid, and Alex was drifting in a haze of good fellowship when it happened. The Falconers were with them on this New Year's Eve, Rane speaking with Caleb and St. John while Claire drifted restlessly from one group to the next. Alex had lost track of her as she spoke with Pen and Caleb's mother.

"You're just like him! The green eyes, those damn green eyes, watching and judging, always watching and judging!" There was no mistaking Claire's target as she came toward Alex, hands curved like claws. "What makes you better . . . what, what? Nothing, fine lady, shopkeeper's daughter, bitch, smiling bitch . . ." The voice gained force as the pitch rose higher like an evil wind, spewing out more venom, and for an instant, everyone in the room was frozen, including Alex.

She threw her arm up just in time to protect her face as Claire's nails raked her bare forearm, drawing blood. Rane sprang forward to grab his wife, and St. John stepped in front of Alex, shielding her from further harm, glaring at the crazed woman as if he would strangle her, though from the look on Rane's face, he would have to wait his turn.

"No! Don't hurt her!" Alex pled. "I'm quite all right, just a bit shaken." Her voice was more tremulous than she intended, but all she could think of was how thankful she was that Claire had not mentioned Morgan and that the Sheldon-Burkes had declined the dutifully offered invitation to the party, for surely they might have roused themselves enough to decide the Carringtons had associations all too strange even for their unwanted child. Her thoughts at that moment seemed scarcely less daft than Claire's, and she covered her mouth, trying in vain to stop the sound as the hysterical laughter rose and overflowed.

St. John put his arm around her and drew her against him. "Hush, love, quiet now. It's all right." He spoke as reassuringly as if she were a child, but she could feel the hectic pounding of his heart. Gratefully she leaned into him, wishing she could block out Rane's white face, Claire's frenzy—the ruin of the lovely evening.

The idea of defeat at the whim of Claire's demons stiffened her spine, and she stepped out of St. John's protective hold.

"Mrs. Falconer is not well." To her great relief she saw that Dr. Cameron had moved to help Rane get Claire out of the room. She wished he could take her away; she didn't even want her staying the night in her home. "The incident is over, and there is nothing we can do. I would appreciate it if you would carry on; we have yet to see the new year in."

It was not the same, but the guests were making a brave attempt at normalcy when, after bidding St. John to remain as host, she left them and went to the kitchen to see to her arm.

Used only as a warming kitchen in the summer, now in winter it was redolent with the smells of various delicacies and the air was comfortingly warm on her chilled flesh. Mavis and Della immediately flanked her like guardian angels, both of them sputtering with rage at Claire's attack.

"She's no better than a wild beast!" Della muttered, and Mavis added, " 'Er ort t' be locked up."

"She can't help it," Alex pointed out, but she found it difficult to say even those brief words. She was suddenly so weary, she swayed on her feet and found herself pressed into a chair, the two women fluttering over her.

Dr. Cameron found them there and took charge, giving her a glass of brandy with a gruff order to drink it while he attended to the bloody runnels, washing them thoroughly before he bound her arm neatly in white linen.

"All this fuss is silly. It will teach me to wear a dress with sleeves or long gloves at least." She tried to make light of it.

"Of course it is silly; that's why you sound as if you're speaking from the bottom of a well," Alastair said. "An attack by a madwoman is, I'm sure, a common occurrence in your life."

His manner made her smile briefly, but then the full weight of Rane's burden descended on her. "Is there nothing that can be done for her?"

"Mr. Falconer has tried everything short of committing her, and that, I predict, will be his only choice in the end. I know I sound unsympathetic, and in a sense I am, or at least I am as sorry for the woman's victims as I am for her. Having expended her malevolent energies on you, Mrs. Falconer is now sleeping peacefully with the help of a small dose of laudanum while you tremble, Mr. Falconer tries to control his despair, and everyone else tries to pretend nothing has happened. I have seen cases like this before, and it is always the same; the mad are scarcely less dangerous than plague carriers, except that they infect other minds rather than bodies." He gave a tired sigh, as if all his own energy had suddenly left him. "I always get angry when I feel helpless."

He fumbled in his coat, as rumpled and badly tailored as his daily garb inevitably was, and brought forth a folded paper. "This is in the nature of a belated Christmas gift, for the welcome I have found here since the first day."

Alex read the contents once and then again before raising incredulous eyes to Dr. Cameron.

"It would not stand up to every scrutiny, certainly not to the owner's, but it will surely give Samson a little more freedom of movement here."

Alex glanced around, relieved to see that Della and Mavis had moved out of earshot and were busy putting the last touches on the food that would be served after midnight. She read the paper yet again. It was a perfect description of Samson and a fictitious history of his sale to St. John by a man on the Eastern Shore of Maryland.

"The man did exist and is now dead. He had few slaves left by the time of his death, having sold them one by one. The ones who did remain were sold at his death. As far as we can determine, none of the slaves from his estate are left in the area. The man was unfriendly and reclusive in his later years, letting his neighbors know very little about his business. It would take hard work to prove this paper false."

"Why?" asked Alex softly, still trying to understand why Alastair should involve himself in such a risky business to give them such a precious gift.

"There are so many sicknesses I cannot cure; hearts that fail, fevers of the lungs, madness like Mrs. Falconer's, so many, and I do not delude myself by thinking that I can cure this horrible illness of slavery that afflicts my country. But I can treat it and mitigate the suffering in a small way, case by case. I have no family and no servants who would suffer were I apprehended in this business. There are others involved who have far more to lose."

"I think you are very brave, no matter how you judge it. And I thank you very much indeed for this." She held the paper reverently. "But one thing discomfits me. How did you know?" She and St. John had told no one, not even the Jenningses, the truth about Samson.

"Don't worry. No one has betrayed him. It is simply that I am often here, and little by little I learned that

Samson had arrived only a short time before my first visit, that he never leaves the place, and that no one speaks of him. You will be glad to know that everyone here is protective of the man. Then I heard the rumor of your husband's purchase of the man and granting of his freedom, though Samson's coming to Wild Swan seemed to have had nothing to do with St. John. It is the sort of situation I have come to notice, though there are woefully few people who would risk sheltering such as Samson, let alone hiring him."

It was Alex's turn to be embarrassed by the praise, and she rose hurriedly, diagnosing herself fit enough to return to her guests. But she secreted the paper in the room they used as a library before returning to the company.

St. John was beside her instantly. "I'm perfectly fine," she whispered. "Alastair plied me with a good dose of brandy."

"A physician after my own heart," St. John returned, his concern easing as he noted the color once more in her cheeks.

She could feel his own start of surprise echo hers as Rane came back into the room, approaching them directly.

"I apologize for my wife's behavior. I should have been watching her more closely. Alex, are you truly all right?" He winced visibly as he stared at the bandage.

"I am far less hurt than you," she said gently. "It was not your fault." She wanted to reach out and smooth away the deep lines of tension on his face.

Abruptly, as if her pity would undo him, he turned away, going to each guest in turn to offer a quiet apology.

"I am glad I do not have to show such courage for the same reason," St. John observed.

"So am I!" Alex agreed fervently, and she had never been more grateful for the orderly working of her own mind.

If they greeted the dawning of 1827 with forced cheerfulness, still they had not allowed Claire Falconer to destroy the gathering altogether.

❧ *Chapter 47* ❧

On January 2, Mabbie produced a beautiful black colt promptly named "Magic Swan" for the crossing of the two lines—Mabbie's with its names of faerie figures and Bay Swan. She had been due to foal in December, and the added time was a gift because now the colt's birth year was 1827 instead of 1826, and he would not have to compete against horses that could have been nearly a full year older.

"I think Beaker did us a favor," St. John said, eyeing the colt critically and still finding nothing but great promise in the long strong lines of the newborn.

Leda was going back to North Carolina to be bred to Sir Archy once again. The old stallion could not go on forever, and his blood had served them well.

This season St. John took Oberon, Swan Song, and Black Swan to the races. And in February Swan started his first season at stud, quickly and cleverly trained by Samson to associate a special halter with breeding. Very soon the otherwise docile stallion was arching his neck and strutting proudly the minute the halter was put on him. It was such a simple device, it was a wonder that everyone did not use it. But then, Samson made everything look simple and logical. Bay Swan was being trained the same way. The only loser was the teaser, a stallion of no particular blood or merit that had been acquired for the specific purpose of testing the mares for readiness or teasing them into it, thus avoiding injury or frustration to the Thoroughbred stallions when the mares were unwilling or even violent in their rejection.

Swan and Bay Swan were first bred to inferior mares;

Swan to one of the farm team and to a few saddle horses brought to him by owners who were anxious for the chance to have a "cocktail," as the half-bred horses were sometimes called. Bay Swan was likewise tried, and both stallions proved themselves manageable and not apt to savage their mares as some were. But even so, there was nothing tame about the process.

Whereas Bay Swan had already mounted a mare, Swan had not, and on his first introduction to the business of breeding, he was clearly puzzled. For years he had been trained to behave well around other horses, including mares in season. It was necessary in order that he be manageable at the race courses. Now he was being told that he was to mate with this mare, not race against her.

Patiently, repeatedly, Samson brought him to the ready female who backed and whinnied and twitched her tail in invitation until the scent of her triggered Swan's response. Once he had gotten through his first few clumsy attempts, Swan came into his own as a stallion.

To watch him mount a mare was to see him completely changed from his usual calm appearance. His neck seemed to grow to become a powerful flex of muscle. His bared teeth and gleaming eyes altered the look of his head completely, making him seem so savage, it was difficult to credit that he ever responded to human command. His screams and low-throated growls were wild music. His whole body became a mass of bulging sinew intent on completing the coupling that had been the heart of life for his species since the dawn of their creation. It was raw sex on such a grand scale, it was no wonder those who had trouble acknowledging the subject in general would find this a spectacle to be forbidden the eyes of women.

With inner laughter, Alex admitted to herself that the stirring sight made her miss St. John intensely. But most of her thoughts about it were of the most practical sort. Only in proving the breeding strength of their horses was there a future for them in this business; winning races was not enough.

In deference to most men's sensibilities, Alex played the role of blind ignorance, welcoming the owners or trainers who brought the mares to Wild Swan and then pretending that she did not know their purpose in coming. It seemed to suit them better than honesty would have done. But sometimes it was just not possible for her to maintain the guise of ignorance, and then she relied on the men's hunger for the bloodline and on their willingness to mark down her eccentricity to her background. At those times she became very, very British, a pose that threatened Samson's impassive façade. For that matter, Samson's own acting amused her as well. Several offers were made to him for employment elsewhere, but his answer was always the same.

"I jus' happy here, yes, I be, kin't go off no place else, all dese hosses be my chilun, kin't be makin' dem sad," he would say fervently, rolling his eyes and shuffling in a very unSamsonlike way. Those who would woo him away with more money found him immovable and soon gave up.

They bred Swan to Mabbie, wanting to see if this combination would produce a foal as promising as Magic Swan. "No betta hosses any place in de worl'," Samson crooned to Swan as he led him back to his own stall.

January had been extraordinarily cold, but February was warmer and even that added to Alex's high spirits. Everything was going so well for them, she sometimes felt as if they were under a benevolent spell. Even the new restrictions on some races in Maryland and the District of Columbia were to their advantage. These rules limited certain races to horses owned and trained north of the York or Pamunkey rivers for at least six months previous to the events, and in some races, only horses raised in Maryland and the District were eligible. Owners in Virginia and North Carolina were particularly outraged as they often brought their horses to these meetings. The reason for the restrictions was simply that most Sir Archy blood lay to the south of Maryland, and Sir Archy horses won most races they entered. It was a rather petty way of insuring more victories for Maryland and District owners. But it presented nothing but advantages to the Carringtons as they had the bloodline as well as their own strong show from England and qualified to compete in all the races.

One of the biggest decisions they had to make was whether or not they would post an entry for the National Colt Stake to be held in May, 1830. It was an act of faith to participate. It meant believing enough in a newly born and unproven colt of 1827 to enter it in a race to be held in three years' time. It was not only the loss of two hundred and fifty dollars—a large amount when one considered that sixty-eight dollars a month was the wage for a hired hand. If the colt was unable to run, it would also be a public admission that the promise of the animal had not been fulfilled, whether by overestimation in the beginning or by injury or illness near race time. The entry had to be made by May of this year of 1827.

St. John and Alex discussed it before he left, and after reviewing all the fine points of Magic Swan's breeding and confirmation, they had let instinct make the final decision. They would enter him because they both felt he was a special animal. St. John more than Alex, but they both possessed it—a talent for judging horseflesh, an instinct that went beyond logical judgment. It was not infallible, but then, nothing was. It could not be taught; one had it or not. Morgan seemed to be possessed of it, and to a lesser degree, Blaine had it. Nigel and Flora seemed to be totally devoid of it, though both were competent riders now.

Samson had the instinct in abundance, and he shared their enthusiasm for Magic Swan, showering the foal with loving attention from the day of his birth.

Samson was still careful about being seen by outsiders, and he and Alex went over the names of horse owners before the mares arrived for breeding so that Samson would have warning were they people he knew. To their relief, it had not yet happened. But the gift of the forged bill of sale from Dr. Cameron and the manumission paper written out by St. John had eased much of Samson's wariness. He understood the papers might be challenged if the worst happened, but he also knew that he was safe under casual scrutiny. He was deeply touched that white men would go to such lengths for him.

There were other changes in the big man. When Alex had handed him the papers and explained, offering to read them to him, he had smiled broadly.

"I reads dem ma own self now." And he had proceeded to do just that, slowly but surely.

"Dat Della, I pays her an' she learns—no, teaches—me."

Alex barely kept her stunned reaction from showing on her face, astonished not that Samson had learned to read, but that Della had taught him. "That's marvelous," she told him warmly, and she sought out Della as soon as she could.

"I think it's wonderful that you've taught Samson how

to read. I could not think of a way to offer without risking his pride," she said directly and saw the woman's pale brown cheeks stain with a blush.

"Oh, it's purely business," she protested. "Samson hired me for the job, wouldn't have it any other way, and that's all it is, a bargain."

"I'm quite sure it is, on both sides," Alex agreed, her eyes twinkling with mischief, causing Della to turn back to her cooking with muttered comments about some people having foolish notions. Alex didn't tease her any more, but she wondered what the future would bring to the two; without being aware of it, they seemed to be meeting on a middle ground, Samson beginning to learn the numbers and letters that meant so much to Della, and Della in turn growing more aware of feelings that had nothing to do with books. Alex tried not to think too much of what Samson's past might mean to his future.

News from St. John was as good as it had been the year before. Oberon was provoking the most interest with his increasingly fierce determination not to be beaten, but Black Swan and Swan Song were also performing well, Song proving over and over again that she could scarcely be beaten at the shorter distances, though four miles would probably always be beyond her. And the overall result of the races was that the horses of Wild Swan were gaining an even better reputation.

In return, Alex sent calm reports of life going smoothly and productively at Wild Swan. For the most part, her accounts were true, but she had long since made it a rule not to bother her husband with minor disasters about which he could do nothing from such a distance. And she learned that the children had adopted somewhat the same policy toward her.

Afterwards she decided that the Fates had offered a compensating kindness in having Alastair Cameron there when Blaine came to find her one late afternoon in March.

"Mama, you mustn't get too upset," Blaine informed her, and his attitude of tightly maintained calm terrified her. "Morgan fell out of a tree, and we think he broke his arm. He's coming along with the others. I came ahead to tell you."

Alastair instantly reached for Alex's hand, gripping it tightly, and she was grateful for his understanding. Despite all her training in healing, nothing made it easier when one of her children was injured. Minor illnesses and tumbles off horses and various other heights they had had, but this was the first broken bone. And Alex could never control memories of Christiana's fatal illness when one of the children was hurt or sick.

Because Alastair was with her, she was able to go out to the children with her panic in check.

Morgan's face was bleached white as bone, his mouth a tight line, his eyes a vividly unnatural yellow-green with shock, but he was walking under his own power, cradling his left arm with his right.

He uttered a little cry when he saw his mother, but then he regained his control as she knelt beside him and inspected his arm. Even when she touched it, he did not make a sound. The break showed clearly between elbow and wrist.

"It looks like a clean break. You did a neat job of it, lad," Alastair said matter of factly. "We'll make you more comfortable in no time. The rest of you, off with you now; we'll let you know when you can see Morgan."

His assumption of authority was accepted by all except Sam. The others moved away, glad to have responsibility lifted from them and glad not to have to watch Morgan suffering any more. But Sam stayed where she was, struggling to get words out past tears that were beginning to roll down her cheeks. "It's m . . . my fault."

"We can talk about it later," Alex told her abstractedly, able to think of nothing except Morgan, already urging him toward the house. But he planted his feet stubbornly. "Not true . . . not . . . Sam's fault." Every word was an effort, but he went on. "Sam, go with the others. I'll be all right."

Desolately, Sam did as he ordered.

Alex deferred to Dr. Cameron automatically, assisting him as he directed, all her energies concentrated on her son. His continued stoicism tore at her heart, and she was hard pressed not to let her own tears fall in place of those he did not shed. In his pale withdrawal into his own strength, he suddenly looked so much like Rane, Alex could hardly bear to look at his face. She cradled him against her breast, wishing she could absorb all the hurt as Alastair manipulated the break, realigning the ends of bone. Alex heard them grate together as Morgan's body flexed against hers and then slumped as the worst of the pain passed.

Alastair made brief, neat work of splinting and wrapping the arm, as Alex went on holding Morgan, brushing his hair softly with her hand, crooning to him as if he were very young again, grateful that he did not reject this treatment.

He could barely keep his eyes open by the time the doctor had finished, and Alastair and Alex put him to bed, both of them relieved to see sleep overcome him instantly.

"It's the best thing for him," Alastair said. "There's no sign of a head wound, so it's not dangerous for him to sleep. He's just worn out by the pain and the shock of the injury. If he's in much pain later on, you might give him a little laudanum or . . . but of course, you know that. One of your brews might even be better for him than the opium. That's a brave son you have."

"He is," she agreed, and her face was so full of love and pride, Alastair had to look away for a moment.

Alex touched his arm. "I cannot tell you how good it was to have you here for this. I am very thankful."

"I would now prescribe a stiff dose of brandy for the mother," he returned gruffly, embarrassed, as always, by gratitude.

"Will a strong cup of tea suffice?" she asked with a smile. "I'd much prefer it."

"I won't dispute my learned colleague's preference," Alastair conceded, and they shared a companionable pot of tea after assuring Della and others that Morgan was going to be fine. Della went to tell the children and returned shaking her head in puzzlement.

"I don't know quite what is going on, but there seems to be a problem with Sam. Blaine says she won't listen to any of them and that she's getting all of her things together. She's out in the schoolhouse. I looked in and called to her, but she pretended she didn't notice me."

"Good lord! I forgot all about her!" Alex gasped, already on her way.

They had converted one of the dependencies into a very comfortable little one-room schoolhouse complete with its own fireplace and two good-sized windows. Alex climbed the short, steep steps, calling to Sam but receiving no answer.

She checked at the sight of the little girl. Sam spent so much time at Wild Swan, she had a good many possessions there, and she had apparently assembled them all in one heap which she was trying to tie into some order so that she could carry her belongings home on her pony.

"Sam, if you're leaving us for good, I would certainly like to know why," Alex said softly, staying where she was near the door.

"Is he dead?" A small whisper of dread.

"Of course he's not dead!" Alex crossed to her then, swinging her around to face her. Sam had more than made up for the tears Morgan had not shed. Her face was blotched and stained from her grief.

"Sweetheart, Morgan has a broken arm, nothing else. He'll be fit in no time at all. Right now, he's sound asleep. Now, what's all this nonsense about your being responsible? Morgan says you're not."

"I am!" Sam declared. "I dared him. I climbed the tree first. Then I came down and dared him in front of everybody. It was very high, and I'm littler than Morgan, so when he did the same thing I did, the branch broke, and he fell."

"Samantha Sheldon-Burke, you listen to me! Daring people to do things is very silly; there's no doubt about that. But Morgan didn't have to accept the dare. He knows better. And he's very agile. He's climbed a lot of trees. He should have had the sense to know the branch wouldn't hold his weight. I hope you've both learnt a lesson, but that's all there is to it. You leave everything here, and we'll ride over to Brookhaven together so you'll have company going home."

It took Sam a moment to believe what Alex was telling her, and then she threw her arms around Alex's neck and hugged so hard, Alex had trouble breathing. "I love you an' Morgan an' everybody here. I'd die if I had to go away forever!" Sam sobbed with all the passionate conviction of her nine years, and Alex was struck by the odd thought that Sam's attachment to Morgan was much like her own had been to Rane. Even as she dismissed it as the fancy of a tense time, she found herself hoping that, if destiny had cast them together, their love would run more smoothly than hers and Rane's.

* * *

Trying to keep Morgan fairly sedentary for the next few days proved to be a challenge. The first day he had slept right through until the next morning. Alex knew his arm must ache quite fiercely, though he made no complaint. But patience with the pain was the only patience he had. Aside from the time spent on lessons, Morgan was accustomed to going at top speed from morning to night. Directing that flashing energy toward quiet activities was like trying to put lightning in a bottle, and it left Alex exhausted. In this, too, he reminded her of his father. Rane, too, was possessed of enormous physical energy. She had ceased to pretend to herself that Rane had not fathered this child. And she gave thanks that she did not have to tell him that Morgan had died in something as senseless as a fall from a tree; she flinched away from the image of the grief that would have added to Rane's sad life.

Sam added her efforts to the project of keeping Morgan from doing himself added injury, doggedly offering to fetch and carry for him and holding herself in readiness to play at draughts or any other game he might suggest.

"I feel like I've got a slave I don't even want," Morgan confided to his mother when Sam had finally gone home on the third day. "Sam's a funny little kid," this from his great advantage of being one year older, "but I like her pretty well. She's a good sport." He looked very thoughtful for a moment, and when he spoke again, his voice was tentative. "Mama, what would you do about someone who cheats?"

"Sam?" Alex asked incredulously.

"No, I just told you she's a good sport," Morgan pointed out impatiently, and Alex could feel him deciding he might as well tell her the whole story. "It's Nigel. He cheats all the time, even at hide-and-seek. He's not very good at games, you see, so he cheats to win. And most of the time, we let him. It sort of evens things out. But I've been thinking that maybe it's not a good idea because what if he does it with somebody else? They might get real angry."

Alex opened her mouth and closed it again, finding she didn't know what to say. She was utterly sure that Morgan had not told her in order to get his brother into trouble. Quite the contrary; he was afraid Nigel would manage to do that by himself if he were not stopped. Cheating: it seemed so unlike her youngest child. He was so bright and so sensitive to those around him, she could not imagine what had driven him to such a shabby course.

"I'll speak to him," she finally managed to say, "and I won't tell him how I found out."

Morgan looked infinitely relieved at that. Tattling was taboo among the children.

When she got Nigel alone, she wasted no time. "I've noticed that you don't always play fairly in outdoor games. In fact, you seem to think it all right to cheat. I would like to know why." She could tell Nigel did not even consider that one of his siblings might have told her; he shared the nearly universal belief among young children that parents had magical sources of information regarding the activities of their offspring.

His eyes suddenly looked big and lost as he gazed at his mother. "I can't win unless I cheat; I'm just not good at those things," he explained earnestly. "And everybody here cares so much 'bout winnin'. If the horses don't win, nobody likes 'em."

Alex's first impulse was to laugh in relief. Here was no evil character flaw, but rather a misinterpretation of values. She controlled her mirth because she realized how important this was to Nigel.

"I can see how you might have thought that," she assured him. "But it isn't so. Cheating to win is no victory at all. Just think how we would feel if we lost a race because another horse was used to cheat us out of the prize." She told him what had happened in the four-mile race Swan had ultimately won in Washington. Your father and I were very angry that such a thing was tried because it was unfair to all the horses that were racing honestly. It's how one comes in first in anything and how one competes, win or lose, that matters, not just taking the prize. And you are not a horse raised to do only one thing, win races. You are my very special son who is so intelligent that even Mr. Whittleby says he has a hard time keeping up with you. It doesn't matter that you don't always win at games; it truly doesn't. They just aren't what you do best. All of us have things we do well and things we don't, especially when we're growing up. It takes time to find out which is which. Does this make sense?"

Nigel considered what she'd told him for a long while, and then the slow, sweet smile so typical of him appeared.

"I'm glad you told me. Cheating is really hard to do right."

With that, Alex did laugh, hugging him to her and tickling him until they were both out of breath.

She reported the results of the interview to Morgan and warned him, "Now just because Nigel quits cheating doesn't mean you must let him win to make him feel better. We all have to learn that we can't always win. And it's a type of cheating to let someone win, even if it is for good motives."

His reluctant nod of agreement told her that he would indeed have let Nigel win had she not cautioned him against it.

She was filled with a love for her children so intense, it was akin to pain. The older they grew and the more she saw of the people they were becoming, the more awed she was by the unique beauty of each of them. She felt a stab of pity for St. John for the little intricacies of each day that he was missing.

∗∾ Chapter 48 ∽∗

St. John arrived home barely in time to take Alex to the races in Washington, but they made it and stayed with acquaintances across Rock Creek in Georgetown.

There were beginning to be more and more one- and two-mile races for younger horses, as if the American system was reluctantly and slowly shifting to the dash race of system of England, and Swan Song was more than capable of demolishing most opponents at these distances. Black Swan and Oberon were formidable at three miles, and St. John thought Oberon would be ready for four miles by autumn. To be able to field three fine horses from one stable and to take them to a good number of races made the Carringtons major owners, and Alex found their increasing status rather dazzling and not altogether comfortable. They were recognized and greeted by a large number of fellow owners, some with wives, some with women of questionable status, these women tending to stay in the background when the men approached the Carringtons. Alex knew she was supposed to adopt somewhat the same attitude when horse breeding was discussed, and she continued to find that delicacy at once frustrating and amusing.

"What do they think goes on at Wild Swan? They must believe I hide inside when the horses are bred. Of course, I have pretended to that so I suppose I deserve this silly show. I wonder if their wives do hide."

St. John grinned wickedly. "I doubt it. Far more likely that their wives know as much about the process as you do; it's a hard spectacle to miss, if you'll pardon the pun. Makes us husbands feel insufficient."

Alex burst out laughing. "You, my love, are wonderfully lecherous. You needn't worry. Sufficient unto the day, as Grandmother used to say."

"Or unto the lay," he amended, loving the sound of her laughter. He reached for her and kissed her soundly. "You delight me, wife."

"It is my pleasure, too," Alex reminded him, nuzzling his ear and running her mouth gently along the hard line of his jaw until she found his lips again. His fingers were busy undoing the buttons down the back of her dress, buttons he had just done up for her. He had been back such a short time, they had not yet satisfied the hunger that had built over the months apart.

"We'll be late for supper, and what will the Harrisons think?" But it was only a halfhearted protest from her, and she agreed with St. John's "Let them think what they will."

St. John loved to watch her face, the sensuality that was always there so heightened by her response to him, the eyes glowing emerald through half-closed lids, the lashes long and thick, and her mouth, lips full and half-parted, her dark hair long and heavy spreading out on the white linen as she lay back, her whole body bidding him welcome.

He was never entirely free of the memories of how he had treated her in the first days. It made him ever con-

523

scious of pleasing her, and he had long since found that by being so concerned, his own pleasure increased immeasurably. The only longing he could not fulfill was an old sorrow now, and its pain was blunted, but still he wished he were able to hold her rightly with two good arms.

He knelt over her, tracing the curves and hollows of her warmth with his lean fingers and his mouth. She shivered with the rippling sensations he evoked in the nerves beneath her skin. She gloried in the care he took in loving her, in the lithe strength that seemed to make so little of his handicap.

"I want you, Sinje, I want you inside now!" she gasped, and she kept her eyes open, watching the taut play of his chest and shoulder muscles as he braced himself with his arm, watching the blue of his eyes deepen as he sank into her with deliberate slowness. She took the initiative then, stroking him with the secret muscles of her sex, clasping him deeper and tighter each time he thrust, wanting the union to go on forever, drawing a husky groan of pleasure from him until her own glory blotted all else from her mind and body.

His body on fire, muscles twitching with the effort, St. John waited until he felt Alex shuddering and heard her cry out before he surrendered to his own sensations and lost his seed in her.

Alex opened her eyes, coming back slowly from that faraway, unthinking place. Even in the throes of his own passion, St. John had rolled to the side, taking her with him before his strength gave out, so that she would not have to bear his weight.

She moved a little away to see him better, feeling him slip from her. "You're shamefully beautiful for a man," she murmured and smiled to see embarrassment color his face. "And I would like to stay like this but I really do think we ought to try again to dress and go downstairs."

They giggled like naughty children as they dressed. It was going to be very difficult to appear prim and proper at supper.

They found they needn't have worried. The Harrisons were a lively middle-aged couple who ran good horses at many of the meets, had a plantation in Virginia and a town house in Georgetown, the venerable old port that had gleaned early riches by being the tobacco inspection station closest to the headwaters of the Potomac as well as the last port a ship could sail to from Chesapeake Bay. Though commerce had diminished, it still boasted houses and shops much superior to the capital's and looked down on the District accordingly.

Martha and Paul were good company and easy hosts. St. John had introduced them to Alex the previous year, and in March they had brought a prize mare to be bred to Swan. Martha had come along to see Wild Swan and to visit with Alex and meet the children.

There was no fuss made over their late appearance. Paul wanted nothing more than to hear about their plans for their horses, while Martha was hungry for news of the children. Alex obliged her, feeling compassion for this woman who would so obviously have liked to have had children of her own. She related the story of Morgan's broken arm, the accident having occurred after the Harrisons' visit, including Sam's claim of blame, and they laughed together over Nigel's pronouncement that cheating was hard work.

Alex's heart gave a queer nervous start at St. John's contribution to the conversation as he left off discussing the finer points of Leda's breeding.

"It's amazing to me how different the children are from each other. Even Flora and Blaine, for all that they are twins. Nigel should grow up to be a diplomat; despite his recent confusion about ethics, he is always anxious that all be peaceful around him. But our son Morgan is most like Alex, and I find myself hard put not to make him my favorite, though I would have none."

His look was so fond, Alex had to swallow hard not to burst into tears. Morgan was as like Rane as he was like her, and yet, St. John had no suspicions. "I only hope he has the kindness of your nature," she managed, and the Harrisons thought how nice it was to see young people so in love.

Alex thought of Rane and his poor, mad wife, and she thought of how blessed she and St. John were in each other and their children.

Martha took Paul's hand and patted it gently. "Mr. Harrison and I longed for children, but it wasn't God's will. We had three little ones, but none of them lived more than a few days."

"I share your sorrow. We lost a little girl before we

came to this country and another while we were in Annapolis," Alex said softly, touched by the trust Martha had shown in telling them. She found herself very pleased with the blossoming friendship with the Harrisons. Both of them were blue eyed and gray haired, but Martha was small and round while Paul was of middle height and lean. I hope St. John and I still love each other as well when we are their age, she thought.

The only shadow on their relationship was that the Harrisons were slave owners. They still spent most of their time on their Virginia property, but when they came to Georgetown, they brought certain slaves with them. They would not have considered traveling without the comfort offered by these possessions.

"You needn't look so furtive," St. John suggested after Alex had turned down the offer made that night by one of the maids to help her undress. "The servants in this house must think you're a very nervous woman; you jump every time one of them tries to do something for you."

"Oh, Sinje! They aren't servants; they're slaves! I'll never grow accustomed to it. It does make me uneasy to know they've been ordered to do something and have no choice."

"Darling, you know I share your views of slavery, but surely it must be possible that many slaves, particularly those as well treated as these, take pride in their work just as the people at Wild Swan do and are pleased to do it well."

With a little sigh, Alex rested her head against his chest. "You're perfectly right, of course, and so much more sensible about it than I. I can't change anything here, and if I accept the Harrisons' hospitality, then I must accept how they live. Sinje, you keep me sane."

"Not too sane, I hope." He tipped her head back so he could kiss her, and she let problems she could not solve slip from her mind as her body responded to his again.

Afterwards she murmured, "I meant what I said, you are the kindest man," and she smiled at the sight of him keeping his eyes open with visible effort against the sin of going to sleep too quickly in the afterglow of loving. "Sleep now, my dear, I love you."

Her smile widened at his relieved compliance, and the passionate ardor of the past moments was replaced by a feeling as maternal as the love she bore the children. St.

John's face had a rare, vulnerable beauty when he slept, his fine aristocratic bones making him appear aesthetic and almost frail. She nearly laughed aloud at the thought, knowing how ill the description went with his recent activity.

Careful not to disturb him, she extinguished the lamp and settled down beside him, utterly content to have him beside her again.

The next day Alex discovered that St. John had more than racing in mind for this trip. Knowing she paid the least possible attention to her wardrobe, he was determined that he would oversee a noticeable expansion of it. She argued against the expense; he pointed out that half of being successful was dressing the part. She declared that she hardly needed an extensive wardrobe for her life at Wild Swan; he argued quite the contrary, that more and more of the horse owners were coming to the place and that she would have an increasing number of social engagements to attend, this trip to Georgetown, for instance. She soon realized that trying to talk him out of it was hopeless, and so they began the round of the fine shops recommended by Mrs. Harrison.

Having won the major battle, St. John was willing to concede the skirmishes over style, and in fact, agreed with Alex. In the last few years, new styles had vanquished the easy graceful freedom of the previous years of the century. Waistlines were dropping from under the bosom to closer to their natural location, but in the process, tight lacing was coming into vogue. Simple sleeves were giving way to leg o'mutton creations, and bonnets were growing apace. Skirts were increasing in circumference and inching upward so that a bit of ankle and frilly pantalettes once confined to little girls' wardrobes were peeking out from underneath.

Alex put her foot down in no uncertain terms. "I will not be bound until I cannot breathe or move. Whoever is doing this to women ought to be shot for making us so helpless. Of course, there are men who corset themselves as well, but I notice you do not, husband. I will not wear pallid colors that make me look ill, nor under-clothing that looks as if it is falling off in pieces. I will not be decked with ribbons, lace, and whatnot to the point of the ridiculous, nor wear bonnets that look as if they have a life of their own. I am a tall, spare woman, and I will not be made to look like a Maypole in skirts."

The dressmaker looked stunned; St. John looked as if he would explode with laughter, but he managed to answer calmly. "I quite agree. And I am sure Madam can meet all of your requirements."

Madam could. Madam was not so stupid as to miss a good sale, and she was recovering enough to be intrigued by the idea of complying with this exotic woman's wishes and showing her own talent at the same time.

Roses, greens, blues, white, even black—all deep clear colors and current styles simplified and softened to suit her; Alex got what she wanted and only belatedly realized that St. John had wanted the same all along.

"You are sly as well as generous," she accused, and he was perfectly willing to plead guilty.

Two of the dresses were delivered to the Harrisons' house on a rush order; the rest would follow shortly to be delivered by messenger to Wild Swan. St. John was wholly pleased with the results of the shopping. Alex's beauty could still strike him so forcefully that it was as if he were seeing her for the first time. And in a room of women, she always seemed to him to be so vividly drawn, the others paled in comparison. The new clothing simply enhanced what had always been there.

In early June, they watched Swan Song win at two miles, beating Florival, Oscar, and Stylla on a heavy course at the Canton races near Baltimore. On the second day, Black Swan triumphed again in two-mile heats. And on the third, Oberon beat the mare, Eliza White, in three-mile heats, both of them running a fine race. Jim Barlow rode in all three races, his riding as pure as the blood of the horses, giving other jockeys no chance to bump or crowd him.

They had taken the meeting by a storm; the horses of Wild Swan had now earned the position of being some of the most desirable horseflesh anywhere in the American racing world. And no one could have been more pleased for the Carringtons than Caleb and Penelope Jennings. The stay with them took on the aspects of one, long riotous party as the Jenningses suspended their own daily routines to attend the races and to celebrate afterward.

"I knew this was a special woman even when I first met her as a breeched boy," Caleb bragged.

He meant it in good part, and Alex took it that way and tried not to wish that Rane were sharing their joy. The Jenningses had seen little of him lately, aside from the business contacts he had with Caleb. Claire had been markedly unstable since the New Year's Eve episode, seeming to have no middle ground any more, veering from nearly catatonic calm to shrieking hysteria. As far as the Jenningses knew, Rane went nowhere that was not required by business. Alex hoped business required him to sail often.

On the morning after their return to Wild Swan, Alex discovered a package waiting for her, shipped from Gravesend and taking many weeks to be delivered. From Baltimore it had gone to Annapolis and then by wagon to Wild Swan. Della was still muttering about the freight charges, but she stopped as she saw all the color drain from Alex's face.

The covering letter was stiffly formal, written by her brother, Paris, to inform her that their grandmother had died peacefully in her sleep and that she had left instructions that the enclosed be sent to Alexandria. Virginia had died in February; the package had been shipped in March and contained the remainder of Virginia's herbals and notes on treatment, and carefully labeled packets of seeds and dried herbs; these last items told Alex that her grandmother must have known her death was near to have left things so neatly organized.

"Every bird and beast, every tree and flower, every man and woman, each and every thing on this earth has its season, and no poor plan we humans make will change that, thank God." Alex almost smiled as she heard the beloved voice, wry and wise. And then the dark cloud closed over her again.

Virginia would have been eighty-six years old this year. It was old indeed. And she had had a long, full life and a kind death. It could not have been expected that she would go on much longer. All this Alex knew, and yet it did not help. She felt utterly alone in the universe. It did not seem possible that Virginia had died in February, had been dead for all those days of late winter and spring when life had been so good at Wild Swan.

She did not know that Della had gone for St. John until he stood beside her. He took the letter from her, and when he had read it, he did not offer any platitudes.

"My love, I am so sorry!" he said, and his voice was heavy with grief of his own. Virginia had had so much to do with the joy he knew now, even to relinquishing her own claims on Alex that he might have her.

He put his arm around her and rocked her gently against him, wishing she would weep, but after a moment she pulled away. "I am going riding." Her face was set in rigid lines.

"Do you want me to come with you?" he asked cautiously.

She shook her head.

But he did go as far as the stable and waited until she was up on Mabbie. Magic Swan was nearly weaned now, so it was possible to take the mare out without the foal and without too much persuasion.

"You will be careful, please?" St. John asked. Again a wordless motion of her head, this time in agreement, but he trusted her instinctive skill in the saddle and was relieved to see that she did not leave in a heedless rush. He watched her out of sight, wanting more than anything to be with her, accepting that she needed to be alone.

When the children had a break from their lessons, he explained what had happened and why their mother was gone for the day. Of all of them, the twins remembered Virginia the best and even their memories were growing dim, but they did know how much the old woman meant to their mother.

"I suppose it doesn't help that she was so very old," Flora ventured, trying to puzzle it out.

"No, it really doesn't," St. John told her. "You see, when you love someone very much, age doesn't seem to matter. You even forget how old the person is. All you know is that you want them to be in your world forever."

Nigel had, unfortunately, been doing a little figuring on his own. "Someday you and Mama will die and leave us alone, won't you?" His voice wavered.

"Not for a very long time, I hope," his father assured him. "But death does come to us all. We can't do anything about that. But we can love each other and treat each other with kindness while we live. And Mama will need us all to be very kind for a while."

The children contemplated this solemnly, prepared to do their part, but also made uneasy by the idea that their always-comforting mother should be in need of their comfort now.

Alex stayed out all day. Afterwards she had very little idea of where she had been except that she must have covered most of Wild Swan. She did not press Mabbie hard, she just wandered the land, waiting for some feeling or reassurance to come from it. The humid heat, to which she had adjusted so readily when she had first arrived in America, now wrapped around her so heavily she felt as if she could not draw a deep breath. Insects whined unpleasantly close to her face, and she could feel sweat trickling down her body. And gradually it came to her that even in heat the land was lovely and fertile again from their care and would provide for them in return for their labor. But it did not offer the solace she needed. St. John was that refuge, waiting for her.

She rode home to the love and compassion that illuminated his face the moment he saw her. Wearily she went to him, and this time she did not draw away when his arm encircled her, and he half supported her as he took her up to their bedchamber.

She was suddenly so exhausted, she could hardly keep her eyes open, but she made the effort to talk because it was important that he understand. "I went looking . . . but it was here . . . because with everything else and everyone else I love, you are the center of my world now, the center of my love." Her eyes closed, but she was aware of St. John's cheek resting against hers and of the warm wetness of his tears. Dimly she explored the strange thought that it was as if even this he did for her, taking the burden of weeping for his own.

The next day, he went with her to turn the hives and to tell the bees of the death, taking the ceremony as seriously as she, and in the days that followed, she found he always seemed to be near when she needed him, reassuring her with a look, a touch, reassuring her in countless small ways. The children, too, went out of their way to be kind, and she knew this, too, came from St. John.

Several times she started to write down things to tell or ask her grandmother in the next letter and then stopped. And she began to understand that in all the essential ways their lives had touched, they touched still. Love and knowledge had been Virginia's greatest gifts to her, the giving begun in a time before Alex could remember. The legacy was as much a part of Alex as the beat of her heart, a living pulse that went on though Virginia was gone. Alex felt it. She felt it in the pleasure everything from books to birds to flowers gave her. She felt it in the wonder her children held for her. She felt it in the way she thought and worked and loved. And she found that the world was not empty, but so crowded with life and sensations, it was nearly impossible to contain it all.

She found herself humming and singing while she went about her tasks, smiling and laughing often, and feeling as if she were so alive, she was going to burst free and fly. St. John understood her reaction and rejoiced in it, loving her more for it.

Often, in years to come, Alex would look back on those days as the happiest of their marriage—as if her grandmother had given one last gift even in death.

✺ Chapter 49 ✺

When Vulcan was delivered to the farm, St. John assumed Alex's reaction to the animal was part of the keen edge of feeling she was living on these days, and briefly, Alex thought so, too.

Vulcan had come up from North Carolina. St. John had taken him as payment of a wager made during the spring racing season, and it had been agreed then that the previous owner would make sure the horse got to Wild Swan sometime during the summer. St. John had nearly forgotten about the horse. The season had been a lucrative one, despite the fact that most people had become cautious about betting against horses from Wild Swan. There had been various purses collected from wins, and there had been unwise wagers; there were always men who thought their luck would triumph over logic.

Vulcan was not the only horse St. John had acquired. There were also a two-year-old filly, Sunrise, and a five-year-old gelding, Gawain. Though they were Thoroughbreds, neither Sunrise nor Gawain had that certain combination of conformation, spirit, speed, and endurance that would make them good race horses. St. John didn't want them for that purpose. He judged they would make good field horses, a cut above most beasts under saddle though not the stuff of racing champions. There was always a market for good riding horses, and he envisioned another profitable business for Wild Swan.

Alex fully agreed with this plan, but she did not want Vulcan to be any part of it. He was a six-year-old stallion of monstrous size, heavily muscled, his coat a dark, sooty gray. Alex hated him on sight.

The men who had brought him were glad to be rid of him. They had had other horses in their charge, horses being sold by various owners to people in Maryland and the District of Columbia, but none had given them as much trouble as Vulcan.

"He's a mean son of a bitch," one of the men said, and then gulped and stammered, "pardon, ma'am," when he caught sight of Alex.

"No apology necessary," she said shortly. "I am quite sure your assessment is accurate."

She repressed her impulse to cause a scene in front of these strangers, but after the horse had been manhandled into a stall and the men had accepted refreshments and gone on their way, she confronted her husband.

"I don't want that horse here."

"I don't plan to race or breed him," St. John pointed out reasonably.

"I don't want you to do anything with him except perhaps shoot him."

St. John looked at her more closely, belatedly realizing she was on the verge of hysteria. "Alex, Sir Arthur is over twenty years old, and while he still serves me well enough, it is time I trained another riding horse."

"You're quite mad! That horse is not fit for riding or for anything else. Sinje, I know what you are thinking; I can see it on your face. You think this is just part of my being overly sensitive or whatever you choose to call it because of Grandmother's death. But it is not that; I swear it! That horse is bad. I can feel it. Nothing good will come of his being here."

He was still regarding her with such intense patience, she felt like slapping his face.

"We'll see how he responds to good training," he offered peaceably, as if he were speaking to a child, and she stalked away before she could say anything she would regret.

She hated the beast even more when she felt the constraint between herself and St. John that lasted even to when they were lying in bed, together, but very, very separate. She heard his breathing slip into sleep, and she felt as alone as she had when news of Virginia's death had reached her.

She got out of bed, taking care not to awaken St. John. Maybe he was right; maybe she was reacting stupidly to the stallion. She didn't bother to dress but wrapped herself in a cloak over her nightgown and quietly left the house, taking a lantern with her for the darkness of the stall.

The moon was shining, lighting the way, and the night was still and singing with the music of myriad insects and rustling nocturnal foragers. But there were other sounds as well; the horses of Wild Swan moving restlessly here and there and nickering uneasily when normally they would be calm and quiet by now. She had no doubt that it was the presence of Vulcan that was upsetting them.

She entered the shed where he was being kept separate from the others. She heard him before she saw him. His stamping grew louder as she neared the stall, and then he kicked at the heavy door blocking his escape, the sound as sharp as the shot of a gun. He gave voice to his rage in low growling pants, more terrifying for the lack of volume than had he been screaming.

It was rage, not fear. She raised the lantern to better see the massive head and stepped back just in time to avoid the flashing teeth as he lashed his neck even further over the door, moving with the speed of a striking snake.

The teeth clicked together in a frenzy of frustration, and his nostrils were flared wide and twitching. But it was his eyes that riveted her. They had none of the liquid willingness of those of the other horses at Wild Swan. These eyes were hard, gleaming red with purpose, narrow pig eyes. He was a perversion of all the splendid virility of the other stallions.

The smell of him enveloped her, hot grass, sweat, and his sex, none of it normally unpleasant, but from him overpowering, and suddenly, she was him—a huge beast of muscle, bone, dim intelligence, and enormous lusting hate. The hate swirled around her, filled her, choked her. Blind unreasoning hate not only for the humans who handled him, but for his own kind, for anything that moved within his range. She staggered back, nearly dropping the lantern, clutching her breast with her other hand as if to keep her heart from tearing from its moorings.

"You are truly evil," she whispered and knew it was true. Perhaps he had been mistreated, perhaps he had been born this way, but whatever the cause, there was no kindness in this beast, only rogue hatred.

She spun around, suddenly aware she was not alone.

"Doan mean t' scare you none, jus' thinkin' somebudy be here."

Samson's eyes were studying her carefully; clearly he had heard what she'd said. There's the difference, she thought. Despite his aloofness in the beginning, despite his vast bulk and strength, despite the abuse he had suffered, there was no meanness in this man, no twisted spirit. She thought of the mad gleam so often in Claire Falconer's eyes. It shows in all of us, beast and human; it shows through the eyes.

"Tell me I'm mistaken. Tell me I'm foolish!" she demanded urgently. He knew everything there was to know about horses; she wanted him to reassure her.

He did not oblige. His thoughts were parallel to hers. "Some men, some beasts, dey jus' bad, an' nothin' goin' change dem. Dis hoss be one of dem."

They stared at each other in the shadowed light, neither saying it but both beginning to realize why St. John wanted to ride this horse. He tested himself in small, constant ways. He had learned to shoot a dueling pistol accurately again; his handwriting was a clear indication of determined effort, as was his riding and the handling of the ribbons when he drove a carriage. So many tasks had become tests of his patience and endurance since he had lost his arm. But Vulcan was the worst test yet.

"I would like to shoot this horse or poison him." She said it very quietly.

"I do it fo' you." The offer was firm.

"I know you would, Samson, and I thank you. But we both know it can't be done. The horse belongs to St. John."

Vulcan was still snorting and stamping when they left him. Alex thought at the very least he should be tied in the box stall, but she was sure this, too, had not been done on St. John's orders, as if to do so would be a violation of some spirit he saw in the beast.

St. John stirred and awakened when she returned to their bed.

"You're so cold! Where have you been?"

She wasn't even aware until then of the chill that seemed to have penetrated her bones though the night was hot. She shivered and moved closer to St. John's warmth.

"I went out to see Vulcan."

She felt his start of surprise. "You went to see Vulcan in the middle of the night? Whatever for?"

She took a deep breath and plunged in. "Because I wanted to be sure, and now I am. Sinje, he's bad blood, dangerous; he's evil clear through! Please get rid of him! Please, for my sake!"

The silence stretched between them. St. John's building anger was tangible, and he moved away from her. She shivered again.

"Too dangerous for a one-armed man to ride? What do you have in mind, a pony cart?" His voice was low, silky, and anger shot through her at the injustice of it.

"He's too dangerous for a man with three arms to ride! He's too dangerous for anyone to ride. You're being stubborn and stupid. How would you feel if I were the one insisting on riding that creature?"

"But you are not, and that is not what we're discussing." The false smoothness in his voice grated against her nerves like broken glass. She felt even colder than before, but she drew as far away from him as she could and turned her back.

St. John started to reach for her, but his own anger stopped him. She was being foolish, and whether she admitted it or not, her worry stemmed from the fact that he was not a whole man. No matter that it came from love, it was an attitude he could not bear.

By morning Alex was resigned. She could not sustain the distance between herself and St. John on account of a renegade horse, and she realized she would only make matters worse by focusing such attention on the issue. Perhaps left to his own devices, St. John would grow weary of fighting the beast. But she felt duty bound to win certain concessions. The children were to stay away from Vulcan, and none of the stablemen was to be required to care for him alone. And he was not to be allowed near any of the racing stock.

St. John gave in easily on these points, knowing the main victory was his. But the victory was not as sweet as it might have been. Though she was determined not to press it any more, he could not miss the taut misery on Alex's face every time he took Vulcan out. It made him more determined than ever to school the horse; St. John's fascination with Vulcan remained undiminished.

He had never before felt such enormous power in a horse. Even when Vulcan had been ridden far beyond the endurance of lesser beasts, even when his nervous pacing had settled down to a walk, even then the huge muscles moved beneath the sleek hide with awesome strength. It was the reason his previous owner had not gelded him, having continued to hope that the horse would eventually prove responsive enough to risk breeding him to produce the same power in better tempered horses.

But Vulcan continued his private war. He was never too tired to take advantage of an opportunity to unseat his rider. He had a keen eye for tree branches that might knock the rider out of the saddle and for deep water that might provide a chance to roll over. Shying violently at the least provocation or none at all was his favorite sport. He didn't mind pain in his mouth as long as there was a chance he could take the bit in his teeth and run. He was ill mannered and wholly undependable. And St. John loved every minute he spent on his back.

A ride on Vulcan provided him with a rare exhilaration. The constant threat of being mastered by the animal made him feel completely alive and whole. Sometimes he found himself laughing aloud for the pure joy of it, and often he felt as young as he had before the war, before the disastrous days of being Florence's husband, when Alex had often been a warm and shining part of his days, though he only realized it now. He was, he admitted, addicted to riding the horse as some men were addicted to the syrup of the poppy or to wild women.

"At least my vice is not secret." Tentatively he teased Alex, but he quickly discovered that despite her forbearance, she found no humor in the subject, and even the children were careful to show their admiration for his riding privately rather than risk their mother's displeasure.

For her part, Alex tried to convince herself that her midnight excursion had been the stuff of fantasy, making her feel things in the horse that did not exist. But her hatred for him persisted, deep and instinctive, and she could see no signs of emerging docility in his nature. Out of deference to her, St. John rode another mount when he rode with her, but that left too many hours of the day when he was on Vulcan. Or being thrown off him.

St. John was a splendid rider, far better than most men with two arms. He had drilled himself relentlessly to regain the skill, but Alex was aware he was losing some of the battles to Vulcan. He did not complain; he was scarcely in a position to do so. But he moved stiffly now and then, and Alex noticed faint bruises. She said nothing until it was too obvious to ignore.

She had seen him come in in the afternoon, his clothing dirt smeared, but he had bathed and changed and appeared for dinner without a word about anything amiss. She watched him covertly, seeing that while he responded patiently to the children, he ate little and moved gingerly, wincing now and again. She discovered how far he intended to carry the charade when they retired for the night.

There had been no false modesty between them since they had overcome their terrible problems in the beginning of their marriage. But tonight St. John was careful to slip quickly into a nightshirt behind the dressing screen. He would have been quick to extinguish the candles, too, had not Alex protested that she wanted to read.

If she hadn't been worried about him, she would have laughed. When they were in bed, she touched him gently, feeling him flinch. "Do you think I notice you so little that I would fail to know when you are hurt? Do you think you've broken anything? Let me see, Sinje." It took her back suddenly to the day she had lost her virginity to him, and she smiled tenderly at the thought of how far they had come since then.

The concern and lack of anger in her voice banished his resistance. He grinned ruefully and took off the nightshirt.

Even expecting something, she gasped at the extent of his bruises. His right side was turning purple black from shoulder to hip; even the stump of his arm showed it.

"My God!" She stopped herself from giving vent to the rush of anger. "My poor love, it's a wonder you can move at all."

"At least I held onto the reins. I hadn't any desire to walk home." He did not mention that as in previous battles with Vulcan, the horse showed more inclination to trample his unseated rider than to bolt for home.

Though it was rather late to do anything to ease him, Alex applied hot and cold compresses for hours into the night, feeling that at least it would take the edge off of Vulcan's latest victory.

Finally St. John sighed with relief as his abused muscles relaxed. "Thank you, sweetheart," he murmured before he slept. But he had not said anything about not riding the horse again, and Alex did not press him.

There were so many other matters to consider—the children, the other horses, all the things that needed daily attention—and Alex knew it was useless to expend so much energy fretting about something she could not change. Swan Song had hooked a foreleg through a fence and thrown herself, wrenching her shoulder; she would not be fit to race in the autumn. And Oberon came up lame after a training run late in the summer. Though Jim Barlow was nearly in tears at the idea that it was his fault, Samson assured him it was not, pointing out that such things happened with these horses, their big bodies carried at such speeds on their slender legs.

Alex and Samson did not think the injury was any more permanent than Swan Song's and doctored Oberon patiently with poultices, but it was doubtful he would be sound enough either to race in the fall. It was a blow because he was the most powerful of the younger horses, but they decided to try Taney, Mabbie's three-year-old bay filly. It was possible that Taney would settle down as she matured, but for now, they had to contend with her erratic nature. One day she might be very calm and concentrated on whatever was asked of her, but on the next she could be so wild-eyed and jumpy, it was nearly impossible to get a good performance out of her. She was not aggressive to other horses or to humans; her starts and frights seemed to be all of her own making. Her saving grace was that when she was in a settled mood, she showed the wondrous speed of her sire, Sir Archy.

Black Swan was not to race but rather to be allowed the lazy life to make her strong for breeding in the new year. Though he had never showed any great will to win, Bay Swan would go because it was worth the chance in order that he might be considered desirable for breeding even if never on a level with Swan.

Swan was seven years old, sound and fit at stud. Putting him back into racing was a risky decision, particularly because he would carry more weight than younger horses, but St. John and Alex decided to do so, as long as the horse did well in training before the autumn season began. Americans raced horses of much greater age than was now popular in England, mostly because of the longer distances for which older horses often had more stamina. And the reason to race Swan once again was simply to keep him in the public eye as a prime breeding animal.

Taney, Bay Swan, and Swan; it was an uneven selection of talent, but they would just have to hope for the best and forfeit the entry fees if the horses couldn't make it to the races.

Alex watched Samson cooling Swan down after a good morning's run, good enough to raise hopes for the races. Samson had taken the saddle off and was walking the horse himself; Swan was a favorite with him. Alex gazed at the horse with pure pleasure, more sure than ever that he would sire a grand line.

She loved the smooth flowing lines of him from the elegant head and neck to the long slender legs and the full, strong chest, the sleek chestnut coat glinting fire in the sunlight. His huge, dark eyes were full of intelligence—no matter what her own intelligence told her about the limited brain power of horses—and willingness, and his nature remained easygoing, despite his new awareness of himself as a stallion. He and Bay Swan had been kept well away from each other and given no reason to compete over the mares during the breeding season, another way of insuring their continued good manners at race courses.

Though she knew she was going to be late for breakfast with St. John and the children, who had already gone in, Alex still leaned against the fence, savoring the soft warmth that was seeping into the day. Later it would be too hot, but now it was a pleasurable caress on her skin. She felt some of the tenseness that had afflicted her since Vulcan's arrival ease.

There was a crashing sound and then a scream so shrill and overwhelming, Alex froze in confusion, having time only to realize that neither Swan nor any of the other horses in the yard had made it before chaos overtook them all.

Still screaming, Vulcan bolted from his stable, scattering horses and people in his wake. He passed so close to Alex, she could smell his hot scent and see the glaring whites of his eyes, but he ignored her and everyone else, streaking toward Swan.

Divining his intention, Alex screamed at Samson, "Let him go!" an unnecessary command as Samson had already seen the danger and had slipped the bridle off Swan.

Vulcan cleared the rail as if it weren't there, and then he knocked Samson out of the way and crashed into Swan.

Swan had made no attempt to flee but watched the advancing monster with an expression of almost human surprise on his face. Aside from harmless mock battles with other foals when he was young, he had never fought against another horse. He had never had to and all his training was against it. He went nearly to his knees under Vulcan's onslaught, and Alex was sure he would be dead in the next moment, sure that Samson already was. Her own screams that they had to get Samson out blended with Vulcan's insane shrieking.

Another voice was raised in the din. Swan had had enough of the unprovoked attack. Vulcan was heavier and had not just been out for a run, but Swan was hard-muscled and quick, and his sudden fierce retaliation startled Vulcan. Swan reared up in unison with his enemy, both of them screaming in horrible, high-pitched bursts of fury, huge yellow teeth bared, hooves slashing. The muscles of his powerful hindquarters bunched with effort, Swan lurched forward, biting at Vulcan's neck as he overbalanced him. Vulcan hit the ground with a tremendous thud and lay there, his labored breathing audible in the sudden cessation of battle cries. Like flame over the smoky gray, Swan pranced nervously as though considering finishing his enemy off, but then with one final clarion call of triumph, he backed off and stood still, sides heaving with exertion.

Suddenly there were cheers all around, and Alex became aware of the watching stablehands. The house staff, the children, and St. John were there, too. There was no doubt who the favorite horse was. Even St. John later had the grace to admit he was glad Vulcan had not inflicted serious damage on Swan.

Samson had gotten his breath back and insisted he was fine. Nothing could deter him from being the one to approach Swan. "Dat ma fine hoss, dat ma bes' boy." Swan responded to the soft, familiar crooning by nuzzling Samson and letting himself be led away.

Vulcan was unsteady, but he got up by himself and stood with his head down, blood running from gashes and bites. Swan had been marked, too, but not nearly as badly, and Alex could almost feel sorry for the beast who had started the fight.

"I'll help you care for him," she offered, and St. John accepted thankfully. Though he had not seen the beginning of the terrible battle, he had no doubt that Vulcan was to blame. And while he was truly relieved to see that the prized Swan was not badly hurt, it gave him an odd inner pang to see Vulcan so humbled.

Though Samson and Swan both moved carefully for the next few days, neither was seriously impaired, and Samson was certain the fight would make no difference in the stallion's racing season.

Vulcan was another matter. He had thrown himself against the door of his stall until it had given way, and that coupled with the battle had left him badly battered. Though nothing was broken, his coat would carry the scars of Swan's teeth and hooves forever, probably in patches of white hair against his soot coat as well as in ridges of flesh, and he was slow to regain his strength. He moped in his stall, balked at exercise, and was off his feed for days. He seemed to be a changed horse. It was as if, like most bullies, he could not withstand courage in another.

Alex would still have preferred that St. John get rid of him, but it no longer seemed so crucial.

❧ *Chapter 50* ❧

St. John was not so foolish as to take Vulcan with him on the racing circuit. Though the horse continued to behave docilely, there was always the chance that he would revert to his former tricks, and St. John did not want to be dumped in the dirt in front of racing enthusiasts. Nor did he want someone else's prize animal to be attacked by Vulcan. Alex did not remark on his decision, but her relief was apparent.

This season Alex not only went to the Washington races with St. John, but in late October, she also made a trip to Virginia by ship down Chesapeake Bay to Norfolk where she watched Taney win the two-mile heats and closed her eyes while Bay Swan lost interest in the three-mile races. But all was redeemed when Swan ran in his full glory to capture the jockey club purse for four-mile heats. He did it in three heats, beating Pirate who took the first, the contest being for two out of three. The time was phenomenal—seven minutes, fifty seconds; seven minutes, forty-five seconds; and seven minutes, fifty seconds, twenty-five seconds less than the now legendary match between Eclipse and Henry.

Virginians were noted for their hospitality in any case, but because of the win, the Carringtons were nearly overwhelmed by pleas that they please stay here, join so and so for dinner there, attend this dance, that reception. They had a marvelous time, and Alex confessed that she was glad her wardrobe was now adequate for such entertainments.

The only drawback was the old hurt; being that much further south was marked by even more evidence of slavery.

Alex felt the oppressive weight of it enough so that she was glad to return to Wild Swan though she had enjoyed the races. At St. John's insistence, Cassie Carter, one of their servants, had accompanied them in order that Alex need not travel alone on her return.

"I am a very settled matron with four children," Alex protested. "Surely I can be trusted to travel alone."

"You I trust, but men between the ages of fifteen and ninety I do not, not once they've seen you," St. John said.

"That is surely the most flattering thing you have ever said to me," she purred, and her kiss led to other things.

On her last night in Virginia, she and St. John were thinking of those other things as they sat through a dinner with other horse owners. The food was good, the wine plentiful, but their hunger lay elsewhere, and though they tried to be discreet, there was more than one envious glance from other couples as the Carringtons made polite excuses for an early departure.

They felt as free as children escaping from studies. Their host and hostess were still at the dinner, so when they arrived back at the house where they were staying, they had nothing to do but to assure the house servants and Cassie that they wanted for nothing and to retire to the privacy of their room.

They undressed slowly, playing a game of discovery. St. John kissed each of Alex's shoulders and then her breasts as they were revealed. In return, she teased his flat male nipples with her mouth and ran her hands through the light sprinkling of blond fur on his chest and batted his hand away so that she could pull his trousers and linen down, laving his taut belly and the sleek skin over his narrow hips. Delicately she paid homage to his swelling manhood until he groaned and pushed her away with a shaky laugh.

"A little more of that, and I will finish before we begin. I seem to be overeager for you tonight. You were all I could think about as we dined. I have reason to be grateful that trousers are not so tight on top as breeches used to be."

Alex gave a peal of laughter. "Under a gown, a woman has more room in that location and less to betray her state, but if we lace too tightly, we have no breath for passionate thoughts. Now you know why I prefer looser clothing."

They fell on the bed, laughter easing their lust so that they could begin again and savor each other longer. And when St. John finally entered her, it was with a long, slow thrust so sweetly controlled Alex felt as if her whole body had become his homing place.

Afterwards they both felt strangely wakeful and reluctant to retreat into their separate selves in sleep, and instead lay for a long time, talking lazily of the children and various projects at Wild Swan.

"This is surely the loveliest part of marriage," Alex murmured, "to be able to find such glory in our bodies and still be so comfortable together in our minds." Their disagreement over Vulcan now seemed foolish and distant.

The next day she and Cassie left for Maryland, and St. John, his men, and the horses prepared to attend other races in Virginia and a few in North and South Carolina where such fine horses as Sally Hope by Sir Archy and Ariel by Eclipse would also be running.

St. John and his entourage arrived home in late November flushed with triumph. Bay Swan had settled down somewhat and won more than he lost. Taney, too, had been steadier than was her wont. But Swan was the star, having triumphed again and again at great speed on various courses in different conditions and weather. More and more horse breeders now looked to his get to rival Sir Archy's.

Two days after St. John returned home, their lives were changed forever.

Vulcan had continued to act subdued through the past months, not even fighting when he was exercised, and Alex had not felt the old leap of fear when St. John had ridden off on him today. But she was outside when Vulcan came back riderless an hour later, and her terror was so instantaneous, she found herself saying aloud, "He is all right. He's just walking home. He'll be very angry. He is all right."

She continued to hold to this image as she organized a rescue party, getting Samson and Jed to hitch up the wagon and sending Polly's husband, Calvin, to find Dr. Cameron. "I'm sure we won't need him, but just in case." She wished her voice didn't sound so thin; she wished the others were making light of her fears instead of looking as concerned as she felt. She was glad the children were at their lessons.

Within a half an hour, they found him, lying face down, and Alex didn't even know she'd dismounted from Mabbie until she realized she was kneeling beside St. John, stroking his head and calling to him urgently. She was sure he was dead, but with a low moan, he opened his eyes and turned his head, trying to see her better.

"Where are you hurt? Tell me so that I make nothing worse."

"My back, but it doesn't hurt that much." His voice had the thready, drifting quality of shock. "Give me a moment. I can't seem to get my legs under me."

She lifted his now ragged coat and shirt so that she could see his back. She closed her eyes, but when she opened them, the evidence was still there, a horrible band of bruising and bloody half-moon hoof marks marring the pale skin above his waist. She jammed her fist into her mouth to keep from screaming, and then she pinched one of his buttocks hard. There was no reaction.

"Sinje, can you move your legs?" She asked it softly, gently.

After a long pause, he said, "I can't seem to feel them at all."

She looked up into Jed's and Samson's faces, black and white, wearing identical expressions of horror.

"I fear your spine has badly been bruised, love. It may be some time before you can get about again." She was proud of the calm sound of her voice.

She got into the wagon, and very carefully, the men lifted St. John and put him in with her, his head cradled in her lap. Samson rode Mabbie home.

St. John was asleep or unconscious for most of the trip home, and looking down at his still face, Alex thought, *this is how he will look when he is dead, like a finely chiseled marble effigy on the tomb of a lord*. She tried to draw her mind back from the abyss but could not until the blue eyes flickered open again.

He frowned, as if he were having difficulty remembering something of great importance, and then he almost smiled as his confused mind sorted out the thought. "You were right all along about Vulcan. In the end, he rode me."

His eyes closed again, but she did not mistake his meaning. She knew Vulcan had thrown him and then trampled him on purpose before fleeing for home.

Once they were back at Wild Swan, Alex felt as if she were under water. Everything around her seemed to move in an oddly blurred way; only St. John remained a clear image.

The children knew now that something awful had happened to their father. "He's a bit dazed," Alex told them. "But Dr. Cameron is on his way, and we'll take good care of your father." *Your father, my husband, my love*; she swam through the murky depths, only dimly aware that Della and Mr. Whittleby had taken charge of the children.

Samson helped her get St. John undressed and in bed; she was vaguely aware of the brown hands helping with infinite tenderness. But when she glanced at his face, she focused on it sharply. His huge dark eyes were brimming with tears that threatened to spill over.

"If you weep, I will not be able to bear it," she whispered very low, and Samson bit his lip savagely to hold back the sobs rising from his gut.

When Dr. Cameron appeared, the protection of the blur was abruptly gone.

He examined St. John thoroughly, his manner gruffly kind but firm as he demanded responses from his patient. Alex could see the relief on his face that St. John did not question him in turn.

When he and Alex were finally face to face and alone, Alastair's professional façade fell away, and he looked at her with stark pain in his eyes. "For the first time since I met you, Alexandria Thaine Carrington, I wish you were not so intelligent, not such a fine healer. Then I could lie. But you know, you know as well as I. There is some small chance that its spine is only badly bruised and that feeling and motion will return to his lower body. But you have seen how savagely the horse attacked him. It is more than a small possibility that the injury is permanent."

"I know enough to torment myself, not enough to help him. Will he be in pain?"

"None of us knows much about such injuries," Alastair growled angrily. "There probably will be pain in the area above the injury, though I cannot be sure. But he is moving his head, his arm, his torso, and he is breathing, which means the paralysis does not extend so far."

"Will he live?"

He did not flinch from the question. "It is not unheard of, but there are many problems. Unless he has control of his bodily functions, he will be as incontinent as an infant or suffer from blockages that could kill him. Infections also afflict such cases. And aside from all these physical problems, he may not have the will to live in such a state." He paused and steeled himself to go on. "I am not sure that I would in his case. He has only one limb left of any use to him; his helplessness would gall any living creature."

"I thought when he lost his arm that nothing worse short of death could ever befall him. I know better now. But still I do not want to lose him. One day at a time; that is all there ever is, no matter how much we want to believe otherwise."

That night while St. John slept and Dr. Cameron watched over him, Alex took a lantern and St. John's dueling pistols, making sure both were primed and loaded, though she intended to need only one.

She felt enormously powerful. She knew no one would see her or stop her; it was part of the spell that nothing impede her progress. This visit to the demon horse was different from the first dark confrontation. Now her rage and hate were immeasurably greater than his.

She hung the lantern close by the stall to illuminate the scene, and very calmly she took one of the pistols from its fitted case, hefting the heavy weight confidently. St. John had insisted she learn how to use them when they had moved out to the country, and now she was glad she had.

Vulcan's stall had been heavily reinforced since his attack on Swan, and he stamped about in it in a frenzy now, emitting husky, panting growls. In the panic of the day, not even Samson had thought to tie him, and Alex thought it all to the good as he thrust his head over the high door. Their eyes met, and Vulcan was suddenly still.

As she had the first time, she felt him so keenly, she knew him from the inside out, but this time she felt fear, stark and primitive, rising in him, overwhelming all else. In that frozen instant, she moved very close, put the pistol to his temple and fired. She felt the bullet slam into his brain, felt it stop the life there, and she was wildly exultant.

The big body collapsed in the stall. Alex did not bother to look at it. Very carefully she put the pistol back in the box and picked up the lantern. She heard them coming, and she stepped out to meet them, seeing Samson in the lead.

"You needn't bother with the carcass tonight; haul it away tomorrow. I should have done this that first night, so long ago," she observed calmly. She, who had been trained by her grandmother from the cradle to alleviate suffering and preserve life, had never felt more satisfied than she did now for having caused death.

She did not hear Samson murmur, "Poor sweet lady, poor chil'."

Dr. Cameron sent word to Annapolis of where he could be found and stayed at Wild Swan for the next few days. He sent other word as well, though she was not at first aware of it.

She was aware of nothing but St. John. Above the spinal injury, his bruised back muscles spasmed and jumped with pain. He could not shift his body to get more comfortable, and Dr. Cameron feared moving him any more than was necessary, not wanting to injure him further. St. John lay much of the time with his jaw clenched and his hand balled into a tight fist, enduring the agony and waiting for the intervals of relief granted by opiates.

Alex cursed the useless pain in his back even as she wished he could feel other things being done to him so that his body might function on its own again. With Alastair assisting and directing, she performed the most intimate indignities on St. John, giving him an enema and drawing off urine with a special tubular metal instrument that made her own body flinch in empathy. But though he knew what they were doing to him, St. John felt none of it, lying with his eyes tightly closed against knowledge of the base invasions.

Alastair and Alex worked with the unspoken understanding that it was necessary that Alex know all that was needed in the care of St. John in case there was no improvement. She did not shy away from the basic nature of the tasks, but from their necessity and the danger. A body that could not feel pain could be so easily damaged.

St. John drifted in an alien place. He almost welcomed the pain in his back because it reminded him that he was alive. He felt as if he were partially buried. He kept thinking that if he could just remember how it felt to think about moving his legs, they would move. But the message would not go through, not yet. He refused to consider the possibility of being like this forever. He ate and drank what he was given, and he tried to ignore the tasks Alex had to do for him. But finally, he could not bear it. In less than a week's time, she had grown pale and haggard, her eyes dull in dark-shadowed sockets.

He lay with his head turned to the side so that he could see her sitting beside the bed.

"May I do something for you?" she asked in response to the intentness of his gaze.

"I don't know how you have been able to carry on this far. How can you stand it? It's . . . disgusting. I am more helpless than an infant." He closed his eyes, suddenly afraid he would weep.

"Sinje, you could have died, but you live; that is all I care about. And your flesh is mine as mine is yours, not only for the good days, but for the bad ones as well. Nothing about your body could ever disgust me. Nothing . . . not ever." She punctuated the words with soft kisses.

It was a long time before she trusted her voice to speak again. "I know you are weary, love; but the children need to see you. May I allow them to come in this evening?"

"Not like this!" It was nearly a shout. Panic gave him strength.

"Please, Sinje. They, like me, think of nothing except that you are alive. But I fear they are beginning to doubt that. I am worried about them." Even though it was true, she felt guilty for using that against him. But she didn't feel she had much choice. She had had little time for the children since the accident, but she had seen how pale and shocked they looked.

Grimly St. John agreed because he didn't have the energy to fight her will.

The visit went no better than Alex had expected. There was unnatural constraint on both sides—the children looking wide-eyed and managing only the briefest words, fearful of saying the wrong thing, while St. John had all he could do not to show his horror of them seeing him like this—but it was a beginning. They would simply have to learn to function as a family again, even if St. John never walked.

It haunted her every waking moment, every moment she tended to him, and in the brief hours she slept, it came in nightmares. The one thing she did not want to consider and could not banish from her mind—the image of St. John condemned to spend the rest of his days as he was, never to walk, or ride, or make love again. She felt guilt for this last image, but she could not rid herself of it. All their careful learning of each other, learning to give and to take with their bodies as an expression of the love in their hearts; it was unthinkable that it should end. Body, mind, heart—they were all part of the loving she and St. John shared. But he is alive, she reminded herself constantly, fiercely.

Alastair had to leave in order to attend to his practice, but he promised to check in often and to come at once if there was any change. A day later Pen and Caleb arrived. Alex gazed at them blankly, not knowing that Dr. Cameron had sent word to them.

Penelope had meant to be strong for her friend, but when she saw how worn Alex looked, her control broke, and she enfolded her in her arms. "Oh, my dear! We are so sorry! Whatever we can do, consider it done." As much as she loved Caleb, Pen did not think she could care for him as Alex was now caring for St. John. The Jenningses had spoken to Alastair before going on to Wild Swan, and they were both shaken by his blunt description of St. John's condition.

Gradually it dawned on Alex that the couple was supposed to be with Caleb's parents in the next few days for the annual party, but when she mentioned it, Caleb brushed it aside. "Alastair's message reached us in Baltimore, I'm sorry it took a little time to arrange everything, but the children are with their grandparents, and you know how much that pleases both parties. We are here for as long as you need us."

Alex was too exhausted to know what she needed beyond St. John's complete recovery. Pen could do nothing about that, but she did try with Della to ease everything else. She encouraged Alex to eat and to sleep, and she spent time with the children, who for all their attempts at bravery were beginning to fall apart. And Caleb spent time with St. John.

"Have you let the Bateses know?" Pen asked.

"No, I told Alastair and Della not to," and I should have told Alastair not to tell the Jenningses either, she thought, but she didn't say it aloud. "Sinje didn't even want to see the children. I know he won't want anyone else to see him as he is." She could think of no polite way to put it.

"Well, he's going to. You've got to have more time away from the sickroom," Pen insisted. "It won't do anyone any good if you fall ill. Caleb is on his way up to St. John right now. And I'm sending word to Timothy and Mavis. They are friends. They have the right to know."

Alex found she lacked the strength to stand in the way of Pen's will. Numbly she agreed.

Caleb did not try to hide his distress with useless and jovial reassurances when he went to see his friend. He went directly to the bed and grasped St. John's hand. "What a hellish business this is! Pen and I came as soon as we could, and we left a message for Rane. He's in New York negotiating to sell the ship being completed in our yard. And with Dr. Cameron's agreement, we've taken the liberty of sending for Dr. Findley from Philadelphia. He's a good man for this sort of injury." He did not make any promises to St. John; Dr. Cameron was quite sure nothing could be done, but he had admitted he would feel better if he knew all possibilities had been tried.

Recovering from the shock of finding Caleb at his bedside, St. John suddenly gave into the despair that had been building day by day. "Christ! I can't even move my own bowels! There's nothing the good doctor can do. It would be better had Vulcan finished the work."

Caleb thought of himself lying there like that and felt the same, but then he thought of Pen. "You're wrong," he said calmly. "If it were Alex in your place, would you want never to see her again?"

St. John turned his head away, but he could not say that he would be glad of Alex's death under any circumstance except were she suffering intolerable physical pain. That was not his case; the pain in his mind was more acute than that in his back.

Pen came to visit him, too, with Caleb so that St. John would not be embarrassed by having a woman other than his wife in the room, and she and Caleb spoke determinedly about everyday things—their children, the political climate of the country, including the dissatisfaction many felt with the Adams administration, and the gradually improving commercial prospect—the conversation designed to remind St. John that he was still a thinking human being.

Most of it he let drift over him, but his interest was caught when Caleb discussed proposed plans for new canals and a railroad. Railroads were now being built in England, but the closest St. John had come to seeing one had been in a newspaper article that had pointed out all the drawbacks of having to lay the rails over various grades and terrains.

"Do you honestly think railroads will ever be built on a scale to be practical?" he asked.

Caleb's eyes sparkled, much more from St. John's show of interest than from anything to do with the subject at hand, but he threw himself into the discussion with vigor, wanting to keep the interest alive in his friend. "I do! I'm not sure how I feel about them personally, for it's rather a horrible idea to consider bands of rails wandering all over the place. But roads are too subject to weather, and canals can only go where adequate water exists. It may well come to railroads, but powered by steam, not by horses. Steam is being used more and more now in ships, and I know it will come to the land as well."

"I'm not sure I like the idea of horses being used less and less," St. John commented with a brief flare of humor.

"But the kind of horses you raise will always be in style," Pen protested. "It's hardly likely that railroads will ever provide so sleek and beautiful a show on a race course." Suddenly she turned ashen, thinking what a dangerous subject this was.

St. John took pity on her. "Pen, I raised the subject, not you. I'll be damned if I'll let one rogue destroy my love of the species. By the way, what has been done with Vulcan?" No one had mentioned the horse to him since the accident, but Pen's startled gasp gave her away.

Caleb saw nothing for it but the truth. "Alex shot him. Della told us she went out by herself the first night and killed him with one ball from a dueling pistol."

St. John thought about that for a long time after they had left him to his rest. He could scarcely picture Alex killing anything in cold blood. And then he thought of how dangerous it had been for her to approach Vulcan alone, and his heart pounded at the too clear image of what might have happened. He wanted to talk to her about it when she came to him, but he found he could not summon the energy. He felt very weak and confused; his thoughts kept wandering.

Alex knew even before she touched his burning skin that something had gone terribly wrong. "Oh, Sinje! My love, don't let go! I'll soon have you better."

He wanted to tell her that she'd got it wrong, this was better, discomfort giving way to a drifting euphoria. He knew he could just float off, and he wanted to.

Alex would not let him do it. For an instant, she was tempted, and then she was angry. Not so soon, not when they really didn't know how much or how little he might improve.

Dr. Cameron was sent for; Pen and Della helped, but it was Alex who brewed white willow, propolis from the bee hives, and herbs, and made St. John swallow the distillations, she who sponged his hot skin continuously until it cooled.

Timothy Bates helped as well as the others. He and Mavis arrived in the midst of the crisis.

"Isn't like I 'aven't done it before, shiftin' and tendin' 'im," Tim declared stoutly, and there was something at once dreadfully familiar and yet comforting about seeing the little man ministering to St. John.

When St. John's fever was very high, he tossed his head restlessly and murmured disjointedly. "Alex, don't hunch in the saddle!" he ordered, and she started at the sound of her name and then realized that he had slipped back to Gravesend and their youth. She had not cried since the accident, but the tears threatened when St. John went on to the sorrow of his days with Florence, pleading with her to tell him how he could make her happy. Alex refused to cry. Her sister had caused them both enough sorrow years before.

"Did I do this to him?" she asked Alastair when he arrived.

"Alex, what we have done to him," he emphasized the "we," "we have done to save his life. There has been no choice."

Alastair was torn. All his training was to save life, but he honestly didn't know whether that was the kindest course in this case. He did know that without Alex's constant care, the high fever and infection would carry her husband away. He decided he still had no choice; he helped her care for St. John. And he rejoiced with her at the change in St. John's body.

"I would not have imagined that incontinence would be

cause for joy," Alex told the doctor, and she had to bite her lip to keep back hysterical laughter.

"Ah, but it is more than that. If those systems begin to work again, who knows what other pathways may again function." Inwardly he cursed anew the lack of knowledge, but he assured himself it was possible, just barely possible that St. John's legs might regain their feeling.

Three days after the fever had begun, St. John opened his eyes and saw Timothy. He frowned. "Waterloo?" he asked, and both Tim and Alex thought he was still delirious until he added, "No, of course not. Wild Swan in Maryland."

Alex stroked his damp hair and gloried in the coolness of his skin. "Welcome back, my love, welcome."

He closed his eyes, not saying anything to that, too tired to decide whether Alex's healing skill was a curse or a blessing. But he, too, was encouraged when he discovered the changes in his body. It was not that he could feel the specific signals and needs as he had before the accident; rather, there were dim, faraway sensations that he soon learned to interpret.

But nothing else happened. His toes didn't move, his legs didn't flex, despite all his concentration. The good doctor from Philadelphia arrived and departed, displaying in the short interim a hearty but distant manner that Alex hated, though she knew he meant well to have made the trip so near Christmas. He assured her that she and Dr. Cameron had given St. John the best of care and that it was a tribute to their skill that he still lived. As for further progress, his eyes slid away from hers as he tried to find encouragement without staking his professional reputation on a lie. Finally he intoned, "Only God knows, madam."

Alex just barely kept her temper.

St. John's brief rise in spirits gave way to deep depression. He did not rail at her or at the children during their timorous visits. He simply seemed to remove himself more and more from everything around him.

"Sinje, you are better than in the beginning," she ventured one day and was immediately sorry.

Hot consuming rage brought an instant flush to his skin and his eyes glittered vivid blue. "Better indeed! I have now progressed to something slightly less than a toddling babe and slightly more than a drooling old man. I now know when to call you to attend to my needs. I would do a jig for the joy of it were I able."

Alex fled from his anger, afraid of saying more to make it worse, and she ran straight into another problem.

Pen and Caleb were going back to Annapolis to spend Christmas Eve with his parents, but Pen felt obliged to share her anxiety with Alex before they left.

"I know how heavy your burden is, my dear, and if I could keep this from you, I would. But Caleb and I just don't know what to do. It's the children, Morgan in particular. One would expect they would react to such a terrible situation; they adore their father. Flora is acting remarkably light-minded, as if nothing at all is wrong. Blaine and Nigel are acting like little old men, as if everything in the world is wrong, and they can't seem to make a decision without Morgan. Morgan is patient with them but not with himself; he is riding out every day as if daring his horse to . . . to do the same thing Vulcan did. No one has dared forbid it. He has stated quite adamantly that he intends to keep on no matter what anyone says."

For a moment, Alex wanted to scream at her that she could bear no more problems, but she was instantly ashamed, aware of how much the Jenningses had done for them. "Thank you. I'll speak to them," she assured Pen wearily.

Pen took her hand with sudden fierce strength. "Alex, what are you going to do? Caleb and I will do anything to help, but it's not enough. I hate to leave you even for so short a time."

"Do?" Alex looked at her blankly, and then straightened her shoulders. "I am going to carry on what Sinje and I have begun." She smiled faintly, remembering. "My grandmother used to say that where there is no choice, there is no decision to be made. There is no choice here. The tavern was never meant to be our life. This land is all we have for the future, and it is St. John's dream. We have good people working for us, and we have some of the finest horses in the country. It is enough to keep us going."

For an instant, Pen saw the old Alex shining through the haggard woman before her and she could do nothing except nod.

❧ *Chapter 51* ❧

It was a ghastly Christmas, all the adults pretending joy for the children, who were devoid of it. Alex felt as if she'd been blind to them, so concentrated had she been on St. John.

Everything Pen had said about the children was true. Though their reactions were true to their characters, still they seemed like strangers to their mother, grown quite out of her control in a few short weeks.

She confronted them after a Christmas dinner they had eaten in awkward tension in their parents' bedchamber so that their father might be included. Flora had giggled and carried on like a spoiled five-year-old, but at least she had provided some relief from her brothers' dull silence.

"I am very sorry," Alex began. "I have been spending so much time with your father, I have neglected all of you. But he needs a great deal of care, so that won't change for a while." She could not bring herself to say forever. "But that does not mean that I am not here for you, too. I would hate to think you could no longer talk to me because of what has happened." She drew a deep breath before she could go on. "I know that each of you has made a decision about riding. And I will not tell you that you must or must not get back on a horse. Riding is dangerous. You have all known that from the beginning. Many things can go wrong. But I don't want you to mistake what happened to your father.

"Vulcan was a rogue animal. He was bad through and through. No human kindness could touch him, and that made him a killer. All of the horses now at Wild Swan are completely different. They are well-trained animals who

557

take joy in pleasing us. It does not mean that accidents can't happen while riding them, but it does mean that they would never savage a rider as Vulcan savaged your father. Not ever. I know that absolutely. They are guiltless. And because that is true, they must not be abused for what Vulcan did." Her eyes held Morgan's. "To put any of them at risk as well as yourself by riding too fast and too hard is foolish and unjust."

"I want to ride again, and at the same time, I don't," Flora said, dropping her abstracted air and getting right to the point.

Nigel and Blaine nodded in agreement, glad their sister had said what they were thinking. Morgan held himself aloof.

"Would it help if I went out with you?" Alex asked. "We could go for a very slow gentle ride, and you could see how you felt about it. It is very difficult to get about if you are not willing to ride." She had not been in the saddle since St. John's injury.

The three thought about it, exchanging signals not even their mother could interpret. Blaine spoke for them. "We'll go."

"And you, Morgan, will you come with us?" She could see that he was about to answer that he wouldn't go on a baby ride, but he swallowed his objection, needing the closeness with his mother and his siblings.

"How did it feel to shoot Vulcan?"

Trust Nigel, Alex thought ruefully, never to lose his curiosity, no matter what the situation.

She considered lying and decided only the truth would do. "It felt wonderful because I knew he could not hurt anyone ever again. But it should never have come to that. Please don't believe that that is any way to solve a problem except in the most extreme circumstance. Killing Vulcan did not make your father better."

Nigel's eyes filled with tears. "Papa isn't going to walk around again, is he?" he whispered.

She nearly repeated the doctor's "Only God knows," but stopped herself in time. It would suit the children no better than it had her. "There is always hope, but I don't think so. Please do not ask your father about it. It is something he must come to know on his own. And if that is the way he is going to be, we are going to have to learn to live with it as he will. He is still the same man though his body is changed. His mind, his heart, his love for me and for all of you, they're all still there."

She did not blame them for their long faces. Since she could barely adjust to the change in their lives, how could she expect them to?

Morgan tarried after the others had gone, and his reason took her totally by surprise.

"What about Sam?" he asked bluntly.

"What about her?" she countered.

His green eyes glittered with angry impatience. "I'm the only one who even noticed! When Sam told her parents what had happened, they said she couldn't come here any more because she'd be too much trouble for you, 'under the circumstances.' " His voice was an uncannily accurate imitation of Mrs. Sheldon-Burke's. "I've been to see her. She's so sad, not like Sam at all! They make her act funny, like a scared little girl."

Alex was appalled. It was bad enough that she had neglected her own children who were surrounded by loving, caring adults even when she was not with them; it was unforgiveable that Sam had been so abandoned. It didn't matter that it was understandable "under the circumstances."

"Morgan, I am so glad she has you to care about her and so sorry that this has happened. What do you say about our ride going in that direction?"

His anger gave way to an engaging grin. "Sort of like knights going to rescue her?"

"Sort of like that. But we had better not let the Sheldon-Burkes know we consider them dragons. They might find that unflattering."

She heard her own laughter join his and was amazed by the sound. It was the first time she had laughed since St. John had been hurt.

When she related the story to St. John, she did not make light of the children's fears—she wanted him to be involved in his family again—but she did include Morgan's image of the medieval rescue planned for Sam.

Even in his preoccupation with his own tragedy, St. John was a compassionate man. He was very fond of Sam and hated the idea of her being confined at Brookhaven as much as Alex did. "Tell her I specifically asked that she come to see me," he said and was rewarded by Alex's brilliant smile.

Alex had not slept in their bed since the accident but rather on a couch nearby, and for an instant, she was tempted to ask him if she could return to their old comfort. But then her courage failed, and she resigned herself to leaving things as they were for a while longer.

The next day they set out in a determined procession. Samson had helped them mount, his face mirroring her own conflict—happiness that the children were overcoming their apprehension, matched by fear that one of them might be injured. She watched them carefully and was relieved by what she saw. Samson and the other stablehands had kept the horses exercised, and the children were all very good riders. The fear was newly learned, and the old habits of a good seat and steady hands on the reins were stronger.

Morgan's problem was quite the opposite. He had to restrain his impulse to gallop off at top speed, testing, always testing. But for Sam, he would do nearly anything.

The last thing the Sheldon-Burkes expected to see the day after Christmas was the mounted troop from Wild Swan, and their faces showed their shock. Sam was as astonished as they, but her reaction was utter joy that left her with shining eyes and an open mouth until Morgan, in his best brotherly manner, suggested she close it.

"Again we have come without warning," Alex said coolly, referring to their first meeting. "But we have missed Sam terribly and have come to ask if we may have her back again. My husband has specifically asked that she be allowed to come visit him."

"But we thought with this . . . this tragedy that . . ."

Alex could not bear to hear the woman's vapid sympathy. "It is a tragedy, but life goes on, day by day for all of us. The children still have lessons to do, and Sam is still welcome." She kept her smile in place with great effort as she watched the transparent chase of emotions across their faces.

Mrs. Sheldon-Burke had not found the presence of Sam any more enjoyable than it had been to her in the days before her stepdaughter had gone to Wild Swan. She wanted the child gone again, but she did not want to appear to be doing the wrong thing. That reminded Alex too painfully of her own mother. Sam's father, on the other hand, looked just the slightest bit unhappy; perhaps he had found that he had some affection for his daughter after all. But his wife still ruled him.

"Since Mrs. Carrington argues so eloquently, I think we must agree," he said. Just for a moment, his eyes met Alex's, and she was shocked by the naked plea in them—be kind to my daughter as I cannot be. It was as if he had spoken the words aloud. She could not approve of his cowardice, but she pitied him. And she was more determined than ever that Sam never again doubt her place at Wild Swan.

Still dazed by her good fortune, Sam nonetheless managed to be ready to leave on her pony in short order. "Thank you, thank you all," she murmured, scarcely able to find the breath to speak because her heart was beating so quickly, but her eyes lingered longest on Morgan.

He reached out and pulled one of her braids. "You're the only one who lets me tease 'em," he told her with a grin, but his eyes were tender, and Alex was struck anew by the special bond between them.

The winter was proving to be particularly warm though they had had their days of rain. Today was bright and shining. Morgan arranged it, Alex thought whimsically, perfect weather for Sam's rescue.

For a while, she listened to the children chatter among themselves catching up on the days when they had been separated from Sam. And then she forced herself to consider what she had told Pen. She did intend to carry on, and in order to do that she had to face their liabilities and assets squarely.

So many things were well begun. Much of the arable land was recovering under a plan of crop rotation that went from turnips (which she had learned from her grandmother made good cattle feed), barley, and clover seed after summer fallow to wheat upon the clover lay, to peas and beans to oats and back again to summer fallow. Dung, soot, and ashes were also added to the soil. The Maryland acres did not seem to mind that the rotation had been devised in England. They now raised enough hay and grain for their livestock and could soon raise enough to sell a surplus. She was already doing a quiet but steady business in herbs and seeds, and soon she was sure some of their apple and pear trees would prove good enough to provide slips to other people who wanted the strains. Plum, cherry, apricot, peach, and nut trees—almonds, hard-shelled and sweet, hazelnuts, walnuts, and others—were maturing now. Some, though not many, had been saved from the days of the previous owner. Vegetables and fruit had sold well in Washington, Georgetown, and Annapolis the previous summer, and they had plans to steadily increase that business.

Alex's practice of healing was limited by the demands of Wild Swan on her time, but still a good number of people came to her for treatment of various ailments, and some of them paid in coin.

The bees produced enough honey so that some could be sold to those who did not keep an apiary, and wax and propolis, or bee glue, came from the hives as well.

In addition, they were producing extra eggs and poultry and enough milk and pork for their own needs. And they had long had plans to build a herd of fine cattle, preferably the red North Devon cattle, English stock noted for providing good milk as well as meat, and for faring well on less rich feed than many other breeds.

But the greatest hope of all still rested with the horses; horses to race and horses to ride. Horses, always the heart of St. John's dream. To give it up, to admit that the dream was over was unthinkable. But though they could exist for a time on the laurels already won by their champions, eventually they would have to enter races again to keep on top. How that was to be done without St. John was beyond her at the moment.

They had built a great deal in a short time, but their liabilities were as real as their assets. There were still thousands of dollars to pay on the land before it would be completely theirs. And raising prime livestock meant being able to purchase prize breeding animals. There were also workers to pay regularly at Wild Swan. They had three more men, added at the end of the summer, on their permanent staff, and there were the extra hands they hired during harvests. Those costs could only increase as the land yielded more. Though they raised much of what they used and augmented their diet with the rich and varied offerings of the wild from fowl to berries, they were not self-sufficient. Coffee, tea, cocoa, sugar, salt, spices, cloth because they did not spin or weave at Wild Swan—the list went on and on, all things that must be purchased. And the children must be clothed and eventually sent away to school. Alex flinched at this last thought; she knew it was necessary, but she hated the idea of them being gone. At least in this, the cost would be defrayed by the money from St. John's trust that had been put away for that specific purpose. Alex was determined it would be used for nothing else.

So much to consider, so much to be done; she felt suffocated, and then she felt pure terror as Nigel cried out.

He was instantly sorry for the panic he had unwittingly caused as the horses shied uneasily at his outcry, but he kept pointing skyward. "I didn't mean to scare everyone, but look, our swans!"

Alex couldn't be angry with him as she saw the flight of swans growing larger until they passed overhead with soft cries and heavy thrumming in their pinions. "They are lovely!" Alex breathed, and she saw that even the moment of fear had served its purpose. All the children had handled their horses well, and no one had come off. They looked more at ease now as they rode along teasing their younger brother for his enthusiasm.

Nigel's next observation, though delivered in a perfectly normal tone, startled Alex far more than his earlier outburst. "I think that's Mr. Falconer coming toward us."

Nigel had the sharpest eyes of any of them, and in a moment, Alex could see that he was right. She shivered, struck by the eeriness of having just seen the swans and then having Rane appear. She felt so many things at once, she could sort nothing out. Wild, childlike gladness flooded her heart; Rane was here, nothing could be wrong in all the world as long as he was here. It broke and crumbled away, a long ago image of days of youth in Clovelly. Rane had a wife crippled in mind. Alex had a husband crippled in body, a husband she loved dearly. What had she and Rane to offer each other except the knowledge of sorrow?

The children rode forward to greet him, telling him of their rescue of Sam, offering other bits of trivia, happy to see one of their favorite adults. Alex followed at a slower pace, giving herself time to collect herself and her thoughts. And still joy welled in her as Rane turned his attention from the children to her. The children moved ahead but kept within their mother's sight.

"Hello, Alex. I would have been here earlier, but the message never reached me in New York. I didn't know until I was back in Baltimore." For a moment, his eyes were shadowed green-black with pain, and suddenly Alex realized it was for her and St. John, not for his own desperate situation with Claire.

"You don't think St. John is going to recover, do you?" he asked softly.

She could not lie to him. Slowly she shook her head. "No one truly knows in these cases, but I think he would have felt something in his legs by now if there was going to be any change."

"What are you going to do?"

Calmly and in detail she told him, speaking aloud her earlier thoughts. "As for racing, I just don't know yet. But I will think of something."

Rane had a mad moment of considering simply carrying her off, stealing her away from all the cares and responsibilities that had already left her looking so worn and pale and would continue to wear away her strength and courage.

"You can't do it all alone!" His voice was sharper than he meant it to be.

"I don't intend to." A note of coolness crept into hers, a warning that she would not tolerate useless pity; he knew how she felt. "I have marvelous people to help me—Della, Samson, the Barlows, and others. And St. John can still think," she added firmly.

"The dream of life in this country has not turned out as we thought, has it?" he observed wearily. It was not a question, but she answered it anyway.

"Tragedies happen to all people everywhere." She did not want to play "what if," wondering whether St. John's life would have been better in England, wondering what would have happened had Henry beaten American Eclipse in that all-important race four years before. Then St. John would have lost the horses, and perhaps the acres of Wild Swan would have been sold to someone else. Useless speculation, all of it.

They forced themselves away from difficult subjects. She asked about the sale of the ship; he said it was satisfactorily concluded. He asked about the autumn racing season; she related how well the horses from Wild Swan had done. But they were uneasy with each other and relieved to catch up with the children.

Rane visited with St. John much as Caleb had done, speaking to him no differently than he had before St. John had become an invalid. It was how Rane would have liked to have been treated in the same case.

Sam had her own approach and managed to be much less ill at ease than the Carrington children.

"I am so sorry you got hurt, Mr. Carrington," she said. "Maybe someday you would like to play checkers, what you call 'draughts.' I played with Morgan when his arm was broken. I could read to you, too. I am much better at it than I used to be, even the big words."

St. John found himself quite happy to see the little girl. Sam had a talent for making people feel they were giving her something while she offered herself. And in a very real sense it was true. Sam was so accustomed to being ignored or to having her presence viewed as an annoyance by her own family, she never took the welcome and attention she received at Wild Swan for granted.

"I think draughts would be a capital idea now and then, to keep my mind sharp," he agreed with a smile. He was allowed to sit propped up in bed now, and he was strong enough to use his arm and torso to shift his body and to roll over. But his legs remained alien. It was as if they were not part of his body at all, useless stage props put there to taunt him.

Rane was still at Wild Swan when the Jenningses came back from Annapolis, and though Pen proposed the idea, Alex felt the force of all three of them behind it.

"Would you let us take the children to Baltimore with us? Just to give you a little time without them to worry about. I think it would be good for them as well."

"Four of them, and then there's Sam. Good God! With your own, you would have enough to open a school! It's out of the question!"

"No, it isn't. Caleb and I love children, and Rane has agreed to help keep them amused; it will be particularly good for him. And Sam will have to come because I don't think she could bear to be separated from the others so soon again. Caleb has already decided on the approach he will take with her parents. Baltimore is to be a splendid outing for the children, a chance to see a world beyond their own. From what I gather, Sam's parents are always ready to do the best for Sam, as long as it's the easiest for themselves."

Alex closed her eyes, trying to decide what she ought to do. It was such a generous offer, and she knew the respite would probably do wonders for both her and the children. But at the same time, she was fearful that it might be wrong to let them escape from a difficult situation. And then grimly she reminded herself that barring a miracle, their father's condition would be the same when they returned as when they left.

"I'm sure you must be considering sending the twins away to school soon in any event," Pen persisted. "Perhaps it would be well if Caleb and I took them to see a few in Baltimore. There are some good ones there, you know. We've already considered several for our John. And were the twins to go there, we could keep an eye on them."

Pen was right. As the Carringtons had long since decided, the children could not be educated here forever. They needed to be exposed to more people their own age and to a wider experience than life at Wild Swan provided.

"You and Caleb must rue the day we came here. Our debt to you is never ending."

"If you continue in that vein, I shall be very angry," Pen objected. "You are our friends, loved for your own sake as I presume you love us. But if we must speak of debt, I would point out that neither Caleb nor I have ever risked the charge of treason for any help we've given you."

Alex was too tired to argue any more; Pen in a determined mood was a powerful force. But she did insist that St. John be consulted.

Pen had the grace to look guilty. "He has been, by Caleb. St. John thinks it a good plan."

St. John was, in fact, relieved to know the children would be gone for a while. Only Sam seemed natural when she visited him; his own were so obviously ill at ease, he found more pain than joy in their visits.

Alex's last objection concerned Rane, and she sought him out and spoke to him with no one else present, still finding it difficult. "I will be thankful for any time you can spare for the children while they are in Baltimore. They are very fond of you. But please, no matter how well she is behaving, I do not want the children to have to deal with Claire; they have enough to cope with as it is." It was the first mention of his wife since he had come to visit.

"Goddamn it, Alex! What do you take me for? I would never subject them to her, not after what happened here last New Year's Eve! She has never been fond of children in any case. Actually, she is not very fond of me either. I've found that keeping out of her way is to keep her more in control." He tried to make his voice light but failed utterly. All the baffled hurt of having offered kindness and having received raving hatred in exchange was there.

Alex reached out and touched him gently on the cheek. "My dear, forgive me. I should not have mentioned it. I know you would never put my children in harm's way." And never, ever your son, she added silently.

Rane took her hand and pressed it briefly to his lips. "We will survive, Alex; we are from strong stock. Your grandmother would be very proud of you. She was a great believer in the blood of the Thaines; your grandfather must have been quite a man to persuade her of that."

Silently Alex blessed him for his gentle way of telling her he knew of Virginia's death without pressing her to speak of it.

"Have you written to Boston about St. John?" he asked, still in the same gentle way, knowing the answer but hoping he was wrong.

"Absolutely not! He is free. He gave us so much help in the beginning. I could not bear to have him return for this."

"I do understand. I would feel the same about Seadon or Elwyn."

Just for a moment, she allowed herself to enjoy the feeling of being with someone who understood her so completely.

She hoped the children would understand as well when she told them about the trip to Baltimore.

Their reactions were in character. Blaine contemplated the plan quietly, looking exactly like his father when St. John was contemplating a new horse. Flora immediately began to prattle about the new sights and beautiful clothes she might see in the city, if she went. Morgan looked rebellious, as if he sensed a trap. Nigel considered it as if he were trying to solve the problem logically as he did his arithmetic or the challenge of identifying a new plant or bird. And Sam was terrified.

But under the surface differences, Alex sensed the same currents; they all wanted to go, and they all felt very guilty for wanting to escape from the new and frightening situation that confronted them at home.

"It is not as if you will be staying with strangers. You all like Mr. and Mrs. Jennings very much; and Mr. Falconer will try to spend time with you as well. And Sam, all of this includes you. I am sure Mr. Jennings will be able to persuade your parents. This is not forever." She paused, looking at each of them in turn. "And it is all right to want to be away for a while. I know you love your father, but things are different now, and it will take time to get used to the change. But I will not force you to go. You must decide."

"Won't you miss us?" Nigel asked.

"Very much." Alex tousled his hair. "Oh, so very much! But I'll know you're coming back, and in the meantime, I'll know you're seeing new things and having a wonderful time. Those thoughts will keep me company until you return."

She let them discuss it among themselves, and Blaine delivered their decision; they would all go, as long as Sam went with them.

Caleb returned from Brookhaven with every bit as much distaste for the Sheldon-Burkes as the Carringtons felt, but he also had permission for Sam to go to Baltimore.

Rane and the Jenningses stayed through New Year's Eve because they could not bear leaving Alex and St. John alone on that particular night. Mavis and Timothy, who had had to return to the tavern previously, came out for the night as well. But no one pretended that it was a celebration of joy.

"What a perfectly horrid end this year has had for Alex, St. John, and Rane," Pen whispered to her husband as the clock chimed in the new year. "We have been very lucky." Her eyes were full of tears. Caleb kissed the salty wetness and held her close.

Rane listened to the beginning of 1828 with no visible expression.

Alex had slipped upstairs to spend the end of the old year and the beginning of the new with St. John. But he was sound asleep. She kept the vigil beside his bed, feeling small, old, and infinitely lonely in a vast universe, longing for the light of morning to come vanquish the darkness in her heart.

✌ Chapter 52 ✂

Though Alex missed the children dreadfully and hoped they were on their best behavior in Baltimore, she found her days too crowded to allow much time for brooding. The winter continued to be so mild that she, Jed, and Samson discussed putting in various vegetables early. And there was the matter of the mares coming to be bred to the stallions. News of St. John's accident was beginning to seep through the racing world, and inquiries about whether or not business at Wild Swan would continue were answered promptly by Alex.

"I can barely keep from pointing out in the rudest terms that it is my husband who is injured, not the horses," she complained to Samson.

He did not have to tell her that it was because a woman was now in charge; had she been hurt, no one would even have questioned the continuation of the business.

Reluctantly but sensibly, Alex had withdrawn their horses from all the spring races in which they had already been entered, in most cases forfeiting the entry fees. It could not be helped, but she told Samson to continue to train the horses and the Barlow boys, who had never lost their eagerness to ride despite St. John's accident.

"Somehow, we will be back on the courses before long. We must be," she told him.

"Mebbe you needs a trainer dat kin go to dem races. You get somebudy else, I unnerstand."

She was infinitely moved by his willingness to relinquish the only security in his life. "Certainly not! Jed is quite competent for that now, and it makes no difference. It's still a matter of the owners being very much involved.

Samson, I do not intend to let what happened to Sinje cripple us all. You are part of Wild Swan. And one way or another, we will find a way to go on."

She wondered if St. John would also find a way. She was beginning to realize that he was being too civilized, too patient and sweet tempered about his condition. It was behavior she had been thankful for, but now she waited for a crack in his shell of indifference. He was by birth and training an undemonstrative man, but he had learned in their life together to express his emotions. The few small outbursts since Vulcan had thrown and trampled him were inadequate. Alex found herself growing more and more tense when she was with him, waiting for something to happen.

Yet when it did, at first she did not recognize the danger.

Daily she rubbed his lean flanks and legs with herb-scented lotion, checking carefully for bedsores and exercising his legs in the vain hope that they would not wither. But already she could feel and see the deterioration. St. John bore this patiently and often sighed in pleasure when her hands moved to ease the tense muscles of his back and chest where he could feel.

Frequently he was asleep when she finished. He escaped a great deal in sleep. But not this day.

"I told you you were right, but I never told you I was sorry, did I?" he murmured. He was lying on his back looking up at her, and automatically she helped him as he struggled into a sitting position.

"Sorry for what?" she asked, still busy fluffing the pillows behind him.

"For bringing Vulcan here, for riding him when you asked me not to. I am sorry."

Her hands froze on the white linen as the image of the stallion came back too clearly, and she thrust it away.

"My love, after what has happened, you owe me no apology. You paid a dear price for that horse, but he no longer exists."

"I know. You killed him. You took a great risk yourself, getting that close to Vulcan."

She had suspected someone had told him, but he had not mentioned it before, and she wondered why he was doing so now. "No, I took no risk. That night I hated so much more than he could, I was invincible."

"Do you love me?" He asked it with such intensity, she could not look away.

She smoothed the tousled hair back from his forehead, unable to read the expression in his eyes. "You know I do. Nothing changes that; nothing ever could."

"Then help me to die! Give me a pistol; my arm is steady enough to do it now. Or poison. You know the herbs to make a man sleep forever. If you truly love me, Alexandria, help me."

Time and earth stopped and a strange new gravity was crushing her body, compressing her lungs until she could not breathe. And in counterpoint to the slowing of her body came the rush of her thoughts.

Finally she accepted that he would never be any better than he was now. He would always be totally dependent on others. A kindness, the ultimate act of love to help him leave with dignity.

With a jolt of terror, she realized she was mirroring his thoughts, not her own. Not leave, die. She would never see him again. The children would never have his wise counsel nor his love again.

"I cannot do it, not now." She could not find the air to speak above a whisper, but she didn't look away from his intense blue gaze. "I don't know what is right, what is wrong in this. I do love you, more than you know, and I cannot bear the thought of being without you. You are so much more than flesh to me, so much more, Sinje, and to the children. You can still think and talk. You still love us—I know you do—and we love you. You are not a horse to be destroyed because you cannot run. You are a man."

She saw him open his mouth to dispute that, and she forestalled him. "It must seem like years to you, but it has not been long enough." She didn't try to defend this arbitrary decision. "And today is so bleak and wet." She was suddenly aware of each separate drop of rain blowing against the windowpanes. "When spring has come again, when the air is soft, and there are flowers, then if you still want it, I will help you to die. I swear it."

Rain was the only sound in the new silence. St. John turned his head away, closed his eyes, and fled into sleep, and Alex felt as lonely as she would be when he was gone. She had won this round, but it came to her that her relentless will would not carry St. John through. It had to be his own, and even that might not sustain his grievously injured body. For the first time in her life, she dreaded the coming of spring. But she would keep her word.

That night, without asking his permission, she crawled into bed beside him. He stirred and jerked awake. "What are you doing?" There was panic as well as anger in his voice.

"I cannot bear to sleep apart from you any longer. I need to feel you beside me at night. You are the one who keeps me from being all alone in the world."

St. John pulled her roughly to his side and buried his face against her neck, his harsh sobs wracking them both. She felt her own well of unshed tears and wished she could release the dull ache of them, but she could not weep. The two of them clung together, a frail barrier of mutual comfort against the desolation sweeping over them. She did not sleep on the couch again.

The next morning she spoke to Samson. "We have been doing St. John a disservice by relieving him of all responsibility. From now on, he will be consulted in the decisions at Wild Swan. Can you do that?"

Indeed he could. Samson could see how helpless brooding could destroy what was left of St. John's spirit, and he was now able to be around his employer without betraying his pity.

Alex pled overwork to St. John and instigated the routine of having Samson come in to discuss various subjects with him every morning. Though St. John suspected his wife's motives, he could not deny that she had enormous responsibilities. And Samson's insistence was difficult to combat. It made no difference that St. John often looked away in the beginning in an obvious attempt to discourage the recital. Samson's grave dignity precluded outright rudeness, and Alex began to notice that St. John was paying attention and offering suggestions in spite of himself. She blessed Samson for his perserverance.

And when the children came home in March, she found unexpected help from that quarter. She had had frequent reports from the Jenningses and scrawled missives from the children, but finally she missed them too much to have them gone any longer. She wrote to the Jenningses and informed Mr. Whittleby that his days of limited classes with the Barlow boys were over. He was genuinely happy at the prospect of having the five back again. Alex was not so sure about St. John.

He had read their letters attentively, but he had made no mention of them coming home. She was sure he dreaded the nervousness they had shown in his presence before they left.

But there was none of that left. They had enjoyed themselves immensely, but they were delighted to come home, and they had changed. They had adjusted to the new image of their father.

Alex noticed it immediately. They were all anxious to go to him the moment they arrived, but when she would have thanked Pen and Caleb, Pen said, "Most of the credit goes to Rane. He was wonderful with them, and somehow they found it very easy to talk to him. Why, seeing him and Morgan together was uncanny. I feel so sorry for Rane; he would have made such a good father."

Alex managed not to betray herself though her heart hammered against her ribs. "Yes, the Thaine blood is very strong indeed in those of us who carry its mark. I expect that Rane's mother and I could easily pass for sisters were we the same age."

It was Morgan who told her how Rane had wrought such a change in her children. "Cousin Rane—he said we could call him that—he took us out in a boat more than once, and oh, Mama, I did like it so! Flora turned a funny color and Nigel threw up the first time, but then they were all right, and Blaine, too. But Sam and me liked it the best. Anyway, we were with him one day on the boat, and Nigel said that Papa didn't seem like Papa any more. You know how Nigel is; he says whatever he's thinking. Cousin Rane said that was very odd because he had a father of his own way back in England and that he couldn't remember what his father's legs looked like, but he'd still know him for the same man. He said he didn't remember talking to his father's legs either, or the legs talking to him, but that maybe children and fathers were different now. It sounded so funny, the way he said it, and pretty soon we were all laughing so hard we were crying. It felt so good, laughing like that. And then after, when we thought about Papa, it just didn't seem to matter that he can't walk any more."

"Cousin Rane is a very wise man," Alex said, and she thought, Bless you, Rane, bless you forever.

The changes in the children were profound. They destroyed the formality of the sickroom by popping in and out all day long to ask their father something or to show him this or that. They all rode their horses, and Morgan no longer set a mad pace, though he was always bolder than the others. But most surprising of all was the change in Flora. She was still lighthearted and gay, but it was as if the protective bubble of extreme foolishness had burst. When she was asked to do something, she did it promptly, and she could often be found in her father's room. She read to him and reported the daily doings at Wild Swan with such an earnest attempt at maturity that St. John was hard put to keep a straight face. And with his lightening mood, the constriction around Alex's own heart began to ease, though she still watched the swans leaving and the redbud quickening, first signs of spring, with dread. She was far less able to discern what St. John was thinking than she had been in the past.

She heard a sweet trill of bird song, as unmistakable a marking of the last border of winter as the shimmering green of new leaves that were succeeding the pink shadows of the redbud in the woods.

She sighed and closed her eyes, gathering the energy to go on with the day. Lessons finished and their father apprised of various subjects, the children had gone off on horseback. St. John had fallen asleep and would probably sleep the afternoon away; there was no point in remaining beside the bed.

"Flora's absolutely correct, and I am a selfish bastard not to have seen it myself." His voice startled her so, she nearly leapt from the chair. "Correct about what?" she asked, trying to gather her wits.

"She says you're looking very tired."

"I'm not . . ."

"Do be quiet," he commanded genially. "It's no use denying it. I'm not blind, whatever else, though I have been, unforgivably so. You're pale as a ghost and not much more substantial." His sudden awareness of her fragility strengthened him; he felt more alive, more aware than he had since the accident. The first months had passed in a gray fog of depression, fear, and anger; only now could he see the changes in himself that had come in the past few weeks.

It was not a way of life he would wish on anyone, not

even on the worst conceivable enemy, but it was life, the only one offered him. That in itself, he realized, was not enough. But he loved his children and knew they needed him. And most of all, he needed and loved Alex. Only now did he understand the courage and love it had taken to return to their bed, to risk his rejection. And until this instant, he had not fully faced cutting his existence off from hers. It was not what he wanted, not what he would ever want. And it would come soon enough.

"It is surely spring," he said, and at first he did not understand why her face had gone even paler than before. And then he did. "You would truly have done it for me. You who love life so fiercely and are trained to preserve it, you would have taken mine to give me ease, wouldn't you?" he asked in wonder.

Fists clenched in her lap, tears so long withheld leaking out of her closed lids in spite of her effort to stop them, it took Alex a moment to understand that he had used the past tense. She opened her eyes and stared at him, his image blurred by her tears.

"Alex, I shall not promise there won't be many days when my courage fails, but you were right, spring is no time to die. And where you are, it is always spring for me. I want to be taken outside where I can feel the sun and see the horses." He stopped, having to swallow hard at the sight of her tremulous smile. "My love, my only love, I will never forget what you would have done for me."

The tense waiting of the past months was over, and her control broke. The tears came faster in a flood of relief, joy, and love.

"Come here," St. John said, his hand reaching out to her.

She went to him, nestling her wet face against him, feeling his hand stroking her back in gentle comfort as he let her cry. She had never felt closer to him than she did now. And for the first time, she honestly believed that they and Wild Swan would survive.

❧ *Chapter 53* ❧

Samson built a comfortable invalid's chair for St. John. It had wheels so that he could be pushed from one place to another once he was outside. It was difficult for him to maneuver himself with only one arm, but he could manage short distances. Samson was able to lift him as if he weighed nothing, and on every fair day, he did it in such a matter-of-fact way that St. John soon got over the embarrassment of accepting his help.

As the days of April warmed into May, St. John spent as much time as possible outside, watching the work of Wild Swan and losing his pallor. He felt as if he had been reborn. The sun on his skin was a tangible benediction, and watching the Thoroughbreds being schooled, far from making him mourn his loss more, instead gave him pleasure in the memories of how it felt to ride a swift, strong horse.

Alex had never complained about the addition to her work load, and had had to handle the first breeding season on her own in any case while he was at the race courses, but St. John quickly realized how much easier it was for her when he was present. With the decision to go outside had come the determination to face all that came with it, including visitors from the racing fraternity. Now when mares were brought for breeding, their owners or handlers were greeted by St. John as well as by Alex. News spread quickly about the accident, but with it went word that Mr. Carrington was still very much part of the operations at Wild Swan. It reassured many who had difficulty with the idea of doing business with a woman, though they would have come anyway because the first colts by Swan were beginning to be born and appeared on all counts to be animals of great promise, while Magic Swan by Bay Swan showed the possibilities of that sire, too.

St. John steeled himself for the unease he expected people to feel when they first saw him in his chair, but he found much less of that than he had dreaded. For the most part, these were people who knew the danger of riding very powerful, highly bred horses. Many of them knew riders who had broken their necks and died. They considered it on the order of a miracle that St. John had sustained such a grievous injury and yet lived. And once they determined that he still knew more about horses than most men, they treated him as they had before, with respect for his knowledge and instinct. And people like Paul and Martha Harrison, Mr. Ralston, and other friends from the race courses came to visit and were generous in their offers of support.

Americans, St. John observed, even those who lived very well, had a tough practicality that set them apart from other people. Alex has it, too, he reflected with tenderness, and perhaps it was part of the reason she has adjusted so well to life in this country.

That she had was more obvious to him by the day. He loved her competence and the laughter that had returned to her. He loved the swift way she moved and the changing green of her eyes that reflected so much of her spirit. Having wanted to embrace death, St. John now found himself feeling peculiarly alive, sensitized to everything around him. He did not mistake its cause. The paradox of the burden of his unresponsive body was that it made him feel light and separate much of the time. He knew with utter certainty that this separate self would not stay in the body for the years upon years Alex envisioned. But he never attempted to talk to her about it; the time would come soon enough when she would have no choice in her acceptance of the truth. He enlisted Alastair's help to make sure his will was in order and would make Alex's inheritance legal and clear.

There was another matter he knew he did have to discuss with her, but he flinched from it until he could avoid it no longer. She made no demands on him to touch her as they lay side by side each night, but he thought of it and of his own conflicting feelings.

Now they spent the time before they fell asleep discussing events of the day, business in general, or the children, and St. John wondered if she were as content with this as she seemed.

Mabbie, true to her old form, had not conceived in the previous year, but Leda had presented them with another colt by Sir Archy, a bay Alex had named "Winter Swan" for the bleakness that had been in her heart at the time.

"I was not far wrong," she explained to St. John as they lay talking after a family celebration of her twenty-eighth birthday. "He is a lovely colt and has been running since the day he was born. But though he is so young, there is a coldness about him. I doubt he will ever lose it. It is not that he is stubborn or misbehaves, it is just that he is so aloof. I think there will be an awful dignity about him when he is older. He will never be the pet Swan is."

"As long as he learns to run on command, I will be content," St. John said, but his mind was not on the horses. Alex's face was softly flushed, her eyes bright from the wine they had had with supper, and her dark hair, left loose, framed her face and tumbled over her shoulders. Though she now wore bedgowns every night, the open neck on this one allowed a tantalizing view of the delicate collarbone and the soft swell of her breasts.

Not even conscious of the old ritual, he reached out and tucked the stubborn strand of hair behind her ear, and then his hand moved down to stroke the smooth skin revealed by the gown. Whatever she had begun to say about another of the horses died unspoken. Her eyes flared wide at the erotic touch, so different from the casual contact they had now.

He read surprise but neither rejection nor demand in her gaze. His hand fell away from her. "Alex, I do think of making love to you. So often, I think of it. My desire for you did not end the day I was thrown. But I cannot; oh, God! I cannot!" His face was agonized as he fought to control his despair.

She saw the image of himself that he was seeing. It was not just that he could not control the hardening of his shaft; the erections came in various degrees without his volition or knowledge, in mockery of his old virility and mastery. Perhaps he could learn to control his sex again as he had other functions, perhaps the old pathway was still open if he but learned to concentrate on what had once been an easy gift. But his fear went beyond that. He had had to learn much to compensate for the loss of his arm, and now his body was more ungainly than ever, a burden to be clumsily shifted this way and that. She knew he imagined too clearly that while she might lavish erotic tenderness on his body, his caresses in return would be minimal and awkward. If he could be content with that, so would she be, but he was not.

"Sinje, I have thought of it, too. I have missed making love with you. But I have found it is not so fierce a need after all." She chose her words with great care. "My body's hunger was in answer to yours and only one of the many ways I love you. I will not waste away for lack of union. We are still together." She was not lying. Steadily her physical need for love had diminished until now when she lay beside him, she seldom craved the old intimacies. She could scarcely remember the self who had hungered so for St. John's body to possess her own.

He was silent for a long time, wanting to believe what she said, yet finding it hard to accept. "I would understand if . . . if you took a lover." He had trouble getting the words out, but he meant them.

"I wouldn't!" Alex replied. "I wouldn't understand at all! I would think I had lost my mind. I will tell you again. I do not need that in my life any more. I have the children, I have you, and I need nothing more." *And I still fear you will realize there was a lover long ago*, she thought.

The anger in her voice convinced him where patience had failed.

She did not tell him that their problem was not as private as he believed. There had been speculative looks that had too plainly shown that some of the men who had brought horses to be bred at Wild Swan were wondering more about the sex life or lack of it of the Carringtons than of the stallions and mares. She didn't like it, but she couldn't blame them for considering it, and there had been no overt rudeness.

She curled against him and let all the problems of their existence slip from her mind, knowing that she would have to take up the burden again in the morning.

Alex began to watch the horses in training with an even keener eye than before as vague ideas gave way to a determined plan. Taney at four, Swan Song at five, and

Oberon, also five years old, were all fit and should go to the fall races. And they would go. She would take them. Jim and Georgy Barlow could ride most of the races; Jed and two of the other men could handle the horses; and Cassie could go as her chaperone. Mabel Barlow had safely given birth to yet another son, Bobby, in early June, so it would not be a case of Jed worrying about her. And though Cassie was being courted, she was, unlike her sister Polly, not married yet so would not be leaving a family if she accompanied Alex. It only remained to convince St. John that it was feasible.

The opportunity to ask him came in a wholly unexpected manner. They were going over the ledgers, kept in Alex's neat hand, when Samson burst in on them.

Alex thought something awful had happened, but then she realized Samson was apologizing for the interruption and was laughing at the same time as he was urging them outside. "Neber sees de like of it, neber! Gots to see it to beliebe!" He was already wheeling St. John out in his chair.

Samson trained all of the horses in the basics of racing on the skinned surface of the half-mile practice track, but he also let the foals play there, claiming that it made them comfortable with the kind of place where they would do the most important work of their lives.

The sight that confronted them certainly seemed to confirm Samson's theory. The two-year-old, Fire Swan, and the yearling, Magic Swan, were staging their own race.

Alex blinked her eyes, at first unable to believe it, but the colts remained in position, lining up side by side and then leaping forward to run as if they were being ridden by invisible jockeys.

"Dey done it one time awready. Dey jus' habin' a good time doin' what dey made fo'. Fire, she bigger, but I swear dis be Magic's idea." Samson's delight was obvious. "An' eben wid a year mo' on Fire, dat Magic pretty much keepin' up."

They saw that it was true. Though the filly, red coat gleaming, was a little ahead, the smaller black colt was not far behind. They had apparently set their own rules, including the distance, slowing when they'd gone twice around the course, then whinnying, bucking, and nipping playfully at each other in an excess of high spirits.

"I have heard of this, but I've never witnessed it before,"

St. John marveled, and he laughed aloud at the colts' antics.

Samson went to praise and collect his charges, and accustomed to his kind handling, they came to him willingly to be rewarded by a nibble of oats from his pocket before he led them away.

"Sinje, our horses are bred for racing. We ought to either sell them or take them to the courses again, and I do not want to sell them. I want to take Oberon, Swan Song and Taney to the fall meetings, just a few here, in Virginia, and perhaps in North Carolina." Very quickly she told him how she would do it and whom she would take with her as help.

He closed his eyes and his face was set in grim, taut lines. He wanted to shout at her that it was out of the question, that it was his duty to take the horses to the races, and that if he could not, the horses could not run. He knew it was petty and childish, but it hurt unbearably to accept the fact that he was no longer able to exercise his chief talent. It made him feel small and shriveled inside. But reality had a habit of doing that to him lately. He swallowed hard before he could trust his voice. "Let me think about it. We will discuss it later."

Alex had the sense not to press him. A week later he had a tentative schedule planned; a meeting in Washington City, one in Baltimore, then in Virginia, the Norfolk, Broad Rock, and New Market races. "North Carolina and other states further south can wait until we see how this works," he finished gruffly.

It was more than she expected. She threw her arms around his neck and hugged him. "You won't be sorry. I've learnt much from you, and you and Samson will still plan the strategy."

Samson was torn between relief at the idea of having the horses compete again and protective horror at the thought of Alex being at the races without her husband. He did a great deal of muttering for several days. And Della's voice seemed so much an echo of his that Alex finally snapped, "Honestly, the two of you make it sound as if I am a small child!"

"The two of us care about you," Della pointed out virtuously, and Alex hid a smile. It was still a touchy subject, but Della had gotten more than used to having Samson around; she deferred to his basic good sense, and her expression always brightened when he came into view. In return, Samson was obviously fond of Della, but there were no signs of his courting her. Alex feared that there was some vestige of his past that prevented it, but hoped it would disappear of its own accord with time.

When Caleb and Pen and their children came to visit toward the end of summer, they were amazed and infinitely pleased by the change for the good in St. John and utterly stunned by Alex's plan to go to the races until she made them see the logic and necessity of it. Typically, once she was convinced, Pen bubbled over with plans to make it work.

"People will be shocked, of course, but you can overcome that by appealing to their sympathies. You are carrying on gallantly for your husband, and Southern gentlemen cannot resist such situations. It makes them feel oh so strong and protective, and while they're feeling so, you can steal the trophies right out from under them. Or rather, the horses can."

She wagged her finger in admonition when Alex wrinkled her nose in distaste at the idea of playing the role of damsel in distress. "Truly nothing else will serve. If you appear too competent, you will threaten them all."

The Jenningses were well versed in American politics, and from them the Carringtons learned a good deal about current affairs. On May 19, the so-called Tariff of Abominations had passed Congress and had been signed by President Adams. Basically, it was designed to protect the manufacturers of the North by placing tariffs on imported manufactured goods, but in the process, it seemed inevitable that the South would be hurt. Because of its agrarian structure, the South had to import most of its manufactured goods and would now have to pay more for anything not made in the United States. In addition, the South exported cotton, tobacco, and rice in exchange for foreign goods, and now there were signs that foreign governments were going to retaliate against the new tariff by applying tariffs of their own to goods from the United States, most of those falling on the raw materials from the South.

There was some reason to believe that the Jacksonian Democrats, hoping to garner support in the Northeast while not losing Southern sympathy, had framed the bill for defeat and had been surprised when it passed. But whatever the truth, the fact was that the tariff was causing outrage in the South and making sectional differences more pronounced.

"Do you think it will come to armed resistance?" St. John asked bluntly, and Caleb answered slowly, obviously having already considered this dire possibility.

"I pray it will not. But it is an old story. It was easier for us to act in unison when we had an outside enemy, England, just as it was easier for England to ignore her internal problems while she was at war with France. But now we are thrown back on ourselves, and we seem to be finding we do not have as much in common from one part of the country to another as we thought. There is more and more talk now of states' rights, as opposed to the right of the Union of those states. It is a thorny question, and I hope we settle it without coming to blows. But I am more convinced than ever that the only hope is for the United States to act as a single entity rather than as numerous principalities. I don't think foreign governments will refrain from causng trouble if we are not united."

He looked so apologetic that Alex said, "You needn't fear to say it. You are quite right. Not only England, but France and Spain as well, would, I believe, be very interested were they to think acquiring territory by conquest was once again possible in this country. Those are old and tired soils; there is much wealth here to tempt them, if the tales of the richness of the earth beyond the mountains are true. And Boston writes that they are."

Caleb nodded. "It will be interesting to see how Andrew Jackson handles all of these problems if he becomes president, and I think he will. So many people are dissatisfied with Adams's administration and want a change. Even the name 'Jacksonian Democrats,' as they call themselves, has appeal to many who think they have too little to say in matters of government." The reservation in Caleb's voice was shared by the Carringtons.

It was not that they thought Jackson was an evil man, but he certainly seemed paradoxical. He was supposed to appeal to factory workers, farmers, and any other men who were not part of the elite, supposed to appeal on the basis of every one of these men having a share in the government, and yet, he was a man of commanding nature who brooked little interference from others and came from a slave state. It was hard for Alex to see how those character traits lent themselves to democracy. But she judged that he was simply the figurehead chosen by the winds of change that seemed to be sweeping the political climate.

The limitations by property ownership and religious belief were being lifted from voting requirements for adult white males. The political parties were realigning and renaming themselves, the Democratic Party superseding the Jeffersonian Party under the banner of equality and denial of privilege in opposition to the National Republican Party. This party had been formed during John Quincy Adams's term and advocated a strong nationalistic program which embraced internal improvements, a national bank, and protective tariffs. The election process was being made more direct by having presidential electors chosen by popular vote rather than by state legislatures, and gaining popularity was the idea of nominating conventions, rather than caucuses and state legislatures, to choose presidential nominees.

The changes seemed very American to Alex and St. John. "It is very like the American demand for oval or circular race courses; everyone wants to see and to be involved," Alex observed. "But at least Mr. Jackson is reputed to be a fancier of fine horseflesh, so he should not make our sport any less popular."

"My practical wife," St. John murmured, but there was affection, not censure in the words.

The summer had seen two events which proved to be significant for the future, and both had occurred symbolically on July 4. In Georgetown, President Adams had turned the first shovelful of earth for the construction of the Chesapeake and Ohio Canal, planned to run westward in competition with the Erie Canal that was giving New York so much of the western trade. And Charles Carroll, a signer of the Declaration of Independence, had been the guest of honor to inaugurate construction of the Baltimore and Ohio Railroad.

The Jenningses had witnessed the latter ceremony, and Caleb confessed, "I had the oddest feeling that I was witnessing the beginning of a future that will move too swiftly for me."

Penelope shook her head in mock despair. "He will consider anything to urge greater speed from a ship, but he does not like to rush about on land."

In all the subjects they discussed, Rane's name did not come up, and finally Alex, sure the omission was deliberate, could not forbear asking Pen about him when they were alone.

"It's such grim news, I thought to spare you," Pen admitted. "You have enough to fret about." She sighed unhappily. "Claire tried to kill herself with a knife. Rane stopped her. She had only a small cut when it was over, but she slashed his arm badly when he put it up to protect his face." She shuddered in distaste and did not notice how white Alex's face had gone. "He's all right now, but he will always have the scar. That woman! She grows more and more uncontrollable. I think Rane ought to have her locked up. But he will not consider it."

"Perhaps she is not so mad after all," Alex said grimly. "Perhaps she made sure he saw her attempt to commit suicide. Perhaps she only meant to frighten or hurt him, rather than herself." She found herself wishing quite coldly that Claire would succeed in killing herself. But her own life had to go on.

She stayed with the Harrisons in Georgetown when Wild Swan's horses raced in Washington; she stayed with the Jenningses for the Canton races at Baltimore, and at each stop in Virginia, she stayed with acquaintances. She remembered Pen's words, and she played the helpless female having to make do as well as she could. And she missed St. John and the children every step of the way. When the horses won, she could hardly stop herself from expecting St. John to be at her side. And when there were problems, she needed him even more.

At Broad Rock, a horse nearly forced Taney off the course. Only strong riding by Jim Barlow kept the mare in the race to win. Alex was quite sure the move had been deliberate, but she checked with Jim first.

He was trembling with rage, totally unlike his normally quiet self. "He done that on purpose! Taney coulda been bad hurt." Mr. Whittleby's grammar lessons fled under the stress.

"More to the point, you might have been injured!" Or killed, she added to herself.

She did not speak to the opposing jockey. She found the horse's owner, Mr. Blockett, a big man who looked coarse despite his well-tailored clothes. His nose was red-veined, his body fleshy from years of overindulgence. She felt like sinking her fists into his soft belly, but instead, she addressed him with exaggerated sweetness.

"I am sure you did not intend for your rider to behave so rudely. Perhaps you ought to improve your training program."

He knew he was at a disadvantage. Alex had made sure there were witnesses within earshot. She was dressed in deep, bright green that made her eyes look particularly vivid. Blockett glanced around nervously and saw the admiring looks Alex was getting as well as the knowing expressions of those who did not believe his jockey's actions had been inadvertent. Still, he could not tolerate being confronted by a woman, particularly since her horse had won and his had lost.

"This is a hardy sport. Perhaps the pressure is too much for you," he sneered.

"The horses of Wild Swan are the best anywhere. They have proved it time and again. And I was not riding, my jockey was. I quite agree that racing is not for the faint of heart. But I would also point out that such tactics as yours do not improve the sport for anyone." She stopped just short of using the word "cheating." "If I see your rider pressing another horse, mine or someone else's, I will make sure the stewards recover the eyesight they so sadly lacked today."

She turned on her heel and left him, secure in the knowledge that she would not be the only one keeping a sharp eye on his jockey. She found that far from judging her unfeminine, most of the other owners applauded her action, many going out of their way to tell her so. It seemed they did not mind steel beneath the flowers in a woman. Though this attitude was to her advantage at the moment, she would not want to play the role for any length of time and was glad St. John did not require it of her.

At New Market, she withdrew Oberon from the four-mile heats. He was not actually limping, but his stride was not quite right, and he had already proven himself vulnerable to injury. It didn't take long for the snide remarks to reach her, all of them to the effect that Oberon was being withdrawn because Alex was acting like a mother hen. Alex understood the true purpose of the gossip; if she could be forced to race a less than sound Oberon, some inferior horses might not only have a better chance of winning the four-mile heats, a chance they were going to have in any case under the circumstances, but one of them would also be able to claim a victory over Oberon, who was now well established as a champion.

Though inwardly Alex's temper boiled, she remained serene on the outside, refusing to be baited into risking the stallion. She knew the pressure was not coming from her friends. And it helped when Allen Ralston, the man who had lost the wager on the Eclipse-Henry match to St. John, sought her out.

"Bravo! You're right to stick to your guns. Your husband would be proud of you," he told her. "I watched Oberon being worked. It's not obvious, but there is something wrong there."

She was grateful for his praise, and they discussed various possibilities of what might be troubling the horse. Alex suspected a strain, though there was no noticeable swelling. She was treating Oberon with rest and poultices and would be relieved when he was back at Wild Swan under St. John's and Samson's knowledgeable eyes.

She wanted comfort for herself as well. She wanted to be home with her children. Most of all she wanted to be with St. John. Even so diminished physically, he was **the** center of her world.

❦ Chapter 54 ❦

Alex arrived home knowing she had acquitted herself well in the first racing season, though she did not forget that the horses and Jim and Georgy Barlow had won the races. St. John was lavish in his praise of all of them and listened avidly to accounts of each race. She glossed over the few difficulties she had had and was relieved when St. John agreed with her assessment of Oberon.

"He's the sort of horse we will always have to watch carefully. His stride is still a bit off. To have raced him would have meant risking not only him, but Jim and the other riders and horses as well."

Though it was late November when she returned, she soon discovered that St. John still spent as much time as possible outside. He looked fit and so alive, it seemed impossible that he could not get up and walk away from his chair. But though he remained unable to walk, his sphere of influence had expanded in her absence.

It took her a startled instant to identify her emotion.

While she was away, the children had learned to turn to St. John for advice and support, and now it was as natural as breathing for them to say, "I'll ask Papa," or "Papa said we could," or "Papa said we couldn't." Even Samantha was part of the pattern, constantly deferring to "Mr. Carrington." And Alex was jealous. It wasn't that the children were trying to hurt her. They obviously still loved her and did not blame her for having gone away because they understood it was necessary. It was just that they needed someone who was available, patient, and loving. St. John had become that for them.

"You can have anything, but you cannot have everything." She could hear her grandmother telling her that when she was very small. It had been over a choice of delights, too many things that had beckoned in one day— bread baking and gardening going on at the same time, as well as hop pickers to watch in the fields and a cat having a litter of kittens. Alex remembered the frenzy she had felt; she had wanted to do everything at the same moment, missing nothing. In the end, she had chosen to work in the garden with Virginia, and because of her grandmother's words, she had felt peaceful about the choice.

Things were no longer as simple as they had been then, but she realized she had already, albeit unknowingly, made a choice. By taking over what had been St. John's role, she had left what had been hers for him to fill. It was as if they had changed places; an odd thought—St. John was becoming the one at home nurturing their offspring.

It was another adjustment to be made, and she knew she should be nothing but grateful that St. John had proven to be so accessible to the children. For the sake of continuity in their lives, she was careful not to usurp St. John's authority, but in the first days it was hard.

Marcus and Octavia, the old slaves who had come with the property, had died within a week of each other while Alex was gone. Marcus had followed his wife as soon as he was sure she had had a proper burial on the place. Dr. Cameron had been called, but there was nothing he could do for them. They had been frail, tired, less and less able to care for themselves, and ready to leave the burdens of living behind.

Though everyone had treated them with kindness, they had never truly entered into the new life of Wild Swan, once Bladensfield. When they died, no one even knew whether they had ever had children or other family; Marcus and Octavia had confided in each other, not in the newcomers.

Here, too, St. John had been adequate to the task of helping the children to understand. The old couple had never been close to the children, and they had been so ancient as to seem beyond life already to the young; still, having death come to Wild Swan was unsettling. But St. John had answered the children's questions honestly and had tried to help them to see the seasonal nature of all life.

"Of course Nigel wanted to know what happens to bodies in the ground," St. John said ruefully, "and I did not indulge that particular curiosity at length."

"There are worse things than being with the person you love for all of your life," Alex said softly. "And worse things than dying nearly at the same time." She felt regret that freedom from slavery had come so late to them as to be meaningless, but the regret was tempered by a sense of fitness. They had managed to create a life for themselves despite their bondage, and they had stayed together and loyal to each other to the end.

St. John did not voice his own thoughts aloud, turning the conversation instead to other things that had occurred at Wild Swan in her absence and to plans for the holidays.

This year they gave a large New Year's Eve party. Alex was proud of St. John for being willing to go through with it. It was a way of asserting their survival and celebrating the new confidence St. John had. Both of them drew strength from the presence of not only Caleb and Pen but the elder Jenningses and other Annapolis friends as well.

And from Rane. Alex had not expected him to come, but she was pleased that he had because his admiration and delight in St. John's improved condition were obvious. She was glad for his own sake as well; he looked so worn and weary when he arrived, but his expression had visibly lightened after a little time with the children.

She saw the tail of the scar from Claire's knife marring the back of his right hand, but she made no mention of it, nor did he.

Much of the talk on New Year's Eve was political. The legislature of South Carolina had adopted a set of eight resolutions declaring the Tariff of Abominations not only oppressive and unjust, but also unconstitutional, and other Southern states were coming out in support of the resolutions. News of the action was traveling swiftly because it was so important, an open example not only of the sectional conflict of interests between the Northern manufacturing and the Southern agricultural states, but also a raising of the question of where power lay—with the federal government or with the states themselves.

Even those at the Carringtons' party who were of avowedly Southern sympathies regarding the tariff question were uneasy at South Carolina's act of defiance, but the talk stayed deliberately away from the possibility of armed conflict, as if speaking of the hideous image would give it strength.

Andrew Jackson had been elected president and would be inaugurated in March. It remained to be seen how he would handle the sectional rivalry. The campaign had been startling in a new intensity and in a good deal of undignified behavior on both sides.

Jackson's supporters had paraded with hickory sticks, symbols of the toughness of "Old Hickory," and hickory brooms to mime sweeping out Adams. Adams, a reserved man, had not been able to control his supporters, some of whom had stooped so low as to call Jackson an adulterer because of a technicality concerning his wife's divorce from a first and loutish husband nearly forty years before. Mr. Jackson had once killed a man in a duel due to a slanderous comment made about Mrs. Jackson, but he could not fight all the wagging tongues of the presidential campaign, and Mrs. Jackson was said to have suffered greatly from the scurrilous remarks. There were, in fact, rumors that she was gravely ill or even dead from the strain. Alex, having known the power of vicious tongues, hoped the rumors were false.

It was easier for everyone when they moved on to lighter subjects, including a toast to Alex, causing her to blush in spite of her effort to accept the accolade calmly. She knew that more than a few of the people there thought of her new work as an eccentric endeavor, but as long as St. John was proud, that was enough.

As 1828 gave way to 1829, Alex spared a thought for Boston and wished him well. She was more peaceful than ever with the decision not to let him or Hugh in England know what had befallen them. Boston's letters came infrequently now as he made his way ever further west, but that was all to the good since he was less likely to run into people who knew about St. John's accident.

"This will be a better year than the last," she whispered to St. John. "I know it will."

The birth of Dreamer in January was a good beginning for the prediction. The previous February when life had been so uncertain and none of the horses had gone to the races, they had bred Black Swan, born in 1821, Leda's daughter by Hugh's English stallion, to Oberon. The result was a lovely black filly with exquisitely long legs, wide dark eyes, and a slip of white on her forehead. Her official name was "Dream Swan" because of her night coloring and the crossing of Mabbie's line with Leda's (still the way the Carringtons designated the two families, though most used the stallion rather than the mare to name a line). The filly had, at Nigel's suggestion, become "Dreamer" to everyone at Wild Swan. The children had long since taken to calling the horses of the Swan line by the first of their names—Black, Bay, Fire, and Winter, with the exceptions of Swan Song who was "Song" to them and Wild Swan who was "Swan" to everyone.

Mabbie had again failed to conceive, but in February she would be bred to Swan in the hope that she would produce a colt the following year. Swan Song and Black Swan were to be bred to Oberon. Fire Swan at three and Taney at five would go to selected races. With neither to run the four-mile heats, and with Fire untested at a formal race meeting, and with Taney's tendency to exhibit erratic temperament, running beautifully one day and badly the next, it was not an impressive offering. But it was enough to keep Wild Swan's name in the forefront among horsemen. And in the fall, if Oberon remained fit as he seemed now, he would again challenge at four miles.

The novelty of traveling to the races had soon paled. They went by ship when possible, by road the rest of the way; Alex rode either Taney or Fire, helping Jim Barlow to keep them exercised. Georgy Barlow wasn't on this trip since the racing was to be so limited. At the courses, Alex either rented an equipage and driver so she'd have a good seat and vantage point or shared the carriages of friends. Jed Barlow and the other handler rode quieter beasts, and Cassie rode pillion with one of the men because she remained terrified of riding alone.

One of the highlights of the trip for Alex was taking Leda to Moorfield in North Carolina for a last breeding to Sir Archy. Not only was the stallion old at twenty-four, but Leda herself was now seventeen. She could not go on producing colts forever, and if they bred her again, they would use Oberon, but they had decided that one more son or daughter by the famous stallion would not be amiss.

Having done so well with their Sir Archy foals, the party from Wild Swan was well received at Moorfield. Alex was excited by the chance to see the famous stud.

Age had marked him. His temples had the hollows of the years, and his big bones were beginning to show in the way of old horses when the body seems to sink in on itself. But the big, dark bay was still magnificent, strength and endurance showing in every line. He had wide intelligent eyes, but he was not a friendly animal. His aloofness reminded Alex of his son, Winter Swan.

People in the racing world were now accepting Alex's presence in place of St. John and were less shocked than they had been in her first season. She was very careful not to give any of the wives reason to resent her presence, and her care was rewarded by the kind treatment she received from most of the women. Even the plainest among them found nothing to envy in a woman whose husband was so disabled.

There were no more shady incidents on the courses. Taney lost slightly more than a quarter of her races despite Jim's expert handling due to her fractious temperament, but the nearly three-quarters that she won kept her listed among the top horses. Fire, though only entered with other three-year-olds in one- and two-mile heat races, won consistently, her bright chestnut coat a beacon as she took the lead in her habitual way, breathtakingly close to the end of each heat. Jim rode as Samson had instructed. Fire liked to run with the others until asked for one great effort. If she were pushed to the front and kept there, she tended to lose interest and heart, as if she disassociated herself from the proceedings. It made the timing delicate for Jim as he had to be careful that other horses did not box Fire Swan in so that she could not make her final move, but she was fast enough so that he could take her out wide rather than hugging the center rail.

Though Georgy Barlow was, at fourteen, a good rider, Jim, a year older, continued to be superior. He communicated in some mysterious way with the beasts he rode so that rider and horse understood the demands being made on each other and came to some silent agreement. Jim had more than fulfilled Samson's prediction of his talent. So far, he had taken few spills and suffered only minor injuries. Alex intended that it remain that way.

The inauguration of Jackson in March provided more gossip than there had ever been before about the presidency. Many of the frontiersmen to whom Jackson so appealed had come to the capital to celebrate with their hero and in the process had displayed not only rough and ready manners, but also muddy boots that tracked through the White House. Though most Southerners would have preferred anyone to the New Englander Adams, many of the horse racing set were of moneyed and privileged backgrounds, and they were not at all certain they liked Jackson's rejection of the elite and his enthusiasm for the uncouth Westerners.

"All of this must seem undignified to an Englishwoman," one woman remarked to Alex as yet another discussion of Jackson began. The woman's tone was friendly and a little embarrassed.

"Not at all," Alex assured her. "You must remember England's present king, George IV, is not noted for his upright character. He had just ascended the throne when my husband and I left England, but his reputation as Prince of Wales was extremely scandalous. And the story of how he humiliated his wife by having her barred from the coronation is widely known, even here, as well as the fact that she died not long after. No, I do not think the English should cast aspersions on President Jackson."

"It's a pity about the president's wife, isn't it? So different from how King George felt about his," the woman commented. "They say he is very bitter about her death and blames Adams's supporters for it."

"I can see how he would. Attacking her character and their marriage was a needless and cruel part of the campaign for votes." The rumors had been true. Rachel Jackson had died in December, leaving her devoted husband of so many years desolate and enraged. She had been buried on Christmas Eve in the dress she would have worn to her husband's inauguration.

In Alex's presence, most people were careful about mentioning that much of President Jackson's popularity came not only from the fact that he was an old Indian fighter who had defeated the Creeks at the Battle of Horseshoe Bend, Alabama, where almost 900 of the 1000 Indians fighting were killed, the Indians having fought with the British in the War of 1812, but also because he was the hero of the Battle of New Orleans. For her part, Alex made no point of it either. It was reasonable that a man should fight savagely to defend his country. The battle was significant to her for reasons of her own history; she had been in Devon with Rane and his family when she had first heard of it. The girl she had been then seemed so distant in time and innocence, she could scarcely recognize her as part of her life and tried not to think about her at all.

Though she and St. John had committed their lives and fortunes to the United States, Alex suspected they would always be regarded as British, particularly when unpleasantness between the United States and England was the subject at hand.

She was profoundly happy to arrive home by late spring, and she discovered that as she had been wont to do for him, so St. John had kept things well under control so that she was not faced with myriad problems when she returned. But she noticed immediately that he was drawn and pale.

"Sinje, no lies," she pled as soon as she had weathered the ecstatic greetings of the children and was alone with her husband. "You don't look well. Is it just too much work or have you been ill while I was away?"

"I hoped to have lost all signs of it before you arrived." He sighed in frustration. "How could I have forgotten how sharp-eyed you are? I had a fever, but Dr. Cameron took good care of me and assured me that he did nothing of which you would not approve."

She put her arms around him and buried her head against his chest, shivering convulsively. "Oh, God, why didn't someone send for me? That's why such a careful schedule was arranged!"

"Sweetheart, it passed very quickly. I was just very tired when it was over."

It passed very quickly; the words wrenched her heart because she knew too clearly what they meant. The crisis of the fever had come too fast for there to be time to summon her. She might have returned too late, returned to find him vanished from her life. She began to sob helplessly. She knew exactly how he had felt when he had come home to her after her miscarriage.

"Hush, love, oh, please don't weep! It's over, and I'm well now."

"I'll never leave you again, never!"

"Yes, you will. It is a difficult adjustment for me, I admit, to have you going to the races in my place, but you are doing a splendid job, and we are prospering far more than we would without your efforts." *And I want you to be as strong and able as you can possibly be to carry on when I am not here,* he added silently. "You may not be able to make the wagers, but the purses are welcome, and more and more mares are being brought here for breeding. And when we are ready to sell some of our stock, we will be able to get high prices for them."

It took her a long time to loosen her compulsive hold on him, and for days she was nervous if he was out of her sight. But he was patient and relentless in his insistence that he was all right and that their plans must go forward.

And among those was the plan to send the twins to school in Baltimore. Blaine and Flora were fourteen years old, and it was time to broaden their education. It was a difficult decision, as both Alex and St. John hated the idea of having the children living away from Wild Swan, but they did not want them to grow to maturity with too narrow a view of the world.

Baltimore was a compromise decision. Georgetown seemed to have better schools by reputation, but the Jenningses lived in Baltimore. Flora was to go to a seminary for young ladies, while Blaine would take classes with other young men. Both of them would attend as day students and live with the Jenningses. It seemed a good way to separate the twins somewhat without removing them completely from each other's influence. In return, the Carringtons would have the Jenningses' children for much of the next summer. John, Elizabeth, and Blake had little familiarity with country living aside from their previous brief visits to Wild Swan, and Caleb and Pen wanted them to know the land as well as the city. The exchange would benefit both sides.

Blaine and Flora were at once excited and apprehensive about this new direction in their lives, but their father had already done much of the groundwork of preparing them to go.

"It's not quite fair," he admitted, "but I think I've convinced them that it's not only a matter of education but also of example to the younger children and of family honor."

Blaine was worried that he would not be adequate to the work.

Alex opened her eyes wide. "You've studied English grammar, Greek and Latin grammar, literature, geography, history, and arithmetic as well as agriculture. Is there something missing from that list?" she asked in a puzzled tone.

Blaine had to grin. "No, I suppose not. Mr. Whittleby would be insulted if he knew how scared I am. I guess I'll just have to see how it goes and do my best." He paused and then offered softly, "Mama if I do well enough in school, I'd like to study the law."

Alex's surprise was no longer feigned. As far as she knew, he had never mentioned this before. There were many in America who seemed to hold the legal profession in contempt, but to Alex's mind it was an honorable one if so practiced. Given Blaine's thoughtful, reasoned approach to daily life, it was not at all odd that he should be attracted to the law. Blaine liked limits and structure; it was why he was so capable of imposing them on his less-disciplined twin.

"I think it is a splendid idea. If you do well in school, I should think you will be ready to apprentice to a lawyer in two years or so." She was pleased to learn that Blaine had chosen to try the idea on her first, and she warned St. John of this development before his son spoke to him, and so Blaine found his father very receptive to the idea. Blaine's confidence climbed steadily.

Flora's qualms were of a different nature. She had a shrewd practicality under the fluff, and she knew very well that her education thus far had been superior to that of the vast majority of girls her age. As far as classes went, she was more worried that she would have to do hours of needlework, which she detested, than that she would have any difficulty with academic subjects. But her basic fears were that she would disgrace herself by being childishly homesick and that she would reveal herself to be a country bumpkin.

"I would be sorry if you didn't miss us once in a while, my love," Alex told her. "But Blaine will be there, too, and the Jenningses are such good friends. I think you will find most of the time there is so much to do and to think about, you won't have time to miss us so much. And as for being a country bumpkin, well, you are from the country, but you are also a lovely young woman with very good manners. I expect there will be many girls at the school who haven't had your advantages, and I am sure you will be kind to them. And remember, Penelope will be there to guide you, and she is every bit a lady." She could see Pen rolling her eyes if she heard that and kept her own expression sober with effort, knowing how important these concerns were to Flora.

In many ways it was harder for the young ones to be left out of the plan than for the twins to go. And though the twins occasionally protested that they were "too old" for this or that, in fact, the five were closer than ever, as if recognizing that a particular part of their childhoods would end when the twins went off to Baltimore.

Alex was aware that they had Sam to thank for helping to make the transition easier. She overheard the little girl saying earnestly to Morgan and Nigel, "But we will have to grow up someday, too, and then we'll have to wear good clothes every day, and we won't be able to get dirty any more or do anything. Poor Blaine and Flora, I bet they won't even be allowed to have adventures in Baltimore."

Morgan, as much as he enjoyed the freedom of life at Wild Swan, was impressed by Sam's argument, and Nigel, who loved his nature studies almost as much as he did his siblings, was content that he would still have the fields and woods and Morgan and Sam.

In the middle of the summer, St. John's surprise arrived—three cows and a prime young bull, their coats a rich distinctive red.

Alex stared at the North Devon cattle and sputtered, "How . . . when . . . ," causing St. John to chuckle in delight at her confusion.

"I wrote to Hugh months ago and asked if his agent could find them for us. His man regularly looks at horses and cattle for Hugh's estates, but Hugh insisted on selecting these beasts himself. He wrote that the honor of England was at stake in the export."

"Oh, Sinje! They're almost as beautiful as the horses!" Alex crowed.

He pretended to view them critically. "A bit cow-hocked for racing, I fear," and they laughed together at the image of the blocky animals running in a match.

Alex didn't mind that St. John had arranged it all behind her back and made the investment without her knowledge. These animals had been part of their plan for the future, and his action seemed a way of confirming that the future would go as they envisioned, despite the trouble that had come to them. She needed desperately to keep on believing that.

❧ Chapter 55 ❧

Despite all of her resolutions not to break down, departure in late September to take the children to Baltimore and to begin the fall racing season was almost more than Alex could bear. She had spoken to Dr. Cameron about St. John's illness and had made him promise to summon her home at the least sign of a repetition.

Alastair had been honest to a point. He told Alex that

St. John had recovered very well and that his strong will to live was much in his favor. What he did not tell her was that he suspected that Vulcan had damaged St. John's kidneys. He couldn't be sure, but St. John had had pain in the area above the spinal injury, and it was possible that some permanent weakness had been caused by the lethal hooves, a weakness that had left St. John even more prone to infection than he might otherwise have been.

Alastair had made his expression bland when he spoke with Alex.

"It is a bond between patient and physician. I do not want Alex chained to my side," St. John had insisted firmly, and when his eyes had met the doctor's, the latter had seen the knowledge and acceptance and had had no choice but to bow to it. Alastair's heart ached for them both; he had long since lost any objectivity about the Carringtons.

"Keep safe, my love. Do not hesitate to send for me if you need me," Alex whispered, her voice strangled by the lump in her throat as she took her leave of St. John.

It was a hard time all around. The children had tears in their eyes, and St. John's were overly bright as he bid the twins good-bye and told them, "I expect you to study hard but to enjoy yourselves as well."

As she traveled in Virginia and North Carolina, Alex had to continually remind herself of how well everything was going. After the first tearful couple of days, the twins had settled into their Baltimore adventure with more maturity than she could have hoped. No word had come of any problem at Wild Swan. And the horses were having a good racing season, particularly Oberon, who was triumphing at the heroic distance in his return to the courses.

As usual, the race meetings were social occasions where all manner of events were discussed. President Jackson in the spirit of "to the victor belongs the spoils," had replaced many government officials with people of his own choosing. That did not seem as reprehensible to Alex as it did to others. In his place, she thought she'd do the same, as it must surely be easier to be surrounded by people who were of one's own persuasion.

She did not express this opinion aloud, aware that many would not find such practical cynicism attractive in a woman. She did not approve as much of what many were calling Jackson's "kitchen cabinet," meaning the advisors he really listened to, as opposed to the titular heads of departments. That seemed rather underhanded, as if there were two goverments—one for public show and one for private use.

A topic of particular interest to the racing world was the *American Turf Register and Sporting Magazine* which had begun publication in Baltimore in August. England had long had a racing calendar, but this was the first of any sort in America. Everyone was talking about it. For the first time, it was possible to find a listing of many future races in one publication as well as the names and records of the best horses. Alex knew she was grinning like an idiot as she read about the horses of Wild Swan in the magazine, but she couldn't help it. It was as if she were reading praise about the children.

But no matter what she was doing, and even when she was forcing herself to watch a hard race start to finish, Wild Swan pulled at her. She slept badly, dreaming of St. John constantly, vague, frustrating dreams wherein she fretted over small, insignificant things while some huge shadow of disaster hovered over him. But for him, she lasted through the full schedule of races they had entered.

She knew the instant she saw him on her return that her worry had not been unwarranted. He assured her that he had been quite well while she was gone, and Della confirmed it without a hint of deception, but St. John looked far less hardy than when she had last seen him. The differences might be undetectable to those who saw him every day, but they were profound to her. He was not only pale, but there was also a new frailty about him. His eyes were shadowed with weariness despite his efforts to deny it, and his skin was stretched too tautly over his bones. She noticed that his hand often trembled by the end of the day and that he was beginning to need long naps again in the afternoon.

She confronted Dr. Cameron but gained no satisfaction. "He's bound to have his good and his bad times, but he had no specific illnesses while you were gone," Alastair told her, gently refusing to acknowledge anything out of the ordinary. "Alex, you must remember, his body has a much harder task to keep fit than does a normally active system."

She would not have had the New Year's Eve party this year, but St. John insisted. The twins were home from

Baltimore for the holidays, and St. John seemed much stronger by Christmas Eve and played the genial host to perfection on New Year's Eve.

Rane had sent a message that he did not think he could come but would try, and in the end he did come, arriving with the Jenningses, young and old, the day before the party.

Alex found herself enjoying the evening after all, and she confessed as much to St. John.

"A gathering of good friends is never amiss," he replied, and inwardly he thought, *remember that you have them, my darling; let them help you through the time to come.*

The only uneasy note of the whole evening came from Rane, and there was nothing Alex could do to help him. After they had toasted the new year and were preparing to eat a last meal before retiring, she saw Rane slip outside. Fearing that he might be ill, she followed him.

It was a chill winter night but clear, and the moonlight illuminated his face and the tears running down his cheeks.

She drew a sharp breath at the sight of him weeping, and he turned to her.

"Rane, I am so sorry! Is there anything St. John or I can do for you?" She was certain the tears were for the agony of his life with Claire.

Claire was the furthest thing from Rane's mind, but he could not betray the cause of his grief. "Nothing, thank you." His voice was rougher than he intended as he fought for control. "I suspect it is just an excess of good brandy, good fellowship, and sentiment."

He took a step away and after hestitating a moment, she left him and went back inside, not wanting to intrude further on sorrow she could not ease.

Within ten days of the party, St. John had a raging fever and all the symptoms of a severe infection. The signs of health he had exhibited during the holidays were stripped away overnight. He slipped quickly into delirium with rare moments of lucidity.

Alex was terrified. She sent for Dr. Cameron immediately and for the twins. And she hung over St. John, dosing him with everything she knew to lower his fever and fight the infection. Alastair had nothing to add to the treatment except his steady presence.

Alex talked to St. John until she was hoarse. "Stay alive, love, stay alive. Flora and Blaine are on their way home. They need you; we all need you." Endless variations on the same theme.

She hardly noticed that the Jenningses and Rane came with the twins. Her children and St. John, they were the only people who existed in her world. She let the children visit their father; she would have let the Devil visit him if it would have helped him live. The children were horrified by their father's condition, but no more than she, and she felt they all owed it to St. John to surround him with their love.

"Take Magic," St. John murmured. It was in the sad, dark hours between midnight and dawn, and Alex was alone with him, candles flickering against the dark.

He had not had a coherent interval for hours upon hours, but ice from the winter store had lowered his fever somewhat. Still, Alex thought his delirium continued.

"Take Magic," he said again, his voice slightly stronger, and she moved a candle so that she could see his face.

His eyes were open and focused. "In May," he added, and then she understood that he was talking about the National Colt Stake they had entered three years before.

"We will decide that when the time comes," she told him, as if it were perfectly normal to be having this conversation in the midst of the crisis.

"No, promise, you take . . . you go on . . . without . . . strong." His eyes closed again.

"Sinje! You'll be well soon! My love, don't give up, please don't give up!" She could hear her own panic.

Suddenly she knew that hope was gone. There was no use in calling Alastair or anyone else. The great shadow of death was in the room, moving closer to St. John, stronger than all of them together.

She climbed onto the bed and cradled St. John's head against her. She smoothed the thick gilt hair back from his forehead. The raging illness had honed his flesh and the proud bones of his face showed even more clearly than they had when he had returned from Waterloo. He looked more aristocratic than his father or his brothers ever would. The beauty she had seen in him even when she was a child struck her anew.

Guilt washed over her. She had brought him to this. No matter that he had chosen to ride Vulcan. It was she who had torn him from England, uprooted him from his heritage. The heritage that had rejected him, a birthright that had given all to his brothers—the thought steadied her.

"We have made a good life here, my love," she whispered. "But without you, I do not want to go on."

She was so sure he was beyond hearing, she started at the rasping sound of his voice. "I would . . . do it . . . all again . . . with you. These years you gave me. You will go on for me, for the children, for Wild Swan, for yourself." The words gathered strength, pouring out in a rush of effort.

Blinded by tears, she leaned over him, cradling him against her breast.

"Always spring. Alexandria, I love . . ." A soft caress from long ago, and he was gone.

You are a bad business, always bringing trouble. You've got too much of your father's and your grandmother's ways and not enough of mine. Her mother's voice sounded around her so loudly, Alex clapped her hands over her ears.

Your mother's got a dry bundle of meanness where she ought to have a heart. It is naught to do with you, child. Grandmother's tart voice overriding her mother's discontent. *It is no use to be human if you cannot dream and love.*

Voices, so many of them in the days that followed. Her own telling the children that their father was dead and making all the dreary arrangements for the burial. Samson's and Della's, Timothy's and Mavis's voices, and the voices of friends and neighbors offering what comfort they could. And she could hear the unspoken words, too: *It's really better this way. Poor man, he was so helpless.*

She wanted to shriek that it was not better to be cold and dead under the earth. Her mind kept wincing away from the image of his body. With Mavis and Della, she had washed and tended the corpse. She could still feel the strange resistance of the dead flesh, could still smell the scent of corruption that had come so soon to taint the air even though it was cold winter. She shuddered, trying to thrust away the memory, succeeding only in raising the image of Christiana dead in England, and the baby girl buried in Annapolis.

She looked up, peering through the shadows of her veil, desperately seeking the comfort of the living.

The green eyes gazed at her across the space. The

sensation was so strong, she felt as if he had reached out and touched her.

Awareness of Rane made her aware of everything else. Of the other people grouped around the open grave, of the old words of the burial service being read from the *Book of Common Prayer* because some marking of the passage was needed, of her hands being held by a child on each side. And then again only of him.

She could feel the comfort Rane was trying to offer, could feel him willing her to know that he was there for her. And beyond that from him came the most gracious gift of all; she knew his grief at St. John's death was genuine, as much because he had come to treasure the man as a friend as for her sake. She knew he did not share the thought that it was just as well that St. John had died. Finally she understood that the tears she had witnessed on New Year's Eve had been for her and for St. John.

Book Five

✍ *Chapter 56* ✍

The Union Course, Long Island, New York, 1830

New York's taverns and hotels were as crowded as they had been for the Eclipse-Henry race in 1823. Of the fifteen colts and fillies that had been entered in their birth year of 1827, only seven had been brought to compete in the National Colt Stake on this, the twenty-fourth of May, 1830. Magic Swan was among them. He shared Sir Archy blood through his sire, Bay Swan. There was only one entry, Price's Hermaphrodite by Duroc out of a Figure mare, that did not have the patriarch's blood. And there had been some debate as to whether this oddly sexed animal should carry the eighty-seven pounds required for a filly or the ninety for a colt. The judges had decided on the latter.

Caleb, Pen, and Rane were with Alex, but she hardly noticed their presence. Dressed in black, she was very noticeable in the gaily-dressed spring crowd. Her face looked bloodless, the only color coming from her green eyes, abnormally large in her thin face. It hurt Rane to look at her.

"Sinje, this is for you, win or lose. Magic Swan will run his best against the best." She carried on the silent monologue as a bugle blew its sweet notes, and the seven entries approached the post. The riders received the traditional admonition from the judges' stand regarding observance of the course rules. The crowd was already noisy in appreciation simply because of the spirit of the day. But for Alex, it was strangely silent. She felt as if she could hear Jim Barlow's heart and Magic's beating in anticipation. Two youngsters from Wild Swan.

"Mount!"

The jockeys obeyed.

"Are you ready? Come up!"

The colts and fillies were led to the starting line and put in their places by grooms who then quickly got out of the way. The starting drum sounded.

Price's Hermaphrodite led the field in the first frantic rush, but Bonnets of Blue, a gray filly and the favorite, was gaining on him as they rounded the first turn. Behind her was Magic Swan, and the other four entries trailed him.

At the half-mile post, Bonnets of Blue passed Hermaphrodite and then Magic passd him, too, and coming in to the second turn, the two were nose to nose, gray and black. Many eyes glanced quickly at the black-garbed figure in the crowd, knowing that Carrington's widow had brought the colt to the race, but Alex was oblivious.

"You're doing well, Jim, just keep him there and ask him at the very last moment to take it. He's like Fire Swan; he likes that last effort. Come on, sweet Magic, you can do it! You were born for this." She said none of it aloud.

They hit the turn at full speed, battling for the lead. The crowd exploded with applause when Magic finished half a length ahead.

Despite her dark, heavy clothing, Alex felt cold as ice, but she had vowed to herself that she would watch every second of this race.

Only Bonnets of Blue, Magic, and Hermaphrodite appeared for the second heat, and by the back stretch, Hermaphrodite was falling far behind while the filly and Magic again dueled for the win, finishing so close that the filly was declared the winner by no more than half the length of her neck.

For the third and final heat, only Bonnets of Blue and Magic Swan came out. Hermaphrodite had been distanced in the last heat and was thus disqualified.

At the drum signal, they both surged forward. For an awful instant, Magic faltered, but he regained his footing and surged after the filly who was nearly a length ahead. And then the filly moved diagonally across the track as Magic was coming up on the inside. It seemed inevitable that the horses would collide, but Jim pulled Magic's head up and jerked him to the right, out of the filly's way, thus averting disaster. The harsh action had put Magic off his stride just enough so that while he fought valiantly to take the lead, he remained just behind the filly. Bonnets of Blue was declared the winner by the smallest margin.

The judges had apparently not seen the foul, but many of the spectators had.

"Every horse that shall fail running on the outside of every pole, or whose rider shall cross, jostle, strike or use any other foul play . . . or who shall take the track before he is clear of every other horse, shall be deemed distanced, and the next best horse declared the winner."

The rule was very clear, and many eyes were fixed on Alex, waiting to see what she would do.

"It was clearly a foul," Caleb growled. "You should protest the decision."

Slowly Alex shook her head. "My position is precarious enough without St. John. Magic acquitted himself very well, and Jim rode brilliantly. That is all that matters. And foul or not, the filly is a magnificent horse. She might have won anyway."

She knew Jim, as well as the others from Wild Swan, was disappointed when she told him the same thing, but he accepted her decision.

"I have never seen any rider perform better than you did today," she added. "Had you not acted so quickly, there could have been injury or death to both horses and riders." She was not the only one who thought so; Jim received many offers from other stables and politely refused them all.

To be declared the second best three-year-old in the nation was no small honor for Magic Swan, and people crowded around Alex, braving the barrier of her widow's weeds to congratulate her. She responded graciously and smiled at the proper moments. Rane saw that the smile never lighted her eyes; she was still far away in whatever place she had fled to when St. John had died.

St. John had left a very simple will; everything was left to Alex. He had made no special provisions for the children. His trust that Alex would do what was best for them had been absolute. And since the day of the burial, Alex had fulfilled all of her duties.

The children had been shocked and desolate, feeling as

if they had been betrayed in some bargain they had made with God or fate. Since they had adjusted to their father's crippled state, they had expected he would live forever or at least until they themselves were very old. Alex had no easy answers to give them, but she made herself available to them, reassuring them that at least one parent was left, and then gradually but inexorably reminding them that the joys and duties of their lives had not ceased with their father's death.

The twins went back to school in Baltimore; Morgan, Nigel, and Sam resumed classes with Mr. Whittleby and the other children at Wild Swan. When Timothy and Mavis tried to comfort Alex, they found themselves comforted instead. All of her friends experienced the same thing.

Dutifully she wrote to St. John's parents, to her brother, Paris, and at much greater length to Hugh and to Boston, emphasizing to Boston that above all else, she did not want him to return to Wild Swan: "There is nothing you can do for us. Wild Swan runs like an efficient clock. It comforts me far more to know you are well and happy in your wandering than it would were you to return here."

No task was neglected at Wild Swan. The breeding season went forward. Within a few weeks of St. John's death, Mabbie produced "Swan's Scion," a chestnut colt who looked exactly like his sire; Leda gave birth to a bay colt, "Dark Swan" by Sir Archy; Swan Song had a chestnut colt by Oberon, named "Puck" for his clumsy mischief in his first days; and Black Swan dropped a black filly, "Sorceress," also by Oberon. And bookings made to Swan, Bay Swan, and Oberon were honored; the mares, often with foals at their sides, received the same fine care as they had before when they came for breeding, having the run of an airy pasture or roomy stalls if the weather was inclement. The only change Alex made was to cancel Wild Swan's entries in the spring races. She had known she could not leave the younger children so soon and had counted on the National Colt Stake to keep Wild Swan in the public eye.

That had been accomplished this day. And still she felt nothing. She had felt nothing since the earth had filled St. John's grave. She had simply existed, doing what others expected of her.

But now decisions of enormous import were looming

ahead, and she just didn't know what she was going to do. Many had disapproved of the Widow Carrington coming to the Union Course, but it could be excused on the basis of the commitment made three years before. To reenter the racing world on a regular basis was not going to be as easy. It was St. John who had belonged to the jockey clubs, not she.

Though she had announced no intention of selling any of the horses, she had already begun to receive offers for them despite the fact that her husband was not six months dead. The letters and, in some cases, the agents' speeches, were all variations on the same theme—all were sorry for her loss and understood what a heavy burden she carried; if she wanted to sell any of the horses, they would be interested. If she could not or did not take the horses back to the races, many would profit by her loss. The horses were of proven racing ability; if she had to sell, many stables would be improved by the addition of Wild Swan's horses.

Dimly she knew that such a thought would have made her furious before, but now she felt only weary, and guiltily she considered how much easier life would be if the horses were sold. She thought of it when she returned to Wild Swan from New York and found more offers waiting. And she thought of it when a farmer from some miles away, a lawyer from Georgetown, and a merchant from Washington came calling. The first two were widowers, both some ten years older than she, while the merchant had never been married and was a fussy little man of nearly fifty years. If she hadn't been so appalled at the idea of having any of them touch her, she would have been amused once she realized they were making early bids for marriage, fearful of waiting the full year of mourning.

"If I were better husband material, I'd ask you to marry me, just to get rid of the idiots that plague you now," Alastair announced angrily, having barely controlled his temper while Alex graciously but firmly got rid of the fat farmer.

"They're harmless; greedy perhaps, but harmless," Alex pointed out flatly. Her eyes were dull and too patient, her movements lethargic, but there was nothing he could do. He knew how shattering it was for many people to lose their mates; some were never the same again. And Alex and St. John had been through much together. But Dr. Cameron continued to visit faithfully and to send reports to the Jenningses and to Rane. Her cousin—that was another sad case, and there was a strong bond between Alex and Rane; Alastair had often felt it, and more than once he had wondered about Morgan who looked so much like Rane. He ceased that useless speculation; Rane was tied to his mad wife, and Alex to her memories.

The children called friendly farewells to him as he left. Alex had insisted that the Jenningses' children come for the summer just as had been planned before St. John's death, and Alastair could see how wise she had been in that. The expanded band of youngsters generated their own energy and joy, and the Carrington children had little time to brood.

Alex was thinking of the children, too, one June afternoon as she watched them head for the coolness of the stream in the woods. "They're not too old to adjust. Perhaps England would be better for them, away from the memories of their father's death," she mused aloud, forgetting that Samson was beside her. Suddenly she was pierced with longing for the familiar sights, smells, and sounds of the land of her birth. The tailored fields, the lush orchards, the ships on the Thames, even the tiny robins—the images flashed before her eyes.

"It so much bedda at dat place 'cross de wada? Den why you leaves in de firs' place?"

Her mind was so far away, at first Samson's drawl made no sense to her, and then the words sorted themselves out. "Better at that place across the water?" She could not judge how calculated his ingenuousness was, but his purpose was achieved. Reality returned. It had not been better there; it had, in the end, been horrible with Christiana dead, their marriage unsanctioned, her mother too close, St. John's family so cold, and their prospects for a settled, prosperous future nonexistent. And now neither her father nor her grandmother were there, nor Boston. Here she and St. John had built a new life, and she'd be damned if she'd let it go.

"Samson, one way or another, Oberon, Fire, and Magic are going to race this autumn, as long as you find them all fit."

"Dey be fit, I has my way!" he answered with alacrity.

She wasn't joyful at the idea of returning to the race

courses, but she was determined, and she did not expect joy any more. She wrote to the Harrisons, to Mr. Ralston, and to various other friends, and shamelessly she asked that they allow Wild Swan's horses to run under their sponsorship. In most cases, this would mean riding under another's colors again, but it was the only way to enter races that were limited to jockey club members. She knew Caleb would help where he could. She did not spare her friends. She stated clearly that she intended to go on with the work her husband had started and had by his express deathbed wish asked her to continue. She could not feel guilt for playing on their sympathies because she was not asking them to sponsor poor horseflesh but rather the best in the land. And none of the people she wrote to were at present fielding so many good horses that there would be a conflict. If one of her friends had one of his own horses entered, then she would race hers under another's colors.

The horses and the children, they were her world, though there was pain as well as the pleasure of seeing the young-sters develop. They were all growing up so swiftly. The fifteen-year-old twins looked so much like St. John that sometimes she could scarcely bear the sight of them, though she was very careful never to let them know that; it was a pain she doubted they would understand. And Nigel had taken over Sir Arthur, explaining that the horse was old and lonely and deserved to have some attention. The big, bay hunter was twenty-five years old, but lately he was behaving as if he were years younger, proving Nigel's assessment. Alex found it difficult to watch the horse trotting off under saddle with a rider other than St. John.

Morgan, as usual, was another matter. At thirteen, he was rapidly acquiring a gangly height, and his voice had begun to prove treacherous. But the changes in him went beyond the physical. He had always been open and much more apt to take action than to brood. Yet now, though he was patient with the other children and with the horses, there was a somberness about him as if all the joy were seeping out of his days. And Alex had seen the tired sorrow on his face when he thought he was unobserved. She understood it for herself, but she did not want it to happen to her children.

Sam served as the catalyst. She was too close to Morgan to have missed his new moodiness, and she came to Alex.

Sam was growing, too, and had reached the delicately awkward stage between child and woman, one moment graceful, the next a tangle of slender arms and legs. But the promise of beauty that Alex had seen on the first day of meeting the child was clearly being fulfilled. With her brown hair shot with golden-red highlights and her wide eyes an ever changing mixture of green, brown, and gold, Sam's appeal was vivid. She still had no awareness of it, dressed badly, and had more in common with the boys than with Flora, but her feminine softness showed in her concern for Morgan.

"I've asked him and asked him what's wrong, and he keeps saying nothing. But I know that's not true. And I don't think it has to do with his father . . . with Mr. Carrington's . . . ," she stuttered to a stop, and Alex reached out and patted her hand.

"It's all right. St. John's death is something that changed us all, and it would be foolish to pretend that it hasn't happened."

Sam nodded and swallowed her tears that so often threatened when she thought of Mr. Carrington, who had been so kind to her. "Anyway, I don't believe that's it. But Morgan isn't the same. He feels so sad."

Sam wasn't conscious of how attuned to Morgan she was, she was so used to it, but when she said that he felt sad, she meant it in the same tangible way she might say that something felt hot from the sun or cold from ice. When Morgan was upset, Sam felt the disturbance as if it were her own.

"I've noticed the change in him, too," Alex told her, "and I hoped he would come to me, but I think this has gone on long enough. I'll speak to him." She sighed, watching Sam leave. Sam was utterly convinced that Alex could solve it all; Alex was not so sure. She missed St. John more than ever. She suspected there were going to be more and more mysteries of young manhood that she would not be able to solve.

But Morgan's problem turned out not to be difficult to understand once he had confessed the source.

She asked him to go riding with her, and none of the other children begged to accompany them, some signal from Sam warning them not to. They all accepted that Morgan was Sam's property.

Alex soon discovered that he was not going to start the

conversation. She decided to come right to the point. "Morgan, we all have days of sorrow, but you are having one after another. There is no joy in anything you do any more. I'm not sure I can help you, but I'd like to try."

For an instant, he was defiant. "You're not happy any more either."

She blinked at the direct hit, and then held his eyes with her own. "I know, and I am trying to change it. I miss your father very, very much. I know you do, too, but I don't think that is your problem, is it?"

His eyes fell, and she could see his face working as he struggled against tears.

"Come," she said gently. "Let's dismount for a while."

When they were settled on a shaded patch of green, she put her arms around him, risking his rejection in her need to give him comfort. He stiffened for an instant, but then he turned his head against her shoulder and wept.

"Oh, Morgan, what is it? Let me help."

He pulled away and scrubbed at his face. "I know I'm supposed to go to school in Baltimore like Blaine and Flora. And then Blaine is going to be a lawyer, a 'solicitor' as you call it." He managed a brief smile as he mimicked her accent. "And I'm better with horses than he is anyway, so I should be the one to help you here. But . . . ," he stopped, shaking his head helplessly.

Alex regarded him in amazement. She had thought she was protecting the children, and now she found that instead they had been planning for her future. "But what? What would you rather do?"

"Ships, I want to be with ships! I want to build them and sail them. I want to see other places. I want to be like Cousin Rane!" The words poured out of him with all the passion that had been lacking in him these past weeks.

Alex felt as if she were falling down a long tunnel. *Cousin Rane.* Oh, not so distant a connection, but rather blood to blood, breath to breath, dream to dream. Morgan, image of his father, and if Morgan were apprenticed to Rane, everyone who saw them would assume they were father and son, even close friends who had never considered it before would consider it then.

None of it mattered. Caleb would not do in this; to Pen's delight, he seldom left Baltimore, his business being mostly at the shipyard, not on the sea. She had weathered gossip before. The sea and ships were Morgan's birthright.

"My son, I did not bear you in order to direct your life as I would wish it. What I want for you is for you to be the best you can be in whatever you chose to do. You, not I. The blood of the Thaines has caused many to love the adventure of the sea. There is nothing unnatural in your desire. What is sad and wrong is for anyone to spend his life doing what he does not love. I think it very possible that Cousin Rane will be willing to teach you as long as you are willing to work hard."

He looked as if the sun had come out after a long darkness. "Work hard? Oh, you bet!" He was suddenly all boy and very American.

It seemed natural, inevitable to send word to Rane. Since St. John's death, Rane had come often to see her and the children. He had not tried to influence her decisions in anything but had simply let her know that he was available if she needed help.

She had not long to wait for his answer. He arrived in person so soon that she wondered if he had set out the moment he received the letter. She wondered, too, if he had interrupted his sailing schedule; it was the busy season for him, but he brushed aside her worries.

"There will be rumors," he said bluntly, his eyes watching her keenly.

"I know," she agreed quietly. "And I will not like them. And Morgan may begin to question his origins. If he does, I will tell him only that he has proof before his eyes in me, in you, that the Thaine blood needs only one parent who looks so to stamp the mark upon the child. I will not tell him anything else. Can you bear that?" She did not flinch from his gaze, and the truth was in her eyes.

"I have always known. Somewhere inside the sure knowledge has been part of me since the day I first saw Morgan." His hands clenched for an instant, and then he relaxed them with visible effort. "But I have never said anything amiss to him and will not now. St. John was a good father to him."

"St. John was his father in every way that matters," she said flatly, and the two pairs of green eyes locked in a silent battle of wills until Rane shook his head.

"Neither of us can win, you know. It is too much like looking in a mirror. But you have my word; Morgan will never doubt his parentage because of me." *Someday he will know it even as I do from some inner source,* he thought, *no one will have to tell him.* Suddenly he found he was appalled at the idea. Any man would be proud of having Morgan for his son, but Morgan had adored St. John and also loved his mother dearly. For an old indiscretion to shatter that love would be a tragedy. An old indiscretion. He felt the familiar pain, as much a part of him as the beat of his heart.

He spoke past the constriction in his throat. "Alex, it is a risk even if neither of us betrays anything. Are you willing to take that risk?"

"I won't deny him the lessons he can learn from you because of it. Year by year I am learning that it is all at best a gamble. One can't expect to win all the time, but it is impossible to win at all if no risk is taken." There was tempered steel in her voice, and Rane loved it as much as he loved the softness still left in her; he wondered if there would ever be anything about her that he did not love.

"If you like, he can go to Baltimore with me now. When he's not on board ship, I know he could live with one of the ship's carpenters from the yard. Mr. Cromb and his wife have no children, though I know they've always wanted them. Then perhaps Morgan could come back here from November to February when the sailings are fewer. He should not lose touch with his life here."

Moving away from the personal, they discussed the situation as if it were an apprenticeship like any other, but Rane was already bracing himself for the first time he would have to say, "No, he is not my son." It had not happened when he had visited with the children in Baltimore, but he knew it would when just he and Morgan were visible for study.

Morgan was ecstatic; Sam was devastated.

"Sam, I know it's all happening too fast, but you must have thought about Morgan going off to school just as the twins have, just as you will if I have anything to say about it." Alex tried to comfort her. "I have already sent a note to your parents asking if I might call on them. I'll try to persuade them to send you to Flora's school next year." She did not tell her that she had already asked Flora if that would be all right. Far from having objections, Flora rather fancied herself in the role of big sister showing the little girl how to get on at the school. It was all very logical. Nigel would go to Baltimore, too. Blaine by then would be ready for his apprenticeship and would live with the lawyer's family. Caleb had already made the arrangements. The one thing Alex was determined to insist upon was that Sam's parents find suitable lodging for her, either at the school or with friends, just as Rane was to find Morgan a place to stay. With Blaine and Flora living with the Jenningses now, and with Nigel and Flora scheduled to live with them next year, it was enough. Despite her love for Sam, Alex did not think she could ask the Jenningses to take her in on a semipermanent basis. With the other children in Baltimore, she knew Sam would not be neglected, even if she did not live in the same household. Very logical, and of no use at all to Sam at the moment.

"I knew it would happen," she confessed in a tiny voice. "But I pretended it would be a long time from now." Her shoulders straightened; the threatening tears receded as she got hold of herself. "Nigel would be very lonesome if all of us were gone. I suppose it's better if I stay until he can come, too." In a flash, she went from little girl to responsible party. And now it was Alex who felt the prickle of tears; Sam was so accustomed to considering what others needed and wanted as being more important than her own desires, Alex sometimes wished she were more selfish just for the sake of survival.

Once his initial excitement had settled a bit and the task of packing for Baltimore was undertaken, Morgan began to consider the reality of leaving Wild Swan for a long period, and Sam was his first concern. Alex described the conversation she had had with the girl, and though Morgan was somewhat relieved, he knew it would be cowardly if he did not talk to Sam directly.

He wished she would cry and behave childishly; he found the sad-eyed maturity that greeted him disconcerting.

"It's not as if I'm going away forever. I'll be back at the end of November for more than two months."

Sam nodded. "I know. But it won't be the same. And that's just the way things are when you're growing up. I know how much you liked going on the ships. It's right for you to learn about them. If I'd been born a boy, I could go with you." Brief anger flared in her at this injustice of nature.

"Well, I'm glad you weren't!" Morgan said fervently, not even questioning why he felt so outraged at the idea.

"Come on, let's go riding. It will be our last chance for a while."

Sam had long since graduated from a pony to a full-size mount, but just for a moment, Morgan pictured her as she had been when he first saw her, and only then did he realize how much she had changed. It gave him a peculiar feeling in the pit of his stomach. Sam was right; they were growing up and changing.

There were those who hoped to change Alex's life as well. The lawyer from Georgetown, ever hopeful despite the fact that Alex never gave him any encouragement, came calling while Rane was still there. Rane had already met the fat farmer on one of his visits but hadn't perceived the man's purpose at Wild Swan. With the lawyer, it was different. The man was obviously prosperous, well spoken, well dressed, and trimly built, despite his forty years or so. And for the way he looked at Alex, Rane wanted to punch him in the mouth.

Seeing the resemblance between Alex and Rane and being told there was kinship between them, the suitor saw no threat to his plan and treated Rane accordingly. Alex finally persuaded the man to leave after listening to all she could stand of his compliments.

The dust of the departure had hardly settled before Rane exploded. "How dare that puffed-up toad come here with his bedraggled flowers and melted chocolates!"

"The heat did wilt and melt his good intentions, but he couldn't help that," Alex protested with a giggle.

"He must find some encouragement here. It is disgusting."

Alex's amusement died abruptly as she realized how angry Rane was, and her own anger rose to meet his. "How dare you! What is disgusting, the fact that a man might find me attractive enough to want to wed me? He is being perfectly civilized about it."

Rane's face was white and drawn. "I didn't mean that. Of course you are an attractive woman, the most beautiful . . . ," he drew back from the edge of the precipice. "I apologize. I meant that he certainly doesn't seem to be the sort of man who would make you happy."

He was so miserable, she could not hold on to her anger though she knew it would be safer to do so. "No, he isn't. I haven't any intention of filling the space St. John has left with someone like that. It would be unfair on both sides." Perversely she could not bring herself to say she would never remarry. Even knowing how dangerous it was to the middle ground they had established, she did not want Rane to think of her as a dried-up stick of a woman who was no longer desirable.

Things were still strained between them when he left with Morgan, but the irony did not escape her. It was an act as intimate as lovemaking for her to trust him with their son.

❧ Chapter 57 ❧

On September 18, a race was staged between a horse and "Tom Thumb," the first locomotive built in America. The locomotive pulled forty passengers over a nine-mile course running from Riley's Tavern to Baltimore, but a leak in the boiler brought it to a standstill, and the horse won.

Having already departed for the Hillsborough races in North Carolina, Alex did not witness the race, but the Jenningses took the twins to watch it, and their glowing accounts of it caught up with Alex in Halifax, Virginia.

"It would be foolish to think horses will always best these machines," Blaine wrote, "for there is enormous power there that doesn't tire like a living beast. But it was splendid to see the horse win this one despite all the fierce huffing and puffing and smoking of the machine."

Flora wrote in a more practical vein: "I shan't ever want to ride on one of those machines, for they are so dirty! Great pieces of ash settled on the passengers. One could catch fire too easily."

Alex laughed over Flora's letter and felt at peace with the world. Oberon, Fire Swan, and Magic Swan were all in fine form, racing under her colors or another's. So far with the help of friends, there had been no challenge of her horses' right to race. She knew she was aided by the fact that women had more of a part in the racing world in America than they did in England. There were always women among the spectators, and more and more festivities were being planned for their entertainment at various courses.

Her pleasure came to an abrupt end after Magic won the one-mile heats for three-year-olds. Blockett's Boy, a big brown colt, had been in the field against him but had been distanced and thus disqualified. Even without the name of the horse, she recognized the jockey and the style of riding. It was the same rider who had fouled Taney the year before and the same owner, the rude Mr. Blockett whom Alex had warned not to cheat again. Blockett's Boy had all the markings of a good race horse, but the jockey had been too rough on him, and the colt had either lost heart or gotten so confused he no longer knew he was being urged to run instead of simply being punished. Alex was sorry for the mishandling of the horse, but as long as other horses were interfered with, it was none of her business. She had hoped to avoid Mr. Blockett altogether, but when she saw him barreling toward her, she knew another confrontation was in the offing.

"Oh, hell!" she swore, and Allen Ralston, who was with her, caught sight of Mr. Blockett.

"You needn't talk to him," he said, starting to step in front of her.

Alex put her hand on his arm. "No, Allen, I won't run from him. He'd enjoy it too much." Still she was glad Allen was beside her. They were on a warm, first name basis now. He had provided the colors for her horses today, and had proved himself a good friend in the time since she had first met him at the Eclipse-Henry match when St. John had won the huge wager from him.

"Some people are importin' English studs again. Some people need 'em. But not me." Blockett was pretending to speak to his cronies, but the remarks were directed at Alex. And she knew he was not talking about the current trend to renew importations of horses from England, a practice that had been at a virtual standstill since the War of 1812. Mr. Blockett was not speaking of horses at all.

Beside her, Allen growled, "The bastard!" and started to

step forward. Again she restrained him. "Please, I need to do this on my own."

She stood her ground, waiting for Blockett to come to her. She detested everything about the man, his condescending attitude, his pig eyes that stripped her naked while his mouth drawled false concern. Most of all, she detested the way he ran his horses.

"I jus' don't think you belong here, you a widow an' all. I'm sure your late husband would appreciate what you've done, little lady, but he wouldn't want you to be goin' on like this, under another man's colors."

"You have no knowledge of what my husband wanted or did not want. You are a poor sport. Your colt lost today and mine won." She glared at him, watching the color rise and fade in his broad face.

"By God, if you were a man, I'd call you out!" he snarled, so intent on her that he did not notice Allen Ralston eyeing him with cold fury.

"If I were a man, you would not be so detestably patronizing," she replied coolly. "Instead of a duel, why don't we have a race? My Magic against your colt—Blockett's Boy, isn't it?" The tone of her voice told him what she thought of the new fashion of some to name their horses after themselves or other people; she could scarcely imagine poorer taste. "Mile heats, half-hour intervals, two out of three heats to win. Winner will have the choice of the losing colt or five hundred dollars. Withdrawal of either colt before the race to be a two-hundred-and-fifty-dollar forfeit. No limits or handicaps beyond not fouling one's opponent. The race to be held the day after tomorrow on Mr. Ralston's training course if he agrees. Are you game?"

She heard Allen make a distressed sound behind her, but she ignored him, concentrating on whether or not Blockett would accept her conditions.

Her friends and his had witnessed the challenge; he had little choice but to accept. He was suddenly aware of Allen and others in Alex's camp. "Maybe Mr. Ralston doesn't want the race on his track," he suggested weakly. It was the only way out Blockett could see, but Allen didn't oblige him. He did not approve, but Alex had made the wager, and he would support her. He admired her courage and her sense of honor as well as the rest of her.

"Mr. Blockett, you and Mrs. Carrington are welcome to

have your race at Windower," he said, as if he was extending a courtesy rather than adding to the insult. "One o'clock in the afternoon, the day after tomorrow?"

Blockett nodded, not trusting his voice, and stalked off.

Alex let her breath out on a long sigh.

"My God, are you sure you want to do this?" Allen asked.

"I am sure I do not," she admitted. "But it is time for me to have the courage and the right to compete."

"But to risk Magic!"

"I do not intend to lose." She could not explain to him, but though her heart was still pounding with the enormity of the wager she had made, she also felt a deep sense of purpose and certainty. St. John would have loved the bet. For the first time, she understood the excitement of risking something one really could not afford to lose.

When she told Jed Barlow what she intended to do, he clearly thought she had lost her mind. "You cain't, jus' cain't! It ain't th' same, ridin' 'im at Wild Swan an' ridin' in a real race. An' t' other, it's a trick, nothin' more; he might not even do it."

"He's accustomed to having me on his back, and he loves to race more than anything on earth," she told Jed firmly. "My only concern is that he will be too tired after the grand race effort he made today."

Honesty and pride in the horse made Jed admit that Magic would be recovered by the time of the match.

Afterward, Alex realized that she had been in a state of shock from the time she offered the wager until she appeared to ride Magic in the first heat. She had drifted through the hours watching the rest of the race meeting, smiling when Oberon won the four-mile heats, responding calmly when asked if it were true that she had challenged Blockett. And none of it had really registered.

But everything focused sharply when she mounted Magic amidst gasps of shock for her appearance in male apparel, let alone her intention to ride.

"You cannot mean to . . . ," Blockett gulped.

Alex cut him off. "Indeed I do. No restrictions regarding riders or weights were put on this match. And there were witnesses. Gentlemen?"

Allen, having decided that nothing would sway Alex from her course, was set to enjoy himself. He had always liked a wild gamble, and he found most people intolerably dull and conservative. Alex Carrington was neither. She was, in fact, the most exciting woman he had ever met. He had a great deal of money staked on her today, and he was serenely confident that he would win. "I heard the terms of the wager. Mrs. Carrington is correct."

Blockett's friends who had witnessed it reluctantly agreed. Not only was what Ralston was saying true, but also, among his talents was his deadly accuracy with a dueling pistol.

The toss of a coin gave Blockett's Boy the inside starting position.

Blockett, still finding no way out of the race, was whispering hurried instructions to his jockey. In addition to the inside position, they had another advantage in that Alex weighed more than Blockett's wiry little rider.

As the two horses were led abreast to the starting post, Alex turned her head and caught the jockey looking at her, his face still registering his shock.

Smiling with false pleasantry, she said, "Understand me; I haven't brought this whip for Magic. He won't need it. But if you foul him in any way, I'll flay you and your horse alive with it. If you can't run a fair race, it would be healthier for you to dismount now."

The jockey's eyes slid from hers, but suddenly she knew that he was at the moment more afraid of what she might do to him during the race than of what Mr. Blockett would do after.

Rumors of the match had brought out quite a few of the racing community even though it was a private affair, but Alex ignored everything except the powerful animal beneath her.

The drum beat sounded like a cannon shot to Alex, and they were off. Magic made a clean start, but so did Blockett's Boy. He was, as Alex judged, a fine horse capable of enormous speed when ridden properly, and his jockey was, at the moment, so taken aback by the turn of events that he was not interfering with the colt's normal ability as he usually did.

They were neck and neck around the first turn, but Alex knew Magic had much more speed in him; he was simply biding his time.

"That's it, my love, that's it, we've got him," she whispered, not caring whether Magic heard her or not, knowing he was conscious of her hands on the reins, her weight balanced in the saddle. Her arms were strong, but not nearly as strong as a jockey's, and already she could feel the enormous strain on them, the ache spreading through her shoulders and clear to the back of her jaw. She saw a flicker in the corner of her left eye and jerked her head in time to see her opponent raise his whip to strike Magic in an attempt to throw him off stride.

"I'll kill you!" she hissed and raised her own whip menacingly.

The jockey couldn't distinguish her words, but he didn't mistake the meaning nor the ferocious intent in her green eyes. He gave up the idea of attacking Magic and immediately began to override his mount.

The pounding of the hooves battered Alex's brain, but she sensed the difference in the other horse and knew the heat was won. As they came around the final turn, she urged, "Now, Magic, now!" and let him have his head. She could feel the primitive joy in him as he pulled away and finished a good two lengths ahead of the other colt.

Blockett's face was livid; Allen Ralston was grinning ear to ear. Jed Barlow was still worried as they cooled Magic out, and Alex was exhausted, her knees shaking from the effort of the ride. But she was also supremely confident. Magic knew the course and his opponent now, and he was not showing the least signs of strain. It helped that Ralston's track was a full mile, so there would be no confusion about how many laps had to be run.

Everyone, including Allen, looked at Alex blankly as she came to stand beside him and Magic was led out by Jed.

"No specification of weight or lack of it, no specification regarding rider or saddle, nothing except that these two colts would race. Gentlemen, Magic is ready to start."

"It's a trick," Mr. Blockett muttered, not sure whether to rejoice because Alex had gone mad—and her colt would surely lose if he even stayed on the track—or to suspect that he was being set up for a truly ignominious defeat.

"She's right; there's no rule against it here," one of his friends murmured.

"Jesus!" Allen Ralston exclaimed involuntarily, seeing his wager lost.

Alex ignored them, watching Jed line Magic up on the inside for this heat and then slip the halter off.

Blockett's jockey looked immensely pleased at the prospect of racing a riderless horse, confident that he could beat him and might even win the heat by default if Magic swerved or in any way fouled him. Alex thought if the man had any sense, he'd be afraid, but he didn't and he wasn't.

It was a perfect start at the tap of the drum, and Alex heard the gasps of wonder around her as the men watched Magic run a perfect race. He ran as if ridden by a superbly skilled jockey. He kept ahead of Blockett's Boy all the way, but not too far ahead, running easily with no weight at all to carry, running his own race with great enjoyment as he had been allowed to do at Wild Swan since the day Samson had seen him instigating the race with Fire Swan. On the homestretch, he unleashed his full power and devoured the ground, leaving lengths of light between himself and the other colt. Magic's talent was enhanced by his opponent's jockey. The man was consistent; he had ridden Blockett's Boy as badly as ever, riding him so hard that by the end of the heat, his mount no longer knew what was required of him.

There was silence as Magic crossed the finish line, slowed, and stopped of his own accord as he sensed the other horse being pulled up. He waited docilely for Jed to approach him. And then there were cheers, even from Blockett's supporters for a feat they knew they would never witness again.

Alex stiffened her knees to keep from collapsing on the ground. Now that it was over, and she'd won, she could think of nothing more mortifying than to faint dead away. She was grateful for the sudden offer of Allen's arm to lean on.

"I thought I was a gambler," he said, "but I don't even qualify. St. John would have enjoyed every minute of this."

"Thank you," Alex whispered, and then she stood straighter as Blockett approached.

"What do you want, the colt or the money?" He looked as if he would rather strangle her than pay his debt.

"I'll take the colt. He's a fine animal. You might have won here today; you might have won other races, too, if you and your jockey knew the first thing about how to run a horse. The colt is fast and willing. But he is ridden so badly, he loses heart and the sense of the race before it's over."

Blockett's hand clenched into a fist, but Allen's voice slipped between them, smooth and deadly.

"Mr. Blockett, Mrs. Carrington is quite right. She's done you a favor. If you take her advice, you might improve your record at the tracks. But in any case, I'll advise you now that if I ever hear of you doing an injury, verbal or otherwise, to Mrs. Carrington, I will kill you. That's a promise I'd be glad to keep."

When Blockett and his party had departed, Allen apologized. "I know how independent you are, but I don't trust that man. I wanted him to know how much trouble he would be in if he threatened you further."

"Allen, it's all right; truly it is. I'm grateful. I may be independent, but I'm not a fool. If I have my way, I will never see Blockett again."

"You wouldn't consider selling the colt, would you?"

"Yes, I would," she replied to his surprise. "We don't really need him at Wild Swan. The only reason I took him instead of the money was to get him away from that man."

Allen was as pleased as a small child who has just discovered Christmas out of season. He had inherited wealth and had increased it with various investments that had succeeded for him in spite of the hard times that had ruined so many. His plantation, Windower, was well kept and productive. And though he liked to gamble, he never risked more than he could afford to lose. He loved the atmosphere at the race courses, and he loved the Thoroughbreds, but he was one of those people who has no instinct for judging horseflesh. He won more bets than he lost only because most of his bets were based on past records; he was quick when it came to figuring the mathematical odds. But he could not look at an untried horse and sense anything special about it. For that reason, many of the horses he brought to the courses were poor performers. He took it in good part, but he was fully aware that the only way he could improve his stable was to pay higher prices for proven stock or to trust another's judgment. Blockett's Boy would be a wonderful addition to his stud, and he promptly offered eight hundred dollars for him.

"I'll take five hundred, and feel greedy at that because you provided the race course plus a great deal of moral support," Alex replied, knowing that Allen would not allow the price to drop below that.

"I have another offer," he said softly as he and Alex shared a meal after the other spectators had left and before Alex had returned to Halifax.

The uncertain note in his voice was her only warning before he continued. "I would be honored if you would consent to be my wife. I have never admired another woman as I admire you, and I am more than fond of you. But I know how much you loved St. John and would not expect the same degree of affection from you. Still, I think we could get along well together. I like your children and . . ."

Alex finally found her voice. "Please, Allen, do stop! I am flattered, truly I am, but I didn't think, I . . ."

"I've embarrassed you. Lord, what a botch I've made of this! Please, my dear, don't look so distressed. Let us forget that the question was ever asked. I do not want to lose your friendship over it." His voice was as steady as ever, but Alex saw the hurt in his eyes and was sorry for it, though she knew nothing could be done to change it. Inwardly she sighed, wondering if she would ever adjust to her changed circumstance. It still seemed unthinkable to be considered marriageable after spending half her life with St. John. The image of Rane's outrage over the lawyer's attention rose in her mind, and she thrust it away.

News of the spectacular match traveled with the high speed reserved for choice gossip, and it accomplished what Alex had hoped it would. She and the horses of Wild Swan were now considered major contenders and an accepted part of the racing world. The match was the stuff of legend, and to most, it no longer mattered that Alex was a woman claiming a place in a man's world; they felt she'd earned it.

❦ *Chapter 58* ❧

By the time she got home, Alex was used to receiving approbation for her race on Magic. Rane's reaction came as a shock.

He and Morgan were at Wild Swan ahead of her, Morgan, like the other children, having been given her schedule and thus knowing when she was due back.

Alex scarcely had time to greet everyone before Rane demanded a private meeting. Thinking it had something to do with Morgan, Alex left Jed to explain the details of the race to Samson and other interested parties and obligingly led Rane into the library.

"What in the hell did you think you were doing?" he exploded without preamble. "News of that damned race has probably gotten all the way to Canada by now!"

"You stop swearing at me, Rane Falconer!" she shouted back. "What I did was my business, and I won. I've brought home five hundred extra dollars. And Magic is mine to wager. It had nothing to do with you! I risked nothing of yours."

He closed his eyes, and his jaw was so tightly clenched, she could see the muscle twitching there. "You risked your life. There is nothing on earth more precious to me," he ground out.

His fear and pain flashed through her, and she reached out to him, putting her hand against his chest, feeling his heart pounding hard. "Oh, Rane, there was no danger; truly there wasn't. I've ridden Magic many times before, and I rode him at top speed for only a one-mile heat." She did not admit that she would have ridden the third heat had Magic not taken the second on his own. "There were witnesses, and I threatened Blockett's jockey that I'd kill him if he fouled us."

Slowly his eyes opened, and he looked down at her. "I believe you did," he said softly, his mouth curving in a reluctant smile. His arms came around her as he bent his head and kissed her.

It began softly, tasting, asking, bridging the more than fourteen years that had passed since they had touched each other as lovers. She was motionless in his arms, and then her mouth opened to his, drinking in his sweetness, accepting the thrust of his tongue. Her body molded against his, as if home had always been there. The heat of desire she had thought never to feel again leapt into bright flame, rushing from the center of her through every nerve and vein.

They pushed away from each other at the same time.

"My God! I never meant . . ."

"It was my fault as much as yours," Alex insisted.

"All these years of control betrayed in an instant," he murmured bitterly, thereby betraying more.

" 'All these years'—you have felt the same through all this time?" The question slipped from her before she thought.

"Yes, goddamn it!" he said savagely. "And you, you felt nothing until now?"

She was too off balance to lie. The words tumbled out. "I thought of you, often and at the oddest times. But you must understand, after the first bad year, Sinje and I built a very good marriage. I loved him, Rane. I will never pretend I did not. I loved him very much, and he loved me. I had something with him that you do not have with Claire, at least not now." There was no way around the brutal truth. "And the kind of loving we had stops the desire for others. I simply ceased being able to see other men in the same way I saw St. John—as a lover. I think it was the same for him. Oh, I'm sure he noticed other women, but I don't think he thought of making love to them. We worked so hard to love each other well with our bodies, with our hearts, with our minds, we just didn't have anything left over for others."

She took another step back from the stark pain on Rane's face and from the impulse to enfold him in her arms. She twisted her hands together nervously. "It is so difficult to explain! But I think we both have to understand so that we hurt no one else. No one else as we have hurt each other." No one—Claire, the children, friends. Rane was a married man, and there were so many others besides the two of them to consider. But she could not leave him so alone and devoid of comfort.

"I did not allow myself to think about it. But my love for you has been part of me for so long, it is there as my blood and bones are there. It is as if I was born with a special part of me loving you."

He took a step toward her, but she shook her head. "Claire is your wife, for better and for worse. The only way you and I can go on seeing each other is as we have for so long, as distant relatives and friends. I don't want to lose that; I don't want you to lose us either. I think my children, all of them, are as important to you as you are to them."

He was tempted to ignore every consequence, to listen only to the demands of his heart and body for this woman. And then the full weight of his responsibility for Claire descended on him again with the further knowledge that Alex meant what she said and was giving him a clear choice. He covered his face with his hands, horrified at the threat of tears rising to choke him. When he looked at her again, his expression was calm, his eyes reserved to the point of coldness.

"It won't happen again. I have never liked you to ride those horses. You know that. The idea that you might have been hurt or killed made me half mad." *And far too sane*, he thought. *It's you I want; you I've always wanted.*

"How has Morgan fared in his new life?" Her voice was only slightly unsteady.

Rane took his lead from her. "Very well indeed. He learns quickly and is marvelously willing." He decided he'd let Morgan tell his mother about the black eyes if he wished to. There had been some baiting about special favors when Morgan had taken his first coastal trading trips and had begun work in the shipyard. There had also been sly remarks about a bastard son. Morgan hadn't the slightest doubt that St. John was his father, and though he liked Rane, he had just taken exception to the slurs on his parentage.

For all his youth, Morgan had always been agile, and Timothy and Samson both had given him instruction on how to defend himself. Morgan soon proved himself more than capable of making a point with his fists when no other way would do. Rane had found it difficult not to intervene. Fatherhood was new to him and secret still, but he remembered how Magnus had allowed him to fight his own battles and knew how angry he would have been had his father interfered.

"Morgan has taken to sail as if born to it." He wished the words unsaid the moment he gave them life. How precarious things had become.

"It's true. I know it and you know it, so you needn't look so horrified for having spoken the truth," Alex said gently and moved on to another subject. "I've heard that whatever the tariff problems here, the West Indies trade is open again. Will that affect you?"

His eyes widened in surprise, and then he started to laugh. "Why have I ever believed I know what you're thinking? You've known all along that I'm involved in free trading, haven't you?"

"Well, not all along, but yes, I've known for a long time."

"And yet you allowed Morgan to go with me."

"I trust you not to put him in unnecessary danger. And you must remember, I had my mind changed about the trade by a certain family in Devon," she told him with a smile, and finally the tension eased between them.

"England's lifting of the restrictions of the West Indies trade will help commerce in general, particularly for the South, but President Jackson doesn't seem to be able to do anything about the Tariff of Abominations, and that has left the door open for a flourishing free trade. But I promise you, I am very careful and most cargoes are legitimate. I just keep my hand in in the old ways." His raffish grin stripped years from him.

But they both sobered as they discussed the continuing dissention over the Tariff of Abominations, which was proving, just as the Southern states had feared, to tax purses in the South more heavily than those in the North, and was above all an example of the increasing sectionalism. In January the now famous Webster-Hayne debates had taken place. They had begun with a difference of opinion over the sale of public lands in the West and had coursed over slavery, tariffs, and other questions, finally evolving into a blazing confrontation over states' rights, with Senator Robert Y. Hayne of South Carolina insisting, "The very life of our system is the independence of the states, and that there is no evil more to be deprecated than the consolidation of this government."

As far as Daniel Webster of Massachusetts was concerned, the states' only areas of sovereignty were those not defined by the Constitution. "Liberty and Union" were "one and inseparable."

"Perhaps the states don't have enough in common to stay together as a country," Rane observed. "Perhaps they will become regional blocks with trade agreements between them. The North, the South, and the West."

"A tidy way to start an endless war!" Alex protested. "It would be just like Europe, wars and tyrants sweeping back and forth like shifting winds. Oh, how I would hate to see that in this country!"

"So would I," he agreed hastily. "I'm not proposing it as a solution, but it might happen. I find it very odd. Some days I feel quite American, and then I feel quite English and distant from what is happening here. Do you ever feel so?"

"Always. Sometimes my own children sound foreign to me, for despite growing up with the Bateses, and Sinje and me, they speak far more like Americans than like the English."

They drifted into talk about their families, subtly but deliberately relegating their feelings for each other to the past. The Falconers were still flourishing despite a decrease in free trading. Rane had more nieces and nephews, children he had never seen.

"I do think of going back to visit, but somehow, I never seem to arrange it. It is such a long journey." He did not need to say that leaving Claire for that amount of time was something he would not do and taking her was out of the question. "I've tried to persuade Mother and Father to come here, but they never will. Nor will my brothers and their wives; their lives and their children are too demanding."

"When I think of Gweneth and Magnus and the others, I remember how kindly all of you treated me. What important days those were for me!"

"Alex, I want you to know that they still love you and wish you well. I wrote to them about St. John's death, and they would have written to you, but I cautioned them against it, thinking it would be too hard for you—for us," he added honestly, and she agreed. The connections already ran too deep and did not need added complications of familial love.

"Do you ever think of returning to England?" he asked.

"There is nothing left for me where I was born," she said flatly. "I won't ever return. Part of me is afraid that if I ever did, I would give up and stay in the emptiness just because it is familiar. Or perhaps, not even that would be true any more. I still correspond with Lord Bettingdon, a friend of Sinje's. He was devastated to hear of Sinje's death, and when he wrote back to me, he was still feeling sad. I expect that's why he wrote more of the bad news of England than he had before. Oh, Hugh continues to flourish; he's very wealthy and astute. But he is also a man of conscience and worries for his country. He sees so many people without work or with work so grueling and poorly paid in the new factories that their lives are hardly worth living. He is not at all surprised by the numbers that are now seeking passage to this country or to Canada."

"Well, I am surprised," Rane admitted. "I remember how few British there were when I arrived, and it still catches my attention to hear the King's English in New York, Philadelphia, and even Baltimore."

"It must be a shock in other areas, too," Alex said with a little laugh. "My brother is now called 'English Boston' in many places where he goes."

"Do you hear from him often?"

"What you mean is did I tell him about Sinje?" she said. "I did only because I thought he might be corresponding now and then with one of the family in Gravesend. But I also told him he would be of no use were he to hurry back here. I asked him to understand that this is my life and that I am managing it very well." In fact, her letter to Boston had been almost severe. The tone of it and the delays before he received it must have worked together to convince him. He had not gotten her late January letter until June, and she had not received his reply until September. Even great tragedies were blunted by such lapses of time.

Rane was aware of the warning to him. Over and over she was insisting that he see her life as her own, to risk on the back of a race horse or any other way she pleased in her pursuit of her own goals. It sat ill with his protective impulses, but he had no right to interfere.

Alex and Rane were careful not to betray the slightest unease in their parting. But that did not stop Alex from listening intently when Morgan told her at length about his new life in Baltimore and included much about Rane.

"The men that work for him like him a lot," Morgan said, "but they feel sorry for him because of his wife. One man said he'd throw her overboard with a weight around her neck. But Cousin Rane never mentions her, and the men know they'd better not, either, when he's around. It's sort of nice, Mama; he looks happier when he's here with us than he ever does in Baltimore. Even the ladies there don't seem to make him happy," Morgan expounded, glad that his idol didn't have feet of clay.

"What ladies?" Alex asked.

"Oh, the men talk about them all the time 'cause they're jealous, the men, I mean. They say that all kinds of women, ladies and not, seek him out." He looked at his mother and blushed, not sure whether he should admit that he was beginning to understand the difference in the definitions, though it still wasn't completely clear.

"Virtue is not absolute," she informed him drily. "It's usually a very personal judgment made by one person about another, and it's better to refrain from that sort of judgment altogether."

Morgan considered this for a moment and nodded. "That makes sense. And anyway, the men think Cousin Rane has a mistress they've never seen and that's why he ignores the other women. I sort of hope it's true. I hope there is someone who makes him happy." Morgan was still in the in-between state where he found the opposite sex more of a bother than an attraction—except for Sam, of course, who didn't count as a female—but he could see what a necessity women were to most men, and he was willing to concede to anything that might make his hero happy.

Alex felt a savage thrust of jealousy that left her quite breathless for a moment as she tried to imagine what sort of woman Rane's mistress might be. And then she reminded herself that it didn't matter, true or not, because as she insisted on directing her own life, so Rane must direct his. He must find relief somewhere from the pain that Claire gave him. It was reasonable and very little comfort, and she resolved not to dwell on it.

The twins were due back soon. The Jenningses would

bring them to Annapolis, and Alex would collect them there when she attended the elder Jenningses' holiday party. She looked forward to going again. So many crises had interrupted attendance in previous years. Though Caleb's parents were ten years older than when she had first met them, they seemed little changed, and Alex did not see them as often as she would like.

Alex expected she would always miss St. John more when special celebrations were in the offing, but she was determined that the children not come to dread those times. They were excited about Christmas, and she let their high spirits enliven her own. Sam, having Morgan home again, needed no addition to her joy. It was a pleasure to look at her, so bright and shining was she in his presence. Alex wondered when it would dawn on her son that Sam was growing into a creature of rare beauty. And yet she was relieved that their awareness of each other was still childish; complications would come soon enough.

Already there was a great deal of whispering and hiding of various projects going on in preparation for Christmas, and Alex wondered what odd gifts would appear. She hoped she had dissuaded Nigel from presenting collections of dried beetles carefully pinned in boxes. As gently as possible she had pointed out that beetles and other insects were not to everyone's liking.

Such cozy domestic concerns were swept away by the arrival of the man from Georgia. He came without prior appointment. Alex was working on the ledgers when Polly announced in her soft drawl that there was a visitor who wanted to see Mrs. Carrington.

It was midmorning, and Alex sighed in annoyance. She had wanted to finish with her clerical duties and then take a long ride, but this interruption would probably cancel that plan.

She disliked Willard Hutchins on sight. He was a fairly tall, well-built man probably approaching fifty years of age. His features were unremarkable, his clothing fine, and yet he reminded her of Mr. Blockett. Because she knew that was unjust, she made herself greet him cordially. But there was something about the way his pale eyes swept over her, something in the too full curve of his mouth that made her uneasy. There was also something familiar about him beyond the comparison to Mr. Blockett, though she could not remember seeing him before.

"How may I help you?" she asked, still sorting through memories, trying to place him.

"I wanna buy that colt of yoahs, Magic Swan. Word of yoah race has spread like summa feva, an' I figa that th' colt is jus' what I need to build up ma stables again. Haven't done so well these pas' few yeahs, but I've still got some fine mares."

"I have no intention of selling Magic," she said. "If someone told you that he was for sale, I am sorry for your trouble. None of the horses here are for sale at this time." And never to you, she thought.

"Ma'am, everythin' has its price, an' I'm willin' t' pay top dolla foah 'im."

His drawl and his false air of bonhomie that was so at variance with the cold glint in his eyes grated on her nerves. "Mr. Hutchins, I repeat, Magic is not for sale, not for any price. And now, if you will excuse me, I have a very busy day ahead of me. I wish you luck in buying horses somewhere else." She started to lead him out of the house, but was stopped by his hand on her arm.

"You haven't even heard ma offa!" His voice was angry, but not as angry as hers.

"Take your hand off my arm! I bid you good day." She jerked away from him and strode purposefully outside, relieved to see Della as well as Polly close by and Jed and another of the men drawing near to the house.

Mr. Hutchins saw that he was outnumbered, but it did not stop him from muttering, "I'll be back afta you've had time t' think on sellin' that colt." Mr. Hutchins was not accustomed to being refused.

When Alex saw how nervously his horse backed from him when he tried to mount, she was more sure than ever that the man was detestable. By the look of it, the horse was no more than a hired hack and thus used to various riders, but it didn't like this man.

She watched him leave, feeling no fear, for the people of Wild Swan had accurately judged the look on her face and were on guard. But still something nagged at her, and then she remembered. "Oh, my God!" she whispered, and her eyes searched frantically for Samson.

Willard Hutchins from Georgia. She knew now why the name had made her uneasy. He was Samson's owner.

She was paralyzed by terror, unable to think coherently.

"Miz Carrington, you all right?" Jed's worried voice steadied her. No one else must be involved.

"What an unpleasant man! And on top of rows of unpleasant figures. I need some fresh air. I think I'll take Magic out for a ride, just to assure him that we have no intention of selling him, for that's what the man wanted." The unnatural high note in her voice escaped Jed's notice in his anger at the idea anyone would think Magic was for sale. But he focused on her again when he realized she meant to saddle the horse herself and ride just as she was, without changing her clothes.

There was so little time. "Jed, I don't have time to stand here arguing with you, and I don't want anyone to go with me. I need to get away alone, now!" She nearly screamed the words, and Jed was suddenly of no mind to question her actions, she looked so fierce. Wordlessly, he helped her saddle Magic, watched her ride off in a burst of speed, and thought how often all of them forgot what an enormous task she had without her husband beside her.

Alex felt as if she were in Samson's mind. He would not confront Hutchins until the man was well away from the house. She was sure of it. And Hutchins, which way had he gone? Even stripped of leaves by winter, the long tree-bordered lane that led to the house did not give a view of which way visitors turned when they departed. Washington City; somehow she was again certain and somehow Samson knew.

She gained the public road and kept Magic at a swift pace, watching for Mr. Hutchins, counting on Magic's speed to make up for the precious lost time. She was beyond the boundary of Wild Swan when she heard the raised voices, audible even over the clip of Magic's hooves.

They were off the road, sheltered by trees, Samson on foot, Mr. Hutchins looming over him on horseback.

"I buy ma fambly back. I pays you all I gots now an' de res' when I earns it," Samson shouted desperately as Hutchins raised his riding crop and brought it down on his head.

"You buy nothin', you no good nigra! I own you!" Hutchins roared. "An' that skinny English bitch'll pay. I know you been workin' foah 'er; that's how you come t'be here."

He brought the whip down again, but this time Samson grabbed it and yanked the man from his saddle.

The men were totally oblivious of Alex's presence. And she was helpless to stop them, for Magic, usually so well mannered, suddenly reared and bucked wildly, pulling to run, terrified by the violence that involved the man whom he knew as a gentle-voiced, gentle-handed trainer.

Even with everything swinging crazily in her vision as she fought to control the colt and stay on his back, Alex saw the finish. There was no fight. Samson smashed his huge fist into the man's temple, felling him with one mighty blow. Hutchins crumpled to the ground, twitched, and lay still. Alex knew he was dead.

Sides heaving from his exertion, Magic stopped plunging beneath her and stood trembling. Samson caught sight of them then and froze in place.

The enormity of it washed over Alex, sucking the air from her lungs. The nightmare had happened. The black man had killed a white man. With savage force, Samson had broken the taboo.

Alex stared at him, green eyes holding the dark brown over the yawning chasm of fear. His fear more than hers. The dark nightmare of the region was not hers.

This was still the same man who had treated every living thing at Wild Swan with complete gentleness since the day he had arrived. The same man who would willingly die for her children or for her. And who would kill for her. She saw the horrific scene again in her mind, saw that Samson had not attacked the man until after Hutchins had made the connection with Wild Swan and threatened her. It might have happened anyway, but that was the way it had happened.

"Samson," she called softly, "will you please come hold Magic so I can dismount? He is still upset."

He came toward them, and Magic backed from his fear and then settled down as Samson reached out to him. The big man buried his face against the horse's neck and his shoulders heaved, but he made no sound.

The last vestige of Alex's fear vanished, leaving in its wake a fierce protectiveness. She had to think fast for both of them.

She slipped from Magic's back and took a firm grip on Samson's arm. "Listen to me; we have very little time. This road is too well traveled. We must make it look like

639

an accident." Only then did she notice that Hutchins's horse had bolted from the scene. "The horse will undoubtedly find his way back to the livery or to somewhere where someone will wonder what has happened."

Slowly Samson raised his head. "You gib me jus' a liddle time; I goes away."

"No, you won't!" she snapped. "Not yet anyway. Right now your only chance is to stay at Wild Swan and know nothing about this. It's my only chance, too; otherwise I may well be accused of harboring a runaway." She didn't fear that for an instant, but she didn't hesitate to use it against him.

"Help me now." Her eyes continued to roam the area, looking for something to aid them, and finally she saw it—a pile of fair-sized stones, probably piled to mark a property line or some dimension of the road.

"He was thrown from his horse and hit his head on those stones," she said calmly. "But his body must be closer to them. pick him up, Samson. Do as I say!"

Shocked to the depths of his soul by what he had done, Samson numbly obeyed her instructions, still only half understanding her intention.

When the body was positioned with the head on the rocks as she had directed, Alex took a deep breath, grabbed the head and smashed the bruised temple as hard as she could against the cairn, becoming in that instant a true accessory to the crime. Her stomach heaved, but she swallowed the rising bile. Very carefully she placed the man's hat nearby where it might have fallen. And then she checked for any signs of struggle, smoothing the hoof prints with her hands and a tree branch.

"Take Magic to the road," she ordered, and again Samson obeyed. As well as she could, she eradicated Magic's tracks, her own, and Samson's, leaving only the confused prints of the rented horse that had pranced around before fleeing.

"Now I am going to ride home. Make your way back and stay off the road. I expect you in the library within the hour. I will tell no one and you will tell no one what happened. Together we will decide what happens next. Do you understand?"

He looked down at her, but he had no words. He handed her up into the saddle as if she were made of spun glass. She did not look back.

She dismounted once, retching violently on the cold earth and feeling better afterward. She mounted with the aid of a tree stump and continued crosscountry. Before she was in sight of the buildings, she pinched her cheeks hard to give them color.

She smiled and assured Jed that the ride had done her a world of good, and she walked steadily into the house and told Della that she would be working again in the library should anyone need her. Both Jed and Della were pleased by the color in Alex's face, and independently they both decided that the peculiar light green brilliance of her eyes was a trick of the stark winter light that flooded the day.

Only when the library door was closed did Alex slump over the desk, shaking uncontrollably though she reminded herself that the course was only half run. When she could control her hands, she poured a healthy dose of brandy from the decanter on a side table and drank it straight down, welcoming the fire of it. And then she waited, wondering if she would ever see Samson again, nearly crying aloud when he appeared.

His skin was sickly gray-brown, his eyes glazed, but he was there. She offered him a glass of brandy, but he shook his head.

"I know who he was," she said. "I remembered his name, though it was almost too late. Samson, I am sure he had no idea you were here until you confronted him. He came here to try to buy Magic, not looking for you. He said as much to you. As long as neither of us betrays what happened, no one will know it was anything but an accident."

"He gots ma babies, ma two liddle boys an' ma wife! Always I plans to go back fo' dem, buy dem o' take dem some ways. When I runs, dey too young to make it an' I hab to go cuz I doan like de way he treats de hosses. He says he beat me 'til I dies I doan do like he wants. So I runs." His voice was so low she had to strain to hear, but she had no difficulty believing him; she had seen the scars.

"Somehow we will find out about your family. But for now, you must stay here, you must. It is the only way. Both of us must go on as if nothing has occurred."

"Why?" he asked, and their eyes met as they had after the killing.

"Because you are part of Wild Swan. Because you are part of our lives. And because you are my friend. I am not at all sure you would have killed him had he not threatened me as well as you. I doubt that you know. And it doesn't matter. He was evil, and he is dead."

There were tears in his eyes as he left, and his step was as heavy as an old man's, but Alex was sure he was not going to bolt.

That night she awakened herself with her own screams as she dreamed of smashing the head again and again against the stones. She lay in the dark, sweating despite the cold and longing for St. John, longing for Rane. The duality of her desire stunned her, and she could not wait for dawn to break.

Behaving naturally around the children and everyone else took enormous effort, but she managed it because there was no choice. It was hardest not to betray anything to Della. Every time Alex looked at her, she thought of Samson's family. No wonder he had never courted Della.

Alex felt relief more than anything else when the authorities arrived the next afternoon. There were two men, and they explained with embarrassed politeness that yesterday a body had been discovered a ways back on the road to Washington. They figured the man had been thrown from his horse, but they wondered if anyone knew anything about him. They were inquiring throughout the area. The man's personal effects identified him as one Willard Hutchins from Georgia.

"Oh, my heavens!" Alex exclaimed, and she gave them a perfect description of the man. "He was here yesterday. He wanted to buy one of our horses, Magic Swan. I told him the horse is not for sale. He was quite rude about it and rode off in a fury. I didn't like him one bit, and would never have sold one of our horses to a man who rode so roughly, but I am certainly sorry he came to such a sad end."

The men were uncomfortable having to discuss such an indelicate subject with Mrs. Carrington. She was obviously a lady, and they knew she had a reputation for fair dealing and for being a good hand at healing the sick. Poor woman, having her husband crippled and then dead like that and having to carry on without him. They had also heard about her famous race and thought Mr. Hutchins must have been a presumptuous fool to think she'd sell the horse. Good riddance to bad rubbish, one of the men thought, but he kept his face carefully somber as befit his duty.

Gratefully the men accepted Alex's offer of warming refreshment against the chill of the day, and they left Wild Swan convinced that the death of Mr. Hutchins was an accident.

In the whole time they were there, Alex did not once look to see if Samson was watching. And she did not seek him out until several hours had passed after the men had left. She knew everyone on the place was talking about the death, but it was idle chatter, nothing more. Only Jed might put the odd bits together and suspect something, but if he had, he was keeping his own counsel.

When Alex finally confronted Samson, she could see that he was beginning to believe it really would be all right. "That part is over," she told him. "And now I ask you to trust me to find a way to free your wife and children."

"I trusts you wid ma life an' wid deyrs," he said, and Alex knew the only other times in her life she had been responsible for trust so precious had been in Clovelly, first when the Falconers had let her stay on and help after her discovery of their involvement in free trading, and then when Caleb Jennings had believed she would help him escape from England.

For a moment she was overwhelmed by the weight of the burden. And then she reminded herself that her grandmother had trained her to minister to the secrets of the human soul as well as to treat the ailments of the flesh because flesh and soul were inextricably bound together. Without her help, Samson might well die by the hangman's rope. Even the thought of failure was intolerable.

❧ Chapter 59 ❧

All Alex could think of was finding help. Despite her protestations of independence, she could not solve Samson's problems alone. There were few people she would even consider trusting with the full story. Caleb and Dr. Cameron; she kept thinking of one and then the other. Alastair, she was certain, continued with his secret work of helping escaped slaves move north, though they never spoke of it. She knew he would help if she asked, but she was loath to put him in even more danger than he was already in. It meant not only a risk to a dear friend but also to the people who depended on him. Caleb, too, she knew would help without hesitation. But he had already done far too much for the Carringtons.

She was still considering the complexities of the situation when the Jenningses' annual Christmas party got under way, and she saw Rane. He never attended social functions any more, and he was the last person she had expected to see. And by the pleased surprise on the Jenningses' faces, she realized they had not expected he would make it either.

Rane had come to Annapolis and to the party for one reason: he had known Alex was going to be there. It was an excuse to see her again though very little time had passed since he had been at Wild Swan. He did not try to deny it to himself. And his breath caught at the sight of her.

She was dressed in black, but with her coloring, it did not make her appear drab. The dress was simply cut with fitted waist and soft billowing skirt, cut low enough at the neckline to show the faintly golden cream of her skin without being too daring. The black of her dress and the dark of her hair served to frame her striking green eyes and her full rosy mouth. At thirty years old, she was far more beautiful than she had been when he had first made love to her and thought she could never be more exquisite.

Alex knew he was her answer, knew that she had been considering him all along. No matter that they had tried to rebuild the walls after the kiss in the library, they were never going to be able to go back to studied indifference. And she knew he could help in the matter of Samson's family. Rane had all kinds of connections; free traders always did.

"What is it? he asked urgently as he came to her, accurately reading the disquiet in her.

"May I speak to you alone?" It already felt as if they were alone, as if the people around them had disappeared.

He led her to the library of the house, and she thought, how strange; I can't even be trusted with him in a room full of musty books and papers. She felt her body stirring with hunger for him as it had at Wild Swan. But her desire died abruptly as she began to recount the story of Willard Hutchins and Samson, leaving nothing out from the time Samson had come to Wild Swan until the authorities had left. Even when she confessed to smashing the head against the stones, her voice trembled only slightly.

"And now I need you to help me find out about Samson's wife and two children. With the man dead, it's more than possible that his slaves might be sold off, the property broken up. Samson says the mistress of the plantation was a discontented woman from New Orleans. Mr. Hutchins treated his wife unkindly, and she thought Georgia was a wilderness. When Samson left there were no Hutchins children, so the woman would have no reason to stay now." She had gotten all the information she could from Samson, including the names of his family. "I don't want you to go yourself. It would be very bad if you did; it is too easy to connect you with me and with Wild Swan. But I thought perhaps you could use someone you trust from free trading to find out about the woman and her children, perhaps even to get them out. To buy them or steal them; I don't care which, as long as neither they nor Samson is endangered. Is it asking too much?"

Rane wanted to tell her that nothing on earth was too much for her to ask except that he cease loving her. "I know exactly the man to serve as agent in this. He is utterly trustworthy because he knows his price. For the right amount, he keeps his bargains." He pictured the nondescript little man who slipped so unobtrusively in and out of various situations, seeming such a dullard while in fact possessed of a fox's wit. Best of all, Rane knew he could get word to him quickly. The man was in Baltimore now, having just provided information on where a cargo of tariff-free goods could be landed, goods Rane was arranging to have brought from England via the West Indies. Rane planned to be aboard the ship waiting off Savannah to take Samson's family aboard one way or another. He would not tell Alex that, but he knew he could make sure that his presence on the water would not endanger the mission. That he would spend Christmas in a tense situation did not concern him; holidays of joy had ceased to exist in his life with Claire, and in her present state of mind, his wife no longer recognized joy at all, let alone which day was which.

Alex knew it was unfair, but she felt soaring relief. Rane had taken the burden from her.

He did not touch her; he knew what would happen if he did. But the current flowed between them more strongly than ever before until Alex remembered that the twins and everyone else might wonder where they had gone. "We must go back," she whispered huskily.

And he thought, if only we could, meaning something entirely different, but he said only, "Of course," and moved to hold the door open for her.

Because she knew Rane was doing his best for her, Alex enjoyed Christmas with the children and everyone else at Wild Swan. Even Samson seemed at peace. She had told him what was being done, and he trusted Rane nearly as much as she did. It did not occur to her that Rane was anywhere except home in Baltimore.

She did not expect him for the small party New Year's Eve at Wild Swan, for when she had mentioned it, he had told her quite definitely that he would not be able to come. Part of her had continued to look out for him, but a more rational element assumed that he simply could not leave Claire for that long. They never talked about her; she had no current knowledge of the woman's state except that it wasn't good.

The older and younger Jenningses, Mrs. Perkins, frail

but still sharp, Dr. Cameron, and the Bateses were the only guests, and so the gathering had the feeling of a family affair. Alex was grateful for it. She needed them there to ease through the memories. A year before, Sinje had been with her, and then so swiftly he had gone forever.

The winter had been fairly cold with snow flurries on and off, but no one was prepared for the great snowstorm that swept in from the southwest with the winds paradoxically blowing a true northeaster on Friday, the fourteenth of January.

The sky had been threatening since dawn, the wind fitful, and in the afternoon, the snow began as the wind grew stronger. The twins were already back in Baltimore, but Alex checked to make sure the others were not tempted to wander too far. Sam had reluctantly agreed to go home early so that her parents would not worry. "As if they would," Morgan had muttered to his mother, and he had escorted Sam to Brookhaven and then returned to Wild Swan.

Alex's next concern was the horses, and along with Samson, she made sure they were all secured. This was an especially critical time for mares in foal and for the newly born. By Oberon, Swan Song had already produced a bay colt, named "Robin Goodfellow" for the elusive and mischievous elf, another Puck, of English lore. Black Swan and Taney had yet to foal. However, Alex soon found she had nothing to fret about. Whatever his personal concerns, Samson would never neglect his charges and had already directed everything to the horses' comfort.

Alex didn't know why she was so nervous. They had weathered storms before. But there was something different about this one, something more menacing in the howling winds that made her as uneasy as the stallions. Swan paced nervously, as if he would go out and fight the wind, and Alex knew how he felt.

Wrapped in her heavy cloak, she was making her way back to the house when she saw the ghostly rider. It was snowing so heavily and blowing so hard, it was difficult to discern anything clearly. She blinked and wiped at her eyes, not sure of the apparition until the horse was close by.

"Easy there, easy, boy," she called, knowing that the horse couldn't see much either.

The muffled rider dismounted slowly and stiffly, obviously nearly frozen. The wind had driven snow against his back, and he looked more like a badly made snowman than a human. But even before she could look into his green eyes, even though his bulky clothing hid his normal silhouette, Alex recognized Rane and went to him, gripping his arms and calling his name over the roar of the wind.

There was no use in trying to talk out in the storm. They moved together, leading his horse to shelter in an empty stall.

"My God! You could have died!" Alex exclaimed when they were inside. "Whatever possessed you to come out on a day like this?"

Rane was too cold and weary for tact. "It wasn't a day like this when I started. We came into Annapolis before the storm hit, and I started for Wild Swan immediately. I had to." His face was grim.

She knew then that he had news of Samson's family, and she knew it was bad.

As they worked to unsaddle Rane's hired mount and rub him down, Samson approached. Rane wished he were not so exhausted, and then he reminded himself that there was no easy way to tell this truth.

With quiet insistence, Samson took over the care of the horse, and Rane watched as if hypnotized, trying to summon the words.

When Samson had finished, he regarded Rane steadily. "Now, you tells me. I knows you gots word of ma fambly."

Rane heard himself babbling about the trip to the Georgia coast, about the reliability of his agent, and he drew himself up short. "Samson, there is no kind way to say this. Your family, your wife and both of your sons, died shortly after you left. They died of some sort of fever that took many of the slaves on Hutchins's plantation."

With one lithe movement, Samson was on him, shaking him violently, as if Rane weighed no more than a child. "You lies, man, you lies! Masta Hutchins, he doan say dat!"

Rane made no move to defend himself, but Alex grabbed at Samson's heaving shoulders. "Stop it! Oh, stop it! Rane risked his life to come here!"

As soon as Samson's hands dropped away, Rane said,

"It's no lie or mistake. An old slave, a man named Abbadias, sent special word; he sent his sorrow to you."

The name meant truth to Samson. "I hurts you?" He sounded as if he were a very old man, and his eyes looked filmed over, blind.

Rane shook his head in negation, his throat too tight for further speech.

Samson slumped to the ground, and then he howled, an agonized bellow of rage and grief that died away to a high, thin mewling as if an animal were caught in a trap. The horses moved uneasily, and the stable echoed with their questioning whickers.

Alex was paralyzed by the sounds that sent shivers up and down her spine, and then she dropped to her knees beside Samson, putting her arms around him, rocking his immense bulk against her.

She went on rocking him until his keening had stopped and she had found her own voice again. "Don't make any decisions now. Give yourself time to grieve. Don't leave us yet, Samson, please don't! I need you; the children need you."

She doubted that he heard her, and she hated to leave him, fearful that he would do himself some hurt, but Samson was a man, and she had to concede his right to deal with his loss and his life as he saw fit.

With Della to help: the thought came to her and took hold. Della loves Samson and knows him. Della can comfort him as I cannot. It was the only light she saw in the darkness.

She was worried about Rane as well. He was shivering with cold and reaction and needed to get warm immediately. As she led Rane out of the stable, she heard Samson murmuring, "All dis time, all de sabin' an' waitin', all dis time dey be dead."

Della gave a gasp of dismay at Rane's sorry state.

"Rane will be all right," Alex told her, "but I'm not sure about Samson." Making sure no one else was nearby to overhear, she gave Della the stark facts. "I'm terrified for him. Will you go to him? Perhaps you can comfort him where I cannot."

Della did not hesitate. Whatever reservations she had had about Samson when he had first come to Wild Swan were long gone. "That poor man. Poor Samson." She was reaching for her cloak even as she crooned the words.

Alex turned her attention to Rane, brushing his clumsy fingers away so that she could help him out of his coat, pulling off his wet boots, leaving him just long enough to fix him a strong cup of tea laced with brandy. His teeth were chattering, and his hands shook so badly that she had to help him hold the cup to drink the brew. Even sitting down he was swaying with exhaustion, his eyes half closed.

"Come on, love, stay awake just a little longer so I can get you up the stairs." She didn't hear her own endearment.

He leaned heavily on her and put one foot before the other as she directed, hardly noticing that she had found Cassie on the way and issued orders for a warming pan. He was so done in, it was all a blur as she helped him strip off the rest of his sodden clothes and slip between the warmed sheets. His eyes closed as soon as his head touched the pillow, though he still shivered.

The guest chamber was clean, kept ready for visitors, but cold, and it would take time for the newly lighted fire to warm it. Alex added extra blankets to the bed, and seeing how damp Rane's hair was, she lifted his head and toweled the thick darkness until it was dry. He did not awaken. She chafed his hands and felt the shudders easing as his body warmed.

She had sent Cassie away, and she didn't give a second thought to the propriety or lack of it of her being alone in the bedchamber with Rane. All that mattered was that he was safe. Her heart had not yet settled from the terror of knowing that he might easily have been lost in the storm for long enough to die of it. The snow and wind were still howling against the house, showing no signs of abating. She left candles burning so that he would not awaken in the dark and be disoriented, and she left brandy and drinking and washing water for his comfort.

She, Cassie, and Polly completed the cooking, fed the children and Mr. Whittleby, and made sure there was enough for anyone who might need a hot meal as the storm raged on. The children had played in the snow early in the day and planned great adventures on the morrow if the wind had decreased and so were tired and went docilely to bed, for which Alex was grateful. The day seemed to have been three times as long as a normal span.

Rane still slept when she checked on him before going

to her own chamber. She put on a nightgown and brushed her hair for a long time, feellng restless despite her own fatigue. Della had not come back to the house, and Alex hoped that meant that Samson had let her share his torment.

She did not want to think of Rane and could not think of anything else. Long and lean, but more broadly, more powerfully built than St. John. How beautiful were the sinews and hollows of his body.

She stood up abruptly and paced her room, trying to banish the image from her mind. The bedchamber seemed more lonely than it ever had since St. John's death. Samson's family, St. John, her grandmother, Christiana and the other baby girl—death was all around, pressing close. She wanted life, bright, coursing, full of chance and change.

She donned a robe over her gown and let herself out into the dark hall, going to Rane's room as if drawn by invisible cords as strong as steel.

His eyes were open, as if he had summoned her with a thought. She could see that he had lighted fresh candles from the guttering stubs of the old, added more wood to the fire, and had helped himself to a glass of brandy. She moved as if in a dream in the silence until she stood over his bed.

"How are you feeling?" she asked softly.

"Warm, thank God and you, and rested." He reached for her hand and brought it to his lips as if it were the most natural gesture in the world. "I have never had a harder task than giving that news to Samson. How is he?"

"I don't know, but Della is with him, and if anyone can help him heal, she can." She shivered, but not with cold, as his fingers manipulated the delicate bones of her hand.

Though he still lay there, the last traces of languor were suddenly gone. "And you, will you help me to heal?" His eyes glittered like dark emeralds, but the pull on her hand was gentle, easily resisted if she so chose.

She did not. In one fluid motion, she sank down on the bed, lying half on top of his hard body.

He pulled the bedclothes away and wrapped his arms around her with a groan. "Alex, my sweet Alex, God, how I want you!" He buried his face in her loose tresses and inhaled the fragrance of her as he ran his hands up and down her back and felt her body melting against his.

He wanted her so much that his body trembled with his need, and he clenched his jaw in an effort to control his response to her.

Alex gloried in the battle he was waging so unsuccessfully. She broke away from him long enough to strip away her robe and gown, hearing him gasp as he saw her nude body. In all her life, she had never felt so completely female, bold and desirable as she did now. She knelt beside him on the bed, pushing him back when he would have sat up. And then she began to explore his body with feathery kisses and caresses, savoring the textures of him, the light mat of dark hair on his chest, arms, and legs, and the fine line of it leading below his waist to the apex of his manhood. His skin tasted of salt and an indefinable essence that was only his. She kissed the hard angle of his jaw, the hollow of his eyes, the curve of his mouth; she traced the savage scar of his arm, Claire's work, mark of his sorrow. No part of his body was worth more than another; all of it was Rane, infinitely precious. The hard upright swell of his shaft proclaimed his ardor before he gasped, "Enough, I cannot bear . . ."

"Then take me, take me now!" she urged, almost laughing with the joy of it.

His patience and control at an end, Rane reached up to hold her, rolling her beneath him, but in that instant before he entered her, she saw what Claire had done to him, saw the fear and uncertainty even as his body urged him on.

It had been more than two years since her body had opened to a man, and as much as she wanted him, there was pain in Rane's first thrusts, but it was part of the pleasure, as if no man had been before him, no children born, as if she came to him a virgin. And then her body blossomed for him, opening warm velvet to sheath him. It was dizzying and strange to have two arms around her, his strong body perfectly balanced even in the throes of lust. She gave herself up to his strength, feeling the flame of him deep inside, letting the fire consume them both.

When it was finished, they rested together for a long time, clinging tightly to each other.

It was Rane who broke the silence. "I love you, Alex. I've loved you since you were a child in Clovelly. And yet I have less to offer you now than I did when I came to you in Gravesend. I cannot take you and the children to Baltimore and provide for you. I can only make your life more difficult . . ."

She put her fingers over his mouth. "Stop! I do not want you to be mistaken in this. Even were you free, I would not leave Wild Swan. This is my home and my work, just as the ships are yours. Sinje and I worked hard for this, and I have no intention of giving it up or losing it. But that has nothing to do with how much I love you. Sweetheart, I fear you are too accustomed to taking care of Claire." She tried to make her voice gentle, but he could hear her tension. "You did not seduce me. I came to you. If you cannot accept my strengths as well as my weaknesses, if you cannot take from me as well as give to me, you cannot love me."

Rane was silent, considering what she said, knowing the truth of it, knowing that one of the things he most loved about her was her strength, and yet knowing as well that he was not always sure of how to live with it. He remembered how furious he had been with her when he had heard about the race. He had truly felt that it was his business; he still did. But he realized now that it was a part of loving arising out of fear for the danger she had put herself in; it was not a right.

"You were afraid, just for a moment, you were afraid to make love to me. Claire has done that to you. I know she has. Will you tell me how? Can you talk about it?" Her voice was uncertain now.

He had never talked honestly about Claire to anyone, but he found himself talking now. There had been a time in his journey to Wild Swan when he had thought he would not survive. After the pain of the cold had eased, he had found himself swaying sleepily in the saddle and had realized how easy it would have been to slip down into the drifting snow forever. Even with the sorrow of his mission, it had seemed utterly fitting that Alex should be the first person he would find, and fitting that his longing should have produced her, real and warm, at his bedside. The silken flesh had celebrated his and welcomed him home. He was she, as she was he. As it had been years before, he was no longer certain where he finished and she began.

"I should never have married Claire. It was unfair to her from the start. Claire has never been able to accept the reality of life. She was raised to believe herself a fairy princess, an other-worldly creature with none of the burdens and none of the pleasures of mortals. I thought her shyness about lovemaking was only that of any virgin who is uninformed. I thought I could teach her the joy of it. I was patient, but it was not enough. I succeeded only in terrifying her. She hated every part of it, and she hated me for wanting it. And yet, she would go through times when she pled that she wanted to learn all the duties of a wife, as if it were a game she could never quite grasp. But then her fear would defeat her again. The more difficult daily life became for her, the more she fled into her own mind. And the worst of it is that she found no peace there but rather demons who give her no rest; and I have become one of them. She is more biddable under opiates, but they make her visions more horrific. Her moans are pitiful. And yet, without the drugs, she is apt to be very strong and destructive. Year by year it has gotten more hellish. You would hardly recognize her now." He drew a deep, shuddering breath, and unconsciously, he touched the knife scar. "Poor Claire, I made her life so much worse."

He felt Alex's head jerk away from his shoulder as she reared up and knelt beside him, sitting back on her heels, heedless of her nakedness and the chill of the air, her fists clenched on her knees.

"You're wrong, so very wrong! I've heard the rumors, and I'm sure they're true. Claire was sick in her mind long before she met you. And her father knew it! He wanted someone else to take care of her; perhaps he even knew he was going to die, but that still doesn't make it right. I know you. I know you in every part of me. And you know how to love, not only physically, but in so many other ways. If any man could have made Claire happy, you would have. Its wicked, what she's done to you! The scars inside are worse than the one on your arm. My sister did the same thing to Sinje; she made him feel guilty for being alive." There was no gentleness in her now, only outrage on his behalf. At that moment, she hated Claire with all of her being.

"But what I did to Claire was far worse," His voice was so low, she had to strain to hear it. "I married her knowing well that I still loved you. I tried to pretend it wasn't true, and in that pretense, I damned both Claire and myself."

Alex's eyes were suddenly wide and strange. She chanted in slow cadence:

Wise child of the wise-woman, you will learn—
You are with him now,
But you won't be then,
Until it's time for him again.

"That's what the gypsy said at Barnstaple Fair. I did not understand, and I forgot the words until now. I did not even recall them when you came to Gravesend. Oh, Rane, I cannot bear to think that Sinje was only a steppingstone on my way to loving you; I cannot, no matter how much I love you, no matter that you have not ever loved Claire."

It would never be easy for him to acknowledge her love for St. John, but it was part of her and part of what he could give her. "Because life and love go on does not make what has been before any less valid," he said softly.

He saw her tears gather and begin to overflow, and he reached for her, drawing her down beside him again, licking the tears from her face, stroking her body reverently, feeling her warm with his touch.

The wonder of it flowed from him to her. This was not Claire's shrinking flesh that he had long since ceased to approach, nor was it the paid willingness of the exclusive whores he sought now and then to slake his lust. This was a woman who loved him as much or more than anyone else ever had or would in his life, a woman who loved him for himself exactly as he was.

He traced delicate circles around the dark roses of her nipples with his tongue, returning to take each in turn in his mouth, sucking gently as he felt her thighs open, giving his hand access between her legs. She moaned deep in her throat, her body shaken by long waves of pleasure as he teased the tight bud of desire and slipped his fingers in and out of her, feeling her welling readiness for him.

Alex felt as if Rane were touching every part of her at once, and she gave herself up to the pleasure of his loving, letting the sensations ripple through her until just when she knew she could bear no more, he sheathed himself in her, stretching and satisfying her.

He thrust in and out with exquisite slowness, watching her face, seeing the response he was causing inside her reflected clearly in the flickering changes in her expression, enjoying her passion more than his own, not losing control until she had begun to buck wildly beneath him.

They fell asleep in each other's arms, and Alex was smiling, hearing her own voice asking, "Can it always be like this?" so long ago.

❧ *Chapter 60* ❧

The blizzard sheltered Alex and Rane, giving them a sense of privacy and respite they would not otherwise have had. The outside world was cut off as the snow continued to fall on and off on Saturday, not finishing until Sunday morning. The children wore themselves out playing in it when the wind was not blowing too hard. The chores took longer to do with the heavy stuff impeding progress, but for the children, even work had a novelty under the circumstances.

Rane was a friend and relation; no one saw anything odd about him being at Wild Swan. Besides Alex, only Della and Samson knew of the grim news he had brought. And perhaps Della suspected what had happened between Alex and Rane, for when the two women had looked at each other on Saturday morning, each had seen herself in the other. There was a certain light that came from loving well, discernible if one was looking for it. But neither woman said anything to the other about it.

On Saturday afternoon, Black Swan gave birth to a black colt. Alex stayed nearby, but the mare did a fine job on her own. Rane shared the wonder and laughter of seeing the long-legged foal take his first rocking steps before he found his mother's teats and began to nurse hungrily. The children were consulted, and the colt was named "Wizard."

"You see, we have more or less established two customs for naming. Leda's line is variations on swan, and Mabbie's, because her real name, Mab's Maid, refers to the fairytale Queen Mab, is mythical. In this case, Oberon is the sire, as he is of Dreamer, Sorceress, Puck, and Robin Goodfellow. Though the lines began with the mares, for the third generation we name mostly for the sires," Alex explained to Rane, and she looked so enthusiastic and earnest, he had all he could do not to kiss her in front of everyone.

Their awareness of each other gave everything a sweeter edge, but they were careful, not wanting to betray themselves, particularly to the children.

On Saturday night, Alex again went to Rane's room, unwilling to love him where the ghost of her life with St. John still lingered, but this time they were careful to lock the door, and as before, she awakened early enough to slip back to her own chamber.

Their second night was calmer than the one before. They were both weary from the upheavals of the past twenty-four hours and that allowed them to come together with leisurely grace, as if they had all the time in the world.

But as they lay savoring the simple pleasure of being with each other and at rest, Rane suddenly sucked in his breath sharply. "Christ! I am like the greenest boy! I have just thought: what if you conceive? It has happened before. Morgan is proof. And I never want to be as frightened for you as I was in Annapolis when you lost your child."

She was silent for a moment, thinking of her two lost daughters, and the sorrow was still in her voice when she answered. "I think I have lost the ability to conceive. I so wanted another daughter, but Sinje and I never managed to have her. If I should be fortunate enough to make a child with you, I would be glad to have our son or daughter, no matter what the consequences." The sadness had turned to defiance.

Rane knew the gossip was nothing to take lightly, no matter what she said, but he could not stop the rush of pride that filled him for her willingness to bear his child. For the first time he faced the idea of divorcing Claire. Always he had cringed away from the cruelty of abandoning her; now he faced the incredible possibility that it might be better for her as well as for him. But he said nothing to Alex about it. It was his problem to solve though it affected her.

"I thought this part of me had died, that I would never desire a man again," she mused.

"What a dreadful waste that would have been." Rane nuzzled her throat. "But I am jealous. I have just realized how much. I have no right, and yet, I cannot bear the idea of your wanting another man."

"I do not think I ever would," she told him with no coyness. "I came alive again because of you."

In the middle of the night, she awakened in panicked disorientation, for a moment knowing only the strangeness of having a man holding her with two arms. She wondered if she would ever grow accustomed to it.

"Is something wrong?" Rane asked, his voice sleepy.

"No, love, nothing," she answered and settled against him again.

On Sunday the storm was over, but there was more than a foot of snow on the ground. Rane stayed until Tuesday. It seemed at once a brief flash of seconds and a lifetime. Everything had changed for them in profound ways, and yet, outwardly nothing had. Rane went back to Baltimore but promised he would return to collect Morgan around the first of February—if the weather permitted.

It had to be accepted and lived as it was, Alex told herself; they both had busy lives in different places. Mares to be bred to Wild Swan's stallions would begin to arrive soon. And she had races to attend. But none of that stopped her from thinking of Rane.

She watched Samson closely, dreading the day when he would come to tell her that he was leaving. He went about his duties efficiently, but he had a vague look, as if he'd lost direction. Indeed he had. The single goal in his life was gone, and she knew there must be savage guilt as well for not having been with his family when they fell ill. But it began to dawn on her that Samson wasn't going anywhere. The only people left in the world whom he loved and who loved him were right here. And above them all was Della. Her surface tartness appeared to be the same toward the big man, but closer observation revealed a new softness. She was no longer flustered in his presence, but her voice gentled when she spoke to him, and her eyes followed him. Gradually Samson responded to it, seeking Della out more often. Alex doubted that they had been lovers since that snowbound night, but she did not think they would remain apart for much longer.

Rane arrived back at Wild Swan at a bad time. After what had seemed a normal course of carrying her foal, Taney was in trouble trying to deliver it.

Rane found Alex and Samson with the mare, and Alex had scarcely more than a glance to spare for him as she and Samson worked, trying to get a rope around the colt's legs so they could pull it out.

It was a gruesome scene. Rane knew as well as they that if a mare did not foal quickly, it meant serious problems. Taney looked too exhausted to labor any longer, and Alex didn't look much better, soaked in sweat in spite of the cold day, her hair falling in tangles around her pale face, blood on her arms and clothing.

"I'll help," Rane said with quiet determination, and Samson threw him a look of gratitude; Alex hadn't wanted anyone else to take her place, but she gave it to Rane.

She cursed softly and bit back tears when the bay filly was finally born dead. With luck, Taney would recover, but Swan's daughter was a loss.

Rane realized that it was not only sentiment that distressed Alex; the get of the champion sires were valuable. It brought home to him more clearly than before that this was a business, and Alex was deadly serious about making it successful.

She could hardly stay awake during the evening meal, and the children were subdued, too, over the loss of the foal. And yet, she went to Rane as soon as she could.

"I am sorry we are so out of sorts here," she began, but he pulled her almost roughly into his arms, hushing her. "Darling, you don't have to perform for me, to pretend that everything is all right when it is not. I love you when you're sad and tired as well as when you are joyful. Now, come to bed, to sleep."

He meant what he said. He rubbed her tense neck and back muscles skillfully until she was so relaxed, she felt as if she was welded to the bed. She fell asleep as he was working the same magic on her feet and legs.

When she awakened, it was still more than an hour before dawn, but she felt completely rested. She found she was cradled spoon fashion, Rane's body against her back, and she knew he wasn't sleeping.

"Have you slept at all?" she asked.

"A little," he lied. "I wasn't very tired." That part was true. He hadn't wanted to waste time sleeping while he could savor the reality of her in his arms, as he had dreamed of her too often since he had left Wild Swan.

And he had been thinking. He hated to admit it even to himself, but he was afraid of Claire now. There was no way she could find out about his mission in Georgia or his affair with Alex, and yet, she had been different when he returned to Baltimore, somehow more alert, more focused, as if she were seeing him clearly for the first time in years. She had spent more time in his presence, had seemed to behave better. Mrs. Calperth, a middle-aged widow and her main attendant, had been very encouraged. Rane had felt chilled to the bone and trapped. Before, it had not mattered; he had had so little that he cared about losing— furniture, clothing, the sort of things Claire liked to destroy, even the fact that she had made him the object of pitying gossip had not mattered once he had grown accustomed to it. But now there was Alex, and to lose her was to lose his own life. He had been so careful for so many years to show no special interest in her, and now he had the eerie feeling that Claire had seen right through the pretense the instant he and Alex had become lovers again, as if Claire had some evil second sight. But he could not bring himself to commit his wife to an asylum in order to satisfy his hunger for another woman.

The thought made him more aware of Alex lying against him. Claire slipped from his mind. He moved restlessly, his manhood swelling as he drew deep breaths of the scent that was uniquely Alex. His hands found her breasts, small, firm, and perfectly shaped despite her childbearing, breasts that fit his hands just so. Alex wiggled against him, and her laugh was husky. "I'm glad you've found something to do with that energy."

But when she would have turned to him, he kept her facing away, pulling her hips toward him, urging her top leg up toward her chest, showing her with his hands and soft words what he wanted from her. "I promise, I will pleasure you this way," he said, and he did, his penetration deep, his hands roaming her breasts and belly and between her legs as he thrust from behind.

It reminded her of the stallions mounting the mares, and that image excited her even more until she was voicing her delight in low, throaty cries.

Rane's own passion was enhanced by the knowledge that this position was new to her, and yet she trusted him to do her no hurt. So many ways of loving; he wanted to show her all of them. Suddenly he saw the stark truth of how limited St. John must have been in some ways from the loss of his arm, let alone the crippling that had finally killed him. He thought of how courageous the man had been, and he thought of the words he and St. John had exchanged, words Alex knew nothing about. Silently, inwardly, he paid tribute to the man. And then he pushed the memories of St. John away. Only he himself and Alex belonged in this bed now.

"I want to come to you while you're in Virginia and North Carolina, away from here, away from Baltimore," he said, liking the idea more by the second.

She had gotten up and was putting on her gown and robe to return to her own room, but she froze at his words. "Oh, Rane, we can't! The slightest breath of scandal, and there are many who would make sure the horses of Wild Swan never race again. I have worked so hard, and so many friends have helped to make it possible for me to go on. And I will not have the children hurt."

"No one would know," he protested. "I am your cousin, after all, and it is perfectly natural that I should be concerned for you." He could not bring himself to say, "now that St. John is dead," but the words were there between them anyway. "Please, my love, I cannot wait so long to see you again."

She could not bear to hear him beg. When he left for Baltimore he took not only Morgan with him but also a list of the races she would be attending.

He sought her out at two of the courses in North Carolina and one in Virginia. It was a dangerous, heady game they played—strictly proper in public, wildly abandoned when they could find time alone. It was rare when they could. The propriety Alex had established by staying with friends and traveling with Cassie and the others from Wild Swan was now a trap that made it difficult for her to find time to be alone with Rane, but they managed brief furtive interludes—once in a house where they were both staying; one afternoon in Rane's lodgings, Alex muffled to the eyes despite the warm day as he smuggled her in; and once in a hired coach, an awkward accommodation that left them both helpless with laughter.

At the courses he saw her dedication and involvement as he never had before. She was tireless in determining the strategies needed against particular horses and in discussing the individual races with the Barlow boys. She checked the horses constantly, seeing to their comfort before she thought of her own. And she was not above using Rane to place wagers for her, an office he fulfilled with good humor that swiftly turned to amazement at her acute judgment.

Something neither of them had considered was the effect the end of Alex's year of mourning would have on the bachelor population and on some who were not free. The men knew Rane was related—anyone could see that—and those who did not know that he was married swiftly sought the information. He was taken for his pose—a concerned relation giving support to the Widow Carrington and nothing more. The lawyer from Georgetown had made the same assumption before Alex and Rane had become lovers again; and now it was even more galling to Rane.

Alex simply ignored the advances, subtle and otherwise, and she was so steady in her refusal to acknowledge the undercurrents or to flirt in return, that most of the men desisted, telling themselves she had not gotten over her husband yet. Few wanted to consider that she simply had no interest in them and never would. But Rane complicated the situation by glowering so fiercely sometimes that she was forced to take him to task.

"An outraged lover is quite different from a protective relative," she pointed out.

He started to disagree and then grinned ruefully. "I know, but I find it difficult to remember that when men are making sheep's eyes at you."

"You surely cannot have missed the arch looks thrown your way," she returned with a smile of her own, but she still feared he would betray them.

And she found he had when Allen Ralston asked politely for a moment of her time at the Halifax races. She thought they had long since come to an understanding and was certain he wanted to talk to her about nothing more than Blockett's Boy, now renamed "Lady's Choice" and running under the Ralston colors with good results. Her eyes found Rane, and she smiled involuntarily, knowing he was making a bet on her behalf. She turned her attention back to Allen.

"You cousin is still married, is he not?" he asked bluntly, and Alex felt the blood draining out of her head all at once.

"Yes, he . . . he is," she stammered.

The anger he had felt dissipated in face of her distress. "Oh, hell! You may rightly point out that this is none of my business, but I do care about you, you know that. And I hate to see you become the target of vicious gossip. Blockett was here today, and he watched you very closely, but you were with Falconer and did not even notice. For God's sake, have a care!"

"Does everyone know?" She did not deny his suspicions. He was too astute, had been too kind, and was too in love with her for pretense to suffice.

She looked so vulnerable and at the same time courageous, he hastened to reassure her. "No, truly they don't know yet. But you must be more cautious. Perhaps one of your other suitors loves you as much as I do, and he will see it, too." He was unflinching in the revelation of the depth of his feeling, driven to it by his urge to protect her.

She reached out and took his hand. "Allen, if things were different, if I were different . . . You are a very special man."

Rane was there in the instant, frowning at both of them.

He was a good deal taller and broader than Allen, but Ralston did not back down. "Have a thought for someone besides yourself, man! It's exactly this kind of behavior I've been warning Alex about. You will pull everything she has built down on top of her if you don't conduct yourself more discreetly."

The two men glared at each other until Alex snapped, "You are both behaving like children!" and stalked away.

"She's right, you know," Allen said, and Rane nodded, his anger evaporating. "Yes, and so are you. Please accept my apology."

"None necessary as long as you protect her. She's worth whatever it takes." This time there was no animosity in the look the men exchanged.

Finally Rane could not ignore the toll the illicit meetings

were taking on Alex. Her eyes were shadowed, her face too finely drawn, and she had gotten so nervous, she often unconsciously twisted her hands together until it seemed they were never still. He could not ask this of her any longer.

Marriage to a divorced man carried its own censure, but it was nothing compared to adultery. His marriage to Claire had been finished before it began. It was time to end it legally. He felt a great sense of relief and peace.

He did not tell Alex of his decision, but she sensed the change in him before he announced that he was returning to Baltimore. They were at a party celebrating the day's fine racing.

"I would like to waltz with you, but I do not trust myself to keep a cousinly distance," he said very low. "My love, take care, I will see you soon at Wild Swan. I leave for Baltimore tonight.

Though she tried to hide it, he could see she was as relieved as she was sorry.

"I would not give up a single minute of our time together," he added, "but I know it has been a strain. Ralston did us a favor."

She was grateful for his understanding. It was better for her reputation, better for the children that he was leaving, better for everyone except the woman he had reawakened inside of her. A touch of his hand, and he was gone. Allen appeared to ask her for the dance, and she let him lead her out on the floor, knowing he was trying to ease the hurt.

She did not watch Rane leave the party but thought instead of when she would see him again.

Rane carried the clear image of Alex with him. Alex was his home. The house in Baltimore seemed colder than it ever had before, but he was not sorry when Claire insisted on dining with him his first night back. The situation had to be faced, and somehow she had to be made to understand that though the marriage would no longer exist, she would be well taken care of. She seemed calm enough and distant.

Very carefully he explained, making no mention of Alex or or any other woman, simply pointing out that he and Claire had made each other unhappy.

He wasn't sure she was listening. Her eyes wandered

around the room, coming back to his face now and then while her hands fiddled nervously with the cutlery.

And then suddenly she focused sharply on him. "You're happy. That's what has changed! You are happy!" She spat the words out as if they were intolerably bitter. "I am miserable, and you are happy! How dare you? I want you to be like me. I will make you like me!" Her voice rose to a piercing shriek, and an amazingly vulgar string of epithets poured forth. She picked up a plate and shied it at his head. He ducked automatically as he advanced on her, pitying her but feeling curiously detached from the whole horrifying scene as Mrs. Calperth rushed in to help, summoned by the racket from her own cosy dinner in the kitchen.

It was all too familiar. Rane helped Mrs. Calperth, a large woman but nearly matched in strength by Claire when his wife was at her peak of hysteria, and together they got Claire into her room.

In one of her lightning shifts of mood, Claire suddenly stopped fighting and screaming, becoming in an instant a sobbing, pathetic child.

Mrs. Calperth shook her head sadly. "She was doing so well, too, calm as you please for days at a time."

"It is undoubtedly my presence that has caused this," Rane said wearily. "Do you need anyone to help you?" The cook and her husband were both strong enough and capable of coping with Claire; it was the main reason they had been hired along with Mrs. Calperth. Their daughter, who helped serve the meals and clean the house, was another matter. She always disappeared at the first sign of trouble from Claire. Rane knew how she felt.

"No, Mr. Falconer," Mrs. Calperth said, refusing help. "She'll be fine now. I'll just give her a little of her medicine, and she'll sleep in no time." Mrs. Calperth had a way of managing Claire without being rough with her. Perhaps for enough money, she and the others could be persuaded to staff Claire's household when he set it up. He was more convinced than ever now that it had to be done. Nothing could be more mad than for one human being to wish sorrow on another she was supposed to love.

He stayed downstairs in the library, a room uniquely his, with none of the fussiness Claire had always favored. He stayed for hours, but he did not drink himself into oblivion as he was wont to do in the past after such episodes. Instead he thought of Alex, of what it would be like to spend the rest of his life with her. He knew there would be problems. She was determined about staying on at Wild Swan, and he could not relinquish his share in the shipyard nor his days on board his ships. Somehow they would manage anyway. They· would just have to make the time they had together count.

He heard the household settling down for the night, the cook's family in their downstairs quarters, Mrs. Calperth upstairs across the hall from his room and Claire's, which were next door to each other. He wished his room were in a different house tonight, but finally he went up. He was exhausted and longed for his bed.

He awakened before dawn with a terrible sense of foreboding. At first he thought it was simply because Alex was not beside him. But then he knew. It was too quiet in the house, much too quiet. This was not Claire's normal pattern. She was always awake by now, sometimes prowling around her room, other times throwing things and screeching. Not even drugs or screaming tantrums like the one she'd had the night before were enough to make her sleep through the darkness until dawn.

He met Mrs. Calperth in the hall. Her broad face reflected worry identical to his. "It's not like her, being this quiet," she said. "But she went to sleep so nice and gentle like. I'm usually up before this, but with no sound from her this morning . . ."

He blocked out the sound of her voice as he entered his wife's room. He smelled it before he saw it. Very carefully he put his candle down on the table beside the bed. He hardly heard Mrs. Calperth's screams filling the room.

Claire's face was very pale and serene, almost as beautiful as when he had first met her, but the bed was soaked with blood where she lay with her arms outstretched, arms slit open elbow to wrist, the left very neatly done, the right not so well gashed but enough for the work of a hand that must have been barely able to hold the razor. One of his razors from a set given to him by his father. It was a true measure of madness that she lay like that, in a mock crucifixion, not curled in on her pain. He wondered if she had felt the pain at all, wondered if in her lesson to him, she had had any realization that death was real and final, or if she had been a child playing the game of "I'll make you sorry," and imagining being there to witness the guilt and remorse. He had seen serious injuries before, but he would never have believed that one body could contain so much blood. The stench of it was suffocating.

He was not thinking clearly and was vaguely aware of that but not enough to do much about it. Mrs. Calperth's continuing hysteria finally registered, and he could not stand the sound. "For God's sake, shut up!" he roared, and the din died to snuffling hiccoughs.

The rest of the household gathered, stunned and horrified though they well knew how insane Claire had been. The next twenty-four hours were crowded with people, officials and friends, as the news spread, and Rane could hold only one thought in his mind—Alex must not be involved in any way.

But Caleb sent word immediately, and it reached her at her next stop in Virginia.

She read the words over and over, not able to believe them at first. She had wanted Claire dead; yes, she had. But the reality of the suicide was hideous. She could feel Rane's agony as if it were her own. Immediately she sent everyone except her maid, Cassie, home to Wild Swan, forfeiting the races still to be run. When she arrived in Baltimore, she went directly to the Jenningses' house.

One look at Pen's face told her how bad it was.

"I am no use at all in this, but Rane looks so beaten!" Pen said, and tears rolled down her cheeks. "There was a brief inquest, but everyone knows how crazy Claire was, and the staff at the house heard her threaten to make him sorry that last night. The verdict was suicide, of course, but it is as if he did kill her, his guilt is so deep. Oh, my dear, perhaps you can make him see the truth!"

He already sees the truth, or at least part of it; his guilt is for loving me, she thought, but she went to him anyway, leaving Cassie at the Jenningses' and instructing her to tell the twins when they returned from school that their mother would see them as soon as possible.

Rane's house was like a mausoleum with the staff creeping about silently. But nothing prepared her for the changes in Rane. His face was ravaged, deeply graven and muddy gray, his eyes shadowed pits. He looked as if he had not slept or eaten since Claire's death. This was far worse than what the snowstorm had done to him; this was killing cold working from the inside out.

"My dear heart," Alex murmured, going to him and putting her arms around him. "My love, I am so sorry."

Just for an instant, he relaxed against her, but then he stiffened and pulled away.

"You should not be here. I want you to leave right now." His voice was hoarse and strange.

"There is no other place I should be. You are so tired as to be ill with it." She stopped listening to his protests, winning the contest by force of will. She found the cook delighted to prepare a tempting meal for her employer; the servants were all worried about Mr. Falconer. Alex set the plate before him, and when he did not begin to eat immediately, she picked up the fork and offered food on it. "I will keep on until you comply," she said, as if she were speaking to a very young child.

An elusive grin touched his face and was gone, but he ate most of the food before him, automatically and without enjoyment, but at least he ate it.

When she led him upstairs, asking which room was his, he roused himself to protest again. "Shouldn't be here; people will know," he mumbled.

"All they will know is that I am your cousin, here to help you."

He was leaning heavily on her by the time she got him into his room. She loosened his clothing and took off his shoes but did not try to undress him.

His eyes closed and then fluttered open briefly. "You are so beautiful, and I love you too much." There was despair, not joy, in the words.

She watched over him as he slept. She did not care what anyone said. His household, in any case, was more grateful than anything else that someone had managed to take Mr. Falconer in charge.

When it grew late, and Rane still had not stirred, Alex left him and asked the cook's husband to take a message to the Jenningses, telling them not to worry and that she would see them and the twins on the following day. She ate the light supper the cook offered and then returned to Rane.

He slept without sound or motion until the early hours of the next morning. And when he opened his eyes, he looked immeasurably better than he had the day before. He saw her, and his eyes seemed to flood with light. "I thought I dreamt you," he said softly. But then the lines hardened again, and she knew the rest she had given him was only momentary.

He did not reach out for her. "If you will wait for me downstairs in the library, I will make myself presentable," he told her, the dismissal firm.

She did as she was bid, still certain that she could reason with him. But as soon as they started talking, she learned how resolved he was.

In measured cadence betraying no emotion, he told her about his argument with Claire and the result. "I should have known what she was planning. After all these years, I should have known."

"How could you?" Alex asked, outraged at his self-condemnation. "I doubt even Claire knew what she was doing, really knew. She just wanted you to be unhappy, and she was damn successful!"

It didn't help Rane that he had had the same thought. "Aside from that, aside from what Claire and I did to each other, I will not subject you to the scandal that would surely come from my continued association with you. Friends might understand, but others will say that you had a hand in her death."

"Association! That's a tidy word for it." Her temper was beginning to soar. "You are determined to punish yourself and me as well. How could there be trouble now? Before you were married. But now you are a widower, and most people, all the people who matter, feel sorry for you and wish you well. They know what a hellish life you had with Claire! Those who would say otherwise are vicious fools. I suffered their like in England and survived; I can do it again."

His eyes were looking right through her, refusing to acknowledge anything she said.

"She knew; somehow she knew," he said.

"She knew only that you were happy; you know that! She couldn't bear it, but there is no way she could have known that your happiness came from our loving. There was no one to tell her except you, and I know you did not! I refuse to blame you or myself for her death, I refuse! My sister Florence did that to St. John and to me; I will not let Claire do it to us. When you come to your senses, come to me."

With him in such a state, she could not find any pity for his dead wife. She left him staring at nothing, certainly not at her.

❧ *Chapter 61* ❧

Alex was absolutely sure that Rane would ride into Wild Swan any day. Instead, she received letters from Penelope and from Morgan. She had seen the twins and Morgan while she was in Baltimore, and they were all very sad for Cousin Rane without knowing their mother's involvement. Morgan was particularly upset as he worshipped the man; Alex had refrained from saying that his hero was behaving like a fool.

The letters were as much of a shock as the one telling of Claire's death had been. Rane had gone back to England, taking passage on a ship from New York rather than on one of his own vessels—an ominous sign as it meant he had no responsibility to return ship and crew to their home port.

"He arranged everything before he left so that I could go on working in the shipyard and going on coastal voyages, so I'm staying on here, but it isn't the same without him. He's the best teacher there is," Morgan wrote. "He didn't say when he would be back, but I hope it's soon."

And Penelope said,

Perhaps it is best that he go away for a while, perhaps it will help him to see things more clearly. But Caleb and I hope that he is not gone for too long or forever. He and Caleb work so well together, it would not be the same at all if Rane were to sell his part of the business to someone else.

Penelope obviously did not suspect that there was anything more than the old cousinly affection between Rane and Alex.

There was precious little of that, Alex thought. He had left without a word to her, left her to find out from other people. Even if he saw it as protection, she did not. Her fury and her hurt were equal. She hated him for re-awakening her desire as a woman and then leaving her to suffer the want of him. She hated him for refusing to accept the comfort she had to give him. And worst of all, the hating was an illusion, nothing more, because even as she tried to hold on to it, she felt the depth of her love for him and the shattering loneliness he had left in his wake.

Everyone saw the change in her, and no one could stop it. She drove herself relentlessly, often taking on tasks others would have performed for her, on the move morning till night. And she started taking more risks as well. She had always had a direct hand in the training of the horses, but now she rode the racing stock more often in practice runs. Samson was dismayed, but could not dissuade her and stopped trying when she said, "Please, I need to feel them running. I need the speed and quickness. It makes me feel alive!"

He was helpless in face of her need. She and Della had given him the strength to go on when he thought all reason for living was gone. And he knew she was feeling the same way now, and even worse than when her husband had died. He wished he could get his hands on Rane Falconer to tell him a thing or two. He was sure the man was the cause of it all.

Della was more blunt than Samson. "What is going to happen to your children if you kill yourself on one of those horses or end up like Mr. Carrington?" she asked.

"Nothing is going to happen," Alex told her flatly. "I'm much too good a rider, and the horses are the best trained anywhere. Vulcan was a rogue." She refused to discuss it further.

When Caleb and Pen brought their children to Wild Swan for the summer, they were shocked by the hectic energy driving Alex. But they had no more effect on her than anyone else.

"It's Rane, you know," Pen told her husband. "It's his leaving like that."

"Well, I suppose it is an awful blow to have St. John dead, her brother gone, and now Rane out of reach, too. Only the Bateses are left here of people who were close to Alex in England."

"My dear husband, for an intelligent man, you are being very thick. In fact, both of us have been for a very long time. Alex and Rane—I think they have loved each other for a very long time, and not as cousins, though I would swear to you that they were always discreet while St. John lived." She thought she was going to have to convince him further of the attraction, but he surprised her.

"I've gotten so used to telling myself it isn't true, I've started to believe my own nonsense. I knew there was something special clear back then in that cave on the Devonshire coast, something beyond being cousins. I suspect I knew it before they did. Alex was very young then, and Rane was very protective of her, to the point of his own detriment."

They stared at each other, reconsidering all the years and seeing countless incidents in a new light. Caleb remembered with particular clarity how stunned the two had been to see each other in Annapolis.

"The snowstorm last January, after that, Rane as a different man, years younger, happier," Caleb murmured, and Pen added in the same low tone, "As he must have been when he fathered Morgan."

They were silent, holding to each other, conscious of how lucky they were to lead lives so uncomplicated compared to those of their friends. And both of them thought that no matter how Rane and Alex had parted in Baltimore, Rane would be the worst sort of idiot if he did not come back to her.

They were still at Wild Swan when Alex took a tumble off a half-bred mare she was training to jump, and once they knew Alex was only bruised, they hoped it would teach her a lesson.

"It was my fault. I should have felt the refusal before it happened. I wasn't paying attention," she said. "I plan to get a good price for this horse when I sell her, and that means she will have to learn that she can't get away with such behavior."

The next day she was riding the horse again with no noticeable added caution.

The only area of her life where moderation seemed to remain was in her dealings with the children. With them, she was a constant of patience and love, as if she was determined they not suffer the same deprivation she was feeling.

"As if their lives wouldn't be ruined if she broke her neck," Pen said, and then wished she had not conjured the image of St. John. "Maybe having our children here as well as her own will keep her busy and out of trouble," she suggested hopefully to Caleb as they traveled to Annapolis to see his parents again before going home.

Caleb didn't look as if he found the idea convincing.

Most of the time, Alex felt as if she were going to climb out of her own skin. No matter how hard she worked her body, she could not banish Rane from her mind. She dreamed of him constantly, often waking herself as she reached out for him and found the bed empty. And sometimes she purposely conjured him, gripping the golden swan necklace until the edges bit into her hands, as if the necklace were a talisman capable of making him appear before her. Every time she had a letter from Morgan, she saw his face and Rane's side by side, young and old of the same. Only when she was riding at great speed, only when all her concentration was demanded by the intricacies of racing was she free of him, mind and heart wiped clean by the pulsing excitement.

She planned a heavy racing schedule for the autumn. It was easier to do now with the turf register magazine providing lists of upcoming races well in advance. She wished she could ride in the races.

She watched the mails, but no word came from Rane. She heard from Boston and she was tempted to write the whole story to him, just to be able to confide in someone. But she feared that would be the final straw that would bring him back to Wild Swan. She knew he still had guilty feelings about not having been there when St. John was hurt and when he died, though Boston had had no way of knowing about it. When she wrote to him, she emphasized how well she was doing and how important it was to her that he continue to live his own life.

Toward the end of August, Fire Swan, Winter Swan, and Magic were put into a program of intensive training. Magic was now four years old, and in spite of his relative youth, Alex and Samson had great hopes for him in the four-mile heats. Fire could be trusted at the intermediate distances. The three-year-old Winter, born in the season of St. John's despair, was the unknown quantity. He had, as Alex had predicted, maintained his aloof temperament. He ran and ran well because it was in his blood, but there were no displays of affection or playfulness with the people who handled him.

"All cold work, dat one," was Samson's judgment, but he accepted the animal for what he was and thought he would have a good chance against others of his age. For that reason, he was a worried man one afternoon when he sought Alex's advice.

"Dat Winter, I jus' doan know. Las' couple a days somepin' jus' not right."

Alex had not seen the morning run and had noticed nothing amiss the day before, but she questioned Jim Barlow closely.

He agreed with Samson. "I can't explain it very well, I really don't know what's th' matter with him. Maybe nothin'. But he feels funny, like his stride is just a little off."

She watched as they walked Winter for her, and she thought she could see what they were talking about, but she wasn't sure. It wasn't anything obvious, more a matter of the tiniest hesitation in his gait now and then. She found no swelling or sign of injury, and his hooves were in good shape.

"I'm going to take him around. Perhaps if I can feel him run, I'll know what the problem is, if there is one at all. He might just have gotten a little lazy. Please saddle him for me while I go change my clothes." Despite the stifling heat, she was more full of nervous energy than ever today; taking the colt out would help her work it off.

Samson didn't even think of crossing her.

She took Winter around the track slowly at first, warming him up and concentrating keenly on feeling every step he took. At one second she thought she sensed something amiss, and in the next he was going as smoothly as ever. It was very frustrating. She brought him to the starting pole.

"I'm going to take him around fast; watch very carefully," she called to Samson and Jim.

At her urging, Winter sprang forward into racing speed. Riding him easily, the air stirring against her in their passage, she felt nothing wrong until it was too late.

* * *

Rane had not even stopped at the front of the house but had ridden around to where the practice track and most of the activity with the horses was. He felt as if he were being pulled by a powerful magnet, though the sensible explanation was that this was where Alex could usually be found when preseason training was going on.

He took it all in at a glance—Samson, Jim, and other hands gathered to watch, the pounding speed of the big bay colt. He even recognized Winter Swan. And not for an instant did he doubt that the rider was Alex. It didn't matter that her hair was tucked up under a cap or that she was riding astride in shirt and breeches and was some distance away, coming around the far turn. He felt the pull of her as if she had reached out. It was exactly as Caleb and Pen had told him; Alex was risking her neck needlessly. Enormous rage rose in him and with it fear like none he had ever known before, so overwhelming that he doubted for an instant that he could stand as he slipped from his horse's back. He clamped his jaw against the impulse to yell at her to stop and instead went to stand beside Samson along the rail. Samson and Jim beside him were so intent on the horse and rider, they didn't even notice Rane.

Alex was such a short distance away. The pounding of the hooves vibrated in Rane's chest; he could hear the deep breathing of Winter and Alex's voice urging the horse on, and then he heard a sharp crack of bone breaking and saw everything in slow motion—Alex trying to keep the horse's head up as she kicked her feet free from the stirrups, getting ready to leap clear. But it was too little too late because, with his right foreleg broken, Winter had no power to right himself and tumbled, doing a horrible ungainly flip, screaming and thrashing helplessly as he crashed into the inner rail.

Rane wanted to see Alex's body thrown clear of the horse, and his eyes searched vainly as he vaulted the close rail with Samson and Jim. But Alex lay tangled with the heaving body of the injured horse.

Rane pulled her clear as Samson and Jim, suddenly possessed of superhuman strength and not waiting for added help, rolled the horse away from her, heedless of the flailing legs. Alex's agonized scream tore through Rane, but at least it told him she lived. Her eyes opened, and she stared at him uncomprehendingly before her eyes rolled back as she fainted in his arms.

Blood, so much of it so fast, not the horse's blood, but Alex's. The wooden railing had shattered as Winter fell on it, and a thick piece of wood had stabbed into Alex's inner left thigh, midway between knee and groin, going through the cloth of her breeches and into her flesh as if it were a knife blade. Even with the wood still in the wound, blood was flowing out at a rapid rate.

Rane's stomach clenched at the sight of the injury, but he started toward the house with her in his arms. He knew it was dangerous to move her, but he wanted to get her inside before she came to again and suffered more from the motion. It was all a blur—Della's scream and a babble of voices—all Rane could think of was that Alex was going to die in his arms.

"Send for Dr. Cameron," he ordered without checking his stride. "Della, bring hot water, bandages, and anything else you think we'll need."

He lay Alex on her bed and stripped away her clothing, using his knife to cut and lift away the material around the leg wound.

When Della appeared with Polly helping her carry her load, neither of the women questioned Rane's right to be there and in charge.

He looked down at Alex and shuddered. The damage was to her left side. He didn't need to be a physician to see the bruising already starting to show on her ribs and the grotesque hunch of the dislocated shoulder. But the leg wound was worst of all.

He looked at Della, but she shook her head, terror in her eyes. "I don't know what to do. She's the healer, not I. But we can't just leave her like this until Dr. Cameron comes; everything will just get worse. I do know that."

He closed his eyes for an instant before he ordered Della and Polly to hold her down. "I'm going to put the shoulder back before it has time to swell."

This he had done before on board ship, and he allowed himself no hesitation now, pulling with steady strength until the joint slipped back in place as Alex screamed.

"I hurt. Oh, Rane, make it stop, ask Gweneth . . ." The little gasping voice faded, and she tossed her head side to side trying to get more air past the fire in her ribcage.

Rane crooned to her helplessly, understanding; not being

able to comprehend that he was here at Wild Swan, she had slipped back in time and thought to Clovelly.

"We can't leave that piece of wood in her. Infection will set in," he said.

Della looked as if she were going to faint, and Polly's eyes were wide and glazed.

"I need you both," he snapped. "Skilled or not, we're all Alex has to help her."

The force of his will got through to them, and they held her leg still as he grappled for a hold on the slippery piece of wood and pulled it free, blood spurting out in its wake. The blood and the fact that Alex didn't seem to feel the rough and ready operation terrified him, and it was Della who poured the strong smelling solution over the wound, muttering, "I know this much. I know she cleans the wound, whatever it is."

But they soon discovered that bandaging was not going to stop the bleeding. Rane made a tourniquet of broad linen strips and twisted it tight and that slowed it, but he knew he couldn't leave it like that for too long or the limb would die. He lost track of everything but the pattern of tightening and loosening the band, watching helplessly as the blood continued to spurt every time the pressure was released, holding a pad of linen so tightly against the wound that sometimes his fingertips were nearly inside the gash.

Della tenderly washed Alex's face and hands, knowing it was a useless gesture, but needing to do something for her. "Polly," she ordered, "you go and watch for the children, make sure they don't come in here. Tell everyone that Mrs. Carrington is hurt but will be all right." When she saw the fear and doubt in Polly's eyes, she hissed, "You tell them that, and you believe it yourself!"

Though Jim Barlow had ridden for Dr. Cameron on Magic and had gotten him back to Wild Swan in record time, to Rane and Della it seemed as if the hours had been days by the time the doctor walked into the room late at night.

Alastair took in the scene before him, and his own face was as grave as theirs. "Poor lass," he said softly, as he set about to assess the damage.

She's bleeding to death, Rane croaked, and when he loosened the tourniquet, Alastair gasped at the pulsing blood. His examination was swift.

"It's not done very often because the risk of infection and failure is so great, but I want to operate. The major artery has been cut, and there's just a chance that I can suture it."

"Do it." Rane had no hesitation in taking authority for her life, and Alastair had none in accepting Rane's right to it.

They put her on the floor so that Alastair would have a firm working surface with enough candles around for light, and Rane discovered the true meaning of hell. Hell was watching Alex suffer and not being able to take the pain from her. The leg still did not seem to be paining her, but her shoulder and ribs the doctor said were broken made her moan even in her unconscious, weakened state. But there was no further sound from her when Alastair cut and probed with quick but delicate movements, Rane following his instructions to mop the blood from the field.

The doctor breathed a sign of relief. "It's little enough for good news, but the artery is torn, not severed clear through. There's hope."

When he was done, they lifted her back onto the bed, and this time she was silent despite being moved. Though he could still see the rise and fall of her chest, Rane thought Alex looked just as dead as Claire had when all her blood had drained away.

"She didn't even feel it when you cut into her leg . . . ," he began, but Alastair interrupted. "It's often that way with so severe an injury. She's lost so much blood, she's deeply unconscious. She'll feel it well enough later, if she lives."

He ran his hand over her flat abdomen. "No sign of internal bleeding, and that's a gift, for there is nothing I could do for that." He bound her ribs and immobilized her left arm to give the shoulder rest and then he covered her carefully, leaving the injured leg exposed so that they would be able to see if massive bleeding started again. His eyes were uncompromising as he gazed at Rane, remembering the first time he had seen and wondered at the resemblance between Rane and Morgan and all it implied. "I have not suspected for these past weeks, but I know it now. You're the one she's been pining for. And you're the one who might keep her here though her will would have her go. You're going to do as I say; otherwise you'll be no use to me or to her. We're going to take turns watching over her, and you will eat and sleep when I tell you to because it is going to be a long vigil." God, I hope it's going to be a long one and not over too soon in death, he thought.

In the end, they compromised; Rane did as Alastair ordered, but only within his own limits. When he slept it was on a pallet in Alex's room, the couch being too short for his long frame. And when he ate, it was usually from dishes brought to him there. He left the room only for short periods of exercise he knew he needed, to wash, and to spend brief moments with the children. They turned to him naturally. He looked like their mother and Morgan; he was a relative; and they liked him for his own sake. He did not try to make the situation less serious than it was, but he also did not steal hope from them.

"It is not like what happened to your father. She is not paralyzed, though she is badly hurt," he told them firmly. "She is getting stronger by the hour." He tried to believe it.

The children were in desperate need of reassurance, and he blessed Samson's kindness to them and added his own promise, "I had to go to England to see my family. But I swear, I will not leave you again." It was as close as he could come to telling them that if something did happen to Alex, he would care for them.

Even when the Bateses arrived from Annapolis and the Jenningses and Morgan from Baltimore, all summoned by messages from Alastair, even when Pen and Mavis took their turns in watching over Alex, Rane did not lessen his hours in the sickroom. He washed her and fed her and cooled her down with precious slivers of ice when her fever soared, hardly noticing the other hands that helped him. He did it all without hesitation or embarrassment, as tenderly as if he were caring for a small child. And no one questioned the propriety of it.

He talked to her constantly, telling her he was there, telling her he loved her though she showed no sign of hearing him. And when she began to drift up through the cushioning layers of unconsciousness, when she began to feel the pain of her injuries, he held her right hand so that she might know she was not alone, and he didn't feel the pain of her nails digging into his flesh.

*　　*　　*

Alex thought she was still trapped beneath Winter's body. His weight was crushing her chest and tearing at her leg. She tried to struggle out from under him.

"Love, be still, please, be still. You're safe, lie quietly now."

She opened her eyes, and with great effort she made the blurred image above her swim into focus. Rane's face. She closed her eyes and opened them again. He was still there. She tried to find the energy to speak but could not.

"Don't try to talk. I'm here at Wild Swan. I came back the day you were hurt. I felt something awful was going to happen. I saw you fall. Alastair, Caleb, and Pen are here, the Bateses as well, and Morgan. The children are all right, just very, very worried about you. Sam, too. I made sure she didn't get stuck at Brookhaven." He thought she almost smiled before her eyes closed again.

She knew there were others caring for her—Alastair told her honestly what her injuries were and about the surgery he had done, knowing how much she would hate it if he talked down to her, and she grew more and more aware that her women friends were helping—but it seemed to be Rane who was always there when she opened her eyes.

"Clovelly?" was the first word she managed to say.

"Is still there and still the same," he answered. "And my family is all well." He hesitated for a moment. "My mother told me I was being a great fool. I told her everything, and she told me to come back here as quickly as I could before I lost you forever. She and my father send their love, and you have always had mine. Am I too late?"

Her eyes were wide and as bright green as summer leaves as she gazed at him. "Never," she said and was pleased that the word was audible. She wasn't sure what he had in mind, and she didn't care at the moment. For now it was enough to feel his love encircling her, dulling the pain, giving her strength.

He waited until she was much stronger before he pressed his suit and his one condition. She gave him the opening by asking about Winter. "It's all terriby confused, but Winter broke his leg, didn't he?" At his nod, she continued, "Poor beast, we had great hopes for him. He must have had a tiny fracture or some other irregularity of bone. We thought his stride was off, but there was no real sign of injury." She didn't have to ask what had been done about the horse; she knew he would have been destroyed with swift kindness.

Rane took her hand, rubbing it gently in his own. "I want to marry you if you'll have me. I wish I'd asked you a century ago in Clovelly. But perhaps it would have changed nothing. I know you loved St. John and always will in a special way. I was a witness to that love and can live with it because I must. And I know you intend to go on with the horses and Wild Swan. I understand now that they are as important to you as ships and the sea are to me. It won't be easy if we marry; our time together won't be as steady as most husbands' and wives', and there will be a world of gossip, at least at first. But there is one thing I will not accept. I cannot live with the idea that you will race again, not in practice, not for a wager, not for any reason. Ride, yes, of course, but racing, never."

She interrupted him. "But it was a freakish accident, nothing more."

His voice remained as gentle and as implacable as before. "You may call it anything you will, but you will never see yourself as I saw you. It was even worse than when you miscarried. I thought you were going to die in my arms. I never want to go through that again or even think I might have to suffer it again. I have considered it very carefully, and I have found that I can bear the thought of never seeing you again more easily than the burden of thinking this or worse might happen. Remember how you felt when St. John was hurt." It was a low blow, but he did not flinch from using it.

Even weak and sore as she was, the old independence rose up, and she nearly told him that she had come too far to tolerate anyone telling her what to do, even him. But then the full realization of what he was offering dawned on her. His life, his fortune, his love for her and for her children, and his respect for her right to do things her own way in everything but this. Himself. No race on earth was worth being without him.

Her smile transformed her face, making her look so soft and young that Rane caught his breath.

"My heart, you are so solemn, so willing to take on all these burdens—four children, five counting Sam, horses you don't particularly care for, and a woman very accustomed to getting her own way. But you have my promise, no more racing. I will have other ways to use my energy now. I need you in my bed, not beside it. I will marry you, gladly, proudly, no matter what rumors rise up." Her smile widened. "It may not be as awful as you fear; Americans seem quite fond of marrying their cousins, many far closer than we are. And there is no prohibition against it." She drew a few careful breaths, still finding her ribs constricting when she talked at length. She wanted enough air for this. "I love you, Rane Falconer."

Very carefully he leaned over and kissed her, and then with a little sigh, he hid his face against the hollow of her throat. Her own throat tightened when she felt the warmth of his tears on her skin. Wordlessly she stroked his soft thick hair and accepted the knowledge that she would never again be complete without him, nor he without her.

✷ Epilogue ✷

Wild Swan, Prince George's County, Maryland, October, 1831

The day of the wedding was perfect as only October can be with the leaves turning and falling, and the smell of woodsmoke sweet in the air that swiftly lost its night chill.

Alex thought that if it were possible to explode with happiness, this would be the day she would do it. What well might have been the biggest obstacle to their marriage had proved to be no obstacle at all. The children had, in their habitual way of making a decision by committee, decided that they approved of the match. In fact, they had made their ruling before Rane had asked Alex to marry him. Though Blaine was a very self-possessed young man, he had the grace to blush when he explained to his mother that he and the others had realized that with all of them growing up, it would be better if their mother had a husband to keep an eye on her. He had obviously considered the idea that husbands did more than that with their wives but was trying not to think of it now, and Alex had had a hard time not laughing though she was also deeply moved.

Rane was handling the children very well, not pressuring them to accept him in St. John's place, but rather allowing them to determine how he fit most comfortably into their lives. The discomfort seemed all on his side, Alex pointed out, but he refused to see it that way. He had asked the boys if they would like to live in his house, giving them a choice, and they had accepted with alacrity. There had been a great many changes in their lives, and suddenly they found it very appealing to think of being together, though Blaine and Morgan both pretended it was for Nigel. Flora and Samantha could thus be together at the Jenningses' house and spend time at Rane's when Alex was there. Caleb and Pen would not hear of having Sam stay anywhere else.

"I warned you that you were taking on a heavy load," Alex teased Rane ruefully when these arrangements were made, but he would have none of that.

"I am enormously pleased that the boys will be coming to be with me," he told her, and he meant it, not only about Morgan, but about the other two as well. He had not realized how truly lonely he had been before. All traces of Claire were being stripped from the house, and he had plans to buy or build a bigger house in the near future. He knew there would be problems now and again with the children, but he did not doubt that together, he and Alex could solve them.

Dutifully Alex had written to her brother Paris about her impending marriage, and with more joy, she had written to Hugh and to Boston, trusting both would wish her happiness. She particularly hoped Boston would understand. It had been more difficult to think of what to write to Gweneth and Magnus, and in the end, the heart of the letter had been the simplest words: "I have loved Rane for a very long time and will love him until the day I die. Thank you for sending him back to me."

Closer to home, she had worried about what the Bateses' reaction would be and found that she had forgotten how accepting they were of life. They had been devoted to St.

John, but they did not believe Alex's life should end because his had. They wanted her to be happy, and they believed Rane would make her so. Neither referred to the shock they had felt when they had first seen Rane Falconer and had noted how much Morgan looked like him. As Mavis said to Timothy, " 'Tis nowt business of ourn."

Today, Alex knew that every time she looked at Rane, she betrayed exactly how much she loved him, and she didn't care. He was so handsome with his tall body simply clothed in a beautifully cut black frock coat and trousers that her heart tended to skitter at the sight of him. He looked young and open to life again, completely different than he had been with Claire. But there was endurance and hard-gained strength marked there, too, and she liked his face at thirty-six even better than the unlined version she had first seen when he was eighteen and she thirteen.

As she smiled and talked to friends, she suffered quite lustful thoughts about Rane. As soon as he was convinced there would be no setbacks in her health, he had gone back to Baltimore to set his affairs in order after his long absence, and he had just returned for the wedding. It had been so long since he had made love to her. This was one bride who had no reservations about the wedding night.

A minister performed the service in the same room that had seen the New Year's Eve parties, both sad and joyful. Alex had no interest in any church after the prohibition that had caused her and St. John so much trouble, but Rane felt differently and wanted their marriage sanctified by more than a clerk. Alex didn't care as long as they were married, but she found herself listening carefully to the vows and meaning them when she spoke her own. And far away in her heart, there was a small voice saying, "Sinje, be happy for me."

She did not know that Rane was thinking of St. John, too. He would never know for certain, but the last time he had seen him, St. John had looked him squarely in the eye and said, "Take care of her when I am gone." Just that. And yet Rane had thought in that instant that St. John knew about his affair with Alex, knew that Morgan was Rane's son. Afterward, he had tried to convince himself that his suspicion was groundless. But now he saw again the steady light in St. John's eyes and came full circle in his belief. He would not, could not feel guilty for those brief days with Alex in Gravesend or for the son who had come from them. Guilt was not what St. John had asked of him; he had asked only that Rane care for the woman they both loved. And that he would do with a glad heart. It was an agreement between gentlemen, something Alex must never know, not after she had worked so hard and suffered so much in her attempt to protect St. John from the truth.

As Rane looked at Alex, his face was shining with the promise of the joy he wanted to bring her.

But though the day was bright, Alex and Rane were aware of shadows moving over the land, shadows they could do nothing to dispel.

As Alex had grown stronger, word of the outside world had trickled in. And then, news of what was being called "Nat Turner's Rebellion" had spread like wildfire. Turner was a fanatical black preacher who on August 21 had led seventy or so slaves on a rampage that resulted in the massacre of fifty-seven whites in Southampton County, Virginia, near the North Carolina border. The militia had moved in, killing about a hundred blacks, and several of Turner's followers had been arrested and would undoubtedly be hanged. Nat Turner had eluded capture but would surely be hunted down and executed.

Already there were cries for more laws to restrict the movement of slaves and to cease any efforts to educate blacks, slave or free. There had been slave rebellions before, but this one had captured the imagination in the most lurid ways. Worst to Alex's mind was the fact that free blacks in Maryland had presented a petition declaring that they had no intention of causing any trouble. It made her sick that they should even have to think of such a measure when they were in no way to blame.

"Though I don't condone the violence, I'm surprised there aren't more rebellions," she had told Rane, and she had insisted that she be allowed to call the people of Wild Swan together and talk to them.

She had been much improved but still moving gingerly and lacking her old energy because she had lost so much blood. Rane had been overly protective due to his fear of a relapse, so they had compromised. Rane had carried her out to address everyone at once and had kept his arm around her when she was standing on her own two feet.

She had gotten right to the point. "I know you have all heard about Nat Turner. Though I've been restricted lately,

I've felt the nervousness and fear, and I want it to stop immediately. Nat Turner has nothing to do with anyone here. He is not going to appear at Wild Swan. It is sad that both black and white people died. But that's an end to it. I would hate to have to apologize every time a white man or woman committed a crime. And I don't want anyone here doing it because a black man committed a crime. Nor will I tolerate fear of each other. Wild Swan is a place where we all have worked well together and will continue to do so. If anyone thinks he or she cannot abide by this, he or she may leave . . . at once."

There had been dead silence for a moment, and then almost tangible relief had swept the small crowd, and the smiles had been genuine and easy for the first time in days. They all treasured the working conditions and relationships they had at Wild Swan and had feared that this outside trouble would somehow alter their lives without their volition.

Alex and Samson had exchanged a brief glance, but it had been enough; hers had told him there was no comparison to Nat Turner in what he had done; his in return had been grateful that she understood the difference. She wanted him to have no doubts to cloud his future, particularly because she was quite sure he and Della would be married before the year was out. Despite the differences in their backgrounds, their lives were growing more intertwined by the day. She had even heard Della murmur, "That man needs someone to care for him," quite tenderly, as if she saw another Samson inside the huge strong man, as if she saw him as he had been when he had learned of the deaths of his family.

More than a few of the guests at the wedding were slave owners, and among them the specter of Nat Turner was still fresh. Slowly but steadily the different sections of the country seemed to be pulling apart from each other, their interests more and more separate. Alex wondered how long they could be held together without coming to blows.

"This might not be the best country to live in in the years to come," she said softly to Rane during a brief respite when they had escaped to her herb garden for a few minutes alone.

"Every country has its problems," he pointed out. "Even England, so long settled, even with her new king and with conditions slowly improving, still there are more every day who are leaving because they cannot earn enough to buy bread. It felt so strange to be there again; at once familiar and yet very foreign. It seemed smaller somehow, as if I had suddenly become aware of the boundaries being so close, the sea pressing in on every side, the plots of land so small and neat and limited. Even the West Country didn't look so wild to me any more. It was you first and last that I came back for, but after you, it was this country as well. For good or for ill, there's a wedding been made there, too. And if you will but notice, our children are American, not English."

She brought his hand to her lips and kissed it, loving him for his commitment to the United States as well as for his dedication to her and to the children. "Perhaps immigrants love a country more than the natives because they choose it."

She thought of her grandmother setting her free and sending her with her blessing to this new land. She thought of the acres, the fields and gardens of Wild Swan, so lovingly brought back to life. She thought of the increasing livestock, and most of all the horses, among the finest anywhere, and all begun from a lame mare and St. John's faith. There would be no racing season for the Carrington lines this autumn, but next spring the children of Leda and Mabbie would compete again.

Life was a series of journeys. Separately she and Rane had traveled far to come home to this place. Her future traveling would be in the mind and the heart with Rane beside her to watch and guide the children's progress, and to be part of this country's growth. Such a proud journey so bravely begun, and what a miraculous country it would become if it could survive the trial of slavery and fulfill its own prophecy of equality, freedom, and justice for everyone. For themselves, for their children, and for their children's children, it was a road worth following.

She heard them before she saw them—a flight of wild swans winging overhead, pursuing their own journey in the cycle of seasons, unaware of the special benediction they bestowed in their passing.

She looked at Rane, and she did not have to tell him that for her, the swans were forever talismans of him. He touched the golden swan necklace ringing her throat and bent his head to claim her mouth with his own.

ABOUT THE AUTHOR

CELESTE DE BLASIS, a native Californian, lives on a ranch high in the Mojave Desert. She is the author of such memorable novels as *The Proud Breed, The Tiger's Woman, The Night Child,* and the acclaimed Swan Trilogy.

DON'T MISS
THESE CURRENT
Bantam Bestsellers

THE LATEST IN BOOKS
AND AUDIO CASSETTES